THE SUMMER GARDEN

By the same author

Tully
Red Leaves
Eleven Hours
The Bronze Horseman
The Bridge to Holy Cross
The Girl in Times Square

PAULLINA SIMONS

The Summer Garden

HarperCollins*Publishers*

HarperCollins*Publishers*
77–85 Fulham Palace Road,
Hammersmith, London W6 8JB

www.harpercollins.com.au

Published by HarperCollins*Publishers* 2005
3 5 7 9 8 6 4

Besame Mucho
Written by Consuelo Velazquez © 1941 & 1943 P.H.A.M., Mexico
Latin-American Music Pub. Co. Ltd., London Controlled in Australia and
New Zealand by Allan & Co. (Pty) Ltd., Australia Used by permission

A catalogue record for this book
is available from the British Library

ISBN 0 00 719368 8

Set in Meridien by Palimpsest Book Production Limited,
Polmont, Stirlingshire

Printed and bound in Australia by Griffin Press, Netley, Australia

For Kevin, my own mystic guide

By the rivers of Babylon, there we sat down,
Yea, we wept, when we remembered Zion.
We hanged our harps upon the willows in the midst . . .
For there, they that carried us away
captive required of us a song,
And they that wasted us required of us mirth, saying,
Sing us one of the songs of Zion.
How shall we sing the Lord's song in a strange land?
Psalm 137

The song of songs, which is Solomon's.
The Song of Solomon

Book One

The Land of Lupine
and Lotus

The Lotos blooms below the barren peak
The Lotos blows by every winding creek . . .
Let us swear an oath, and keep it with an equal mind,
In the hollow Lotos-land to live and lie reclined
On the hills like gods together, careless of mankind

Alfred, Lord Tennyson

CHAPTER ONE

Deer Isle, 1946

The Carapace

Carapace n. a thick hard case or shell made of bone or chitin that covers part of the body of an animal such as a lobster.

Once upon a time, in Stonington, Maine, before sunset, at the end of a hot war and the beginning of a cold one, a young woman dressed in white, outwardly calm but with trembling hands, sat on a bench by the harbor, eating ice cream.

By her side was a small boy, also eating ice cream, his a chocolate. They were casually chatting; the ice cream was melting faster than the mother could eat it. The boy was listening as she sang "Shine Shine My Star" to him, a Russian song, trying to teach him the words, and he, teasing her, mangled the verses. They were watching for the lobster boats coming back. She usually heard the seagulls squabbling before she saw the boats themselves.

There was the smallest breeze, and her summer hair moved slightly about her face. Wisps of it had gotten out of her long thick braid, swept over her shoulder. She was blonde and fair, translucent-skinned, translucent-eyed, freckled. The tanned boy had black hair and dark eyes, and chubby toddler legs.

They seemed to sit without purpose, but it was a false ease. The woman was watching the boats in the blue horizon single-mindedly. She would glance at the boy, at the ice cream, but she gawped at the bay as if she were sick with it.

Tatiana wants a drink of herself in the present tense, because she wants to believe there is no yesterday, that there is only the moment here on Deer Isle—one of the long sloping overhanging islands off the coast of central Maine, connected to the continent by a ferry or a thousand-foot suspension bridge, over which they came in their RV camper, their used Schult Nomad Deluxe. They drove across Penobscot Bay, over the Atlantic and south, to the very edge of the world, into Stonington, a small white town nested in the cove of the oak hills at the foot of Deer Isle. Tatiana— trying desperately to live only in the present—thinks there is nothing more beautiful or peaceful than these white wood houses built into the slopes on narrow dirt roads overlooking the expanse of the rippling bay water that she watches day in and day out. That is peace. That is the present. Almost as if there is nothing else.

But every once in a heartbeat while, as the seagulls sweep and weep, something intrudes, even on Deer Isle.

That afternoon, after Tatiana and Anthony had left the house where they were staying to come to the bay, they heard loud voices next door.

Two women lived there, a mother and a daughter. One was forty, the other twenty.

"They're fighting again," said Anthony. "You and Dad don't fight."

Fight!

Would that they fought.

Alexander didn't raise a semitone of his voice to her. If he spoke to her at all, it was never above a moderated deep-well timbre, as if he were imitating amiable, genial Dr. Edward Ludlow, who had been in love with her back in New York—dependable, steady, doctorly Edward. Alexander, too, was attempting to acquire a bedside manner.

To fight would have required an active participation in another human being. In the house next door, a mother and daughter raged at each other, especially at this time in the afternoon for some reason, screaming through their open windows. The good news: their husband and father, a colonel, had just come back from the war. The bad news: their husband and father, a colonel, had just come back from the war. They had waited for him since he left for England in 1942, and now he was back.

He wasn't participating in the fighting either. As Anthony and Tatiana came out to the road, they saw him parked in his wheelchair in the overgrown front yard, sitting in the Maine sun like a bush while his wife and daughter hollered inside. Tatiana and Anthony slowed down as they neared his yard.

"Mama, what's wrong with him?" whispered Anthony.

"He was hurt in the war." He had no legs, no arms, he was just a torso with stumps and a head.

"Can he speak?" They were in front of his gate.

Suddenly the man said in a loud clear voice, a voice accustomed to giving orders, "He can speak but he chooses not to."

Anthony and Tatiana stopped at the gate, watching him for a few moments. She unlatched the gate and they came into the yard. He was tilted to the left like a sack too heavy on one side. His rounded stumps hung halfway down to the non-existent elbow. The legs were gone *in toto*.

"Here, let me help." Tatiana straightened him out, propping the pillows that supported him under his ribs. "Is that better?"

"Eh," the man said. "One way, another." His small blue eyes stared into her face. "You know what I would like, though?"

"What?"

"A cigarette. I never have one anymore; can't bring it to my mouth, as you can see. And they"—he flipped his head to the back—"they'd sooner croak than give me one."

Tatiana nodded. "I've got just the thing for you. I'll be right back."

The man turned his head from her to the bay. "You won't be back."

"I will. Anthony," she said, "come sit on this nice man's lap until Mama comes back—in just one minute."

Anthony was glad to do it. Picking him up, Tatiana placed him on the man's lap. "You can hold on to his neck."

After she ran to get the cigarettes, Anthony said, "What's your name?"

"Colonel Nicholas Moore," the man replied. "But you can call me Nick."

"You were in the war?"

"Yes. I was in the war."

"My dad, too," said Anthony.

"Oh." The man sighed. "Is he back?"

"He's back."

Tatiana returned and, lighting the cigarette, held it to Nick's mouth while he smoked with intense deep breaths, as if he were inhaling the smoke not just into his lungs but into his very core. Anthony sat on his lap, watching his face inhale with relief and exhale with displeasure as if he didn't want to let the nicotine go. The colonel smoked two in a row, with Tatiana bent over him, holding the cigarettes one by one to his mouth.

Anthony said, "My dad was a major but now he's a lobsterman."

"A captain, son," corrected Tatiana. "A captain."

"My dad was a major *and* a captain," said Anthony. "We're gonna get ice cream while we wait for him to come back to us from the sea. You want us to bring you an ice cream?"

"No," said Nick, leaning his head slightly into Anthony's black hair. "But this is the happiest fifteen minutes I've had in eighteen months."

At that moment, his wife ran out of the house. "What are you doing to my husband?" she shrieked.

Tatiana scooped Anthony off the man's lap. "I'll come back tomorrow," she said quickly.

"You won't be back," said Nick, gaping after her.

Now they were sitting on the bench eating ice cream.

Soon there was the distant squawk of gulls.

"There's Daddy," Tatiana said breathlessly.

The boat was a twenty-foot lobster sloop with a headsail, though most fishing boats were propelled by gas motors. It belonged to Jimmy Schuster, whose father, upon passing on, passed it on to him. Jimmy liked the boat because he could go out in it and trawl for lobsters on his own—a one-man job, he called it. Then his arm got caught in the pot hauler, the rope that pulls the heavy lobster traps out of the water. To free himself, he had to cut off his hand at the wrist, which saved his life—and him from going to war— but now, with no small irony, he needed deckhands to do the grunt work. Trouble was, all the deckhands had been in Hürtgen Forest and Iwo Jima the last four years.

Ten days ago Jimmy had got himself a deckhand. Today, Jimmy was in the cockpit aft, and the tall silent one was standing pin straight, at attention, in orange overalls and high black rubber boots, staring intently at the shore.

Tatiana stood from the bench in her white cotton dress, and when the boat was close enough, still a bay away, she flung her arm in a generous wave, swaying from side to side. Alexander, I'm here, I'm here, the wave said.

When he was close enough to see her, he waved back.

They moored the boat at the buyers' dock and opened the catches on the live tanks. Jumping off the boat, the tall man said he would be right back to off-load and clean up and, rinsing his hands quickly in the spout on the dock, walked up from the quay, up the slope to the bench where the woman and the boy were sitting.

The boy ran down to him. "Hey," he said and then stood shyly.

"Hey, bud." The man couldn't ruffle Anthony's hair: his hands were mucky.

Under his orange rubber overalls, he was wearing dark green army fatigues and a green long-sleeved army jersey, covered with sweat and fish and salt water. His black hair was in a military buzz-cut, his gaunt perspiring face had black afternoon stubble over the etched bones.

He came up to the woman in pristine white who was sitting on the bench. She raised her eyes to greet him—and raised them and raised them, for he was tall.

"Hey," she said. It was a breathing out. She had stopped eating her ice cream.

"Hey," he said. He didn't touch her. "Your ice cream is melting."

"Oh, I know." She licked all around the wafer cone, trying to stem the tide but it was no use, the vanilla had turned to condensed milk and was dripping. He watched her. "I can never seem to finish it before it melts," she muttered, getting up. "You want the rest?"

"No, thank you." She took a few more mouthfuls before she threw the cone in the trash. He motioned to her mouth.

She licked her lips to clean away the remaining vanilla milk. "Better?"

He didn't answer. "We'll have lobsters again tonight?"

"Of course," she said. "Whatever you want."

"I still have to go back and finish."

"Yes, of course. Should we, um, come down to the dock? Wait with you?"

"I want to help," said Anthony.

Tatiana vigorously shook her head. She would not be able to get the fish smell off the boy.

"You're so clean," said Alexander. "Why don't you stay here with your mother? I'll be done soon."

"But I want to help you."

"Well, come down then, maybe we'll find something for you to do."

"Yes, nothing that involves touching fish," muttered Tatiana.

She didn't care much for Alexander's job as a lobsterman. He reeked of fish when he returned. Everything he touched smelled of it. A few days ago, when she had been very slightly grumbling, almost teasing, he said, "You never complained in Lazarevo when I fished," not teasing. Her face must have looked pretty crestfallen because he said, "There's no other work for a man in Stonington. You want me to smell like something else, we'll have to go somewhere else."

Tatiana didn't want to go somewhere else. They just got here.

"About the other thing . . ." he said. "I won't bring it up again."

That's right, don't bring up Lazarevo, their other moment by the sea near eternity. But that was then—in the old bloodsoaked country. After all, Stonington—with warm days and cool nights and expanses of still and salty water everywhere they looked, the mackerel sky and the purple lupines reflecting off the glass bay with the white boats—it was more than they ever asked for. It was more than they ever thought they would have.

With his one good arm, Jimmy was motioning for Alexander.

"So how did you do today?" Tatiana asked him, trying to make conversation as they headed down to the dock. Alexander was in his big heavy rubber boots. She felt impossibly small walking by his side, being in his overwhelming presence. "Did you have a good catch?"

"Okay today," he replied. "Most of the lobsters were shorts, too small; we had to release them. A lot of berried females, they had to go."

"You don't like berried females?" She moved closer, looking up at him.

Blinking lightly, he moved away. "They're good, but they have to be thrown back in the water, so their eggs can hatch. Don't come too close, I'm messy. Anthony, we haven't counted the lobsters. Want to help me count them?"

Jimmy liked Anthony. "Buddy! Come here, you want to see how many lobsters your dad caught today? We probably have a hundred lobsters, his best day yet."

Tatiana leveled her eyes at Alexander. He shrugged. "When we get twelve lobsters in one trap and have to release ten of them, I don't consider that a good day."

"Two legals in one trap is great, Alexander," said Jimmy. "Don't worry, you'll get the hang of this. Come here, Anthony, look into the live-well."

Keeping a respectful distance, Anthony peered into the tank where the lobsters, already banded and measured, were crawling on top of one another. He told his mother he didn't care much for their claws, even bound. Especially after what his father told him about lobsters: "They're cannibals, Ant. Their claws have to be tied up or they would eat each other right in the tank."

Anthony said to Jimmy, his voice trying not to crack, "You already *counted* them?"

Alexander shook his head at Jimmy. "Oh, no, no," Jimmy quickly said. "I was busy hosing down the boat. I just said approximately. Want to count?"

"I can't count past twenty-seven."

"I'll help you," said Alexander. Taking out the lobsters one by one, he let Anthony count them until he got to ten, and then carefully, so as not to break their claws, placed them in large blue transfer totes.

At last Alexander said to Anthony, "One hundred and two."

"You see?" said Jimmy. "Four for you, Anthony. That leaves ninety-eight for me. And they're all perfect, as big as can be, right around a five-inch carapace—which means shell, bud. We'll get 75 cents a piece for them. Your dad is going to make me almost seventy-five dollars today. Yes," he said, "because of your dad, I can finally make a living." He glanced at Tatiana, standing a necessary distance away from the spillage of the boat. She smiled politely; Jimmy nodded curtly and didn't smile back.

As the buyers started to pour in from the fish market, from the general store, from the seafood restaurants as far away as Bar Harbor, Alexander washed and cleaned the boat, cleaned the traps, rolled up the line, and went down dock to buy three barrels of bait herring for the next day, which he placed into bags and lowered them into the water. The herring catch was good today, he had enough to bait 150 lobster traps for tomorrow.

He got paid ten dollars for the day's work, and was scrubbing his hands with industrial-strength soap under the water spout when Jimmy came up to him. "Want to wait with me and sell these?" He pointed to the lobsters. "I'll pay you another two dollars for the evening. After, we can go for a drink."

"Can't, Jimmy. But thanks. Maybe another time."

Jimmy glanced at Tatiana, all sunny and white, and turned away.

They walked up the hill to the house.

Alexander went to take a bath, to shave, to shear his hair, while Tatiana, placing the lobsters in the refrigerator to numb them, boiled the water. Lobsters were the easiest thing to cook, 10–15 minutes in salted boiling water. They were delicious to eat, breaking the claws, taking the meat out, dipping them in melted butter. But sometimes she did think that she would rather spend two dollars on a lobster in a store once a month than have Alexander spend thirteen hours on a boat every day and get four lobsters for free. Didn't seem so free. Before he was out of the bathroom, she stood outside the door, knocked carefully and said, "You need anything?"

There was quiet inside. She knocked louder. The door opened, and he towered in front of her, all fresh and shaved and scrubbed and dressed. He was wearing a clean green jersey and fatigues. She cleared her throat and lowered her gaze. Barefoot she stood with her lips level with his heart. "Need anything?" she repeated in a whisper, feeling so vulnerable she was having trouble breathing.

"I'm fine," he said, walking sideways past her. "Let's eat."

They had the lobsters with melted butter, and carrot, onion and potato stew. Alexander ate three lobsters, most of the stew, bread, butter. Tatiana had found him emaciated in Germany. He ate for two men now, but he was still war thin. She ladled food onto his plate, filled his glass. He drank a beer, water, a Coke. They ate quietly in the little kitchen, which the landlady allowed them to use as long as they were either done by seven or made dinner for her, too. They were done by seven, *and* Tatiana left some stew for her.

"Alexander, does your . . . chest hurt?"

"No, it's fine."

"It felt a little pulpy last night . . ." She looked away, remembering touching it. "It's not healed yet, and you're doing all that trap hauling. I don't want it to get reinfected. Perhaps I should put some carbolic acid on it."

"I'm fine."

"Maybe a new dressing?"

He didn't say anything, just raised his eyes to her, and for a moment between them, from his bronze-colored eyes to her sea-green passed *Berlin, and the room at the U.S. Embassy where they had spent what they both were certain was their last night on earth, when she stitched together his shredded pectoral and wept, and he sat like a stone and looked through her—much like now. He said to her then, "We never had a future."*

Tatiana looked away first—she always looked away first—and got up.

Alexander went outside to sit in the chair in front of the house on the hill overlooking the bay. Anthony tagged along behind him. Alexander sat mutely and motionlessly, while Anthony milled about the overgrown yard, picking up rocks, pine cones, looking for worms, for beetles, for ladybugs.

"You won't find any ladybugs, son. Season for them's in June," said Alexander.

"Ah," said Anthony. "Then what's this?"

Tilting over to one side, Alexander looked. "I can't see it."

Anthony came closer.

"Still can't see it."

Anthony came closer, his hand out, the index finger with the ladybug extended.

Alexander's face was inches away from the ladybug. "Hmm. Still can't see it."

Anthony looked at the ladybug, looked at his father and then slowly, shyly climbed into his lap and showed him again.

"Well, well," said Alexander, both hands going around the boy. "Now I see it. I sit corrected. You were right. Ladybugs in August. Who knew?"

"Did you ever see ladybugs, Dad?"

Alexander was quiet. "A long time ago, near a city called Moscow."

"In the . . . Soviet Union?"

"Yes."

"They have ladybugs there?"

"They *had* ladybugs—until we ate them all."

Anthony was wide-eyed.

"There was nothing else to eat," said Alexander.

"Anthony, your father is just joking with you," said Tatiana, walking out, wiping her wet hands on a tea towel. "He is trying to be funny."

Anthony peered into Alexander's face. "*That* was funny?"

"Tania," Alexander said in a far away voice. "I can't get up. Can you get my cigarettes for me?"

She left quickly and came out with them. Since there was only one chair and nowhere for her to sit, she placed the cigarette in

Alexander's mouth and, bending over him, her hand on his shoulder, lit it for him while Anthony placed the bug into Alexander's palm.

"Dad, don't eat this ladybug." One of his little arms went around Alexander's neck.

"I won't, son. I'm full."

"*That's* funny," said Anthony. "Mama and I met a man today. A colonel. Nick Moore."

"Oh, yeah?" Alexander looked off into the distance, taking another deep drag of the cigarette from Tatiana's hands as she was bent to him. "What was he like?"

"He was like you, Dad," Anthony replied. "He was just like you."

Red Nail Polish

In the middle of the night, the boy woke up and screamed. Tatiana went to comfort him. He calmed down, but would not let her leave him alone in his bed, even though it was just across the nightstand. "Alexander," she whispered, "are you awake?"

"I am now," he said, getting up. Moving the nightstand out of the way, he pushed the two twin beds together so Anthony could lie next to his mother. They tried to get comfortable, Alexander against the wall spooning Tatiana spooning Anthony, who instantly fell asleep in his mother's arms. Tatiana only pretended to fall back to sleep. She knew that in a moment Alexander would get up and leave the bed.

And in a moment, he was gone. She whispered after him. *Shura, darling.* After a few minutes, she got up, put on a robe and walked outside. He wasn't in the kitchen or the yard. She looked for him all the way down to the dock. Alexander was sitting on the bench where Tatiana usually sat waiting for him to come back from the sea. She saw the flare of the cigarette in his mouth. He was naked except for his skivvies, and he was shivering. His arms were crossed over himself, and his body was rocking back and forth.

She stopped walking.

She didn't know what to do.

She never did know what to do.

Turning around, she stumbled back to their room and lay in bed blinkless, staring beyond Anthony's sleeping head until Alexander came back, icy and shaking, and fitted in behind her. She didn't move and he said nothing, made no noise. Just his cold arm went around her. They lay there until four when he got up to go to work. As he ground the coffee beans in the pestle, she buttered a fresh roll for him, filled his water containers and made a sandwich for him to take on the boat. He ate, drank his coffee, and then left, his free hand traveling under her chemise for a moment to rest on her bare buttocks and then between her legs.

They had been on Deer Isle exactly five minutes, breathing in the salt water of the afternoon and seeing the lobster boats returning to shore, and already Tatiana said that a month would not be long enough to spend here. Their agreement was just a month in every state and then onward. Forty-eight states, forty-eight months, beginning with Deer Isle. "A month won't be enough here," she repeated when Alexander said nothing.

"Really?" And nothing more.

"You don't think it's great here?"

A small ironic something crossed his silent mouth in reply.

On the surface, Stonington had everything they needed: a general store, a variety store, a hardware store. The general store sold newspapers, magazines and, most important, cigarettes. It also sold coffee beans and chocolate. On North and South Deer Isle, there were cows—thus milk, cheese and butter—and chickens that laid eggs. Grain was shipped in by the shipload. There was plenty of bread. Plenty of apples, peaches, pears, corn, tomatoes, cucumbers, onions, carrots, turnips, radishes, eggplant, zucchini. There was cheap and plentiful lobster, trout, sea bass, pike. There even was beef and chicken, not that they ever ate it. Who'd ever believe the country had been through a Depression and a world war?

Alexander said ten dollars a day wouldn't be enough to live on.

Tatiana said it would be plenty.

"What about high-heeled shoes? Dresses for you? Coffee? My cigarettes?"

"Definitely not enough for cigarettes." She forced a smile, seeing his face. "I'm joking. It's enough for everything."

She didn't want to mention that the amount he was spending on cigarettes was nearly what they were spending on food for the week for all three of them. But Alexander was the only one working. He could spend his money on whatever he liked.

She had been talking English to him as she drank her Sunday coffee. He was responding in Russian to her as he smoked his Sunday cigarettes and read his Sunday paper.

"There's trouble brewing in Indochina," he said in Russian. "The French owned it, and lost it to the Japanese during the war. The Japanese lost the war, but they don't want to leave. The French, rescued by the victors and thus on the side of victory, want their colony back. The Japanese are protesting. While staying neutral, the U.S. are helping their ally France, but they're really between a rock and a hard place since they're also helping Japan."

"I thought Japan is no longer allowed to have an army?" Tatiana asked in English.

And he replied in Russian, "They're not. But they had a standing army in Indochina, and short of the U.S. forcing them out, the Japanese refuse to lay down their arms."

She asked in English, "What's your interest in all this?"

He replied in Russian, "Ah. In all this—because there just isn't enough trouble—Stalin for decades has been courting a peasant farmer named Ho Chi Minh, paying for his little educational trips to Moscow, feeding him vodka and caviar, teaching him the Marxist dialectic by the warm fire and giving him some old Shpagins and mortars, and some nice American Lend-Lease Studebakers while training and educating his little band of Vietminh right on Soviet soil."

"Training the Vietminh to fight the Japanese whom the Soviets fought and hate?"

"Believe it or not, no. To fight the former Soviet allies, the colonial French. Ironic?" Alexander stubbed out his cigarette, put down his paper. "Where's Anthony?" he said in a low voice in English, but before he could even reach for her wrist, Anthony walked into the kitchen.

"I'm here, Dad," he said. "What?"

They needed a room for just themselves, but Anthony didn't think so, and besides, the old landlady didn't have one. The choice was one tiny room next to the kitchen in a vertical house overlooking the bay—with two twin beds, and a bath and toilet down the hall—or their camper with one full bed, and no bath and no toilet.

They had looked at other houses. One had a family of five living in it. One had a family of three. One a family of seven, all women. Generations and generations of women, filling up the white houses, and old men going out on the boats during the day. And younger men—sometimes whole, sometimes not—trickling back from war.

Mrs. Brewster lived alone. Her only son was not back, though Tatiana didn't think he was out with the troops. Something in the way the old lady said, *oh he had to go away for a little while*. She was sixty-six years old and had been a widow for forty-eight of them: her husband died in the Spanish-American War.

"In *1898*?" Tatiana whispered to Alexander.

He shrugged. His heavy hand was squeezing her shoulder, telling her he didn't much like Mrs. Brewster, but Tatiana was happy to have his hand on her in any capacity. "This is your husband, right?" Mrs. Brewster had said suspiciously before she rented out the rooms to them. "He's not just some . . ." She waved her hand around. "Because I won't have that in my house."

Alexander stood mute. The three-year-old said, "Have what?"

The landlady narrowed her eyes at Anthony. "This your father, boy?"

"Yes," said Anthony. "He is a soldier. He was in a war *and* in prison."

"Yeah," said Mrs. Brewster, looking away. "Prison's hard." Then she narrowed her eyes at Tatiana. "So where's your accent from? Doesn't sound American to me."

Anthony began to say, "Russ—" but Alexander pulled his son behind him, pulled Tatiana behind him. "Are you going to rent us the room or not?"

She rented them the room.

But now Alexander asked Tatiana, "Why did we buy the Nomad if we're not going to stay in it? We might as well sell it. What a waste of money."

What would they do when they got to the deserts of the west? she wanted to know. To the wine hills of California? To Hell's Canyon in Idaho? Despite his sudden frugality, Alexander didn't sell the camper, the dream of it still so fresh. But this was the thing about him: though Tatiana knew he liked the *idea* of the camper— he was the one who wanted to buy it—he didn't particularly like the reality of it.

Tatiana got the impression he felt that way about a number of things in his new civilian life.

The camper had no running water. And Alexander never stopped washing one part or another of his body. Living too close for too many years to men at war had done this to him. He washed his hands obsessively; true, much of the time they had fish on them, but there wasn't enough soap or lemons and vinegar in all of Maine to get Alexander's hands clean enough for his liking. They had to pay Mrs. Brewster an extra five dollars a week for all the water they were using.

He may have liked the idea of a son, but the reality of a three-year-old boy being with them every waking moment, never leaving his mother's side, sleeping in the same room with them! coming into bed with them at night! was too much for a soldier who had never been around children.

"Nightmares are hard for a little boy," Tatiana explained.

"I understand," he said, so polite.

Alexander may have once liked the idea of a wife, but the reality of one, Tatiana wasn't so sure about either. Maybe he was looking for Lazarevo in every day that they lived, though from the way he acted, she fully expected him to say, "What's Lazarevo?"

His eyes, once like caramel, were now hard copper, nothing liquid or flowing in them. He turned his polite face to her, and she turned her polite face back. He wanted quiet, she was quiet. He wanted funny, she tried funny. He wanted food, she gave him plenty. He wanted to go for a walk, she was ready. He wanted newspapers, magazines, cigarettes, she brought them all. He wanted to sit mutely in his chair; she sat mutely on the ground by his side. Anything he wanted, she was ready at any moment to give him.

Now, in the middle of a sunny afternoon, Tatiana stood barefoot in front of the mirror in a yellow, slightly sheer muslin dress, a peasant-girl dress, appraising, assessing, obsessing.

She stood with her hair down. Her face was scrubbed, her teeth were clean and white. The summer freckles on her nose and cheeks were the color of malt sugar, her green eyes sparkled. She rubbed cocoa butter into her hands to make them softer in case he wanted to take her hand as they walked down to Main Street after dinner. She rubbed a bit of musk oil behind her ears, in case he bent to her. She put some gloss on her sulky lips and pressed them together to make them softer, pinker. She stood, looked, thought. Smiled a nice fake smile to make the lips less sulky, and sighed. A little bit of this, a little bit of that.

Her hands went inside her dress and cupped her breasts. Her nipples hardened. Ever since Anthony was born, her body had changed. That, and the American food—all those nutrients. The post-nursing, American-fed breasts hadn't lost their weightiness, their full-bodied heartiness. The few bras Tatiana owned were all too loose around and made her jiggle. Instead of a bra, Tatiana sometimes wore tight white vests, tight enough to restrain her breasts, which tended to sway when she walked, attracting the eyes of men. Not her husband, necessarily, but other men, like the milk boy.

She slowly lifted up her dress to see her slim rounded hips in the mirror, her smooth belly. She was slight, but everything on her seemed to have been curved by Anthony's birth—as if she stopped being a girl at the point of his entry into the world.

But it was the girl-child with breasts that the soldier man with the rifle on his back had once crossed the street for.

She pulled down her sheer panties to see her patch of blonde hair. She touched herself, trying to imagine what he might have felt once when touching her. Seeing something in the mirror, she looked closer, then bent her head to look at her legs. On the insides of her thighs were small fresh bruises—thumbprints from his hands.

Seeing them gave Tatiana a liquid throb in her loins, and she straightened out, adjusted herself and, with a flushed face, started brushing out her hair, debating what to do with it. Alexander had never seen her hair this length before, down to the small of her back. She thought he would like it, but distressingly he seemed indifferent to it. She knew the color and texture of the hair weren't quite normal. She had colored it black eight months ago, before she went to Europe, then painstakingly leached the black out of it last month in Hamburg, and now the hair was dry and limp. It wasn't silk anymore. Is that why he wasn't touching it? She didn't know what to do about it.

She put it into its usual braid, leaving the fronts out and the tuft long in the back, threading the braid with a yellow satin ribbon, in case he touched the hair. Then she called for Anthony, who was outside playing with dirt, and cleaned him, making sure his shorts and shirt weren't stained, pulling up his socks. "Why do you play with dirt, Anthony, right before we go see Daddy? You know you have to be tidy for him." Alexander liked order in his wife and son when they came to meet him at the docks. She knew he liked how neat they looked, how put-together, how summery. The flowers in Stonington were breathtaking, the tall shimmering lupines purple and blue; she and Anthony had picked some earlier and now Tatiana put some in her hair, the purple, like lilac, to contrast with the hair, like gold, because once he had liked that, too.

She studied her fingernails to make sure there was nothing

underneath them. They both hated dirty fingernails. Now that Tatiana stopped working—and Alexander was with her—she kept her nails a little longer, because, though he never said anything, he wordlessly responded to the light back and forth of her nails on him. Today she had a few minutes and painted them red.

He said nothing that day about the nails. (Or the lilac lupines, the satin in the hair, the lips, the hips, the dress, the breasts, the sheer white panties.) The next day he said, "They sell such dazzling nail polish at the Stonington store?"

"I don't know. I brought this one with me."

He was quiet so long, she thought he hadn't heard her. And then: "Well, that must've been nice for all the invalids at NYU."

Ah, some participation. Not great—but a start. What to say to that, though? *Oh, it wasn't for the invalids.* She knew it was a trap, a code for, *since nurses aren't allowed to wear nail polish, what'd you have nail polish for, Tania?*

Later that evening at the kitchen table, she took the polish off with acetone. When he saw it was gone, he said, "Hmm. So other invalids rate the red nails but not me?"

She lifted her eyes at him standing over her. "Are you joking?" she said, the tips of her fingers beginning to tremble.

"Of course," he said, without a glimmer of a smile.

Tatiana threw away her red New York nail polish, her flirty postwar ruched and pleated New York dresses, her high-heeled New York greenbelt brilliant Ferragamo shoes. Something happened to him when he saw her in New York things. What's the matter, she would ask, and he would reply that nothing was the matter, and that would be *all* he'd reply. So she threw them *all* out and bought herself a yellow muslin dress, a floral chintz dress, a white cotton sheath, a blue wrap dress—from Maine. Alexander still said nothing, but was less quiet. Now he talked to her of other things, like Ho Chi Minh and his band of warriors.

She tried, *tried* to be funny with him like before. "Hey, do you want to hear a joke?"

"Sure, tell me a joke." They were walking up a Stonington hill behind a huffing Anthony.

"A man prayed for years to go to paradise. Once, going up a narrow path in the mountains he stumbled and fell into the precipice. By a miracle he grasped some sickly bush and started crying: 'Anybody here? Please, help! Anybody here?'

"After some minutes of silence the voice answered: 'I am here.'

"'Who are *you*?'

"'I am God.'

"'If you are God, then do something!'

"'Look, you asked me for so long to be brought to paradise. Just unclench your hands—and immediately you will find yourself in paradise.'

"After a small silence the man cried: 'Anybody ELSE here? Please—help!'"

To say that Alexander didn't laugh at that joke would have been to understate matters.

Tatiana's hands trembled whenever she thought of him. She trembled all day long. She walked through Stonington as if she were sleepwalking, stiff, unnatural. She bent to her son, she straightened up, she adjusted her dress, she fixed her hair. The churning inside her stomach did not abate.

Tatiana tried to be bolder with him, less afraid of him.

He wouldn't kiss her in front of Jimmy, or the other fishermen, or anybody. Sometimes in the evenings, as they walked down Main Street and looked inside the shops, he would buy her some chocolate, and she would turn up her face to thank him, and he would kiss her on the forehead. The forehead!

One evening Tatiana got tired of it and, jumping up on the bench, flung her arms around him. "Enough with the head," she said, and kissed him full on his lips.

His one hand on the cigarette, the other on Anthony's ice cream, he couldn't do more than press against her. "Get down," he said quietly, kissing her back, without ardor. "What's gotten into you?"

Ladies and gentlemen of the jury, I give you man o' war!

Alone with Anthony, in their daily wanderings up and down the hills of Stonington, Tatiana made friends with the women who ran the stores and the boys who brought the milk. She befriended a farm woman in her thirties up on Eastern Road, whose husband, a naval officer, was still in Japan. Every day Nellie cleaned the house, weeded the front garden and waited for him on the bench outside, which is how Tatiana met her, just skipping by with her son. After talking to her for two minutes, Tatiana felt so sad for the woman, viscerally remembering grieving for Alexander, that she asked Nellie if she needed help with the farm. Nellie had an acre of potatoes and tomatoes and cucumbers. Tatiana knew something about these things.

Nellie gladly agreed, saying she could pay Tatiana two dollars a day from her husband's army check. "It's all I can afford," she said. "When my husband comes back I'll be able to pay you more."

But the war ended a year ago, and there was still no news of him. Tatiana said not to worry.

Over coffee, Nellie opened up a little. "What if he comes back and I won't know how to talk to him? We were married such a short time before he went to fight. What if we find out we're complete strangers?"

Tatiana shook her lowered head. She knew something about these things too.

"So when did *your* husband come back?" Nellie asked with envy.

"A month ago."

"So lucky."

Anthony said, "Dad didn't come back. Dad was never coming back. Mama left me to go find him."

Nellie stared dully at Anthony.

"Anthony, go play outside for a minute. Let Nellie and me finish up." Tatiana ruffled Anthony's hair and ushered him outside. "Kids these days. You teach them to speak and look what they do. I don't even know what he's talking about."

That evening Anthony told Alexander that Mama got a job. Alexander asked Anthony questions, and Anthony, happy to be asked, told his father about Nellie and her potatoes and tomatoes and cucumbers, and her husband who wasn't there, and how Nellie ought to go and find him, "just like Mama went and found you."

Alexander stopped asking questions. All he said after dinner was, "I thought you said we were going to be all right on ten dollars a day."

"It's just for Anthony. For his candy, his ice cream."

"No. I'll work at night. If I help sell the lobsters, it's another two dollars."

"No!" Tatiana quickly lowered her voice. "You work plenty. You do plenty. No. Anthony and I play all day anyway."

"That's good," he said. "Play."

"We'll have time for everything. He and I will be happy to help her. And besides," said Tatiana, "she is so lonely."

Alexander turned away. Tatiana turned away.

The next day Alexander came back from the boat and said, "Tell Nellie to stuff her two dollars. Jimmy and I worked out a deal. If I catch him over a hundred and fifty legal lobsters, he'll pay me an extra five dollars. And then five more for every fifty legals above one fifty. What do you think?"

Tatiana thought about it. "How many traps on your trawl?"

"Ten."

"At two legal lobsters per trap . . . twenty at most per trawl . . . one trawl an hour, hauling them up, throwing most of them back . . . it's not enough."

"When it comes to me," he said, "aren't you turning into a nice little capitalist."

"You've sold yourself short, Alexander," Tatiana said to him. "Like a lobster."

Jimmy must have known it, too—the market price for lobsters increasing, and Alexander receiving many job offers from other boats—because he changed the terms without even being asked, giving Alexander five dollars extra for every *fifty* legals above the first fifty. At night Alexander was too tired to hold a glass of beer in his hands.

Tatiana marinated Nellie's tomatoes, made Nellie potato soup, tried to make tomato sauce. Tatiana had learned to make very good tomato sauce from her friends in Little Italy, almost as if she were Italian herself. She wanted to make Alexander tomato sauce, just like his Italian mother used to make, but needed garlic, and no one had garlic on Deer Isle.

Tatiana missed New York, the boisterous teeming marketplace of the Saturday morning Lower East Side, her joyous best friend Vikki, her work at Ellis Island, the hospital. The guilt of it stung her in the chest—longing for the old life she could not live without Alexander.

Tatiana worked in the fields by herself while Nellie minded Anthony. It took her a week to dig up Nellie's entire field—one hundred and fifty bushels of potatoes. Nellie could not believe there was so much. Tatiana negotiated a deal with the general store for 50 cents a bushel, and made Nellie seventy-five dollars. Nellie was thrilled. After twelve hours on the boat, Alexander helped Tatiana carry all hundred and fifty bushels to the store. At the end of the week, Nellie still paid Tatiana only two dollars a day.

When Alexander heard this, his voice lost its even keel for a moment. "You made her seventy-five dollars, we carried all the fucking bushels down the hill for her, and your so called *friend* still only paid you your daily wage?"

"Shh . . . don't . . ." She didn't want Anthony to hear the soldier-speak, kept so carefully under wraps these days.

"Maybe you're not such a good capitalist after all, Tania."

"She has no money. She doesn't make a hundred dollars a day like that Jimmy does off you. But you know what she did offer us? To move in with her. She has two extra bedrooms in her house. We could have them free of charge and just pay her for the water and electric."

"What's the catch?"

"No catch."

"There's a catch. I hear it in your voice."

"Nothing." She twittered her thumbs. "She just said that when her husband came back, we'd have to go."

Across the table, Alexander stared at Tatiana inscrutably, then got up and took his own plate to the sink.

Tatiana's hands trembled as she washed the dishes. She didn't want to make him upset. No, perhaps that was not quite true. Perhaps she wanted to make him *something*. He was so exceedingly polite, so exceptionally courteous! When she asked him for help, he was right there. He carried the cursed potatoes, he took the trash to the dump. But his mind was not on the potatoes, on the trash. When he sat and smoked and watched the water, Tatiana didn't know where he was. When he went outside at three in the morning and convulsed on the bench, Tatiana wished she didn't know where he was. Where was she within him? She didn't want to know.

When she was done clearing up, she came outside to sit on the gravel by his feet. She felt him looking at her. She looked up. "Tania . . ." Alexander whispered. But Anthony saw his mother on the ground and instantly planted himself on her lap, displayed for her the four beetles he had found, two of them fighting stag beetles. When she glanced up at Alexander, he wasn't looking at her anymore.

After Anthony was asleep and they were in their twin bed, she whispered, "So do you want to—move in with Nellie?" The bed was so narrow, they could sleep only on their sides. On his back Alexander took up the whole mattress.

"Move in until her husband comes back and she kicks us out because *she* might actually want some privacy with the man who's back from war?" Alexander said.

"Are you . . . angry?" she asked, as in, *please be angry.*

"Of course not."

"We'll have more privacy at her house. She's got two rooms for us. Better than the one here."

"Really? Better?" Alexander said. "Here we're by the sea. I get to sit and smoke and look at the bay. Nellie's on Eastern Road, where we'll just be smelling the salt and the fish. And Mrs. Brewster is deaf. Do you think Nellie is deaf? Having Nellie at our bedroom door with her young hearing and her five years without a husband, do you think that would spell more privacy for us? Although," he said, "do you think there could be *less* privacy?"

Yes, Tatiana wanted to say. Yes. In my communal apartment in Leningrad, where I lived in two rooms with Babushka, Deda, Mama, Papa, my sister, Dasha—remember her?—with my brother, Pasha—remember him? Where the toilet down the hall through the kitchen near the stairs never flushed properly and was never cleaned, and was shared by nine other apartment dwellers. Where there was no hot water for four baths a day, and no gas stove for four lobsters. Where I slept in the same bed with my sister until I was seventeen and she was twenty-four, until the night you took us to the Road of Life. Tatiana barely suppressed her agonized groan.

She could not—would not—she *refused* to think of Leningrad.

The other way was better. Yes, the other way—without ever speaking.

This bloodletting went on every night. During the day they kept busy, just how they liked it, just how they needed it. Not so long ago Alexander and Tatiana had found each other in another country and then somehow they lived through the war and made it to lupine Deer Isle, neither of them having any idea how, but for three o'clock in the morning, when Anthony woke up and screamed as if he were being cut open, and Alexander convulsed on the bench, and Tatiana thrashed to forget—and then they knew how.

Tainted with the Gulag

He had such an unfailing way with her. "Would you like some more?" he would say, lifting the pitcher of lemonade.

"Yes, please."

"Would you like to take a walk after dinner? I heard they're selling something called Italian ices by the bay."

"Yes, that would be nice."

"Ant, what do you think?"

"Let's go. Let's go now."

"Well, wait a second, son. Your mother and I have to finish up."
So formal. *Mother.*

He opened doors for her, he got jars and cans for her off the
high shelves in the kitchen. It was so handy him being tall; he
was like a step stool.

And she? She did what she always did—for him first. She cooked
for him, brought the food to his plate and served him. She poured
his drink. She set and cleared his table. She washed his clothes,
she folded them. She made their little beds and put clean sheets
on them. She made him lunch for the boat, and extra for Jimmy
too, because one-handed Jimmy didn't have a woman to make
him a sandwich. She shaved her legs for him, and bathed every
day for him, and put satin ribbons in her hair for him.

"Is there anything else you would like?" she asked him. Can I
get you something? Would you like another beer? Would you like
the first section of the newspaper or the second? Would you
like to go swimming? Perhaps raspberry picking? Are you cold?
Are you tired? Have you had enough, Alexander? Have—you—
had—enough?

"Yes, thank you."

Or . . .

"No, I'll have some more, thanks."

So courteous. So polite. Straight from the Edith Wharton novels
Tania had read during the time of his absence from her life. *The
Age of Innocence* or *The House of Mirth* (ironic).

There were times when Alexander wasn't unfailingly polite.

Like one particular afternoon when there was no wind and
Jimmy was hung over—or was it when Jimmy was hung over and
there was no wind? In any case, Alexander had returned early
when she wasn't expecting him and came looking for her when
she was still in Nellie's potato fields. Anthony was inside the house,
having milk with Nellie. Tatiana, her hands grimy from the earth,
her face flushed, her hair in tangles, stood up in the field to greet
him in her sleeveless chintz summer dress, tight in the torso, slim
down the hips, open down the neckline. "Hey," she said with happy
surprise. "What are you doing back so early?"

He didn't speak. He kissed her, and this time it wasn't calm and it wasn't without ardor. Tatiana didn't even have a chance to raise her hands in surrender. He took her deep in the fields, on the ground, covered in potato leaves, the dress becoming as grimy as her hands. The only foreplay was his yanking the dress off her shoulders to bare her breasts to his massive hands and pulling the dress up over her hips.

"Look what you did," she whispered afterward.

"You look like a peasant milkmaid in that dress."

"Dress is ruined now."

"We'll wash it." He was still panting but already distant.

Tatiana leaned to him, murmuring softly, looking into his face, trying to catch his eye, hoping for intimacy. "Does the captain *like* his wife to look like a peasant milkmaid?"

"Well, obviously." But the captain was already getting up, straightening himself out, giving her his hand to help her off the ground.

Since Alexander came back, Tatiana had become fixated on his hands, and on her own by contrast. His hands were like the platter on which he carried his life. They were large and broad, dark and square, with heavy palms and heavy thumbs, but with long thick flexible fingers—as if he could play the piano as well as haul lobster trawls. They were knuckled and veined, and the palms were calloused. Everything was calloused, even the fingertips, roughened by carrying heavy weapons over thousands of miles, hardened by fighting, burning, logging, burying men. His hands reflected all manner of eternal struggles. You didn't need to be a soothsayer, or a psychic or a palmreader, you needed not a single glance at the lines in the palms but just one cursory look at the hands and you knew instantly: the man they belonged to had done everything—and was capable of anything.

And then take Tatiana and *her* own square hands. Among other things, her hands had worked in a weapons factory, they had made bombs and tanks and flamethrowers, worked the fields, mopped floors, dug holes in snow and in the ground. They had pulled sleds along the ice. They had taken care of dead men, of wounded men, of dying men; her hands had known life, and strife—yet *they* looked like they soaked in milk all day. They were tiny, unblemished, uncalloused, unknuckled, unveined, palms light, fingers slender. She was embarrassed by them—they were soft and delicate like a child's hands. One would conclude that her hands had never done a day's work in their life—and *couldn't*!

And now, in the middle of the afternoon, after touching her

in places unsuitable to the genteel propriety of Nellie's cultivated
potato fields, Alexander gave her his enormous dark hand to help
her off the ground, and her white one disappeared into his warm
fist as he pulled her to her feet.

"Thank you."

"Thank you."

When they first got to Deer Isle, in the evenings, after Anthony
was finally asleep, they climbed up the steep hill to where their
Nomad was parked off road near the woods. Once inside,
Alexander took the clothes off her—he insisted she be bare for
him—though most of the time he did not undress himself,
leaving on his T-shirt or his sleeveless tank. Tatiana asked once.
Don't you want to undress, too? He said no. She didn't ask again.
He kissed her; with his hands he touched her to soften her; but
never said a word. He never called her name. He would kiss her,
clasp her body to him, present himself to her eager mouth—
sometimes too forcefully, though she didn't mind—and then he
would deliver himself unto her. She moaned, she couldn't help
herself, and there had once been a time when he lived for her
moaning. He himself never made a sound anymore, not before,
not during, and not even at the end. He aspirated at the end;
made an H. Sometimes not even a capital H.

Many things were gone from them. Alexander didn't use his
mouth on her anymore, or whisper all manner of remarkable things
to her anymore, or caress her from top to bottom, or turn the
kerosene light on—or even open his eyes.

Shura. Naked in the Nomad was the only time in their new life
Tatiana called him by that beloved diminutive now. Sometimes she
felt as if he wanted to put his hands to his ears so he wouldn't
hear her. It was dark in the camper, so dark; there was never light
to see anything. And he wore his clothes. *Shura. I can't believe I'm
touching you again.*

There were no Edith Wharton novels in the camper, no *Age of
Innocence*. He took her until she had nothing more to give, but still
he took her until there was nothing.

"Soldier, darling, I'm here," Tatiana would whisper, her arms
opened, stretched out to him in helplessness, in surrender.

"I'm here, too," Alexander would say, not whispering, getting
up, getting dressed. "Let's go back downhill. I hope Anthony is
still sleeping." That was the afterglow. Him giving her his hand to
help her up.

She was defenseless, she was starved herself, she was open. She would give it to him any way he needed it, but still . . .

Oh, it didn't matter. Just that there was something so soldierly and unhusbandly about how silently and rapaciously Alexander needed to still the cries of war.

Near tears one night, she asked him what was the matter with him—with *them*—and he replied, "You have become tainted with the Gulag." And then they were interrupted by a child's maniacal screams from down below. Already dressed Alexander ran.

"Mama! Mama!"

Old Mrs. Brewster had trotted into his room, but she only terrified Anthony more.

"MAMA! MAMA!"

Alexander held him, but Anthony didn't want anyone but his mother.

And when she ran in, he didn't want her either. He hit her, he turned away from her. He was hysterical. It took her over an hour to calm him down. At four Alexander got up to go to work, and after that night Tatiana and Alexander stopped going to the camper. It stood abandoned in the clearing up the hill between the trees as they, both clothed, and in silence, with a pillow or his lips or his hand over her mouth to stifle her moaning, danced the tango of life, the tango of death, the tango of the Gulag, creaking every desperate bedspring in the twin bed across from Anthony's restless sleeping.

They tried to come together during the day when the boy wasn't looking. Trouble was, he was always looking. By the end of long napless Sundays, Alexander was mute with impatience and discontent.

One late Sunday afternoon Anthony was supposed to be in the front yard playing with bugs. Tatiana was supposed to be cooking dinner, Alexander was supposed to be reading the newspaper, but what he was actually doing was sitting beneath her billowing skirts on the narrow wooden chair that leaned against the wall of the kitchen, and she was standing astride him. They were panting, her legs were shaking; he was supporting her shifting weight with his hands on her hips, moving her in spasms. Near the moment of Tatiana's greatest distress, Anthony walked into the kitchen.

"Mama?"

Tatiana's mouth opened in a tortured O. Alexander whispered *Shh*. She held her breath, unable to turn around, overwhelmed by the stillness, the hardness, the fullness of him so thoroughly inside her. She dug her long nails into Alexander's shoulders and tried not to *scream*, and all the while Anthony stood behind his mother.

"Anthony," said Alexander, his voice almost calm. "Can you give us a minute? Go outside. Mommy will be right there."

"That man, Nick, is in his yard again. He wants a cigarette."

"Mom'll be right there, bud. Go outside."

"Mama?"

But Tatiana could not turn around, could not speak.

"Go outside, Anthony!" said Alexander.

In the short term, Anthony left, Tatiana took a breath, Alexander took her to the bedroom, barricaded the door, and resolved them, but in the long term she didn't know what to do.

One thing they *didn't* do is talk about it.

"Would you like some more bread, some more wine, Alexander?" she would ask with open hands.

"Yes, thank you, Tatiana," he would reply with lowered head.

The Captain, the Colonel, and the Nurse

"Dad, can I come on the boat with you?" Anthony turned his face up to his father, sitting next to him at the breakfast table.

"No, bud. It's dangerous on a lobster boat for a little boy."

Tatiana studied them both, listening, absorbing.

"I'm not little. I'm big. And I'll be good. I promise. I'll help."

"No, bud."

Tatiana cleared her throat. "Alexander, if I come, um, *I* can look after Ant."

"Jimmy's never had a woman on his boat before, Tania. He'll have a heart attack."

"No, you're right, of course. Ant, you want some more oatmeal?"

Anthony's head remained down as he ate his breakfast.

Sometimes the wind was good, and sometimes it wasn't. Windward, leeward, when there was no wind, it was difficult to trawl, despite Jimmy's valiant efforts to set the sail. With just the two of them on the boat, Alexander loosened the staysail and while the sloop floated in the Atlantic, they sat and had a smoke.

Jimmy said, "Good God, man, why do you always wear that shirt down to your wrists? You must be dying of heat. Roll it up. Take it off."

And Alexander said, "Jimmy, man, forget about my shirt, why don't you get yourself a new boat? You'd make a heap more money. I know this was your old man's, but do yourself a favor, invest in a fucking boat."

"I got no money for a new boat."

"Borrow it from a bank. They're bending over backwards to help men get on their feet after the war. Get a fifteen-year boat mortgage. With the money you'll make, you'll pay it back in two years."

Jimmy got excited. Suddenly he said, "Go halves with me."

"What?"

"It'll be *our* boat. And we'll split the profits."

"Jimmy, I—"

Jimmy jumped up, spilling his beer. "We'll get another deckhand, another 12-trap trawl; we'll get a 1300-gallon live tank. You're right, we'll make a heap."

"Jimmy, wait—you have the wrong idea. We're not staying here." Alexander sat with the cigarette dangling from his fingers.

Jimmy became visibly upset. "Why would you be leaving? She likes it here, you keep saying so. You're working, the boy's doing all right. Why would you go?"

Alexander put the cigarette back in his mouth.

"You'll have the winters off to do what you want."

Alexander shook his head.

Jimmy raised his voice. "So why'd you get a job if you were just going to raise anchor in a month?"

"I got a job because I need work. What are we going to live on, *your* good graces?"

"I haven't worked full time like this since before the war." Jimmy spat. "What am I going to do after you leave?"

"Plenty of men are coming back now," Alexander said. "You'll get someone else. I'm sorry, Jim."

Jimmy turned away and started untying the rope from the stay-sail. "Just great." He didn't look at Alexander. "But tell me, who else is going to work like you?"

That evening, as Alexander was sitting in his chair, showing Anthony how to tie a hitch knot through the marlinspike in his hands while they were waiting for Tatiana to go for their evening walk, there was shouting, and what was unusual this time was that a male voice was participating.

Tatiana came out.

"Mama, do you hear? He's fighting back!"

"I hear, son." She exchanged a glance with Alexander. "You two ready?"

They walked out the gate and started slowly down the road—all of them trying to hear the words instead of just the raised voices.

"Odd, no?" Alexander said. "The colonel arguing."

"Yes," Tatiana said in the tone of someone who was saying, *isn't it fantastic.*

He glanced puzzled at her.

They strained to listen. A minute later, the mother came barreling out of the backyard, pushing the wheelchair with Nick in it through the tall grass. She nearly knocked herself and her husband over.

Thrusting the chair into the front yard, she said, "Here, sit! Happy now? You want to sit here all by yourself in the front so that passersby can gawk at you like you're an animal in a zoo, go ahead. I don't care anymore. I don't care about anything."

"That much is obvious!" the colonel yelled as she stormed away. He was panting.

Tatiana and Alexander lowered their heads. Anthony said, "Hi, Nick."

"Anthony! Shh."

Anthony opened the gate and went in. "Want a cigarette? Mama, come here."

She looked at Alexander. "Can I have a cigarette for him?" she whispered.

But it was Alexander who went to the colonel—his body and face slightly twisted—took out a cigarette from his pack, lit it, and held it to the colonel's mouth.

The man inhaled, exhaled, but without his previous fervor with Tatiana. He didn't speak.

Tatiana put her hand on Nick's shoulder. Anthony brought him a stag beetle, a dead wasp, a raw old potato. "Look," he said, "look at the wasp."

Nick looked, but said nothing. The cigarette calmed him down. He had another one.

"Want a drink, Colonel?" Alexander asked suddenly. "There is a bar down on Main Street."

Nick nodded in the direction of the house. "They won't let me go."

"We won't ask them," Alexander said. "Imagine their surprise when they come out and find you gone. They'll think you wheeled yourself down the hill."

This made Colonel Nicholas Moore smile. "The image of that is worth all the screeching later. OK, let's go."

Swezey's was the only bar in Stonington. Children weren't allowed in bars.

"I'm going to take Anthony on the swings," Tatiana said. "You two have fun."

Inside Alexander ordered two whiskeys. Holding both glasses, he clinked them, and put the drink to Nick's mouth. The liquor went in one gulp. "Should we order another one?"

"You know," said Nick, "why don't you order me a whole bottle? I haven't had a drink since I got hit eighteen months ago. I'll pay you back."

"Don't worry," Alexander said, and bought Nick and himself a bottle of Jack Daniel's. They sat in the corner, smoking and drinking.

"So what's the matter with your wife, Colonel?" Alexander asked. "Why is she always so ticked off?"

They were leaning toward each other, the colonel in a wheelchair, the captain by his side.

Nick shook his head. "Look at me. Can you blame her? But not to worry—the army is going to get me a round-the-clock nurse soon. She'll take care of me."

They sat.

"Tell me about *your* wife," Nick said. "She's not afraid of me. Not like others around here. She's seen this before?"

Alexander nodded. "She's seen this before."

Nick's face brightened. "Does she want a job? The army will pay her ten dollars a day for my care. What do you say? A little more money for your family."

"No," Alexander said. "She was a nurse long enough. No more nursing for her." He added, "We don't need the money, we're fine."

"Come on, everyone needs money. You can get yourself your own house instead of living with crazy Janet."

"And what's she going to do with the boy?"

"Bring him, too."

"No."

Nick fell quiet, but not before making a desperate noise. "We're on a waiting list for a nurse, but we can't get one," he said. "There aren't enough of them. They've all quit. Their men are coming back, they want to have babies, they don't want their wives to work."

"Yes," said Alexander. "I don't want my wife to work. Especially not as a nurse."

"If I don't get a nurse, Bessie says she's going to send me to the Army Hospital in Bangor. Says I'd be better off there."

Alexander poured more needed drink down the man's throat.

"They'll certainly be happier if I'm there," Nick said.

"They don't seem like a happy pair."

"No, no. Before the war, they were great."

"Where d'you get hit?"

"In Belgium. Battle of the Bulge. And there I was thinking colonels didn't get hit. Rank Has Its Privileges and all that. But a shell exploded, my captain and lieutenant both died, and I was burned. I would've been fine, but I was on the ground for four-teen hours before I got picked up by another platoon. The limbs got infected, couldn't be saved."

More drink, more smoke.

Nick said, "They should've just left me in the woods. It would've been over for me five hundred and fifty days ago, five hundred and fifty nights ago."

He calmed down by degrees, helped by whiskey and the smokes. Finally he muttered, "She is *so* good, your wife."

"Yes," said Alexander.

"So fresh and young. So lovely to look at."

"Yes," said Alexander, closing his eyes.

"And she doesn't yell at you."

"No. Though I reckon she sometimes wants to."

"Oh, to have such restraint in my Bessie. She used to be a fine woman. And the girl was such a loving girl."

More drink, more smoke.

"But have you noticed since coming back," said Nick, "that there are things that women just don't know? Won't know. They don't understand what it was like. They see me like this, they think this is the worst. They don't know. That's the chasm. You go through something that changes you. You see things you can't unsee. Then you are sleepwalking through your actual life, shell-shocked. Do you know, when I think of myself, I have legs? In my dreams I'm always marching. And when I wake up, I'm on the floor, I've fallen out of bed. I now sleep on the floor because I kept rolling over and falling while dreaming. When I dream of myself, I'm carrying my weapons, and I'm in the back of a battalion. I'm in a tank, I'm yelling, I'm always screaming in my dreams. This way! That way! Fire! Cease! Forward! March! Fire, fire, fire!"

Alexander lowered his head, his arms drooping on the table.

"I wake up and I don't know where I am. And Bessie is saying, what's the matter? You're not paying attention to me. You haven't said anything about my new dress. You end up living with someone who cooks your food for you and who used to open her legs for you, but you don't know them at all. You don't understand them, nor they you. You're two strangers thrown together. In my dreams, with legs, after marching, I'm always leaving, wandering off, long gone. I don't know where I am but I'm never here, never with them. Is it like that with you, too?"

Alexander quietly smoked, downing another glass of whiskey, and another. "No," he finally said. "My wife and I have the opposite problem. She carried weapons and shot at men who came to kill her. She was in hospitals, on battlefields, on frontlines. She was in DP camps and concentration camps. She starved through a frozen, blockaded city. She lost everyone she ever loved." Alexander took half a glass of sour mash into his throat and still couldn't keep himself from groaning. "She knows, sees, and understands everything. Perhaps less now, but that's my fault. I haven't been much of a—" he broke off. "Much of anything. Our problem isn't that we don't understand each other. Our problem is that we do. We can't look at each other, can't speak one innocent word, can't touch each other without touching the cross on our backs. There is simply *never* any peace." Another stiff drink went into Alexander's throat.

Suddenly Tatiana appeared in the dark corner. "Alexander," she whispered, "it's eleven o'clock. You have to be up at four."

He looked up at her bleakly.

She glanced at Nick, who was staring at her with a knowing, full expression. "What have you been telling him?"

"We've just been reminiscing," said the colonel. "About the good old days that brought us here."

Slightly slurred, Alexander said he would be right back and stood up, knocking over his chair and swaying away. Tatiana was left alone with Nick.

"He tells me you're a nurse," Nick said.

"I was."

He fell silent.

"What do you need?" She placed her hand on him. "What is it?"

His moist eyes were pleading. "Do you have morphine?"

Tatiana straightened up. "What's hurting?"

"Every single fucking thing that's left of me," he said. "Got enough morphine for that?"

"Nick . . ."

"Please. Please. Enough morphine so that I never feel again."

"Nick, dear God . . ."

"When it gets unbearable for your husband, he's got the weapons he cleans, he can just blow his brains out. But what about me?"

Nick couldn't grab her, but he threw his body forward to her. "Who is going to blow my brains out, Tania?" he whispered.

"Nick, please!" Her hands were propping him up, but he'd had too much to drink and was listing.

Alexander came back, unsteady on his feet. Nick stopped speaking.

Tatiana had to wheel Nick up the steep hill herself because Alexander kept releasing the handlebars and Nick kept rolling back down. It took her a long time to get him to his house. Nick's wife and daughter were purple with ire. The shrieking would have been sweeter for Tatiana had the colonel not spoken to her, but since he had, and since Alexander himself was too drunk to react to the histrionics of the two women, and since Nick Moore was also in a stupor, the punchline of the joke—a quadruple amputee in a wheelchair vanishing from the front lawn—went unappreciated by all parties, except for Anthony the following day.

The next morning Alexander had three cups of black coffee, staggered to work hung over, could put down only three traps at a time instead of the usual twelve, and came back with barely seventy lobsters, all of them chickens or one-pounders. He refused his pay, fell asleep right after dinner and never woke up until Anthony screamed in the middle of the night.

In the evening after supper, Tatiana went outside with a cup of tea, and Alexander wasn't there. He and Anthony were with Nick in the next yard. Alexander had even taken his chair. Anthony was looking for bugs, and the two men were talking. Tatiana watched them for a few minutes and then went back inside. She sat down at the empty kitchen table and, surprising herself, burst into tears.

And the next night, and the next. Alexander didn't even say anything to her. He just went, and he and Nick sat together, while Anthony played nearby. He started leaving his chair on Nick's front lawn.

After a few days of not being able to stand it, Tatiana made a long distance call to Vikki before breakfast.

Vikki screamed into the phone with joy. "I can't believe I'm finally hearing from you! What's *wrong* with you? How are you? How is Anthony, my big boy? But first, what is *wrong* with you? You are a *terrible* friend. You said you'd be calling every week. I haven't heard from you in over a month!"

"It hasn't really been a month, has it?"

"Tania! What in heaven's name have you been doing? No, no, don't answer that." Vikki giggled. "How has everything been?" she said in a low, insinuating voice.

"Oh, fine, fine, how's it with you? How have you been keeping?"

"Never mind me, why haven't you called me?"

"We've been—" Tatiana coughed.

"I know what you've been doing, you naughty girl. How is my adored child? How is my beloved boy? You don't know what you've done to me. Tania giveth him and Tania taketh him away. I really miss looking after him. So much so that I'm thinking of having my own baby."

"Unlike mine, Gelsomina," said Tatiana, "your own child you're going to have to keep forever. No giving him away like a puppy. And he's not going to be as nice as Antman."

"Who ever could be?"

They talked about Vikki's nursing, about Deer Isle, about the boats, and the swings, and Edward Ludlow, and about a new man in Vikki's life ("An *officer*! You're not the only one who can take up with an officer") and about New York ("Can't walk any street without getting your shoes dirty with construction debris") about her grandparents ("They're fine, they're trying to fatten me up, they say I'm too tall and skinny. Like if they feed me, I'll get shorter") and about the new short teased haircuts and new stilettos, and new fandango dresses and suddenly—"Tania? Tania, what's the matter?"

Tatiana was crying into the phone.

"What's the matter? What is it?"

"Nothing, nothing. Just . . . nice to hear your voice. I miss you very much."

"So when are you coming back? I can't live without you in our empty apartment," said Vikki. "Absolutely can't. Can't do without your bread, without your boyzie-boy, without seeing your face. Tania, you've ruined me for other girls." She laughed. "Now tell Vikki what's wrong."

Tatiana wiped her eyes. "Are you thinking of moving out of the apartment?"

"Moving, are you joking? Where am I going to find a three-bedroom in New York? You can't imagine what's happened to apartment prices since the war ended. Now stop changing the subject and tell me what's the matter."

"Really. I'm fine. I just . . ." Anthony was by her feet. She blew her nose and tried to calm down. She couldn't speak aloud about Alexander in front of his son.

"You know who's been calling for you? Your old friend Sam."

"What?" Tatiana instantly stopped crying. She became alert. Sam Gulotta was her contact at the State Department for the years she had been trying to find Alexander. Sam knew very well Alexander had been found; why would he be calling for her? Her stomach dropped.

"Yes, calling for you. Looking for Alexander."

"Oh." Tatiana tried to keep her voice careless. "Did he say why?"

"He said something about the State Department needing to talk to Alexander. He was *adamant* that you call him. He's been adamant every time he called."

"How many times, um, has he called?"

"Oh, I don't know, try . . . every day?"

"Every *day*?" Tatiana was stunned and frightened.

"That's right. Every day. Adamant every day. That's too much *adamant* for me, Tania. I keep telling him, as soon as I hear from you, I'll give him a call, but he doesn't believe me. Do you want his number?"

"I have Sam's number," she said slowly. "I've called him so many times over the years, I have it committed to memory."

When Alexander first returned home, they had gone to Washington to thank Sam for helping with Alexander's return. Sam had mentioned something about a mandatory debriefing by the State Department, but he had said it calmly and without haste, and added that it was summer and vital people were away. When

they had left Sam at the Mall near the Lincoln Memorial, he didn't
say another word about it. So why such urgency now? Did this
have anything to do with the reversal of friendly relations between
two recent war allies, the United States and the Soviet Union?

"Call Sam, please, so he stops calling *me*. Although . . . ." Vikki's
voice lowered a notch into flirtation territory. "Perhaps we should
let him continue calling me? He's a cutie-pie."

"He's a 37-year-old widower with kids, Vikki," said Tatiana. "You
can't have him without becoming a mother, too."

"Well, I've always wanted a child."

"He has *two* children."

"Oh, just stop it. Promise you're going to call him?"

"I will."

"Will you give our boyzie-boy a kiss from me the size of
Montana?"

"Yes." When Tatiana went to Germany to search for Alexander,
it was Vikki who took care of Anthony. She had grown very
attached to him. "I can't call Sam right away," Tatiana said. "I have
to talk to Alexander about it first when he comes home tonight,
so do me a favor, if Sam calls again, just say you haven't spoken
to me yet, and you don't know where I am. All right?"

"Why?"

"I just . . . I need to talk to Alexander, and then sometimes we
can't get the phone to work. I don't want Sam to panic, so hang
tight, okay? Please don't say anything."

"Tania, you're not very trusting, that's your problem. That's
always been your problem. You've always been suspicious of
people."

"I'm not. I'm just . . . suspicious of their intentions."

"Well, Sam wouldn't do anything to . . ."

"Sam's not running the State Department, is he?" said Tatiana.

"So?"

"He can't vouch for everyone. Haven't you been reading the
papers?"

"No!" Vikki said proudly.

"The State Department is afraid of espionage on all fronts. I must
talk to Alexander about this, see what he thinks."

"This is *Sam*! He didn't help you get Alexander back home just
to accuse him of espionage."

"I repeat, is Sam running the State Department?" Tatiana felt
apprehension she could not explain to Vikki. In the 1920s

Alexander's mother and father belonged to the Communist Party
of the United States. Harold Barrington got himself into quite a bit
of trouble stateside. Suddenly Harold's son was back in America
just as tension between the two nations was escalating. What if
the son had to pay for the sins of the father? As if he hadn't paid
enough—and by the looks of him indeed he had. "I have to run,"
Tatiana said, glancing at Anthony and squeezing her hands around
the phone. "I'll talk to Alexander tonight. Promise you won't say
anything to Sam?"

"Only if you promise to come and visit me as soon as you leave
Maine. "

"We'll try, Gelsomina," said Tatiana, hanging up. I will try
someday to make that promise.

Shaking, she called Esther Barrington, Alexander's aunt, his
father's sister, who lived in Massachusetts. She called ostensibly to
say hello, but really to find out if anyone had contacted Esther
about Alexander. They hadn't. Small relief.

That evening over lobsters, Anthony said, "Dad, Mama called Vikki
today."

"She did?" Alexander looked up from his plate. His eyes probed
her face. "Well, that's great. How is Vikki?"

"Vikki is good. Mama cried though. Two times."

"Anthony!" Tatiana lowered her head.

"What? You did cry."

"Anthony, please, can you go and ask Mrs. Brewster if she wants
some dinner now or if I should keep it in the oven for her?"

Anthony disappeared. Acutely feeling Alexander's silence,
Tatiana got up to go to the sink, but before she could utter a word
of defense for her tears, Anthony reappeared.

"Mrs. Brewster is bleeding," he said.

They rushed upstairs. Mrs. Brewster told them her son, newly
returned from prison, beat her to get the rent money Alexander
was paying. Tatiana tried to clean up the old lady with rags.

"He's not staying with me. He's staying down the road with
friends." Could Alexander help her with her son? Since he'd been
in prison too, he should understand how things were. "I don't
see you beatin' your wife, though." Could Alexander ask her son
not to beat her anymore? She wanted to keep her rent money.
"He's just going to spend it on filthy drink, like always, and then
get hisself into trouble. I don't know what you was in for, but

he was in the pen for assault with a deadly weapon. Drunken assault."

Alexander left to go next door to sit with Nick, but late that night he told Tatiana he was going to talk to Mrs. Brewster's son.

"No."

"Tania, I don't like her either, but what kind of a fucked-up loser beats his own mother? I'm going to talk to him."

"No."

"No?"

"No. You're too tightly wound."

"I'm not tightly wound," Alexander said slowly, into her back. "I'm just going to talk to him, that's all, man to man. I'll tell him beating his mother is not acceptable." They were whispering in the dark, the beds pushed together, Anthony lightly snoring by Tatiana's side.

"And he says to you, screw you, mister. Stay out of my business. And then what?"

"Good question. But perhaps he'll be reasonable."

"You think so? He beats his *mother* to take her money!" Sighing, Tatiana twitched in the middle between her two men.

"Well, we can't just do *nothing*."

"Yes, we can. Let's not ask for someone else's trouble." We've got plenty. She didn't know how to bring up Sam Gulotta, cold terror gluing his name to her throat. She tried to keep thinking about someone else's troubles. She didn't want Alexander *near* that woman's son. But what to do?

"You're right," Tatiana finally said with a throat clearing. "We can't do nothing. You know what? I think *I'll* go and speak to him. I'm a woman. I'm little. I'll talk to him nicely, the way I talk to everybody. He's not going to get rough with me."

She felt Alexander stiffen behind her. "Are you joking?" he whispered. "He beats his *mother*! Don't even *think* of coming close to him."

"Shh. It'll be okay. Really."

He turned her around to face him. "I'm serious," he said, his eyes on her unblinking and intense. "Don't take one step in his direction. Not one *step*. Because a syllable out of him against you, and he won't be speaking to anyone ever again, and I'll be in an American prison. Is that what you want?"

"No, darling," she said softly. He was talking! He was animated. He had raised his whispering voice! She kissed his face, kissed him and kissed him, until he kissed her back, his hands pacing over her nightgown.

"Have I mentioned how much I *hate* you wearing clothes in my bed?"

"I know, but there's a little boy with us," she whispered. "I can't be naked next to him."

"You don't fool me," Alexander said heavily.

"Darling, it's the boy," she said, avoiding his eyes. "Besides, my slip is made of silk, not burlap. Have you noticed I'm naked underneath?"

Alexander slipped his hands under. "Why were you crying with Vikki?" Something cool and unwelcome got into his voice. "What, you miss your New York?"

Guiltily Tatiana glanced at him. Lonely she glanced at him. "Why do you keep going next door every night?" she whispered, moaning lightly.

Alexander took his hands away. "Come on. You've seen Nick's family. I'm the only one he can talk to. He's got nobody besides me."

Me neither, Tatiana thought, the hot hurt of it burning her eyes.

She couldn't say anything to Alexander about Sam Gulotta and the State Department. There was no more room on his cold plate of anguish.

The next evening Anthony wandered back by himself after only half an hour outside with his father and the colonel. The sun had set and the mosquitoes were out. Tatiana bathed him, and as she was applying Calamine lotion to his bites, she asked, "Ant, what do Daddy and Nick talk about?"

"I don't know," Anthony said vaguely. "War. Fighting."

"What about tonight? Why did you come back so early?"

"Nick keeps asking Dad for something."

"What does he keep asking Dad for?"

"To kill him."

A crouching Tatiana staggered backward, nearly falling on the floor. "*What*?"

"Don't be upset with Dad. Please."

She patted him. "Anthony . . . you're a good boy."

Seeing the crashed look on his mother's face Anthony began to whimper.

She took him in her arms. "Shh. Everything is going to be all right, son."

"Dad says he doesn't want to kill him."

Tatiana quickly dressed the boy for bed. "You wait here, you promise? Don't go outside in your nightshirt. Stay in your bed and look at your book of boats and fish."

"Where are you going?"

"To get daddy."

"Are you going to . . . come right back after you get Dad?" he said uncertainly.

"Of course. Anthony, of course. I'll be right back."

"Are you going to yell at him?"

"No, son."

"Mama, please don't be mad if he killed the colonel."

"Shh. Look at your book. I'll be right back."

Tatiana got her nurse's bag from the closet. It took her a few minutes to compose herself, but finally she walked determined down the road.

"Uh-oh," said Nick when he saw her. "I think there's going to be some hollerin'."

"There isn't," Tatiana said coldly, opening the gate.

"It's not his fault," Nick said. "It's mine. I've kept him."

"My husband is a big boy," she said. "He knows when enough is enough." She looked at Alexander accusingly. "But he does forget that his son speaks English and hears every word the adults say."

Alexander got up. "On that note, good night, Nick."

"Leave the chair," said Tatiana. "Go. Ant is by himself."

"You're not coming?"

"I'm going to talk to Nick for a minute." She looked steadily at Alexander. "Go on. I'll be right along."

Alexander didn't move. "What are you doing?" he said quietly.

She could see he wasn't going to go and she wasn't going to argue in front of a stranger. Though an argument would've been nice. "Nothing. I'm going to talk to Nick."

"No, Tania. Come."

"You don't even know what—"

"I don't care. Come."

Ignoring his outstretched hand, she sat down in the chair and turned to the colonel. "I know what you're talking to my husband about," Tatiana said. "Stop it."

Nick shook his head. "You've been at war. Don't you understand anything?"

"Everything," she said. "You can't ask this of him. It's not right."

"Right?" he cried. "You want to talk about what's right?"

"I do," said Tatiana. "I've got a few things I'm trying to set right myself. But you went to the front, and you got hurt. That's the price you paid to keep your wife and daughter from speaking German. When they stop grieving for you, they'll be better. I know it's hard now, but it will get better."

"It'll never get better. You think I don't know what I was fighting for? I know. I'm not complaining about it. Not about *that*. But this isn't life, not for me, not for my wife. This is just bullshit, pardon my language." Because he could do nothing else, Nick heaved himself out of his chair onto the grass. Tatiana gasped. Alexander picked him up, put him back into his chair. "All I want is to die," Nick said, panting. "Can't *you* see it?"

"I see it," she said in a low voice. "But leave my husband alone."

"No one else will help me!" Nick tried to throw himself on the ground again, but Tatiana kept a firm arm on him.

"He won't help you either," she said. "Not with this."

"Why not? Have you asked him how many of his own men he had shot to spare them agony?" Nick cried. "What, he hasn't told you? Tell her, Captain. You shot them without thinking twice. Why won't you do it for me now? Look at me!"

Tatiana stared at a darkly grim Alexander and then at Nick. "I know about my husband at war," she said, her voice shaking. "But you leave him alone. He needs peace, too."

"Please, Tania," Nick whispered, bending his head into her hand. "Look at me. My revels now are ended. Have mercy on me. Just give me the morphine. It's not violent, I'll feel no pain. I'll just drift off. It's kind. It's right."

Tatiana looked questioningly up at Alexander.

"I'm begging you," said Nick, seeing her vacillation.

Alexander pulled Tatiana up out of the chair. "Stop this, both of you," he said, in a voice that brooked no argument, not even from the colonel. "You two have lost your minds. Good night."

Later, in bed, they didn't speak for a long while. Tatiana was scooped narrowly into him.

"Tania . . . tell me, were you going to kill him so that I wouldn't spend any more time with him?"

"Don't be ridi—" she broke off. "The man is dying. The man wants to be dead. Can't you see that?"

With difficulty came Alexander's reply. "I see it."

Oh God.

"Help him, Alexander," said Tatiana. "Take him to Bangor, to the Army Hospital. I know he doesn't want to go, but he *needs* to go. The nurses are trained to take care of people like him. They will put the cigarettes in his mouth, they will read to him. They will care for him. He will live." That man can't be around you. You can't be around him.

Alexander stopped talking. "Should I go to Bangor Hospital, too?" he asked.

"No, darling, no, Shura," she whispered. "You have your own nurse right here. Round the clock."

"Tania . . ."

"*Please* . . . shh." They were whispering desperately, he into her hair, she into the pillow in front of her.

"Tania, would you . . . do it for me, if I asked? If I was . . . like him—" He broke off.

"Faster than you can say Sachsenhausen."

Click click somewhere, crickets crickets, bats and wings, Anthony snoring in the silence, in the sorrow. There was once so much Tatiana could help Alexander with. Why couldn't she do it anymore?

Soundlessly she cried, only her shoulders quaking.

The next day Alexander took the colonel to the Bangor Army Hospital, four hours away. They left in the early morning. Tatiana filled their flasks, made them sandwiches, and washed and ironed Alexander's khaki fatigues and a long-sleeved crew.

Before he left he asked, crouching by Anthony's small frame, "You want me to bring you something back?"

"Yes, a toy soldier," replied Anthony.

"You got it." Alexander ruffled his hair and straightened up. "What about you?" he asked Tatiana, coming close to her.

"Oh, I'm fine," she said, purposefully casual. "I don't need anything." She was trying to look beyond his bronze eyes, into somewhere deeper, somewhere that would tell her what he was thinking, what he was feeling, trying to reach across the ocean waters she could not traverse.

Nick was already in the camper, and his wife and daughter were milling nearby. Too many people around. The backs of Alexander's fingers stroked her cheek. "Be a good girl," he said, kissing her hand. She pressed her forehead into his chest for a moment before he stepped away.

When he was near the cab of the Nomad, he turned around. Tatiana, standing still and erect, squeezed hard Anthony's hand, but that was the only indication of the turmoil within her, for to Alexander she presented herself straight and true. She even managed to smile. She blew him a kiss. Her hand went up to her temple in a trembling salute.

Alexander didn't come back that night.

Tatiana didn't sleep.

He didn't come back the next morning.

Or the next afternoon.

Or the next evening.

She searched through his things and saw that his weapons were gone. Only her pistol remained, the German-issue P-38 he gave her in Leningrad. It was wrapped in a towel near a large wad of bills—extra money he had made from Jimmy and left for her.

She slept in a stupor next to Anthony in his twin bed.

The next morning Tatiana went down to the docks. Jimmy's sloop was there, and Jimmy was doing his best to repair some damage to the side. "Hey, little guy," he said to Anthony. "Your dad back yet? I gotta go and get me some lobsters or I'm gonna go broke."

"He's not back yet," said Anthony. "But he's going to bring me a toy soldier."

Tatiana wavered on her calf legs. "Jim, he didn't say anything to you about how many days he was going to take off?"

Jimmy shook his head. "He did say if I wanted to, I could hire one of the other guys coming here looking for work. If he doesn't come back soon, I'm gonna do it. I gotta get back out there."

The morning was dazzling.

Tatiana dragging Anthony by the hand, practically ran uphill to Bessie's and knocked until Bessie woke up and came miserably to the door. Tatiana, without apologizing for the early call, asked if Bessie had heard from Nick or from the hospital.

"No," Bessie said gruffly. Tatiana refused to leave until Bessie called the hospital, only to find out that the colonel had been admitted without incident two days ago. The man who brought him stayed for one day and then left. No one knew anything else about Alexander.

Another day passed.

Tatiana sat on the bench by the bay, by the morning water, and watched her son push himself on a tire swing. Her arms were twisted around her stomach. She was trying not to rock like Alexander rocked at three o'clock in the morning.

Has he left me? Did he kiss my hand and go?

No. It wasn't possible. Something's happened. He can't cope, can't make it, can't find a way out, a way in. I know it. I feel it. We thought the hard part was over—but we were wrong. Living is the hardest part. Figuring out how to live your life when you're all busted up inside and out—there is nothing harder. Oh dear God. Where is Alexander?

She had to go to Bangor immediately. But how? She didn't have a car; would she and Ant go there by bus? Would they leave Stonington for good, leave their things? And go where? But she had to do something, she couldn't just continue to sit here!

She was clenched inside, outside.

She had to be strong for her son.

She had to be resolute for him.

Everything was going to be all right.

Like a mantra. Over and over.

This is *my* vicious dream, Tatiana's entire body shouted. I thought it was like a dream that he was with me again, and I was right, and now I've opened my eyes, and he's gone like before.

Tatiana was watching Anthony swing, looking beyond him, dreaming of one man, imagining only one other heart in the vastness of the universe—then, now, as ever. She still flew to him.

Is he still alive?

Am I still alive?

She thought so. No one could hurt this much and be dead.

"Mama, are you watching me? I'm going to spin and spin and spin until I get dizzy and fall down. Whee! Are you watching? Watch, Mama!"

Her eyes were glazed over. "I'm watching, Antman. I'm watching."

The air smelled so August, the sun shone so brightly, the pines, the elms, the cones, the sea, the spinning boy, just three, the young mother, not even twenty-three.

Tatiana had imagined her Alexander since she was a child, before she believed that someone like him was even possible. When she was a little girl, she dreamed of a fine world in which a good man walked its winding roads, perhaps somewhere in his wandering soul searching for her.

On The Banks of the Luga River, 1938

Tatiana's world was perfect.

Life may not have been perfect; far from it. But in the summer, when the day began almost before the last day ended, when the crickets sang all night and cows mooed before dreams fled, when the smells of summer June in the village of Luga were sharp—the cherry and the lilacs and the nettles in the soul from dawn to dusk—when you could lie in the narrow bed by the window and read books about the Grand Adventure of Life and no one disturbed you—the air so still, the branches rustling and, not far, the Luga River rushing—then the world was a perfect place.

And this morning young Tatiana was skipping down the road, carrying two pails of milk from Berta's cow. She was humming, the milk was spilling, she was hurrying so she could bring the milk back and climb into bed and read her marvelous book, but she couldn't help skipping, and the milk couldn't help spilling. She stopped, lowered the rail over her shoulders onto the ground, picked up one pail and drank the warm milk from it, picked up the other and drank some more. Replacing the rail around her shoulders she started skipping again.

Tatiana was one elongated reedy limb from toe to fingers, all one straight line, feet, knees, thighs, hips, ribs, chest, shoulders, a stalk, tapering off in a slender neck and expanding into a round Russian face with a high forehead, a strong jaw, a pink smiling mouth and white teeth. Her eyes glinted green with mischief, her cheeks and small nose were drowned in freckles. The joyous face was framed with white blonde hair, just wispy feathers falling on her shoulders. No one could sit by Tatiana without caressing her silky head.

"TATIANA!" The scream from the porch.

Except maybe Dasha.

Dasha was always shouting. Tatiana, this, Tatiana, that. She is going to have to learn to relax and lower her voice, Tatiana thought. Though why should she? Everyone in Tatiana's family hollered. How else could one possibly be heard? There were so many of them. Well, her gray quiet grandfather managed somehow. Tatiana managed—somehow. But everyone else, her mother, her father, her sister, even her brother, Pasha—what did *he* have to shout about?—shouted as if they were just coming into the world.

The children played noisily and the grown-ups fished and grew vegetables in their yards. Some had cows, some had goats; they bartered cucumbers for milk and milk for grain; they milled their own rye and made their own pumpernickel bread. The chickens laid eggs and the eggs were bartered for tea with people from the cities, and once in a while someone brought sugar and caviar from Leningrad. Chocolate was as rare and expensive as diamonds, which was why when Tatiana's father—who had left for a business trip to Poland recently— asked his children what they wanted for gifts, Dasha instantly said chocolate. Tatiana wanted to say chocolate, too, but instead said, *maybe a nice dress, Papa?* All her dresses were hand-me-downs from Dasha and much too big.

"TATIANA!" Dasha's voice was now coming from the yard.

Turning her reluctant head, Tatiana leveled her bemused gaze at her sister, standing at the gate with her exasperated arms at her large hips. "Yes, Dasha?" she said softly. "What is it?"

"I've been calling you for ten minutes! I'm hoarse from shouting! Did you hear me?" Dasha was taller than Tatiana, and full-figured; her unruly curly brown hair was tied up in a ponytail, her brown eyes indignant.

"No, I didn't hear," Tatiana said. "Next time, maybe shout louder."

"Where have you been? You've been gone two hours—to get milk from five houses up the road!"

"Where's the fire?"

"Stop it with your fresh lip this instant! I've been waiting for you."

"Dasha," said Tatiana philosophically, "Blanca Davidovna says that Christ says that blessed are the patient."

"Oh, you're a fine one to talk, you're the most impatient person I know."

"Well, tell that to Berta's cow. I was waiting for it to come back from pasture."

Dasha took the pails off Tatiana's shoulders. "Berta and Blanca fed you, didn't they?"

Tatiana rolled her eyes. "They fed me, they kissed me, they sermonized me. And it's not even Sunday. I'm fed and cleansed and one with the Lord." She sighed. "Next time you can go get your own milk, you impatient heathen."

Tatiana was three weeks from fourteen, while Dasha had

turned twenty-one in April. Dasha thought she was Tatiana's second mother. Their grandmother thought she was Tatiana's third mother. The old ladies who gave Tatiana milk and talked to her about Jesus thought they were her fourth, fifth and sixth mothers. Tatiana felt that she barely needed the one loud exasperated mother she had—thankfully in Leningrad at the moment. But Tatiana knew that for one reason or another, through no fault of her own, women, sisters, other people felt a need to mother her, *smother* her more like it, squeeze her in their big arms, braid her wispy hair, kiss her freckles, and pray to their God for her.

"Mama left me in charge of you and Pasha," Dasha declared autocratically. "And if you're going to give me your attitude, I won't tell you the news."

"What news?" Tatiana jumped up and down. She loved news.

"Not telling."

Tatiana skipped after Dasha up the porch and into their house. Dasha put the pails down. Tatiana was wearing a little-girl sundress and bouncing up and down. Without warning she flung herself onto her sister, who was nearly knocked to the floor before she caught her footing.

"You shouldn't do that!" Dasha said but not angry. "You're getting too big."

"I'm not too big."

"Mama is going to kill me," said Dasha, patting Tatiana's behind. "All you do is sleep and read and disobey. You don't eat, you're not growing. Look how tiny you are."

"I thought you just said I was too big." Tatiana's arms were around Dasha's neck.

"Where's your crazy brother?"

"He went fishing at dawn," Tatiana said. "Wanted me to come too. *Me* get up at dawn. I told him what I thought of that."

Dasha squeezed her. "Tania, I have kindling that's fatter than you. Come and eat an egg."

"I'll eat an egg if you tell me your news," said Tatiana, kissing her sister's cheek, then the other cheek. Kiss kiss kiss. "You should never keep good news all to yourself, Dasha. That's the rule: Bad news only to yourself but good news to everybody."

Dasha set her down. "I don't know if it's *good* news but . . . We have new neighbors," she said. "The *Kantorovs* have moved in next door."

Tatiana widened her eyes. "You don't *say*," she said in a shocked voice, grabbing her face. "Not the *Kantorovs*!"

"That's it, I'm not speaking to you anymore."

Tatiana laughed. "You say the Kantorovs as if they are the Romanovs."

In a thrilled tone, Dasha continued. "It's rumored they're from Central Asia! *Turkmenistan*, maybe? Isn't that *exciting*? Apparently they have a girl—a girl for you to play with."

"*That's* your news?" said Tatiana. "A Turkmeni girl for me to play with? Dasha, you've got to do better than that. I have a village-full of girls and boys to play with—who speak Russian. And cousin Marina is coming in two weeks."

"They also have a son."

"So?" Tatiana looked Dasha over. "Oh. I see. Not my age. *Your* age."

Dasha smiled. "Yes, unlike you, some of us are interested in boys."

"So really, it's not *my* news. It's *your* news."

"No. The girl is for you."

Tatiana went with Dasha on the porch to eat a hard-boiled egg. She had to admit she was excited, too. New people didn't come to the village very often. Never actually. The village was small, the houses were let out for years to the same people, who grew up, had children, grew old.

"Did you say they moved in *next* door?"

"Yes."

"Where the Pavlovs lived?"

"Not anymore."

"What happened to them?"

"I don't know. They're not there."

"Well, obviously. But what happened to them? Last summer they were here."

"Fifteen summers they were here."

"Fifteen summers," Tatiana corrected herself, "and now new people have moved into *their* house? Next time you're in town, stop by the local *Soviet* council and ask the Commissar what happened to the Pavlovs."

"Are you out of your mind, such as it is? I'm going to the *Soviet* to ask where the Pavlovs went? Just eat, will you? Have the egg. Stop asking so many questions. I'm tired of you already and it's only morning."

Tatiana was sitting, cheeks like a chipmunk, the whole egg uneaten in her mouth, her eyes twinkling. Dasha laughed, pulling Tatiana to herself. Tatiana moved away. "Stay still," said Dasha. "I have to rebraid your hair, it's a mess. What are you reading now, Tanechka?" she asked as she started unbraiding it. "Anything good?"

"*Queen Margot*. It's the best book."

"Never read it. What's it about?"

"Love," said Tatiana. "Oh, Dasha—you've never dreamed of such love! A doomed soldier La Môle falls in love with Henry IV's unhappy Catholic wife, Queen Margot. Their impossible love will break your heart."

Dasha laughed. "Tania, you are the funniest girl I know. You know absolutely nothing about anything, yet talk in thrall of words of love on a *page*."

"Obviously you've never read *Queen Margot*," Tatiana said calmly. "It's not words of love." She smiled. "It's a *song* of love."

"I don't have the luxury of reading about love. All I do is take care of you."

"You leave a *little* time for some nighttime social interaction."

Dasha pinched her. "Everything is a joke to you. Well, just you wait, missy. Someday you won't think that social interaction is so funny."

"Maybe, but I'll still think *you're* so funny."

"I'll show you funny." Dasha knocked her back on the couch. "You urchin," she said. "When are you going to grow up? Come, I can't wait for your impossible brother anymore. Let's go meet your new best friend, Mademoiselle Kantorova."

Saika Kantorova.

The summer of 1938, when she turned 14 was the summer that Tatiana grew up.

The people who moved in next door were nomads, drifters from parts of the world far removed from Luga. They had odd Central Asian names. The father, Murak Kantorov, too young to be retired, mumbled that he was a retired army man. But his black hair was long and tied in a ponytail. Did soldiers have long hair like that? The mother, Shavtala, said she was a non-retired teacher "of sorts." The nineteen-year-old son, Stefan, and the fifteen-year-old daughter, Saika, said nothing except to pronounce Saika's name. "Sah-EE-ka."

Was it true that they came from Turkmenistan? Sometimes. Georgia? Occasionally. The Kantorovs answered all questions with vagueness.

Usually new people were friendlier, not as watchful or silent. Dasha tried. "I'm a dental assistant. I'm twenty-one. What about you, Stefan?"

Dasha was already flirting! Tatiana coughed loudly. Dasha pinched her. Tatiana wanted to make a joke, but there didn't seem to be any room for jokes in the crowded dark room where too many people stood awkwardly. The sun was blazing outside, yet inside, the unwashed curtains were drawn over the filthy windows. The Kantorovs had not unpacked their suitcases. The house had been left furnished by the Pavlovs, who seemed not so much to have left as to have stepped out.

There were some new things on the mantel. Photos, pictures, strange sculptures and small gilded paintings, like icons, though not of Jesus or Mary . . . but of *things with wings*.

"Did you know the Pavlovs?" asked Tatiana.

"Who?" the father said gruffly.

"The Pavlovs. This was their house."

"Well, it's not their house anymore, is it?" said the raven mother.

"They *won't* be back," said Murak. "We have papers from the *Soviet*. We are registered to stay here. Why so many questions from a child? Who wants to know?" He pretended to smile.

Tatiana pretended to smile back.

When they were outside, Dasha hissed, "Stop it! I can't believe you're already starting with your inane questions. Keep quiet, or I swear I'll tell Mama when she comes."

Dasha, Stefan, Tatiana and Saika stood in the sunlight.

Tatiana said nothing. She wasn't allowed to ask questions.

Finally Stefan smiled at Dasha.

Saika watched Tatiana guardedly.

It was at that moment that Pasha, little and fast, ran up the steps of the house, shoved a bucket with three striped bass into Tatiana's body and said loudly, "Ha, little smart Miss Know-it-nothing, look what I caught today—"

"Pasha, meet our new neighbors," interrupted Dasha. "Pasha—this is Stefan, and Saika. Saika is your age."

Now Saika smiled. "Hello, Pasha," she said.

Pasha smiled broadly back. "Well, *hello*, Saika."

"And how old are *you*?" Saika said, appraising him.

"Well, I'm the same age as this one over here." Dark-haired Pasha pulled hard on Tatiana's blonde braid. She shoved him. "We're fourteen soon."

"You're twins!" exclaimed Saika, looking at them intently. "What do you know. Obviously not identical." She smirked. "Well, well. You seem so much older than your sister."

"Oh, he *is* so much older than me," said Tatiana. "Nine minutes older."

"You seem older than that, Pasha."

"How much older do I seem, Saika?" Pasha grinned. She grinned back.

"Like *twelve* minutes older," Tatiana grumbled, stifling the desire to roll her eyes, and "accidentally" tripping over the bucket, spilling his precious fish onto the grass. Pasha's attention was loudly and properly diverted.

To wake up and be still with the morning, to wake up and feel the sun, to not do, to not think, to not fret. Tatiana lived in Luga unbothered by the weather, for when it rained she read, and when it was sunny she swam. She lived in Luga unbothered by life: she never thought about what she wore, for she had nothing, or what she ate, because it was always adequate. She lived in Luga in time-less childhood bliss without a past and without a future. She thought there was nothing in the world that a summer in Luga could not cure.

The Last Snow, 1946

"Mama, Mama!"

Shuddering she came to and swirled around. Anthony was run-ning, pointing to the sloping hill, down which walked Alexander. He was wearing the clothes he left in.

Tatiana got up. She wanted to run to him too, but her legs wouldn't carry her. They couldn't even support her standing. Anthony, the brave boy, jumped straight into his father's arms.

Carrying his son, Alexander walked to Tatiana on the pebbled beach and set him down.

"Hey, babe," he said.

"Hey," she said, barely able to keep her composed face.

Unshaven and unclean, Alexander stood and stared at her with gaunt black rings under his eyes, with a barely composed face of his own. Tatiana forgot about herself and went to him. He bent deeply to her, his face pressed into her neck, into the braids of her hair. Her feet remained on the ground and her arms were around him. Tatiana felt such black despair coming from Alexander that she started to convulse.

Gripping her tighter, his arms surrounding her, he whispered, "Shh, shh, come on, the boy . . ." When he released her, Tatiana didn't look up, not wanting him to see the fear for him in her eyes. There was no relief. But he was with her.

Tugging on his father's arm, Anthony asked, "Dad, why did you take so long to come back? Mama was *so* worried."

"Was she? I'm sorry Mommy was worried," Alexander said, not looking at her. "But, Ant, toy soldiers aren't easy to come by." He took out three from his bag. Anthony squealed.

"Did you bring Mama anything?"

"I didn't want anything," said Tatiana.

"Did you want this?" He took out four heads of garlic.

She attempted a smile.

"What about this?" He took out two bars of good chocolate.

She attempted another smile.

As they were walking up the hill, Alexander, carrying Anthony, gave Tatiana his arm. Putting her arm through his, she pressed herself against him for a moment before walking on.

Alexander was cleaned, bathed, shaved, fed. Now in their little narrow bed she was lying on top of him, kissing him, cupping him, caressing him, carrying on, crying over him. He lay motionless, soundless, his eyes closed. The more clutching and desperate her caresses became, the more like a stone he became, until finally, he pushed her off himself. "Come on now," he said. "Stop it. You'll wake the boy."

"Darling, darling . . ." she was whispering, reaching for him.

"Stop it, I said." He took her hands off him.

"Take off your vest, darling," Tatiana whispered, crying. "Look, I'll take off my nightgown, I'll be naked, like you like . . ."

He stopped her. "No, I'm exhausted. You'll wake the boy. The bed creaks too much. You're making too much noise. Stop crying, I said; stop carrying on."

She didn't know what to do. Caressing him until he was swollen in her hands, she asked if he wanted something from her. He shrugged.

Trembling, she put him in her mouth but couldn't continue; she was choking, she was so sad. Alexander sighed.

Getting off the bed, he brought her down to the plank wood floor, turned her on her hands and knees, told her to keep quiet, and took her from behind, holding her at the small of her back with one hand and at her hip with the other to keep her steady. When he was done, he got up, got back into bed, and never made a sound.

After that night, Tatiana lost her ability to talk to him. That he wouldn't just tell her what was going on with him was one thing. But the fact that she couldn't find the courage to ask was wholly another. The silence between them grew in black chasms.

For three subsequent evenings, Alexander wouldn't stop cleaning his weapons. That he had the weapons was troubling enough, but he wouldn't part with any of the ones he brought back from Germany, not the remarkable Colt M1911 .45 caliber pistol she had bought for him, not the Colt Commando, not even the 9mm P-38. The M1911, the king of pistols, was Alexander's favorite—Tatiana could tell by how long he cleaned it. She would go to put Anthony to bed, and when she returned outside, he would still be sitting in the chair, sliding the magazine in and out, cocking it, putting the safety on it and back again, wiping all the parts with cloth.

For three subsequent evenings Alexander wouldn't touch her. Tatiana, not knowing, not understanding, but desperately wanting to make him happy, stayed away, hoping that eventually he would explain, or evolve back into what they had. He evolved so slowly. On the fourth night Alexander pulled off all his clothes and stood in front of her naked in the dark, as she sat on the bed, about to get in. She looked up at him. He looked down at her. *You want me to touch you?* she whispered uncertainly, her hands rising to him. *Yes,* he said. *I want you to touch me, Tatiana.*

He evolved a little but never explained anything in the dark, in their little room with Anthony sleeping.

The days became cooler, the mosquitoes left. The leaves started changing. Tatiana didn't think there was breath left in her body to sit on the bench and watch the hills of cinnabar and wine and gold reflect off the still water.

"Anthony," she whispered. "Is this so beautiful or what?"

"It's or what, Mama." He was wearing his father's officer's cap, the one Dr. Matthew Sayers had given her years ago off a supposedly dead Alexander's head. *He has drowned, Tatiana, he is dead in the ice, but I have his cap; would you like it?*

The beige cap with a red star, too big for Anthony, made Tatiana think of herself and her life in the past tense instead of in the present. Sharply regretting having given it to the boy, she tried to take it from him, to hide it from him, to put it away, but every morning Anthony said, "Mama, where is my cap?"

"It's not your cap."

"It is so. Dad told me it was mine now."

"*Why* did you tell him he could have it?" she grumbled to Alexander one evening as they were ambling down to town.

Before he had a chance to reply, a young man, less than twenty, ran by, lightly touching Tatiana on her shoulder, and said with a wide, happy smile, "Hi there, girly-girl!" Saluting Alexander, he continued downhill.

Slowly Alexander turned his head to Tatiana, who was next to him, her arm through his. He tapped her hand. "Do I know him?"

"Yes, and no. You drink the milk he brings every day."

"He's the milkman?"

"Yes."

They continued walking.

"I heard," Alexander said evenly, "that he's had it off with every woman in the village but one."

"Oh," Tatiana said without missing a beat, "I bet it's that stuck-up Mira in house number thirty."

And Alexander laughed.

He laughed!

He laughs!

And then he leaned to her and kissed her face. "Now *that's* funny, Tania," he said.

Tatiana was pleased with him for being pleased. "Will you explain to me why you don't mind the boy wearing your cap?" she asked, squeezing his arm.

"Oh, it's harmless."

"I don't think it's so harmless. Sometimes seeing your army cap prevents me from seeing Stonington. That isn't harmless, is it?"

And what did her inimitable Alexander say to that, strolling down a sublime New England autumn hill overlooking the crystal ocean waters with his wife and son?

He said, "What's Stonington?"

And a day later Tatiana *finally* figured out why this place was so close to her heart. With its long grasses and sparkling waters, the field flowers and the pines, the deciduous smells coupled with the thinness in the air—it reminded her of Russia! And when she realized this—the minutes and hours of claret and maroon maples, the gold mountain ash and swaying birches piercing her heart—she stopped smiling.

When Alexander came home from the boat that evening and went up to her, as usual sitting on the bench, and saw what must have been her most unresponsive face, he said with a nod, "Ah. And there it finally is. So . . . what do you think? Nice to be reminded of Russia, Tatiana Metanova?"

She said nothing, walking down to the dock with him. "Why don't you take the lobsters, go on up?" he offered. "I'll keep the boy while I finish."

Tatiana took the lobsters and flung them in the trash.

Alexander bit his amused lip. "What, no lobsters today?"

She strode past Alexander to the boat. "Jim," she said, "instead of lobsters, I made spaghetti sauce with meatballs. Would you like to come have dinner with us?"

Jimmy beamed.

"Good." Tatiana turned to go, and then, almost as an after-thought, said, "Oh, by the way, I invited my friend Nellie from Eastern Road to join us. She's a little blue. She just found out she lost her husband in the war. I hope you don't mind."

Jimmy, as it turned out, didn't mind. And neither did a slightly less blue Nellie.

Mrs. Brewster was beaten for her rent money again. Tatiana was cleaning the cut on her hand for her, while Anthony's eyes, as somber as his father's, stared at his mother from the footstool at her feet.

"Mama was a nurse," said Anthony reverentially.

Mrs. Brewster watched her. There was something on her mind. "You never told me where you come from, the accent. It sounds—"

"Russian," said the three-year-old whose father wasn't there to stop him.

"Ah. Your husband a Russki, too?"

"No, my husband is American."

"Dad is American," said Anthony proudly, "but he was a cap-tain in the—"

"Anthony!" Tatiana yanked his arm. "Time to go get Dad."

The next day Mrs. Brewster expressed the opinion that the Soviets were nasty communists. This was her son's view. She wanted another seven dollars for the water and electric. "You're cooking all the time on my stove there."

Tatiana was rattled at the shakedown. "But I make dinner for you."

Mrs. Brewster said, patting the bandage Tatiana had wrapped around her hand, "And in the spirit of communism, my son says he wants you to pay thirty dollars a week for the room, not eight. Or you can find another collective to live on, comrade."

Thirty dollars a week! "All right," said Tatiana through her teeth. "I'll pay you another twenty-two a week. But this is just between us. Don't mention it to my husband." As Tatiana walked away, she felt the glare of someone who'd been beaten by her son for rent money and yet still trusted him more.

No sooner had they met Alexander on the dock than Anthony said, "Dad, Mrs. Brooster called us nasty communists."

He glanced at Tatiana. "She did, did she?"

"She did, and Mama got upset."

"She did, did she?" He sidled up to her.

"No, I didn't. Anthony walk ahead now, I have to talk to your father."

"You did, you did," Anthony said. "You get that tight mouth when you get upset." He tightened his mouth to show his father.

"Doesn't she just," said Alexander.

"All right you two," Tatiana said quietly. "Will you go on ahead, Anthony?"

But he lifted his arms to her, and she picked him up.

"Dad, she called us communists!"

"I can't believe it."

"Dad?"

"Yes?"

"What are communists?"

That night before dinner, of lobsters ("Oh, not again!") and potatoes, Anthony said, "Dad, is twenty-two dollars a lot or a little?"

Alexander glanced at his son. "Well, it depends for what. It's a little money for a car. But it's a lot of money for candy. Why?"

"Mrs. Brooster wants us to pay twenty-two more dollars."

"Anthony!" Tatiana was near the stove; she didn't turn around.

"No, the child is *impossible*. Go wash your hands. With soap. Thoroughly. And rinse them."

"They're clean."

"Anthony, you heard your mother. Now." That was Alexander. Anthony went.

He came up to her by the sink. "So what's going on?"

"Nothing."

"It's time to go, don't you think? We've been here two months. And soon it's going to get much colder." He paused. "I'm not even going to get started on the communists or the twenty-two dollars."

"I wouldn't mind it if we never left here," she said. "Here on the edge of the world. Nothing intrudes here. Despite . . ." she waved her hand to Mrs. Brewster upstairs. "I feel safe here. I feel like no one will ever find us."

Alexander was quiet. "Is someone . . . *looking* for us?"

"No, no. Of course not." She spoke so quickly.

He placed two fingers under her chin and lifted her face to him. "Tania?"

She couldn't return his serious gaze. "I just don't want to go yet, okay?" She tried to move away from his hand. He didn't let her. "That's all. I like it here." She raised her hands to hold on to his arms. "Let's move to Nellie's. We'll have two rooms. She has a bigger kitchen. And you can go for a drink with your pal Jimmy. As I understand, he's been coming around there a little." She smiled to convince him.

Letting go of her, Alexander put his plate in the sink, clanging it loudly against the cast aluminum sides. "Yes, let's," he said. "Nellie, Jimmy, us. What a fine idea, communal living. We should have more of it." He shrugged. "Oh, well. Guess you can take the girl out of the Soviet Union, but you can't take the Soviet Union out of the girl."

At least there was *some* participation. Though, like Tatiana kept saying, not great.

They moved to Nellie's. The air turned a little chilly, then a lot chilly, then cold, particularly in the night, and Nellie, as they found out, was Dickensianly cheap with the heat.

They may have paid for two rooms, but it was all never mind to Anthony, who had less than no interest in staying in a room all by himself. Alexander was forced to drag his twin bed into their room, and push the beds together—again. They paid for two rooms and lived in one.

They huddled under thick blankets, and then suddenly, in the middle of October, it snowed! Snow fell in balls out of the sky, and in one night covered the bay and the barely bare trees in white wool. There was no more work for Alexander, and now there was snow. The morning snow fell, they looked out the window and then at each other. Alexander smiled with all his teeth.

Tatiana finally understood. "Oh, you," she said. "So smug in your little knowledge."

"So smug," he agreed, still smiling.

"Well, you're wrong about me. There is nothing wrong with a little snow."

He nodded.

"Right, Anthony? Right, darling? You and me are used to snow. New York had snow, too."

"Not just New York." The smile in Alexander's eyes grew dimmer, as if becoming veiled by the very snow he was lauding.

The stairs were slippery, covered with four inches of old ice. The half-filled metal bucket of water was heavy and kept spilling over the stairs as she held on to the banister with one hand, the bucket with the other and pulled herself up one treacherous step at a time. She had to get up two flights. At the seventh step, she fell on her knees, but didn't let go the banister, or the bucket. Slowly she pulled herself back to her feet. And tried again. If only there were a little light, she could see where she was stepping, avoid the ice maybe. But there wouldn't be daylight for another two hours, and she had to go out and get the bread. If she waited two hours there would be no bread left in the store. And Dasha was getting worse. She needed bread.

Tatiana turned away from him. It was morning! There was no dimming of lights at the beginning of each day; it was simply not allowed.

They went sledding. They rented two Flexible Flyers from the general store, and spent the afternoon with the rest of the villagers sledding on the steep Stonington hill that ran down to the bay. Anthony walked uphill exactly twice. Granted, it was a big hill, and he was brave and good to do it, but the other twenty times, his father carried him.

Finally, Tatiana said, "You two go on without me. I can't walk anymore."

"No, no, come with us," said Anthony. "Dad, I'll walk up the hill. Can you carry Mama?"

"I think I might be able to carry Mommy," said Alexander.

Anthony trudged along, while Alexander carried Tatiana uphill
on his back. She cried and the tears froze on her face. But then
they raced down, Tatiana and Anthony on one sled, trying to beat
Alexander, who was heavier than mother and son, and fast and
maneuvered well, unhampered by fear for a small boy, unlike her.
She flew down anyway, with Anthony shrieking with frightened
delight. She almost beat Alexander. At the bottom she collided into
him.

"You know if I didn't have Ant, you'd never win," she said,
lying on top of him.

"Oh, yes, I would," he said, pushing her off him into the snow.
"Give me Ant, and let's go."

It was a good day.

They spent three more long days in the whitened mountain ash
trees on the whitened bay. Tatiana baked pies in Nellie's big
kitchen. Alexander read all the papers and magazines from stem
to stern and talked post-war politics to Tatiana and Jimmy, and
even to indifferent Nellie. In Nellie's potato fields, Alexander
built snowmen for Anthony. After the pies were in the oven,
Tatiana came out of the house and saw six snowmen arrayed
like soldiers from big to little. She tutted, rolled her eyes and
dragged Anthony away to fall down and make angels in the
snow instead. They made thirty of them, all in a row, arrayed
like soldiers.

On the third night of winter, Anthony was in their bed rest-
fully asleep, and they were wide awake. Alexander was rubbing
her bare buttocks under her gown. The only window in their
room was blizzarded over. She assumed the blue moon was
shining beyond. His hands were becoming very insistent.
Alexander moved one of the blankets onto the floor, silently;
moved her onto the blanket, silently; laid her flat onto her
stomach, silently, and made love to her in stealth like they were
doughboys on the ground, crawling to the frontline, his belly to
her back, keeping her in a straight line, completely covering her
tiny frame with his body, clasping her wrists above her head with
one hand. As he confined her, he was kissing her shoulders, and
the back of her neck, and her jawline, and when she turned her
face to him, he kissed her lips, his free hand roaming over her
legs and ribs while he moved deep and *slow!* amazing enough by
itself, but even more amazingly he turned her *to* him to finish,

still restraining her arms above her head, and even made a brief noise not just a raw exhale at the feverish end . . . and then they lay still, under the blankets, and Tatiana started to cry underneath him, and he said *shh, shh, come on*, but didn't instantly move off her, like usual.

"I'm so afraid," she whispered.

"Of what?"

"Of everything. Of you."

He said nothing.

She said, "So you want to get the heck out of here?"

"Oh, God. I thought you'd never ask."

"Where do you think you're going?" Jimmy asked when he saw them packing up the next morning.

"We're leaving," Alexander replied.

"Well, you know what they say," Jim said. "Man proposes and God disposes. The bridge over Deer Isle is iced over. Hasn't been plowed in weeks and won't be. Nowhere to go until the snow melts."

"And when do you think that might be?"

"April," Jimmy said, and both he and Nellie laughed. Jimmy hugged her with his one good arm and Nellie, gazing brightly at him, didn't look as if she cared that he had just the one.

Tatiana and Alexander glanced at each other. April! He said to Jim, "You know what, we'll take our chances."

Tatiana started to speak up, started to say, "Maybe they're right—" and Alexander fixed her with such a stare that she instantly shut up, ashamed of questioning him in front of other people, and hurried on with the packing. They said goodbye to a regretful Jimmy and Nellie, said goodbye to Stonington and took their Nomad Deluxe across Deer Isle onto the mainland.

In this one instant, man disposed. The bridge had been kept clear by the snow crews on Deer Isle. Because if the bridge was iced over, no one could get any produce shipments to the people in Stonington. "What a country," said Alexander, as he drove out onto the mainland and south.

They stopped at Aunt Esther's for what Alexander promised was going to be a three-day familial visit.

They stayed six weeks until after Thanksgiving.

Esther lived in her big old house in a quaint and white Barrington with Rosa, her housekeeper of forty years. Rosa had known

Alexander since birth. The two women clucked over Alexander and his wife and child with such ferocity, it was impossible to leave. They bought Anthony skis! They bought Anthony a sled, and new boots, and warm winter coats! The boy was outside in the snow all day. They bought Anthony bricks and blocks and books! The boy was inside all day.

What else would you like, dear Anthony?

I'd like a weapon like my Dad has, said the boy.

Tatiana vehemently shook her head.

Look at Anthony, what an amazing boy he is and he talks so well for a three-and-a-half-year-old, and doesn't he look just like his father did? Here's a picture of a baby Alexander, Tania.

Yes, Tatiana said, he was a beautiful boy.

Once, said Alexander, and Tania nearly cried, and he was never smiling.

Esther, seeing nothing, continued. Oh, was my brother ever besotted with him. They had him so late in life, you know, Tania, and wanted him so desperately, having tried for a baby for years. Never was a man more besotted with his child. His mother too. I want you to know that, Alexander, darling, the sun rose and set on you.

Cluck, cluck, cluck, for six weeks, wanting them to stay for the holidays, through Easter, through the Fourth of July, maybe Labor Day, for all the days, just stay.

And suddenly, late one evening in the kitchen, when Alexander, exhausted from playing in the snow with Anthony, fell asleep in the living room, and Tatiana was clearing up their tea cups before bed, Aunt Esther came into the kitchen to help her, and said, "Don't drop the cups when you hear this, but a man named Sam Gulotta from the State Department called here in October. Don't get upset, sit. Don't worry. He called in October, and he called again this afternoon when you three were out. Please—what did I tell you?—don't shake, don't tremble. You should have said something when you called in September, given me a warning about what was going on. It would have helped me. You should have trusted me, so I could help *you*. No, don't apologize. I told Sam I don't know where you are. I don't know how to reach you, I know nothing. That's what I told him. And to you I say, I don't want to know. Don't tell me. Sam said it was *imperative* that Alexander get in touch with him. I told him if I heard from you, I'd let him know. But darling, why wouldn't you tell me? Don't you know I'm on your side, on Alexander's side? Does he know that Sam is calling for him? Oh. Well. No, no, you're right of course. He's got enough to worry about. Besides, it's the government; it takes them years just to send out a veteran's check. They're hardly going to be on top of this. Soon it will go into the inactive pile and be forgotten. You'll see. Tell Alexander nothing, it's for the best. And don't cry. Shh, now. Shh."

"Aunt Esther," said Alexander, walking into the kitchen, "what in the world are you telling Tania *now* to make her cry?"

"Oh, you know how she is nowadays," Aunt Esther said, patting Tatiana's back.

On Thanksgiving, Rosa and Esther talked about having Anthony baptized. "Alexander, talk some sense into your wife. You don't want your son to be a heathen like Tania." It was after a magnificent dinner during which Tania gave thanks to Aunt Esther, and they were sitting late in the deep evening, with mulled apple cider in front of a roaring fire. Anthony had been long bathed and fussed over and adored and put to sleep. Tatiana was feeling sleepy and contented, pressed against Alexander's sweatered arm. It reminded her throbbingly of another time in her life, sitting next to him, like this, in front of a flickering small stove called the *bourzhuika*, feeling calmed by his presence despite the apocalyptic things going on just steps from her in her own room, in her own apartment, in her own city, in her own country. And yet, she sat like this with him and for a fleeting minute was comforted

"Tania is not a heathen," Alexander said to Esther. "She was dunked into the River Luga promptly after birth by Russian women so old they looked as if they lived in the times of Christ. They took her from her mother, babynapped her, you might say, and muttered over her for three hours, summoning the love of Christ and the Holy Spirit onto her. Tania's mother never spoke to the old women again."

"Or to me," said Tatiana.

"Tania, is this true?"

"Alexander is teasing, Esther. Don't listen to him."

"That's not what she asked, Tatia. She asked if it was true." His eyes were twinkling.

He was teasing! She kissed his arm, putting her face back against his sweater. "Esther, you mustn't fret about Anthony. He is baptized."

"He is?" said Esther.

"He is?" said Alexander with surprise.

"He is," Tatiana said quietly. "They baptized all the children at Ellis Island because so many of them used to get sick and die. They had a chapel, and even found me a Catholic priest."

"A Catholic priest!" Catholic Rosa and Protestant Esther raised their hands to the heavens in a loud interjection, one happy, one slightly less so. "Why Catholic? Why not even Russian Orthodox, like you?"

"I wanted Anthony," Tatiana said timidly, looking away from Alexander's gaze, "to be like his father."

And that night in their bed, all three of them, Alexander didn't go to sleep, lightly keeping his hand on her. She felt him awake behind her. "What, darling?" she whispered. "What do you need? Ant's here."

"Don't I know it," he whispered back. "But no, no. Tell me . . ." his voice was halting, "was he . . . very small when he was born?"

"I don't know . . ." she replied in a constricted voice. "I had him a month early. He was quite little. Black-haired. I don't really remember. I was in a fever. I had TB, pneumonia. They gave me extreme unction, I was so sick." She clenched her fists to her chest, but groaned anyway. And so alone.

Alexander told her he couldn't stay in wintry Barrington any longer, couldn't do snow, winters, cold. "Never again—not for one more day." He wanted to go swimming for Christmas.

Whatever Anthony's father wanted, Anthony's father got. *The sun still rises and sets on you, husband,* she whispered to him.

Sets mainly, he whispered back.

They said a grateful good-bye to Esther and Rosa, and drove down past New York.

"Aren't we stopping to see Vikki?"

"We're not," Tatiana said. "Vikki always goes to visit her mentally ill mother in California during Christmas. It's her penance. Besides, it's too cold. You said you wanted to go swimming. We'll catch her in the summer."

They drove through New Jersey and Maryland.

They were passing Washington DC when Alexander said, "Want to stop and say hello to your friend Sam?"

Startled she said, "No! Why would you say that?"

He seemed pretty startled by *that.* "Why are you getting defensive? I asked if you wanted to stop and say hello. Why are you talking to me as if I asked you to wash his car?"

Tatiana tried to relax.

Thank goodness he dropped it. In the past, he never used to drop anything until he got his answer.

Virginia, still in the thirties, too cold.

North Carolina, in the high forties, cold.

South Carolina in the fifties. Better.

They stayed in cheap motels and had hot showers.

Georgia in the sixties. Not good enough.

St. Augustine in Florida was in the seventies! on the warm ocean. St. Augustine, the oldest city in the United States, had red Spanish tile roofs and was selling ice cream as if it were summer.

They visited the site of Ponce De Leon's Fountain of Youth, and bought a little immortal water, conveniently in bottled form.

"You know it's just tap water, don't you?" Alexander said to her, as she took a drink from it.

"I know," Tatiana said, passing him the bottle. "But you have to believe in something."

"It's not tap water I believe in," Alexander said, drinking half of it down.

They celebrated Christmas in St. Augustine. Christmas Day they went to a deserted white beach. "Now this is what I call the dead of winter," said Alexander, diving into the ocean water in swimming shorts and a T-shirt. There was no one around him but his son and wife.

Anthony, who didn't know how to swim, waded at the edge of the water, dug holes that looked like craters, collected seashells, got burned, and with his shoulders red and his hair sandy, skipped on the beach, singing, holding a long stick in one hand, and a rock in the other, moving his arms up and down to the rhythmic beat of the tune while his mother and father watched him from the water.

"*Mr. Sun/ Sun/ Mr. Golden Sun/ please shine down on/ please shine down on/ please shine down on me . . .*"

After weeks in St. Augustine, they drove south down the coast.`

CHAPTER TWO

Coconut Grove, 1947

The Vanishing

Miami in January! Tropics by the sea. It was eighty degrees
and the water was seventy-five. "Better," said Alexander, smiling.
"*Much* better. Now we stay."

Sprawled near the calm aqua waves of the Atlantic and Biscayne
Bay, Miami Beach and South Beach were a little too . . . grown
up for them with a small boy, with the rampant gambling casinos,
the made-up, dressed-up women walking the streets, and the
fanned, darkened 1930s Art Deco hotels on the ocean that looked
as if men with mortal secrets lived there. Perhaps such hotels
were rightful places for the Tatianas and Alexanders of this world—
but she couldn't tell him that. She used Anthony's moral well-
being as her excuse to leave. From South Beach, they drove twelve
miles south to Coconut Grove, where it was calmer and neater.
Cocoanut Grove, as it was called before the roads and the trains
and the tourist trade came in 1896, was just a little town on
Biscayne Bay with twenty-eight smart elegant buildings, two large
stores doing whopping business, and a luxury hotel. That was
then. Now the prosperity was like the sunshine—abundant and
unabated. Now there were parks and beaches, marinas, restaurants and stores galore, all etched on the water under the fanning palms.

They stayed at a motel court inland but every day kept drifting
out to the bay. Tatiana was worried about the money running
through their fingers. She suggested selling the camper. "We can't
stay in it anyway. You need to wash—"

"I'll wash in the ocean."

"I need somewhere to cook your food."

"We'll eat out."

"We're going to go broke."

"I'll get work."

She cleared her throat. "We need a *little* privacy . . ."

"Ah, now you're talking. But forget it, I won't sell it."

They were strolling along Bayshore Avenue, past moorings that fingered out into the water. He pointed to a houseboat.

"You want to rent a boat?"

"A *house*boat."

"A what?"

"A boat that is also a house."

"You want us to live on a *boat*?" Tatiana said slowly.

Alexander called to his son. "Anthony, how would you like to live in a house that is also a boat?"

The child jumped up and down.

"Anthony," said his mother, "how would you like to live in a snowy mountain retreat in the north of Canada?"

Anthony jumped up and down.

"Alexander, see? I really don't think you should be making all your life decisions based on the joy of one small boy."

Alexander lifted Anthony into his arms. "Bud," he said, "a house that is moored like a boat and sways like a boat, but never moves from the dock, right on the ocean, doesn't that sound great?"

Anthony put his arms around his father's neck. "I said yes, Dad. What more do you want?"

For thirty dollars a week—the same money they didn't want to pay Mrs. Brewster—they rented a fully furnished houseboat on Fair Isle Street, jutting out into the bay right between Memorial Park and the newly broken construction site for Mercy Hospital. The houseboat had a little kitchen with a small stove, a living room, a bathroom with a toilet—And two bedrooms!

Anthony, of course, just like at Nellie's, refused to sleep by himself. But this time Tatiana was adamant right back. She stayed with her son for an hour, lay down in the bed with him until he was asleep in his own bed. The mother wanted a room of her own.

When an utterly bare Tatiana, without even a silk nightgown, lay down in a double-size bed in front of Alexander, she thought she was a different woman making love to a different man. It was dark in the bedroom, but he was also naked, no tank tops, no shirts, no battle gear. He was naked and on top of her, and he actually murmured a bit to her, things she hadn't heard in a very long while, he took it a little slower, slower than he had in a very long while, and for that Tatiana rewarded him with a breathless climax, and a shy plea for a little more, and he obliged, but in a way that was too much for her, holding up her legs against his upright arms and moving so intensely that small thrilling cries of pain and pleasure drowned her parchment throat, followed by a less shy plea for some more . . . and he even opened his eyes briefly, watching her mouth moaning for him, *Oh my God, Shura.* She saw his searching face; he whispered, *You like that, do you?* He kissed her, but Tatiana unclasped from him and began to cry. Alexander sighed and closed his eyes again, and there was no more.

Alexander got ready to go look for work, Tatiana got ready to take their clothes to the Laundromat. There was no Laundromat nearby. "Maybe we should have rented a house closer to the Laundromat."

He stopped getting his cigarettes and his money and stared at her. "Just so we're clear," he said, "a houseboat on the Atlantic, dawn over the water like you saw this morning, or living by the Laundromat? Are you opting for the latter?"

"I'm not opting," she said, chastised and blushing. "But I can't wash your clothes in the Atlantic, can I?"

"Wait for me to come back and we'll decide what to do."

When he returned in the late afternoon he said, "I found work—Mel's Marina."

Tatiana's face was so crestfallen, Alexander laughed. "Tania, Mel owns a marina right on the other side of Memorial Park, a ten minute walk from here down the ocean promenade."

"Does Mel have one hand like Jimmy?" asked Anthony.

"No, bud."

"Does Mel smell like fish like Jimmy?" asked Tatiana.

"Nope. Mel rents boats. He's looking for someone to maintain them, and also do a tour-ride twice a day around Key Biscayne and South Miami Beach. We go around, look at the sights and then we come back. I get to drive a motor boat."

"But Alexander," said Tatiana, "did you tell Mel you don't know how to drive a motor boat?"

"Of course not. I didn't tell you I didn't know how to drive a camper either."

She shook her head. He was something else.

"Seven thirty to six," he said. "And he's paying me *twenty* dollars. A day."

"Twenty dollars a day!" Tatiana exclaimed. "Double the money in Deer Isle, and you don't have to smell like fish. How can he afford to pay you so much?"

"Apparently rich lonely ladies love to take boat rides to far away beaches while waiting for their husbands to return from the war."

Tatiana turned away from him so he wouldn't see her face.

From behind, his arms went around her. "And if I'm very good to the ladies," continued Alexander, moving her braid away to kiss her neck and brushing his groin against her, "sometimes they tip the captain."

Tatiana knew he was trying to amuse her, to be light with her, and even as a tear ran down her cheek, she said, patting his hand, "Well, if there's one thing you know how to do, Alexander, it's be good to the ladies."

In the morning, at seven, as Alexander was about to leave for the marina, he said to Tatiana, "Come by to see me just before ten. That's when we go out for our morning tour." He picked up Anthony, who was still in his pajamas. "Bud, I'm going to take you on the boat with me. You'll be my co-captain."

Anthony's face shined. "Really?" Then his face fell. "I can't go, Dad."

"Why?"

"I don't know how to steer a boat."

"Neither do I, so we're even. "

Anthony kissed his father on the mouth.

"Am I coming, too?" Tatiana asked.

"No. You are going to walk a mile to the store and buy food, and do laundry. Or suntan." He smiled. "Do whatever you like. But come at twelve thirty to pick him up. We can have lunch together before I have to go out again at two."

Tatiana kissed her husband on the mouth.

He took his boy with him! What happiness, what joy for Anthony. Tatiana did laundry, bought food and a Cuban cookbook, and sandwich meat, and potato salad and rolled everything back home in a newly purchased wooden cart. She opened all the windows to smell the ocean breeze while she made lunch as strings playing the Poco Allegretto from Brahms's Third Symphony filled her houseboat from the kitchen radio. She loved that piece. She'd heard it played on Deer Isle, too.

Then she ran through Memorial Park to bring her two men food.

Anthony was apparently a hit on the boat. "He was so busy making friends, he forgot to help his dad steer," said Alexander. "And believe me when I tell you, I needed his help. Never mind, bud. Maybe tomorrow?"

"I can come again with you tomorrow?"

"If you're a good boy for your mother, how about every day?"

Anthony leaped and hopped all the way home.

For dinner she made plantains and beef brisket from a recipe in her new cookbook.

Alexander liked it.

Tatiana set about cooking in every conceivable way what she called "the greatest New World creation since corn"—plantain. Not soft, not sweet, but otherwise banana-like, it went with everything. She bought flounder and fixed it with Mexican salsa and tomatoes and pineapples. But the plantains were the centerpiece of the plate. Tatiana had never had corn or bananas or plantains until she came to America.

"Heavenly plantains with rum," she said, theatrically lighting a match and setting the plantains and frying pan on fire. Alexander was worried *and* skeptical until she spooned them over vanilla ice cream; the plantains were mixed with butter, dark brown caramelized sugar, heavy cream—and rum.

"Okay, I'm sold. Heavenly," he said. "Please. Just a little more."

The oven didn't work properly; it was hard to make real bread in it. It wasn't like the great big oven she had in her apartment in New York. Tatiana managed small challah rolls, from a recipe she had got from the Ukrainian Jews on the Lower East Side. It had been *four months* since her last conversation with Vikki. Her stomach went cold every time she thought of her and of Sam. She didn't want to think about them. She forced herself not think of them.

Tatiana was good at forcing herself not to think of things.

Alexander liked the puffy and slightly sweet rolls. "But what, no plantain salad?" he teased when the three of them were eating their lunch on one of the picnic tables under the moss oaks and pines in Memorial Park.

She bought Alexander white cotton and linen shirts with white cotton slacks. She knew he was most comfortable in khaki or green fatigues and long sleeve crews—but he had to look like a boat captain.

Maintaining the boat took most of his time between tours—he learned to make repairs to the hull, the engine, the bearings, the fittings, the bilge pumps, the plumbing, the safety gear, the rails. He repainted the deck, replaced broken or cracked glass, changed the oil. Whatever it was, if it needed fixing, Alexander fixed it, all in his captain's whites and shirtsleeves down to his wrists in the sweltering sun.

Mel, terrified of losing Alexander, gave him a raise to twenty-five dollars a day. Tatiana, too, wished she could give Alexander a raise, for the same reason.

In Miami there was a large Spanish population, and no one heard Tatiana's Russian accent, no one knew her name was Russian. In Miami, Tatiana fit right in. Though she missed the smallness and the tightness and the smells of Deer Isle, though she missed the largesse, the expanse, the blaze of New York, she liked the Miami vanishing.

She made stuffed cabbage, which she knew Anthony liked from their time in New York. Alexander ate it, but after dinner said, "Please don't cook cabbage again."

Anthony got upset. He loved cabbage. And there was even a time when his father enjoyed cabbage pie.

But Alexander said no cabbage.

"Why?" she asked him when they were outside on their boat deck, bobbing above the water. "You used to like it."

"I used to like a lot of things," he replied.

You certainly did, Tatiana thought.

"I saw cabbage that grew as big as three basketballs on the mountain heaps of human ashes and remnants of bones in a death camp called Majdanek in Poland," said Alexander. "It was freak cabbage like nothing you've ever seen, grown out of the ashes of dead Jews. You'd never eat cabbage again either."

"Not even cabbage pie?" she said softly, trying to lure him away from Majdanek and into Lazarevo.

"Not even cabbage pie, Tania," replied a not-to-be-lured Alexander. "No more cabbage pie for us."

Tatiana didn't cook cabbage anymore.

Anthony was told he was not allowed to leave the table unless his plate was empty.

"I'll leave when I want," said Anthony.

Alexander put down his fork. "What did you say?"

"You can't tell me what to do," said Anthony, and his father got up from the table so swiftly that Anthony knocked over his chair to run to his mother.

Taking him out of Tatiana's arms, Alexander set him firmly down. "I can and I will tell you what to do." His hands were on his son's shoulders. "Now we're going to try it again. You will not leave when you want. You will sit, you will finish your food, and when you're done, you will ask to leave the table. Understand?"

"I'm full!" Anthony said. "Why do I have to finish?"

"Because you have to. Next time, Tania, don't give him so much."

"He said he was hungry."

"Give him seconds. But today he will finish his food."

"Mommy!"

"No, not Mommy—*me*! Now finish your food."

"Mom—"

Alexander's hands squeezed around Anthony. Anthony finished his food *and* asked to leave the table. After dinner, Tatiana went outside on the narrow deck where Alexander was sitting and smoking. She crouched carefully, uncertainly by his side.

"You've been too soft on him," he said. "He has to learn. He will learn."

"I know. He's so little, though."

"Yes, when he is my size, it'll be too late."

She sat on the floor of the deck.

After a while Alexander spoke. "He can't leave food on his plate."

"I know."

"Do you want me to tell you about your brother starving in Catowice?"

She barely suppressed her sigh. "Only if you want to, darling." Only if you need to. Because, like you, there are many things I would rather never talk about.

In the POW camp in Catowice, Poland, where the Germans threw Alexander, his lieutenant, Ouspensky, and Pasha into the Soviet half— which meant the death half—Alexander saw that Pasha was weakening. He had no fuel to feed the shell that carried his life. It was worse for Pasha because he had been wounded in the throat. He couldn't work. What they gave the Soviet men was just enough to kill them slowly. Alexander made a wood spear, and when he was in the forest cutting down trees for fire- wood, he caught three rabbits, hid them in his coat and, back at camp,

cooked them in the kitchen, giving one to the cook, one to Pasha, and split-
ting one between himself and Ouspensky.

He felt better, but he was still starving. From Tatiana, during Leningrad's
blockade, he learned that as long as he constantly thought about food—
about getting it, cooking it, eating it, wanting it, he was not a goner. He'd
seen the goners—then in Leningrad, now in Catowice—the last-leggers, as
they were called, the men unable to work, who shuffled through the camp's
trash eating what scraps they could find. When one of the goners had died,
Alexander, about to dig a grave, found Pasha and three others eating the
remains of the dead man's slops by the fire at the outskirts of the barracks.

Alexander was made a supervisor, which did not endear him to his
peers, but it did allow him to get a larger food ration, which he shared
with Pasha. He kept Pasha and Ouspensky with him, and they moved into
a room that housed only eight people instead of sixty. It was warmer.
Alexander worked harder. He killed the rabbits and the badgers, and occa-
sionally he didn't wait to bring them back to camp. He built a fire and
ate them on the spot, half cooked, tearing at them with his teeth. It wasn't
making much of a difference even to him.

And Pasha suddenly stopped being interested in rabbits.

Tatiana's head was folded over her knees. She needed a better
memory of her brother.

In Luga, Pasha is stuffing blueberries into Tatiana's open mouth. She
is begging him to stop, trying to tickle him, trying to throw him off her,
but in between mouthfuls of blueberries for himself, he is tickling Tatiana
with one hand, stuffing blueberries into her mouth with the other, and
pinning her between his legs so she can't go anywhere. Tatiana finally
heaves her small body hard enough to throw Pasha off, onto the pails
of blueberries they just brought freshly picked from the woods. The buckets
tip over; she screams at him to pick them up and when he doesn't, she
takes handfuls and mashes them into his face, painting his face purple.
Saika comes from next door and stares blankly at them from the gate.
Dasha comes out from the porch and when sees what they've done, she
shows them what real screaming is all about.

Alexander smoked, and Tatiana, on weakened legs, struggled up
and went back inside, hoping that when Anthony was older they
could tell him in a way he would understand, about Leningrad,
and Catowice, and Pasha. But she feared he would never understand, living in the land of plantains and plenty.

* * *

In the *Miami Herald* Tatiana found an article about the House of

Un-American Activities Committee investigations into communist infiltration of the State Department. The paper was pleased to call it "an ambitious program of investigations to expose and ferret out Communist activities in many enterprises, labor unions, education, motion pictures and most importantly, the Federal Government." Truman himself had called for removal of disloyal government employees.

She became so engrossed that Alexander had to raise his voice to get her attention. "What are you reading?"

"Nothing." She slammed the newspaper shut.

"You're hiding things in newspapers from me? Show me what you were reading."

Tatiana shook her head. "Let's go to the beach."

"Show me, I said." He grabbed her, his fingers going into her ribs and his mouth into her neck. "Show me right now, or I'll . . ."

"Daddy, stop teasing Mommy," said Anthony, prying them apart.

"I'm not teasing Mommy. I'm tickling Mommy."

"Stop tickling Mommy," said Anthony, prying them apart.

"Antman," said Alexander, "did you just . . . call me *daddy*?"

"Yes. So?"

Bringing Anthony to his lap, Alexander read the HUAC article. "So? They've been investigating communists since the 1920s. Why the fascination now?"

"No fascination." Tatiana started to clear the breakfast plates. "You think there are Soviet spies here?"

"Rampaging through the Government. And they won't rest until Stalin gets his atomic bomb."

She squinted at him. "You know something about this?"

"I know something about this." He pointed to his ears. "I listened to quite a bit of chatter and rumor among the rank and file outside my door in solitary confinement."

"Really?" Tania said that in a mulling tone, but what she was trying to do was to not let Alexander see her eyes. She didn't want him to see Sam Gulotta's anxious phone calls in her frightened eyes.

When they didn't talk about food or HUAC, they spoke about Anthony.

"Can you believe how well he's talking? He is like a little man."

"Tania, he comes into bed with us every night. Can we talk about *that*?"

"He's just a little boy."

"He needs to sleep in his own bed."

"It's big and he gets scared."

Alexander bought a smaller bed for Anthony, who didn't like it and had no interest in sleeping in it. "I thought the bed was for you," said Anthony to his father.

"Why would I need a bed? I sleep with Mommy," said Anthony Alexander Barrington.

"So do I," said Anthony Alexander Barrington.

Finally Alexander said, "Tania, I'm putting my foot down. He can't come into our bed anymore."

She tried to dissuade him.

"I know he has nightmares," Alexander said. "I will take him back to his bed. I will sit with him as long as it takes."

"He needs his mother in the middle of the night."

"*I* need his mother in the middle of the night, his naked mother. He's going to have to make do with me," Alexander said. "And *she* is going to have to make do with me."

The first night, Anthony screamed for fifty-five minutes while Tatiana remained in the bedroom with a pillow pressed over her head. Alexander spent so long in the boy's room, he fell asleep on Anthony's bed.

The following night Anthony screamed for forty-five minutes.

Then thirty.

Then fifteen.

And finally, just whimpers coming from Anthony, as he stood by his mother's side. "I won't cry anymore, but please, Mama, can *you* take me back to my bed?"

"No," said Alexander, getting up. "I will take you back."

And the following afternoon as mother and son were walking back home from the boat, Anthony said, "When is Dad going back?"

"Going back where?"

"The place you brought him from."

"Never, Anthony." She shivered. "What are you talking about?" The shiver was at the memory of the place she had brought him from, the bloodied, filth-soaked straw on which he lay shackled and tortured, waiting not for her but for the rest of his life in the Siberian resort. Tatiana lowered the boy to the ground. "Don't ever let me catch you talking like that again." Or your nightmares now will pale compared to the ones you will have.

*   *   *

"*Why* does he walk as if he's got the weight of the whole world on his shoulders?" Alexander asked while walking home. The green and stunning ocean was to their right, through the bending palms. "Where does he get that from?"

"I can't imagine."

"Hey," he said, knocking into her with his body. Now that he wasn't covered with lobster he could do that, knock into her. Tatiana took his arm. Alexander was watching Anthony. "You know what? Let me . . . I'll take him to the park for a few minutes while you fix dinner." He prodded her forward. "Go on now, what are you worried about? I just want to talk to him, man to man."

Tatiana reluctantly went, and Alexander took Anthony on the swings. They got ice cream, both promising conspiratorially not to tell Mommy, and while they were in the playground, Alexander said, "Ant, tell me what you dream about. What's bothering you? Maybe I can help."

Anthony shook his head.

Alexander picked him up and carried him under the trees, setting him down on top of a picnic table while he sat on the bench in front of him so that their eyes were level. "Come on, bud, tell me." He rubbed Anthony's little chubby legs. "Tell me so I can help you."

Anthony shook his head.

"Why do you wake up? What wakes you?"

"Bad dreams," said Anthony. "What wakes *you*?"

His father had no answer for that. He still woke up every night. He had started taking ice cold baths to cool himself down, to calm himself down at three in the morning. "What kind of bad dreams?"

Anthony was all clammed up.

"Come on, bud, tell me. Does Mommy know?"

Anthony shrugged. "I think Mommy knows everything."

"You're too wise for your own good," said Alexander. "But I don't think she knows *this*. Tell me. *I* don't know."

He cajoled and prodded. Anthony's ice cream was melting; they kept wiping up the drips. Finally Anthony, looking not at his father's prying face but at his shirt buttons, said, "I wake up in a cave."

"Ant, you've never been in a cave. What cave?"

Anthony shrugged. "Like a hole in the ground. I call for Mom. She's not there. Mommy, Mommy. She doesn't come. The cave starts to burn. I climb outside, I'm near woods. Mommy, Mommy.

I call and call. It gets dark. I'm alone." Anthony looked down at his hands. "A man whispers, *Run, Anthony, she is gone, your mommy, she is not coming back.* I turn around, but there is no one there. I run into the woods to get away from the fire. It's very dark, and I'm crying. Mommy, Mommy. The woods go on fire too. I feel like somebody's chasing me. Chasing and chasing me. But when I turn around, I'm all alone. I keep hearing feet running after me. I'm running too. And the man's voice is in my ear. *She is gone, your mommy, she is not coming back.*"

The ice cream dripped through Alexander's fingers, through Anthony's fingers. "That's what you dream about?" Alexander said tonelessly.

"Uh-huh."

Alexander stared grimly at Anthony, who stared grimly back. "Can you help me, Dad?"

"It's just a bad dream, bud," Alexander said. "Come here." He picked up the boy. Anthony put his head on Alexander's shoulder. "Don't tell your mom what you just told me, all right?" he said in a hollow voice, patting the boy's back, holding him close. "It'll make her very sad you dream this." He started walking home, his gaze fixed blinklessly on the road.

After a minute, he said, "Antman, did your mother ever tell you about her dreams when she was a little girl in Luga? No? Because she used to have bad dreams, too. You know what she used to dream about? Cows chasing her."

Anthony laughed.

"Exactly," Alexander said. "Big cows with bells and milk udders would go running down the village road after your young mother, and no matter how hard she ran, she couldn't get away."

"Did they go moo?" said Anthony. "Here moo, there moo, everywhere moo-moo."

"Oh, yes."

In the night Anthony crawled to his mother's side, and Alexander and Tatiana, both awake, said nothing. Alexander had just come back to bed himself, barely dry. Her arm went around Anthony, and Alexander's damp icy arm went around Tatiana.

The Body of War

As it began to stay lighter later, they would go swimming when the park beaches emptied. Tatiana hung upside down on the monkey bars, they played ball, they built things in the sand; the beach, the bars, the breaking Atlantic were good and right as rain. Alexander sometimes even took off his T-shirt while he swam in the languid evenings—slowly, obsessively trying to wash away in the briny ocean typhus and starvation and war and other things that could not be washed away.

Tatiana sat near the shoreline, watching father and son frolic. Alexander was supposed to be teaching Anthony how to swim, but what he was doing was picking the boy up and flinging him into the shallow waters. The waves were perfect in Miami for a small boy, for the waves were small also. Son jumped to father, only to be thrown up in the air and then caught again, thrown up in the air very high and then caught again. Anthony squealed, shrieked, splashed, full of monumental joy. And there was Tatiana nearby, sitting on the sand, hugging her knees, one of her hands out in invocation, *careful, careful, careful*. But she wasn't saying it to Alexander. She was saying it to Anthony. Don't hurt your father, son. Be gentle with him. Please. *Can't you see what he looks like?*

Her breath burned her chest as she furtively glanced at her husband. Now they were racing into the water. The first time Tatiana had seen Alexander run into the Kama River in Lazarevo, naked except for his shorts—like now—his body was holy. It was gleaming and woundless. And he'd been in battles already, in the Russo-Finnish War; he'd been on the northern rivers of the Soviet Union; he had defended the Road of Life on Lake Ladoga. Like her, he had lived through blighted Leningrad. Why then, since she had left him, had this happened to him?

Alexander's bare body was shocking to see. His back, once smooth and tanned, was mutilated with shrapnel scars, with burn scars, with whip marks, with bayonet gouges all wet in the Miami sun. His near-fatal injury at the breaking of the Leningrad blockade was still a fist-sized patch above his right kidney. His chest and shoulders and ribs were defaced; his upper arms, his forearms, his legs were covered with knife and gunpowder burn wounds, jagged, ragged, raised.

Tatiana wanted to cry, to cry out. It wasn't fair! It wasn't right that he should carry Hitler and Stalin on his whole body, even here in Miami where the tropical waters touched the sky. The colonel had been right. It wasn't fair.

And because all the other iniquities were not enough, the men that guarded Alexander tattooed him against his will, as punishment for escape, as a warning against possible transgressions, and as an ultimate slur against his future—as in, if you have a future at all, you will never have an unblemished one.

Tatiana watched him and her pitying heart rolled around the concrete drum of her insides.

On Alexander's upper left arm was a black tattoo of a hammer and sickle! It was burned into him by the depraved guards at Catowice—so they would know him by his marks. Above the hammer and sickle, on his shoulder there was a mocking tattoo of a major's epaulet, taunting that Alexander had spent too much time in solitary confinement. Under the hammer and sickle was a large star with twenty-five points on it—one point for each of the years of his Soviet prison sentence. On the inside of his right forearm, the numbers 19691 were burned in blue—the Soviets learned to use the Nazi torture implements with glee.

On his right upper arm a cross was tattooed—Alexander's only voluntary mark. And above the cross, he was branded with an incongruous SS Waffen Eagle, complete with a swastika, as a symbol of grudging respect from the ill-fated guard Ivan Karolich for Alexander's never having confessed to anything despite the severe beatings.

The concentration camp numbers were the hardest to hide, being so low on his arm, which was why he didn't often roll up his sleeves. Jimmy in Deer Isle had asked about the numbers, but Jimmy hadn't been to war, and so when Alexander said, "POW camp," Jimmy didn't follow up and Alexander didn't elaborate. The blue numbers now, post Holocaust, screamed of Jewish suffering, not Soviet suffering, of someone else's life, not Alexander's. But the hammer and sickle, the SS insignia!— all alarms on his arm, ringing to be explained—were impossible to explain away in *any* context. Death camp numbers *and* a swastika? There was nothing to do about any of it, except cover it from everyone, even each other.

Tatiana turned to watch a family strolling by, two small girls with their mother and grandparents. The adults took one glimpse at Alexander and gasped; in their flustered collective horror, they shielded the eyes of the little girls; they muttered, they made the sign of the cross—on *themselves*, and hurried on. Tatiana judged them harshly. Alexander, lifting and throwing Anthony, never noticed.

Whereas once, certainly in Lazarevo with Tatiana, Alexander looked god-like, it was true now, the strangers were right— Alexander was disfigured. That's all anyone saw, that's all anyone could look at.

But he was so beautiful still! Hard still, lean, long-legged, wide-shouldered, strapping, impossibly tall. He'd gained some of his weight back, was muscular again after hauling all those lob-ster traps. On the rare occasions he laughed, the white of his teeth lit up his tanned face. His sheared head looked like a black hedgehog, his milk chocolate eyes softened every once in a while.

But there was no denying it, he was damaged—and nowhere more noticeably than in this, his American life. For in the Soviet Union, Alexander would have been among millions of men who were maimed like him, and he might have thought no more of it as they sent him out in his sheepskin parka to log in their woods, to mine in their quarries. Here in America, Tatiana sent him out in public, not in a parka but in linen, covering him from his neck to his ankles, to man their boats, to fix their engines.

During lovemaking Tatiana tried to forget. What needed to be whole and perfect remained whole and perfect. But his back, his arms, his shoulders, his chest: there was nowhere for her to put her hands. She held onto his head, which was marginally better. There was a long ridge at the back of the occipital lobe, there were knife wounds. Alexander carried war on his body like no one Tatiana had ever known. She cried every time she touched him.

Tatiana couldn't touch Alexander at night and prayed he didn't know it.

"Come on, you two," she called to them weakly, struggling to her feet. "Let's head home. It's getting late. Stop your horsing around. Anthony, please. What did I tell you? Be careful, I said!" *Can't you see what your father looks like?*

Suddenly her two men, one little, one big, both with the straight posture, the unwavering gazes, came and stood in front of her, their legs in the sand, each in an A, their hands on their hips like kettles.

"Ready to go then?" she said, lowering her gaze.

"Mommy," said her son firmly, "come and play."

"Yes, Mommy," said her husband firmly, "come and play."

"No, it's time to go home." She blinked. A mirage in the setting sun made him disappear for a second.

"That's it," said Alexander, lifting her into his arms. "I've had just about enough of this." He carried her and flung her into the water. Tatiana was without breath and when she came up for air, he threw himself on her, shaking her, disturbing her, implacably laying his hands on her. Perhaps he wasn't a mirage after all, his body immersed in water that was so salty he floated and she floated, too, feeling real herself, remembering cartwheeling at the Palace of the Tsars for him, sitting on the tram with him, walking barefoot through the Field of Mars with him while Hitler's tanks and Dimitri's malice beat down the doors of their hearts.

Alexander picked her up and threw her in the air, only pretending to catch her. She fell and splashed and shrieked, and scrambling to her feet, ran from him as he chased her onto the sand. She tripped to let him catch her and he kissed her wet and she held on to his neck and Anthony jumped and scrambled onto his back, *break it up, break it up*, and Alexander dragged them all deeper in and tossed them into the ocean, where they bobbed and swayed like houseboats.

Alexander's Favorite Color

"Tania, why haven't you called Vikki?" Alexander asked her at breakfast.

"I'll call her. We've only been here a few weeks," she said. "Where's the fire?"

"Try eleven."

"Eleven weeks? No!"

"I know how much rent I've paid. Eleven."

"I didn't realize it's been that long. Why are we still here?" Tatiana muttered, and quickly changed the subject to Thelma, the nice woman she met in the store a few mornings ago. Thelma's husband had recently come back from Japan. Thelma was looking for something to entertain him with as he seemed a bit down in the dumps. Tatiana had suggested a boat ride, and Thelma had sprung at the idea.

Thelma apparently didn't make it to the boat that afternoon, nor the next, though all afternoons were equally blue-skied and acceptable. When Tatiana ran into her at the store a few days later, Thelma muttered an excuse but said she and her husband were hoping to get to the boat *this* afternoon for sure. She asked Tatiana if she came on the boat. Tatiana said no, explaining about her son's nap and her husband's dinner and other home things. Thelma nodded in sisterly understanding, doing the home things herself that morning. She was making a hot apple cobbler. Apparently men returning home from the war liked that.

Alexander had been bringing home astonishing amounts of money. One dollar, two dollars, five dollars, *twenty dollars*.

"Even *my* math is failing me," Tatiana said, sitting at the kitchen table with a stash of singles and fives in front of her. "I can't count this high. Did you make a—*hundred* dollars today?"

"Hmm."

"Alexander, I want to know what you're doing to these women for a hundred dollars a day."

When he smoked and grinned and didn't reply, she said, "That was not a rhetorical question. Your wife would like an answer."

He laughed, and she laughed, ha ha, but the next day when she went to pick up Anthony from the boat, who should she see but Thelma, nattily dressed standing at a distance Tatiana deemed to be too close to her barely salvaged husband. She wasn't even sure it *was* Thelma, for in the grocery store Thelma was sans makeup and wore grocery store clothes. Here, her wavy dark hair was curled and teased, she had makeup on . . . she . . . .Tatiana wasn't even sure what it was that was provocative— perhaps the tightness of the skirt around the hips, the bareness of leg under-neath, perhaps the wine trollop lips in the middle of a torrid noon, perhaps even the smiling tilt of the coquettish, slatternly head.

"Thelma?" Tatiana said, coming up the plank. "Is that you?"

Thelma snapped around as if she'd heard a voice from the grave. "Oh! Hi."

"Oh, hi," said Tatiana, stepping between her and Alexander. She turned to face the woman. "I see you've met *my* husband. Where's *your* husband?"

High-heeling away, Thelma waved her off. "He couldn't make it today."

Tatiana said nothing—then. But she asked Anthony the next morning, in full hearing of a certain husband having breakfast, about the nice woman on the boat, and Anthony told her that she'd been coming every morning for some time.

"Is that so?"

"No, that is not so," intervened a certain husband.

"And, Anthony, does the nice woman's husband come with her?"

"Oh no. She doesn't have a husband. She told Daddy her husband ran away. She said he didn't want to be married after the war."

"Oh, *really?*"

"Yes, and, Mommy," said Anthony, licking his lips, "she brought us an apple cobbler to eat. It was *so* yummy!"

Tatiana said nothing else. She didn't even look up. Alexander tilted his head across the table to get her attention, saying nothing himself. When he went to kiss her, he cupped her face and made her look up at him. His eyes were twinkling. He kissed her nice and open, making the lava pit in her stomach nice and open too, and left for work.

When Tatiana went to pick up Anthony at noon, Thelma wasn't there.

"Mommy," Anthony whispered. "I don't know what Daddy said to her this morning, but she ran from the boat in *tears!*"

Thelma was never seen again, not even in the grocery store.

At home Alexander said, "You want to come with me tomorrow for the morning ride, for the afternoon ride? You know you can come on the boat with me any time you want."

"Can I now?"

"Of course. Any time. You haven't expressed any interest." He paused. "Until now."

There was something slightly . . . Tatiana didn't know . . . *pointed* in his remark. Something accusing. But accusing her of what? Of cooking and cleaning and washing for him? Of braiding her hair and shaving and scrubbing herself pink, and putting on gauzy dresses and sheer panties and musk oil to come to meet him in the evenings? Of letting him have an hour or two with his boy in the mornings?

She contemplated making an issue of it. But an issue of what? She studied him, but he was already past it, as he was past most things, reading the paper, drinking, smoking, talking to Anthony.

Tatiana did come on the boat ride the next morning.

"Your hair is in a crew cut," a girl murmured to him after she sauntered to stand by his side while Tatiana sat quietly nearby, Anthony on her lap. "Almost like you're in the army," the girl persisted when Alexander didn't reply.

"I was in the army."

"Oh that's great! Where did you serve?"

"On the Eastern Front."

"Oh, wow. I want to know everything! Where is this Eastern Front, anyway? I've never heard of it. My father was in Japan. He's still there." The girl, who looked to be in her late teens, continued nonstop. "Captain, you're driving the boat *so* fast, and it's getting *so* windy, and I'm wearing this flouncy *skirt*. You don't think it'll be a problem, do you? The wind isn't going to kick the skirt *up*, in an immodest sort of way?" She giggled.

"I don't think so. Ant, do you want to come, help me steer?"

Anthony ran to his father. The girl turned around to glance at Anthony and at Tatiana, who smiled, giving her a little wave.

"Is this your son?"

"Yes."

"Is that, um . . . ?"

"My wife, yes."

"Oh. Excuse me. I didn't know you were married."

"I am, though, nonetheless. Tania, come here. Meet . . . sorry, I didn't catch your name."

As Tatiana walked past the girl to get to Alexander, she said, "Excuse *me*," and added evenly, "I think the wind might indeed kick *up* that immodesty you were talking about. Better grab on to the skirt."

Alexander bit his lip. Tatiana stood calmly next to him, her hand on the wheel.

That evening walking home, he said, "I either continue to invite questions or I can grow out my hair." When she didn't say anything—because she didn't think her husband with a head full of shiny black hair would be repellent enough—he prodded her to tell him what she was thinking.

She chewed her lip. "The constant female attention . . . um . . . wanted or unwanted?"

"I'm indifferent, babe," he said, his arm around her. "Though amused by you."

Tatiana was quiet when Alexander came home the following evening.

"What's the matter? You're more glum than usual," he asked after he came out from the bath.

She protested. "I'm not usually glum." Then she sighed. "I took a test today."

"What test?" Alexander sat down at her table. "What does the husband want for dinner?"

"The husband wants plantains and carrots and corn and bread, and shrimp, and hot apple cobbler with ice cream for dinner."

"Hot apple cobbler?" Alexander smiled. "Indeed. Indeed." He laughed, buttering his bread roll. "Tell me about this test."

"In one of my magazines. *Ladies Home Journal*. There's a test. 'How Well Do You Know Your Husband?'"

"*One* of your magazines?" His mouth was full. "I didn't know you read *any* magazines."

"Well, perhaps it would behoove you to take that test, too, then."

He was twinkling at her from across the table, buttering another roll. "So how did you do?"

"I failed, that's how I did," Tatiana said. "Apparently I don't know you at all."

"Really?" Alexander's face was mock-serious.

Tatiana flung the magazine open to the test page. "Look at these questions. What is your husband's favorite color? I don't know. What is his favorite food? I don't know. What sports does he like best? I don't know. What is his favorite book? His favorite movie? His favorite song? What's his favorite flavor ice cream? Does he like to sleep on his back or his side? What was the name of the school he graduated from? I don't know anything!"

Alexander grinned. "Come on. Not even the back or side question?"

"No!"

Continuing to eat his roll, he got up, took the magazine out of her hands and threw it in the trash. "You're right." He nodded. "There is nothing to be done. My wife doesn't know my favorite ice cream flavor. I demand a divorce." He raised his eyebrows. "Do you think a priest will give us an annulment?" He came up to her, sitting dejectedly in the chair.

"You're making fun," Tatiana said, "but this is serious."

"You don't know me because you don't know what my favorite color is?" Alexander sounded disbelieving. "Ask me anything. I'll tell you."

"You won't tell me anything! You don't talk to me at all!" She started to cry.

Wide-eyed, flummoxed, stopped in mid-laugh, Alexander speechlessly opened his hands. "A second ago, this was all kind of funny," he said slowly.

"If I don't even know a simple thing like your favorite color," Tatiana said, "can you imagine what else I don't know?"

"*I* don't know my own favorite color! Or movie, or book, or song. I don't know, I don't care, I never thought about it. Good God, is this what people are thinking about after the war?"

"Yes!"

"Is this what *you* want to be thinking about?"

"Better than what *we've* been thinking about!"

Anthony, bless his small ways, came out of his bedroom, and, as always, prevented them from *ever* finishing any discussion until he was well asleep. All the things they talked about had to involve him, be compelling to him. As soon as he heard his mother and father talking in animated tones, he would come and take one of them away.

But later, in their bed, in the dark, Tatiana, who still had on her glum face, said to Alexander, "We don't know each other. It occurs to me now—perhaps a little belatedly—that we never did."

"Speak for yourself," he said. "I know how you've lived and I know how you like to be touched. You know how I've lived and you know how I like to be touched."

Oh. Alexander may have known theoretically, intellectually, how Tatiana liked to be touched, but he certainly never touched her that way anymore. She didn't know why he didn't, he just didn't, and she didn't know how to ask.

"Now, can I make love to you *once* without you crying?"

Certainly she didn't want to *make* him touch her.

"Just once, and please—don't tell me you're crying from happiness."

She tried not to cry when he made love to her. But it was impossible.

The goal was to find a way to live and touch where everything that had happened to them to bring them here could be put away somewhere safe, from where they could retrieve *it*, instead of *it* retrieving them any time *it* felt like it.

In the bedroom they were night animals; the lights were always off. Tatiana had to do something.

*   *   *

"*What* is that god-awful smell?" Alexander said when he came home from the marina.

"Mommy put mayonnaise in her hair," said Anthony with a face that said, *Mommy washed her face with duck poop.*

"She did *what*?"

"Yes. This afternoon she put a whole jar of mayonnaise in her hair! Dad, she sat with it for hours, and now she can't get the water hot enough to rinse it out."

Alexander knocked on the bathroom door.

"Go away," her voice said.

"It's me."

"I was talking to you."

Opening the door, he came in. She was sitting bedraggled in the bath with her hair wet and slick. She covered her breasts from him.

"Um—what are you doing?" he said, with an impassive face.

"Nothing. What are *you* doing? How was your afternoon?" She saw his expression. "One wrong word from you, Alexander . . ." she warned.

"I said nothing," he said. "Are you going to . . . come out soon? Make dinner, maybe?"

"The water is lukewarm, and I just can't get this stuff out. I'm waiting for the tank to reheat."

"It takes hours."

"I got time," she said. "You're not hungry, are you?"

"Can I help?" Alexander asked, working very, very hard at a straight face. "How about I boil some water on the stove and wash it out?"

Mixing boiling water with the cold, Alexander sat shirtless at the edge of the tub and scrubbed Tatiana's head with shampoo. Later they had cheese sandwiches and Campbell's tomato soup. The tank reheated; Tatiana washed the hair again. The smell seemed to come out, but when the hair dried, it still smelled like mayonnaise. After they put Anthony to bed, Alexander ran the bath for her and washed her hair once more. They ran out of shampoo. They used heavy duty soap. The hair still smelled.

"It's like your lobsters," she said.

"Come on, the fish weren't this bad."

"Mom almost smells like herself again," said Anthony when Alexander came home the next day. "Go ahead, Dad, smell her."

Dad leaned down and smelled her. "Mmm, quite like herself," he agreed, placing his hand on her hair.

Tatiana knew that today her hair, down to her lower back, glowed gold and was silken and shiny and exceedingly soft. She had bought strawberry shampoo that was berry fresh and washed her coconut-suntan-lotioned body with vanilla scented soap. Tatiana sidled against Alexander, gazing up up up at him. "Do you like it?" she asked, her breath catching.

"As you know." But he took his hand away and only *glanced* down down down at her.

She got busy with steak and plantains and tomato roulade.

Later, out on the deck, he said quietly, "Tania, go get your brush."

She ran to get the brush. Standing behind her—as if in another life—Alexander slowly, carefully, gently brushed out her hair, running his palm down after each stroke of the brush. "It's *very* soft," he whispered. "What in the world did you put mayonnaise in it for?"

"The hair was dry from the coloring, the leaching and then the ocean," Tatiana replied. "Mayonnaise is supposed to make it smooth again."

"Where did you hear that?"

"Read it in a beauty magazine." She closed her eyes. It felt so good to have his hands in her hair. Her hot liquid stomach was pulsing.

"You need to stop with the magazines." Bending, Alexander pressed his mouth into the back of her head, running his lips back and forth against her, and Tatiana groaned, and was embarrassed that she couldn't stop herself in time.

"If I don't read them, how else am I going to know how to please my husband?" she said thickly.

"Tatia, *you* don't need to read any magazines for that," he said.

We'll have to see about that, she thought, in trepidation at her own anticipated audacity, turning around and stretching out her tremulous hand to him.

His hands behind his head, Alexander lay naked in bed on his back, waiting for her. Tatiana locked the door, took off her silk robe and stood in front of him with her long blonde tresses down over her shoulders. She liked the look in his eyes tonight. It wasn't neutral. When he reached to switch off the light she said, no, leave the light on.

"Leave the light *on*?" he said. "This is new."

"I want you to look at me," Tatiana said, climbing on top of his stomach, spanning him. Slowly she let her hair fall down onto his chest.

"How does it feel?" she murmured.

"Mmm." His hands on her hips, Alexander arched his stomach into her open thighs.

"Silky, right?" she purred. "So soft, silky . . . velvety . . ."

And Alexander groaned.

He *groaned*! He opened his mouth and an unsuppressed sound of excitement left his throat.

"Feel me, Shura . . ." she murmured, continuing to rub herself ever so lightly against his bare stomach, her long loose hair fluttering along with her flutters. But it was stirring her up too much; she had to stop. "I thought maybe if the hair was silky," she whispered, moving her head from side to side as the cascading mane feathered him in silk strands across his chest, "you'd want to put your hands in it . . . your lips in it again."

"My hands *are* on it," he let out.

"I didn't say on it. I said *in* it."

Alexander stroked her hair.

She shook her head. "No. That's how you touch it now. I want you to touch it like you touched it *then*."

Alexander closed his eyes, his mouth parting. His gripping hands pulled her hips lower on him, while he pulled himself higher. Tatiana felt him so geared up and searching for her that in one second all her grand efforts with mayonnaise were going to come to the very same end that had already been happening in their bed for months.

Quickly she bent to him, moving herself up and away. "Tell me," she whispered into his face, "why have you stopped caring how I keep my hair?"

"I haven't stopped."

"Yes, you have. Come on. You're talking to *me*. Tell me why."

Falling quiet, Alexander took his hands away from her hips and rested them on her knees.

"Tell me. Why don't you touch me?"

Alexander paused heavily, looking away from her searching eyes. "The hair is not mine anymore. It belongs to the other you, the you of New York and red nail polish and high-heeled dancing, and Vikki, and building a life without me when you thought I was dead—as you absolutely should have. I'm not against you. But that's what it reminds me of. I'm just telling you."

Tatiana put her hand on his cheek. "Do you want me to cut it? I'll cut it all off right now."

"No." Alexander moved his face away. They were quiet. "But nothing is ever enough, have you noticed?" he said. "I can't touch you enough. I can't make you happy. I can't say anything right to you. And you can't take away from me a single thing I've fucked up along the way."

She became deflated. "You're here, and you're forgiven for everything," she said quietly, sitting up and closing her eyes so she wouldn't have to look at his tattooed arms and his scar-ribbon chest.

"Tell *me* the truth," Alexander said. "Don't you sometimes think it's harder—*this*—and other stuff like the magazines quizzes— harder for the two of us? That magazine quiz just points up the absurdity of us pretending we're like normal people. Don't you sometimes think it would be easier with your Edward Ludlow in New York? Or a Thelma? No history. No memories. Nothing to get over, nothing to claw back from."

"Would it be easier for you?"

"Well, I wouldn't hear you cry every night," Alexander said. "I wouldn't feel like such a failure every minute of my life."

"Oh my God! What are you talking about?" Tatiana yanked to get off him, but now it was Alexander who held her in place.

"You know what I'm talking about," he said, his eyes blazing. "I want amnesia! I want a fucking lobotomy. Could I please never think again? Look what's happened to us, *us*, Tania. Don't you remember how we used to be? Just look what's happened."

His long winter's night bled into Coconut Grove through all the fields and villages in three countries Alexander plundered through to get to the Bridge to Holy Cross, over the River Vistula, to get into the mountains, to escape to Germany, to save Pasha, to make his way to Tatiana. And he failed. Twenty escape attempts—two in Catowice, one ill-fated one in Colditz Castle, and seventeen desperate ones in Sachsenhausen, and he never got to her. He had somehow made all the wrong choices. Alexander knew it. Anthony knew it. With the son asleep, the parents had hours to mindlessly meander through the fields and rivers of Europe, through the streets of Leningrad. That was not to be wished upon.

"Stop it," Tatiana whispered. "Just stop it! You didn't fail. You're looking at it all twisted. You stayed alive, that was all, that was *everything*, and you know that. Why are you doing this?"

"Why?" he said. "You want it out while sitting naked on top of my stomach with your hair down? Well, here it is. You don't want it out? Then don't ask me. Turn the light off, keep the braid in, get your"—Alexander stopped himself—"get off me, and say nothing."

Tatiana did none of those things. She didn't want it out, what she *wanted*, desperately, was him to touch her. Though the aching in her heart from his words was unabated, the aching in her loins from her desire for him was also unabated. She remained on him, watching his face watching her. Gently she stroked his chest, his arms, his shoulders. Bending to him, she flickered her moist soft lips over his face, over his neck, and in a little while, when she felt him calm down, she whispered to him. *Shura . . . it's me, your Tania, your wife . . .*

"What do you want, Tania, my wife?" His hands grazed up her thighs, up her waist, to her hair.

She was so ashamed of her craving. But the shame didn't make her crave it any less.

His hands traveled down to her hips, holding her, pulling her open. "What are you clamoring for?" Alexander whispered, his fingers clamoring at her. "Tell me. Speak to me."

She moved a little higher, rubbing her breasts over his mouth.

Cupping them into his face, Alexander groaned again, his mouth opening underneath them.

Moaning, Tatiana whispered, "I want you to stroke my hair . . . rub it between your fingers, knead it like you used to. I used to *love* that, you touching me." Her body was quivering. "Hold it tight, so tight . . . *yes!* like *that* . . . touch my blonde hair that you used to love . . . do you remember? Don't you remember?"

Very slowly Tatiana moved up on his chest, and up and up and up, until she was kneeling over Alexander's panting parted mouth. *Please, please, darling, Shura*, whispered Tatiana, *touch me . . .* grasping on to the headboard and lowering herself slightly. *Please . . . touch me like you used to . . .*

This time, Alexander, with no breath left in his lungs, did not have to be asked again. When she felt his hands spreading her open and his warm soft mouth on her for the first time since their return to America, Tatiana nearly fainted. She began to cry. She couldn't even hold herself up; if it weren't for the headboard and the wall, she would have surely pitched forward.

"Shh . . . Tatiasha . . . shh . . . I'm looking at you . . . and what do you know, it turns out that blonde . . . is my favorite color."

She couldn't last three gasping breaths, milling into his mouth, trying to remain upright. Crying, crying, from happiness, from arousal, *Please don't stop, darling, Shura, don't stop* . . . pulsing into his lips, moaning so loudly the heavens were about to open up . . . *Oh God, oh, yes . . . Oh Shura . . . Shura . . . Shura . . .*

The next morning before work, when he came to the kitchen to get his coffee, Tatiana said to him, deeply blushing, "Alexander, what would you like for breakfast?"

And he, taking her into his arms, lifting her, setting her down on the kitchen counter in front of him, embracing her, madness in his eyes, said, "Oh, now that it's morning, I'm Alexander again?" His open lips were over her open lips.

Lovers Key

On a moist Sunday—after spring boiled over into summer— Alexander borrowed a one-mast sailboat from Mel and took them out to the bay where they thought the breezes would make them cooler. The humid breezes just made them muggier, but because they were alone out at sea, Alexander undressed to his swimming trunks, and Tatiana wore her bikini swimsuit, and they floated peaceably under the zenith of the Tropic of Cancer sun. Alexander brought two fishing lines and some worms. The wind was good. The headsail was up. *Come with me*, she murmured, *and I will make you fishers of men*. They sailed on the serene waters around Key Biscayne, and down south to Lovers Key, where he dropped anchor so they could have some lunch. Anthony fell asleep after helping his dad loosen the ropes on the jib. He had been leaning on his mother and just keeled over. Smiling, Tatiana adjusted the boy, holding him closer, more comfortably. "I know how he feels. This is quite soothing." She closed her eyes.

Raising anchor, Alexander let the boat float and flounder as he went to sit by her on the white bench at the rudder. He lit a smoke, gave her a drink; they sat and swayed.

The Russian they spoke reminded them of another time. They

spoke softer, often they spoke English, but this Sunday on the boat, they were Russian.

"Shura? We've been here six months."

"Yes. It hasn't snowed."

"We've had three hurricanes, though."

"I'm not bothered about the hurricanes."

"What about the heat, the mugginess?"

"Don't care."

She considered him.

"I'd be happy to stay," Alexander said quietly. "This is fine with me."

"In a houseboat?"

"We can get a real house."

"And you'd work the boats and the girls all day?"

"I've taken a wife, I don't know what girls are anymore." He grinned. "I admit to liking the boats, though."

"For the rest of your life? Boats, water?"

His smile rather quickly disappearing, he leaned away from her.

"Do you recall yourself in the evenings, at night?" Tatiana asked gently, bringing him back with her free hand. The other held the boy.

"What's that got to do with the water?"

"I don't think the water is helping," Tatiana said. "I really don't." She paused. "I think we should go."

"Well, I don't."

They stopped talking. Alexander smoked another cigarette.

They floated in the middle of the tropical green ocean with the islands in view.

The water *was* doing something to Tatiana. It was dismantling her. With every flutter of the water she saw the Neva, the River Neva under the northern sun on the sub-Arctic white night city they once called home, the water rippled and in it was Leningrad, and in Leningrad was everything she wanted to remember and everything she wanted to forget.

He was gazing at her. His eyes occasionally softened under the sticky Coconut Grove sun.

"You've got new freckles, above your eyebrows." He kissed her eyelids. "Golden, soft hair, ocean eyes." He stroked her face, her cheeks. "Your scar is almost gone. Just a thin white line now. Can barely see it." The scar she got escaping from the Soviet Union.

"Hmm."

"Unlike mine?"

"You have more to heal, husband." Reaching out, she placed her hand on Alexander's face and then closed her eyes quickly so he couldn't pry inside her.

"Tatiasha," he called in a whisper, and then bent to her and kissed her long and true.

It had been a year since she had found him shackled in Sachsenhausen's isolation chamber. A year since she dredged him up from the bottomdwellers of Soviet-occupied Germany, from the grasping hands of Stalin's henchmen. How could it have been a year? How long did it seem?

An eternity in purgatory, a hemidemisemiquaver in heaven.

His boat was full of women, old women, young women, widowed women, newly married women, and now there were pregnant women. "I swear," said Alexander, "I had *very* little to do with that." Also returning war veterans. Some were foreigners. One such man, Frederik, with a limp and a cane and a heavy Dutch accent, liked to sit by Alexander as he looked out on the sea. He came in the mornings, because the afternoon tour was too hot for him, and he and Anthony stayed by Alexander's steering wheel. Anthony would frequently sit on Frederik's lap. One day, Anthony was playing a clapping game with Frederik and said, "Oh, look you have blue numbers on your arm, too. Dad, look, he's got numbers on him, just like you."

Alexander and Frederik exchanged a look. Alexander turned away but not before Frederik's eyes welled up. Frederik didn't say anything then, but at noon after they docked, he stayed behind and asked Tatiana if he could talk to Alexander in private. Casting an anxious look at Alexander, she reluctantly left all the sandwiches and took Anthony home for lunch.

"So where were you?" Frederik asked, prematurely old though he was only forty-two. "I was at Treblinka. All the way from Amsterdam to Treblinka. Imagine that."

Alexander shook his head. He lit a smoke, gave one to Frederik, who shook his head. "You have the wrong impression," Alexander said.

"Let me see your arm."

Rolling up his white linen sleeve, Alexander showed him.

"No wrong impression. I'd know these anywhere. Since when are American soldiers branded with German numbers?"

The cigarette wasn't long enough, the smoke wasn't long enough. "I don't know what to tell you," Alexander said. "I was in a concentration camp in Germany."

"That's obvious. Which camp?"

"Sachsenhausen."

"Oh. It was an SS-training camp."

"That camp was many things," said Alexander.

"How did you get there?"

"Long story."

"We have time. Miami has a large ex-pat Jewish community. You want to come with me tonight to our meeting? We meet on Thursdays. Just a few of us, like me, like you, we get together, talk, drink a little bit. You look like you sorely need to be around other people like yourself."

"Frederik, I'm not Jewish."

"I don't understand," Frederik said haltingly. "Why would the Germans brand you?"

"The Germans didn't."

"Who did then?"

"The Soviets. They ran that camp after the war."

"Oh, the pigs. I don't understand anything. Well, come with me anyway. We have three Polish Jews—you didn't think there were any left, did you?—who were imprisoned by the Soviets after Ukraine went from Soviet to German back to Soviet hands. They're debating every Thursday which occupation was worse."

"Well," said Alexander, "Hitler is dead. Mussolini is dead. Hirohito deposed. Fascism has suddenly gotten a bad name after being all the rage for twenty years. But who's stronger than ever? The answer should give you a clue."

"So come, give your two cents. Why would the Sovietskis do that to you if you weren't Jewish? They didn't brand American POWs; they were fighting on the same side."

"If the Soviets knew I was American, they would've shot me years ago."

Frederick looked at him suspiciously. "I don't understand . . ."

"Can't explain."

"What division did you say you served in?"

Alexander sighed. "I was in Rokossovsky's Army. His 97th penal battalion."

"What—that's not the U.S. Army . . ."

"I was a captain in the Red Army."

"Oh, my God." On Frederik's face played sharp disbelief. "You're a *Soviet* officer?"

"Yes."

Frederik careened off the plank with his cane so fast, he nearly tipped himself over. "I got the wrong impression about you." He was wheeling away. "Forget we ever spoke."

Alexander was visibly upset when he came home. "Anthony!" he said as soon as he walked through the door. "Get over here. I told you this before, I'm going to tell you again, but for absolutely the *last* time—stop telling strangers about me."

The boy was perplexed.

"You don't have to figure it out, you just have to listen. I told you to keep quiet, and you still continue as if I hadn't made myself clear."

Tatiana tried to intervene, but Alexander cut her off. "Ant, as punishment tomorrow you're not going on the boat with me. I'll take you the next day, but if you ever speak about me to strangers again, you'll be off the boat for good. You got it?"

The boy cried.

"I didn't hear you, Anthony."

"I got it, Dad."

Straightening up, Alexander saw Tatiana watching them silently from the stove. "Wouldn't it be nice if you could put a long-sleeve linen shirt on Anthony's mouth like you do on my body," he said, and ate dinner by himself out on the deck.

After Tatiana put Anthony to bed, she went outside.

The first thing Alexander said was, "We haven't had meat in weeks. I'm as sick of shrimp and flounder as you were of lobsters. Why can't you buy some meat?"

After hemming and hawing, Tatiana said, "I can't go to the Center Meat Market. They've put a sign in the window—a little war souvenir."

"So?"

"Sign says, 'Horse meats not rationed—no points necessary.'"

They both fell mute.

Tatiana is *walking down Ulitsa Lomonosova in Leningrad in October 1941, trying to find a store with bread to redeem her ration coupons. She passes a crowd of people. She is small, she can't see what they're circling. Suddenly the crowd opens up and out comes a young man holding a bloodied knife in one hand and a hunk of raw meat in the other, and Tatiana can see the opened flesh of a newly killed mare behind him. Dropping his knife on the ground, the man rips into the meat. One of his teeth falls out and he spits it out as he continues to chew frantically. Meat!*

"You better hurry," he says to her with his mouth full, "or there won't be any left. Want to borrow my knife?"

And Alexander was remembering *being in a transit camp after Colditz. There was no food for the two hundred men, who were contained within a barbed wire rectangular perimeter with guards on high posts in the four corners. No food except the horse that every day at noon the guards killed and left in the middle of the starving mess of men with knives. They would give the men sixty seconds with the horse, and then they would open fire. Alexander only survived because he would head immediately for the horse's mouth and cut out the tongue, hide it in his tunic and then crawl away. It would take him forty seconds. He did it six times, shared the tongue with Ouspensky. Pasha was gone.*

Tatiana stood in front of Alexander, leaning against the rail of the deck and listening to the water. He smoked. She drank her tea.

"So what's the matter with you?" she asked. "Why did you eat by yourself?"

"I didn't want to be eating dinner with you looking at me with your judging eyes. Don't want to be judged, Tania"—he pointed at her—"most of all by you. And today, thanks to Ant, I had an unpleasant and unwanted conversation with a crippled Jewish man from Holland who mistook me for a brother in arms only to learn I fought for a country that handed over half of the Polish Jews and all of the Ukrainian Jews to Hitler."

"I'm not judging you, darling."

"I'm good for nothing," Alexander said. "Not even polite conversation. You may be right about me not being able to rebuild my life working off Mel's boats, but I'm not good for anything else. I don't know how to be anything. In my life I've had only one job—I was an officer in the Red Army. I know how to carry weapons, set mines in the ground, drive tanks, kill men. I know how to fight. Oh, and I know how to burn down villages wholesale. That's what I know. And I did this all for the Soviet Union!" he exclaimed, staring into the water, not looking at Tatiana, who stood on the deck, staring at him. "It's completely fucked up," he went on. "I'm yelling at Anthony because we have to pretend I'm not what I am. I have to lie to deny what I am. Just like in the Soviet Union. Ironic, no? There I denied my American self, and here I deny my Soviet self." He flicked his ash into the water.

"But, Shura, you've been other things besides a soldier," Tatiana said, unable to address the truth of the other things he was saying to her.

"Stop pretending you don't know what I'm talking about," he snapped. "I'm talking about living a life."

"Well, I know, but you've managed before," she whispered, turning her body away from him to herself look out onto the dark bay. Where was Anthony to interrupt the conversation she realized belatedly she didn't want to have? Alexander was right: there were many things she would rather not have out. He *couldn't* talk about anything, and she didn't want to. But now she was in the thick of it. She had to. "We lived a life in Lazarevo," she said.

"It was a fake life," said Alexander. "There was nothing real about it."

"It was the realest life we knew." Stung at his bitter words, she sank down to the deck.

"Oh, look," he said dismissively, "it was what it was, but it was a month! I was going back to the front. We pretended we were living while war raged. You kept house, I fished. You peeled potatoes, made bread. We hung sheets on the line to dry, almost as if we were living. And now we're trying it in America." Alexander shook his head. "I work, you clean, we dig potatoes, we shop for food. We break our bread. We smoke. We talk sometimes. We make love." He paused as he glanced at her, remorsefully and yet— accusingly? "Not Lazarevo love."

Tatiana lowered her head, their Lazarevo love tainted by the Gulag.

"Is any of it going to give me another chance to save your brother?" he asked.

"*Nothing* is going to change what cannot be changed," she replied, her head close to her knees. "All we can do is change what can be."

"But, Tania, don't you know that the things that torture you most are the things you cannot fix?"

"That I know," she whispered.

"And do I judge *you*? Let's see," said Alexander, "what about taking ice away from the borders of your heart? Is that change-able, you think? No, no, don't shake your head, don't deny it. I

know what used to be there. I know the wide-eyed joyous sixteen year old you once were."

Tatiana hadn't shaken her head. She bowed her head; how
different.

"You once skipped barefoot through the Field of Mars with me.
And then," said Alexander, "you helped me drag your mother's
body on a sled to the frozen cemetery."

"Shura!" She got up off the deck on her collapsing legs. "Of all
the things we could talk about—"

"On the sled *dragged*," he whispered, "your entire family! Tell
me you're not still on that ice in Lake—"

"Shura! Stop!" Her hands went over her ears.

Grabbing her, removing her hands from her head, Alexander
brought her in front of him. "Still there," he said almost inaudibly,
"still digging new ice holes to bury them in."

"Well, what about you?" Tatiana said to him in a lifeless voice.
"Every single night reburying my brother after he died on your back."

"Yes," Alexander said in his own lifeless voice, letting her go.
"That is what I do. I dig deeper frozen holes for him. I tried to save
him and I killed him. I buried your brother in a shallow grave."

Tatiana cried. Alexander sat and smoked—his way of crying—
poison right in the throat to quell the grief.

"Let's go live in the woods, Tania," he said. "Because *nothing* is
going to make you skip next to me again while walking through
the Summer Garden. I'm not the only one who's gone. So let's go
make fish soup over the fire in our steel helmet, let's both eat and
drink from it. Have you noticed? We have one pot. We have one
spoon. We live as if we're still at war, in the trench, without meat,
without baking real bread, without collecting things, without
nesting. The only way you and I can live is like this: homeless and
abandoned. We have it off with the clothes on our back, before
they start shooting again, before they bring reinforcements. That's
where we still are. Not on Lovers Key but in a trench, on that hill
in Berlin, waiting for them to kill us."

"Darling, but the enemy is gone," Tatiana said, starting to shake,
remembering Sam Gulotta and the State Department.

"I don't know about you, but I can't live without the enemy,"
said Alexander. "I don't know how to wear the civilian clothes
you bought to cover me. I don't know how not to clean my
weapons every day, how not to keep my hair short, how not to
bark at you and Anthony, how not to expect you to listen. And I

don't know how to touch you slow or take you slow as if I'm not in prison and the guards are coming any minute."

Tatiana wanted to walk away but didn't want to upset him further. She didn't lift her head as she spoke. "*I* think you're doing better," she said. "But you do whatever you need to. Wear your army clothes. Clean your guns, cut your hair, bark away, I will listen. Take me how you can." When Alexander said nothing, nothing at all, to help her, Tatiana continued in a frail voice, "We have to figure out a way that's best for *us*."

His elbows were on his knees. Her shoulders were quaking.

Where was he, her Alexander of once? Was he truly gone? The Alexander of the Summer Garden, of their first Lazarevo days, of the hat in his hands, white-toothed, peaceful, laughing, languid, stunning Alexander, had he been left far behind?

Well, Tatiana supposed that was only right.

For Alexander believed his Tatiana of once was gone too. The swimming child Tatiana of the Luga, of the Neva, of the River Kama.

Perhaps on the surface they were still in their twenties, but their hearts were old.

Mercy Hospital

The following afternoon at 12:30, she wasn't at the marina. Alexander could usually spot her from a great distance, waiting for them on the docks, even before he entered the no wake zone. But today, he pulled up, he docked, let the women and the old men off as Anthony stood by the plank and saluted them. He waited and waited.

"Where's Mommy?"

"Good question, son." Alexander had relented; she had asked him this morning to forgive Anthony, and he did and took the boy with him, admonishing him to keep to himself. Now Ant was here, and his mother wasn't. Was she upset with him after yesterday's excruciating conversation?

"Maybe she took a nap and forgot to wake up," said Anthony.

"Does Mommy usually sleep during the day?"

"Never."

He waited a little longer and decided to bring the boy home. He himself had to be back by two for the afternoon tour. Anthony, his joy in life unmitigated by external circumstance, stopped and touched every rust spot, every blade of glass that grew where it wasn't supposed to. Alexander had to put the boy on his shoulders to get home a little faster.

Tatiana wasn't home either.

"So where's Mommy?"

"I don't know, Ant. I was hoping you'd know."

"So what are we gonna do?"

"We'll wait, I guess." Alexander was smoking one cigarette after another.

Anthony stood in front of him. "I'm thirsty."

"All right, I can get you a drink."

"That's not the cup Mommy uses. That's not the juice Mommy uses. That's not how Mommy pours it." Then he said, "I'm thirsty *and* I'm hungry. Mommy always feeds me."

"Yes, me too," said Alexander, but he made him a sandwich with cheese and peanut butter.

He thought for sure she would be back any minute with the laundry or with groceries.

At one thirty, Alexander was running out of options.

He said, "Let's go, Antman. Let's take one more look, and if we can't find her, I guess you'll have to come with me."

Instead of walking left to Memorial Park, they decided to walk right on Bayshore, past the construction site for the hospital. There was another small park on the other side. Anthony said sometimes they went there to play.

Alexander saw her from a distance, not at the park, but at the Mercy Hospital construction site, sitting on what looked to be a dirt mound.

When he got closer, he saw she was sitting motionless on a stack of two-by-fours. He saw her from the side, her hair in its customary plait, her hands laid tensely in a cross on her lap.

Anthony saw her and ran. "Mommy!"

She came out of her reverie, turned her head, and her face wrinkled in a contrite scrunch. "Uh-oh," she said, standing up and rushing to them. "Have I been a bad girl?"

"On so many levels," Alexander said, coming up to her. "You know I have to get back by two."

"I'm sorry," she said, bending to Anthony. "I lost track of time. You okay, bud? I see Daddy fed you."

"What are you doing?" Alexander asked, but she was pretending to wipe the crumbs off Anthony's mouth and didn't reply.

"I see. Well, I have to go," he said coldly, bending to kiss Anthony on the head.

That evening they were having dinner, almost not talking. Tatiana, trying to make light conversation, mentioned that Mercy Hospital was the first Catholic hospital in the Greater Miami area, a ministry of the Roman Catholic Church, and it was being built in the shape of a cross, when Alexander interrupted her. "So this is what you've been doing with your free time?"

"Free time?" she said curtly. "How do you think you get food on your table?"

"I didn't have food on my table this afternoon."

"Once."

"Was that the first time you were sitting there?"

She couldn't lie to him. "No," she admitted. "But it's nothing. I just go and sit."

"Why?"

"I don't know. I just do, that's all."

"Tatiana, let me understand," Alexander said, and his voice got hard. "You have the Barnacle House to visit, the Vizcaya Palace, the Italianate Gardens, there is shopping, and libraries, there's the ocean, and swimming and sunbathing, and reading, but what you do with the only two hours you have to yourself all day is go and sit in a dust bowl, watching construction workers build a *hospital*?"

Tatiana didn't say anything at first. "As you well know," she said quietly, "the way you are toward me, I have much more than two hours to myself all day."

Alexander didn't say anything.

"So why don't you call Vikki and ask her to come down and spend a few weeks with you?" he said at last.

"Oh, just *stop* forcing Vikki on me all the time!" Tatiana exclaimed in a voice so loud it surprised even her.

Alexander stood up from the table. "Don't raise your fucking voice to me."

Tatiana jumped up. "Well, stop talking nonsense then!"

His hands slammed the table. "What did I say?"

"You left me and were gone for three days in Deer Isle!" she yelled. "*Three days!* Did you ever explain to me where you were? Did you ever tell me? And do *I* bang the table? Meanwhile I sit for five minutes a block away from our house and suddenly you're all up in arms! I mean, are you even serious?"

"TATIANA!" His fist crashed into the table and dishes rattled off to the floor.

Anthony burst into tears. Holding his hands over his ears, he was saying, "Mommy, Mommy, stop it."

Tatiana threw up her hands and went to her son. Alexander stormed out.

Inside the bedroom Anthony said, "Mommy, don't yell at Daddy or he'll go away again."

Tatiana wanted to explain that adults sometimes argued but knew Anthony wouldn't understand. Bessie and Nick Moore argued. Anthony's mom and dad didn't argue. The child couldn't see that they were getting less good at pretending they were both made of china and not flint. At least there was actual participation, though as with all things, one had to be careful what one wished for.

Many hours later Alexander came back and went straight out on the deck.

Tatiana had been lying in bed waiting for him. She put on her robe and went outside. The air smelled of salt and the ocean. It was after midnight, it was June, in the high seventies. She liked that about Coconut Grove. She'd never been in a place where the nighttime temperature remained so warm.

"I'm sorry I raised my voice," she said.

"What you should be *sorry* about," Alexander said, "is that you're up to no good. That's what you should be sorry about."

"I'm just sitting and thinking," she said.

"Oh, and I was born yesterday? Give me a fucking break."

She went to sit on his lap. She was going to tell him what he needed to hear. She only wished that just *once* he would tell her what *she* needed to hear. "It's nothing, Shura. Really. I'm just sitting. Mmm," she murmured, rubbing her cheek against his. His cheek was stubbly. She loved that stubble. His breath smelled of alcohol. She breathed it in; she loved that beer breath. Then she sighed. "Where've you been?"

"I walked to one of the casinos. Played poker. See how easy that was? And if you wanted to know where I'd been back in Deer Isle, why didn't you just ask me?"

Tatiana didn't want to tell him she was afraid to know. She had gone missing for thirty minutes. He had been lost, gone, missing and presumed dead for years. She wished sometimes he would just think, *think* of the things *she* might feel. She didn't want to be on his lap anymore. "Shura, come on, don't be upset with me," Tatiana said, getting off.

"You, too." He threw down his cigarette as he stood up. "I'm doing my level best," he said, heading inside.

"Me, too, Alexander," she said, head down, following him. "Me, too."

But in bed—she naked, holding him, he naked, holding her, nearly there, nearly at the very end for him—Tatiana clutched him as she used to, feverishly clutched his back and under her fingers, even at the moment of her own breaking abandon, felt his scars under her grasping fingers.

She could not continue. Could not, even at that moment. *Especially* at that moment. And so she found herself doing what she remembered *him* doing in Lazarevo when he couldn't bear to touch her: Tatiana stopped him, pushed him away, and turned her back to him.

She put her face in the pillow, raised her hips and cried, hoping he wouldn't notice, hoping that even if he did notice, he would be too far gone to care.

She was wrong on all counts. He noticed. And he wasn't too far gone to care.

"So *this* is what your level best looks like, huh?" Alexander whispered, out of breath, bending over her, lifting her head off the pillow by her hair. "Presenting your cold back to me?"

"It's not cold," Tatiana said, not facing him. "It's just the only part that's taken leave of *all* its senses."

Alexander jumped off the bed—shaking and unfinished. He turned on the lamp, the overhead light, he opened the shades. Unsteadily she sat up on the bed, covering herself with a sheet. He stood naked in front of her, glistening, unsubsided, his chest heaving. He was incredibly upset.

"How can I even *try* to find my way," he said, his voice breaking, "if my own wife recoils from me? I know it isn't what it used to be. I know it isn't what we had. But it's all we have now, and this body is all I've got."

"Darling—please," Tatiana whispered, stretching out her hands to him. "I'm not recoiling from you." She couldn't see him through the veil of her sorrow.

"You think I'm fucking blind?" he exclaimed. "Oh God! You

think this is the *first* time I noticed? You think I'm an idiot? I notice every fucking time, Tatiana! I grit my teeth, I wear my clothes so you don't see me, I take you from behind, so nothing of me touches you—*just like you want.*" He enunciated every syllable through his teeth. "You wear clothes in bed with me so I won't accidentally rub my wounds on you. I pretend not to give a shit, but how long do you think I can keep doing this? How much longer do you think you're going to be happier on the hard floor?"

She covered her face.

He swept his hand across and knocked her arms away. "You are my wife and you won't *touch* me, Tania!"

"Darling, I *do* touch you . . ."

"Oh, yes," he said cruelly. "Well, all I can say is, thank God, I guess, that my tackle is not maimed, or I'd never get any blow. But what about the rest of me?"

Tatiana lowered her weeping head. "Shura, please . . ."

He yanked her up and out of bed. The sheet fell away from her. "*Look* at me," he said.

She was too ashamed of herself to lift her eyes to him. They were standing naked against each other. His angry fingers dug into her arms. "That's right, you *should* be fucking ashamed," he said through his teeth. "You don't want to face me *then*, and you can't face me now. Just perfect. Well, nothing more to say, is there? Come on, then." He spun her around and bent her over the bed.

"Shura, please!" She tried to get up, but his palm on her back kept her from moving until she couldn't move if she wanted to. And then he took his palm away.

Behind her, leaning over her, supporting himself solely by his clenched fists on the mattress, Alexander took her like he was in the army, like she was a stranger he found in the woods whom he was going to leave in one to-the-hilt minute without a backward glance, while she helplessly cried and then—even more helplessly, was crying out, now deservedly and thoroughly abased. "And look—no hands, just like you like," he whispered into her ear. "You want more? Or was that enough *lovemaking* for you?"

Tatiana's face was in the blanket.

Himself unfinished, he backed away, and she slowly straightened up and turned to him, wiping her face. "Please—I'm sorry," she whispered, sitting down weakly on the edge of the bed, covering her body. Her legs were shaking.

"You cover me from other people because you don't want to

look at me yourself. I'm surprised you notice or care that other women talk to me yourself." He was panting. "You think they'll run in horror, like you, once they catch a glimpse of me."

"What—no!" Her arms reached for him. "Shura, you're misunderstanding me . . . I'm not frightened, I'm just so *sad* for you."

"Your pity," he said, stepping back from her, "is the absolute last fucking thing I want. Pity yourself that you're like this."

"I'm so afraid to hurt you . . ." Tatiana whispered, her palms openly pleading with him.

"Bullshit!" he said. "But ironic, don't you think, considering what you're doing to me." Alexander groaned. "Why can't you be like my son, who sees everything and never flinches from me?"

"Oh, Shura . . ." She was crying.

"Look at me, Tatiana." She lifted her face. His bronze eyes were blazing, he was loud, he was uncontrollable. "You're terrified, I know, but here I am"—Alexander pointed to himself, standing naked and scarred and blackly tattooed. "Once again," he said, "I stand in front of you naked and I will try—God help me—one *more* fucking time." Flinging his fists down, he was nearly without breath left. "Here I am, your one man circus freak show, having bled out for Mother Russia, having desperately tried to get to you, now on top of you with his scourge marks, and you, who used to love me, who has sympathized, internalized, normalized every-thing, you are not *allowed* to turn away from me! Do you under-stand? This is one of the unchangeable things, Tania. This is what I'm going to look like until the day I die. I can't get any peace from you *ever* unless you find a way to make peace with this. Make peace with me. Or let me go for good."

Her shoulders rose and fell. "I'm sorry," Tatiana said as she came to him, putting her arms around him, kneeling on the floor in front of him, holding him, looking up into his face. "Please. I'm sorry."

Eventually she managed to sooth him back on the bed. Alexander came—not willingly—and lay down beside her. She pulled him on top of her. He climbed where he was led as her hands went around his back. She wrapped her legs around him, holding him intimately and tight.

"I'm sorry, honey, husband, Shura, dearest, my whole heart," Tatiana whispered into his neck, kissing his throat. With heart-broken fingers she caressed him. "Please forgive me for hurting your feelings. I don't pity you, don't turn it that way on me, but I cannot help that I'm desperately sad, wishing so much—for your sake only, not mine—that you could still be what you once were—before the things you now carry. I'm ashamed of myself and I'm sorry. I spend all my days regretting the things I cannot fix."

"You and me both, babe," he said, threading his arms underneath her. Their faces were turned away from each other as Alexander lay on top of her, and she stroked the war on his back. Naked and pressed breast to breast they searched for something they had lost long ago, and found it briefly, in a fierce clutch, in a glimmer through the barricades.

The Sands of Naples

Alexander came home mid-morning and said, "Let's collect our things. We're leaving."

"We are? What about Mel?"

"This isn't about Mel. It's about us. It's time to go."

Apparently Frederik had complained to Mel that the man who was running his boats full of war veterans and war widows was possibly a communist, a Soviet spy, perhaps a traitor. Mel, afraid of losing his customers, had to confront Alexander, but couldn't bring himself to fire the man who brought him thousands of dollars worth of business. Alexander made it easy for Mel. He denied all charges of espionage and then quit.

"Let's head out west," he said to Tatiana. "You might as well show me that bit of land you bought. Where is it again? New Mexico?"

"Arizona."

"Let's go. I want to get to California for the grape-picking season in August."

And so they left Coconut Grove of the see-through salt water and the wanton women with the bright colored lipstick, they left the bobbing houseboats and Anthony's crashing dreams, and the mystery of Mercy Hospital and drove across the newly opened Everglades National Park to Naples on the Gulf of Mexico.

Alexander was subdued with her, back to Edith Wharton polite, and she deserved it, but the sand was cool and white, even in scorching noon, and the fire sunsets and lightning storms over the Gulf were like nothing they'd ever seen. So they stayed in the camper on a deserted beach, in a corner of the world, in a spot where he could take off his shirt and play ball with Anthony, while the sun beat on his back and tanned the parts that could be tanned, leaving the scars untouched, like gray stripes.

Both he and the boy were two brown stalks running around the white shores and green waters. All three of them loved the heat, loved the beach, the briny Gulf, the sizzling days, the blinding sands. They celebrated her twenty-third birthday and their fifth wedding anniversary there, and finally left after Anthony's fourth birthday at the end of June.

They spent only a few days in New Orleans because they discovered New Orleans, much like South Miami Beach, was not an ideal city for a small boy.

"Perhaps next time we can come here without the child," said Alexander on Bourbon Street, where the nice ladies sitting by the windows lifted up their shirts as the three of them strolled by.

"Dad, why are they showing us their boobies?"

"I'm not sure, son. It's a strange ritualistic custom common to these parts of the world."

"Like in that journal where the African girls put weights in their lips to make them hang down past their throats?"

"Something like that." Alexander scooped up Anthony into his arms.

"But Mommy said the African girls make their lips big to get a husband. Are these girls trying to get a husband?"

"Something like that."

"Daddy, what did Mommy do to get you to marry her?" Anthony giggled. "Did Mommy show you her boobies?"

"Tania, *what* are you reading to our child?" said Alexander, flipping a squealing Anthony upside down by his legs to get him to stop asking questions.

"*National Geographic*," she said, lightly batting her eyes at him. "But answer your son, Alexander."

"Yeah, Dad," said Anthony, red with delight, hanging upside down. "Answer your son."

"Mommy put on a pretty dress, Antman." And for a fleeting moment on Bourbon Street in the French Quarter, Tatiana and Alexander's eyes made real contact.

They were glad they had the camper now in their quest, in their summer trek across the prairies. They had cover over their heads, they had a place for Anthony to sleep, to play, a place to put their pot and spoon, their little dominion unbroken by pungent hotel rooms or beaten-up landladies. Occasionally they had to stop at RV parks to take showers. Anthony liked those places, because there were other kids there for him to play with, but Tatiana and Alexander chafed at living in such close proximity to strangers, even for an evening. After Coconut Grove they finally discovered what they liked best, what they needed most—just the three of them in an unhealed but unbroken trinity.

CHAPTER THREE

Paradise Valley, 1947

Bare Feet and Backpacks

Alexander drove their Nomad through Texas, across Austin, down to San Antonio. The Alamo was a fascinating bit of history—they all died. He couldn't get around that fact. Despite the heroism, the bravery, they all died! And Texas lost its battle for independence and continued to belong to Santa Ana. Death to *all* wasn't enough for victory. What kind of a fucked-up life lesson was that for Anthony? Alexander decided not to tell his son about it. He'd learn in school soon enough.

Western Texas was just flat road amid the dusty plains as far as the eye could see. Alexander was driving and smoking; he had turned off the radio so he could hear Tatiana better—but she had stopped speaking. She was sitting on the passenger side with her eyes closed. She had been telling him and Anthony soothing stories of some of her pranks in Luga. There were few stories Alexander liked better than of her child self in that village by the river.

Is she asleep? He glances at her, squeezed in around herself in a floral pink wrap dress that comes down to a V in her chest. Her glistening, slightly tender, coral nectar mouth reminds him of things, stirs him up a little. He checks to see what Anthony is doing—the boy is lying down facing away, playing with his toy soldiers. Alexander reaches over and cups a palmful of her breast, and she instantly opens her eyes and checks for Anthony. "What?" she whispers, and no sooner does she whisper than Anthony turns around, and Alexander takes his hand away, an aching prickle of desire mixed with frustration all swollen behind his eyes and in his loins.

Their hostilities in Coconut Grove have been yielding some significant crops for him. Just a small measure of his subsequent closed-mouthedness has been making Tatiana trip over herself to show him that his bitter accusations against her were not true. It doesn't matter. He knows of course they were true, but he doesn't mind in the least her cartwheels of palpitating remorse.

At night in the tent, he leaves the flaps open, to feel the fire outside, to hear Anthony in the trailer, to see her better. She asks him to lie on his stomach, and he does, though he can't see her, while she runs her bare breasts over his disfigured back, her nipples hardening into his scars. *You feel that*? she whispers. Oh, he does. He *still* feels it. She kisses him from the top of his head downward, from his buzz-cut scalp, his shoulder blades, his wounds. Inch by inch she cries over him and kisses her own salt away, murmuring into him, *why did you have to keep running? Look what they did to you. Why didn't you just stay put? Why couldn't you feel I was coming for you?*

You thought I was dead, he says. *You thought I had been killed and pushed through the ice in Lake Ladoga.* And what really happened was, I was a Soviet man left in a Soviet prison. Wasn't I dead?

He is fairly certain he is alive now, and while Tatiana lies on top of his back and cries, he remembers *being caught by the dogs a kilometer from Oranienburg and held in place by the Alsatians until Karolich arrived, and being flogged in Sachsenhausen's main square and then chained and tattooed publicly with the 25-point star to remind him of his time for Stalin*, and now she lies on his back, kissing the scars he received when he tried to escape to make his way back to her so she could kiss him.

As he drives across Texas, Alexander remembers himself in Germany lying in the bloody straw after being beaten and dreaming of her kissing him, and these dreams morph with the memories of last night, and suddenly *she is kissing not the scars but the raw oozing wounds, and he is in agony for she is crying and the brine of her tears is eating away the meat of his flesh, and he is begging her to stop because he can't take it anymore. Kiss something else*, he pleads. *Anything else.* He's had enough of himself. He is sick of himself. She is tainted not just with the Gulag. She is tainted with his whole life.

Does it hurt when I touch them?

He has to lie. Every kiss she plants on his wounds stirs a sense memory of how he got them. He wanted her to touch him, and this is what he gets. But if he tells her the truth, she will stop. So he lies. *No*, he says.

She kisses him past the small of his back, down to his legs, to his feet, murmuring to him something about his perfect this and that, he doesn't even know, and then climbs up and prods him to turn over. She lies astride him, holding his head in her arms while he holds her buttocks in his (now *they're* perfect), and kisses his face, not inch by inch but centimeter by centimeter. As she kisses him, she murmurs to him. He opens his eyes. *Your eyes, do you want to know what color they are? They're bronze; they're copper; they're ocher and amber; they're cream and coffee; cognac and champagne. They are caramel.*

Not crème brûlée? he asks. And she starts to cry. *All right, all right*, he says. *Not crème brûlée.*

She kisses his scarred tattooed arms, his ribboned chest. Now he can see her face, her lips, her hair, all glowing in the flickering fire. His hands lie lightly on her silken head.

Mercifully few wounds on your stomach, she whispers, as she kisses the black line of hair that starts at his solar plexus and arrows down.

Yes, he groans back. *Do you know what we call men with wounds on their stomachs? Corpses.*

She laughs. He doesn't laugh, *his very good Sergeant Telikov dying slowly with the bayonet in his abdomen. There wasn't enough morphine to let him die free of pain. Ouspensky had to mercy-shoot him—on Alexander's orders, and this one time Alexander did turn away.* The flinching, the stiffness, the dead, the alive, all here, and there is no morphine, and there is no mercy. There is only Tatiana.

She murmurs, she purrs. *A corpse, that's not you.*

He agrees. *No, not me.*

Her breasts press into his rigid with tension—

He is rupturing. *What else do you like? Come on, I'm going to implode. What else?* She sits between his legs and her small healing hands finally take him. She rubs him between her palms like she's about to set him on fire. Her warm hands softly milk him, softly climb rope on him. He is stacked in her clasped fingers when she bends her head to him. *Shura . . . look at you . . . you are so hard, so beautiful.* He desperately wants to keep his eyes open. Her long hair feathers his stomach in rhythm to her motion. Her mouth is so soft, so hot, so wet, her fingers are in rotating rings around him, she is naked, she is tense, her eyes are closed and she moans as she sucks him. He is set on fire. He is in bondage through and through. And now, well past it but utterly within it, he keeps quiet during the day while his hands stretch out in a shudder for her yoke of contrition, for her blaze of repentance at night.

But night isn't nearly enough. As he keeps telling her, nothing is enough. So now he is trying not to crash the camper.

She sits looking ahead at the sprawling fields, and then suddenly straight at him as if she is about to tell him something. Today her eyes are transparent with sunny yellow rays beaming out from the irises. When they're not misted or jaded by the fathomless waters of rivers and lakes left behind, the eyes are entirely pellucid—and dangerous. They are clear in meaning, yet bottomless. And what's worse—they allow all light to pass through. There is no hiding from them. Today, after deeming him acceptable, the eyes turn back to the road, her hands relaxing on her lap, her chest swelling against the pink cotton fabric. He wants to fondle her, to feel her breasts in his hands, feel their soft weightiness, to have his face in them—how long till night? She is so sensitive, he can't breathe on her without her quivering; in her pink nipples seem to center many of the nerve endings in her body. She has amazing, unbelievable breasts. Alexander's hands grip the wheel.

Peripherally he sees her look of concern—she thinks he is tormented. Yes, he is made stupid by lust. She leans over slightly and says in her corn husk of a breath, "A penny for your thoughts, soldier."

Alexander composes his voice before speaking. "I was thinking," he says calmly, "about freedom. You come, you go, and no one thinks twice about you. Any road, any country road, any state road, from one city to another, never stopped, never checked. No one asks for your internal passport, no one asks about your business. No one cares what you do."

And what did his wife do? She sat, motionless and—was it tense?—listening to him, her hands no longer relaxed but clenched together, and then pulled open her dress, pulled down her vest and leaning back against the seat, smiled and shut tight her eyes, sitting pushed-up and topless for him for a few panting moments. O Lord, thank you.

Has the sun set? Yes, *finally*, and the fire is on, and Anthony is asleep, and that's good, but what Alexander really wants is to see

Tatiana in the daylight, without shadows on her, when he can look at her with diurnal lust unadorned by war, by death, by his agonies that pursue him like he pursues her in the choppy black-and-white frames of the used movie camera she made him buy in New Orleans (he's learned she has a weak spot for new gadgets). Just once, a song in the daylight with nothing else but lust. She too has not been happy, that he knows. Something weighs upon her. She often can't face him, and he is too fractured to pry. He used to be stronger but not anymore. His strength has been left behind—thousands of miles east, in the christening Kama, in the gleaming Neva, on the icy Lake Ladoga, in the wooded mountains of Holy Cross, in Germany with the blackguard Ouspensky, his lieutenant, his friend, betraying him for years in cold blood, left behind on the frozen ground with the barely buried Pasha. God! Please, no more. He shudders to stave off the fevers. This is what night does to him. But wait—

She stands in front of him, as if she is trying to determine what he wants. Isn't it obvious? DAYLIGHT! He sits without moving, without speaking and rages inside his burning house. He used to need nothing and want nothing but his stark force upon her open body—and still does—but Tania has given him something else, too. At last, she has given him other things to dream about. She stands glimmering in front of him blonde and naked, trembling and shy, the color of opalescent milk. He already can't breathe. She is supple and little, creamy-smooth, her bare body is finally in his groping hands, and her gold hair shimmers down her back. She shimmers. He tears off his clothes and pulls her into his lap, fitting her onto himself while he sucks her nipples as he caresses her hair. He cannot last five minutes with her like that, hard nipples in his mouth, warm breasts in his face, silk hair in his hands, all curled up and molten honey around him, slightly squirming, fluttering, tiny, soft and satiny in his avid lap. Not five minutes. O Lord, thank you.

In New Orleans, on stinging nostalgic impulse, he had bought her a dress he saw in a shop window, an ivory frothy, thin-netted and muslin dress with a slight swing skirt and layers of stiff silk and lace. It was pretty, but regretfully too big for her: she was swimming in muslin snow. The shop didn't have a smaller size. "Your wife is very petite, sir," said the corpulent sales woman with a frowning, disapproving glare—either disapproving of Tania for being petite or disapproving of a man Alexander's size for marrying someone who was. They bought the dress anyway, judgmental beefy sales lady notwithstanding, and that night in their seedy and stifling hotel room, with Anthony in their bed and the fan whooshing the heat around, Alexander silently measured out her smallness—consoling himself with math instead of love, with circumference instead of circumfusion. Her ankles *six* inches around. Her calves, *eleven*. The tops of her very bare thighs below the sulcus, *eighteen and a half*. The tape measure dropped, his hands ringed her thigh, the entire length of his left index finger burning. Her hips, the tape clasped just above the blonde down, *thirty-two*. Her waist, *twenty-one*. The tape measure dropped, his hands ringed her waist. Anthony is in the bed, she whispered, Anthony is unsettled.

Her chest, *thirty-six*. With the nipples erect, *thirty-six and a half*. Tape measure dropped for good. Anthony is stirring, Shura, *please*, and the room is tiny and broiling, and just outside the open windows, the sailors below will hear. But math did not suffice that time. Gasping kneeling piety in the corner of the creaking floor just feet away from sleeping Anthony and the laughing sailors barely sufficed.

Now, on the road, he is thirsty, hungry, profoundly aroused; he glances back to see what Anthony is doing, to see if the boy is busy with his bugs, too busy with his bugs to see his father grope blindly for his mother. But Anthony is on the seat behind her, watching him.

"What'ya thinkin' about, Dad?"

"Oh, you know your dad. A little of this, a little of that." His voice creaks, too.

Soon they'll leave western Texas, be in New Mexico. He casts another long look at her clavicle bones, slim shoulders, straight upper arms, *eight*, at her graceful neck, *eleven*, her white throat that needs his lips on it. His eyes drift down to her bare feet under her thin cotton skirt; white and delicate as her hands; her feet *six*, her hands *five*, less by *three* than his own—but it's her feet he's stuck on; why?—and suddenly he opens his mouth to let out a shallow anguished breath of a deeply unwanted memory. No, no, not that. Please. His head shudders. No. *Feet—dirty, large, black-nailed, bruised, lying motionless underneath a raggy old brown skirt attached to the dead body of a gangraped woman he found in the laundry room. It is Alexander's job to drag her by the feet to the graves he's just dug for her and the three others who died that day.*

He fumbles around for his cigarettes. Tatiana pulls one out, hands it to him with a lighter. Unsteadily he lights up, *pulling up the woman's skirt to cover her face so that earth doesn't fall on it when he shovels the dirt over her small part of the mass grave. Under her skirt the woman is so viciously mutilated that Alexander cannot help it, he begins to retch.*

Then. Now.

He puts his hand over his mouth as the cigarette burns, and inhales quickly.

"Are you okay, Captain?"

There is nothing he can say. He usually remembers that woman at the worst, most inopportune moments.

Eventually his mouth stops the involuntary reflex. Then. Now. Eventually, he sees so much that he becomes dead to everything. He has inured himself, hardened himself so that there's nothing that arouses a flicker of feeling inside Alexander. He finally speaks as they cross the state line. "Have a joke for me, Tania?" he says. "I could use a joke."

"Hmm." She thinks, looks at him, looks to see where Anthony is. He's far in the back. "Okay, what about this." With a short cough, she leans into Alexander and lowers her voice. "A man and his young girlfriend are driving in the car. The man has never seen his girl naked. She thinks he is driving too slow, so they decide to play a game. For every five miles he goes above fifty, she will take off a piece of her clothing. In no time at all, he is flying and she is naked. The man gets so excited that he loses control of the car. It veers off the road and hits a tree. She is unharmed but he is stuck in the car and can't get out. 'Go back on the road and get help,' he tells her. 'But I'm naked,' she says. He rummages around and pulls off his shoe. 'Here, just put this between your legs to cover yourself.' She does as she is told and runs out to the road. A truck driver, seeing a naked crying woman, stops. 'Help me, help me,' she sobs. 'My boyfriend is stuck and I can't get him out.' The truck driver says, 'Miss, if he's that far in, I'm afraid he's a goner.'"

Alexander laughs in spite of himself.

In the afternoon after lunch, Tatiana manages to put Anthony down for an unprecedented godsent nap, and in the canopied seclusion of the trees at the empty rest area grounds, Alexander sets Tatiana down on the picnic bench, pulls high her watercolor skirt, kneels between her legs in the glorious daylight and lowers his head to her fragile and perfect perianth, his palms up, under her. She has given him this, like manna from heaven. O Lord, thank you.

He is driving through the prairies and he is thirsty. Tania and Ant are playing road games, trying to guess the color of the next car that passes them. Alexander declines to participate, saying he doesn't want to play any game where Tatiana *always* wins.

It's very hot in the camper. They've opened the top hatch and all the slotted windows, but it's just dust and wind blowing at them at forty miles an hour. Her hair is getting tangled. She is flushed; a few miles back she had taken off her blouse and now sits in the slightly damp see-through white vest that cannot constrain her. Being around her all day and night like this is getting to be no good for him. He is becoming slightly crazed by her. All he wants is more. But unlike Lazarevo, where his desire like a river flowed into the sea extempore, here the river is dammed by their seedling who sits awake from morning till night and plays road games.

Ant says a word, like "crab," and she says one that follows into her head, like "grass." Alexander doesn't want to play that game either. Should they stop, have lunch? *German dead* crabgrass *in the middle of the camp, in the middle of February. Beaten, lashed, blood oozing down his back, he is made to stand in the cold grass for six hours and what he thinks about for six hours is that he is thirsty.*

He glances at her sitting serenely folded over. She catches him looking and says, "Thirsty?"

Does he nod? He doesn't know. He knows that she gives him a drink.

Tank, says Anthony, continuing the game.

Commander, says his mother.

Alexander blinks. The camper lurches.

Shura, watch the road, or we'll crash.

Did she just say that? *He's commanding his tank, and they're in the middle of the Prussian fields, they're almost in Poland. The Germans have mined the meadow in retreat, and one of the S-mines has just gone off, in full view of Alexander. It lifted up to his engineer's lurching chest, paused as if to say, looky who's here, and exploded. Ouspensky has dug the hole where the engineer fell, and they buried him in it—him and his backpack. Alexander never looks through the backpacks of the fallen, because the things they contain make it impossible for him either to walk away or to continue forward. As the soldier's outer wear—his uniform, helmet, boots, weapon—contain the outer him, the backpacks contain the inner him. The backpacks contain the soldier's soul.*

Alexander never looks. Unopened it is buried with the timid engineer who had a large blue tattoo of a cross on his chest that the Nazi mine ripped open because the Nazis don't believe in Jesus.

"Where's your backpack?" Alexander said to Tatiana.

"What?"

"Your backpack, the one you left the Soviet Union with. Where is it?"

She turned to the passenger window. "Perhaps it's still with Vikki," she said. "I don't know."

"My mother's *Bronze Horseman* book? The photos of your family? Our two wedding pictures? You left *them* with Vikki?" Alexander was incredulous.

"I don't know," she repeated. "Why are you asking?"

He didn't want to tell her why he was asking. The killed land-mine engineer had a sweetheart in Minsk—Nina. Pictures of her, letters from her had filled his pack. Ouspensky told Alexander this, even though Alexander had asked him not to. After he knew, he felt bitterly envious, blackly jealous of the amorous letters the meek engineer was sent by a Nina from Minsk. Alexander never got any letters. Once long ago he received letters from Tatiana, and from her sister, Dasha. But those letters, the cards, the photographs, Tania's white dress with red roses were all at the bottom of the sea or had turned to ashes. He had no more things.

"The letters I wrote you—after I left you in Lazarevo," said Alexander, "you don't—you don't know where *they* are? You've . . . left *them* with Vikki?" Perhaps things remained that stirred *some* feeling in him.

"Darling . . ." her voice was soothing. "What on heaven's earth are you thinking about?"

"Can't you just answer me?" he snapped.

"I have them. I have it all, they're with me, buried deep in my things. The whole backpack. I never look through it, but I'll get it for you. I'll get it when we stop for lunch."

Relief heaved out of his chest. "I don't want to look through it either," he said. He simply needed to know that she is not like him—that she has a soul. Because Alexander's backpack during his penal battalion days was empty. If Alexander had died and Ouspensky, before burying him, looked through it, he would have found cards, smokes, a broken pen, a small Bible—Soviet-issue, distributed to the Red Army late in the war with false piety—and that is all. If Alexander had died, all his men would have seen that their commander, Captain Belov, had no soul.

But had they looked through the backpack a little more carefully, in the cracking parchment of the New Testament, they would have found a soiled small black-and-white picture of a young girl, maybe fourteen, standing toes turned in like a child, in white braids and a sundress, with a broken and casted arm, next to her dark brother. He was pulling her hair. Her good arm was around him. Pasha and Tania, two striplings. They were laughing—in Luga, a long time ago.

Ninety-Seven Acres

New Mexico. Santa Fe Mountains. Arizona. Tonto Mountains.

Seven thousand feet above sea level the air is thinner, drier. In Santa Fe, Anthony had slept almost through the night. Only a whimper from him at dawn. They all felt it was progress and stayed a little longer, hoping to continue the improvement, but it didn't last.

The Tonto Mountains were breathtaking, the air so transparent Tatiana could see over the vistas and the valleys and the sloping hills clear to the sun, but they've left them behind now, and the air has become like the land, bone-dry, overbaked and opaque with stodgy molecules of heat. She has unbuttoned her blouse, but Alexander is focused on the road. Or is he just pretending he is focused on the road? She has noticed a small but palpable change in him recently. He still doesn't talk much, but his eyes and breath during the day are less impassive.

She offers him a drink, a cigarette. He takes it all but is not distracted by her this time. She wonders when they can stop, break camp, maybe find a river, swim. The memories of swimming in the Kama prickle her skin with pain, and she stiffens, trying not to flinch and, pulling down her skirt, forces her hands to lie still on her lap. She doesn't want to think of then. It's bad enough she has to think of *now*, when she keeps expecting the police to stop them at every intersection and say, *Are you Alexander Barrington, son of Harold Barrington? What, your wife didn't tell you that at your last campsite when you dared to leave her alone for just a moment, she*

*called her old roommate in New York? Your wife, Mr. Barrington, seems
not to tell you many things.*

That's right. Tatiana called long distance through an operator,
but Sam Gulotta picked up the phone. She got so frightened, she
hung up and she didn't have enough time to call Aunt Esther too,
but now she is terrified that the operator told Sam where in New
Mexico she had called from. *People with nothing to hide don't run,
Alexander Barrington,* the police will say when they stop the Nomad.
*Why don't you come with us, and your wife and son can stay here at the
intersection of souls and wait for you to come back as they have been doing,
as they're doing still, waiting for you to return to them. Tell them you
won't be long.*

It's a lie. They will take the casement that is his body, they will
take his physical self, for that's almost all that remains of him
anyway, and Tatiana and Anthony will be at that intersection forever. No. It's better to have him here, even like this—withdrawn,
into himself, silent, occasionally fevered, fired up, occasionally
laughing, always smoking, always deeply human—than to have
just a memory. For the things he does to her at night, they're not
memories anymore. And his sleeping with her. She fights her own
sleep every night, tries to stay awake long after he has gone to
sleep just so she can feel his arms around her, so she can lie completely entombed and surrounded by the ravaged body he barely
saved that now comforts her as nothing else can.

He measures her to order her. He gets upset when she won't
respond in kind, but she wants to tell him that he cannot be
ordered by Aristotelian methods or by Pythagorean theorems. He
is what he is. All his parts are in absolute proportion to his sum,
but even more important, all are in relative proportion to her sum.
Cardinal or counting numbers don't help. Ordinals or ranking numbers help so long as she stops at 1. Archimedes's principle won't
help. Certainly she can't and won't measure what is measureless,
what neither terminates nor repeats, what is beyond even the tran-
scendental of π—though *he* doesn't think so—what is beyond poly-
nomials and quadratic formulas, beyond the rational and irrational,
the humanist and the logical, beyond the minds of the Cantors
and the Dedekinds, the Renaissance philosophers and the Indian
Tantrists, what falls instead into the realm of gods and kings, of
myth, of dawn of man, of the mystery of mankind—that there is
a space inside her designed solely for him and despite clear
Euclidian impossibilities not only does everything, in plenary

excess, cleave like it's meant to, but it makes her feel what math cannot explain, what science cannot explain. What nothing can explain.

And yet, inexplicably, he continues to measure her, tracing out fluents of curves and slopes of tangents. His two hands are always on her—on top of her head, against her palms, her feet, her upper arms, ringing her waist, clasping her hips. He is so desperately endearing. She doesn't know what he thinks π will give him.

Playing with Anthony. Is that not real? Anthony having his father? The dark boy sitting on his lap trying to find the ticklish spot and Alexander laughing, is *that* not real, not math nor a memory?

Alexander has nearly completely forgotten what it's like to play, except when he's in the water, but there had been no water in Texas, barely any in New Mexico, and now they're in Arid Zona.

Anthony tries land games with his father. He perches on Alexander's lap, holds the tips of his index fingers together, and says, "Daddy, want to see how strong I am? Hold my fingers in your fist, and I'll get free."

Alexander stubs out his cigarette. He holds Anthony's fingers lightly, and the boy wriggles free. The delight of freeing himself from his daunting father is so great that he wants to play the game again and again. They play it two hundred times. And then the reverse. Alexander holds his index fingers together while Anthony clenches his tiny four-year-old fist over them. When Alexander is unable to get free, Anthony's joy is something to behold. They play *that* two hundred times while Tatiana either prepares lunch or dinner, or washes or tidies, or just sits and watches them with a gladdening heart.

Alexander takes Anthony off his knee and says in a throaty, nicotine-stained voice, "Tatia, want to play? Put your fingers into my fist and see if you can wriggle free. Come." Not a muscle moves on his face, but her heart is no longer just gladdening. It's quickening, it's maddening. She knows she shouldn't, Anthony is right there, but when Alexander calls, she comes. That's just how it is. She perches on his lap and touches together the tips of her slightly trembling index fingers. She tries not to look into his face, just at her fingers, over which he now places his enormous fist, squeezes lightly, and says, "Go ahead, wriggle free." Her whole body weakens. She tries, of course, to get free, but she knows this: while as a father Alexander plays one way with Anthony, as a husband, he plays the opposite way with her. She bites her lip to keep from making a single sound.

"Come on, Mommy," says the uncomprehending child by her side. "You can do it. *I* did it! Wriggle free."

"Yes, Tatiasha," whispers Alexander, squeezing her fingers tighter, looking deep into her face as she sits on his lap. "Come on, wriggle free."

And she glimpses the smiling soul peeking out.

But when he drives, he is often silent and sullen. She hates it when he reduces himself like this to the worst of his life—it's hard to draw him away, and sometimes even when he wants to be drawn, he can't be. And sometimes Tatiana is so full of fears herself of the imminent danger to Alexander at every stop sign that she loses the weapons she needs to draw him away, herself reduced to the worst of her life.

She wishes for something else to swallow them, where the road wouldn't apprehend her, where his soul wouldn't apprehend him. Perhaps if they were less human.

She was leading him to Phoenix, but Alexander was too hot; he almost wanted to drive straight on to California. "I thought you wanted to see the ninety-seven acres I bought with your mother's money," she said to him.

He shrugged, drank some water. "What I want," he said, "is to feel water on my body. That's what I want. Will we get that in Phoenix?"

"Not if I can help it."

"Exactly. I am thus reluctant."

It took them a day to get from Arizona's eastern border to Phoenix. They had stopped at a camping site that evening near the Superstition Mountains. Alexander lay down on the wooden deck under the water spout with the cold water pouring down onto his chest and face. Anthony and Tatiana stood at a polite distance and watched him. Anthony asked if his dad was all right.

"I'm not sure," said Tatiana. "I'd say the odds are fifty-fifty." Had Alexander insisted a little harder, she would've been easily persuaded to keep moving until they reached the Pacific. Not because she didn't want to show him their desert property, but because she thought there was a possibility that Federal agents would be waiting for them in the only place that belonged to them. Vikki might have mentioned the land to Sam Gulotta. Tatiana suspected she might have mentioned it to Sam herself. She and Sam had developed a friendship over the years. What if they were waiting? The thought was sickening her. But unfortunately Alexander didn't protest hard enough. Tatiana already knew what she wanted to do—unthinkable though it was: to sell the land! Just sell it at whatever price, take the money, go far into another state, maybe into the vastness of Montana, and never be seen again. She had no illusions: Sam's allegiance was hardly going to be to her and Alexander. Sam wasn't Aunt Esther. Tatiana was mute as she thought of these things while her husband lay on the deck drowning himself with running water.

The following morning, they took the Superstition Freeway. "It's very flat here," Alexander said.

"Well, it *is* called Mesa," said Tatiana. "It means flat."

"Please tell me the land is not here."

"Okay, the land is not here." There were stone mountains in the far distance across the flatlands. "This is too developed."

"*This* is too developed?" he said. There were no stores, no gas stations, just farmland on one side, untouched flat desert on the other.

"Yes, this is Tempe," Tatiana said. "Quite built up. Scottsdale, where we're headed, is a little western town. It's got a few things— a store, a market. You want to see it first? Or . . ."

"Let's see this mythical promised land first," he said.

They continued to drive north through the desert. He was thirsty. She was frightened. The paved road ended, and a gravelly Pima Road began that separated the Phoenix valley from the Salt River Indian Reservation that stretched for miles to the McDowell Mountains. It wasn't as flat anymore, the blue dusty mountains rising up on all sides far and near, low and wide, in the apocalyptic heat.

"Where are these mountains you told me about?"

"Shura, don't tell me you don't see them!" Tatiana pointed straight ahead. The ranges did loom rather large and monolith-like across the saguaros, but Alexander was in a good mood this morning and wanted to tease her.

"What, those? Those aren't mountains. Those are rocks. I know, because I've seen mountains. The Tontos we passed yesterday, those were mountains. The Santa Fe, those were mountains. Also I've seen the Urals, I've seen the Holy Cross Mountains, completely covered by coniferous forest. *Those* were mountains." His mood became less good.

"Now, now . . ." Tatiana said, reaching over and easing him away with her hand on his thigh. "These are Arizona's McDowell Mountains. Sedimentary rock on top of granite rock formed from lava two billion years ago. Precambrian rocks."

"Aren't you a little geologist." Alexander grinned. "A capitalist and a geologist." She was in yellow gingham today, white bobby socks and ballet slipper shoes, her hair pulled back in a braided bun. She didn't have a bead of perspiration on her face, looking almost serene if only Alexander didn't look down on her lap and notice her fingers pressed so stiffly against each other, they looked as if they were breaking.

"All right, all right," he said with a slight frown. "They're mountains."

They chugged along north, kicking up dirt with their dusty tires. The McDowell Mountains drew closer. The sun was high. Alexander said they were idiots, *morons* for taking a trip across the hottest part of the country during the hottest part of the year. If they were smart they would have left Coconut Grove early, driven up to Montana to spend the summer, then carried on to California for the grape-picking.

"You didn't want to leave Florida, remember?"

"Hmm," he assented. "Coconut Grove *was* quite nice for a while."

They fell quiet.

It was another forty-five minutes of unpaved frontier road with not a house, a fruit stand, a gas station, a storefront, or another soul around before Tatiana told him to make a right on a narrow dirt path that sloped upward.

The path was called Jomax.

Jomax ended in a sun-drenched rocky mountain, and that's where Alexander stopped, a mile above the valley. Tatiana, her fingers relaxed, a toothy, happy smile on her face, exclaimed, "Oh God! There is nobody here!"

"That's right," Alexander said, turning off the ignition. "Because everyone else is in Coconut Grove in the ocean."

"There is *nobody* here," she repeated, almost to herself, and hopped out of the trailer.

Anthony ran off but not before Tatiana stopped him, saying,

"Remember what I told you about the cholla, Ant? Don't go anywhere near it. The wind blows the puffs of needles right under your skin and I won't be able to get them out."

"What wind? Let go of me."

"Anthony," said Alexander, looking for his lighter, "your mother tells you something, you don't tell her to let go. Tania, hold on to him for another two minutes until he understands that."

Tatiana made a face at Anthony, pinched him, and quietly let him go. Alexander's lighter was in her hands. She flicked it on for him, and he cupped her hand as he lit his cigarette. "Stop being so soft with him," he said.

Walking away from her to explore a little, Alexander looked north and south, east and west, to the mountains, to the expanse of the entire Phoenix valley lying vast beneath his gaze, its farms all spread out in the overgrown rolling Sonoran Desert. This desert wasn't like the Mojave he vaguely remembered from childhood. This wasn't gray sand with gray mounds of dirt as far as the eye could see. This desert in late July was covered in burned-out, abundant foliage. Thousands of saguaro cacti filled the landscape, their brown-green spiky towering pinnacles and their arms reaching thirty, forty feet up to the sun. The mesquite trees were brown, the palo verdes sepia. The underbrush and the motley overbrush were all in hues of the taupe singed earth. All things grew not out of grass, but out of clay and sand. It looked like a desert jungle. It was not at all what Alexander had expected.

"Tania . . ."

"I *know*," she said, coming up against him. "Isn't it *unbelievable*?"

"Hmm. That wasn't *quite* what I was thinking."

"I've never seen anything like it in my whole life." Her voice became tainted with *something*. "And wait till you see this place in the spring!"

"That implies that we would see it in the spring."

"Everything blooms!"

"And you know this how?"

"I know this," Tatiana said with funny solemnity, "because I saw pictures in a book in the library."

"Oh. Pictures in a book. Do these books mention water?"

She waved her hand dismissively. "The Hohokam Indians back hundreds of years ago saw what I see and wanted to live in this valley so much that they brought water here by a series of canals that led from the Salt River. So back when the mighty British

Empire was still using outhouses, the Hohokam Indians were irri-
gating their crops with running water."

"How do *you* know?" he exclaimed.

"The New York Public Library. The white man here still uses the
Hohokam canals."

"So there *is* a river around here then?" He touched the dry sand
with his hands

"Salt River, but *far*," Tatiana replied. "With any luck, we'll never
have to see it."

Alexander had never experienced this kind of stunning heat.
Even in Florida, all was tempered by the water. No temperance
here! "I'm starting to boil from the inside out," he said. "Quick,
show me our land before my arteries melt."

"You're standing on it," said Tatiana.

"Standing on what?"

"The land." She motioned around. "This is it. Right here, all of
it, at the very top of this hill. From this road due southeast, *ninety-
seven acres* of the Sonoran Desert flush into the mountain. Our
property is two acres wide, and—you know—about forty-nine acres
deep. We'll have to get a surveyor. I think it may open up in a
pie shape."

"Kind of like Sachsenhausen?"

Tatiana looked as if she'd been slapped. "Why do you do that?"
she said quietly. "This isn't your prison. This is your freedom."

Slightly abashed, he said, "You *like* this?"

"Well, I wouldn't have bought it if I didn't like it, Shura." Tatiana
paused. Once again strange trouble passed over her face.

"Tania," Alexander said, "the place is going to set itself on fire."

"Look," she said, "we'll go, we'll get it appraised. If the price is
right, we'll sell it. I have no problem selling it. But . . . don't you
see!" she exclaimed, coming up to him. "Don't you see the desert?
Don't you see the mountains?" She pointed. "The one right next
to ours is Pinnacle Peak; it's famous. But ours has no name. Maybe
we can call it Alexander's Mountain." She raised her eyebrows, but
he wasn't playing at the moment, though he noted her mischief
for later.

"I see the desert," Alexander said. "There's not a single green
thing growing anywhere. Except cacti and they don't need water.
I'm not a saguaro. I need water. There is no good river and no
lakes."

"*Exactly!*" she said, all energized. "No *rivers*. No Nevas, Lugas,

Kamas, Vistulas. No lakes. No Lake Ilmens, no Lake Ladogas. No fields. No clearings. No pines, no pine needles, no birches, no larks, almost no birdsong. Sometimes the swallows come in the summer. But there are no forests over the mountains. There's no snow. You want those things, you can go into the Grand Canyon in the winter. The Ponderosa pine grows a mile above the ice cold Colorado." Standing close, she put her intimate hands on him. "And you are a little bit like the mighty saguaro," she murmured.

Okay, Alexander was noting the playing, he was coming back to it very shortly. "I won't live anywhere without water, Tatiana Metanova." He stamped out his cigarette and his arms went around her. "I don't care what you're trying to get away from."

"It's Tatiana Barrington, Alexander Barrington," said Tatiana, slipping out of his hold. "And you don't know *anything* about what I'm trying to get away from."

He blinked at her. "I think even here in Arizona there might be a moon. Maybe a crimson moon, Tatia? A large, low, harvest crimson moon?"

She blinked back. "Why don't you put on your sixty pounds of gear and pick up your weapons, soldier." Backing away with a swirl, she walked back to the Nomad, while Alexander remained like a post in the sand. In a moment she returned with some water, which he gulped gladly, then went to look for Anthony, finding him near the prickly pears, deeply immersed in a study of rocks. Turned out it wasn't rocks, it was a lizard, which the boy had pinned to the ground with a sharp cactus needle.

"Ant, isn't that the cactus your mother told you to stay away from?" Alexander said, crouching by his son and giving him some water.

"No, Dad," Anthony replied patiently. "Cholla is bad for playing with lizards."

"Son," said Alexander, "I don't think that lizard is playing."

"Dad, this place is *swarming* with reptiles!"

"Don't say that as if it's a good thing. You know how afraid your mother is of reptiles. Look how you're upsetting her."

They peeked out from the prickly pears. The upset mother was leaning back against the Nomad, eyes closed, palms down, sun on her face.

After a while, he returned to her, splashing water on her. That made her open her eyes. Alexander paused to take her in, her square-jawed flushed face, outrageous freckles, serene seaweed

eyes. He appraised the rest of her up and down. She was so arous-
ingly *tiny*. And bewildering. Shaking his head, Alexander hugged
her, he kissed her. She tasted as though plums had dried on her
lips.

"You are out of your mind, my freckle-faced tadpole," he said,
eventually stepping away, "to have bought this land in the first
place. I honestly don't know *what* in the world possessed you. But
now the die is cast. Come on, Arizona-lover, cholla-expert, before
we go see the appraiser, let's eat. Though we'll have to go somewhere else to put water on our bodies, won't we?"

They brought out their flasks, their bread, their ham. Earlier
that morning they had bought plums, cherries, tomatoes,
cucumbers at a farm stand. They had so much to eat. He rolled
out the canopy, they sat under it, where it was a hundred in the
shade, and feasted.

"How much did you say you paid for the land?" he asked.

"Fifty dollars an acre."

Alexander whistled. "This is near Scottsdale?"

"Yes, Scottsdale is only twenty miles south."

"Hmm. Is it a one horse town?"

"Oh, not anymore, sir!" said a real estate agent in Scottsdale. "Not
anymore. There's the army base, and the GIs, like you, sir, they're
all comin' back from the war and marrying their sweethearts. You
two are newlyweds?"

No one said anything, as the *four*-year-old child sat near them
lining up the real estate brochures in neat rows.

"The housing boom is something to behold," the realtor went
on quickly. "Scottsdale is an up-and-coming town, you just watch
and see. We had nobody here, almost as if we weren't part of the
Union, but now that the war is over, Phoenix is exploding. Did
you know," he said proudly, "our housebuilding industry is number
one in the country? We've got new schools, a new hospital—
Phoenix Memorial—a new department store in Paradise Valley.
You would like it here very much. Would you be interested in
seeing some properties?"

"When are you going to pave the roads?" asked Alexander. He
had changed into clean beige fatigues and a dry black T-shirt.
Tattoos, scars, blue death camp numbers, no matter—he could not
wear a long-sleeve shirt in Arizona. The real estate man kept trying
not to glance at the long scar running up Alexander's forearm into

the blue cross. The realtor himself was wearing a wool suit in which he was sweating even in air conditioning.

"Oh, every day, sir, new roads are being paved every day. New communities are being built constantly. This is changing from farm country to a real proper town. The war has been very good for us. We're in a real boom. Are you from the East? I thought so, by your wife's accent. Much like your Levittown communities, except the houses are nicer here, if I may be so bold. May I show you a couple of—"

"No," said Tatiana, stepping forward. "But we would be interested in finding out the going price of our own property here. We're up north, off Pima Road, near Pinnacle Peak."

The realtor's face soured when he heard they weren't in the market. "Where, near Rio Verde Drive?"

"Yes, a few miles south of there. On Jomax."

"On what? They just named that road. You have a house there? There's nothing up there." He said it as if he didn't believe her.

"No house, just some property."

"Well," he said with a shrug. "My appraiser is out to lunch."

An hour later, the appraiser and the realtor's faces were trying to maintain their poker expressions, but it wasn't working. "*How* many acres did you say you have?" the appraiser said, a short man with a small head, a large body and an ill-fitting suit.

"Ninety-seven," repeated Tatiana calmly.

"Well, that's impossible," said the appraiser. "I know all the land bought and sold here. I mean, the town of Scottsdale is just now thinking of incorporating—do you know how many acres?—Sixty hundred and forty. Three and a half square miles. A smart man bought them last century for three and a half dollars an acre. But that was then. You're telling me you have ninety-seven acres? A sixth of the land of our whole town? No one sells in large parcels like that. No one would sell you ninety-seven acres."

Tatiana just stared at him. Alexander just stared at him. He was trying to figure out if this was a ploy, a game, or whether the guy was actually being rude, in which case—

"Land's too valuable," stated the appraiser. "Around here we sell one acre, two at most. And up there, there's nothing but desert. It's all owned by the Federal Government or the Indians."

So it *was* a ploy. Alexander relaxed.

Tatiana was silent. "I don't know what to tell you. You don't think I can count to ninety-seven?"

"Can I see the deed, if you don't mind?"

"Actually, we do mind," Alexander said. "Are you going to tell us what the land is worth or do we have to go somewhere else?"

The appraiser finally spluttered that being all the way out there, all the way out in the boonies where no one wanted to go, the land now would probably be worth about $25 dollars an acre. "It's a good price for it—there's nothing up there, no roads, no electricity. I don't know why you would buy land in a location so isolated."

Tatiana and Alexander exchanged a glance.

"Like I said, it's *worth* twenty-five dollars," said the appraiser quickly. "But this is what I can do for you. If you sell, say, ninety-five of those acres, keeping two for yourselves, we can give you a one time deal, take it or leave it, of . . . forty dollars an acre."

"Mister," said Alexander, "we'll gladly leave it. We paid fifty an acre for that land."

The appraiser wilted. "You vastly overpaid. But . . . to get your business, I'll be glad to give you fifty. Imagine all that money in your pocket. You could buy yourself a brand new house with that. For cash. We have an outstanding development near here in Paradise Valley. You only have the one boy? But perhaps more in your future? How about if I show you some new communities?"

"No, thanks." Alexander prodded Tatiana to go.

"All right, wait," said the appraiser. "Sixty dollars an acre. That's nearly a thousand dollar profit on your original investment. Half a year's salary to some people."

Nodding vigorously, Tatiana opened her mouth to speak, but Alexander squeezed her hand to cut her off. "I made that in three weeks driving a boat in Miami," he said. "We're not selling our land for a thousand dollar profit."

"Are you certain about that?" The appraiser glanced at Tatiana beseechingly, looking for her support. Alexander mock-glared at her. She stayed impassive. "Well then, I'm going to tell you something," said the appraiser. "If you don't take your money out of the land now, in a year's time, it won't be worth twenty-five an acre. You wait until your boy starts school, you won't be able to sell your ninety-seven acres for three dollars and fifty cents. All the way up there past the Indians? Forget it. No one of sound mind will want to live north of the reservation. Go ahead, you wait a while. Your land will be worthless by 1950."

Alexander ushered his family out. They stood on a dusty Western street. They didn't talk about what the appraiser told them. Alexander wanted to get a cold beer. Tatiana wanted to go to the general store on the corner and buy some ice cream. Anthony wanted a cowboy hat. In the end, Alexander didn't get a cold beer, because he wouldn't take his family into a saloon, but Tatiana did get an ice cream, and Anthony did get a hat. They walked around the town square. Alexander didn't know why, but he liked it, liked the Western feel of it, the frontier expanse and yet the small town intimacy of it. They drove around in their Nomad, saw that much of the farmland around the town square was being turned into housing developments. For dinner they had steak and baked potatoes and corn on the cob at a local restaurant with sawdust on the floor.

He asked her what she wanted to do and she said that perhaps they ought to take one more look at the land before they made a final decision.

It was seven in the evening, and the sun was arching downward. Because the sun was a different color, their mountain turned a different color—the rocks now glowed in three-dimensional orange. Alexander appraised the land himself. "Tania, what are the chances that you had been prescient when you bought this land?" he said, bringing her to him after they walked around a while.

"Slim to none," Tatiana said, her arms going around his waist, "and Slim has already left town. We definitely should sell it, Shura. Sell it as quick as we can, take our money, go someplace else nice and not as hot."

Leaning down, he placed his lips on her moist cheek. "*You're* so nice and hot, babe," he whispered. She smelled of vanilla ice cream. She tasted of vanilla ice cream. "But I disagree. I think the appraiser is lying. Either there is a housing boom, or there isn't. But a housing boom means land *in*creases in value."

"He's right, though," she said. "It's very out of the way."

"Out of the way for what?" Alexander shook his head. "I really think we can make a little money here. We're going to wait a while, then sell it." He paused. "But Tania, I'm confused about your motives. One minute you want to sell the land for pennies to the lowest bidder. The next you're breathlessly talking about spring."

Tatiana shrugged. "What can I say? I'm conflicted." She chewed her lip. "Would you ever consider . . . living here?" she asked carefully.

"Never! Feel the air. Feel your face. Why, do *you* want to live here—" Suddenly Alexander broke off, his eyes widening.

Do you *want to live in Arizona, Tatia, the land of the small spring?*

He had asked this of her—in another life. "Oh, come now," he said slowly. "You don't—you aren't—no, come on . . . Oh no!" Alexander let out an incredulous laugh. "I *just* got it! *Just.* Oh, I'm good. I'm sharp. I don't know how we ever won the war. Tania, come on! Recall when I said it."

"I'm recalling it as if you're saying it to me now," she said with crossed arms.

"Well, then surely you know I meant it metaphorically. As in, would you like to live somewhere that's warm. I didn't actually mean *here*!"

"No?" Her no was so quiet.

"Of course no! Is *that* why you bought the land?"

When Tatiana didn't reply, Alexander became speechless. There were so many baffling things he didn't understand about her, he simply didn't know where to look for answers. "We're in the middle of an iced over, blockaded, heatless Leningrad," he said. "The Germans are denying you even the unleavened cardboard and glue that you're eating instead of bread. I briefly mention a vague warm place I barely remember that I had once driven through with my parents. Damn, I should've said Miami. Would you have then bought land there?"

"Yes."

"You're *not* serious. Anthony, come here, stop chasing rattle-snakes. Do *you* like it here?"

"Dad, this is the funnest place in the whole world."

"What about this cholla? Is that fun?"

"So fun! Ask Mommy. She says it has evil spirits. She calls it the cactus from hell. Tell him, Mama—it's worse than war." He ran off with joy.

"Yes," said Tatiana, "stay away from the cholla, Alexander."

He furrowed his brow. "I think the heat has done something to both of you. Tania, inland, we're so far inland, the air doesn't even carry water on the wind!"

"I know." She took a hot gulp of air.

They disengaged, spread out, thinking their separate thoughts. Anthony was picking dried-out fruit off the prickly pear cactus. Tatiana was pulling the dried-out red flowers off the cattail-like ocotillo. And Alexander was smoking and looking at the land and the mountain and the valley below. The sun set peacefully, and as the light of the sun changed once more, the rock hills transformed into a blaze. They put down a blanket, sat shoulder to shoulder, knee to knee and watched the sunset while Anthony played.

Alexander thought Tatiana had been thinking of how to convince him to sell the land or not to sell the land, but what she said to him was more perplexing. She said: "Shura, tell me, in Lazarevo, when you were going to go back to the front . . . we used to look at the Ural Mountains like this. Tell me, why didn't you just stay?"

Alexander was taken aback. "What do you mean, *stay*?"

"You know." She paused. "Why didn't you just . . . not go back?"

"Not go back to my command post? You mean—*desert*?"

She nodded. "Why didn't we just run—into the Urals? You could have built us an *izba*, we could've settled there, in the forest, found some precious stones, bartered them, grown things to eat. They would've never found us."

Alexander shook his head, his hands opening in deep question. "Tatiana, what in the name of God," he said, "are you thinking? What in the world is going through your mind, and more important, why?"

"It's not a rhetorical question. I would like an answer."

"An answer to what? Why didn't I desert the Red Army? For one, my commander, Colonel Stepanov, that nice man—remember him, who let me have twenty-nine Lazarevo days with you—would've gone to the firing squad for having a deserter in his brigade. So would my major, and all the lieutenants and sergeants I served with. And you and I would've been on the run for the rest of our short, doomed lives. On the run! And they would've found us, like they find everybody. Remember I told you about Germanovsky? They found him in Belgium after the war, and he'd never even set foot in the Soviet Union. He was born in France. His father was a diplomat. Germanovsky was given ten years hard labor for not returning when he turned eighteen—*fourteen* years earlier! That would have been us. Except they would have found us in five minutes, the first time we tried to barter some of that precious Ural malachite to match your eyes. It would've been over like lightning, and the five extra minutes we would have had would've been spent with one eye looking over our shoulder. In other words, *prison*. That's what you wanted—?"

Without letting him finish, she jumped up and walked away. What was she *thinking*? But at the same time, the sun was on fire, and Alexander had spent too long in dark places below ground, and so he didn't go after her but sat and finished his cigarette, watching the desert sunset up from a hill.

When Tatiana came back to the blanket she said. "It was just a silly question." She knocked into his shoulder. "I was musing, not serious."

"Oh, that's good. As opposed to what?"

"Sometimes I think crazy thoughts, that's all."

"The crazy part, absolutely. What thoughts?" Alexander paused. "How it all might've been different?"

"Something like that," she said staring into space. Then she took his hand. "Sunset's nice, isn't it?"

"Sunset's nice," said Alexander.

She leaned against him. "Shura, this all might look burned and brown now, but in the spring," she said in a breathy voice, "the Sonoran Desert is *reborn*! With pale blue delphinium, white thistle, flame poppy, red ocotillo, blue and yellow palo verdes, and scarlet bugle. We can even plant some lilac sand verbena. You know how much you like lilac," she cooed. "And prickly pears and pincushion cacti grow here . . ."

Alexander squeezed her little hand and raised his eyebrows. This was a *much* better conversation. "Babe," he said, lowering his voice, and glancing around to make sure Ant wasn't nearby, "in my lewd soldier's world *pincushion* means only one thing, and you can be sure it's not cacti."

Tatiana tutted in mock shock, pulled to get away, but Alexander grabbed her, pulled her down onto her back on the blanket, bent over her, and said huskily, "Tell me, is there pussy willow in the desert, too?" watching her flush red, and forgetting all about flame poppy and scarlet bugle.

He let her shove him, scramble up, and run from him. He chased her, he chased Anthony.

He is making a silent movie with her, and she is moving in broken frames, animated and choppy, to the sound of the jerking crank. Her arms do a little flapper dance from side to side; her teeth are gleaming, she is tousle-haired and sunny, she runs after Anthony, her taut hips curve and swivel, she runs back to Alexander, her bouncy breasts bob and sway; she stands in front of him, holding her hands out to him, come, come, but he is holding the shaking camera, he can't come. Her exquisite mouth puckers, her mouth in black and white—it's a bow, a blow, a kiss, a gift that keeps on giving—and suddenly, a broken reel. *Shura! Shura! Can you hear me?* she squeals, and he puts the camera down and chases her, and somewhere in the Siberian juniper he catches her. She bats her eyes that squint upward catlike when she laughs, she parts her mouth and pleads falsely and merrily for release. Someday perhaps they will look back at the movies of this time, movies that will have captured the illusion, the fleeting joy that is their youth. Just as Soviet cameras once captured the snapshots of another her, another him, on the stone steps of wedding churches or near their long lost brothers.

Covered in sweat and sand, Alexander and the boy took off their shirts and fell down on the nylon tent covering while Tatiana dipped a towel into a bucket of water and cooled their chests and faces. Once he had only a soaked towel on his face as he dreamed of her. Now he had a soaked towel *and* her. He reached out, like a bear—and pawed her. She *is* here.

"I want the Biscayne Bay now . . ." croaked Alexander. "The Gulf of Mexico now."

He got darkness now, and a sleeping son. The stars were *all* out, even Jupiter. She came out to him after putting Anthony to bed inside the camper, and he was sitting in a plastic folding chair, smoking. Another chair stood by his side.

She started to cry.

"Oh, no," he said, covering his face.

Patting his shoulder, her voice low, she said with a sniffle, "Thank you." And then climbed into his lap and held his head to her.

"You understand *nothing*," he said, rubbing his cropped hair into her neck. "The lap was always so much better."

Alexander had pitched a tent for them and built a small careful fire surrounded by stones right in front of it. "You know how I lit the kindling?" he said. "I held it to a rock for five seconds."

"All righty, now," she said. "Enough of that."

They sat facing west, wrapped around each other, looking out onto the dark valley.

"When you weren't with me," said Tatiana, "and when I thought you were never going to be with me again, I bought this land on top of the hill. For you. Because of the things you taught me. Just like you always taught me. To be on high ground."

"That rule is only for floods and war, Tatia. What are the chances of either here?" He stared into the blackness.

"Husband . . ." she whispered, "you see nothing down there now, but can you imagine in a few years' time, all the twinkling lights from streets, from houses, from shops, from other souls in the valley? Like New York is lit up, this valley will be lit up, and we could sit here like this and watch it below us."

"You said a second ago we were selling the land tomorrow!"

"Yes." Tatiana was warm, open, until a part of her shut off, became tense like her fingers. Her wistful desire to see the desert bloom in the sometime spring was strong, but the trouble in her clenched hands was strong also. "Just a dream, Shura, you know? Just a silly dream." She sighed. "Of course we'll sell it."

"No, we're not selling it," Alexander said, turning her to face him. "And I don't want to talk about it anymore."

She pointed to the tent. "We're sleeping there?" Her palms went around his neck. "I can't. My bravery is fake, as you know. I'm scared of scorpions."

"Nah, don't worry," said Alexander, his hands tight around her ribs, his lips pressing into her pulsing throat, his eyes closing. "Scorpions don't like loud noises."

"Well, that's good," Tatiana murmured, tilting her head upward. "Because they won't be hearing any."

She was so wrong about that . . . christening their ninety-seven acres, and Pinnacle Peak and Paradise Valley, and the moon and the stars and Jupiter in the sky with their tumultuous coupling and her ecstatic moans.

The next morning as they raised camp and packed up to go north to the Grand Canyon, Alexander looked at Tatiana, she looked at him, they turned around and stared at Anthony.

"Did the boy not wake last night?"

"The boy did not wake last night."

The boy was sitting at the table doing a U.S. puzzle. "What?" he said. "You *wanted* the boy to wake last night?"

Alexander turned to the road. "Well, isn't that interesting," he mused, reaching for his pack of Marlboros. "Something calm to make us sane."

Missing Time

At Desert View, they stood over the ageless rim of the Grand Canyon and stared west into the blue haze horizon and far down to the snake of the Red River. They drove a few miles west and stopped at Lipan Point and then at Grandview Point. At Moran Point they sat and gawked and walked in silence, even the normally chatty Anthony. They walked along the rim on a wooded path under the Ponderosa pines to Yavapai Point, where they found a secluded spot to sit and watch the sunset. Anthony came too close to the edge, and both Alexander and Tatiana jumped and yelled, and he burst into tears. Alexander held him in a vise, finally relenting and releasing him only after literally drawing a line in the sand and telling the boy not to step an inch over it if he didn't want a military punishment. Anthony spent the sunset building up that line into a barricade with pebbles and twigs.

The sun in the indigo sky set over the Canyon, painting crimson blue the greening forests of cottonwoods and juniper and spruce. Alexander stopped blinking, for while the sun was setting, the hues of the Canyon had changed, and he could not catch his breath in the silence while the cinnabar heat fell like rust iron mist over two billion years of ancient temples of layered clays and fossiled silt, and from its cream Coconino to its black Vishnu schist, all the ridges and Redwalls and cliffs and ravines, and the Bright Angel shales and the sandstones and limestones from Tonto to Tapeat, all the pink and wine, and lilac and lime, and the Great Unconformity: the billion years of missing time—*all* was steeped in vermilion.

"God is putting on some light show," he finally said, taking a breath.

"He's trying to impress you with Arizona, Shura," murmured Tatiana.

"Why do the rocks look like that?" asked Anthony. His barricade was nearly a foot high.

"Water, wind, time erosion," replied Alexander. "The Colorado River below started as a trickle and became a deluge, carving this canyon over millions of years. The river, Anthony, despite your mother's aversion to it, is a catalyst for all things."

"It is precisely because of this catalysis that the mother is averse to it," said the mother as she sat under his arm.

Alexander finally stood up and gave her his hand. "At the end of His geological week, God surveyed His rocks in the most Grand of all the Canyons in all the Earth He had created and all the life that dwelt upon them and behold, it was very good."

Tatiana nodded in her approval of Alexander. "Who said that? You know what the Navajos say, who live and walk and die in these parts?" She paused trying to remember. "*With beauty in front of me, I walk,*" she said, stretching out her arms. "*With beauty behind me, I walk. With beauty below me, I walk.*" Not a sound came from the Canyon below. "*With beauty above me, I walk.*" She spoke quietly. "*It is finished in beauty.*" She raised her head. "*It is finished in beauty.*"

"Hmm," said Alexander, taking one long inhale of his cigarette, eternally in his mouth. "Substitute what you most believe in for the word beauty," he said, "and then you've really got something."

In the eerily soundless night at the Yavapai campsite, Anthony was restlessly asleep in one of the two tents, while they kept listening to his stirrings and whimperings, waiting for him to quieten down, sitting huddled under one blanket in front of the fire, a mile from the black maw of the Canyon. They were shivering, their icy demons around the worsted wool.

They didn't speak. Finally they lay down in front of the fire, face to face. Alexander was holding his breath and then breathing out in one hard lump.

He didn't say anything at first. He didn't want to talk to her about things that could not be changed. And yet, pain he could not forget kept creeping in and prickling his heart in a thousand different ways. He imagined other men touching her when he was dead. Other men near what he was near, and her looking up at them, taking their hands to lead them into rooms where she was widowed. Alexander didn't want the truth if it wasn't what he wanted to hear; he didn't know how he would bear the unwelcome truth, and he hadn't asked her in all the time he'd been back, but here they were, lying together at the Grand Canyon, which seemed like a rightful place for mystical confessions.

He took a breath. "Did you love to go dancing?" he asked.

"What?"

So she wasn't answering. He fell silent. "When I was in Colditz, that impenetrable fortress, whittling away my life, I wanted to know this."

"Looks like you're still there, Shura."

"No," he said. "I'm in New York, a fly on the wall, trying to see you without me."

"But I'm here," she whispered.

"Yes, but what were you like when you were *there*? Were you gay?" Alexander's voice was so sad. "I know you didn't forget us, but did you want to, so you could be happy again like you once were, dance without pain?" He swallowed. "So you could . . . love again? Is that what you were thinking sitting on the planks at Mercy Hospital? Wanting to be happy again, wishing you were back there, in New York, reciting Emily Bronte to yourself? *Sweet love of youth, forgive if I forget thee . . .*"

He was leading her to temptation of clarity. But he could see she didn't want clarity. She wanted a jumble that she could deny.

"Okay, Shura, if we're talking like this, having these things out, then tell me what you meant when you said I was tainted with the Gulag. Tell me what happened to you."

"No. I—forget it. I was—"

"Tell me what happened to you when you went missing for four days in Deer Isle."

"It's getting longer and longer. It was barely three days. First tell me what you were thinking at Mercy Hospital."

"Okay, fine, let's not talk about it."

He pressed his demanding fingers into her back. He put his hands under her cardigan, under her blouse, into her bare shoulders.

He turned her on her back and kneeled astride her, the fire, the maw behind them. No comfort, no peace, he guessed with a sigh, even in the temples of the Grand Canyon.

Anthony's whimperings turned into full scale miseries. "Mama, Mama!" Tatiana had to rush to him. He calmed down, but she stayed in his tent. Eventually, Alexander crawled in and fit in sideways behind her in the little tent on the hard ground.

"It's just a stage, Shura," said Tatiana, as if trying to assuage him. "It too will pass." She paused. "Like everything."

Alexander's impatience and frustration also burned his throat. "You wouldn't say that if you knew what he dreams about."

Tatiana stiffened in his arms.

"Ah!" Alexander raised his head to stare at her in the dark. He could barely see the contours of her face, as the fire diffused muted light through the slightly raised flaps. "You *know*!"

Tatiana sounded pained when she nodded. Her head remained down. Her eyes were closed.

"All this time you knew?"

She shrugged carefully. "I didn't want to upset you."

After a stretch of conflicted silence, Alexander spoke. "I know you think, Tatiana," he said, "that everything will turn out well, but you'll see—it won't. He's never going to get over the fact that you left him."

"Don't say that! He will. He's just a small boy."

Alexander nodded, but not in agreement. "Mark my words," he said. "He won't."

"So what are you saying?" she said, upset. "That I shouldn't have gone? I found you, didn't I? This conversation is just ridiculous!"

"Yes," he whispered. "But tell me, if you hadn't found me, what would you have done? Returned to New York and married Edward Ludlow?" He was indifferent to her stiffness and her tutting. "Anthony for one, rightly or wrongly, thinks that you would have never come back. That you'd still be looking for me in the taiga woods."

"No, he doesn't!" Turning sharply to him, Tatiana repeated, "No. He doesn't."

"Did you listen to his dream? His mother had a choice. When she left him, she knew there was a very good chance she was leaving him for good. She knew it—and still, she left him. That is his dream. That is what he knows."

"Alexander! Are you being deliberately cruel? Stop!"

"I'm not being cruel. I just want you to stop pretending that's not what he's going through. That it's just a small thing. You are the big believer in consequences, as you keep telling me. So when I ask you if he's going to get better, don't pretend to me you don't know what I'm talking about."

"So why ask me? Obviously you have all the answers."

"Stop it with the snide." Alexander took a breath. "Do you know what's interesting?"

"No. Shh."

"I have nightmares that I'm in Kolyma," Alexander said dully. "I'm sharing a cot, a small dirty cot with Ouspensky. We're still shackled together, huddling under a blanket. It's viciously cold. Pasha is long gone." Alexander swallowed past the stones in his throat. "I open my eyes and realize that all this, Deer Isle, Coconut

Grove, America, had been the actual dream, just like I feared. This is just another trick the mind plays in the souls of the insane. I jump out of bed and run out of the barracks, dragging Ouspensky's rotting corpse behind me into the frozen tundra, and Karolich runs after me, chasing me with his weapon. After he catches me—and he always catches me—he knocks me in the throat with the butt of his rifle. 'Get back to the barracks, Belov,' he says. 'It's another twenty-five years for you. Chained to a dead man.' When I get out of bed in the night, I can't breathe, like I've just been jabbed in the throat."

"Alexander," Tatiana said inaudibly, pushing him away with shaking hands. "I begged you, *begged* you! I don't want to hear this!"

"Anthony dreams of you gone. I dream of you gone. It's so visceral, every blood vessel in my body feels it. How can I help *him* when I can't even help myself?"

She groaned in remonstration.

He lay quietly behind her, cut off mid-sentence, mid-pain. He couldn't take it anymore. He couldn't get out of the tent fast enough. He said nothing, just left.

Tatiana lay inside by Anthony. She was cold. When the boy was finally asleep, she crawled out of the tent. Alexander was sitting wrapped in a blanket by the fading fire.

"Why do you always do that?" he said coldly, not turning around. "On the one hand you draw me into ridiculous conversations and are upset I won't speak to you, but when I speak to you about things that actually gnaw at me, you shut me down like a trap door."

Tatiana was taken aback. She didn't do that, did she?

"Oh, yes," he said. "Yes, you do do that."

"I didn't mean to upset you."

"Then why do you?"

"I'm sorry," she said. "I can't help that I can't talk about Ant's unspeakable dreams. Or yours." She was terror-stricken enough.

"Well, run along, then, back in the tent." He continued to sit and smoke.

She pulled on him. He jerked away.

"I said I was sorry," Tatiana murmured. "Please come back inside. I'm very cold, and you know I can't go to sleep without you. Come on." She lowered her voice as she bent to him. "Into *our* tent."

In the tent he didn't undress, remaining in his long johns as he climbed inside the sleeping bag. She watched him for a few moments, as she tried to figure out what he wanted from her, what she *should* do, what she *could* do. What did he need?

Tatiana undressed. Bare and unprotected, fragile and susceptible, she climbed into the sleeping bag, squeezing in under his hostile arm. She wanted him to know she wasn't carrying any weapons.

"Shura, I'm sorry," she whispered. "I know all about my boy. I know all about the consequences of my leaving him. But there is nothing I can do now. I just have to try to make him better. And he does have both his parents for my trouble and his trouble. I'm hoping in the end, somewhere down the line, that will mean something to him, having his father. That the balance of things will somehow be restored by the good that's come from my doing the unforgivable."

Alexander didn't say anything. He wasn't touching her either.

Putting his hand under his crew, she rubbed his stomach. "I'm so cold, Shura," she whispered. "Look, you've got a cold nude girl in your tent."

"Cold is right," he said.

Pressing herself against him, Tatiana opened her mouth and he cut her off half-murmur. "Stop this whole speaking thing. Just let me go to sleep."

She sucked in her breath, held her other words back, and tugged at him, opening her arms to him, but he remained unapproachable. "Forget about comfort, forget about peace," he said, "but even what kind of *relief* do you think I'm going to get from you when you're all clenched up and upset like this? The milk of kindness is not exactly flowing from you tonight."

"What, and you're not upset?" she said quietly.

"I'm not bothering *you*, am I?"

They lay by each other. He unzipped the bag halfway on his side and sat up. After opening the tent flaps for some air, he lit a cigarette. It was cold in the Canyon at night. Shivering, she watched him, considering her options, assessing the various permutations and combinations, factoring in the X-factor, envisioning several moves ahead, and then her hand crept up and lay on his thigh. "Tell *me* the truth," Tatiana said carefully. "Tell me here and now, the years without me . . . in the penal battalion . . . in the Byelorussian villages—were you really without a woman like you told me or was that a lie?"

Alexander smoked. "It was not a lie, but *I* didn't have much choice, did I? You know where *I* was—in Tikhvin, in prison, at the front with men. I wasn't in New York dancing with my hair down with men full of live ammo."

"My hair was never down, first of all," she said, unprovoked, "but you told me that once, in Lublin, you did have a choice."

"Yes," he said. "I came close with the girl in Poland."

Tatiana waited, listened. Alexander continued, "And then after we were captured, I was in POW camps and Colditz with your brother, and then Sachsenhausen—without him. First fighting with men, then guarded by men, beaten by men, interrogated by men, shot at by men, tattooed by men. Few women in that world." He shuddered.

"But . . . some women?"

"Some women, yes."

"Did you . . . taint yourself with a Gulag wife?"

"Don't be absurd, Tatiana," Alexander said, low and heavy. "Don't divide my words by your false questions. You know what I said to you has nothing to do with that."

"Then what did you mean? Tell me. I know nothing. Tell me where you went when you left me in Deer Isle for four days. Were you with a woman then?"

"Tatiana! God!"

"You're not answering me."

"No! For God's sake! Did you see me when I came back? Enough of this already, you're degrading me."

"And you're not degrading me by your worries?" she whispered.

"No! You believed I was dead. In New York you weren't betraying me, you were continuing your merry widowed life. Big fucking difference, Tania."

Hearing his tone, Tatiana moved away from the verbal parrying, though what she wanted to say was, "Obviously *you* don't think it's such a big difference." But she knew when enough was enough with him. "Why won't you tell me where you went in Maine?" she whispered. "Can't you see how afraid I am?" She was upset he wasn't willing to comfort her. He was never willing to comfort her.

"I don't want to tell you," Alexander said, "because I don't want to upset you."

Tatiana became so scared by his hollow voice that she actually changed the subject to other unmentionables. "What about my brother? Did he have a prison wife?"

Alexander smoked deeply. "I don't want to talk about him."

"Oh, great. So there's nothing you want to talk about."

"That's right."

"Well, good night then." She swirled away. Really a symbolic gesture, swirling away, turning your narrow naked back to an enormous dressed man next to whom you're still lying in one sleeping bag.

Alexander sighed into the smoke, inhaled it. With one arm, he flipped her back to him. "Don't turn away from me when we're like this," he said. "If you must have an answer, a laundry girl in Colditz fell in love with Pasha and gave it to him for free."

Tears came to Tatiana's eyes. "Yes. He was very good at having girls fall in love with him," she said quietly. She settled as close as she could into Alexander's unwelcoming side. "Almost as good as you," she whispered achingly.

Alexander didn't say anything.

Tatiana tried hard to stop shivering. "In Luga, in Leningrad, Pasha was always in love with one girl or another."

"I think he was mistaking love for something else," said Alexander.

"Unlike you, Shura?" she whispered, desperately wishing for some intimacy from him.

"Unlike me," was all he said.

She lay mutely. "Did you have yourself a little laundry girl?" Her voice trembled.

"You know I did. You want me to tell you about her?" Throwing his cigarette away, he leaned over her, putting his hand between her thighs. Just like that. No kissing, no stroking, no caressing, no whispering, no preamble, just the hand between her thighs. "She is maddening," he said. "She is mystifying. She is bewildering, and infuriating." His other hand went under her head, into her hair.

"She is true." Tatiana tried to stay still. She was feeling not mystifying but sickly vulnerable at the moment—naked and small in complete blackness with his overwhelming clothed body, too strong for its own good, over her; with his heavy soldier hand on her most vulnerable place. She forgot her mission, which was to bring him comfort from the things that assailed him. "And she gives it to you for free," she whispered, her hands grasping his jersey.

"You call this free?" he said. Miraculously his rough-tipped fingers were caressing her exceedingly gently. *How* did he do this? His hands could lift the Nomad if they had to, he had the strongest hands, and they weren't always gentle with her, but they did tread ever so lightly in a place so sensitive it shamed her before his fingers made her senseless. "You don't fool me, Tatiana, with your reverse questions," he said. "I know exactly what you're doing."

"What am I doing?" she said thickly, trying not to move or moan.

"Turning it around to me. If I, an irredeemable sinner stayed clean, then you certainly did."

"Obviously, darling, you are not irredeemable . . ." Her head angled back.

"One less wrong move by burly Jeb, and you would've given yourself to him," said Alexander, pausing both in word and deed. The pause made Tatiana only less steady. "One more right move by Edward, one more forward move by Edward"—Tatiana couldn't help it, she moved, she *gasped*—"and you would have given it to him for free."

She was having trouble speaking. "That's not true," she said. "What, you think I couldn't have?" She turned her face into his chest, her body stiff. "I could have. I knew what they wanted. But I . . ." She was having trouble thinking. "I didn't."

Alexander was breathing hard and said nothing.

"Is this why you are so detached from me?"

"What's detached, Tania?"

It was ironic at the moment to accuse him of this. The soft rhythmic skates and slips of his fingers became too much for her; clutching him, she whispered inaudibly, *wait, wait,* but Alexander bent and sucked her nipple into his mouth, slightly increasing his pressure and friction on her, and she had no more inaudible *wait, wait,* but a very audible *yes, yes.*

When she could speak again, Tatiana said, "Come on, who are *you* talking to?" She pulled on his crew. "Look at me, Shura."

"It's dark, fire's out, can't see a thing."

"Well, I can see *you.* You're so bright, you're burning my eyes. Now look at me. I'm your Tania. Ask me, ask me anything. I don't lie to you." She stopped speaking. I don't lie to my husband. I do *keep* some things from my husband. Like: *there are men coming up the hill again, coming after you, and I have to do everything in my power to protect you, and so I can't comfort you as well as I would like to because at the moment I'm attacked in more ways than you know.* "In Lazarevo," she said, reaching for that comfort, for that truth he wanted, feeling for his face above her, "you broke my ring and I gave you my hand, and with it my word. It's the only word that I keep."

"Yes," he whispered, his smoky breath beating to the tense drum of his heart. "I did break your ring once upon a time." His fingers lightly remained on her. "But in New York you thought I was dead."

"Yes, and I was mourning you. Perhaps in twenty years' time I may have married the local liege, but I hadn't. I wasn't ready and I wasn't happy and I wasn't gay. *Your* son was in the bedroom. Though I may have danced a few times, you know better than anyone I did not forget my sweet love of youth," she whispered, adding nearly inaudibly, "I left our little boy because I did not forget and could not forget."

His apologetic palm was warm and comforting on her. Oh, so he *was* willing to comfort her.

"No apologies necessary," she said. "You're anxious, aren't you? But I told you the truth back in Germany. I don't lie to you. I won't lie to you. I wasn't touched, Shura. Not even in New York as your merry widow." She moaned for him.

He was staring at her through the black night, tense, tight. Haltingly he whispered, "Kissed, Tatiana?"

"Never, darling Shura," she replied, lying on her back, her arms around him. "Never by anyone but you. Why do you flagellate yourself over nothing?"

They kissed raptly, tenderly, openly, softly. "Well, look at the idiotic questions you keep asking me," he said, throwing off his crew and his long johns like a large bristly hedgehog in a small sack. "Worrying about women in Byelorussia, in Bangor. It's not nothing, is it? It's *everything*." He climbed on top of her in the unzipped sleeping bag. Her hands went above her head. His hands went over her wrists. His lips were on her.

"And finally," Alexander said, after he was sated, and her palms were on his back, "there is a little *blessed* relief."

The cigarette long stubbed out, she lay in his arms and he continued to caress her. Were they close to sleep? She thought he might be, his hands on her back were getting slower. But here at Yavapai, over the silent shrines of God's fluvial Canyon carved centimeter by centimeter by a persistent and unyielding and course-changing Red River, was as good a time as any for Tatiana's own slight erosion of the carapace that covered Alexander.

"Shura, why am I tainted with the Gulag?" she whispered. "Please tell me."

"Oh, Tania. It's not you. Don't you understand? I'm soiled by the unsacred things I've seen, by the things I've lived through."

She stroked his body, kissed his chest wounds. "You're not soiled, darling," she said. "You're human and suffering and struggling . . . but your soul is untouched."

"You think?"

"I *know*."

"How do you know?"

"Because," she whispered, "I *see* it. From the first moment I touched you on our bus, I saw your soul." She pressed her lips to his shoulder. "Now tell me."

"You won't want to hear it."

"I will. I do."

Alexander told her about the gangrapes and the deaths on the trains. Tatiana almost said then that he had been right—she did not want to hear it. The savagery didn't happen that often, he said; it didn't need to in the camps. On the transport trains, these assaults and consequent deaths had been a daily occurrence. But at Catowice, Colditz, Sachsenhausen, most of the women either sold it, or bartered it, or gave it away free to strangers—quickly, before the guards came and beat them and then took some for themselves.

He told her about the women at Sachsenhausen. When Tatiana said she didn't remember any women at Sachsenhausen, Alexander replied that by the time she came they had all gone. But before she came, the guards who hated Alexander put him in charge of building a brick wall to replace the barbed-wire fence that separated the women's two barracks from the men's sixteen. The guards knew it would put Alexander's life in danger to build a wall to replace the existing barbed wire—which was so facilitating in the barter of sexual favors. The women backed up to the barbed wife on their hands and knees as if they were washing the floor, while the men kneeled on the ground, careful not to pierce themselves on the rusty protrusions.

Tatiana shivered.

So he built the wall. At five feet tall, it was not tall enough. At night the men skipped over the wall, and the women skipped over the wall. A watch tower was put up and a guard remained there round the clock to prevent connubial activity. The skipping over the wall continued. Alexander was told to make the wall seven feet. One afternoon during construction he was cornered in the barracks by eight angry lifers. They came to him with logging saws and axes. Alexander wasted no time talking. He swung the chain he was holding. It hit one of the men across the head, breaking open his skull. The other men fled.

Alexander finished the wall.

At seven feet, the wall was still not tall enough. One man would stand on another man's shoulders and hop up onto it, then pull the standing man up. The prison guards electrified the top of the wall and put up another watch tower.

The men sustained some electrical shock damage to their bodies—but continued to climb over to get to the women on the other side.

Tatiana asked why the guards didn't increase the electrical charge at the top of the barrier to instantly kill the man who touched it. Alexander replied they had to preserve their work force. They would have no one left to fill the logging quotas if they made the charge lethal. Also it took too much electricity. The guards had to light their own barracks. "At the commandant's house, Karolich had to eat and sleep in comfort, didn't he, Tatia?"

"He did, Shura. Not much comfort for him now."

"The motherfucking bastard."

Tatiana's hand was on his heart. Her face was pressed into the muscles in his chest, into his Berlin shrapnel scar that was always under her mouth when she lay in his arms.

Alexander was told to build the wall to twelve feet.

One of his helpers said, "They were ready to maim you for a seven-foot wall. For a twelve-foot wall, they'll kill you for sure."

"Let them try," said Alexander, never walking anywhere without the chain wrapped around his right hand. For extra protection he had attached nails to it in the metal shop. He had to use it again—twice.

The wall grew to twelve feet. And still the men climbed over. The electrical wire ran along the top. And still they climbed over. The barbed wire ran along the electrical wire. And still they climbed over.

Venereal diseases, fatal miscarriages, but worse, continuing pregnancies—the most incongruous thing of all—were making it impossible to run the prison. Finally the women were all put into trucks and carted a hundred kilometers east to the tungsten mines. Alexander found out there was a collapse of the mine during one of the explosions and all the women died.

The men stopped climbing over and began to get sick, to attempt suicidal escapes, to hang themselves with sheets, to fall down mine shafts, to cut each other's throats in petty arguments. The production quotas were still going unfilled. The guards ordered Alexander to knock down the wall and start digging more mass graves.

He stopped speaking. Tatiana lay heavily by his side. She felt suddenly like she was two hundred pounds, not one hundred.

"During the years I'd been away from you, I used to dream of touching you," Alexander said to Tatiana. "Your comfort is what I imagined. But during this period, all I saw was women being brutalized, and you, instead of staying sacred, diminished, and my thoughts of you became torture. You know how it goes— I lived oxen, so I dreamed oxen. And then you vanished altogether." He paused, and nodded in the dark. "And that's what I mean by tainted. And suddenly—after you fled me even in memories—I saw you in the woods, a vision of a phantom very young you. It wasn't a dream. I saw you! Real like you are now. You were laughing, skipping, seraphic as always, except you had never sat on our bench in Leningrad, you had never worn your white dress the day Hitler invaded the Soviet Union. I had patrolled somewhere else, or you had gone somewhere else, and I had no one to cross the street for. And so in these woods, you were looking at me as if you had never known me, as if you had never loved me." He broke off. "It was then that I began to attempt my own suicidal escapes, all seventeen of them. It was those eyes of yours that pursued me through Sachsenhausen," said Alexander in a dead voice. "I may have felt nothing, but I could not live, could not last a minute on this earth believing you had felt nothing too. Your meaningless eyes were the death of me."

Tatiana was crying. "Oh, God . . . Shura, husband . . ." she whispered, her arms, her legs going around him. She climbed on top of him in the sleeping bag. She couldn't hold him close enough to herself. "It was just a vile dream. My eyes are never meaningless."

He stared at her, near her face. "Then why do you keep looking at me as if you're missing something, Tania?"

She couldn't return his pained gaze, even in the black of night. Taking a breath, she said, "I'm not missing anything. I'm just looking for you. Looking for you in the taiga woods. Looking for the Alexander I left behind a million miles away on the pine needle banks of Lazarevo, or in the critical care tent in Morozovo. That's what I was thinking of at Mercy Hospital."

That wasn't the only thing she had been thinking at Mercy

Hospital. Having called Esther that morning, she had found out just how determined, how grave, and how unrelenting Sam Gulotta remained. Her good sense was devoured by fear and she went missing and forgot to keep time. Tonight she swallowed and went on. "What could I do then that I can't seem to do now? That's what I think about. What can I do to bring you back? What can I do to make you happy? What can I do to help you? Where are you?"

Alexander fell quiet. He pulled her off him. She lay behind him, kissing him softly on a ridged scar over his spine, hearing his heart thunder out through his shoulder blades.

After a while he spoke. "You want to know where I was in Maine?"

"No."

"I was trying to find that man."

"Did you," asked Tatiana in a faltering voice, putting her forehead on his back, "find him?"

"Obviously not," Alexander replied. "I felt I had fucked it up, that it was all a bust. I didn't know who I was. I too didn't recognize the man who came back with you from Berlin. You had wanted the boy you met in 1941, the boy you loved, the boy you married. I couldn't find him—but I couldn't find *you* either behind your searching eyes. I saw other things there—worry for me, concern. The eyes of compassion you had for Colonel Moore, it's true, you had in spades for me. But as you know, I didn't want your pity eyes, your pity hands. The wall between us seemed a hundred feet, not twelve. I couldn't take it. You had done so nicely for yourself while I had been gone and now I was damned and ruining it. The colonel and me, we both needed to be in that military hospital. He went, but there was no place for me. No place for me there, and not with you either. There was no place for me anywhere in this world," said Alexander.

He had taken his weapons with him, and left her his money. Tatiana was breathing hard into her hands, trying to keep from completely breaking down. "I can't believe you're telling me this," she said. "I can't believe you're saying these things out loud to me. I don't deserve them."

"I *know*," Alexander said. "That's why I didn't tell you. Our son needed you. He has his whole life to set right. I thought you could still help him, save *him*."

"Oh my God—but what about you?" Tatiana asked. "Shura, you

desperately needed my help." And still do, she wanted to add. She tried to wipe her face, but it was useless.

He turned to her, lay on his side in front of her. "I know." He touched her eyes, her lips, her heart. "That's why I came back," whispered Alexander, his palm fanning her face. "Because I wanted to be saved, Tatiasha."

Tatiana slept terribly, like *she* was being repeatedly hit in the throat with the butt of his rifle. They were hoping time would help them. A month here, a month there, a month without mosquitoes and snow, time was like fresh dirt on the shallow graves. Pretty soon the sound of the cannons might mute, the rocket launchers might stop whistling off the ground. Not yet though. *On the run for the rest of our short, doomed lives. In other words, prison.*

I wanted to be saved, Tatiasha.

"*Nearer to thee,*" he whispered to her last night before he fell asleep. "*Even though it be a cross/that raiseth me.*"

Up, up, up, on the run, unsaved, through Desolation Canyon, through the salt flats of Utah, through the Sunrise Peak Mountains, to where there was wine in the valley.

CHAPTER FOUR

Vianza, 1947

Bisol Brut Bobbing Bubbly

And was there ever wine in the valley.

Chardonnay, Cabernet, Merlot, Pinot Noir, Sauvignon Franc and Sauvignon Blanc. But sparkling wine was the most delicious of all, creamy, nutty, fruity, exploding with flavors of green apple and citrus, its bubble trapped in the bottle for maximum fizz and maximum joy.

It was the Italians that drew them in, the Sebastianis, running their tiny California winery on a foggy, winding, tree-canopied, hilly road nestled between other vineyards stretching from the Mayacamas Mountains to the east and the Sonomas to the west. The Sebastianis ran their winery as if they lived in Tuscany. Their yellow stucco Mediterranean house looked like something out of Alexander's mother's old country. Alexander could barely whoa the horse and drop the reins, before he was hired on the spot by Nick Sebastiani, who whisked Alexander away at four in the afternoon. It was late August and harvesting season, and the grapes had to come off the vine instantly or something terrible would happen to them, some overripening acidity. They had to be "cooled," "threshed," "separated from their skins," "crushed in steel drums." That's what Nick told Alexander as Tatiana remained with Anthony in the unpaved parking lot, trying to figure out what to do next.

Holding his hand, she ambled over to the winery and said hello to Jean Sebastiani, and fifteen minutes later found herself not only drinking and admiring the unfamiliar but pleasant tastes, but accepting a *job* as a wine server for the outdoor patio area!

Tatiana muttered something about Anthony, and Jean said, "Oh, no, the boy can be your helper. We'll get even more customers, you'll see."

People indeed loved the little helper—and were not entirely averse to the mother helper either. Tatiana continued to constrain herself in vests one size too small while her white limbs peaked out from her white sleeveless dresses as she hurried from table to table. While Alexander worked the fields picking acres of grapes, making seven bucks a day for his twelve hours of trouble, Tatiana was tipped like she was working for the emperors.

Short of quitting, there was nothing Alexander could do—there were too many men willing to work for even less. So Alexander continued to work like he worked and when Nick Sebastiani saw it, he gave him a raise to ten a day and put him in charge of twenty other migrant hand harvesters.

Temporarily they stayed in their camper near the barracks to use the shower facilities. Sebastiani wanted Alexander to live in the barracks with the rest of the workers. Alexander refused. "I'm not staying in the barracks with my family, Tania. What is this, Sachsenhausen? Are you going to be my little labor camp wife?"

"If you wish."

They went off site to live, renting a room on a second floor of a bed and breakfast two miles down the road. The room was expensive—five dollars a day—but very large. It had a bed the size of which they'd never seen before. Alexander called it a brothel bed, for who else would need a bed this size? He would have been happy with a Deer Isle twin bed, it had been so long since they'd slept in one. Anthony had his own rollaway in the far corner. There was a bath with a shower down the hall, and the dining room downstairs served them breakfast and dinner so Tatiana didn't have to cook. Alexander and Tatiana both didn't love that part.

Alexander said as soon as it got cold, they would leave. September came and it was still warm; he liked that. Better still, not only was Tatiana making them a little money, she was drinking some sparkling wine, some Bisol Brut, for which she developed a bit of a taste. After work, she would sit with Anthony, have bread and cheese, and a glass of sparkler. She closed the winery, counted the money, played with the boy, waited for Alexander to finish work, and sipped her drink. By the time they drove to the B&B, had dinner, chocolate cake, more wine, a bath, put

Anthony to bed, and she fell down onto the goose down covers, arms flung above her head, Tatiana was so bubbled up, so pliant, so agreeable to all his relentless frenzies, and so ceaselessly and supernally orgasmic that Alexander would not have been a mortal man if he allowed anything to come between his wife and her Bisol Brut. Who would do a crazy thing like quit to go into dry country? This country was flowing with foaming wine, and that is just how they both liked it.

He started whispering to her again, night by night, little by little.

Tania . . . you want to know what drives me insane?

Yes, darling, please tell me. Please whisper to me.

When you sit up straight like this with your hands on your lap, and your breasts are pushed together, and your pink nipples are nice and soft. I lose my breath when your nipples are like that.

The trouble is, as soon as I see you looking at me, the nipples stop being nice and soft.

Yes, they are quite shameful, he whispers, his breath lost, his mouth on them. *But your hard nipples also drive me completely insane, so it's all good, Tatia. It's all very very good.*

Anthony was segregated from them by an accordion room partition. A certain privacy was achieved, and after a few nights of the boy not being woken up, they got bolder; Alexander did unbelievable things to Tatiana that made her sparkler-fueled moaning so extravagant that he had to invent and devise whole new ways of sustaining his usually impeccable command over his own release.

Tell me what you want. I'll do anything you want, Tania. Tell me. What can I do—for you?

Anything, darling . . . anything you want, you do . . .

There was nothing Gulag about their consuming love in that enchanted bed by the window, the bed that was a quilted down island with four posters and a canopy, with pillows so big and covers so thick . . . and afterward he lay drenched and she lay breathless, and she murmured into his chest that she should like a soft big bed like this forever, so comforted was she and so very pleased with him. Once she asked in a breath, *Isn't this better than being on top of the hard stove in Lazarevo?* Alexander knew she wanted him to say yes, and he did, but he didn't mean it, and though she wanted him to say it, he knew she didn't want him to mean it either. Could anything come close to crimson Lazarevo where, having been nearly dead, without champagne or wine or bread or a bed, without work or food or Anthony or any future other than the wall and the blindfold, they somehow managed for one brief moon to live in thrall sublime? They had been so isolated, and in their memories they still remained near the Ural Mountains, in frozen Leningrad, in the woods of Luga when they had been fused and fevered, utterly doomed, utterly alone. And yet!—look at her tremulous light—as if in a dream—in America—in fragrant wine country, flute full of champagne, in a white quilted bed, her breath, her breasts on him, her lips on his face, her arms in rhapsody around him are so comforting, so true—and so real.

You want me to whisper to you, Alexander whispers on another blue night on the quilt, blue night now but heather dawn already much too near. She is on her back, her arms above her head, her gold hair smelling freshly washed of strawberry shampoo. He is propped up over her, loving her taste of chocolate and wine, kissing her open lips, her throat, her clavicles, licking her breasts, her swollen nipples.

Maybe not just whisper? she moans.

He moves lower, happier, presses his face into her stomach, on his knees in front of her; he kisses lingeringly the femoral flesh, listening to her whispering pleas. To draw out his time with her, he caresses her as lightly and arhythmically as he can. When she starts to cry out, he stops, giving her a breath to calm down. She is not becalmed. He pours a little bubbly wine on her—it fizzes, she curves—and licks it off her, softly kisses it off her, softly sucks it off her. She is gasping, she is clenching the quilt. *Please, please,* she whispers.

His palms are over her inner thighs, so exquisitely open, so alive. *Do you know how sweet you are?* He kisses her. *You're so soft, so slippery . . . Tatia, you are so beautiful.* His mouth is on her, adoring her.

She gasps, she clutches, she cries out and out and out.

I love you.

And Tatiana cries.

You know that, don't you? Alexander whispers. *I love you. I'm blind for you, wild for you. I'm sick with you. I told you that our first night together when I asked you to marry me, I'm telling you now. Everything that's happened to us, everything, is because I crossed the street for you. I worship you. You know that through and through. The way I hold you, the way I touch you, my hands on you, God, me inside you, all the things I can't say during daylight, Tatiana, Tania, Tatiasha, babe, do you feel me? Why are you crying?*

Now that *is what I call a whisper.*

He whispers, she cries, she comes to him in unconditional surrender and cries and cries. Deliverance does not come cheap, not to her, not to him, but it does profoundly come at the price of night.

And in the gray-purple morning, Alexander finds Tatiana by the basin in the bedroom, washing her face and arms. He watches her and then comes to stand behind her. She tilts her head up to him. He kisses her. *You're going to be late*, Tatiana says with a small smile. His chest is bursting with the night, aching for her. Saying nothing, he hugs her from behind and then slips her vest down from the shoulders, lathering up and running his wet soapy hands over and around her breasts, cupping them, fondling them. *Shura, please*, she whispers, quivering, her raw pink-red nipples standing straight out, piercing his palms.

Anthony's awake. Alexander pulls the wet vest back over her, and she says, well, now *that's* useless, isn't it. Not completely useless, says Alexander, stepping away, watching her in the mirror as she finishes washing, the breasts full, the vest see-through, the nipples large and taut against it. She dances all day in his heart and in his drunken, unquenchable loins.

Something has awakened in him here in the wine valley of the moon. Something that he thought had died.

Perhaps a young woman who was being made love to so thoroughly in the night, who was lavished with such ardent caresses, could not walk around in daylight without all the pores of her skin glistening, exuding her nocturnal exuberance. Perhaps there was no hiding her small sensual self, because the clientele sure beat against her wine trays. They came from everywhere and sat outdoors at her little patio tables, and she, with Anthony by her side, would shimmy up to them, her perpetually pulpy, slightly bruised mouth smiling the words, "Hi. What can I get you?"

Alexander didn't think it was his son that the city dwellers kept creeping back to in their gray flannel suits on weekdays. Alexander knew this because he himself crept up from the fields one day to have lunch at one of her tables. Actually what he did was sit down at one of her tables, and Anthony came running to him and sat on his lap, and they waited and waited and waited and waited, as their mother and wife flitted about, humming like a

hummingbird, laughing, joking with the customers like a come-
dienne—particularly with two men in pressed suits who took off
their trembling hats to speak to her, gawking open-mouthed into
her bedroom lips as they ordered more wine. Their expressions
made Alexander look down onto his son's head and say carefully,
"Is Mommy *always* this busy?"

"Oh, Dad, today is a slow day. But look how much *I* made!" He
showed his father four nickels.

Alexander ruffled his hair. "That's because you're a good boy,
bud, and they all see it."

Anthony ran off and Alexander continued to watch her. She was
wearing a white cotton sheath tank dress, straight, sleeveless and
simple, empire-waisted and hemmed just below the knee. One of
the men in the flannel suit looked down and said something,
pointing to the pink bubble gum toes she had painted, naked for
Alexander last Sunday afternoon while Anthony lay sleeping.
Tatiana jingled out a little laugh. The flannel man reached up and
brushed some strands of hair out of her face. She backed away, her
smile fading, and turned to see if Alexander noticed. Oh, he noticed,
all right. And so finally she made her way to *his* table. He sat cross-
armed in the round metal chair with spindly legs that scraped across
the stone tiles every time he moved.

"Sorry, I took so long," Tatiana murmured sheepishly to him,
with a smile now even for him, in his dungaree overalls, not in a
suit. "See how busy I am?"

"I see everything," Alexander said, studying her face a few
moments before he took her hand, turning it palm up, and kissed
it, circling her wrist with his fingers. Not letting go, he squeezed
her wrist so hard that Tatiana let out a yelp but did not even try
to pull away.

"Ouch," she said. "What's that for?"

"Only one bear eats from this honey pot, Tatia," he said, still
squeezing her.

Blushing, bending to him, she said in a low mimicking sing-
song voice, "Oh, Captain, here's your apple cobbler, Captain, and
is my dress going to blow above my head because you're going
so fast, Captain, and have you noticed my bobbing boobs,
Captain?"

Alexander laughed. "Bobbing boobs?" he said quietly, delight-
fully, kissing her hand again and releasing her. "Oh, I've noticed
those, babe."

"Shh!" She ran to bring him food and then perched down by his side, while Anthony climbed on his lap.

"You have time to sit with me?" he said, trying to eat with one hand.

"A little. How's your morning been?" She brushed a grape twig out of Alexander's hair. "Anthony, come here, sit on Mommy, let Daddy eat."

Alexander shook his head, eating quickly. "He's fine. But I've been better. We were getting a shipment of grapes from another vineyard, and half a ton of it fell off my truck."

"Oh, no."

"Ant, do you know how much half a ton of grapes is?" Alexander said to his son. "A thousand pounds. I went over a bump in the road." He shrugged. "What can I tell you? If they don't want the grapes to fall, they should rebuild the road."

"Half a ton! What happened to the grapes?" Tatiana asked.

"I don't know. By the time we noticed and came back for them, the road was picked clean, obviously by unemployed migrants looking for food. Though why anyone would be unemployed is beyond me, there's so much work."

"Did Sebastiani yell at you?" asked Anthony, turning around to look at Alexander.

"I don't let anybody yell at me, bud," replied Alexander, "but he wasn't happy with me, no. Said he was going to dock my pay, and I said, you pay me nothing as it is, what's to dock?" Alexander looked at Tatiana. "What?"

"Oh, nothing. Reminds me of that sack of sugar my grandmother found in Luga in the summer of 1938."

"Ah, yes the famous sack of sugar." Dipping a small piece of bread in olive oil, Alexander put it into Tatiana's mouth. "Not very pleasant, what happened to your grandparents, but I'm suddenly more interested in the truck driver who dropped the sack of sugar in the first place."

"He got five years in Astrakhan for being cavalier with government property and helping the bourgeoisie," she said dryly, as he got up to go.

"Aren't you going to kiss me?" she asked, lifting her face to him.

"In front of the flannel lepers so they can see your lips open? Never," he replied, running his hand lightly down her braid. "Stay away from them, will you?"

As he was walking past the two men, he knocked into their table so hard their glasses of wine spilled.

"Hey, man, easy!" one of them said, glancing up at Alexander, who slowed down, stopped, and leveled him with such a stare that the man instantly looked away and called for the check.

October warmly came and warmly went. Though foggy at the day's edges, November remained mild. Alexander didn't work in the fields anymore or drive trucks; now he was down in the cellars. He hated being in the dark basement all day, for when he started work it was barely light and when he finished it was just after dark. He worked at the steel fermenting drums or the oak barrels, riddling the sparkling wine behind closed cellar doors and dreaming of sunshine. The night visions still ground him down. He stopped trying to figure them out; their mysticism was beyond his scope and his mystic guide was busy navigating through her own unstill waters. Anthony still crawled in next to her toward dawn.

The three of them looked forward to Sundays when they had a whole day to themselves. On Sundays they drove around the Bay area. They saw Sacramento and Montecito, and Carmel by the Sea, so blissful and briny—which was a good way to describe Tania also. It was there that she asked him if he wanted to leave Napa and go to Carmel, but Alexander declined. "I like Napa," he said, taking her hand across the table as they sat in a small café, eating New England Clam Chowder out of a bread bowl. Anthony was having French fries, dipping them into Tania's soup.

But Tatiana liked Carmel. "It has no weather. How could you not like a place that has no weather?"

"I like a *little* weather," Alexander said.

"For weather we can go south to Santa Barbara."

"Let's just stay put for a while, okay?"

"Shura . . ." Leaving Anthony to her soup, she got up and moved to sit close to Alexander in the booth, holding his hand, caressing his palm, kissing his fingers. "Husband . . . I was thinking . . . maybe we could stay in Napa for good?"

"Hmm. Doing what? Harvesting grapes for ten bucks a day? Or," Alexander said with a small—very small—smile, "selling wine to men?"

Tatiana's grin was wide. "Neither. We sell our Arizona land, we buy some land here and open our own winery. What do you think? We wouldn't see any profits for two years while the grapes grew, but then . . . we could do what the Sebastianis do, just smaller. You already know so much about the business. And I could count the money." She smiled, her sea eyes foaming. "I'm a very good counter. There are so many little vineyards around here; we could grow to be successful. We'd have a little house, another little baby, live above the winery, and it would be ours, all *ours*! We'd have a great view of real mountains, like you want. We could go a little north to a place called Alexander's Valley"—she kissed his cheek— "see, it's already conveniently named after you. We could start with two acres; it would be plenty to make a living. Hmm? How does that sound?"

"So-so," said Alexander, his arm going around her, bending to her exalted, turned-up face.

Vanishing Dreams of the Valley of the Moon

Alexander left every morning at six thirty. Tatiana didn't have to be in until nine. She and Anthony walked the two miles to the winery. After he left, Tatiana sat by the window, paralyzed with fear and indecision. She desperately needed to call Vikki. But the last time she called, Sam had picked up Vikki's phone.

This morning Tatiana was bent over the sink, retching. She knew she had to call, she *needed* to know if Alexander was safe, if they were safe—to stay, to begin to live their little life.

She called from a public phone near the common dining room downstairs, knowing it was still five thirty in the morning in New York, and Vikki would be asleep.

The voice on the other end of the line was groggy. "Who is this?"

"It's Tania, Vik." She held the phone receiver so tensely in her fingers, she thought it would break. Her mouth was pressed to the mouthpiece, and her eyes were closed. *Please. Please.*

There was scrambling, dropping of the receiver, sharp cursing. Vikki didn't say what happened, but the things she did say when she finally got back to the receiver were quite sharp and cursy themselves.

Tatiana backed away from the mouthpiece, seriously contemplating hanging up before she heard another word. She could tell that everything was not all right.

"Tatiana! What is *wrong* with you?"

"Nothing, we're fine. Anthony says hello." But this was said in a low, defeated voice.

"Oh my God. Why haven't you called Sam, Tania?"

"Oh, that. I forgot."

"YOU WHAT?"

"We've been busy."

"They sent Federal agents to your aunt's house in Massachusetts! They've been talking to her, to me, to Edward, to the whole hospital. They've been looking for you in New Mexico where you called from, and in that stupid place you bought your stupid land; Phoenix, is it?"

Tatiana didn't know what to say. She was losing her breath.

Federal agents on the path called Jomax.

"Why didn't you just call him as you promised? "

"I'm sorry. Why was he there last time I called?"

"Tania, he's practically moved in. Where are you?"

"Vik, what do they want?"

"I don't know! Call Sam, he's dying to tell you. Do you know what Sam said to me when I told him I was going to change my telephone number? He told me I'd be arrested for conspiracy because it could mean I was protecting you!"

"Conspiracy to what?" Tatiana said in a small voice.

"I can't believe Alexander is allowing this."

There was silence from Tatiana.

"Oh, my God," Vikki said slowly. "He doesn't *know*?"

Silence from Tatiana. Her choices were narrowing. What if there was a wiretap on Vikki's phone? They'd know where she was, at which B&B, in which valley. Unable to speak any longer, she just hung up.

She called Jean and said she wasn't feeling well. Jean complained—money talking—and insisted that Tatiana come in regardless of how she was feeling. They had words. Tatiana said, "I quit," and hung up on her, too.

She couldn't believe she just quit. What in the world was she going to tell Alexander?

She and Anthony took a bus to San Francisco, where she thought she would be anonymous, but as soon as she heard the streetcar's stop bell, she knew the sound would be pretty distinct, even to someone living in Washington DC. She went to a wet cold park on the shores of San Francisco Bay, where there were no rails and no clanging, just screaming sea gulls, and from a payphone during the late morning called Sam who was still at home.

"Sam?"

"Who is this?"

"It's me, Sam."

"Oh my God. Tania."

"Sam—"

"OH. MY. GOD."

"Sam—"

"Oh my God."

"Sam . . ."

"Seventeen months, Tania! Do you know what you've done? You're costing me my job! And you're costing that husband of yours his freedom!"

"SAM—"

"I told you both when he first came back—a debriefing. So simple. Tell us about your life, Captain Barrington. In your own words. A two-hour conversation with minor officials, so easy, so nice; we stamp his file closed, we offer him college tuition, cheap loans, job placement."

"Sam."

"And instead? During this unbelievably tense time—have you not been reading the papers?—his file, his *OPEN* file has traveled from my desk, up to the Secretary of State, across to Secretary of Defense, across to the Justice Department. He's got J. Edgar Hoover himself looking for him! This Alexander Barrington, who was a *major* in the Red Army, whose father was a Communist—who let him in? You can't be a commissioned officer in the Red Army without a being Soviet citizen and a member of the Communist Party. How did a person like that get a U.S. passport? *Who* approved that? Meanwhile, Interpol is looking for an Alexander Belov . . . they say he killed sixty-eight of their men while escaping from a military prison. And even HUAC got into this. Now you've got them on your back, too! They want to know, is he theirs or ours? Where is his allegiance— now, then, ever? Is he a loyalty risk? Who *is* this man? And no one can find him even to ask him a simple question—why?"

"Sam!"

"Oh, what have you done, Tatiana? What have you—"

She hung up the phone and sank to the ground. She didn't know what to do. For the rest of the morning, she sat catatonically on the dewy grass in the fog of the San Francisco Bay while Anthony made friends and played on the swings.

What to do?

Alexander was the only one who could lead her out of this morass, but he would not run from anything. He was not on her side.

And yet he was the only one on her side.

Tatiana saw herself opening the windows on Ellis Island, the first morning she arrived on the boat, after the night her son was born. Not since then had she felt so abandoned and alone.

After extracting a solemn oath from Anthony not to tell his father where they had been, she spent two hours after they got back to Napa poring over the map of California, almost as if it were a map of Sweden and Finland that the Soviet soldier Alexander Belov once pored over, dreaming of escape.

She had to steel herself not to shake. That was the hardest thing. She felt so unsound.

The first thing Alexander said when he walked through the door was, "What happened to you? Jean told me you quit."

She managed a nice pasty smile. "Oh, hi. Hungry? You must be. Change, and let's go eat." She grabbed Anthony.

"Tania! Did you quit?"

"I'll tell you at dinner." She was putting on her cardigan.

"What? Did someone offend you? Say something to you?" His fists clenched.

"No, no, shh, nothing like that." She didn't know how she was going to talk to him. When Anthony was with them, it was impossible to have a serious conversation about serious things. Her work was going to have to be quick and subtle. So it was over dinner and wine in the common dining room, at a withdrawn table in the corner, with Anthony coloring in his book that she said, "Shura, I did quit. I want you to quit, too."

He sat and considered her. His brow was furled.

"You're working too hard," she said.

"Since when?"

"Look at you. All day in the dank basement, working in cellars . . . what for?"

"I don't understand the question. I have to work somewhere. We have to eat."

Chewing her lip, Tatiana shook her head. "We still have money— some of it left over from your mother, some of it from nursing, and in Coconut Grove you made us thousands carousing with your boat women."

"Mommy, what's carousing?" said Anthony, looking up from his coloring.

"Yes, Mommy, what's carousing?" said Alexander, smiling.

"My point is," Tatiana went on, poker-faced, "that we don't need you to break your back as if you're in a Soviet labor camp."

"Yes, and what about your dream of a winery in the valley? You don't think that's back-breaking work?"

"Yes . . ." she trailed off. What to say? It was just last week in Carmel that they'd had that wistful conversation. "Perhaps it's too soon for that dream." She looked deeply down into her plate.

"I thought you wanted to settle here?" Alexander said in confusion.

"As it turns out, less than I thought." She coughed, stretching out her hand. He took it. "You're away from us for twelve hours a day and when you come back you're exhausted. I want you to play with Anthony."

"I do play with him."

She lowered her voice. "I want you to play with me, too."

"Babe, if I play with you any more, my sword will fall off."

"What sword, Dad?"

"Anthony, shh. Alexander, shh. Look, I don't want you to fall asleep at nine in the evening. I want you to smoke and drink. I want you to read all the books and magazines you haven't read, and listen to the radio, and play baseball and basketball and football. I want you to teach Anthony how to fish as you tell him your war stories."

"Won't be telling those any time soon."

"I'll cook for you. I'll play dominoes with you."

"Definitely no dominoes."

"I'll let you figure out how I always win." A Sarah Bernhardt-worthy performance.

Shaking his head, he said slowly, "Maybe poker."

"Absolutely. Cheating poker then."

Rueful Russian Lazarevo smiles passed their faces.

"I'll take care of you," she whispered, the hand he wasn't holding shaking under the table.

"For God's sake, Tania . . . I'm a man. I can't not work."

"You've never stopped your whole life. Come on. Stop running with me." The irony in that made her tremble and she hoped he wouldn't notice. "Let me take care of you," Tatiana said hoarsely, "like you know I ache to. Let me do for you. Like I'm your nurse at the Morozovo critical care ward. Please." Tears came to her eyes. She said quickly, "When there's no more money, you can work again. But for now . . . let's leave here. I know just the place." Her smile was so pathetic. *"Out of my stony griefs, Bethel I'll raise,"* she whispered.

Alexander was silently contemplating her, puzzled again, troubled again.

"I honestly don't understand," he said. "I thought you liked it here."

"I like you more."

CHAPTER FIVE

Bethel Island, 1948

Tilting at Windmills

They said farewell to the bittersweet sickly heady scent of ripened effervescent grapes, got into their Nomad and left. Tatiana navigated them south and east of Vianza to lose themselves in the flatness of a thousand square miles of the California Delta, amid the islands that were so close to sea level, some would get flooded every time it rained. A hundred miles from the valley of the wine, at the mouth of the Sacramento and San Joaquin Rivers, they found tiny Bethel Island and that's where they stopped.

Bethel Island. Surrounded by river channels, levees, and antediluvian marsh. Nothing moved in any direction except the herons. The canals were made of glass. The cold November air was still as if it were about to storm.

It didn't even seem like part of the same country, yet unmistakably was America. On Dutch Slough they rented a wood shack with an long L-shaped dock that jutted out onto the canal. The house had what they needed. A room of their own, and a bathroom. Across the canal was nothing but plains of fields and the horizon.

"Looks like Holland," Alexander said as they unpacked.

"Would you like to go to Holland someday?" she asked, busy nesting.

"I'm never under *any* circumstances leaving America. How did you find this place?"

"Looked at a map."

"So now you're a cartographer, too?" Alexander grinned.

"Would you like a glass of wine, my little geologist, capitalist, cartographer?" He had brought a case of bubbly with them.

The next day at precisely eight in the morning, the mailman on a passing boat barge hooted his horn into their bedroom window. Introducing himself as Mr. Shpeckel, he asked if they would be getting any mail. They said no. But perhaps Aunt Esther wanted to send Anthony a Christmas present? Tatiana said no. They would call Esther at Christmas; that would have to be good enough.

Even though there was going to be no mail, Shpeckel still came by every morning at eight, tooting his horn into their windows just to let them know they had no mail—and to say hello to Alexander, who in his usual military manner was already up, washed and brushed and dressed, and out on the deck with a fishing line. The canals harbored prehistoric sturgeon and Alexander was trying to catch one.

Shpeckel was a 66-year-old man who had lived in Bethel for twenty years. He knew everyone. He knew their business, he knew what they were doing on his island. Some were lifers like him, some vacationers, and some were runners.

"How do you know which are which?" asked Alexander one afternoon when Shpeckel was done with his water route. Alexander had invited him in for a drink.

"Oh, you can always tell," Shpeckel replied.

"So which ones are we?" Alexander asked, pouring him a glass of vodka, which Shpeckel had admitted to never having before.

They clinked and drank. Alexander knocked his back. Shpeckel carefully sipped his like a mug of tea.

"You are runners," said Shpeckel, finally downing his and gasping. "Egads, man, I wouldn't drink this stuff anymore. It's going to set you on fire. Come to the Boathouse with us on Friday night. We drink good old beer there."

Alexander politely declined. "But you're wrong about us. Why do you say we're runners? We're not runners."

Shpeckel shrugged. "Well, I've been wrong before. How long are you staying?"

"I have no idea. Not long, I think."

"Where's your wife?"

"Hunting and gathering," he said. Tatiana had gone alone to the store to buy food. She always went alone, dismissing Alexander's offers of help. "I didn't catch any sturgeon today."

There were other fish in the waters. Striped bass, black bass, catfish—and perch. The perch was a Russian fish—here all the way from the Kama River, Alexander thought with amusement as it trembled on his line. Tatiana didn't mention the existence of Russian perch in American waters as she cleaned it and cooked it and served it. And Alexander didn't mention that she didn't mention it.

He did mention, however, what Shpeckel had said to him. "Imagine that, calling us runners. We're the most rootlessly rooted people I know. We tool around, find a spot, then don't move from it."

"He *is* being silly," she agreed.

"Did you get me a newspaper?"

Tatiana said she had forgotten. "But the Czech Foreign Minister Jan Masaryk was just killed in a 'fall' from his office window following the Communist coup in Prague." She sighed.

"Now my gloomy wife is also a newscaster and a Czechophile. What's your interest in Masaryk?"

Downtrodden, Tatiana said, "A long time ago, in 1938, Jan Masaryk was the only one who stood up for his country when Czechoslovakia was about to be handed over to Hitler on a plate. He was hated by the Soviets, while Herr Hitler was admired by everyone. Then Hitler took his country, and now the Soviets took his life." She looked away. "And the world has stood on its head."

"I wouldn't know," Alexander said. "We don't even have a radio in the house. Did you get a radio as I asked? I can't keep going outside into the Nomad."

She forgot that, too.

"Did you get me *Time* magazine?"

"Tomorrow, darling. Today I got you some nice American books from the 19th century. *The Wings of the Dove* from Henry James, ghost stories from Poe and the complete works of Mark Twain. If you like something a little more current, here is the excellent *The Everlasting Man* from 1923."

The isolation was complete on their last frontier. The house they were living in had a name—on a plaque. It was called *Free*. The dock they fished on was called *My Prerogative*. The skies remained gunmetal gray with no sunshine day after day, and the blue herons hid behind the reeds in the fields across the canal, and the swans flew away in lonely formations. The stillness as far as the eye could see was vertical and horizontal.

Well, perhaps not horizontal, for they had a room of their own and a case of sparkling wine.

They drifted through the winter like river rats in the lost world downstream from Suisun Bay.

One March morning in 1948, Shpeckel, with a salute, said after sounding his bugle, "I guess I was wrong about you and your wife, Captain. I'm surprised. Few women can live this life, day in and day out."

"Well, you have to know who you are," Alexander called back, a cigarette in his mouth and his fishing rod in the water. "And you don't know my wife."

And Tatiana, who heard the exchange from the window, thought that perhaps Alexander didn't know his wife either.

The boy was remarkable. The boy was so dark haired, so dark eyed, growing so lean. He went on boats; now *he* was fearless. On Bethel Island, they taught him how to read, in English *and* Russian, how to play chess, cards, how to make bread. They bought bats and gloves and balls, and spent the cold days outside. The three of them went to the nearby field and in their winter jackets—because the temperature was in the forties—kicked a soccerball, threw a football, hit a baseball.

Anthony learned how to sing—in English *and* Russian. They bought him a guitar, and music books, and in the long winter afternoons, they taught him notes and chords and songs, and how to read the bass clef and the treble clef, the tones and the semitones. Soon he was teaching them.

And one afternoon, Tatiana, to her horror, watched Anthony change the magazine cartridge in his father's Colt M1911 in six seconds.

"Alexander! Are you out of your mind?"

"Tania, soon he will be five."

"Five, not twenty-five!"

"Did you see him?" Alexander was beaming. "Do you see what he is?"

"Do I ever. But you don't want to be teaching him that."

"I teach him what I know."

"You're not going to teach him *everything* you know, are you?"

"Oh, sauce in the winter! Come here."

They hibernated, ate berries, slept, waiting for the ice to melt. Underneath Tatiana was mute. Even to herself she seemed disabled in her dread. For her son, for her husband, she put on her bravest face, but she feared it wasn't brave enough.

Sitting next to each other, Alexander and Anthony had finished fishing; it was the end of a quiet day, before dinner, and their rods were down. Anthony climbed into Alexander's lap and was touching the hair on his face.

"What, son?" He was smoking.

"Nothing," Anthony said quietly. "Did you shave today?"

"Not today, not yesterday." He couldn't remember the last time he shaved.

Anthony rubbed Alexander's face, then kissed his cheek. "When I grow up, am I going to have black stubble like you?"

"Unfortunately yes."

"It's so bristly. Why does Mommy always say how much she likes it?"

"Mommy sometimes likes strange things." Alexander smiled.

"Am I going to be tall like you?"

"Sure, why not?"

"Big like you?"

"Well, you *are* my son."

"Am I going to . . . *be* like you?" Anthony whispered.

Alexander took a careful look at the boy's upturned blinkless gaze. Leaning down he kissed him. "Maybe, bud. You and only you will decide what kind of man you want to be."

"Ticklish, like you?" Anthony pulled up his father's flannel shirt-sleeve and tickled his forearm and the inside of his elbow. He tickled him under the arms.

Alexander put the cigarette out. "Watch out," he said, holding the boy to him, "because in a minute there'll be no mercy for you."

Anthony squealed, his arms around Alexander, whose arms were around Anthony. The chair was nearly falling over. Suddenly Anthony pressed his head to Alexander's ear. "Daddy, don't turn around, because this will frighten you, but Mommy is standing behind us."

"Is Mommy looking particularly frightening this evening?"

"Yes. She's crying. Don't turn around, I said."

"Hmm," Alexander said, "What do you think it is?"

"I don't know. Maybe she's jealous we're playing?"

"No," said Alexander. "She is not a jealous mom."

He whispered to Anthony, who nodded and slowly climbed

down from his father. They both turned around to face her. She stood there blankly, her face still wet.

"One two three—go!" said Alexander. They ran, and she ran from them; they chased her into the house, and brought her down onto the carpet, and she was laughing and she was crying.

Alexander was sitting outside down the long dock, in his quilted patchwork winter jacket, smoking, fishing. He hadn't shaved in weeks, and his hair had grown shaggy. Tatiana knew if she drew attention to it, ran her hands through it, looked at it too long, he might cut it. So she watched him from behind as he sat on his little chair, with a rod in the water and a cigarette in his mouth, humming. He was always humming when he was trying to catch that prehistoric sturgeon.

Tatiana couldn't help herself. Wiping her face, she walked down the dock to his chair, pressed her face to his head, kissed his temple, his bearded cheek. "What's this for?" he asked.

"Nothing," she whispered. "I like your pirate beard."

"Well, your Captain Morgan will be done soon. I'm trying to catch us a fish."

"Don't make me cry, Shura."

"All right, Tania. You too. You with your kissing. What is it with you and the boy lately?"

She held his head to her, in the space at her neck. "Come inside, darling," she whispered. "Let's go in. Your bath is hot and ready." Her lips were on his hair.

"It's really grown out, hasn't it?" he said absent-mindedly. But when he came back inside he *didn't* cut it.

Later that night, in complete darkness, after a hot conjugal bath, after love, Alexander asked her, breathed out to her, "Babe, *what* are you so afraid of?"

Tatiana couldn't tell him. "We're hanging in there," he said. "Ant's doing great."

"You shouldn't have told me your dream," Tatiana said dully. "That's what I think about now—I'm awake and in Germany watching you being dragged away by Karolich." She was glad it was dark and he couldn't see her face. "What if this little life, us, is all just an illusion. And will soon be gone."

"Yes," was all he said.

Restlessly they slept, and then settled down again, to blessed silence.

Lost in Suisun Bay

"How long do you plan to keep me here?" It was spring, they had been in Bethel six months. She couldn't stop herself from twitching. "Day in, day out, weeks, months, years? Tell me. Is this where we're staying? Is this what I'm doing? Should I get Shpeckel's job when he dies? Should I put in for it now, in case there's a waiting list?"

"Shura."

Alexander was contemplative. "Are you hiding me from myself? Are we *here* because you think I can't function out *there*?"

"Of course not."

"So why are you hiding me?"

"I'm not, darling." Tatiana rubbed his back, feathered his scars. "You're worrying yourself for nothing. Go to sleep."

But Alexander wasn't sleepy. "What? You can't imagine me in an office?" he asked. "In a suit all day, sitting at a desk, selling stocks, bonds, insurance, going to visit you in a winery in my drab flannel suit, coming from my city office?"

She was all coiled up inside. "I can imagine you visiting me."

"My father wanted me to be an architect," Alexander said. "A fine thing—an architect in the Soviet Union. He wanted me to build with the Communists, bridges, roads, workers' houses."

"Yes."

"And I spent my life blowing up fucking houses. Perhaps I can be in demolition work."

"No, not you." Please could it be the end of this conversation. "Don't worry. You'll figure it out."

But Alexander continued. "Is that what I'm doing here? Figuring it out? Who I am? I spent my whole life asking myself this question. There in the Soviet Union, here in Suisun Bay. No easy answers to that one, me with SS Eagles, and hammer and sickles on my arms."

You are an American, Alexander Barrington, Tatiana wanted to say to him. An American, who fought in the Red Army and married a Russian girl from Leningrad who can't live without her soldier. That's who you are.

"My mother and father knew who they were."

It was the absolute *last* thing Tatiana wanted to talk about. Her body was a spring; in a minute she was going to catapult away from him.

"They have nothing to do with you," she said, and *couldn't* say anymore.

"The Communist and the radical feminist, the Soviet émigrés, oh, they knew who they were." Alexander sat up and lit a cigarette. "You can only hope in today's climate, no one will find out about my mother and father, because who then is going to give me permanent work? I might as well be a murderer out on work release." He blew smoke rings above the bed.

Tatiana couldn't endure it, she coiled away. "Jimmy hired you, Mel hired you, Sebastiani hired you . . ."

"Yes, until just one man says: what are the numbers on your arm, Alexander? and we're off. I don't know what happened back in Vianza, but something did because it was a slice of heaven, but we didn't stay, did we? What are we going to do? Every time someone asks us a question, we run? Where in the army did you serve, Alexander? and we go right in the bunker, Tania? Is that how we're going to live?"

Tatiana didn't know how they were going to live. She didn't know if they would ever get to have a normal life, like other people, like other married couples, simple, calm, small, nice. What was a normal life for the two of them? She didn't know how long she could keep him remote in a bunker, in splendid isolation, secluded from all men.

Stepping Out For Love

Alexander wanted to see Idaho, Hell's Canyon. He wanted to see Mount Rushmore, Yosemite, Mount Washington, Yellowstone National Park, the wheat fields of Iowa.

No, she kept saying, let's stay here just a little longer. Weeks passed. I'll come to the store with you. Help you with shopping.

No, stay here, catch us a fish, Shura.

I'm going to go to the Boathouse, have a drink with the postman.

Let's go to Sacramento on Sunday. Find a Catholic church, have brunch afterward at the Hyatt Regency, walk on Main Street, show Anthony the Capitol building, have ice cream.

I don't want to. I have things to do. I have to wash-clean-cook-bake-peel-scale. I want you to build me a chest for my knick-knacks, a bench to sit on, fix the posts in the fence, planks on the dock. Let's go for a boat ride on the canals instead.

Her reluctance to leave reminded him of wintry Deer Isle—it's *snowing* and she is still not saying, let's go. This is how it still was. Metaphorically snowing, and she was staying put.

He didn't mind it in the beginning, this slowness. It left him alone with himself while he fished and listened to the call of the herons, and taught Anthony to row a boat and to play baseball and soccer, while Anthony read to him from his children's books as Alexander held the fishing line. The soul was repairing itself little by little. And it was on Bethel Island, with his mother and father twenty-four hours by his side, watching over him, talking to him, playing with him, that Anthony stopped waking up with nightmares in the middle of the night and settled down to silence inside himself.

And it was on Bethel Island that Alexander stopped needing ice cold baths at three in the morning—the hot sudsy dimly lit baths, with her soapy hands and soapy body in the late evening sufficing.

But eventually, one Sunday morning in July 1948, Alexander said, let's go to Sacramento, and he wasn't asking.

They went to Sacramento. They went to a Catholic mass and then had brunch at the Hyatt Regency.

In the late afternoon they were strolling down Main Street, window shopping, when a police car pulled up to the curb and out jumped two officers and ran toward—

For a second it was unclear what they were running toward, and in that second, Tatiana stepped out in front of Alexander, covering half of him with her small body. Paying no attention to the Barringtons, the police officers ran into the grocery store.

Tatiana stepped away. Alexander, after a double take, his eyes widening, continued to stare at her.

When they were having an ice cream soda at a drug store, he was sitting across from her, studying her, waiting for her to volunteer.

"Tania . . ." he drew out.

She was chatting to Ant, not meeting Alexander's eye, volunteering nothing.

"Yes?"

"What *was* that back there?"

"What?"

"Back there, with the police."

"I don't know what you're referring to. I stepped out of their way." Still not looking at him.

"You didn't step out of their way. You stepped out in front of *me*."

"I had nowhere else to go."

"No. You stepped in front of me, as if . . ." Alexander didn't even know how to say it. His eyes narrowed, his heart narrowed, he saw something, understood a little bit, not much, but something. "Did you think they were coming for . . . *me*?"

"That's silly." Studying her soda. "Anthony, you want whipped cream?"

"Tania, why did you think they were coming for me?"

"I didn't think so at all." She tried to smile.

He took her face into his hands. She averted her gaze.

"You won't *look* at me? Tania! What's happening?"

"Nothing. Honest."

He let go of her. His heart was doing odd things in his chest.

That evening Alexander found her in the back of the house—when she thought he was having a bath—cocking and recocking his P-38. She was grimly aiming it from the shoulder, her legs apart, holding it with both hands.

Alexander backed away, stumbled to the dock, sat in his chair, smoked. When he came back inside, he stood in front of her. She had put away his weapon. "Tania," he said. "What the *fuck* is going on?"

His voice was too loud in the house, with Anthony just steps away in his bedroom.

"Nothing, nothing at all," she said quietly. "Please, let's just—"

"Are you going to tell me?"

"There is nothing to tell, honey."

He grabbed his jacket and said he was going out. "By the way, you forgot to lock the magazine catch on the P-38," he said coldly. "It's at the bottom of the grip." He left without giving Tatiana a chance to reply.

Alexander came home hours later. There was no food on the stove, and she was sitting stiff, like a board bent in the middle, at the little kitchen table.

She jumped up when he walked in the door. "My God! Where have you been? It's been four hours!"

"Wherever I've been, I'd be coming home hungry," was all he said.

She made him a cold chicken sandwich, heated up some soup while he stood silently near the stove. He took his plate and his cigarette outside. He thought for sure she would follow him out but she didn't. After quickly eating he came back in the house, where she was still sitting behind the kitchen table.

"You don't want to have this conversation in the house with Anthony," Alexander said. "Come outside."

"I'm not having this conversation."

In two strides he was near her, pulling her up from the table.

"Okay, okay," she whispered, before he even opened his mouth. "Okay."

Outside on the deck Alexander stood before her in the growing darkness, silent but for the hushed rippling off the water, the distant rustle of trees from a small cool wind.

"Oh, Tatiana," said Alexander. "What have you *done*?"

She said nothing.

"I called Aunt Esther," he said. "She wasn't an easy egg to crack. Then I called Vikki. I know everything."

"You know everything," she said without inflection, stepping away from him and shaking her head. "No. You know *nothing*."

"I've been wondering why in two years you haven't called your friend. Why you're poring over maps. Why you're shielding me from officers of law. Why you're practicing with my weapon." Alexander spoke low and pained. "Now I know."

Abruptly she turned away, and he grabbed her and spun her back to him. "Two years ago —two years!—we could've stopped in DC on the way to Florida. What are you proposing we do now?"

"Nothing," Tatiana said, pulling away from his hands. "We do *nothing* now. *That's* what we do."

"You do see how from their point of view it looks as if we've been on the run?"

"I don't care how it looks."

"We're not fugitives. We have nothing to hide."

"No?"

"No! One conversation with the generals at Defense and the diplomats at State would've put this whole thing behind us."

"Oh, Alexander," said Tatiana with a shake of her head, "you once saw through so much. Since when did you become so naïve?"

"I'm not naïve! I know what's going on, but since when did you become so cynical?"

"They already talked to you in Berlin. Why do you think they want to talk to you again?"

"It's procedure!" he yelled.

"It's not procedure!" she yelled back. Their voices carried down the black canals, echoing down the water tunnels. She lowered her voice. "Don't you understand *anything*? Interpol is looking for you, too."

"You know this how?"

"Because Sam told me, that's how."

Alexander fell back in his chair. "*You* talked to Sam?" he said aghast. "You knew this, and you didn't tell me?"

"I didn't tell you a lot of things."

"Obviously. When did you talk to him?"

She wouldn't say.

"When?" He raised his voice. "Tania! When? Hard way or easy way, you're going to tell me. You might as well tell it to me easy."

"Eight months ago," she whispered.

"Eight *months* ago!" he yelled.

"Oh, why did you have to call Esther? Why?" Tatiana threw her arms down in defeat.

"Is this why we left Napa? Oh my God. " He glared at her with sharp reproach. "All this time, moving from place to place, wringing your hands, falling silent on me, asking me about desertion to the Urals. What games you played, knowing this." Alexander was so disappointed, he was forced to look away from her. How could the Tatiana he thought he knew keep secrets from him *so* well? And what was so wrong with him that he never prodded, never pursued, never pushed, even though he sensed and suspected that something was wrong? Alexander couldn't look at her.

Tatiana continued to stand in front of him and not speak.

"We're leaving tomorrow morning," he said finally. "We're leaving and going to Washington."

"No!"

"*No?*"

"That's right, no. Absolutely under no circumstances. We stay put. We go nowhere. Unless it's to the woods in Oregon."

"I'm not going to the woods in Oregon," said Alexander. "I'm not hiding out in the Urals. Or Bethel Island."

Tatiana bent to him, raising her voice, carrying it far. "We're not going, and that's *it*," she said. "We're not going anywhere."

He frowned at her angry face. "Well, *I'm* going."

Her mouth trembled as she straightened up. "Oh, that's just perfect, *you're* going, *you*, like you're all by yourself, only you. Returning to the front, are you? Well, then, you're going to have to go without me, Alexander. This time if you go, you go alone. Anthony and I aren't coming with you."

He got up so furiously he knocked the chair down behind him and the plates and the glasses and his cigarettes. Tatiana backed away, her hands up; he took one lunging step toward her. "Oh, that's just fucking priceless!"

"Shura, stop!"

He loomed too close to her on the dock. "You're threatening me with *leaving?*"

"I'm not threatening you with leaving!" she yelled. "You're the one who's telling me you're going by yourself. I'm telling you we're not going!"

"We are!"

"No!"

Anthony came out, having been awakened by their raised voices, and stood warily on the edge of the dock. Raggedly panting, they stared at each other. Then Tatiana took the boy inside and didn't come back out.

After a long while Alexander returned to the house to find her under the covers. He sat on the bed, and she turned away in a coil.

"What, that's it?" he said. "You walked away, in the middle, got into bed, and that's *it?*"

"What more is there?" she said tonelessly.

"My own government is looking for me," he said. "I won't have it."

Tatiana shuddered.

"Don't you understand—they're going to come for me, Tania," said Alexander. "One day, they'll find me, working on a farm some- where, picking grapes, making wine, driving a boat, catching lobster, and the statute of limitations won't run out on me."

"Yes, it will," she said, "After ten years it will."

"Are you joking?" he whispered into her back. "Ten *years*? What are you talking about? What am I, in espionage? I've done nothing wrong!"

"Well, if you go back, they're going to cuff you and put you away for obstructing justice, for running from the law, or even for treason. You'll be in prison though you did nothing wrong. Or worse—they'll . . ." She was speaking into the pillow, Alexander could barely hear her.

"So what do you propose?" he said. "Living your life hoping

you're going to stay one step ahead of the United States Government?"

"I can't have this argument with you, Shura," said Tatiana. "I just can't."

Alexander turned her to face him, she turned back. He moved her to him, she moved away, pulling the blankets over her head. He removed all the pillows, all the blankets and threw them on the floor, leaving her naked on the empty sheet. She covered her body from him. He pulled her hands away; she struggled against him. He bent to her bare stomach, to the soft gold space below her navel, pressed his mouth to it, whispering to her, *touch me, touch my head.* She was shaking and didn't. He lay on top of her naked body in all his clothes, flat on her, but since there was no peace inside her, there was no peace for him. Piercing her sadness with his sadness, barely undressing, he made deaf mute love to her and then they lay deaf mute, unable to utter the things that were piercing them—he thought he had made himself so clear, and she thought she hadn't made herself clear enough.

Her back was to him. His back was to her. "I won't live like this," said Alexander. "This was my life in the Soviet Union, trapped, running, lying, afraid. This can't be my life in America. This can't be what you want for us."

"I just want you," she said. "I'll take you in the Ural Mountains, I don't care how many men you kill with your desertion. I know, it's unforgivable, but I don't care. I will take you running and trapped and lying. I will take you any way. I don't care how difficult it will be. Everything has been difficult."

"Tania, please. You don't mean it."

"Oh, yes, I do," she said. "How little you know me. Better take that magazine quiz again, Shura."

"That's right," he said, "I obviously don't know you at all. How could you have kept this from me?"

Tatiana didn't reply; a gasp was all that came from her.

Alexander unrolled her out of her fetal ball, holding her wrists away from her face. "All this time you deceived me, and now you say you won't come with me?"

"Please," she whispered. "Please, you are so blind! I'm begging you, begging you, please see reason. Listen to me. We can't go to them."

"I lived in a prison already," said Alexander, squeezing her wrists, bearing down on her. "Don't you understand? I want a different life with you."

"See, that's the difference between us. I just want a life with you," said Tatiana, not struggling against him at all, lying fragile and open under his hands. "I told you this back in Russia. I didn't care if we lived in my cold Fifth Soviet room with Stan and Inga at our door. All I wanted was to live there with you. I don't care if we live here on Bethel Island, or in one small room on Deer Isle. Soviet Union, Germany, here—it doesn't matter. I just want it with you."

"On the run, hiding out, forever scared?" he said. "That's how you want it?"

"Any which way," she said, crying. "Just with you."

"Oh, Tania," he said, letting go of her.

She crawled to him, grabbed him by the shoulders and shook him. "Not now, not in Russia, not *ever*," she said with sobbing anger, "did you *ever* protect yourself for my sake, for Anthony's sake!"

"Shh," he said, opening his arms. "Come here. Shh."

But she wouldn't come, her hands clenched in supplication. "Please, let's not go," she said. "For Anthony. He needs a father."

"Tania . . ."

"For me," she whispered.

Frozen in time they remained on the bed in a November Leningrad embrace.

"I swore to myself in Berlin," she said into his chest, "that they would never have you again."

"I know," Alexander said. "So what are you going to do? Inject me full of morphine like you planned to, kill me like you wouldn't kill Colonel Moore?" He extended his upturned forearm to her, tapping on his tattooed blue numbers. "Go ahead. Right here, Tatiana."

"Oh, stop it, just *stop* it!" she whispered madly, slapping his arm away.

They didn't speak the rest of the night.

In the morning, without saying a word to each other and barely one to Anthony they packed their things and left Bethel Island. Mr. Shpeckel waved good-bye to them from his boat, a regretful look about him in the pale sunrise. "What did I tell you, Captain?" he called after Alexander. "I always knew you were runners."

After a traveling day of stunning silence, somewhere in the drifting sands of Nevada, Alexander whispered, cradling her in the sleeping bag, "They won't have me again. I promise you."

"Yes," she said. "Not them, not me."

"Come on, I'll take care of it. Trust me."

"Trust you?" Tatiana said, "I trusted you so much I believed your lying face and left the Soviet Union, pregnant, thinking you were dead."

"You weren't alone. You were supposed to be with the doctor," he whispered. "Matthew Sayers was getting you out."

"Yes. You didn't count on him getting suddenly dead." She took a breath. "Don't speak to me. You want me to do what you want, I'll do what you want, but don't speak to me, don't try to make it better."

"*I* can't make it better," he said. "I want *you* to make it better."

He knew that beyond Sam Gulotta and the irate Americans, she was afraid of the Soviets most of all. He was not blameless, he was not innocent. She had reason to be afraid.

He couldn't see her face. "Tania," said Alexander, quietly, non-challengingly, caressing her, "you want to fix us? Help me set this right. I know you don't want to live with this debilitating fear. You've been unable to think straight. Help us. Please. Make yourself free. Make me free."

On another black night near Hell's Canyon in Idaho, Alexander said to her, "How could you have kept something like this from me? Something this big, this grave? We are meant to go through this together, hand in hand. Like lovers." He was in the sleeping bag, lying on top of her back, tethered to her, their hands threaded.

"Go through what together?" she said, her voice muffled by the pillow. "Your surrender to the authorities? Which is what you're doing after the first second you heard they were looking for you? Gee, I wonder why I didn't tell you. It's a mystery."

"Had you told me, we would have fixed it back then, instead of trying to plug up the hole in the Titanic now."

"The Titanic was doomed as soon as it hit that iceberg," said Tatiana. "Nothing could've saved it. So you'll excuse me if I tell you that I hate your metaphors."

Finally Tatiana gave Alexander Sam Gulotta's number. Alexander called from a public phone booth, Sam called back and they spent a tense hour on the phone, Tatiana listening to Alexander's end of the conversation and biting her nails. When he hung up, he said Sam agreed to meet them in ten days in Silver Spring, Maryland.

Anthony, sensing that something was remiss, made barely any demands on his washed-out parents. He read, he played his guitar, he drew pictures and played with his soldiers. But in the middle of the night, he started to wake up again and crawl into the tent with his mother. She had to start putting her nightgown on again.

Without stories, or laughing, or joking, they meandered through their America, north through the rivers of Montana, south through the Black Hills of Wyoming and the Badlands of South Dakota. Grimly through the days they drove across the country, they lived in the tents, they cooked over fires, ate out of one bowl. They fastened together and then slept fitted together, one metal bowl inside the other, she buried in his chest, pressed into his heart, swallowed by his ruined body. He didn't know what was happening. He felt all his instincts were abandoning him, he couldn't find his way out of the blind mire of her terror. They were exhausted by their demons, by the worry in the day, by the fears in the night. They prayed for sleep, but when it came it was broken and black. They prayed for sun, but each sun just got them closer to the Washington DC of their nightmares.

CHAPTER SIX

Jane Barrington, 1948

Sam Gulotta

Silver Spring, Maryland, just north of DC, Tatiana said, "Stop the camper." He did stop—at the designated meeting point, at a gas station. They got out; he filled the tank, went to go get them Cokes, cigarettes, candy for Anthony, who was running around raising dust. They were meeting Sam at eight in the morning; it was seven-thirty.

Tatiana had put on the sheer ivory muslin and tulle dress Alexander had bought for her in New Orleans; she had taken it in herself on Bethel Island; after all, her mother had been a seamstress. She had brushed out her hair and left it down. In the summer morning breeze, the diaphanous dress floated up slightly and the wisps of her sundried hair blew around her face.

"Thank you for looking so lovely for me," said Alexander.

She managed a "You're welcome." She tried to speak to him, but her voice wouldn't work. It was unseemly in the zenith of a bright God-like summer morning to be filled with so much anxiety. He lit a cigarette as they waited. He was wearing his U.S. captain's Class A dress uniform he had been given by the U.S. consul in Berlin. He had shaved and cropped short his hair.

Tatiana had at first insisted she was going to be by Alexander's side through everything. Trouble was, there was no one to leave the boy with. She said she would call Vikki and ask her to come help, but as soon as Anthony, who was milling nearby, obviously listening to adult conversations, had heard the name Vikki in conjunction with his own, he started to cry and clinging to his mother's leg, said please, please, don't leave me alone with Vikki.

And though Tatiana was horrified, she was not so horrified as
to *not* want to call her friend. It was Alexander who put his foot
down. They were not going to both leave Ant now when he needed
his mother again.

Standing at the camper, Tatiana said bitterly, to no one in particular, "I can't believe we're subjecting ourselves to this. Who
would have found us in our vast America? We'd have been lost
forever."

"How many times do you intend to step out in front of me,
Tatiana," Alexander asked, "to hide me from the Communists?"

"The rest of my life, if that's what it takes."

He turned to her, and something in his eyes opened and
cleared and focused on her. He stared into something he was
obviously trying very hard to understand. "What did you just
say?"

She turned her upset face away from his questioning gaze.

"Oh, I am *such* a fucking idiot," said Alexander—as Sam Gulotta
drove up in his old Ford sedan.

Sam shook Alexander's hand, and then stood in front of Tatiana
without speaking. He was wearing an atypically rumpled suit, and
his face was weary. His curly hair had started to go gray at the
edges and thin on top; he looked less sturdy though he had coached
his sons' baseball games for many years. "You look well, Tatiana.
Very well." He cleared his throat, and looked away. Sam, who
never noticed her, looked away! "Marriage obviously agrees with
you," he said. "I got married again myself." His first wife had died
in a plane crash at the start of the war, bringing supplies to the
troops. Tatiana wanted to say that the second marriage didn't seem
to agree with him quite so well but of course didn't. Her arms
were crossed on her chest.

Sam said, "So finally you saw reason."

"Not me," she retorted.

"Well, since he's the one who's going have to pay for your
shenanigans, I'm glad one of you had some sense."

"I'm not paying for her shenanigans," said Alexander.

Tatiana waved them both off. "Sam, don't pretend you don't
understand why in today's climate I might not be completely forthcoming with bringing you my husband."

"Yes," said Sam. "But why were you not forthcoming with
bringing me your husband back in 1946?"

"Because we were done with all of you!" Tatiana exclaimed.

"And he's already talked this to *death* in Berlin. That's not in his file for all to see?" Alexander put his hand out to quieten her. Anthony was nearby.

"It *is* in his file," Sam said evenly. "But I told you, the military tribunal in Berlin had their own protocol and we have ours. After he got here he had to talk to *us*. Which part of that didn't you understand?"

"Oh, I understood. But why can't you leave him alone?" She stepped in front of Alexander. "A hundred million people—don't you have something better to do? Who is he bothering? You know he is not in an espionage ring, collecting information for the Soviets. You know he's not hiding. And you know perfectly well that the last thing *he* of all people needs is to have your little State Department get their hooks in him."

Alexander put his hands on Tatiana's shoulders to stop her from heaving. Sam stood powerlessly in front of her. "Had you called me two years ago," Sam said, "this would've been behind you. Now everybody in three government departments is stuck on the fact that he's been hiding!"

"Traveling, not hiding. Do they know the difference?"

"No! Because they haven't debriefed him. And Defense *really* needed to debrief him. It's only because of your obstinacy that it's snowballed to this level."

"Don't blame it on me, you with your incessant phone calls to Vikki! What did you think I was going to think?"

Alexander fixed his hold on Tatiana's shoulders. "Shh," he said.

"No shh. And you know what, Sam?" Tatiana snapped, still under Alexander's hands. "Why don't you spend less time looking for my husband and a little more time looking at your State Department? I don't know if you've been reading the papers the last few years, but all I'm saying is, you might want to first clean your own house before searching all over the country to clean mine."

"Why don't you come and talk to John Rankin of the House of Un-American Activities Committee," Sam said impatiently. "Because he's waiting for you. Perhaps you can illuminate him about what you know about our State Department. He loves to talk to people like you."

Alexander's hold constricted around her. "All right, you two," he said. He turned Tatiana to him. "That's enough," he said quietly, staring her down. "We have to go."

"I'm coming with you!" Tatiana exclaimed. "I don't care what I promised. I'll take Ant with me—"

"Sam, excuse us for a minute," Alexander said, pulling Tatiana with him behind their camper. She was panting in desperation. He brought her flush against him and took her face in his hands. "Tatia, stop," he said. "You told me you were going to stay calm. You promised. Come on. The boy is right here."

She was shaking.

"You're going to wait here," he said, his steadying hand spreading around her gauzy back, holding her close, comforting her. "As you promised me, God help me. Just sit and wait. No matter what happens, we will come back. This is what Sam said. One way or another, I'm going to come back, but you have to wait. Don't go off. The boy is with you now, and you have to be good. Now swear to me *again* you'll be good."

"I'll be good," she whispered. She only hoped her face wasn't showing him what she was feeling. But then Anthony jumped between them and was in her arms, and she was forced to pretend to calm down.

Before they left, Sam ruffled Anthony's hair. "Don't worry, buddy. I'll do my best to take care of your dad."

"Okay," said Anthony, his arm around his mother's neck. "And I'll take care of my mom."

Tatiana backed away. Alexander nodded. She nodded. They stood for a moment. She saluted him. He saluted her. Anthony's hands were around his mother. "Mommy, how come you salute Dad first?"

"He's higher in rank, bud," she whispered.

Her face must have been so contorted that Alexander's words failed him. He just said, "Dear God, have a little faith, will you?" But he said it to her turned and squared back. The boy was in her arms.

"When did she become this overwrought?" Sam asked as they drove to the State Department in his sedan. He shook his head. "She used to be so much calmer."

"Really?"

Sam obviously wanted to talk about her. "Absolutely. You know when she first came to me, she was a stoic. A young petite widowed mother, spoke in a low voice, polite, never talked back, barely knew how to speak English. As time went on and she kept calling, she remained polite and quiet. She would come to DC sometimes, we would have lunch, sit quietly. I mean, she was so placid. I guess the only thing until the end that should have given me a clue was that she called every single month, without fail. But toward the end, when I got word about you in Colditz, she transformed into . . . into—I don't even know. A *completely* different woman."

"No, no," said Alexander. "Same woman. The quiet and polite is a ruse. When it's going her way, she is quiet and polite. Just don't cross her."

"It's true, I've seen that! The consul in Berlin has seen that. Did you know the man asked to be reassigned after she dealt with him?"

"The U.S. Consul to Berlin?" said Alexander. "Try the Soviet Communist Party-trained Commandant to the Special Camp at Sachsenhausen. I don't even want to guess what happened to him after she was done with his little special camp."

Soon they were driving along the Potomac, heading south. Alexander turned to the window, fanning out his hand over the glass.

On the fourth floor of the State Department on C Street, a block north of Constitution Avenue and the Mall, Sam introduced Alexander to a brand-new, just-out-of-law-school lawyer named Matt Levine, who had the smallest office known to man, smaller than the prison cells Alexander spent so much time in, a six by six cubicle with an imposing wooden desk and three chairs. The three men huddled together so close and uncomfortable that Alexander had to ask Levine to open the small window for an illusion of space.

Even in a suit, Matt Levine looked barely old enough to shave, but there was a certain short-stop look about him that Alexander liked. Also it didn't hurt that the first thing he said to Alexander was, "Don't worry. We'll lick this thing," even though he spent three subsequent hours reviewing Alexander's file and telling him that they were completely fucked.

"They'll ask about your uniform." Levine appraised him admiringly.

"Let them ask."

"They'll ask about your parents. There are some unbelievably damning things about them."

"Let them ask." This part he wished he could avoid.

"They'll ask why you haven't contacted State."

That Tania.

"Did you know Gulotta here thinks we can blame the whole thing on your wife?" Levine grinned.

"Does he?"

"But I told him old soldiers don't like to blame their troubles on their women. He insisted though."

Alexander looked from Sam to Levine and back again. "Are you guys fucking with me?"

"No, no," Sam said, half-seriously. "I really considered blaming it all on her. It's not even a lie: you actually didn't know we'd been looking for you—though ignorance is not a legal defense. But she can plead spousal privilege since she can't testify against you, and we're done. What do you think?"

"Hmm," Alexander drew out. "What's plan B?"

They didn't have a plan B.

"I will object to everything. That's my plan B." Levine smiled. "I just passed my bar exam. I'm retained by State as legal counsel. You're only my second case. But don't worry, I'm ready. Remember, don't be riled." He squinted his eyes at Alexander. "Are you . . . easily riled?"

The guy was scrappy. "Let's just say I'm not *not* easily riled," Alexander replied. "But I've been provoked by tougher men than these." He was thinking about Slonko, the man who interrogated his mother, his father, and finally—years later—himself. It hadn't gone well for Slonko. Alexander decided not to tell the just-passed-the-bar-exam Levine about the intricacies of Soviet NKVD interrogation—half naked in a freezing dark cell, starved and beaten, without witnesses, being pummeled with vicious insinuations about Tatiana.

Alexander was perspiring in his heavy uniform. He was not used to being this close to other people. He stood up, but there was nowhere to go. Sam was nervously chewing his nails in between tying and retying his tie.

"Some hay will almost certainly be made over your citizenship issue," Levine told Alexander. "Be careful of those questions. You'll see. There'll be some dueling between the departments."

Alexander mulled a question of his own. "Do you think"—he didn't want to ask—"that extradition might, um, come up?"

Sam and Levine exchanged fleeting frank glances, and Levine

mumbled, all averted, "I shouldn't think so," and Sam, also averted, said, "If all fails, we're reverting to plan A: Save your ass, blame your wife."

Sam told him the hearing would be conducted by seven men: two from State ("One of whom will be me"), two from Justice (one Immigration and Naturalization, one FBI), and two from Defense ("One lieutenant, one old colonel; I think you might like young Tom Richter; he's been very interested in your file") and the most important person at the hearing—Congressman John Rankin, the senior member from the House of Un-American Activities Committee, who would come to determine if Alexander had ties to the Communist Party at home or abroad. After the session was over, the seven men would put the question to vote by majority. John Rankin would be the one to cast the tie-breaker— if it came to that.

"He'll also be the one to determine whether or not you need to be investigated by the full HUAC," Sam said. "I don't have to tell you," he added, telling Alexander nonetheless, "at all costs, try to avoid that."

"Yes," said Levine, "if you go on to meet with HUAC, you're fucked. So no matter how rude anyone is, be polite, apologize and say, yes, sir, absolutely, sir, and I'm sorry, sir."

"You're very lucky in some respects," Sam said (Alexander agreed), "you really couldn't be getting a hearing at a better time."

"Oh, yeah?" Alexander desperately needed a smoke, but he didn't think there was enough oxygen in the office to light one small cigarette.

"HUAC is about to launch an explosive investigation into one of our own," said Levine. "Count your blessings. Alger Hiss, you heard of him?"

Alexander had. Alger Hiss had been the director of a committee presiding over the founding of the United Nations. Hiss had been leading the charge on the U.N. since 1944. He nodded.

"Hiss was at Yalta with Roosevelt and Churchill, he was the President's adviser, and now he's been accused by a former communist colleague of being a Soviet spy—since the 1930s!"

"That's one high-up man facing some high-up charges," noted Alexander.

"No shit," said Sam. "Point is, HUAC is busy with much bigger fish than you, so they want you, *need* you, to be square and on the up and up. So be on the up and up, will you?"

"Yes, sir," said Alexander, standing up and heading for the door, out of the stifling room. "Absolutely, sir. I'm sorry, sir, but I have to have a fucking smoke, or I'm going to die, sir."

Lieutenant Thomas Richter

Alexander was grateful that the room in which he met with the representatives of State, Defense and Justice across the National Mall was bigger than Matt Levine's office. The room in a Congressional testimonial room on the second floor of the Old Executive Building near the Capitol was narrow and long, with a row of tall open windows to his right that overlooked trees and gardens. The half-pack of cigarettes he smoked en route from State to Old Executive calmed him but did not quell his hunger or thirst. It was mid-afternoon.

He downed a glass of water, asked for another, asked if he could smoke, and sat tensely—and smokelessly—behind a small wooden table across from a raised wooden platform. Soon seven men filed in. Alexander watched them. They took their places, took a long good look at him, who was standing in front of them, appraised him, sat. He remained standing.

They were serious and well-dressed. Four of the men were in their fifties, two looked to be Alexander's age and one was 39-year-old Sam, who could've used a smoke himself. And Sam said Tania was overwrought. Tania was a woman—what was Sam's excuse? The two from Defense, one young, one old, were in full military dress. There were microphones in front of everyone. A stenographer, a court reporter, a bailiff were present. The bailiff said there would be no chair at the hearing and the members were therefore allowed to direct questions to Alexander and to each other.

After Alexander raised his right hand and swore to tell the truth and the meeting was called to order, but nearly before he finished saying, "So help me God," the young soldier from Defense opened his mouth.

"Lieutenant Thomas Richter," the soldier said. "Tell me, why are you wearing a *U.S.* military uniform? Officer's dress greens no less?"

"I'm a military man," Alexander said. "I own no suit. The dress greens were given to me by Mark Bishop, the U.S. Military

Governor of Berlin." It was better than lobstering dungarees. Or a Red Army uniform. He liked Richter's question. It was as if Richter had invited Alexander to set himself slightly outside the order of this civilian committee.

"So what do you call yourself nowadays?" Richter continued. "Do we refer to you as Commander? Captain? Major? Judging from your file, you seem to have had a number of ranks."

"I was major for only a few weeks," said Alexander. "I was wounded and arrested, after which I was demoted back to captain as punishment. I served as commander of a Railroad Patrol in General Meretskov's 67th Army and of a penal battalion in General Rokossovsky's 97th Army—as captain in both capacities. Upon my last conviction in 1945, the Red Army stripped me of my rank and title."

"Well, you seem like a military man to me," remarked Richter. "You say you served as an officer from 1937 to 1945? I see you received the Hero of the Soviet Union medal. There is no higher military honor in the Red Army. As I understand, it's the equivalent of our Congressional Medal of Honor."

"*Mister* Barrington," interrupted an elderly, desiccated man, introducing himself as Mr. Drake from the Department of Justice. "Major, Captain, Mister. Medals, years of service, titles, ranks—none of these things are at issue or our concern or the purpose of this meeting, frankly."

"I beg the pardon of the gentleman from Justice," said Richter. "But the establishment and verification of Captain Barrington's military history is of *prime* concern to the members of Defense at this meeting, and is the reason we're here. So if you'll excuse me . . ."

"Could the gentleman from Defense allow me to ask just *one* question, if I may. Just *one*," Mr. Drake said sonorously. "Mr. Barrington, as I'm sure you're aware, this committee is very troubled that you came to this country two years ago on special asylum privilege from the U.S. Government, and yet this is the first time we're meeting you face to face."

"State your question, Mr. Drake," said Alexander.

Richter suppressed a smile.

Drake coughed. "I see no record of your asylum application."

"State your question, Mr. Drake," repeated Alexander.

"Objection!" That was Matt Levine. "You see no record of my client's asylum application because my client did not come to this country on asylum. He returned to the country of his birth as a

U.S. citizen with a full passport and all his rights as a citizen intact. Mr. Barrington, tell the Court how long your family had resided in Massachusetts prior to 1930."

"Since the 1600s," said Alexander. He went on to explain that there were indeed some special and sensitive circumstances surrounding his return, but that he believed he had fulfilled his obligations after meeting in July 1946 with Sam Gulotta, the details of which were in the public record.

Mr. Drake pointed out that it was also in the public record that Alexander Barrington's file was open until the final *formal* debriefing—which had not taken place.

Sam said into his microphone, "I wish to elaborate on Mr. Barrington's statement. I did indeed meet and speak at length with him, and had not made the urgency and necessity for a full debriefing clear. I apologize to the members of this hearing for my oversight."

Tania was right about Sam.

"Mr. Gulotta is correct," Alexander said. "As soon as I was aware that the State Department needed to speak to me, I contacted him and returned immediately."

"I will attest to that," Sam said. "Mr. Barrington voluntarily, without an arrest or a subpoena, returned to Washington."

"Why have you not contacted us earlier, Mr. Barrington?" asked Drake. "Why were you in hiding?"

"I have been traveling," Alexander said. "I was not in hiding." He was being hidden—a vital difference. "I was not aware I had outstanding business with the U.S. Government."

"*Where* have you been traveling?"

"Maine, Florida, Arizona, California."

"By yourself?"

Alexander very nearly lied. If seven copies of his file were not lying in front of the men behind the long table, he would have. "No, not by myself. My wife and son are with me."

"Why did you hesitate, Mr. Barrington?" asked the man from State sitting next to Sam. He had not introduced himself, though it was his first question. He was portly and in his fifties, with beads of perspiration gluing his combed-over slick hair to his wet scalp. His brown tie was to one side; his teeth were bad.

"I hesitated," Alexander replied, "because my debriefing here today has nothing to do with my family."

"Doesn't it though?"

Alexander blinked, taking half a breath. "Not with my wife and son, no."

The man from State cleared his throat. "Mr. Barrington," he said, "tell me, please, how many years have you been married?"

Something from Slonko came to him—Slonko, standing just three feet away in Alexander's cell, holding the specter of a defenseless pregnant Tatiana over Alexander's head. After another slight pause Alexander said, "Six."

"So—you got married in 1942?"

"Correct," Alexander said tersely. He hated being questioned about Tatiana. Slonko had inferred that well, which is why he kept pushing. A little too far, as it turned out.

"And your son—what is his name?"

Alexander thought he had misheard. "You want to know my *son's* name?"

"Objection! Relevance!" Levine rattled the windows yelling out that one.

"Withdrawn," said the man from State. "How old is your son?"

"Five." Alexander said through his teeth.

"Born in 1943?"

"Correct."

"But Mr. Barrington, you just told us you didn't return to this country until 1946."

"Yes."

"Well, that's only *two* years ago. And your son is *five*?"

"Objection!" exclaimed Levine. "*How* is this relevant?"

"I'll tell you how it's relevant," said the man from State. "Things are not quite adding up. Am I the only one who can count? Mr. Gulotta, are Mr. Barrington's wife and son American citizens?"

"Yes, they are," said Sam, his eyes steady on Alexander, as if to say, *it's all right. But remember? Yes, sir, absolutely, sir. I'm sorry, sir.*

"So *where* could Mr. Barrington, a soldier in the Red Army, have possibly married a U.S. citizen in 1942 to have a child by in 1943?" A mulling silence fell over the room. "This is why I was inquiring as to the name of the boy. Pardon me for the indelicacy of my next question, Mr. Barrington, but . . . is it *your* child?"

Alexander was frigid. "My wife and child are none of your business, Mr.—"

"Burck," said the man. "Dennis Burck. Foreign Service. Principal Deputy Assistant Secretary for Eastern European and Soviet Affairs. *Where* in the world did you marry your American wife, Mr. Barrington, that she could have become with child in 1942?"

Alexander pushed away from table, but Levine, elbowing him, jumped up. "Objection! The wife and child are *not* under a subpoena from this committee. They do *not* fall under the jurisdiction of these proceedings, therefore I ask that all questions regarding them are to be excised from the record! I request a recess. If the hearing members want to learn more about Mr. Barrington's wife, they are welcome to subpoena her!"

"All I'm trying to ascertain here, Counsel," said Mr. Burck, "is the veracity of Mr. Barrington's statements. After all, the man *has* been in hiding for two years. Perhaps he has reasons to hide."

"Mr. Burck," said Levine, "if you have proof regarding my client's veracity, or lack thereof, by all means, bring it to the attention of this hearing. But until then, I request that no more scurrilous aspersions be made and that we move forward."

"Why can't Mr. Barrington answer my simple question?" Burck persisted. "I know where I married my wife. Why can't he tell me where he married his—in 1942?"

Alexander had to hide his clenching hands under the table. He had to protect himself. He didn't understand this man Burck, he didn't know the man, and perhaps these questions were harmless and just the normal order of operations. Perhaps. But he understood himself, and he knew himself. And he had spent too long being interrogated along these lines when it wasn't normal and it wasn't harmless, when her name, her safety, her security, her life was flung over his neck like a noose. *Tell us who you are, Major Belov, because your pregnant wife is in our custody. She is not safe, she is not in Stockholm, she is with us, and we have ways of making her talk.* And now here—did he hear Burck correctly, or was he just paranoid: *We know who your wife is. We know how she got here. She is here on our privilege.* There was simply nothing that could make Alexander lose reason quicker than explicit or implicit threats against Tatiana. He had to protect himself—for her sake. He didn't want Burck to know she was his Achilles heel. He sat up square-shouldered and with a force of his will placed his hands flat down on the table.

"My wife is not here to defend herself, Mr. Burck," Alexander said in a low voice. "Nor is she being debriefed. I will not answer any further questions regarding her."

Lieutenant Richter, sitting erect and unperspiring in his uniform, leaned into his microphone. "With all due respect to the other members, we're not here to assess the length and quality of Captain Barrington's marriage. This is not one of the questions put before this committee. This is an executive closed session to assess the security risk this man poses to the United States. I second the counsel's request for a recess."

The members took recess to confer. While waiting, Matt Levine whispered to Alexander, "I thought you said you weren't going to get riled?"

"*That* was riled?" said Alexander, taking a long drink. That wasn't riled.

"Don't you understand, I *want* them to subpoena your wife," Levine said.

"Not me."

"Yes. She'll plead spousal privilege to every single fucking question and we'll be out of here in an hour."

"I need to smoke. Can I smoke now?"

"They told you no."

The seven men returned to the order of business. They concurred with counsel, and Dennis Burck was forced to move on.

But he didn't move far.

"Let's return to *your* record then, Mr. Barrington," said Burck. Didn't anyone else have any questions for Alexander? "I had a chance to review your Military Tribunal papers from Berlin in 1946. Fascinating bit of business."

"If you say so."

"So then, just to assert, as per the record, Alexander Barrington and Major Alexander Belov are one and the same man?"

"They are."

"Why then did you describe yourself as a civilian man, Mr. Barrington, when your record clearly states that you were a Red Army major who escaped a military prison and killed a number of Soviet soldiers after a protracted battle? Are you aware that the Soviets want you extradited?"

"Objection!" yelled Levine. "This meeting is not concerned with the demands of Soviet Russia. This is a U.S. committee."

"The Soviet Government says this man falls under their jurisdiction, and that this is a military matter. Now, once again—Mr. Barrington, are you or are you not aware that the Soviets want you extradited?

Alexander was silent. "I am aware," he said at last, "that the

Red Army stripped me of my rank and title in 1945 when they sentenced me to twenty-five years in prison for surrendering to German forces."

Richter whistled. *Twenty-five years,* he mouthed.

"No," said Burck. "Your record states that you were sentenced for desertion."

"I understand. But the rank and title is removed upon conviction for desertion *or* surrender."

"Well, perhaps the title was not removed," said Burck with a gentle expression, "because there was no conviction."

Alexander paused. "Pardon me, but then why was I in the Soviet prison, if there was no conviction?"

Burck's demeanor stiffened.

"My point is," said Alexander, "I cannot be a deserter in 1945 and a major in 1946." He took a breath, not wanting to leave his name besmirched with desertion. "Just for the record," he said, "I was neither."

"Your record says you are a Red Army major. Are you saying your record is wrong, Mr. Barrington?" said Burck. "Incomplete? Perhaps less than truthful?"

"I've already explained I was a major for only a few weeks in 1943. My direct statement to the tribunal in Berlin regarding my years in the Red Army is clear and unequivocal. Perhaps we need to go over it."

"I move to go over the commander's record," joined in Richer, opening his notes, and then proceeded to ask *two hours* of questions about Alexander's years in the Red Army. He was single-minded and relentless. He was interested in Alexander's war experience, in the weapons the Soviets used, in their military campaigns in and around Leningrad, and through Latvia, Estonia, Byelorussia and Poland. He asked about Alexander's arrests, interrogations, and years in the penal battalion without supplies or trained soldiers. He asked so many questions about the Soviet activities in Berlin that Burck, who was otherwise quiet, finally piped up with an exasperated request that they move on to the order of business.

"This *is* our order of business," said Richter.

"I just don't see how these alleged Soviet activities in Berlin are relevant to the assessment of the man before us," said Burck. "I thought we were trying to determine if this man is a communist. When do you think we could begin determining that?"

That was when John Rankin from HUAC finally leaned into his microphone and spoke for the first time. He was a tall stiff gentleman in his sixties, who spoke with a deep Southern accent. A Democrat, Rankin had been a member of Congress since the twenties. He was grave, purposeful, and humorless. Alexander thought Rankin was a military man himself, something about his no nonsense demeanor as he had sat and listened.

"I'll answer Mr. Burck," Rankin said, addressing the whole committee. "The looting of atomic laboratories, the Soviet rampage in a closed Berlin for eight days, the transformation of Nazi concentration camps into Soviet concentration camps, forced repatriation—in light of the blockade of Berlin by the Soviet Union that is going on even as we speak, does the gentleman from State really think that Soviet activities in Berlin are *irrelevant* to this hearing?" He smiled.

Alexander looked down at his hands. Rankin was definitely military—and perhaps not so humorless.

"*Alleged* activities," corrected Burck. "It's all hearsay—from a man who the honorable Congressman suspects of being a loyalty risk."

"I have not asked Mr. Barrington a single question," said Rankin. "The gentleman from State should not postulate what I'm suspecting."

Clearing his throat, Richter interjected. "Just for the record, there is nothing alleged about the Soviet blockade of Berlin." He changed the subject back to the POW camp at Catowice and at Colditz. During Alexander's recounting of the escape from Sachsenhausen, the entire room full of men and one female stenographer, fell mute. The only thing Alexander omitted from this version was Tatiana. He didn't know if it was perjury, but he figured if they weren't meticulous enough to sift through his tribunal transcript and ask, he certainly wasn't going to volunteer.

"Well, well, Captain Barrington," said Rankin when Alexander had finished. "I agree with Lieutenant Richter—as a former soldier in WWI, I don't know what to call you myself after what we've just heard. I think perhaps 'mister' is not entirely appropriate. But we do need to go a little further back in your history than Sachsenhausen."

Alexander held his breath. Perhaps they sifted through his record more meticulously than he had hoped.

"Do you have Communist sympathies, Captain Barrington?"

"No," he replied.

"What about your mother and father?" Rankin wanted to know. "Harold and Jane Barrington? Would you say *they* had Communist sympathies?"

"I don't know if they had sympathies," said Alexander. "But they *were* Communists."

A chill ran through the long room. Alexander knew his parents were fair game, but he noticed that Burck clammed up.

Rankin fixed his gaze on Alexander. "Please continue. You were about to tell us about your Communist background, I believe."

He was? "We moved to the Soviet Union in 1930, when I was eleven," he said. "My parents and I were ultimately arrested during the Great Purge of 1937-38."

"Well, hold *on* here," said Burck, *un*clamming. "Let's not use the term the Great *Purge* the same way we use the term the Great Depression. It's just propagandistic words, meant to scare and confuse. Often what is a purge to one is simply the execution of applicable laws to another. The record on whether or not there was something called a 'purge' is extremely unclear." He paused. "Much like *your* record, Mr. Barrington."

Alexander silently narrowed his eyes at Burck.

"And may I point out," continued Burck, "that, since you are sitting before us, you are actual proof that you were not purged."

"I wasn't purged because I escaped on the way to Vladivostok," said Alexander. "What does that prove?"

"Which escape was this, Mr. Barrington?" said Burck pleasantly. "There seem to be so many."

Drake, from Justice, took the opportunity to intervene. "When you escaped were you already a Soviet citizen?"

Here it was. More murkiness. "Yes," said Alexander. "When I was conscripted at age sixteen, I automatically became a Soviet citizen."

"Ah! And when you became a Soviet citizen, your American citizenship was automatically revoked," said Drake with cooped-up delight, finally given the chance to uphold the immigration and naturalization laws of the United States.

"Objection!" said Levine, "Mr. Drake, I will repeat again, my client *is* an American citizen."

"But, Counsel, your client just stated for the record that he was a Soviet citizen. He cannot be a citizen of both the United States and the Soviet Union," Drake said. "Not then—and *certainly* not now."

"Yes," said Matt Levine. "But his American citizenship cannot be revoked if he became the citizen of the Soviet Union involuntarily. And I would posit that *conscription*, by its very definition, infers *involuntary* citizenship. Once again, my client is a natural-born citizen of the United States."

"Unlike someone who was a naturalized citizen after, say, receiving asylum?" said Burck, looking only at Alexander. "Like a refugee coming into one of our ports—oh, say, Ellis Island, during war?"

Alexander's hands did not move from the table this time; he had had a chance to prepare himself. Only his teeth ground in his mouth. He had been right to be on guard. It was exactly as he had suspected.

Matt Levine said, "That's right, nothing like that. Can we move on?"

They moved on—to Harold and Jane Barrington.

For another hour, maybe longer, the man from FBI, along with Congressman Rankin kept on and on.

"Objection! Already asked. Eight times."

"Objection. Already asked. Ten times."

"Objection."

"Objection."

"Objection."

"His parents' history and his own seditionary activities speak to relevancy here, Counsel," said Rankin.

"What seditionary activities? He was a minor! And his parents are not here to defend themselves. We *really* need to move on."

"It says here that Anthony Alexander Barrington was arrested at the age of ten in Washington DC during unrest at a pro-revolutionary radical demonstration," said Rankin. "That's *his* history. So did he or did he not have some Communist sympathies of his own? He went to the Soviet Union? Lived there, went to school there? Joined the Red Army? Did he become a member of the Communist Party to be in the officer corps? My understanding was that all officers had to be card-carrying party members."

"That is not true," said Alexander. "*I* wasn't. Which was fortunate for me because almost all card-carrying officers of the Red Army were shot in 1938 during"—he paused, coldly staring at Burck—"the *execution of applicable laws.*"

There was stiffness on Burck's face and satisfaction on Rankin's. "Answer my question, Captain," he said.

Levine started to object, but Alexander cut him off. "There were many questions, Congressman Rankin. Starting with the first, you are right, I had been many times by my father's side when I was a boy." Alexander took a small breath. "I participated in a number of demonstrations with him. I was arrested three times during some turbulence. He was a Communist, but he was also my father. None of this is in dispute."

"Mr. Barrington, at the very crux of what is in dispute," said Rankin in his Mississippi drawl, "is whether or not *you're* a Communist."

"And I have answered you a number of times, Congressman," said Alexander. "I said I was not."

"Just so you're clear about the Congressman's line of questioning, Mr. Barrington," said Burck with unrestrained derision, "in the now famous opinion of John Rankin, and I quote, 'the real enemy of the United States all along has been not the Axis Powers but the Soviet Union.'"

"And is this something in *this* day and age that the honorable gentleman from State would like to go on record as *disputing*?" said Rankin with his own unconstrained derision.

Alexander looked from one man to the other and said nothing. He wasn't being asked a question. Tania was right. He needed to be very careful. Talk about dueling agendas. His head was swimming. The Immigration Department wanted him to be a Soviet citizen without asylum, whom they could deport. The FBI wanted him to be a spy, Soviet or American, they weren't choosy. Rankin wanted him to be a Communist *and* an American, so he could be charged with treason. Burck, Alexander thought, wanted him to be a Communist *and* a Russian so he could be deported. And Richter just wanted him to be a soldier with a fuckload of information about the enemy. That's how the forces were lined up at the frontline across from Alexander's trench.

"Was your father part of any underground espionage network?" asked Rankin.

"Objection," Levine said in a tired voice.

"Popular Front perhaps? Comintern? The Red Brigade?" Rankin continued.

"Perhaps," replied Alexander. "I really don't know."

"Was Harold Barrington involved in espionage activities for the Soviet Union when he was still in America?"

"Objection, objection, objection . . ."

"Objection noted. Please answer the question, Captain Barrington."

"I don't know. I doubt it," said Alexander.

Rankin said, "Did your father run to the Soviet Union because his cover as a spy for them was blown in his own country and he feared for his safety?"

"My father didn't run to the Soviet Union," said Alexander slowly. "We moved to the Soviet Union with the full knowledge and assent of the U.S. Government."

"He didn't run to escape arrest on espionage charges?"

"No, he did not."

"But wasn't his U.S. citizenship revoked?"

"It was not revoked as punishment. It was revoked when he became a Soviet citizen."

"So the answer would be yes?" said Rankin politely. "It was revoked?"

"Yes," said Alexander. "It was revoked." He almost wanted to voice his own objection.

"Captain Barrington, did your father commit treason," asked Rankin, "against his own country, the United States, by spying on it for the Soviet Union?"

"No, Congressman," said Alexander. "He did not." He forced his hands to remain steady. Oh, Dad, look what you've left behind for me.

They stopped questioning him to take another short recess.

"What happened to Harold and Jane Barrington after they were arrested in 1936 in Leningrad?" asked Rankin when the meeting resumed.

"They were executed in 1937." Alexander gave Burck a look that said, *this is what I think of your "record is unclear," gentleman from State.*

"On what charges?"

"Treason. They were convicted of being American spies."

There was a pause. "*Convicted*, you say?" said Rankin. "Of being American spies?"

"Yes. Arrested, tried, convicted, shot."

"Well, we know for a fact," said Rankin, "that they were not spying for the *United States* Government."

"With all due respect, Congressman," said Burck, "there is *nothing* in Mr. Barrington's record that shows the details of his parents' alleged conviction. There is only his account of it, and he, by his own admission, was not present at their trial. And the Soviet Government exercises the privilege of not releasing information about its own citizens."

"Well, they released plenty of information about a certain Alexander Belov, Mr. Burck," said Mr. Rankin.

"As is also their privilege with regard to their own citizens," said Burck and quickly went on before Levine could object. "I think we must keep perspective on why we're here, which is not—despite the Congressman's best efforts—to re-examine the Soviet Union's role in world conflict, but simply to ascertain whether Mr. Barrington is who he says he is and whether he poses security concerns for us here in the United States. There are two vital questions of order before this hearing. One, is Mr. Barrington an American citizen? Two, is Mr. Barrington a Communist? I, for one," Burck went on, "think that we should look a little more closely at the former and not the latter, for I think it is very easy to see witches everywhere"—he paused and coughed—"particularly in today's political climate. However, as to the first point of order, Mr. Barrington does not deny that he was a Soviet citizen. The Soviets to this day are maintaining that he is still a Soviet citizen. Perhaps we should rely on concurring information."

"The gentleman's own State Department established Mr. Barrington's American birthright two years ago when they granted him safe passage from Berlin," said Rankin. "Is this something the gentleman would like to dispute with his own department?"

"All I'm saying," said Burck, "is that the Soviet Union is disputing it. That is all."

"The Soviet Union that executed his parents?" said Rankin. "His parents who surrendered their U.S. citizenship, became Soviet citizens and then were tried and shot? I am not in complete agreement with the gentleman from State with regard to the Soviet Union's *reliability* on matters of Captain Barrington's lineage."

"We don't know for a fact his parents were executed, Congressman," retorted Burck. "Was Captain Barrington present at their execution? It's just speculation, frankly."

"Mr. Burck is correct," said Alexander. "I was not present at their execution. However, I was present at my own arrest. I am not speculating on my own ten-year sentence to hard labor."

"Wait, wait," said Thomas Richter, looking into his notes. "Captain, you said before you were sentenced to twenty-five years."

"That was the third time, Lieutenant," said Alexander. "The second time, I was sentenced to the penal battalion command. The first time it was to ten years. I was seventeen."

There was silence in the room.

"I think," Richter said slowly, "that it's probably safe to conclude that Captain Barrington is *not* a Communist spy."

"Only according to the words of Captain Barrington himself," said Burck. "We have no way of verifying the truth of his statements, except to check it against the records of the country where he lived, where he maintained his citizenship, and in whose army he served for eight years."

"Correct me if I'm wrong," said Rankin incredulously, "but is the gentleman from State contending to the chairman of HUAC that Captain Barrington *is* a Communist?"

"No, no, a Soviet citizen," rejoined Burck hastily.

Sam and Alexander exchanged glances. Matt Levine, dumbfounded, asked in a slow voice if anyone had any further questions for his client.

"I'm wondering, Captain Barrington," said Rankin, "if you would be so kind as to answer two questions for *me*, please, *sua sponte*, two questions that I had posed to William Bullitt, this country's first ambassador to the Soviet Union."

"Objection!" And that was Burck!

Alexander didn't know what was going on. *Sua sponte?* He stared questioningly at Sam, who waved his hand slightly, to say, *yes, sir, yes, sir, yes, sir.*

Rankin turned slowly to face the man from State. "I believe only counsel is allowed to object." Turning back to Levine, he said, "Do you have any objections to my asking your client two questions, Counsel?"

"Well," Levine replied, "my client hasn't heard the *sua sponte* questions. I would rather not object in principle."

"Except *I* know the questions the honorable Congressman posed to Ambassador Bullitt last year in a public session," said Burck. "We *all* know them, everyone in this room knows them, and they are completely irrelevant to these proceedings. Are they going to help you determine if this man is a loyalty risk, Congressman?"

"*I* don't know them," said Alexander.

"The answers will tell me where his heart is," said Rankin. "After all, *out of the abundance of the heart, the mouth speaks.*"

Congressman Rankin was right. Tania fully believed that.

Levine said quietly to Alexander, "*Sua sponte* means of your own accord. Choose to answer or not answer."

"I'd like to answer the Congressman," said Alexander.

"Captain Barrington," said Rankin, lowering his drawling voice, "is it true what we heard—that they eat human *bodies* over there in Russia?"

Not expecting it, Alexander flinched. It was a good ten seconds before he opened his mouth to answer. "I think, Congressman," he said slowly, "that we don't need to invent horrors about the Soviet Union. What *is* true is that during the great famine in the Ukraine in 1934, and during the blockade of Leningrad from 1941 to 1944, there have been instances of people killed for their flesh."

"As compared, say, with the ongoing blockade of the American sector of Berlin," said Rankin, "during which no one is eating anyone's flesh?"

"Because the U.S. Government is air-dropping all the food and supplies its citizens need." Alexander sat stiffly. His voice was curt. "The instances you heard about are in no way a reflection of the Russian people. These are extenuating circumstances. After all the horses and rats are gone, there is nothing left. It's impossible to fully represent to this hearing what it is like for three million people in a large, civilized, modern, cosmopolitan city to starve to death. Really, it cannot *bear* any more discussion." He lowered his head momentarily, looking at his balled-up hands.

Burck stared at Rankin with unconcealed glee. "Oh, please," he drew out, "can the Congressman from Mississippi proceed with his next question to Captain Barrington, who obviously knows a *great* deal about the Soviet Union."

After pausing gravely, Rankin spoke. "On further consideration," he said, "I have no more questions for Captain Barrington." Looking thoughtfully at Alexander, he closed his notebook.

Burck's smile was irrepressible. "Does anyone else have any more *sua sponte* questions for Captain Barrington? Anyone? No? Then does counsel wish to conclude?"

After looking in his notes for a couple of minutes, Levine stood up. "Yes. Our stipulation is that Captain Alexander Barrington is a man who went to the Soviet Union as a minor, changed his name to save his life, joined the Red Army because he had no choice, and is now back home as an American citizen. His two-year absence from a debriefing, while troubling, is not sufficient evidence of any espionage activities or communist sympathies. And since there is no other evidence against him, I motion that these proceedings be called to end and that my client's name be cleared of all charges." He sat down.

Rankin moved to adjourn and the seven men got up and left the room.

Alexander and Levine were left alone.

"What did Rankin ask Bullitt last year?" Alexander wanted to know. "What was his second question?"

"Rankin asked the ambassador if people were just like slaves in Russia," Levine said. "Bullitt apparently replied that they were."

Alexander said nothing.

"So how do you think it went?" he asked Levine after a short silence.

"As good as can be expected," Levine said, closing his notes. "But perhaps we should have gone with plan A."

"I'm beginning to think so myself," said Alexander.

"Richter quite liked you. Is that a soldier thing? You have Sam's vote. That's two. All you need is two more. Probably won't be getting Burck's. Maybe the mute colonel's? That's three right there. And Rankin? I think he would've been happier if you had told him publicly and for the record that mothers eat their little children with glee in that live slave beast pit, the Soviet Union. But there you go."

"Yes," said Alexander. "But you did very well, Counsel. No one could have done better. Thank you."

"Thank *you*, Captain. Thank you very much." Levine beamed and left to go get Alexander more cigarettes.

As Alexander remained alone in the executive room, waiting for seven strangers to decide on his life, he tried to focus on things from which he could draw sustenance at a time like this: Sundays on Nantucket, sitting on boats, smelling the ocean, picking sea shells, playing with his friends. Memories of himself as a happy American boy, just a few years older than Ant. But he couldn't drum up any of those memories now, that breath of sunshine he needed as he drummed tensely on the table.

Levine came back with cigarettes, asked him to stop drumming. Alexander walked to the open window, sat on the ledge and smoked instead; o mercy. He inhaled deeply, held the smoke in his throat, the cymbals of nicotine clanging into his lungs.

All things considering, he couldn't complain. Many times the vicissitudes of life had gone in his column. When he jumped off a moving train into the Volga River, he did not hit boulders and smash his head open. His column. When he got typhus, he did not die. His column. When a shell exploded and ripped open his back, and an angel flew over him and poured her blood into him. His column.

But he was not thinking of his column. Night had long fallen. He was thinking of the other column.

He thought about Tatiana's brother, Pasha, about carrying him on his back for three days, Pasha so hot he couldn't breathe.

Alexander held snow to Pasha's head, bandaged his oozing leg wound, pleading, praying, disbelieving. I didn't find him in the mountains of Holy Cross to watch him die. Find him, save him, perform a frontline tracheotomy on him—

"Pasha. Can you hear me?"

"I can hear you."

"What's wrong? What's hurting? I cleaned your leg. What's the matter?"

"I'm burning up."

"No, you're fine."

"I can't feel my legs."

"No, you're fine."

"Alexander, I'm not . . . dying, am I?"

"No. You're fine." Alexander looks right at him. He doesn't blink. If he can look straight and narrow, brave and indifferent, into Tatiana's pregnant face and lie to send her forever away, to give her her only dim chance of survival, he can find the strength to look at her brother before he is forever away. Though he must admit, he doesn't feel quite as strong. Pasha is half lying, half sitting on the ground, propped up against Alexander.

"Why do I feel like I'm dying?" says Pasha, his breathing lower, more shallow. He is rasping. Alexander has heard this rattle a thousand times, the rattle of a dying man. But this is Pasha! He cannot die!

"You're not, you'll be fine."

Pasha whispers, "You're lying to me, you bastard."

"I'm not."

"Alexander," he rasps, "I can see her!"

"Who?" Alexander nearly drops Pasha to the ground.

Tears trickle down Pasha's face "Tania!" Pasha cries, extending his hand. "Tania. Come, swim with me one more time. Just once more across the Luga. Run with me across the meadow to the river, just like you did when we were kids. You are my sister." He stretches out his arm to some-

thing near Alexander, who is like an apparition himself, shellshocked and ashen. He actually turns to look. Pasha is smiling. "We are in the Lake Ilmen boat. She is sitting by my side," he whispers.

That's when Alexander knows—the impossible is true.

Alexander carries Pasha dead on his back for one more day in winter Germany, refusing to believe what could not be believed, refusing to bury him in the frozen ground.

Now, sitting on the windowsill in the Old Executive Building, Alexander admitted that a world in which Tatiana's vanished brother could die because he got his trouser leg caught on a rusty nail, was a world in which armed forces sometimes did not go into your column.

Inhaling the nicotine, Alexander closed his eyes. He did not see her by his own side—at least that was something. Tatiana, who always sat by the dying, was not here with him.

At Catowice, a supervisor had died, and was buried in a casket! Some of the men complained, including Ouspensky, including Pasha. Alexander had been digging one or two mass graves a day for the last several weeks, and here was a man buried by himself in a casket. Grumbling over his bowl of oats and boiled carrot shavings, Pasha said to Alexander that maybe they should complain. "Yes, you go ahead," Alexander said. "But I tell you what—you're not working hard enough. That man has been here for three years. He was a respected work supervisor and a favorite of all the prison chiefs because he made their jobs easier."

That evening, Pasha drew up twenty leaflets by hand regarding the man buried in the coffin. "REMEMBER! WORK HARD!" his leaflet said. "IF YOU WORK HARD ENOUGH, YOU TOO CAN BE BURIED IN A WOODEN CASKET!"

"Now isn't that encouraging?" said Pasha with a big grin as he distributed the handmade leaflets. And Alexander agreed with a smile of his own that it was.

The seven men came back. Alexander stood at attention.

The vote on the questions put before the committee was four to three, with Rankin casting the deciding vote—that Alexander Barrington be cleared of all suspicion against him.

It had taken Alexander seven hours with two breaks to sing for his freedom.

When Sam came over, he looked nearly happier than Alexander. "John *Rankin*, chairman of HUAC, voted to clear you of communist conspiracy charges!" he exclaimed. "Is Tania going to think that's fantastic, or what?"

"Ironic is more like it." Alexander didn't notice the deep tension in his shoulders until he breathed out when the gavel struck. He shook Sam's hand.

"I swear, if Rankin asked one more question about your parents, I was going to become a communist myself just to spite him," Levine said.

"Oh, *that* would spite him," Sam said. "He lives for that. You know what he said, Alexander? It was the question about the cannibals that decided it for him."

"*Really?*" That was surprising.

Sam shook his head. "That's what I said. But Rankin said, *out of the abundance of* your *heart, the mouth spoke.*"

Sam introduced Tom Richter to Alexander. Richter saluted him. The lieutenant was tall, good-looking in that athletic, light-haired American sort of way, well-built, brash. He had a strong handshake, and in the hall, he laughed. "So what did you think? A nail-biter or what? Walked into a den of wolves, didn't you?"

"No shit."

"What you don't know," said Richter, "is that the graying graceful Southern gentleman John Rankin is second in popularity only to Satan among the members of State. Isn't it true, Mr. Gulotta?" He was loud and unapologetic.

"Not true, Lieutenant Richter," said Sam, only a little quieter. "Satan is much more popular." You could tell Sam and Richter were friends.

The four men stood in the hall and had a nice long smoke. Richter was thirty, a year older than Alexander. He had been with MacArthur in Japan during the war, and was likely to be joining him again now that certain troubles were brewing at the 38th parallel between North and South Korea.

Richter said he only came to the hearing because he had heard so much about Alexander from Sam. "Defense is very interested in the mechanics and hierarchy of the Red Army, and your command of Russian and knowledge and understanding of Soviet activities." He smiled. "Nice touch there, keeping quiet about your wife."

"Yes," said Alexander. "I do not speak about my wife to her enemies."

"Well, that Sachsenhausen story was pretty remarkable even without her. I think if you mentioned that your unarmed Donut Dolly of a wife was in the trees with you and had helped you escape, those men would have had a fucking heart attack."

Alexander laughed then, comfortable with Richter, and relieved.

"You might not know about us," said Richter, "but we at Defense know quite a bit about you." He asked if Alexander would be interested in getting a security clearance so he could do some limited military intelligence analysis for the U.S. Army. "Very rare to find a fluent bilingual speaker." Richter said there was so much rapid-fire international activity going on—the Communist insurgencies in Greece, in Yugoslavia, the ongoing near-collapsed negotiations with Mao in China, and the acquisitions of classified documents from the USSR regarding their atomic program, that to get periodic analysis on raw data from someone like Alexander would be a tremendous boon to the Armed Services Committee, and the Military Intelligence arm of the U.S. Army. "Consider the last eight hours part of your security interview." Richter grinned.

Alexander wasn't sure how it was going to work. Carefully he said that plunging back into the military was not going to be in his best interest. Tatiana would go through the roof.

"Who's plunging back into the military?" Richter said calmly. "You could be commissioned as a reserve officer. Just two days a month of your time. Earlier this year, the President passed legislation for drill pay for reservists. You'll have to pass formal clearance," he went on. "It's not going to be easy——Red Army are incendiary words these days—as you've just witnessed. But I'll help you. I *really* think you should do it. Where you are living?"

Alexander said nowhere at the moment, they were still trying—.

"Well, it doesn't matter," said Richter. "Wherever you are in the States, you can get onto an army base, look over the raw data we send and prepare a finished intel report for us. It'll be sporadic work, but it'll more than satisfy your annual active duty requirement, and give you other options. You can train, or you can do combat support."

Sam Gulotta thought it was a great opportunity for Alexander. Richter said the position could be expanded to serve Alexander's interests. If he wanted to live in Washington, he could work for Army Intelligence right here and be permanently employed by the Department of Defense.

Alexander said, "I'll let you know. Not likely about living in DC, though."

"What, Missus Commando doesn't like Washington?" asked Richter.

"She doesn't like war," said Alexander. "She's not going to be happy with any of it."

"Bring her to the Pentagon tomorrow." Richter smiled broadly. "I'll change her mind. I'll convince her to move here. You'll see— I'll convince her to move to Korea with you."

"Oh, much luck with that."

"I picture your Russian wife," Richter said, slapping Alexander on the back, "the woman who single-handedly took on the Red Army in Germany on your behalf as someone who, built like an ox, used to pull her own plow in the Russian collective fields, sowing and reaping for the proletariat." He laughed.

"Well, that's about right, isn't it, Alexander?" said Sam.

"Just about." Alexander smiled back, finishing up his smoke. He needed to get back to the Russian ox-built serf, who was no doubt now summoning a county militia to snatch him from the iron grip of the U.S. State Department.

As they were walking down the corridor, Dennis Burck came out of one of the offices and stopped them in the hall. He wondered if he could have "simply a minute" of Alexander's time.

Richter said good-bye and left. Sam tried to pull Alexander aside, Matt Levine wanted to come inside the chamber, but Burck said, "No, no, you'll have him back in thirty seconds, you can speak all night to him." He cited the smallness of his office and the absence of extra chairs. "Just wait for him outside," Burck said amiably. "I will leave the door open, and we won't be but a moment."

Burck was more senior than Sam Gulotta. Sam had to stay behind. Alexander went into an office that was even smaller than Matt Levine's. Invited to sit, Alexander opted to stand. Burck began by saying that one of his many responsibilities at the State Department being a deputy liaison between State and Interpol. Alexander half listened half politely. Burck continued in the same genial tone. "I know you didn't want to mention it to the committee, but we know, of course, that your wife was also a Soviet subject, who escaped, leaving a dozen Soviet troops dead on the border with Finland."

Alexander's mouth was tight. "The dead border troops had nothing to do with her," he said. "And my wife is now an American citizen. Now, will there be anything else?"

"Oh, that wasn't what I wanted to talk to you about, Mr. Barrington." On Burck's desk lay a thick file that was the Barrington State Department documents since 1917. "Let me get right to my point. I have information about your mother."

Alexander thought he had misheard. "What did you say?"

Burck buried his gaze and his hands in the file. "You were told your mother was executed in 1938. Who told you this?" He glanced up.

"I have no idea what you're talking about, Mr. Burck."

Burck got up. "Would you mind if I closed the door, Mr. Barrington, so we could have a little privacy?"

"Privacy for what?"

Burck went around Alexander and shut the door on Sam and Levine.

When he sat back down at his desk, in a voice so low Alexander had to strain to hear, Burck said, "Now listen carefully. Your father, it is true, was executed, but . . . *your mother is still alive.*"

Alexander stood stonelike, his face a concrete mask.

Burck pressed on. "It's true. She is still alive! She is in Perm-35. Do you know where that is?"

Alexander spoke with difficulty, but he became more calm, not less, all his senses sharpened as if he were in battle. "I have credible information my mother was killed," he said in a dull voice. "I heard it four different ways from four different people."

"You're hearing it another way from me."

Alexander's fists clenched as he tried to keep his composure. "I don't believe you," he said.

"It's my business to know. And it is the truth. This is objectively verifiable information. She has been in the labor camp near the Urals for the last eleven years. She is old and not in the best of health, but she's still alive. Her name is on the prison rolls."

Alexander's fists started to shake.

"Would you like to see?" Burck started to leaf through a long thick sheaf of serrated papers he'd taken from the folders.

Taking a step back, a small stagger back, Alexander stumbled against a chair.

His voice a sibilant excited whisper, Burck exclaimed, "*You* can help your mother. It's up to you. *You* can bring her back home."

Alexander needed to sit down. He stood. He said nothing. If he asked how he could do that, it would mean he believed Burck, that it was true, she was alive.

"Since the war, many people, especially women, have been released and rehabilitated. You'll see, the Soviets will help us. And your mother has not been well."

"Why would they listen to you?"

"My Foreign Office is in constant contact with the Soviet attaché and with Cominform. I am also close to the Commissar of People's Affairs, who often commutes sentences for prisoners based on recommendations."

"The Commissar of People's Affairs? You mean Lavrenti Beria?"

Burck went on without replying. "We can leave for Turkey next week. From Istanbul we will fly across the Black Sea to Yalta, and then—with Soviet permission, of course—drive in a special convoy arranged by them north through the country up the River Volga to the camp. In the meantime, I will begin negotiating for her release."

Alexander backed away.

"I have incentives to sway them. These are very troubled times. We often exchange influence—"

The chair crashed over and fell against the bookshelves.

"Mr. Barrington, wait!"

Alexander was already in the corridor through the flung-open door. "Let's go," he said to Sam and Levine. "Now."

They walked quickly, almost running, down the corridor and into the stairwell. "What did he say?" Levine kept asking. "What did he say?"

Sam said nothing.

Alexander didn't reply, but like a grim statue, said good-bye to Levine and then sat mutely in Sam's car on the way back to Silver Spring, asking for a few moments to himself so he could still the cries of his heart.

They got back to the Nomad well after ten in the evening. Tatiana had been sitting outside on the little steps of the camper, holding a sleeping Anthony on her lap. Alexander couldn't say a word to her for many minutes while she stood in his arms, sobbing, buried in his chest. In his pajamas, Anthony, having been suddenly awoken, was pulling on her dress.

"Mom, come on, stop it, let go; Mama, let go of him."

Sam took the boy away to give them a minute. "So how was your mother today?" he said, picking him up.

"Terrible," said Anthony. "She said herself she was a train wreck of a mother. I'm hoping she'll be better tomorrow."

"Indeed, Ant, I think she will be," said Sam. "Everything is going to be all right. And tomorrow your dad is going to take you to a special place where soldiers work. It's called the Pentagon."

Anthony beamed.

Five yards away, near the door of the Nomad, Tatiana was whispering against Alexander's chest. "Darling, I'm sorry, I can't stop crying."

He stood stiffly, his arms around her.

"So it's okay? It went okay?"

"It went okay."

She immediately heard it, caught it, looked up at him, through her wet eyes. "What?" she said, wiping her face. "What happened?"

"Nothing. I'll tell you later."

Finally he let her disengage from him and Anthony jumped to his dad. Sam said he had to be going. His own wife was going to kill him for coming home this late. Despite feeling completely wiped out, a grateful Alexander didn't want to let Sam go, asking him to stay, perhaps have dinner together.

"Yes," Tatiana said, more composed. "Please stay, Sam. I'll make something quick."

"Last thing you need is me around here," said Sam. "You rest up. Tomorrow, I'll take the three of you out to lunch. We have to go to the Pentagon anyway. Tania, tomorrow you're going to meet your husband's new boss and his new lawyer. I think I'll call your friend Vikki, see if she wants to take the train and come down and join us."

"No, no! Not Vikki," said Anthony, reaching for his mother.

"My husband has a boss *and* a lawyer?" said Tatiana, reaching for Alexander, taking the boy.

They stood in the dusty bowl of a yard by the gas station, and Sam told her about the hearing. Alexander, his powers of speech draining away, said nothing.

"Thank you, Sam," Tatiana said. "Once again—you have been very good to me."

Patting her gently, Sam said with affectionate reproach, "Your husband did all the work. Thank him. *You* nearly lost me my job, missy. All because you wouldn't trust me. You knew I'd help you if I could."

"I'm sorry," she whispered. "I was so afraid." She didn't look at Alexander as she spoke.

She fussed and murmured over him after Sam left. He was shattered and in no condition to drive at night searching for a campsite. They were right by the side of the road and there was nowhere to pitch a tent, to have a little privacy, but they reluctantly stayed. She warmed up some water on their little Primus stove for him to wash with, fed him canned Spam, some bread, cucumbers, a beer. Anthony fell asleep on the floor of the camper.

After she put Ant in his bed, Tatiana went outside and stood in front of Alexander. He couldn't look at her. "Tania, I simply can't speak any more. I'll tell you everything tomorrow."

"No, darling, tell me tonight."

There was a long nicotine-stained silence. Then Alexander told Tatiana about Dennis Burck.

Tatiana, sitting on his lap, held him to her, tried to calm his frantic heart, but now she was the one who was shaking, having taken some of the frenzy he had been feeling onto herself. "Husband," she said, "it's not true."

He instantly became defensive. He pushed her away and raised his voice. "How do *you* know?"

"Alexander, you don't want to believe your mother survived eleven years in the worst prison the Soviets have built."

"It's not the worst prison," he said by way of expiation. "It's not bitterly cold there. Don't you remember? It's near Lazarevo." His voice broke.

"Shura!" She grabbed him, brought him to her off the chair, her arms went around his shaking back. "It's not true! She's not there. She is not in their prison." Her eyes were blazing. "Don't you see why Burck is telling you this? So you will go back with him. As soon as you enter their territory, with their Soviet-permitted convoy, *you*'ll be taken to Perm-35. The convoy is for you. It's a ruse, it's fraud, it's lies. It's *meant* to enslave you."

"Yes," he said, feeling enslaved. "I know it doesn't *seem* like it's true. But, Tania . . . what if it is?"

"Darling," she whispered, her begging eyes on him, "it's not true."

"It's my mother!"

"It's not true!"

In the camper next to a sleeping Anthony in their only bed, lying on his back, Alexander said quietly to her, "Maybe you're right— Burck is not to be trusted. But don't you think there is a *chance* that he could be telling the truth?"

"No."

She was so sure. How could she be so sure?

"Four people told you she had died. One of them was Slonko. Don't you think when monstrous Slonko was alone with you in your jail cell that he, to get you to admit you were Alexander Barrington, would have told you your mother was alive? 'Tell me you're the American we've been looking for, and I will personally let you see your mother?' Wouldn't he have said that?"

"It could've been bluster." Alexander put his arm over his face.

Tatiana took it away, putting her face over his, climbing on top of him.

"A man is talking to another man about his mother! Tell us who you are, Major Belov, and we will let your mother live. That's bluster?"

"Yes." He couldn't help himself; he pushed her off him. She climbed right back.

"Burck wants you to acknowledge that what he's saying *might* be true. He wants you to say it's possible, and then he will immediately know you by your words. That for the silence of your own heart you will sell out everything you believe. And return to the Soviet Union with them. Don't you remember Germanovsky in Sachsenhausen? Please. You don't want to give them this, we're done with them."

"Are we?"

"Aren't we?" she said ever so faintly.

He wanted to turn his face from her, but she wouldn't let him. They stared at each other in the dark.

Alexander spoke in a depleted voice. "If I went back, how could I help her?"

"You couldn't. You would be dead. But you should comfort yourself with knowing he told you lies."

"I have *no* fucking comfort. And you don't know everything. You don't. You wouldn't be so cavalier if it were your mother."

"I'm not cavalier," Tatiana said. "Don't hurt me. I'm never cavalier."

His eyes stinging, Alexander wanted to apologize but couldn't.

Tatiana whispered, "In my family I was closest to Pasha, not my mother. And I'll tell you this—if Burck told me Pasha was still alive and was with the enemy in the Polish woods, I would have left him to God. I would not have sent *you* to go find him."

"That's a good thing, because as you know, I fucked it up."

"You didn't, darling," Tatiana whispered. "You did all you could to rage against fate. Like I did to try to save Matthew Sayers. But every once in a blue while," she continued, her voice barely an aching breath, "what we do, unfortunately, is just not enough."

They fell quiet; struggling, stuporous but not quite asleep.

His mother, Gina Borghese, was seventeen when she left Italy to come to America to find a life fit for a modern, progressive young woman. She met Harold Barrington, as American as the Pilgrims; they fell in love—that fine-looking Italian and that fast-talking radical—fell in love, so unprogressive; they married, even worse. She changed her name, became Jane Barrington. They changed. She put away her abiding Catholicism. They became Communists. It felt so right. She was thirty-five when she finally had Alexander, her desperately wanted baby; it seemed less right to want something personal so badly. She was forty-six when they left for the Soviet Union. She was fifty-two when she was arrested. Now she would have been sixty-four. Could she live out twelve years in Perm-35, a feminist, a Communist, an alcoholic, a wife, Alexander's mother? He had seen his father in his dreams. He had seen Tatiana. He had never seen his mother, not even as a ghostly breath on someone else's voice to whisper to him, *She is gone your mother. She is never coming back.* He thought she was buried so deep in the recesses of his heart, and yet it took a shabby little man like Burck one word to uncover Alexander's mother from her shallow grave.

Deep in the night Tatiana suddenly said, "You're breathing so raw, Alexander. Don't torture yourself. Can't you see past the lies?"

"I can't," Alexander whispered, nearly breaking down. "Because I want it desperately to be true."

"No, you don't. Oh, Shura . . ."

"You should understand that better than anyone," he said. "You who left our only child to go and find *me* when you thought I might be alive, because you wanted it desperately to be true. You didn't leave *me* in the German woods."

Her eyes were glistening. "It actually *was* true. You sent me word."

"Oh come on. Orbeli? You told me what you thought of my Orbeli."

Her hands gripped his shoulders. "You said Orbeli, but the word was *faith*. I went because I believed. But this isn't even your mother's *one* vague word. This is the lying word of a lackey who's betraying his country."

He held her in desperation. "I just can't see the truth of anything anymore."

"Sometimes I can't either." She looked into his face in the blue of night. "You and your lying face and your damn Orbeli," she whispered.

Alexander moved her off him, lay her down, was over her, was pressed into her, crushing her. Anthony was right there, he didn't care, he was trying to inhale her, trying to absorb her into himself. "All this time you were stepping out in front of me, Tatiana," he said. "Now I finally understand. You hid me on Bethel Island for eight months. For two years you hid me and deceived me—to *save* me. I'm *such* an idiot," he whispered. "Wretch or not, ravaged or not, in a carapace or not, there you still were, stepping out for me, showing the mute mangled stranger *your* brave and indifferent face."

Her eyes closed, her arms tightened around his neck. "That stranger is my life," she whispered. They crawled away from Anthony, from their only bed, onto a blanket on the floor, barricading themselves behind the table and chairs. "You left our boy to go find me, and this is what you found . . ." Alexander whispered, on top of her, pushing inside her, searching for peace.

Crying out underneath him, Tatiana clutched his shoulders.

"This is what you brought back from Sachsenhausen." His movement was tense, deep, needful. *Oh God. Now there was comfort.* "You thought you were bringing back *him*, but, Tania, you brought back *me*."

"*Shura* . . . you'll have to do . . ." Her fingers were clamped into his scars.

"In you," said Alexander, lowering his lips to her parted mouth and cleaving their flesh, "are the answers to all things."

All the rivers flowed into the sea and still the sea was not full.

Alexander didn't get in touch with Burck. The next day they met with Tom Richter, who could not hide his astonishment when he shook the delicate hand of Alexander's ox-pulling wife, his slight, slim, unassuming, soft and smiling wife.

"I told you," Sam said quietly to Richter. "Not what you expected."

"It's not possible! She looks like she'd be scared of a mouse! And look at her—she's the size of a peanut!"

"Gentlemen," said Alexander, coming from behind them and putting his hands over their shoulders, "are you *whispering* about my wife?"

The size of a peanut she might have been and certainly scared of mice, but the promise Tatiana extracted from Tom Richter was the size of the Giza Pyramid—her husband could join the reserves to go to a quiet army base and translate classified documents in a room; military intelligence behind secure closed doors was fine with her, combat support, if necessary, in the form of intel analysis, perhaps a little training and exercise, but not under any circumstances, for any reason, in any universe could he be pulled up to active duty. She said the wounds he and she received in his ten years at war rendered *her* incapable of *his* active combat.

Richter agreed and Alexander spent a month being interviewed and probed and classified and tested and trained at Fort Meade, Maryland, while waiting for the final reserve paperwork to go through. Finally he got a security clearance card and a commission as a captain in the U.S. Army Officer Reserve Corps. Richter even managed to get a sparkly replica of a Congressional Medal for Anthony to whom he had taken a real shine—and even more of a shine to a fantastically flirty though engaged-to-someone-else Vikki who had come to see her Tania and her boyzie-boy.

They had long dinners with Sam and Matt Levine and their wives, went sailing on the Chesapeake with Richter and Vikki. Whittaker Chambers and Alger Hiss was all anyone talked about. And Dennis Burck quietly and without a trace left the Federal Government.

After two months with Richter, Tatiana and Alexander went on their way—to Wisconsin, South Dakota, Montana, to the woods in Oregon—through the land of lupine and lotus, to find their way.

First Interlude

Saika Kantorova, 1938

We children live in a frightening time for Russia.

Alexander Blok

Pasha

Pasha Metanov always cleaned his own fish, even when he was a little boy. He didn't ask Babushka to clean it, nor even Mama, who would've cleaned his fish, his teeth, his feet and his britches for the rest of his life if he let her—because Pasha was Mama's only son. He didn't ask Tania to clean it because he knew she wouldn't—and didn't know how. When he was five he asked Deda to show him how to clean the fish, and from then on, he took care of his own dirty work.

The evening after meeting Saika they were having fish soup made out of Pasha's bass, just the three of them. Pasha caught it and cleaned it and Dasha cooked it. Tania, who neither caught nor cleaned nor cooked, read.

The three siblings were by themselves. Deda, their grandfather, had gone fishing alone while it was still light, and Babushka, their grandmother, was visiting Berta and her mother, Blanca, down the street. "So what do we think? Do we like our new neighbors?" Dasha asked. "Stefan is such a nice boy."

"He could have no teeth, Dasha, and you'd think he was a nice boy," said Pasha. "Saika, now *that's* a nice girl." He smiled.

Tatiana said nothing. She was picking the bones out of the fish.

"Oh, no," said Pasha. "Oh no, oh no, oh no. Dasha, she's already quiet. What is *wrong* with her? What is wrong with you?" he boomed. "You don't like them?"

Tatiana's mind on this windy June evening was full of the Catholic Queen Margot sacrificing her life to an arranged marriage to the Protestant Henry Navarre to unite the French Catholics and the French Protestants, believing she would never in her life find true love in the prison in which she lived. But Tatiana knew she would—and how. She wanted to get back to Margot and La Môle.

Her brother and sister stopped eating and stared at her.

"Did I say anything? I said nothing."

"Your silence is screaming to us," said Pasha.

"And *now* she says nothing," Dasha said. "Before you couldn't shut up with your stupid questions."

"Oh, leave her alone, Dash. She's just jealous." Pasha grinned, banging Tatiana on the head with a wooden spoon.

The spoon flew out of his hands, hit by Tatiana's quick, no-nonsense fist. "Pasha, if I was jealous of every girl you said hello to, I'd be green all day long."

With a flare to her dancing brown eyes, Dasha said, "So what was with the inquisition earlier?"

"Just wanted to know where the Pavlovs went, that's all," said Tatiana.

"What do *you* care?"

"I wanted to know. What if I end up where they're at?"

"I saw a large portrait of a blue peacock in their house!" exclaimed Pasha. "It struck me kind of funny."

Tatiana jumped on top of the dining table and sat down on it cross-legged. Dasha yelled at her to get off. Tatiana didn't move. "Exactly, Pasha!" she said. "They haven't unpacked, they haven't taken down Pavlovs' things, but they put up a portrait of a *peacock*. Funny indeed. You think maybe they're ornithophiles?"

"Stefan is a little like a peacock." Dasha smiled. "With that *fine* tail to draw me in like a peahen."

"What about Mark, your boss?" Tatiana said casually. "Does he have a fine tail?"

Oh how Pasha laughed. Indignantly red, Dasha pushed Tatiana off the table. "What do you know about anything? Stay out of adults' business. I like it better when you're buried in your silly books."

"I bet you do, Dasha," said Tatiana, hitting a laughing Pasha with the flat of her hand as she went to fetch *Queen Margot*. "I just bet you do."

Who is Saika?

Saika was an arresting girl with dramatic overemphasized features, as if her creating artist drew her too fast with a charcoal pencil and then slapped on some undiluted paint. Her hair and eyes were the color of char and coal tar, her lips were ruby red and her teeth polar white. The cheekbones were high, the chin pointed, the forehead broad, the nose sharp. It all was sort of right, well-shaped, slick, but all of it together had the effect of too much on too small a canvas that you were standing too close to. You couldn't look away, but for some reason you wanted to.

The next morning, Saika was by Tatiana's window. "Hello," she said, sticking her head in with a smile. "I'm unpacked. Want to come out and play?"

Was she serious? Tatiana never got out of bed in the morning.

"Can I climb in?" Saika asked. "I'll help you get dressed."

Tatiana, who slept cool and comfortable in just her under-wear was ready to tell Saika to come on in, but something in the girl's glance stopped her. What was it? Saika's eyes were too black to discern a dilation of the pupil, and her skin was too dark to blush, but there was something in the unblinking of the almond eye and the parting of the large mouth that puzzled Tatiana. "Uh . . . I'll be out in five minutes." Tatiana drew the shabby window curtain. She slept by herself in a tiny alcove near an old unused stove. Her family hung a curtain across the opening so she could pretend it was a bedroom and not a boarded-up kitchen. She didn't care. It was the only time in her life she slept by herself.

When she was dressed and brushed, Tatiana ambled with Saika down the morning village road in the fragrant air. She took Saika to Berta's house. Berta had a cow that needed to be milked. Saika immediately asked why Berta couldn't milk the cow herself.

"Because she is ancient. She is like *fifty*! Also she has arthritis. She can't grasp the udders."

"So why does she have a cow if she can't take care of it? She can sell that cow for fifteen hundred rubles."

Tatiana turned her head to Saika. "Because then she'll have fif-teen hundred rubles and no milk. What would the point be?"

"She can buy the milk."

"The money will be gone in three months. The cow will pro-duce milk for another seven years."

"I'm just saying. Why have a cow if you can't take care of it?"

Berta was very surprised to see Tatiana so early in the morning, throwing up her arthritic hands and exclaiming, "*Bozhe moi!* Who died? Even my mother is still sleeping." She was a small, round, dark-haired woman, with sharp button eyes, "Not fifty, you impossible child," she said, "but sixty-six." Her hands may have been crippled, but she still made Tatiana and Saika tea and eggs, and while the girls ate, her gravel hands sifted through the grains of Tatiana's soft hair. Saika watched it all.

They brought the fresh milk back to Dasha and then went out into the fields, on the outskirts of Luga, across the long grasses. Tatiana said to Saika that she imagined that's what the prairies in America must look like—long grasses on rolling fields out to the horizons.

"Are you dreaming of America, Tania?" Saika said, and Tatiana, flustered, said no, no, not dreaming, just imagining prairies.

Saika told Tatiana she didn't know where she was born (how could she not?) but she spent her last few years in a small town called Saki in northern Azerbaijan in the Caucasus Mountains. Azerbaijan was a tiny republic nestled under Georgia and above Iran. Iran! It might as well have been a prehistoric universe full of ferns and mastodons, that's how remote it was from Tatiana's understanding. "And from there, we came by train to here. After the summer my father's new post will be north in Kolpino."

"New post? What does he do?"

Saika shrugged. "What *do* adults do? He leaves in the morning. He comes home in the evening. My mother asks how his day was. He says it was fine. The next day it starts again. Sometimes he travels." She paused. "Does your father travel?"

"Yes," Tatiana said proudly, as if her father's traveling was a reflection of her personal glory, as if she was just *fantastic* for raising a father who traveled. "He has gone to Poland for a month. He is going to bring me back a dress!"

"Oh, a dress," said Saika, as if she couldn't care less. "We haven't been to Poland, but we've been to a few other places. Georgia. Armenia. Kazakhstan. To Baku on the Caspian Sea."

"My, you've been all over," Tatiana said with a touch of white envy. She didn't want Saika *not* to have traveled. She just wished she had traveled a bit herself. All she'd ever seen was Leningrad and Luga.

They sat on a rock in the field, and Tatiana showed Saika how to eat the sweet meat out of a clover flower. Saika said she had never eaten it before.

"They don't have clover in the Caucasus Mountains?" asked Tatiana, surprised that Saika could have lived without once touching the ubiquitous three-lobed weed.

"We lived on a farm in the mountains, herded sheep. I don't know, maybe there was clover."

"You were shepherds?"

"Of sorts."

There was that vague qualification again. "What does *that* mean?"

Saika smiled. "I don't think we were very good shepherds. We kept herding the sheep into the wolf's mouth." Tatiana turned to get a better look at Saika, who was smiling as she said it. "Just joking. It wasn't sheep, Tania. We actually herded goats." She made a derisive sound. "I don't want to talk about it. I hate goats. Disgusting filthy animals."

Tatiana didn't reply. She never thought much about goats—but she smelled something suddenly that made her slide away from Saika. Embarrassed at her reaction—but there was that odor again!— Tatiana forced herself to sit still as she looked down at Saika's hands, which were oddly unwashed for so early in the morning. Tatiana wanted to ask about the dirt under the nails, and the darkened tint to some of the pores of the skin, the rough brown texture of the ridges and grooves of Saika's fingers, but then glanced further down and noticed too the unwashed feet in the sandals and wondered what Saika could have been doing at seven in the morning to have gotten herself into such a filthy state. Then Saika spoke, and the breath left Saika's mouth and traveled across the summer meadow air to Tatiana's nose and Tatiana realized that the smell that made her move away was Saika's sour breath.

Tatiana got up. Saika walked in front of Tatiana, and as she did so, the whiff of her body got into Tatiana's nose. Saika smelled of mold and ammonia. A baffled Tatiana looked at Saika, whose hands were raised above her head as she stretched. Yet Saika's hair was shiny as if it had just been washed, and her face was not dirty. She wasn't actually unwashed, she just smelled and looked unwashed.

The two girls stood in front of each other. The dark-haired girl wore an indigo dress. The blonde-haired girl wore a pale print dress. Saika was a head taller and her feet were one and a half times larger, and as Tatiana looked closer she noticed that the second and third toes on Saika's feet grew out in a V. She stared inappropriately long and finally pointed. "Huh. I never saw that before. What is that?"

Saika glanced down. "Oh, that. Yeah. I have a fused joint." She shrugged. "My father jokes that I have cloven feet."

"Cloven feet?" Tatiana said faintly. "What does he mean by that?"

"I don't know. You sure do ask a *lot* of questions, girl. Let me ask *you* a question. Can we go play with Pasha?"

Slowly they started walking back to Luga. "Tell me about him. What do you all do for *fun* around here?"

"What do kids do in the summer? Nothing," Tatiana replied. When Saika laughed, Tatiana said, "No, really. *Nothing.* Last week, for example, we spent two days seeing how long a blueberry string we could make. Turned out about ten meters. Other times we fish. We swim, we argue."

"Argue about what?"

"Europe, mainly. Hitler. Germany. I don't know."

"Come on," Saika said. "You must do something else around these parts other than argue about Hitler and swim." She raised her eye brows.

Like what? Tatiana wanted to ask. And what did the raising of the eye brows mean? "No, not really," she said slowly.

"Well, we're going to have to change that, won't we?" said Saika.

Tatiana coughed slightly as they walked to the river to the other kids, attempting to steer the conversation back to how the children fished or berry-picked or idly spent their hazy summers.

How Idle Children Spend their Hazy Summers

Anton Iglenko was Tatiana's best friend and he played great football and constantly begged for Tatiana's small Leningrad-bought supplies of chocolate. Anton had three older brothers, Volodya, Kirill, and Alexei, all of them Pasha's friends and all under direct nonnegotiable orders from Pasha to stay away from Tatiana, all except for Volodya's friend Misha, who didn't leave Tatiana's side and *hated* Anton. There was also Oleg, who never played anything.

The only other girl in their group was Natasha with long brown hair, a bookworm even worse than Tatiana, always trying to engage Tatiana in one conversation or another about who was a better writer, Dumas or Dickens, Gogol or Gorky. Cousin Marina, who was not a reader, was coming in two weeks and would inflate the girl numbers and equalize the games.

Tatiana stood politely to the side while the new raven-haired girl held court among the eager-for-a-new-face throng, who had all known each other since birth.

"Who is the boy sitting under the tree?" Saika whispered, pointing. "He hasn't come over to say hello to me."

Tatiana glanced over. "That's Oleg," she said. "I told you about him. He is not in a playing mood."

"When will he be in a playing mood?"

"When Hitler is dead," Tatiana replied lightly. "He is a bit over-wrought about—well, you want to see? I'll show you. Oleg!" She called to the skinny brown boy nestled under the birches.

Reluctantly, as if it were a great effort, Oleg stood up and walked over. He nodded to Saika, he did not shake hands, and when Tatiana, poking him in the ribs, asked if he wanted to play hide and seek, he said, "Oh, great, yes, go ahead, play your little games. Czechoslovakia is about to fall, but you go ahead and play," and went back under the trees.

Tatiana stared at Saika with a *you see?* "Oleg," she explained, as they followed him to his hiding spot, "is distraught not only at the crisis in international relations, but—"

"I'm distraught only at your lack of interest in the outside world," Oleg exclaimed.

"We're very interested," Tatiana said. "We're interested in the fish in the river, and in the blueberries in the woods, and in the potatoes in the fields and in the amount of milk the cow brings us because that will determine whether we can have sour cream next week."

"Go ahead. Make fun. Foreign Minister Masaryk and I only hope that sacrificing his fledgling country will be the *only* price the world pays for peace."

Saika said she found him delightful. Tatiana replied that yes, they all took frequent delight in Oleg, who put up with them for only so long and then spat and ran the other way.

"Not too far, though," Saika said. "Just under the tree."

"He wants to save our immortal souls." Tatiana smiled. "He can't be doing that all the way from his *dacha*."

"Oh, the immortal soul is such a bourgeois concept," said Saika dismissively. "Oleg," she said, "what are you afraid of? There will be no war. No one will go to war for little Czechoslovakia."

"So how big does a country have to be before someone will go to war to defend it from Hitler?" asked Oleg.

Saika laughed. "Bigger than Czechoslovakia."

"No one will go to war for Austria either."

"Why would anyone want to?" Saika said. "The Austrians

wanted the Germans in. Didn't you see the results of the referendum they had two months ago? Ninety-nine percent of all Austrians welcomed Hitler."

"The referendum was rigged," said Oleg.

A shrugging Saika continued, "And now in the Sudetenland elections, the Germans won many votes. Did you hear what Herr Hitler said when he argued for the annexation of Sudetenland? 'It is intolerable,' he said, 'to think of a large portion of our people exposed to the democratic hordes who threaten us.' Herr Hitler also has no patience for democracy, like our Comrade Lenin."

"Czechoslovakia is *not* his people," said Oleg, frowning. "And Herr Hitler, as you reverentially call him, is amassing his troops along the Maginot line. Tell me, after Austria and Czechoslovakia, what's next?"

"France!" Saika happily exclaimed. "Belgium, Holland. Spain will go to Franco soon—he's winning that silly civil war against the factioned communists."

"Now there's a house divided against itself," said Tatiana.

Saika shrugged. "Never heard of that expression," she said, "but sounds right. Spain is Franco's. Italy is already in Germany's pocket. France will be next."

"Do you think England will go to war for *France*?" Oleg asked caustically.

Saika laughed. "Certainly not for France," she said.

"Exactly. France will fall. And then?"

"And then what?" Saika asked with a benign smile.

"Is Hitler going to be facing *west* during his entire expansion?" asked Oleg. "You don't think he'll turn east? To the Soviet Union?"

"Oh, he might turn east," Saika said, crouching near Oleg who moved away from her warily. "But so what?"

"When he mobilizes his troops along the Ukraine and Byelorussia, will you still say, so what?"

"Yes, I will still say so what," said Saika. "He will not step one foot into the Soviet Union. He is afraid of the Red Army. So who cares about what's going on in the rest of the world?"

"I care," said Oleg, glancing at Tatiana. "I care that Mussolini is firing Jews from top government posts. I care that the British are reneging on their promise to the Jews for a national home. I care that Anthony Eden quit over what he perceives as Chamberlain's weakness."

"Chamberlain is not weak," said Saika. "He just doesn't care either—like me. He wants the British boys to stay alive for their mothers. He has seen Verdun—a million young men lost for nothing. He wants no part of another war. Do you? Don't you want to stay alive for your mother, Oleg?"

"Oleg's mother died last year," said Tatiana from behind.

"That explains everything." Saika got up. "Come, Oleg. Take the load off your shoulders. Let's go swim. You think because you worry, the generals will behave differently?"

"I'm not going anywhere," Oleg said. "I cannot engage in pointless fun when the world is in chaos. When the future of the world is at stake."

Tatiana pulled Saika away, and when they were walking back to the bank of the river, she said with an impressed whistle, "How do you know so much?"

Leaning into her, Saika said, "I make it my business, Tania, to know *everything*."

Why did that send a small shiver on a hot day down Tatiana's spine?

The Swim Race to the Swift

The lazy day passed, searching for hornets' nests and playing cat's cradles, with two football games and one fall from a tree. There was a poetry reading from Blok (*"For the last time/old world/we bid you/come."*) and a nap. There was some blueberry eating, there was a war game in the woods, and then it was late afternoon. The boys were arm wrestling, while the girls were braiding each other's hair. The boys were fishing—with homemade sticks instead of fishing lines. Oleg and Saika engaged in another fiery discussion on whether a command economy—such as National Socialism in Germany or Communism in the Soviet Union—could perform as well in times of peace as it could in times of war (Saika thought it definitely could—and would).

And Pasha said, "Tania, let's race."

"Don't want to." Tatiana was sitting cross-legged on the ground, playing a cat's cradle string game with Natasha.

"Does Tatiana even know how to swim?" Saika teased, leaving Oleg alone.

Tatiana didn't want to explain. She had no bathing suit and

didn't want to be swimming in her underwear and vest today in front of Saika—which was ironic, since she never thought twice about swimming in front of Anton or Misha or Oleg.

But Pasha was coaxing her and Saika was coaxing her and Misha, who didn't think she could win today, was coaxing her, and then they were all softly laughing, except Saika who was loudly laughing. And so Tatiana, never one to shy away from one of Pasha's challenges undressed to her underwear and vest. Was she imagining it, or was that a smirk on Saika's face? The afternoon tide filled the air with fresh water and leaning wet white cherry blossoms, and the sun was high and reluctant in the sky.

Tatiana and Pasha climbed down the slope to the bank. The object was to fling yourself wholeheartedly into the river on "THREE!" and then swim fifty meters to the other side.

And then you raced back.

Tatiana saluted him as they stood facing the Luga. "I'll see you on the other side, brother," she said.

He saluted her. "Yes, I'll look back and there you'll be."

"Onetwothree!"

Pasha, oh Pasha, small, strong, swift, laughably competitive, trying to trip his smaller, weaker sister. She wasn't as strong, not as a runner, not as a swimmer. Her legs were not as muscular. Tatiana had slender girl thighs; she was a tiny lean foal.

They ran in—leaped in—with joy, and then swam as fast as they could, front stroke, breast stroke, frog stroke, doggy-paddle stroke. The current in the afternoon moved swiftly, the river was almost on full, the flow was strong.

Pasha was winning at the twenty-meter mark, but the relentless Tatiana, a few meters behind him, called out, "Don't forget to breathe, Pasha."

"Don't forget to lose, Tania," he called back, gaining half a meter on her. But at the thirty-meter mark, his lead began to slip. Tatiana didn't even increase her tempo. Trying not to swallow water, she kept moving. Pasha was slowing down; his kicking, splashing legs were near Tatiana's head—on purpose, she knew. At the forty-five-meter mark, taking a deep breath, she propelled herself forward past him, touched bottom, and ran out, jumping up and down jubilantly, dripping, panting and breathless, her wet hair clinging to her delighted face.

Pasha was less jubilant. "I cannot tell you how annoying you are," he said calmly, shaking himself off.

"Says the vanquished." Tatiana jumped on him, and they fell into the water, and a laughing Pasha said, "Get away from me. I can't breathe."

She got off him. "Race back?"

"Forget it."

"Next time, Pasha."

"That's right. Next time, Tania."

They swam slowly back across, on their backs, just their legs kicking. Tatiana was looking up at the cloudless sky and the distant pale June sun. Reaching out, she took hold of Pasha's hand.

"What?"

"Nothing." She moved to let go. He didn't let go.

Their friends were gathered in a cluster on the pebbly needly banks. Saika said, "All right, Tania. Now I'll race you."

"Yeah, Tania," said Oleg. "Go ahead. Girls' war. Sort of like Belgium against France. Even I want to see. Natasha here never races."

"I'm a reader, not a racer," said Natasha proudly, clutching her Gogol (*Dead Souls*). "Besides, the girls can't win against Tania."

"We'll see about that." Without a word, Saika threw off her dress. And then her bra. And then her underwear. And then she was naked.

The children for a moment stopped playing. Even Natasha looked up from Councilor Chichikov's exploits with the souls of the deceased village peasants. Tatiana quickly averted her eyes but not before she noted Saika's well-developed body, the sloping breasts, the dark nipples, the prominent mound of thick black hair, the widening hips. She had hair under her arms, and Tatiana just began to think that Saika at fifteen looked as advanced as Dasha at twenty-one when Saika turned around to walk to the river, and the boys and girls inhaled in a collective gasp.

Saika's back was ruined with raised thick coiled white scars, crisscrossing her back like ropes from her shoulder blades into the small of her spine.

Tatiana's quickened breath must have given her away. Saika stopped walking and turned around. "What?"

It was Pasha who broke the shocked and nervous silence. "What happened to your back, Saika?"

"What? Oh, that? Nothing."

"Must have gone and done something pretty bad," said Oleg.

"I must have. Tania, are you just going to stand there gaping or are you going to race?"

Tatiana gave her brother a troubled look before going down to the waterline. She no longer thought about her vest or her smallness. Racing suddenly seemed offensive. "Saika, maybe we should do this another day."

"Why? Another day my back will be just as scarred." There was no emotion in her voice.

Tatiana looked back at Pasha, Anton, Oleg, Natasha, Misha, Kirill, Volodya. No one knew what to feel. They were embarrassed and uncomfortable. Tatiana frowned.

"If you're not up to it . . ." Saika drew out.

"No, no, I'm always up to it," Tatiana said. "On three then?"

"On three."

But it wasn't quite on three. It was more on two and a half. Before Tatiana could utter the word "three" Saika ran into the water, all shaking flesh and hair.

Tatiana sprinted and dived in head first, literally flying past Saika, who stopped instantly and said, "Wait, that's not fair."

Tatiana stopped reluctantly.

"I didn't know you could leap in like that."

"I didn't know *on* three meant right *before* three," Tatiana rejoined, swimming back. "You didn't hear me complaining."

"Well, you should've complained if you didn't like it."

"It didn't matter."

"It's not fair," Saika repeated, rubbing her wet breasts.

"All right," said Tatiana. "Let's do it again."

They did it again. This time *almost* on three, and this time, Tatiana didn't long-jump in.

Saika was strong and she was fast. But she was also heavier than Tatiana, and that body must have weighed her down, because Tatiana had to slow down at the twenty-meter mark, and again at the thirty-meter mark, and by the time they were at forty meters, Tatiana was swimming so slowly that she thought she could float on her back faster than Saika was swimming, spluttering in the water, out of breath, panting, wheezing. Tatiana stopped using her arms. Then she started dog-paddling but stopped using her legs. Her breathing was three beats above normal. Finally she let Saika stagger out of the water first and collapse on the shore. "That was hard won," Saika panted. "But a good race."

Still in the water, Tatiana bent backwards and dunked her head to slick back her hair and then came out and sat next to Saika.

Saika said, "You did really well for such a small thing." She couldn't get her breath.

"Thank you," Tatiana said quietly.

"When you're ready we'll swim back."

"How's now then?"

"Let's wait a second." Saika was still panting.

It took them a long time to make it back. Saika could barely move her legs and kept floating downriver in the current.

"Saika, if you're not careful, you'll end up in the Baltic Sea," Tatiana said. "Look how far we've gotten away from the others. Let's swim a little harder."

Saika couldn't swim a little harder.

The first thing Pasha said when they finally stepped on the bank was, "Tania, what happened to you in that race? You looked like you died out there."

Saika swirled to look at Tatiana for one dark and icy blink. The unholy expression fast passed from Saika's face but not from Tatiana's memory.

"Put on your clothes, Saika," Tatiana said, turning away. "I have to go home."

Something about Tatiana

Walking back home from the river, wet, hungry and tired, they passed a flock of old women in long robes, Bibles in their hands. The women's faces lit up at Tatiana, who smiled, sighed slightly and hid behind Pasha.

"What's wrong?" asked Saika, but before she could say anything else, the old women were upon them. They extricated Tatiana from Pasha, their crinkled hands all over her, stroking her hair, putting the sign of the cross on her forehead, kissing her hands.

"Tanechka," they cooed, "how is our darling this evening?"

"Your darling is fine," answered Pasha for Tatiana, yanking her away.

Tatiana introduced Saika. The women nodded but did not shake hands with the girl, nor did Saika offer her own hand. They stood awkwardly, Tatiana still in their midst, in their fold, in their skirts.

Pasha explained to Saika that these women had baptized him and Tania in 1924.

"Baptism is so provincial, ladies," said Saika to the women. "Our new laws of 1929 clearly state—no religious instruction of young children until they are of age. Do you *still* go around baptizing children who cannot choose for themselves?" Everyone fell quiet. "Do you?" she repeated, undaunted by their silence.

"Well, no, not anymore," replied one of the women.

After an unsuitable silence, Tatiana spoke. "Are you baptized, Saika?"

"No, I do not belong to the cult of Christ," Saika replied. "My ancestors used to be something called the Yezidi. We did not baptize."

The women's mouths opened. "Not the *Yezidi*!"

"Ah, informed village women," said Saika. "Well, well. Yes, but I'm not really part of that anymore, ladies. Now I'm a Pioneer."

"Are you in a League of Militant Atheists?" Pasha smiled. "Or are you a member of the Group of Godless Youth?"

"No, but when I turn eighteen I will become a Comsomol—a vigorous, modern, free-thinking member of the new world."

Immensely curious, Tatiana pulled herself away, calling for Saika, who stared down the old women before she caught up to the Metanovs, kicking up the dirt road with her worn brown sandals as they walked in silence. "What is it, Tania?" Saika asked. "Why are the old so enamored with you? That Berta this morning couldn't keep her hands off you, why?"

"Tell her, Tania."

"Pasha, shut up."

"All the old people in Luga think Tania can save them from death."

"Pasha, shut *up*!"

Pasha was, as always, undeterred. "Saika, seven years ago, there was a fire in one of the village huts. Blanca Davidovna, the oldest person in the village, was alone in it. Her daughter Berta, whom you saw this morning pawing Tania, was in Leningrad. And our Tania ran into that house and got Blanca out, while the hut burned to the ground. Of course when our mother found out, she nearly killed Tania for going in there." Pasha laughed. "That would've been ironic, wouldn't it, Tanechka?" Pasha leaned in to his sister and tickled her damp neck.

"Pasha, will you please stop it," Tatiana said in a stern voice.

"How did you get her out, Tania?" asked Saika.

"I don't know. I don't remember. I was barely seven."

"But why did you go in there in the first place?"

"I don't know. I don't remember. I was barely seven. I thought I heard her calling."

"Yes—from the other side of the village!" Pasha laughed. "You should hear Blanca Davidovna tell that story." Pasha's eyes went all aglow as he mimicked the older woman. "Oh, our Taaaaanechka, she just took my *hand* and led me—*led* me, I tell you, *out* of my burning house! If you think those old women were bad, wait till you see Blanca with Tania."

"Pasha, I swear, if you don't stop it . . ."

Telling Saika about the incident filled Tatiana with uncharacteristic anxiety. The mystery of the fire, of her seven-year-old self running into that house, had been bizarre even to her, considering how easily frightened she was of all kinds of uncontrollable things. She didn't like to talk about it, she didn't like to think about it, and she certainly didn't like the way Saika kept staring at her. Tatiana firmly felt that she didn't want Saika knowing things about her that Tatiana couldn't understand or explain, even to herself.

Something About Saika

That evening in the hammock in their small weed-covered yard, Saika played the lute for them. It made Pasha speechless. Saika was a girl of many talents, Tatiana was realizing. Saika held the three-string *panduri*, and played it as if she were born to it. She played them national Georgian tunes they'd never heard of, many Azeri melodies, and then some Soviet war marches.

"Very fine, Saika," said Pasha with a whistle. "Very fine indeed."

Saika laughed coquettishly. Tatiana glanced at Pasha. Could her brother still be besotted with a malodorous girl who couldn't swim and had such marks on her back? No, she decided. He didn't look particularly besotted anymore.

"You do play nicely, Saika," Tatiana said.

"And when I play, I get into people's hearts," Saika said. "I made quite a bit of pocket money playing my lute in Saki."

Tatiana was swinging her feet and listening to the crickets when Saika, also swinging in the hammock, said, "My mother is a fortune teller, you know."

"A what?"

"You know, a lady who tells the future. You don't have them here in Luga? I thought every village had them. I thought it was a requirement."

Pasha and Tatiana said nothing. Blanca Davidovna, deeply religious and fully believing she was sinning, still occasionally looked at the palms and the tea leaves. Did that count?

Saika jumped up from the hammock. "Come to my house right now," she said. "My mother is the best. She'll tell you your future."

Tatiana shook her head. "It's getting late, Saika," she said. "Maybe another time."

"No. Come now. What are you, afraid? Pasha, you gonna let your sister cow you down?"

A curious Pasha could never resist a challenge, and he dragged Tatiana with him. Pasha was *very* curious. Leaning into him, Tatiana whispered, "If only you knew how to read, you would right now recall the story of Bluebeard. Idle curiosity, my dear Pasha, often leads to deep regret."

"Yes, well, when I'm a silly woman, I'll worry about it," he whispered back.

"Pasha, don't you smell her?"

"What are you talking about?"

"She smells so *sour*. Every time you go near her, you don't want to hold your nose?"

"Tania, you've gone mad. Really, you have. She smells fine. Be quiet."

Inside Saika's house, the mother, Shavtala, was nowhere to be found. The doors to the bedrooms were closed. The children perched on the sofa in the dark living room that smelled heavily of smoke, and waited. "She'll be out any minute," said Saika. "I see you're looking at our books, Tania. What kind of books do you like?"

"All kinds." The Kantorovs had odd things up on their shelves. Tatiana couldn't take her eyes off the picture of large blue peacock over the mantel.

"You don't like the books we have, Tania?" Saika shrugged. "Well, your Dickens, your Dumas do not write about anything I'm interested in. I like Gorky. I like Mayakovsky. I like Blok."

"Yes, I see," said Tatiana, reluctantly drawing her gaze away from the vivid bird. "Gorky is dead. Mayakovsky dead. Blok dead. What about Osip Mandelstam? You like him? He's the best we've got, and he's not dead—yet."

"Who?"

Through one open casement window, Tatiana heard the click of the crickets, the rustling of the leaves—and then through the air, above the crickets and over the leaves . . . came a wailing howl.

She looked at Pasha.

Saika said quickly, "Tell me about Mandelstam."

Tatiana lowered her voice. "Where is Mandelstam? The official word is that he has pneumonia and is on his deathbed. But my Deda says very soon they will say he killed himself after poetic torments." Tatiana said the word Deda reverentially.

Saika's eyes flared. "Your grandfather says that, does he? And who is *they*?"

The howls continued.

Tatiana was puzzled by them. "Saika . . . ?" she said.

"Tania, shh." That was Pasha.

"I thought your grandfather was a math teacher," said Saika, "not a rumormonger."

The piercing sounds were making it difficult for Tatiana to carry on a normal conversation. "Oh, dear!" she finally exclaimed. "What *is* that? Is that coming from *this* house?"

Pasha stared down at the unswept wood floor.

"I don't know," Saika said calmly. "Look, it's stopped now. But tell me—what does your grandfather know about the traitor Mandelstam?"

"Who said he was a traitor?" Tatiana lowered her voice. "All that gorgeous poetry he wrote around the time of the revolution and then later in exile—gone, excised! And he is excised, too. As if he never existed." Almost in a whisper herself, Tatiana said, *"Perhaps my whisper/ was already born/ before my lips."*

"That's how enemies of the state are treated," said Saika. "Excised as if they never existed. Not even a *whisper* left. Nothing left."

"The poet Mandelstam is an enemy of the state?" Tatiana said with surprise.

"Of course," said Saika. "He is a man who believes in the self more than he believes in the State. The self is dead! The Writers' Union expressly told him, told everyone, Socialist Realism only. No personal poetry. He went directly against all precepts and laws set forth in the doctrine. For that he became an enemy of the State."

It was Tatiana's turn to be silent. "Saika, I thought you didn't know who Mandelstam was."

Saika said carelessly, "Oh, I know *something* about him."

"Yes," Tatiana said, "for a goat herder's daughter, for someone who lived in the mountains, who did not read books or newspapers, you sure do know a lot about . . . a lot of things." In Tatiana's tone was a flickering sparrow of darkening confusion, but in Saika's tone as she answered was a swollen puff of peacock pride.

"I told you, Tania. I make it my business to know everything. Which is why I want Mama to read your fortune."

Loud high-pitched inhuman cries resumed suddenly.

Pasha jumped up. "You know what? We have to go."

"No, no, stay," said Saika. "She'll be out in a minute."

"No. Come on, Tania." He grabbed her hand, pulling her up.

"Saika, what *is* that sound?" said Tatiana. "Those beastly cries will wake the dead! Please tell me that's not your *mother*."

"Tania, let's go!"

"Pasha is right, Tania," said Saika, sitting quietly on the couch. "You really should run along."

Pasha yanked on Tatiana's arm. But she was concerned, worried. She stared at the closed doors, at the open windows. "No . . . it's . . . out there . . . it sounds like . . . caterwauling."

"Must be cats then," said Saika. "Or coyotes."

"*Coyotes* . . ." Tatiana repeated. "Carnivorous canines? In Luga?" She turned to her brother. "Do we have wolves in Luga, Pasha?"

"I don't *know*, Tania." Pasha was headed outside, dragging Tatiana behind him. "You with your questions. Will you *ever* stop?"

"Another time then," Saika called after them. "My mother will read your fortune another time."

They were out in the night air. It was no better outside. The shrieks *were* coming from the Kantorov house, and they were knife-like. Across the weedy yards, over the broken fence and the overgrown grass, in their little summer *dacha*, Dasha and Babushka were peering outside, muttering obscenities and slamming shut all the crusty windows. When Tatiana and Pasha came inside their house, small and compact Deda, still like smooth and clear glass, was sitting calmly, his magnificent head of salt-and-pepper hair focused over his tangled fishing lines. He sat in his chair on the screened porch almost as if he were deaf.

Babushka was not deaf. Larger than him, gray and imperious, after slamming the windows and muttering, "Indecent! Simply indecent!" over and over, she ran out of words. She put on the little radio, turned the sound up high. They caught only static.

No one knew what to say. Except for Deda who was busy with his lines, everyone kept casting nervous glances toward Tatiana.

Babushka said, "Do we have any mountain ash? Some superstitions believe that the rowan tree or mountain ash drives away evil spirits."

"Anna!" That was Deda atypically raising his voice to Babushka. "Have you got nothing, *nothing* else to do? Mountain ash?"

Tatiana laughed.

Late that night, after Babushka and Deda were long in bed, Dasha, Pasha, and Tatiana were sitting on the small porch around the kerosene lamp talking about Saika and her scars. "She got completely *naked* in front of all of you?" Dasha said incredulously. "Tomorrow I will tell her not to do that again. Or I swear, I will tell her mother."

Pasha coughed. Dasha coughed.

Tatiana smiled. "Her mother, the, um, loud fortune teller?" she said.

Oh, such coughing from her brother and sister!

"Come on, Tania, aren't you a little interested?" said Pasha, shifting the subject slightly. "A real fortune teller! I mean, that's exciting, no? Someone who sees through unfathomable things to the future, to the path of your life? We've never met anyone like that. Blanca Davidovna and her tea leaves don't count. Aren't you curious?"

"No," Tatiana replied. "Not in the slightest." She was sitting on the floor between Dasha's legs, watching Pasha shuffle cards, while Dasha was braiding her hair, splitting it, kneading it, caressing her head, tying up the white-gold down feathers with satin ribbons. As her hands moved across Tatiana's head, Tatiana closed her eyes, feeling sleepy in the late night with her brother and sister.

"Why not?" said Pasha.

"Yeah, Tania," said Dasha. "Even I'm interested in hearing what she has to say."

A relaxed and murmuring Tatiana said, "*Beware* of false prophets, who come to you in sheep's clothing, for inwardly they are ravening wolves . . ." Amused at her own joke, at her reference to wolves, at her funny family, Tatiana laughed.

Pasha and Dasha didn't laugh. "Who says she is a false prophet?" said Dasha. "Where did you hear that?"

"Blanca Davidovna."

"Um, but, do you have any questions, Tania?" Pasha said with another one of his peculiar coughs, like he had a fish bone stuck in his throat. "For me . . . or, say, for Dasha?"

"Well, if you two clever-clogs have the answers," Tatiana said, blinking at him with amused affection, "why are you running to the loud fortune teller?"

A Fateful Visit

Mama came for the weekend on Friday night from Leningrad. But Mama did not come alone. Mama brought Mark with her. Mark! Dasha's dentist boss.

When Tatiana saw them through her window coming down the dusty road, she jumped from her bed and ran to the porch on the other side of the house, where she shook her sister, who was reading a newspaper, and hissed, "Mama brought Mark, Dasha. *Mark*!" What a mire. And by Dasha's horrified face, it looked as if Tatiana didn't know the half of it. And perhaps she didn't, but she did know that in the last week, after all the chores and the housework and the dinner and the cleaning were done, Dasha fixed herself up, put on nice clothes, and disappeared for long walks in the woods with Stefan.

Mark came in, still in his suit, a balding man in his thirties. There was awkward confusion. Dasha fussed, bleated, giggled— and finally offered him a cup of tea. Babushka offered him something stiffer. Deda, as always, said nothing.

They had dinner. The conversation was stilted and broken. Dasha and Mark made small talk about the weather, and Leningrad, and white nights, and work. Deda and Mark made small talk about Hitler and Italy and Abyssinia and Spain. Tania stayed quiet. An exhausted Mama sat near Pasha and asked quiet questions only of him. How was he feeling? How was he sleeping? How was he fishing? How was Tatiana behaving?

At ten in the evening, when it seemed much too late for social visits, Tatiana heard a knock on the porch door. Deda sent Tania. Stefan and Saika stood outside.

Dasha nearly groaned out loud.

Tatiana stood quietly in front of them and said nothing. Finally it was Babushka who came forward and said, "Tatiana Georgievna!

What in the world is wrong with you? Tell your friends to come in. Come in, please. Come in."

Tatiana sighed, going to sit next to Dasha, who had moved a little away from Mark. Dasha struggled to her feet as Saika and Stefan came in.

Poor Dasha looked so flummoxed that Deda was forced to intercede with the introductions. And unsmiling Stefan shook hands with a smiling Mark.

For a few minutes Deda sat constitutionally quiet and then said he was going to bed, dragging Babushka with him. "Leave the young ones alone, Anna," he said. "They'll work it all out. They always do."

Tatiana didn't think so. She asked if anyone wanted to play dominoes. Her family usually refused to play dominoes with her, but Mark absent-mindedly played six times. And lost six times. Pasha to make him feel better said he would never win even if he was rapt on his tiles.

The conversation they made was wretched. Mark kept repeating that for him this was a rare weekend off. He was a dentist and Dasha worked for him when it wasn't summer. He must have noticed Stefan's cold stares at Dasha because he clammed up, and then conversation *really* ground down. Not soon enough, Stefan got up and said they had to be going.

That's when Saika handed Dasha her shawl and said, "You left it in our house, Dasha, the other night after you came back from your walk with Stefan."

Tatiana, deeply frowning, looked away. It was a train wreck. What was Saika doing? Tatiana excused herself and disappeared to her room, and in a moment Saika knocked on her window, asking if she wanted to sneak outside. Tatiana did not.

After the light was turned off and she was nearly asleep, she heard voices in the yard. At first she thought it was Saika again, but it was Dasha and Mark, she trying to be quiet, he trying to be loud.

Tatiana didn't want to hear a single word, but since she couldn't shut her window without proclaiming her wakefulness, she put a pillow over her head and started humming. Only when Dasha's voice became louder, did curiosity and sadness for her sister get the better of Tatiana, and she removed the pillow to listen.

"*Why* did I come here?" Mark was saying. "I came here because I wanted to be with you, Dasha. And I *thought* you wanted to be with me."

"This is a dead end between us," said Dasha. "I know you think we're having quite a romance, and I'm certainly not expecting more, I'm not asking you for more. Staying late after work in your office is enough for me in Leningrad. But I didn't realize you felt I owed you even in Luga."

Tatiana started humming. Mark said something.

"That's what you want, right?" Dasha said. "Me to give myself to you for fifteen minutes during our lunch break, or between patients, on the reception sofa before you run home to your wife, while I go home to sleep in bed with my sister? Is there more, Mark? Because I didn't realize there was. I thought that we were pretty much squeezing every drop out of the dry rag that is our relationship."

Hummm . . .

Mark said something. It sounded like, "But I love you."

"Did you love me when I got pregnant last year"—

Oh no! HUMMMMMMMMMMMMMMMMMMM!

—"What did you say to me then? You must have been saying I love you, but what I heard was, Dasha, there's *nothing* we can do. We have nowhere to go. That must have been your I love you. And I knew you were right. Did I complain? Did I ask you to come with me to the clinic? No. I went by myself after work, and stood in line like all the other women, and afterward, another woman, a complete stranger, helped me walk home. The next day, I came into work. You and I went on as before. Oh, and by the way, I love you, too, Mark." Dasha was crying.

Hummm . . .

"I'm resigned to my life," Dasha said. "Resigned to my life at twenty-one." Tatiana couldn't hum loud enough to drown out her sister's breaking voice. "But you know what? I think I prefer five hot minutes in the woods with Stefan to two years on that freezing sofa with you."

"I love you, I do," Mark said faintly. "I came to tell you I'm planning to tell my wife I'm leaving."

"You better do more than figure out how to tell her, Mark," said Dasha. "You better figure out how to leave her."

"I thought we could stay in the office until the council found us a new place."

"In the office? What, on the couch?" Dasha paused. Quietly they said some things Tatiana blessedly couldn't hear. Then Dasha said, "Why can't you just tell her she has to go live somewhere else? Tell her *she* has to leave, not you. Why does *she* get to stay?

It's your apartment. It's registered to you. It's her problem if there's nowhere for her to live."

Mark said something Tatiana couldn't hear, but what she did hear was Dasha's subsequent, "Are you kidding me? Oh my God! Oh my God!"

"She just told me last week," Mark said quickly. "I didn't know. She says it's illegal now anyway to get rid of it."

"Now, *there's* a reason to keep a baby!" yelled Dasha.

"Well, she said she didn't *want* to get rid of it."

"She told you she was going to have a baby and you're standing here under the cherry blossoms with me figuring out a way to leave her?"

Tatiana heard struggling, wrestling, slaps, footsteps, tears, heard Dasha walking away, crying, saying, "You are such a prize, Mark. You are such a fucking prize."

Mark stayed outside smoking. Tatiana heard him even through the pillow over her head, kicking branches, muttering, lighting cigarette after cigarette.

He left to go back to Leningrad the following foggy morning at dawn. No one saw him go except Tatiana who watched his stooped back and his bag in his hand as he shuffled down the road. She watched him until he disappeared from sight and the cows went out to pasture, their bells clanging.

Tatiana could not even read her book, lying on her side, pitying her poor sister.

After going with Dasha to the women's public baths at the *banya* that Saturday night, she and Dasha walked quietly back home, all bathed and clean, and flushed and red. Saika, who had not gone to the baths, asked if Tatiana wanted to come out and play, but Tatiana again refused. At home Dasha made Tatiana a fresh egg yolk and sugar milk shake, and after drinking it, Tatiana lay her head on Dasha's lap on the porch sofa.

"Dashenka, sister, Dasha?"

"Yes?" She sounded so sad.

Tatiana swallowed. "Want to hear a funny story?"

"Oh, yes, please. I need a funny story to cheer me up. Tell me, darling."

"Stalin as Chairman of the Presidium went in front of the Houses of Parliament to make a short speech that lasted maybe five minutes. After the speech there was applause.

"The plenum stood on its feet and applauded. For a minute. Then another minute. Then another minute.

"They stood and applauded. But—

"Another minute. Still applauded. They were standing up, and still applauding, as Stalin stood in front of the lectern and listened with a humble smile on his face, the epitome of humility. Another minute. And still applauded.

"No one knew what to do. They waited for a signal from the Chairman to cease, but no such signal came from the humble and diminutive man. Another minute went by. And still they stood and applauded.

"It had now been eleven minutes. And no one knew what to do. Someone had to stop applauding. But who?

"Twelve minutes of applause.

"Thirteen minutes of applause. And still he stood there. And still they stood there.

"Fourteen minutes.

"Fifteen minutes.

"Finally, at the fifteen-minute mark, the man in the front, the Secretary of Transportation, stopped. As soon as he stopped, the entire auditorium fell mute.

"The following week the Secretary of Transportation was shot for treason."

"Tania!" exclaimed a startled Dasha. "That was supposed to be *funny*?"

"Yes," said Tatiana. "Funny, as in, cheer up, things could be worse. You could be the Secretary of Transportation."

"You are insane!" Dasha moved Tatiana off her and got up to go get a cigarette. "Where in the world do you hear this stuff from?"

"Blanca. Berta. Oleg. Deda. Everyone just loves to tell me things."

"I forbid you to talk to them."

"Who are you, my mother?"

Dasha fell mute as she lit up.

Tatiana patted her arm. "I'm sorry. When *is* Mama leaving, by the way? She punished me again, you know. I can't go out for four days."

"You deserve it, digging holes in the ground for her to fall in."

"Hole wasn't meant for her, was meant for Pasha."

"I didn't see Pasha sticking up for you as Mama was beating you with the stinging nettles."

Tatiana rubbed her sore legs. She didn't know what else to say. "Dasha . . . are you upset?"

"Why should I be upset?" Dasha looked so upset when she said it.

Tatiana didn't reply, studying her sister.

"Stay out of adults' business, Tanechka, all right?" Dasha whispered. "We'll figure it out without you."

Tatiana cleared her throat. "Can I ask you a question?"

"What?"

"Do you think I'm going to start developing soon? Growing . . . things?"

The sadness gone from Dasha's eyes, the twinkle back, Dasha chuckled and said, "Girly-girl, come outside." They went down the steps to the yard. "Come into the hammock," Dasha said, "and climb on me."

Happily Tatiana climbed in and lay in the crook of her sister's arm while Dasha swung them back and forth. "Tanechka," Dasha asked fondly, "what's your hurry?"

"Oh, no, no, you misunderstand," said Tatiana. "Just the opposite. I'm wondering how many decent years I've got left."

"What—"

"Well, yes. Look at the magnificent swamp *you're* in, all because you have boobs and dark hair on your body. I'm just wondering how much longer before the good life is over for me, too."

Dasha hugged her. "Tania," she said, "you are the funniest girl." She laughed. "Who in the world is going to give you dark hair? You'll be lucky to get any hair at all, but it's never going to be dark, is it?"

"I already have a little hair," Tatiana said defiantly. "And you don't know. Mama said that when she was young she had blonde hair—and look at her now."

"Yes, Mama said that. However, I'm skeptical. And Babushka said that when she got married she weighed only *forty-seven* kilo."

"Stop it right now," said Tatiana. The sisters laughed quietly. They lay in the hammock in the dark, swinging and swaying.

"I just want to find some love, Tanechka," Dasha whispered. "Can you hear me? That's all. Some real love."

The dim kerosene light from the porch was flickering out. The crickets were loud, the air was fresh. Tatiana had fallen asleep, unworried, unfettered, untainted, untouched, and young.

Two Girls in the Trees at Night

"Tania, are you sleeping?" It was Saika.

Tania *was* sleeping. Happily in her bed. She groaned. Oh, no, not again.

"Come on. Come outside with me."

When would the girl stop lurking at her window? "What time is it?"

"Late. Come on. They'll never know."

"Are you joking? They check on me every five minutes. Besides I'm punished."

"Why are you asleep so early? I thought you were reading."

Saika wanted her asleep late, awake early. Was Tatiana *ever* going to get any peace? Reluctantly she lifted her head.

"Climb out. We'll go in my yard."

"And do what?"

"Nothing. Talk. I got something."

Tatiana slept in her underwear *and* vest now that Saika knocked at her window every morning and night. She slipped on a dress and climbed out. They crossed the yard, and flitted through the nettles and the broken fence pieces. They climbed a tree. In the tree Tatiana sat on a thick branch above Saika who perched on a lower one. She pulled out two cigarettes and handed one to Tatiana. "I stole these from Mama. Come on, take one."

"You stole from your *mother*?"

Saika laughed. "She doesn't care; it's just cigarettes. It's not her immortal soul as you put it."

"So you do draw the line then." Tatiana did not take the offered cigarettes.

"Oh, come on. Don't be a ninny. Everybody does it."

"What, steal from their mothers?"

"No, smoke." Proudly she lit up and added, "I've been smoking since I was nine."

"That's great." Why was she in the trees? Truth was . . . curiosity about the scars brought Tatiana out. Saika's scars were not just a punishment gone wrong. They were not an overzealous parent disciplining a wayward child. No, Saika was not beaten— she was branded. Her back was her *fleur de lis*. It was her brand of monstrous dishonor; no one who saw those could ever *not* think with a frightened heart of what a young girl could possibly have done to have warranted such a cicatrix of shame.

Night was quiet. The leaves in the trees where they sat smelled of woodsy acorns. From above, Tatiana watched Saika inhale and exhale, ash falling on her thighs. Cigarette smoke, blossoms, fresh water and moist earth, moist grass. Maybe it was things like pinching cigarettes from her mother that got Saika into trouble. Tatiana didn't know. She didn't want to speculate, she wanted to ask outright. She was curious herself, and Pasha had been prodding her for days. "Come on, Tania. She likes you. She's always Tania this and Tania that. She'll tell you anything. You can't just not ask."

Dasha said, "He's right. It's rude not to ask. The worst thing that's happened to a girl, and you don't even ask?"

"Wouldn't she tell me herself if she wanted me to know?" Tatiana had said.

"No! Asking shows you're interested."

Even Babushka said to ask. (Mama didn't care, but Mama, to her credit, didn't care about much.) Only Deda, reading quietly on the couch, stayed out of it until the end when he glanced up and commanded, "Tania, stay out of it. It's not your business."

So Deda decreed. And now Tatiana sat in the tree and tried to forget Deda's words because she *really* wanted to ask. She heard Saika laugh softly. "Do you think I disconcerted your friends the other day? Haven't they ever seen a girl naked? *You* go naked in front of them, don't you, Tania?"

"I'm a child."

"Do you want to stay a child?" Saika whispered.

"*What*?"

Shaking her head, Saika smoked, while Tatiana carefully formulated her questions.

"Well?" Saika said. "What do you want? Do you want to touch them?"

Now, *Tatiana* was disconcerted. "Touch what?" she asked faintly.

"The scars, silly." Saika laughed, pulling down her dress to expose her bare back.

Reaching down, Tatiana gently touched one of the rough-hewn ridges, but when she did, Saika flinched and moved away. Tatiana reached out again to put her palm on Saika's back, to comfort her with her hand, but Saika flinched again, emitted a tiny groan and moved farther away, nearly off the branch, far enough so that no part of Tatiana could touch any part of her.

"What's the matter?" Tatiana said. "I'm not . . . hurting you, am I?"

"No, no," Saika said. "Just . . ." But before she pulled up her dress, she turned around to Tatiana, her breasts rising with her heavy breath. "Do you want to touch them?" she said throatily, and now it was Tatiana's turn to move uncomfortably away.

"No." Tatiana swallowed. "But . . . how did you get those scars, Saika?"

Sighing, Saika pulled up her dress, covered herself. "I did something my father didn't like."

"What?"

"Just . . . I was bad . . ."

"Is that why you came here? Why you left Saki?"

Saika looked at Tatiana with surprise. "You think because of a small personal matter my father would abandon his post?"

"His post as a *goat-herder*?" Tatiana rejoined with equal surprise.

Her eyes dark, Saika said, "Our leaving had nothing to do with this. This didn't happen in Saki, anyway, it happened right before. But when our work was done, we left and went where there was work. Nothing to do with this."

Tatiana waited. "What small personal matter?" she said at last.

"I took up with a local boy," said Saika casually. "My father was upset with me."

"You took up with a local boy," Tatiana repeated without inflection.

"Yes."

"And your father beat you like that?" Tatiana *tried* to say it without inflection. She failed.

Saika smiled. There was no emotion in her eyes. "What do you think *your* father would do to you, Tania," she asked, "for taking up with a local boy?"

"I don't know," Tatiana replied dully. "He might not be very happy with the local boy."

"Who says *my* father was happy with the local boy?"

When Tatiana didn't speak—when Tatiana was speechless—Saika said, "What surprises you, here, Tanechka? My taking up with the local boy? Or the beating?"

Tatiana was very careful when she answered. "It's the reaction to the action that surprises me," she said slowly, still thinking. "I really like physics, Saika. Like my grandfather's math, classical physics is a good, concrete science, with good absolute laws that govern matter—solid things that have mass and occupy space. Things you can touch and see. There is a law in physics that says that for every action there is an equal and opposite reaction. I like that law a lot." Tatiana broke off. She listened to too many adult conversations these days and she didn't want to say to Saika that this made her think of human *justice* more than she wanted to. "Almost as if Newtonian *science*," she continued excitedly, "was founded, was sprung whole from principles that govern things that are not science, that are things we can't touch and see. Invisible, irrational things that govern human stories, that rule over myth and legend and fairy tales and our behavior. Things like: All our actions have meaning—and therefore have consequences."

"That's right," said Saika. "Well, that makes sense. I did wrong and I was punished. Perfect Newton. An eye for an eye."

"I don't think your father was trying to punish you," Tatiana said. "I think he was trying to kill you."

Saika sat up straighter in the tree. "Are you *judging* him for treating me too harshly?"

"I'm not judging at all, no."

"Oh, Tania." Shrugging, Saika lit another cigarette. "You might understand physics, but you clearly don't understand many things about human beings. You don't understand Azeri justice."

Tatiana was looking at the branches and not at Saika. "Is Azeri justice unique?"

Saika smiled her knowing smile again. "How do you know," she said, "that it *wasn't* an eye for an eye?"

After a moment of stunned silence, Tatiana said, "You know what? I've got to get back. Or *I'll* be beaten without mercy."

"Is *that* what you think?" Saika's tone suddenly changed. It became cold, almost menacing. "Is *that* how you think I was beaten—without mercy?"

Tatiana didn't say anything. Clearly that is how Saika had been beaten.

"Where in your little Newtonian theories does it say anything about *mercy*?" Saika persisted acidly. "Who tempers his physics with mercy, Tatiana?"

Tatiana was quiet, prickles of fear crawling on her back like venomous ants.

"I disgraced and dishonored my family and was appropriately punished," said Saika.

"Okay, Saika." Tatiana's gaze was on the ground below.

"How do you know my father's justice wasn't steeped in mercy?" Saika leaned in. "My father says he *had* mercy on me. What do you think of that? Judge that, why don't you?"

"I'm nobody. I'm judging no one," Tatiana said, jumping off the tree, two meters down, to Saika's gasp and subsequent applause. Without turning around, she clambered through the fence and the nettles and climbed through her window. She wished she could lock it.

Sleep would not come for a long time to Tatiana.

A Small Matter of a Large Cherry Tree

Pasha heard Tatiana before he saw her. Volodya and Kirill Iglenko were standing at the foot of a large cherry tree at the end of the village road. Tatiana's voice was chiming, "Ready? Catch!" Volodya and Kirill were looking up with their mouths gaping open. Pasha saw something small and red fall from the tree. Kirill caught it with his hand and popped it into his mouth. Another cherry fell. Volodya caught it, popped it into his mouth. They never stopped looking up at Tatiana. Pasha, as he came closer, could see her bare legs propped up on two branches half a meter apart. He shook his head and quickened his step, cursing under his breath. When he got to the bottom of the tree, without even looking up at his sister, without saying a word to her, or to them, he shoved them hard out of the way of the falling cherries, pushed them away even though they were bigger, and said, "*What* are you doing?"

"What? Nothing. She's getting us cherries," said Volodya, blinking innocently.

"Get the hell out of here." Pasha lowered his voice. "Who are you talking to? I'm not Tania. I told you and told you, stay away from her. Now go."

"Pasha—"

"I said *go*!"

They slowly walked away, regretfully waving to Tatiana.

"Pasha," Tatiana called to him, "what did you say to poor Volodya? Why did you shoo him like a fly?"

Pasha paused and then looked up. He looked up quickly, in the hope that maybe he was wrong, maybe this one time, his sister's dress was not hitched to her hips, maybe she had tucked it under herself, maybe her bare white panties and the whites of the insides of her thighs were not exposed to two teenaged boys as they stood gawking up at her while she dropped cherries into their mouths.

But he was not wrong.

"Tania, get down," Pasha said, looking away with a sigh.

"Why? Come up here. Want some cherries?"

"No!"

She threw some down to him anyway, and he swatted them away and said resignedly, "Just get down, will you?"

She jumped down like a cat in a floral sundress, landing on the balls of her feet with bent knees, with hardly a noise when she touched the ground. As she straightened up, she looked into Pasha's face. "What's wrong with *you*?"

"Nothing," he said. "Tania, when will you—" He broke off. Her face was flushed and smiling and happy and he just could not.

"When will I what?"

"Forget it, nothing. Let's go. Dasha is making potatoes."

"Oh, potatoes! Well, let me run. I've never had that delicacy before. Wherever did she get them?"

"Go ahead, mock. Can't eat mock for dinner, Tania."

"I'll eat cherries instead," said Tatiana, shoving her brother but he was not in a playful mood.

When they got home, Tatiana disappeared to her room to read, and Pasha went to Dasha who was outside peeling potatoes into the bushes. He slumped down by her. "Dasha, what are you planning to do about Tania?"

"Oh, no, what did she do now?"

"You know where I found her again?"

Dasha laughed. "In the cherry tree?"

Pasha nodded with exasperation.

"So talk to her, Pasha." She smiled.

"You're her sister. That conversation is much better left to the girls."

"You think *I* should talk to her?"

"She is fourteen next week! She *can't* be that oblivious anymore. She is not a child."

Dasha was still smiling when she said quietly, "But Pasha, she *is* a child."

"Well, it's not appropriate."

"So talk to her."

"I can't. You talk to her."

"You want her to listen to someone? Have Deda talk to her."

And Deda's strong voice sounded from the cucumber beds where Dasha and Pasha had not seen him. "I will *not* be talking to her." He came out from the cucumber leaves, holding rope in his hands, his thick gray hair disheveled. "I think if you should be talking to anyone, Pasha, it should be to your two friends. After all, it is not Tatiana who is behaving inappropriately."

Dasha and Pasha said nothing.

Deda studied the two of them for a few moments and then said, "Have you two got nothing better to do? Once you talk to her, she won't be able to be friends with them anymore. You want to ruin her summer? Oh, and also—she'll never horseplay with you, or tickle you, or swim in the river with you, or tie you up, or kiss you unexpectedly or sit on your lap again. She will never again do any of the things she does, because she will have eaten from your cursed cherry tree. Is that what you want?"

They said nothing.

"I didn't think so. Your sister," said Deda, "knows everything she needs to. Dasha, why don't you ask her to tell *you* how to behave. Better yet, leave the child alone. And Pasha, talk to the wild beasts you call your friends—or I will."

"Talk to the wild beasts about what?" said Tatiana, coming down the porch steps.

"Nothing, nothing," said Dasha. Deda kissed the top of Tatiana's head and went back to stringing up his cucumbers on their supports.

Pasha asked her if she had heard them talking.

"I heard you shouting, yes."

"Did you hear what we were shouting about?"

"If I listened to what this family shouted about every time they shouted, I'd never read a word of anything." Tatiana grinned. "Tell me what were you shouting about."

"Nothing," said Dasha. "Go set the table, will you, and slice the bread. Don't forget to give me the thickest piece, right near the crust."

"You can have all the bread you can eat and then you'll get nice and fat, Dasha," said Tatiana, skipping inside.

In the evening after dinner, Deda and Dasha watched Tania and Pasha playing loud dominoes. Tania was loud-winning as always and Pasha was loud-sore-losing, as always. They played fifteen, sixteen games, and Pasha lost every one. "How! Tell me, how do you do that! How do you always win at this! You do something, you cheat, I know you do! Deda, play Tania, let me see if you can beat her."

"I beat her in chess, that's enough for me," said Deda, smiling at Tatiana.

Leaving Pasha to his bitter defeat, Dasha sat with her grandfather on the bench outside in the overgrown garden. Moving over slightly, Deda said, "Dasha, don't blow your cigarette smoke into my face."

"What are you going to tell your Tania when she starts smoking?" Dasha said, moving away.

"I'll tell her not to blow her smoke in my face."

Dasha sighed. Why did she suspect that though Deda loved her, he slightly disapproved of her, as if somehow her conduct in life was less to his liking than, say, Tania's. Pasha, as the only male child, was beyond reproach. Why not Dasha, too? What did she do or not do? Didn't she cook and clean and take care of the urchins as if she were their mother?

Deda put his arm around Dasha, and she threw away her cigarette. "I struggle, Dedushka," Dasha said quietly. "I struggle all the time."

"Dasha, dear, it's good to have conflict inside you. Struggle away."

Dasha wanted to know what specifically Deda was referring to. Stefan and Mark? Dasha was not married, and she was young. She just wanted to have a bit of fun. Was that so wrong?

"Does Tania struggle?" she asked.

"She doesn't think about things she can't understand."

"How convenient," said Dasha. "Can I be that blind? But she reads more than anyone, how can she read Stendhal's *The Red and the Black* and not see the corruption, the immorality, the lust underneath all those proper skirts and trousers the ladies and gentlemen of France wear? How can she read so much yet see nothing?"

"Tania sees nothing?" said Deda, turning his surprised gaze at Dasha.

"That's the whole problem, isn't it? If she saw, you think she'd be up in that tree in her dress?"

Deda shook his head. "What a miracle," he whispered, kissing Dasha. "Granddaughter, I didn't know you too were so funny. Despite your problems, you are growing up to be a fine and funny young woman. But willfully or inadvertently, you're misunderstanding your sister."

"I am?"

"Of course. Haven't you figured out by now," Deda said, "that Tania sees through everything, right from the start?"

"She doesn't see through Kirill and Volodya."

"She does. She knows they're harmless. So don't worry about her. Worry only about your own life."

"What's to worry about?" said Dasha, her face falling. "We are all fish swimming in the same water. We don't know we can't breathe in the air."

"You're right, our choices are slightly blunted," agreed Deda. "But we don't all live the same life. Do you see the Kantorovs? You think they swim in the same water we do?"

"Yes."

Deda was quiet.

"What, you don't like them *either*? Tania keeps saying the Saika girl is no good."

Without answering, Deda said, "You know who I like?"

"Tania?"

"No. Your grandmother. Her I like. Her I have an opinion on. Otherwise, I refrain from all judgment."

But Dasha did not think he was refraining. "Dedushka, what am I supposed to do?" she said plaintively, suddenly in the confessional. "I don't want to be playing these games with my boss, but what are my alternatives?"

"You're telling your grandfather too much," said Deda.

"His pregnant wife will have nowhere to go after he kicks her out," Dasha continued.

"Dasha, stop!"

Dasha stopped, briefly.

"They still live with his mother, in one room," she said quietly. "But where's he going to go? Can he come and live with us? Can he sleep in one bed with me and Tania?"

Deda did not reply.

"This is what I mean about my choices," Dasha said. "You see I'm trying. Just trying to find a little love, Dedushka. Like you and Babushka. Did you have a place to live, to be alone, when you fell in love, when you married?"

"It was at the turn of the century," said Deda, "and we had a great big apartment in the center of town, near Aleksandr Pushkin's house on Moika Canal." Wistfully he smiled. "We had your father and your Aunt Rita there. We lived happily and well for many years."

Dasha listened intently.

"Things changed," he continued. "But even after the Revolution, when your grandmother and I were evacuated for two years during the Civil War—during all that strife and famine and chaos—we hid out and lived in a little fishing village called Lazarevo on the river Kama, near Molotov, and if you ask your grandmother, Dashenka, she will tell you that those two years in Lazarevo were the happiest two years of her life." Dasha gazed at him as Deda closed his eyes and tilted back his head just a little, as if he had leaned into some hidden away gilded tresses of his long memory and touched gladness that made the heart lighter.

"So don't fret so much," he said when he spoke again. "Even in this life, joy is possible. Have fun, darling. Go dancing, smoke, laugh, be young. Be young when you can. It will all be over soon enough. Then you'll have plenty of time to muddle yourself with married dentists."

"Is this what you talk to Tania about?" Dasha whispered. "Lazarevo?"

Deda laughed. "Your sister hasn't *once* sat on this bench asking *me* for guidance."

"No, she's too busy swinging like a freckled monkey off the trees," grumbled Dasha.

"That's right. And you want it to end so she can sit here glum like you?"

Dasha fell silent. She liked her grandfather's arm around her, and he did not take it away.

"Protect her, Dasha," whispered Deda. "It'll be gone for her soon enough."

In the house, Tatiana was on top of her bed, buried in her book. She didn't stir, not when Dasha came in, not when she sat on the edge of the bed, not when she slapped her sister's behind with her open hand. What Tatiana said without missing a breath was, "Hmm."

"Tania."

"Hmm."

Dasha swiped the book out of her hands. "You're *still* reading *Queen Margot*?"

"I'm *re*reading it." Tatiana turned over on her back.

"Why?" Dasha leafed through it indifferently. "Does it have a happy end?"

"Hardly happy. To save the Queen, La Môle sacrifices his life, is so horribly tortured that he sweats blood, and is then beheaded as she weeps."

"She never forgets him?"

"I don't know. The story ends with his death."

"Does she love again?"

"I don't know," Tatiana said slowly. "The story ends with his death."

Dasha smiled. "Is that the kind of love you want, Tanechka? Great passion, short-lived, ending with his torture and death?"

"Hardly," Tatiana muttered, staring with confusion at Dasha. "Is that the kind of love *you* want?"

Dasha laughed. "Tania," she said, "I'd settle for anything but what I've got at the moment. Now go to sleep. Are you ready for bed?"

"I'm in bed, aren't I?" Tatiana stretched out.

"Did you wash? Brush your teeth?"

"Yes, Dasha," said Tatiana solemnly. "I did what I'm supposed to. I'm not a child, you know."

"No?" said Dasha, gently touching Tatiana's barely budding chest.

"Oh, stop it," Tatiana said easily without moving away. "What do you need from me?"

"Who said I need anything from you?"

Tatiana sat up. Her clear eyes on Dasha, she sat, blinked twice, twice again, placed her hand on Dasha's face and said, "What? What is it?"

Sighing, Dasha kissed her hand and stood up. "Lights out. I don't care what Queen Margot is getting up to with her Protestant lover."

In the middle of the night, Dasha was woken up by whimpering coming from near her bed. She opened her eyes to find Tatiana crawling to her bedside.

"What's the matter?" Dasha whispered. Tatiana found the corner of the blanket. Dasha helped her by lifting it. Tatiana was still whimpering.

"Had a bad dream. Very bad dream. That Saika just won't leave me alone, even in my nightmares." Softly crying, she crept in. Dasha turned on her side and opened her arms. Tatiana's warm frightened body curved against her. Dasha's arms went around Tatiana, who pushed her spine as far as she could into Dasha, curled up, her head on Dasha's arm and whispered, "When are they going to stop?"

"Never," said Dasha. "You just become scared of different things.

What was the dream about?"

But Tatiana didn't answer. Pasha was snoring in the catty-cornered bed by the window. Dasha lay awake, feeling Tatiana's blonde body rise and fall in the pale moon light of night. Tatiana, she whispered, curl up against me, press yourself against me, and sleep in my arms where I have missed you these days in Luga, so used I am to sleeping with you in our bed in Leningrad. Rise and fall and tell me why it is that when you crawl in to seek comfort by me and find your sleep, I, instead, am comforted by you. Tell me that as you rise and fall.

And your head of hair so silk and your heart so light and your breath like a baby's, and your golden halo around you as you tread and read and speak, and our hearts become lighter when we hear your voice when we know you are near. We worry less about ourselves when you are here, and your spirit trickles out drop by drop and stills our restless hearts.

Book Two

Ithaca

Who led thee through that great and terrible wilderness, wherein were fiery serpents, and scorpions, and drought, where there was no water; who brought thee forth water out of the rock of flint.

Deuteronomy 8:15

CHAPTER SEVEN

Conjugal Compromises

Where To?

In the hammock in Key West, above the sand, near the ocean, in the heart of the tropics, tanned, freckled, scarred, together they lay, Alexander on his back, legs splayed, and Tatiana on top of him, on her back, legs together, staring up into the overhanging moss oaks. He was wearing his white swim trunks; she, a white bathing bottom and a bandana kerchief tied in a bow around her chest. His jet hair was longer and spiky; he was darkly tanned. She was golden but looked like snow in his arms by comparison. Once in a while his hands would drift languidly to fondle her breasts. His lips were rubbing against her briny ocean hair. She smelled of salt and coconut suntan lotion, which always made him a little light-headed.

They were talking about states. It was the deep summer of 1949. "Shura, be good. If you touch my breasts again, this conversation will be over."

"This is supposed to stop me?"

"Come on, where were we?"

"We were crossing off states and caressing your . . ."

"Oh, yes. We were having a trivial conversation about where to spend the rest of our life." They had returned to Miami for the winter, to work the boats again, and then travelled south to the Keys for the summer.

"Shura!"

"Okay, okay. Where were we? You said snow states are out. So no DC? Richter won't be happy," Alexander said. "You know how he likes me right by his side. And your Vikki won't be happy. You know how she likes you right by hers."

"They'll have to move where we are, won't they? Now then. No snow. So—no Maine, New Hampshire, Vermont, Massachusetts, Rhode Island, Connecticut, New Jersey, New York"—Tatiana sighed theatrically but longingly—"Pennsylvania, Ohio, Illinois, Wisconsin, Michigan, Minnesota, South Dakota, North Dakota, Montana, Wyoming, Idaho, Washington. They're all out."

"Also no Iowa, Kansas, Colorado, Nebraska," Alexander added. "Is that all?"

"Wait, West Virginia. Maryland. Virginia."

"It doesn't snow in Virginia," Tatiana said.

"Tell that to General Sherman," said Alexander.

"Fine. Twenty-one states left."

"Aren't you a good little counter. A capitalist, a geologist, a cartographer, and a mathematician, too." He laughed, bending his head, trying to see the expression on her face.

She turned her face up to him. "The Oregon woods are out," she said softly. "Because it rains all the time. Also, it's on the water."

"Are we excluding water states?"

"You don't have to," she said. "But nothing is going to sway back and forth in my home state except a hammock."

"So no California? No Napa Valley?" He smiled. "No more champagne?" Pulling down her bandana top, he played with her bouncy stand-up swell and swelling breasts.

"You can buy me all the champagne you like," she murmured, her hips lightly rubbing into him. "I hear they sell it in all forty eight states. So no California. Or North Carolina, South Carolina, Georgia, Florida—"

"Hold on there. We're reserving Florida. That's my one peremptory challenge."

"Fine. No Alabama, Louisiana, Missouri, Mississippi—"

"Wait," Alexander said, "Mississippi is on the water?"

She tilted her head back. "You're joking, right?"

"Oh, come on, we don't have to live right on the river."

"The state *is* the river."

"Oh, fine."

"Moving right along. Texas."

"Texas is on the water?" he said with surprise.

"Have you never heard of the Gulf of Mexico?"

"We'll live in Abilene, which has never heard of the Gulf of Mexico."

"Moving right along. What does that leave?"

"Europe, I think," Alexander muttered.

"Nevada. Nevada is out because I'm not living in a state where the only thing my husband will be able to do for a living is play poker in cathouses."

Alexander laughed. "Really?" he said. "You don't think my playing poker in cathouses fits your definition of a normal life?"

"Moving right along. Utah . . . mmm, a possibility. The mountains are real."

"Tatiasha? In Utah, can I get myself one more wife?"

"Utah's out."

He tweaked her, kissed her, rubbed her, pressed her to him, ground against her for good measure. She absorbed it all. "Oklahoma is out," she finally said, "just because."

"So what are we left with?"

"New Mexico, Arizona, Florida," she said. "Florida is out. Too much sway."

"Arizona is out then," he said. "Not enough."

"Well, the choice is clear. New Mexico it is."

They fell quiet.

He wanted Miami.

She wanted Phoenix. "Shura, come on—no rivers!"

"Salt River."

"No winter."

"No oceans either."

"Nothing familiar, nothing old. And other soldiers live in Phoenix."

"You want me to associate with other soldiers?"

"It's the last thing I want, but they at least understand things. You say, I was at war, and they nod their heads, and say no more because they don't need to. They know. No one wants to talk about it. That's what I want," she said. "Not to talk about it."

"Is there a military base in Phoenix?"

"No, but there's a training facility in Yuma, two hundred miles away, and an actual army intelligence base at Fort Huachuca, near Tucson, also two hundred miles away."

"I see my topless tadpole has done a little background work," he said, his thumbs kneading her. "Two hundred miles away? Once a month?"

"We'll all go with you, spend the weekend," she said. "We'll stay in married quarters." She squirmed away from his fingers. "Ant and I will sightsee and you can debrief, translate, evaluate dossiers and documents to your and Richter's hearts' content."

"It's too hot in Phoenix," Alexander said.

She gave him a look. It was 93°F in Key West that morning.

"It's too hot *and* there is no ocean," he said.

"There'll be lots of work."

"I'm not convinced," he said. "I can work anywhere."

"Yes, but you've already smelled like lobsters. You already carted young ladies around on boats. You've picked apples and grapes and corn. What about something good for yourself, Shura?"

He didn't have a flip response to that, though he was thinking of one.

"Phoenix was an ancient Roman bird," she said, "that set fire to itself, burned down, and then rebuilt itself anew out of its own ashes. Phoenix reborn."

"Hmm."

"Did I mention it doesn't get cold?"

"Once or twice," he said. "Miami doesn't get cold either."

"I know you love your water, but we can build a pool. In Phoenix there is no past. That's how I want to live. As if I have no past."

"I'll be in Phoenix. Hard to forget the past when me and my tattoos are on top of you, Tania." His long legs wrapped around her.

Picking up his dark hand off her white breast and kissing it, she pressed it to her face. "Yes, I've learned that lesson well. For better or worse, Alexander," she said, "you're the ship I sail on— and go down with."

"Did you say go down with or on?"

She pulled his forearm hair. "You I take with me—to our ninety-seven acres of America. We have nothing else to do but live there and die there. And when we die, we can be buried on the land by our mountain." She almost smiled. "Not in the ice, not in the frozen earth, but near a sunset. We can call it our Riddarholm Mountain, like that place in Stockholm, and we can be buried there like kings and heroes in our own Temple of Fame."

"You're daydreaming of dying then?" asked Alexander. "Is this how you always get what you want?"

"I don't always get what I want. If I got what I wanted," said

Tatiana, staring up into the moss oaks, "we wouldn't be orphans, you and I."

They went to Phoenix.

Double Wide or Triple Wide?

"Let's buy a mobile home and put it on our property." That was him.

"You mean a *trailer*?" That was her.

"Not a trailer," Alexander said patiently. "A mobile home. Have you noticed your Temple of Fame-y ninety-seven acres have no house? Where would you like to live while we save up for one? In the tent?"

They were sitting cross-legged opposite each other in the clay sand on their land on top of Jomax. Anthony was chasing Gila monsters or collecting cholla blooms. The electricity had finally been run on their unpaved upwardly sloping road. A mile down near Pima someone had built two small homes. The desert was singed; it was scorching July. Alexander sat palms out with Tatiana's little palms flat on top of his.

"Shura," she said, "we just lived in a trailer. For three years. I don't want to live in a trailer anymore. I want a real house."

"A mobile home is a real home. And it won't cost as much as a regular house. We won't need a mortgage—ah, you like that." He smiled. "I thought so. We have enough money, we can buy it outright. We'll get a couple of cars, I'll build a deck for the back, so we can sit and watch the sun over your little valley, and I'll find work. We'll save money and then build exactly what we want."

Tatiana frowned. "What cars?"

He smiled. "I want to get a truck. And you need your own car."

She shook her head. "No, no, your truck will do. You can drive me."

"I'll drive you anywhere you want to go, babe," he said, squeezing her hand, "but unless you plan to grow your cucumbers like your grandfather in Luga, you're going to have to go food-shopping once in a while. Besides, I'm a carnivore." He grinned. "I need meat. I can't live your Luga life of potatoes and onions."

She was unconvinced. "Two vehicles is too extravagant for us."

"Tania, this isn't Coconut Grove. No Laundromat a mile away. You're going to want to go to a department store. Maybe buy yourself some high heels?" He poked her. "An electric can-opener?"

"So we have to spend even more money?" she asked. "This—um, trailer, will it be bigger than our Nomad? Will it be on wheels? Will it have even one bedroom? And what about a bathroom? You can't live five minutes without water on your body."

Alexander stared at her incredulously and then laughed. Jumping up, he gave her his hand, pulling her up. "Come, my communal-apartment-living Russian princess. I'll show you what I mean. Anthony, let's go!"

He drove them to Pacifico Mobile Home dealer on Thomas. After two hours of wandering around the lot full of mobile homes and comparing sizes and prices, Tatiana said, "All right. It's not bad. But we don't need a large one. A small one will do."

"A minute ago you wouldn't live in one at all because you were afraid it would be too small, now you want one the size of a closet," said Alexander. "Where are you going to put your books and can openers, Tatia?"

The mobile homes came in three widths: the single wide, the double wide, and the triple wide. Tatiana was opting for the single wide—the least expensive. It was 14 feet wide, 30 feet long. It had two bedrooms, one bathroom and a tiny kitchen. "The price is right. And it's plenty for us," she said. "We need so little."

Alexander sighed in mock exasperation. "Here, let me show you something." Stepping inside the home, he bent his head to get in and then, once inside, stood nearly touching the ceiling. "You don't see a problem here?" The model was six and a half feet tall.

She stepped in the little house without bending or touching anything and stood comfortably, saying, "No."

"I know you barely clear five feet, but I'm six three," Alexander said. "Am I going to have to live with my head permanently bent to the side like this?"

Tatiana said first of all, she cleared five feet by nearly a full inch and a half, and second she didn't know what the big deal was. "It's just for a little while. You said so yourself. We'll save more money this way."

"It's not about the price," said Alexander, stepping back outside into the heat and crossing his arms. "It's about the life. What if we have to live in it for a couple of years? Don't you want to be comfortable?"

"It doesn't matter to me," she said, coming close to him. "As you know—a shack with no roof, as long as it's with you."

Alexander covered her face with his open hand and then kissed her nose through his spread apart fingers. "Well, at least with no roof," he said, "I won't get a crick in my neck." He pulled her to the triple-wide home, where Tatiana said timidly, "You know we can just sell ten of our acres and build ourselves a proper house."

Alexander shook his head. "Wife, for someone who's supposed to have second sight, you sure are completely unprescient. You want to sell our land? If we sell ten acres, then right next to us someone will build twenty homes. Maybe thirty. You want to live that close to other people?"

"No," she admitted, sheepishly.

"Exactly. And second, you bought the land six years ago for fifty dollars an acre. It's now worth $500 an acre. I don't know about you, but I'm seeing a trend."

"The realtor said—"

Alexander lowered his voice. "Fuck the realtor."

He tried not to smile. He crossed his arms and waited while she wrestled with herself.

"Fine fine," she said. "But a triple wide is a colossal waste of money. We don't need a trailer that big."

"What about our squad of offspring? Where are we going to put them?"

"When we have a squad then we'll upgrade to a triple wide."

"Now *that's* a colossal waste of money."

It was Tatiana's turn to cross her arms. Alexander gave in and in the spirit of matrimonial harmony, they compromised—which is, neither got what they wanted.

The double wide home, 24 feet wide, 60 feet long and 8 feet tall, had a front door, a back door, and a large open area in the center with a kitchen, a dining area and a living room. To the right of the living room was a master bedroom with its own attached bathroom! And a shower! "What a country," said Tatiana. On the opposite side of the mobile home were two more bedrooms, the bigger one for Anthony and a smaller one for "a nursery," said Alexander. "A guest room for Vikki and Tom," said Tatiana. There was another bathroom in the hall and a laundry room.

"Shura, no more washing clothes in rivers!" she said happily.

"That's good," he said, "considering there's no water for three states."

The home had black and white linoleum in the kitchen and dining area, and wall-to-wall carpeting throughout the rest of the house. "Wall-to-wall carpeting, Tatia," Alexander said, suggestively reminding her of Lazarevo wood floors gone by, but Anthony was near and Tatiana wasn't playing, though she was blushing.

They paid for the home in cash and in two days the workmen delivered it and set it up on cement blocks on the edge of their property, up on the hill, with the front of the trailer facing the road. They couldn't look in any direction without seeing the desert or the mountains or the valley.

"We finally have a home!" Anthony kept yelling, running through the empty house. "We're not nomads, we're not gypsies! We have a home!"

All three of them painted the trailer—the bedroom cream-yellow, Anthony's room cream-blue. The living room and kitchen walls were the color of crème brûlée, though when Alexander called it that, Tatiana cried. "Why, *why* do you say such awful things, Dad?" asked Anthony, patting his mother.

Tatiana hung sheer white curtains, she bought stainless-steel pots and pans. "No more eating out of the same bowl, Shura?"

"Forever out of the same bowl, Tania."

Alexander bought himself a truck. He spent a week picking out just the right one. Finally he decided on a 1947 electric blue Chevy light truck, 3/4-ton with a roomy cab, chrome grille and sideboards. He bought Tatiana a brand new 1949 sage green Ford sedan.

He bought lumber and started building a shed where he could work and keep his tools. "If you're very good," Alexander said to Tatiana in a low voice, "I'm going to build a work table in the shed that will be just the right height for you—to peel potatoes on, that is." Anthony was near so Tatiana wasn't playing, though she was profoundly blushing.

They bought a round dining table with extra leaves for when guests came, ("Like King Arthur's," he said, "so we can discuss the business of our life here"), a comfy couch and three radios. Alexander, with Anthony's help, built Tatiana two bookshelves, a knick-knack shelf, though she had no knick-knacks, and himself a utility table.

They bought a Napa-sized, brothel-worthy brass bed. It didn't have a canopy but it had a box spring and a thick cushy mattress, and was nicely high off the floor. Tatiana spent more woman-hours picking out sheets for the bed than she spent painting and furnishing the rest of the house—though slightly less time than Alexander spent picking out his truck.

"What color sheets would you like?" she asked him. They were out back in the heat.

"I don't care, anything you want." He had a saw in his hands. He and Anthony were laying out two-by-fours on the ground for their rear deck. Alexander was making it king-size, despite her protestations.

"Alexander."

"What? I don't care. Anything you want." His back was to her.

She pulled him away from Anthony. "It's our marriage bed. It's the first real bed you and I have ever had. This is very, *very* important. We need sheets that reflect this paramount gravity."

"That's a lot to ask of poor sheets." He went back to sawing the two-by-fours, telling Anthony to keep his little hands away.

"What color?"

"I don't care."

"Fine. Pink then?"

"No, not pink."

"Polka dotted? Striped? Black?"

"Anything's fine."

"Pink then?"

"Not pink I said."

"Mommy, how about something with dinosaurs?"

"What about roosters, Mommy?" Alexander grinned. "Maybe rutting ruminants?"

Tatiana took the saw out of Alexander's hands, pulled him up again, and made him write down his three top choices on a piece of paper. He put down white, white, and white. She tore up his piece of paper and made him do it again. He wrote down cream, cream, and cream. She held his hand to the paper and made him write down other words. He was laughing until he couldn't breathe. "I. Don't. Care," he kept saying. "Which part of I don't care don't you understand? Please yourself. Make yourself happy."

"You are going to have to make love to your wife every night looking at these damn sheets," she whispered into his ear, "so you better start to care, because you're going to care in a week."

All grimy and sweaty, Alexander drew her to him, his palms on her back, and bending to her and tilting his head, whispered into her mouth, "Tatiasha, I know you won't believe this, but if I'm looking at the sheets when I'm making love to you, we've got bigger problems than what damn color they are." He kissed her like it wasn't daylight.

She pulled away from him, gave the pencil back to Anthony, and huffed away. "That's it, I'm not playing with you anymore."

Finally Tatiana came back with quilts, pillows and blankets, and spent another day washing and ironing them. After she made the bed, she made Alexander close his eyes before she led him inside. "Okay, now open."

Alexander opened his eyes. The mass of pillows, the down quilt, the sheets were white. The patchwork quilted bedspread was light cream, almost like *white*, with satin stitching and velvet crimson buds all over. She'd bought new curtains, too—gauzy with velvet blue and yellow pansies. He stood silently, looking at the bed.

"Well," she said eagerly, squeezing his hand. "What do you think?"

"Eh," he said with a shrug.

She burst into tears.

Laughing, he lifted her into his arms. "Oh, no! The wife has lost her bawdy sense of humor." He kicked the door shut behind them.

Their six-year-old Anthony was down the road playing at Francesca's house with six-year-old Sergio Garcia. There weren't many children born in 1943; Sergio's father and mother recently came from Mazatlán, Mexico. Sergio spoke Spanish. Anthony spoke Russian. They were instant best friends. While they played, Alexander made love to Tatiana on their new sheets, and afterward said, "Honestly, I barely noticed them."

But she had just been loved and was in no laughing mood.

"I'd like an armchair for the bedroom," he murmured.

"What do we need an armchair in the bedroom for?" she said. "We have a couch outside."

"Buy the chair and I'll show you."

After the chair was delivered, he undressed her and kneeled between her legs upraised on the chair arms. Afterward she agreed it was money well spent.

When Anthony started school they suddenly had their new house all to themselves. They had tomblike daylight privacy. They had DAYLIGHT! They walked Ant downhill to the school bus stop on the corner of Jomax and Pima, in front of Sergio's house, saw him off, said hello to an always smiling non-English-speaking Francesca, who was pregnant with her second, and then spent the mornings

in their plush, downy, soft white bed with crimson buds. Day, daylight, empty house. They christened every room (except Ant's). The
kitchen counters, the kitchen table, the kitchen chairs, the comfy
couch, the carpets, the linoleum floors, the baths (with water and
without), Alexander's truck (bench and back of pick-up), Tatiana's
sedan—front and back (and hood). In between, they drove down
south once to the Fort Huachuca base, he finished the rear deck
and she planted lilac sand verbena and baked bread. The deck was
fabulous. They christened that too. They had a wonderful August.

And then they ran out of money.

Every penny they had made and earned and saved had gone—
into their home and their cars.

"Now what?" she asked.

"I think I might need to get a job," he replied.

She sent him off with a packed lunch. He got work on a painting
crew on a large commercial account. But when the gig was over,
the work was gone. He got another gig; that was soon gone. It
took a while to get paid. Tatiana stopped buying meat. "Buy the
meat," Alexander said. "We're fine."

"Next week there'll be no work again," she said.

The problem wasn't just the unsteady work, it was the enor-
mity of the labor force and the paucity of the wages. Alexander
may as well have been picking grapes in Napa. "Tania, quit worrying. I'll get new work," he assured her. "And my reserve check
will be coming in any day." But the small check wasn't enough to
live on, to pay their overwhelming electric bills with the air con-
ditioners being on day and night. Tatiana started anxiously turning
off the AC, conserving water, foregoing lunch, making him two
sandwiches instead of three. She told him he could smoke only
two packs a day. "Two packs? That's how you know everything is
going to hell in a handbasket," said Alexander, lighting up.

Dreaming Oxen

One night in September Alexander came home from painting,
and the house was cool! Tatiana had made *Beef* Stroganoff. A bottle
of wine was open on the table, on the stove a cherry pie was
cooling. She came out from the bedroom to greet him wearing a
soft dress, her hair down.

"Oh, no," he said, in his overalls, covered with barely dried paint. "Is it our anniversary?" He had taken off his boots and left them outside. They were too filthy to bring into his clean house.

"Mommy got a job," said Anthony, running up to Alexander.

"Anthony!" Tatiana exclaimed. "Go to your room right now."

Turning around, Anthony stared at her blankly.

"In the hospital, Dad."

"Anthony!"

Alexander stood bleakly by the door. "Ant," he said, "you heard your mother. Go to your room."

"And do what?"

Throwing his keys on the side table, Alexander ushered Anthony to his room and shut the door to his plaintive, "What did I do?"

He walked back to the kitchen.

"Sit, darling, are you tired?" Tatiana said, pulling out a chair for him. "Or do you want to wash first? Are you thirsty?" She got him a drink, a beer, opened it for him, poured it for him.

"Are you going to drink it for me, too?" Alexander said, downing it. "What's going on?"

"Why don't you go change, wash? Dinner will be ready in a few minutes."

"I'm suddenly not hungry. You got a job?"

"It's just to help us a little, like in Napa, remember? Until we get back on our feet." She was fidgeting.

Alexander took her by the hands and sat her down in the chair next to him. "You got a job at a hospital?"

"*The* hospital. There's only one. Phoenix Memorial. It's downtown on Buckeye, just a few miles from here."

"Buckeye? It's forty miles from here!"

"Thirty-seven. You can come and meet me for lunch."

"Please tell me you got a job washing floors. Please—please don't tell me you got a job as a nurse."

She didn't say anything.

Letting go of her hands, he shook his head and stood up. "No."

Tatiana started fretting again, shifting her eyes. "It's only three days a week. Darling, please. We need it."

"No, we don't."

"Yes, we do."

He looked at her grimly. "If you think we need money so badly, why didn't you get yourself a job at a restaurant in Scottsdale?"

"You want me to be a waitress? You want me to serve food to men?"

"Don't twist things to make this about me, Tania."

"Please don't be upset. I'm just trying to help our family."

"Help our family by staying home."

"We're so broke," she whispered.

"I'll make enough."

"I know. Shura, what, you don't think I know? You work harder than anybody. But it's not steady. We're still broke."

"You're saying I can't make enough for us to get by?"

Her hands opened to him. "Please. I'm not saying that. This is just for a little while. It's a regular job, and it pays okay. This way you don't have to take the first stupid thing that comes along just to buy food. You can choose wisely, look around, see what's out there that's good for you, that's right for you. And then when we're both working, we'll be able to save money. We can get on our feet so much faster."

Alexander was still standing, looking at her. Anthony opened the door. "Can I come out now?" he asked.

"No!" they both yelled.

Anthony slammed the door.

"Let's sell ten acres of our land," said Alexander, sitting back down. "I'd rather sell the land and live close to other people than have you work."

Tatiana looked at him aghast. "Shura, you don't mean that."

"With all my heart." He stared into her face. "Remember Coconut Grove?" he asked, bringing her to sit on his lap. He was still so messy, and she in her light dress was so perfect. "You stayed on the boat, and brought me lunch at the marina, and put mayonnaise in your hair, and when I came home from work, you were happy, excited, rested. Anthony was fed and clean and played with. You were so eagerly waiting for me, serving me your . . . plantains. Wasn't it beautiful?"

"It was," she whispered. "We just lived it. You can't already be feeling nostalgic for it."

"I am, though," he said. "That's what I want here. That's all I need. I want to hunt and gather, and you to stay home. I don't want you to work. Certainly, certainly," Alexander said, "not in a fucking hospital!"

"Shh!" They both glanced at Anthony's closed door.

He lowered his voice. "It'll suck the soul right out of you."

"It won't. You'll see."

"There'll be nothing left for me."

"That'll never be true."

"Do you see me dragging you to Huachuca? I can get an active reserve post there any time. Do you want that to be my work?"

"But then we won't be here, in our own little house, on our land," she whispered.

"That's not my point."

"You don't want to go back into that life."

"Then why do *you*?"

"I don't. I just want to help our family—and," she said, "it's the only thing I know how to do. Perhaps I can find a weapons factory, make tanks, like at Kirov? I know how to do that, too."

"Tania, I thought the whole point of Phoenix was that we were going to try to do something we don't know how to do," Alexander said. "Which is live regular. Because would you like me to remind you of all the things *I* can do? I know you don't want me doing them. Richter, though, would love to have me with him in Korea doing them."

"Alexander," she said, "it's hardly the same thing, now is it? I work three days a week in a peacetime hospital, and I'm home in bed with you every night. We go to Korea, and men who want to kill you throw very big things that explode right into your bunker. You do see a small difference, no?"

"That's exactly my point," said Alexander. "We're trying to build a new life here. *New* being the operative word. What is it with you? You haven't seen enough bloodshed?"

"It's going to be okay," she said beseechingly.

"Really? There are shootings, stabbings, assaults, bar fights, murders, car accidents, heart attacks. Death. What the hell do you want to surround yourself with that for?" He broke off, backing slightly away from her, still sitting in his lap. Her eyes were contrite and pleading, her mouth was agitating. And suddenly he understood. As he carried himself wherever he went, she carried herself wherever she went. How could he stop her from being what she was? The only thing he said after that, in great resignation, was, "Hasn't anything I've gone through shown you that if you live oxen, you dream oxen?"

"No, not me. I put it all away." Her lips trembled just a little. "I put it *all* away," she whispered. "And in a little while, I'll get some seniority," she continued soothingly. "I'll move to the obstetric ward. I'll deliver babies."

"Start with delivering your own baby, then move on to other

people's, how would that be?" With a short groan, Alexander got up to wash, change. "I'm not even going to ask where in the hospital you're going to be working," he said as he walked away. "Because I know it's not the baby wing. Maternity ward, yeah, sure. Babies, sweetness, happiness, God forbid. No. You've got that terminal-care-ward-in-Morozovo look about you. You're either in ER or ICU."

"ER," she said, o so guiltily.

"That's right, of course. ER," he said, already in the bedroom, taking off his clothes.

She came in after him.

"It's going to turn out badly, Tatiana," Alexander said. "Unlike you, I have an uncanny ability to see the future."

"So funny. It's just to help us, darling."

"Don't try that line with me. Don't talk to me like I don't know you—Leningrad hospital during the blockade, terminal wings, the frontline, refugees at Ellis Island. But it's not just about you anymore. You have a family to consider now, a husband, a son."

The son called from his half of the house. "Dad, can I come out now?"

"Yes, Anthony," Alexander called back, clothes off, walking into the bathroom and turning on the shower. "The conversation is over. Mommy's in the terminal ward."

She followed him into the bathroom.

"I don't know why you're so against Korea, Tania," he said, taking off his watch. "It'll be perfect for you. It's just where you need to be."

"Please, Shura," she whispered, throwing her arms around his waist before he got in. "It's just for a little while, until we get things together."

Alexander sighed deeply, his hand on top of her head.

"How about this?" she cooed, kissing his chest. "I'll make you a deal. As soon as I get pregnant, I'll quit. I promise. Okay?"

"I'm not holding my breath," he said, standing naked against her, squeezing her.

"Careful. I could be pregnant already." She smiled at him. He was more careful. But she wasn't pregnant. She was a nurse.

CHAPTER EIGHT

The House that Balkman Built

The Man with the Broken Hand

Oh, she was good. Three days at the hospital, she told Alexander. What she didn't tell him was that they were three twelve-hour shifts, seven to seven. She had to leave the house by six and wasn't home until nearly eight. She had to be up at five in the morning. She didn't go fishing in Lazarevo at five in the morning, and now she was up at five putting on her girdle and nurse's uniform!

But at least now that Tatiana was working her "part time," "only three little days" hospital gig, Alexander didn't have to take the first thing he found. He looked for more permanent work with the homebuilders around Scottsdale. He concentrated on custom builders only: he liked their quality and they paid better. He spent weeks trying to figure out where he would fit best. He didn't quite know what he was looking for; he would know when he found it. Unlike his crazy wife, he was trying to get away from what he was, not rushing headlong into it.

After receiving half a dozen offers to train to be a framer, a roofer, and an electrician's apprentice, he finally got two job offers that interested him—from G.G. Cain Custom Homes and Balkman Custom Homes. G.G.'s business was small: five or six well-built homes a year, because that's what suited serious, laconic G.G., who wanted a living, not an empire. But it didn't quite suit Alexander, who thought there was not enough living there for him, too. Besides, soon Tania would have another baby and they would have to go back to living on one salary.

That's when he met Bill Balkman. Balkman Custom Homes was

a bigger business than G.G.'s; they built ten true custom homes a year but also some moderately priced template homes and cheap homes for the college kids in Tempe.

Balkman's office was in his own brand new stucco spec home, built on old farmland on Camelback that he bought from "an old peasant" and subdivided into forty plots.

"The template houses have the highest profit margin," Balkman said. "I build them cheap and sell them high." But he was looking for a new custom home foreman as his previous one had suddenly quit for reasons Balkman didn't go into. What he did go into, with a big wide smile, was how perfect he thought Alexander would be for the job.

Balkman was a talker, a toucher, a hand-shaker, a laugher. He took to Alexander like he was a prodigal son come home. G.G. had been markedly more reserved. Balkman offered Alexander a promise for growth as well as a good salary. When Alexander told him he had no experience as a foreman, Balkman slapped him on the back and said, "Did you say you were in the army? Well, then, you can do anything."

"Yes, if it involves shooting people."

Balkman liked that. He was in his early fifties, and had a funny drooping moustache, a well-pressed suit and an easy going manner. Coming around the desk in his panelled, well-appointed office, he shook Alexander's hand again. "I think we're going to get along fine, just fine," he said. "Come down the street with me. I want you to meet my son. He's my other custom foreman. I think you two will get along splendidly."

As they stood up to leave, Alexander glanced at Balkman's wall display of framed degrees and letters from satisfied customers. Next to them a large color postcard of a topless woman was pinned to the panelling. "Viva Las Vegas!" the postcard said.

Alexander said nothing as his neutral gaze met Bill's. "By the way," Balkman said, smiling, "I forgot to ask. Are you married?"

"I am," replied Alexander.

Balkman slapped him on the back again. "Oh well," he said, "no one's perfect. But don't worry—we're willing to overlook that."

"I'm not willing to overlook that," said Alexander.

The builder laughed. "Just kidding. You'll see. We kid big around here."

They walked four unpaved blocks to the construction site where his son was working. Balkman was telling Alexander that to be a foreman, one had to be an architect, mixed with a bit of an engi-neer, a plumber, an electrician, a manager, a hand-holder, and a psychologist. He smiled. "Think you can handle that?"

Alexander didn't think he'd be a very good hand holder. Maybe Tania should be a foreman. "Absolutely," he said.

"And we work hard around here, Alexander," said Balkman, "but we also play hard."

Alexander agreed that work and play were both important.

Steve Balkman looked remarkably clean for someone who was supervising a construction site, as if he spent the whole time watching the men from his spit-polished car. Steve was young and well-groomed—spit-polished. The hair was in place, the face was fresh shaven, he was wearing cologne, his fingers looked mani-cured—well, the fingers on his left hand, anyway, with which he awkwardly shook Alexander's hand. Steve's right arm was in a cast from his elbow to the tips of his fingers. Aside from his busted arm, he was a pretty boy, a dandy, all fine and confident and smooth and smiling. Casual, friendly, open like his father. "Good to meet you," said Steve. "You going to be working for us?"

"Don't know yet."

"What do you mean, you don't know? Of course you are!" Balkman boomed with another hearty slap on Alexander's back. "I won't take no for an answer. When can you start? Because we're breaking ground tomorrow just around the block, and I might as well baptize you by fire."

Alexander made note of the attempts at military analogies.

"Stevie, Alexander was in the army, like you."

Alexander took a long look at Steve.

"Steve was stationed in England," Balkman said proudly. "He was wounded in the leg, not seriously, thank God, and came home because of it. Only saw action for four months."

"Pop," said Steve, "I was wounded in friendly fire, behind the lines. Some guy got careless with his weapon. I never saw any action. What about you, Alexander? See any action?"

"Here and there," Alexander said.

"Ever wounded?"

"Nothing serious," he said, the words themselves forming a neurotransmitter electrical connection that shot across the bil-lions of synapses of his brain, down the spine, firing pain right into the closed fist of a hole in his lower back. One question, instant memory, and this in Phoenix!

Balkman suggested that Alexander might want to take a few courses in structural or civil engineering at Arizona State College in Tempe. "A degree in architecture is very useful in this business. My Stevie is thinking of going, too, now that the war is over. Aren't you, Stevie?"

Alexander wanted to point out that the war had been over for four years.

And Steve said in a tired voice, "I'm thinking about it, Pop."

"I think college is a very good idea," said Alexander, taking out his cigarettes. Balkman flicked on the light for him. "My father wanted me to become an architect."

"You see!" a beaming Balkman exclaimed to Steve.

"Where's your old man now?" asked Steve.

"He's not around anymore," said Alexander, without a flicker even in his cigarette.

"By the way," Balkman said to his son, sounding *much* less friendly, "the building inspector called me this afternoon, all worked up because he waited for you for an hour and you never showed. He had to leave for another appointment. Where were you?"

"I was there, Pop. I thought our meeting was at two, not one."

"It clearly said one o'clock in the appointment book."

"My book said two. Sorry, Pop. I'll meet him tomorrow."

"See, the problem is, he can't tomorrow. He can't till next week. It's going to delay the ground breaking and cost us two hundred bucks to smooth it over with the plumbing and the cement crew who were ready to start. They gave up other work, and now I have to explain it to the homeowners . . . ." He shook his head. "Ah, forget it. I'll have Alexander meet with the building inspector. I'll give him this project to work. Alexander, so you think you can start tomorrow?"

Alexander took the job. Words of engineering and architecture courses, of responsibility, of learning the house building business from the ground up, images of Bill Balkman congenially patting his back whirled in his head.

A thought flowed through that perhaps he should've talked to Tania first, but he was certain of her approval from twenty miles away.

Steve asked him to go for a quick drink. At Rocky's down on Stetson in Scottsdale, they sat behind the bar and ordered beers, and Steve said, "Boy, Pop must really like you. He *never* hires the married ones."

Alexander looked at him puzzled. "How many single men can he find after the war?" he said. "I'd guess not many."

"Well, I'm single," said Steve, grinning, "and it's after the war." He sighed. "I got engaged last year."

Alexander was pleased that Steve had no interest in discussing the war with him; made it easier not to have to lie. "So what'd you get engaged for if you're sighing?"

Steve had a good laugh over that one. "I did it because all I heard was when, when, when," he said. "So I gave her a ring, and now that keeps her quieter. Not quiet, but quieter. You know what I mean?"

Alexander took a drink of his beer and didn't answer, drumming his fingers on the bar counter.

"I'm only twenty-four, Alexander," said Steve. "I'm not ready to settle down yet. You know? Haven't sowed all them wild oats yet. When did you get circled?"

"At twenty-three."

Steve whistled. "Were you still in the army?"

"Of course."

"Wow. Alex—can I call you Alex?—I'll tell you, I don't know how you did it. Married at twenty-three *and* in the army? What about the oats?"

"All sowed beforehand." Alexander laughed, raising his eyebrows and his beer glass. "*All* sowed beforehand."

And Steve laughed right back, clinking with him. "Well, at least we understand each other. Man, the girls are everywhere, aren't they? Restaurants, clubs, hospitals—I met one the other week at the hospital—you've never seen *anything* like her."

"Speaking of hospitals," said Alexander, "how'd you bust your arm?"

"Oh, I was an idiot. Tripped on a ladder at one of the houses and fell."

Steve's shoes and clothes didn't look like he'd been up any ladders. Maybe that was why he fell.

"I keep telling Pop I'm not cut out for this business," Steve said merrily, "but he doesn't want to hear it." He alternated swigging his beer and smoking his cigarette. "Which is why I am so flipping glad you came along. You're taking a lot of pressure off me, frankly."

"Well, always glad to help out," Alexander said, shaking Steve's hand, and getting up to go. He couldn't wait to tell Tatiana.

They celebrated that night with a late dinner and champagne after Anthony had gone to bed. "I'm sorry I didn't talk to you first about it," he said, "but it just felt so right. What kind of feeling are you getting about them?"

"What, from twenty miles away?" They smiled. "If you're happy, I'm happy, Shura." She was lying in the crook of his arm, but looking at him thoughtfully. "What did you say the name of the company was again?"

"Balkman Custom Homes."

"Balkman, huh," she intoned. "Must be a common name around here. I've heard the name before." She frowned.

Alexander was flying high, wired and excited. He told her about going to college starting January. "I'm going to get Richter to help me get a GI loan to pay for the tuition. Yes, yes, I know it's a loan, but it's Richter, it's for my degree, and it's worth it. What do you think?"

"It's wonderful," Tatiana said, kissing his chest scar under her mouth.

"And after I figure out what I'm doing, I'll build a house for you." He put his palms on her. "With these bare hands. So start thinking about what you want your dream house to look like."

"I'm still thinking about what I want my promised potato countertop to look like," she said, pressed into him.

The next morning Alexander left home at six thirty. He spent all day with Balkman. He met with the building inspectors and city construction supervisors, he met with the two architects, with the plumbers, foundation layers, electricians, roofers, plaster and brick and stucco guys, painters and cabinet makers, the crown molding guys and the door crew. He sat in on a meeting in Balkman's office with prospective home buyers, he smoked three packs of cigarettes, he barely ate, and he came home at nine in the evening, starved and too tired to speak.

But at home he fell into the kitchen chair and Tatiana served him chicken stew in red chile wine sauce over onion rice, with warm bread; she lit his cigarettes and poured his drink and then sat with him on the quiet couch and caressed his head until he fell asleep and she had to wake him to come to bed.

She told him that on the three days she also worked late, Francesca gladly agreed to take Anthony home with her after school in return for a little money and Tatiana teaching her English.

"You teaching *her* English?" said Alexander. "You don't see the ironies there?"

"I see ironies everywhere," said Tatiana.

On Friday Steve asked Alexander out for a drink with another foreman, Jeff, who worked on middle-income houses in Glendale, and Alexander went and didn't get home until eleven. Saturday he worked all day into the evening. Balkman asked him to come in for a few hours on Sunday, but Alexander said no. "I don't work Sundays, Bill." On Monday, Bill asked him to stay late to sit in on a meeting with prospective clients. On Tuesday, he had an early morning meeting, a lunch meeting, and another late meeting. The painter quit over a pay dispute, so Alexander had to finish painting one of the houses himself.

Leaving home early, coming home late, he was exhausted but exhilarated. And he liked Steve and Jeff. When they got a few drinks in, they turned into Lewis and Martin. Balkman trained Alexander himself, donning dungarees and going on the construction sites. One day over lunch, Balkman mentioned the training seminars where they learned about new construction materials, techniques, developments in air conditioning and roofing. "A few times a year, we go to these various conventions, builders' shows. In Las Vegas." Balkman paused significantly, his smile broad. "The foremen learn a tremendous amount, and the boys play a bit after a hard day's work."

"I'm sure they do." Alexander smiled back.

"One's coming up in two weeks."

Alexander put down his fork. "Bill, I won't be able to go."

Balkman nodded sympathetically. "I know—married men have a harder time getting away. Have to smooth it over with the missus? I understand. Tell her it's just for a weekend."

"Yes, Bill. But in two weeks, I have to go to Tucson for the weekend. I'm a commissioned reservist for the United States Army. I give them two days a month."

Bill also put down his fork. "A reservist? Oh, that's going to be awkward. On the weekends?"

"Two days a month. Weekends seem easier."

"Saturdays are our busiest day, Alexander, you know that."

Alexander didn't point out that Bill wanted him to be in Las

Vegas on a Saturday. "I know. I'll make up the work. I'm not going to let you down. But I have to go."

"Is this going to be an ongoing thing?"

Alexander squinted. "As opposed to what? The ongoing Las Vegas commitments?"

"But a commission means you can resign after a certain time, can't you?"

"*Resign* my commission?"

"Just think about it, is all I'm asking. You're going to be very valuable to my business, Alexander. I want to give you every opportunity to succeed."

Anthony ran to him at the door. Tatiana walked up with less than her full smile, a wooden spoon in her hand. "Hey."

"Hey." He kissed her.

"You smell like beer," she said.

"I went out for a drink with Stevie," he said, sinking down at the table.

"Oh. How was it?" She turned to the stove. "Ant, time for bed, like we agreed."

"But Mom—!"

"Now, Anthony," said Alexander.

Grumpily Anthony got up to go. As he was walking away, Alexander circled his little wrist. "Ant," he said, "when your mother tells you to do something, you just do it. No need for grumpy. Got it?"

After the boy left the room, Alexander watched Tatiana's back to him as she focused on the stove. She was making chicken molé enchiladas and cilantro lime rice. Tania was teaching Francesca English, and Francesca was teaching Tania Mexican food. It was a fine barter of services.

"Are you upset because I went out for a drink?" he asked at last. "I'm just trying to be friendly."

Coming to him with a plateful of food, leaning over and kissing his head, she said, "I'm not upset with you, darling. Though I wouldn't mind if you called to tell me when you'd be coming home so I know when to make dinner ready for you." She gave him more rice, bread, filled his glass, then stood quietly by him, pressing her body against his. His hand automatically went around her and under her skirt to touch her nylon stockings. Tracing up the seam, he stopped on the space of bare flesh suspended just under her open girdle. He loved that space. "I know it's been crazy," he said. "It's not going to be that way forever. I won't let it be that way. I'll—I'll take care of it. But what else is wrong?"

She sighed.

"Oh, sighs are so unpromising."

Anthony ran out to tell them what was on the radio, and Alexander took his hand away from Tatiana and said, "Not radio. Bed, Anthony. Now."

But after Anthony disappeared inside his bedroom, Alexander sighed himself. Telling Tatiana he'd be right back, he went into Anthony's room, where the boy was silently putting on his pajamas. Alexander watched him for a few moments, then helped him turn the top right way out, took him to the bathroom, helped him with his teeth and face, brought him back, settled him under the covers, and sat on the bed.

"What's up, bud?" Alexander asked. "Everything okay? School okay? Sergio okay? Mommy okay? What are you glum for?"

"I'm tired," Anthony said, turning on his side, away from Alexander. "I got school tomorrow."

Turning off the light, Alexander bent over the bed, his arms flanking the boy. "Your dad's working too much," he said quietly. "I know. No one's used to it anymore." They barely worked the last two years they had been travelling, just enough to get by. "But remember when you were three, and I was on the lobster boat? I left the house at four in the morning, and came back at five in the evening? That was a long day."

"I don't remember," said Anthony. "But in that place with the long-necked birds and the canals you didn't work at all, not even picking apples. We just kept trying to catch that fish. What was it called?"

"Prehistoric sturgeon. Didn't do such a great job, did we, Antman?"

"Should have stayed there longer," said Anthony. "We would've caught him. Mommy said he swam all the way from that river where you got married so you could catch him."

"Your mommy is very funny." Alexander pressed his lips to Anthony's head. "You played me nice songs on your guitar on the deck of that canal," he whispered. "This Sunday, you're going to help me finish our front deck. I'm going to need your help, bud, okay?"

"Okay, Dad." And the boy's arm went around his neck.

After dinner, during which she remained quiet, he went outside for a smoke. Tatiana followed him. The darkened mountains were calming in the moonlight, but not as calming as Tatiana hands on him. He pulled her to sit on his lap. She sat briefly, pressing her cheek to his cheek, and then got up. That was less calming.

"You don't want me to sit on your lap when I tell you what I'm about to tell you," she said, chewing her lip in agitation.

He studied her. "What are you doing? Are you . . . weighing your words?"

"Yes," she said. "I'm having trouble—look, it's like this." She sighed. "Your Steve Balkman is a young man? A handsome fella with a bit of a swagger? Has a broken right arm?"

"Yes . . . how did you—"

"He was brought into ER late one night a while back and I was the one who helped set his arm when I came in to work next morning."

He frowned. "So? He broke his arm falling off a ladder."

There was a silence. "No, he didn't," said Tatiana. "He broke it in a drunken brawl."

"What?" Alexander got testy. Her face was making him testy. It was asking for a reaction he didn't want to give. "All right, so?"

Tatiana backed away to the railing. "Two men came in together, both injured. The police came. This Steve Balkman apparently had been making inappropriate comments about the other man's girlfriend." She paused. "The problem was, the other guy was badly busted up, and his family was going to press charges. In the end, William Balkman came—is that your new boss?—he came in, talked to the cops, to the other man's family, smoothed things over, and no charges were filed." She took a deep breath, adding quietly, "I think the injured guy had been Balkman's other foreman."

Alexander glared at her until she looked away. "Okay," he said. "You didn't want to tell me, and now you've told me. It's fascinating. Thank you for sharing that. But so what? He's hardly going to be telling the new guy he was in a bar fight. *I* wouldn't."

"In a bar fight with his previous foreman over inappropriate comments."

"Tania," said Alexander, "are you worried about my safety? Afraid for me? That something might happen to me if I go for a drink with him? I tell you what, worry about all kinds of things, but don't worry about that."

She tried to say something, but he didn't want to hear it. Talking to her about Las Vegas or resigning his army commission was clearly out of the question. "You're making a big deal out of absolutely nothing," he said, getting up.

In bed he said, "Don't you understand? This place is going to be my career and my future. I'm going to be an architect, Tania. I'm going to build houses."

"I know. The work *is* perfect for you. But there are hundreds of home build—"

"NO!" he yelled.

Alexander was shouting. He raised his voice, was upset, so upset he yelled at her while they were both naked, under covers, in their bed. They had not had loud words in the bedroom since Coconut Grove and that was—not this. Not knowing how to deal with it, Tatiana, her lips a nerve-ending away from trembling, said in her quietest voice, "Shh. I'm sorry. We won't mention it again." She reached for his face.

"*This* job is perfect for me," he said, jerking away from her. "If you can't understand why, I can't and won't and *refuse* to explain it to you."

"Darling, you don't have to explain anything."

"That's right. I don't. I want us to go out to dinner with Steve and his fiancée, so you can see for yourself he's all right."

"He has a fiancée?"

"I don't understand why *that* would surprise you!"

Her lip bitten she said nothing.

Alexander was breathing hard. "What?" he said. "What? What? What?" He turned to her, glaring. "Tell me right now before I—"

Tatiana opened her mouth to speak.

"I don't want to hear it!"

Tatiana closed her mouth.

"What's wrong with you?" he said. "How can you judge him? You haven't even met him!"

"Oh, I met him, all right," Tatiana said. "I set his arm, remember? But I'm not judging anyone. You're right. I'm just being—a ninny. Let's not talk about it anymore. It's so late." She forced a smile. She rubbed his chest. She stroked his face. "It's fine. Shh. And you're right. This isn't the Gulag, this isn't Catowice."

After Alexander fell asleep, Tatiana put on her silk robe and went to sit at the kitchen table, putting her face down on her arms. What could she do? It was clear that whatever Alexander needed from her, he didn't need or want to hear about the Balkmans. She didn't tell him that Steve came back to the hospital three times looking for her, came back even after she told him she was married, not interested, not keen on him. "Come out with me—you're finer than *all* the girls in Vegas, and I've seen them all. Come out with me"—arched eyebrows, slick suggestive grins—"You *won't* regret it." She hoped her grim stare told him she didn't get the filthy joke he shared with her.

Not only this, but he recently had made another trip to the hospital, broken arm and all, following another drunken brawl. He and his buddies had stripped a man naked and kicked him repeatedly. Carolyn Kaminsky, the nurse on duty who told her about this, described the arrival of Bill Balkman, after which the police and the beaten man once again quietly dropped the charges and went away. Tatiana wanted to tell Alexander but he didn't want to hear it. I've heard worse in the army. That would be his answer. And perhaps he was right. Alexander would know better than she what a man like Steve might say to a woman like Tatiana.

She was still sitting when Alexander staggered out of the bedroom half an hour later looking for her. "I hate it," he said, "when you sit in the middle of the night and fucking fret at the kitchen table like you did on Bethel Island. My whole life flashes before my eyes. Come to bed."

The Nurse is In, the A Side

The following evening, a depressed Tatiana rushed home after work. She tried very hard to be home before Alexander so she could start dinner and get things in order before he came home hungry and tired. Anthony was having pizza for Sergio's birthday. She had to pick him up at nine.

To her surprise Alexander's truck was already outside. It was only quarter of eight. Usually Friday nights he was home later. She came up the steps and opened the door. He was sitting on the couch, his head tilted to the side. Tatiana barely noticed the bouquet of flowers on the table. "Shura?"

He groaned.

She rushed to him. "What's wrong?"

He was spread out on the sofa in his long johns, a wet towel over his face. She pulled the towel off. His eyes were closed. He was listless. He shook from side to side. "I don't know. I'm sick . . ."

"Oh, dear, what's the matter?"

"My whole body hurts, I can't move . . ."

She threw her nurse's bag to the floor.

"No, no," he said. "Bring the bag."

With the bag she came, bending over him solicitously. She kneeled on the couch by his side to feel his head, his face. His eyes remained closed. He was damp from the towel. "I don't think you have a fever . . ."

"I need a nurse . . ." he muttered.

"Darling, I'm here," she said.

"Are you in uniform?"

"Of course. I just came home from work."

"Is your hair up in a tight bun?"

"Of course. Shura, open your eyes."

"Your white shoes, your white stockings all on?"

"Yes, yes, what are you doing?"

"I need a nurse . . ." he muttered again.

There was silence from Tatiana.

"Hmm," she finally said in an officious tone. "It does appear as if you're gravely ill. I need to give you a full check-up before I make my diagnosis."

"Whatever you think is best, Nurse Metanova."

From her bag, she procured a stethoscope. "Can you take off your crew? I need to listen to your lungs."

The stethoscope was deliciously cold on his chest.

When he opened his eyes her expression was solemn. She had put her nurse's hat back on and undone the top buttons of her uniform, revealing her soft cleavage. "I need to check you for ill humors," she said, pulling off his long johns. "Please sit very still and don't move. This can be dangerous. We must proceed with caution." She unhooked her front closing bra, undid her uniform all the way, leaving fastened only the button under her breasts, now pushed together and spilling out. She was exposed to him, coral hardening nipples, cream stomach, her light open girdle gartering her sheer white stockings. She kneeled on the carpet between his legs. "Hmm," she said again, taking hold of him. "Ill humors indeed. But I think we may be able to fix it, Captain Belov."

Retrieving a little mineral oil from her bag, she rubbed it on herself, then on him, and put him slippery between her breasts, sliding back and forth on him.

He couldn't take it. "I think I've got a severe case," he said, groaning, struggling not to close his eyes. "I'm sick to the core."

Nodding her head in somber agreement, she caressed him, pulsing and engorged, slowly up, slowly down with her slick hands. "Ill humors are serious things, Captain. There are no guarantees."

His hands went into her hair; her cap fell off. He heaved himself off the sofa, bent to her and kissed her. "I'm sorry about yesterday, Tatia," he whispered. "The silly shouting. I just don't want you to worry. Please trust me on this. Please."

"Captain!" she said, her fingers tightening their spiral stroke around him, rendering him speechless. "Please. You mustn't speak. It's for your own good."

"Is there a treatment for ill humors?" Alexander asked, falling back on the couch.

"Well, in the olden days, the remedy," Tatiana replied calmly, "was to have them sucked out of you."

He wasn't calm when he said, "I see. Do you think that treatment will work today? Modern medicine seems to have progressed so far beyond that."

"You're right, but all we can do is try. Now sit still and don't move. The mouth shall know no restraint. It is our only hope."

The mouth never knew restraint. He tried to stop her at the end, he really wanted her on top of him in that uniform and the insanity-inducing open girdle, but she whispered, "Captain, you want to be cured? Then come in my mouth. Like you love." Stopping her was obviously completely impossible.

Alexander's response to Tatiana's white nurse's outfit and her tight bun became so Pavlovian that he found himself becoming aroused at the first sight of her on work mornings, then during the occasional afternoons they met for lunch, and then at the glimpse of the uniform hanging in the closet, ironed and ready for next day. The nadir was his starched tumescence at just the *thought* of the white uniform. After a while she pronounced him terminal and said there was absolutely no hope for him.

He joyously agreed.

But still she made every excuse known to Alexanderkind not to go out to dinner with Steve and his fiancée.

Dinner with Steve and his Fiancée

Coming home late, he was speeding up Pima, knowing she was home with Ant and they were waiting for him. It was their first Christmas season in Arizona. Alexander had hung Christmas lights around the house and now they sparkled multi-colored like a city of dreams from down the road. He could see his little lit-up house shining on the hill as soon as he turned right on Jomax, still a mile downstream. The tension of the frenetic day began to leach out of him. After he parked his truck, he lingered on the front deck for a moment so he could see her through the window.

She has nested peace all through the house; everything is dusted and spotless. They have books and magazines and newspapers, and shoes and baseball bats, and sofa blankets and Christmas holly, but everything has a place, everything looks like comfort. The table lamps are on dim, the stove is on, the white snowflakes are patched on the windows. He will tell her to draw the shades in the future, but tonight he's happy to watch her without her seeing him. He feels as if he is standing behind the lilac tree in the summer of their Lazarevo. Her hair is piled high on top of her head and she is hiding her body in one of his worn army crews—which means when he picks it up, it will smell like her. He must remember to ask her not to wash it. He keeps telling her, she is a true Alberto Varga girl: she could be wrapped in a rug and still look naked. She is getting butter for the bread; she's made sugar cookies, they're cooling on the rack. His gaze drifts to his son, who is sitting at the table pretending to do his homework. Actually what Anthony is doing is following her with his eyes. Wherever she moves, his venerating gaze follows. Anthony says something, and she laughs, throwing back her head, and then comes over and kisses him. Alexander watches his son's face being kissed by her, then hers as she kisses him.

He opened the door, and they came to him. The tree was twinkling, the house smelled of pine, the stew smelled great, the warm bread and the sugar cookies even better.

"Dad's home!" said Anthony, taking his keys.

"Daddy's home," echoed Tatiana, lifting her face to him. "So late."

Alexander kissed her mouth, her neck. Cookies and musk. "Nice," he whispered.

Over dinner he said, "We're going out with Steve this Friday."

"No, I can't this Friday."

"I don't want to hear it. Tania, I've been working for Bill four months! You've never met him or Steve."

"I wouldn't say I've never met Steve," she said dryly. "But I know what you mean."

"Stop that. I'm completely out of excuses."

"I'm not though."

"They think I'm making you up."

"Oh, listen," she said breezily. "We'll go in the New Year."

"Yes, then, too. But Bill is having a Christmas party next week."

"Sorry, can't make it. Vikki and Tom are coming next week. Aunt Esther and Rosa are coming. Did you forget? We have a full house for the holidays. Anthony and I have a lot to do to get ready."

"Oh no, does Vikki *have* to come?" Anthony said plaintively.

"Yes, Anthony, be nice. She loves you. She's buying you a bike."

"Aunt Esther already bought me a bike."

"Well then, you're going to have two and be grateful."

"Ant, you are going to help on Saturday," said Alexander. "Because on Friday as it turns out, your mother is busy."

In a small, exclusive, Italian-American restaurant in Scottsdale called Bobo's, Alexander sat at the table with Steve and Amanda, waiting. As always, Tatiana was late. She was consistently late absolutely everywhere. He didn't know how she kept her job. Did he not buy her a watch three months ago to help her keep time? She got off work at seven, but here it was after eight. Alexander tried not to feel impatient. The bread came, the menus. Amanda was a young, pretty, light-brown-haired gal, coiffed and made up, who looked like she might run to heavy with age. She was easy to talk to, and Alexander hoped that Tania liked her; everything would be so much easier if the four of them could be friends.

He chatted with Steve and Amanda, but eventually even Steve said, "You think everything is all right?"

Nodding, Alexander motioned for the wine menu. Bobo, the owner, brought it over himself. "Señor Alexander, where is our señora?"

"Late again, Bobo." Alexander smoked, smoked, smoked, drumming, drumming, drumming.

And then, even before he raised his head and saw her, he knew she had arrived because there was a slight change in the restaurant air, as if a small breeze had swept through.

Bobo brought her over himself. Alexander and Steve stood up.

She was wearing a fitted embroidered lavender dress he had not seen before, and her hair was in a Russian peasant braid with a few strands falling around her cheeks. She had on light mascara and pink lip gloss.

"Thank you, Bobo, for such personal service." Alexander turned to Steve and Amanda. "Bobo's been secretly in love with my wife for months."

"What do you mean secretly, señor?" said a delighted, cue-ball-headed, bull-necked, short, black-doe-eyed Bobo in a thick Italian accent. "Openly, openly. Señora, if he doesn't treat you right, you know where to go."

"Thank you, Bobo," said a shining Tatiana. "He's been on his best behavior, but it's always good to keep him on his toes." After melting, Bobo reluctantly left. Tatiana raised her face to Alexander. "Hey," she said with a smile. "Sorry I'm late." He did not kiss her in public and wasn't going to start tonight. Touching her braid, he turned her to his friends and, with his hand on her shoulder, said, "Amanda, Steve, this is Tania—my wife."

After slightly flinching at the sound of a man saying "my wife" with such happiness, Amanda politely shook Tatiana's hand. Alexander saw that Tatiana barely offered her hand to Steve, who didn't look directly at her, his face flushed.

Well, Tania did look quite glossy. Alexander was flushed himself.

They all sat down. Amanda in a composed and friendly tone, said, "Tania, it's so nice to finally meet you. Alexander's told us so much about you."

"Has he?"

"Oh, yes. I can't believe he's been working with my Stevie for so long and we just met."

"Oh, no, Steve and I already met," Tatiana said evenly. "I took care of his arm at PMH a few months ago."

"Stevie, you never told me!" squealed Amanda.

Steve's face was impassive. "Well, I didn't know it was her, did I?" he said, pouring himself some wine. Lifting his gaze from the glass, flip and smiling toothily, he said with a shrug, "Sorry, I really don't remember meeting you."

"No?" said Tatiana.

"Tania, would you like a glass of wine?" Alexander asked, so cool, without even raising his eyebrows!

"Oh, yes, thank you, Alexander. I do enjoy a glass of wine now and again." She said it with a short cough but without blushing. He leaned into her a little when he clinked his glass against hers.

"How was work?" he asked quietly.

"Not too bad today." Just as quietly.

"Where's your watch?"

"Oh." She let out a sheepish laugh. "Must have left it home."

"Not very useful at home, is it?"

He poured her a little more wine, offered her bread, opened the menu for her. She said, thank you very much. And he said, you're welcome. So refined. Like characters from Edith Wharton. Alexander smiled, wondering if fine *fin-de-siècle* manners could hide their profound conjugal ease.

When he looked across the table, Amanda was staring at him. "So how long have you two been married?" she asked quickly, looking embarrassed at being caught out staring.

"Seven years," replied Tatiana.

"Seven years, wow." Amanda raised her brows at Alexander. "No seven-year itch for you, huh, Alexander?"

"Not very likely," he said. Tania smelled like lilac and looked dressed in lilac from the Field of Mars, the tops of her breasts swelling over the lavender fabric of the low, scalloped neckline. She was so lush and bosomy, so blonde and sparkling, Alexander didn't know how anyone could be talking about anything when his wife looked like this.

"You have such long hair, Tania. I've never seen hair that long," said Amanda, whose hair was fashionably short, like all the women's now—short, teased, sprayed, coiffed in a bouffant. "They let you wear it like that in the hospital?"

"No, it's up in a bun when I go to work."

"You really should cut it," Amanda advised in a helpful tone.

"Oh, I know—I'm hopelessly out of style. But what to do?" Tatiana smiled. "The husband likes it long."

Amanda turned to Steve. "Which way do you like it, Stevie?"

"As you know, I like it any way, Mand." And they both laughed. Tatiana glanced at Alexander. He knocked her leg.

Steve told a joke, everyone enjoyed it, even Tatiana, and thus encouraged, Steve told another and another. He told stories of his time stationed in England, about meeting Amanda at one of his houses, about his father pushing him into college. He was gregarious, funny, could tell a good story. Amanda sat close, listening to every word. Then she tried to ask Tatiana questions, but no one knew the cardinal rule about human beings better than Tatiana: that everyone wanted most to talk about themselves. So, after vaguely telling Amanda that she had lived in New York, that she and Alexander got married and then he went to the front (none of which was, strictly speaking, untrue), Tatiana swerved the conversation away from herself, and Amanda began her own account of growing up in quiet Phoenix when it was all farmland, and the Indians would come into the center of an unpaved town for the Saturday market on Indian School Road. Tatiana remarked that she still went to that very crowded morning market. Yes, it was shocking how many people lived in Scottsdale now! Amanda said. Did New York have even more people? She couldn't imagine it. She'd never been anywhere but Phoenix and was so jealous of Steve who had been to exotic England and now was going to Vegas practically every month.

"Stevie," she said, "promised to take me to Vegas with him." She tilted her plaintive head. "I'm still waiting, baby."

"Soon, baby, soon."

"Steve and his dad have been trying for months to get Alexander to go to Vegas with them."

"Have they?" This from Tatiana.

Alexander tried to change the subject, because Vegas was a sore subject at his house. But Amanda steamrollered ahead, asking if Tatiana had ever been to Vegas and when Tatiana curtly said no, Amanda exclaimed, "Oh, you're like me, you've never been anywhere!"

Alexander laughed.

"What's so funny?" Amanda for some reason didn't look as if she found his laughter remotely amusing.

"Nothing, excuse me." He tried to turn serious. "Tania, you've never been to Sweden?" His eyes were unserious. "Finland, perhaps?"

Her leg knocked into his. "No," she said.

"What about Russia?"

Her leg knocked into his harder. "No," she said. "You?" Turning to Amanda, Tatiana said, "Before we came to Phoenix we travelled the United States, so we did actually see a bit of America. And we spent some time in Nevada," she added, "but decided not to go to Las Vegas, because we didn't think it would be a good place for our small boy."

"Oh, that's certainly true!" said Steve. "Only big boys in Vegas." Amanda tittered uproariously.

Tatiana had on a nice pasty smile.

Alexander changed the subject to business: the houses under construction, new architecture designs in Phoenix, and then the imminent war with Korea. Steve was singularly uninterested in Korea despite Alexander's best efforts to steer his friend to the topic. Steve would not be steered. "Don't have the stomach for politics, man, you know that. Even less when I've had a few." He ordered a beer for himself. "I like jokes. I have another one about Vegas. Want to hear?"

"Steve-o, ladies present," Alexander said. "No stupid drunk jokes."

Amanda told Alexander not to worry, she'd heard them all.

"Manda, you haven't heard this one," said Steve. "You'll think it's hilarious." He took a swig of his beer. "A man comes home to find his wife with a packed suitcase. She tells him she's leaving and going to Vegas, because she heard she can make $100 a night doing what she gives him for free. The man thinks about it and then starts packing his own suitcase. The wife asks him where he is going, and he replies, 'I'm going to Vegas, too.' When she asks him why, he says, 'Because I want to see how you're going to live on $200 a year.'"

Oh, how Amanda and Steve laughed.

Alexander laughed too, but Tatiana wasn't laughing. He sighed slightly, but fortunately the food came. He gave Tatiana some of his steak, took some of her lasagna, poured her some more wine.

Suddenly Amanda said, "Stevie and I are getting married in the spring. Right, Stevie?"

"Absolutely," Steve said, draping his arm around Amanda, dangling it over her shoulder very close to her breast.

Alexander glanced at Tatiana's moist but compressed mouth. "Congratulations," said Tatiana in a tone that said, Lord have mercy on you.

"And when we get married I'm not going to work. Am I, Stevie?"

"Of course not, doll. You can stay home and eat bonbons all day in your robe and slippers."

Was Amanda trying to stir things up? Alexander was obtuse when it came to things like this, but by the look on Tatiana's face, he had his answer, and then, as if to prove it, his wife asked, "How long have you two been engaged?"

Amanda didn't reply and Steve said, "Nearly four years."

"Ah," said Tatiana. "Four years." Without inflection.

"What about you?" Amanda asked.

Tatiana waved her hand casually. "Oh, it was war. Things weren't the same then. Everything had to be so quick."

"Everything?" Amanda said, with a giggle. "So how long?"

When Tatiana still didn't reply, Alexander said, "Two days."

"Two days!" exclaimed Amanda, peering at Alexander and then falling quiet.

"He was going to the front," Tatiana hastily explained.

"Obviously not so hastily," Amanda said. "So you have just the one boy, Tania? Are you thinking of having more?"

"We're thinking about it."

"Are you thinking about it, or doing something about it?" Amanda said, and Steve laughed into his food, and Tatiana, whose job it was to become friendly with Amanda so the four of them could do things together, was instead like the tetchy building inspector, obviously not willing to give the certificate of occupancy to anyone without additional incentives. Alexander pulled on her braid lightly.

"I'm sorry," Amanda said when she stopped laughing. "I hope I don't offend you, Tania, the way I talk."

"Not at all."

"Hang around too long with Stevie and his buddies, and you can't help it. He's simply *ruining* me." She said it with delight. "You should have heard the joke he told me the first time he met me. No, it's too horrid to repeat in public, isn't it, hon?"

"I don't remember the joke, Mand. I'm sure it was awful, knowing me."

"Remember, the 'just like a baby' joke?" She giggled wildly, and even blushed!

"Steve," said Tatiana in a withering tone, "I love a good joke. Let's hear it." Her cold eyes never left Steve's face.

Steve laughed. "Nah," he said. "You don't want to hear that joke, Tania. It'll make a truck driver blush."

"Indeed," said Tatiana.

Frowning, remembering something too distant for clarity, Alexander looked at Tatiana's face, and then across at Steve, who was shaking his head, not looking at Tatiana, examining the remains of the cold steak on his plate. It occurred to Alexander that Steve, during the whole dinner, had barely addressed Tatiana, barely spoken to her directly; in fact, though very much himself in all other ways, he acted as if she were not sitting at their table.

"We're inviting you to our wedding," Amanda went on, wonderfully oblivious. "The invitations go out right after Christmas. Scottsdale Country Club, *very* exclusive. Jeff and his fiancée Cindy want to get married there, too, but between you and me, it's not going to happen. Jeff is simply not ready to get married yet. We're inviting two *hundred* people. It's going to be an extravaganza." She gurgled. "Tania, you probably didn't have a big wedding. Sounds like you didn't have a lot of time to prepare."

"You're right, we didn't," Tatiana replied. "Our wedding was tiny. Just us, the priest, and the couple we paid to be our witnesses."

Amanda looked at Tatiana incredulously. "You got married and didn't even invite your families?"

Alexander and Tatiana said nothing.

Amanda went on. "What about a wedding reception? You didn't have any food? Any music? How can there be no food or music at a wedding?"

It was Alexander who answered her. "There was music," he said. "Oh, how we danced on the night we were wed."

An odd hush fell over the table. "But I can't remember if we had any food." He paused. "Did we have food, Tania?" He didn't look at her.

"I don't think so, Shura." She didn't look at him.

"What did she just call you?" asked Amanda.

"Just a nickname she has for me." He couldn't take one more second of Amanda watching them, not one more. He stood up, pulling Tatiana up, too and motioning to Bobo, who instantly had the band start to play "*Bésame Mucho*." On the dance floor Alexander drew her to him. "Tania, come on, they're all right. Lighten up. You're not being very good."

"But, Shura, you tell me I'm *so* good," she murmured against his chest, blinking up at him.

Alexander threaded his large fingers through her small ones. "Stop that right now," he said, gazing down at her and squeezing her hands.

"Tell me, why won't your buddy Steve marry that poor girl?"

"Why buy the cow," said Alexander, "when you can get the milk for free?"

He was expecting her to laugh, but she didn't. She said with a straight face, "You think she's giving him free milk?"

"And cheese and butter too."

And then she laughed.

Bésame, bésame Mucho . . .

"All I want to do," he said, "is kiss the top of your breasts. Right *now.*"

Como si fuera esta noche la ultima vez . . . She lifted her face to him. "Let's go home and you can kiss me all over." *Que tengo miedo perderte, perderte despues . . .*

When they got back, Alexander called for the bill and Tania excused herself to go to the ladies' room. Amanda went with her. The girls were barely a yard away from the table when Alexander said, "Stevie, you crazy bastard, did you say something inappropriate to my wife when she was setting your arm? She's acting as if you killed her dog."

Steve shrugged. "Alex, I'm sorry, man, I know she says she set it, and I'm sure she's right, but I honestly don't remember ever meeting her."

"Stop bullshitting me. You told me four months ago you met someone at the hospital, remember? It was her, wasn't it?"

"I don't think so." Steve lowered his voice. "I meet so many goils."

"In the hospital? How many times do you go to the fucking hospital?"

"If I said anything to her, I apologize. I didn't know she was your wife or I never would have said anything, ever. You know that, man. Here, let me have that. Dinner's on me. I insist."

The following Friday Alexander was back at Bobo's, once again waiting for her, this time with Vikki and Richter. They had just flown in; he picked them up at Sky Harbor, got them set up at home, left Ant at Francesca's, and now they were all waiting. When Tatiana finally arrived, only forty minutes late ("Oh, for Vikki, you're almost on time!"), it was Vikki not Bobo who jumped up and squealed, throwing her arms around Tatiana.

They spent the next four uncompressed, unstilted, unmannered hours, eating, drinking, smoking, swearing, dancing, even rude-joking.

Vikki and Richter were a good-looking couple, young and tall, in love and all charged up. Nearly all conversation at the table, directed entirely by two soldiers, revolved around Korea. Vikki and Tatiana couldn't get a word in. "In fact, you're not allowed to speak," Richter said to Vikki. "I know all you want to do is complain about me, and I'm not going to let you spoil a perfectly good evening of hearty man talk about war."

"Well, if you didn't do so many things wrong, Tom, I wouldn't have to complain about you."

Richter was aghast that the U.S. troops had just been ordered to pull out of South Korea, since the intentions of the Communist North were so clearly to cross the 38th parallel. Five months earlier, in July 1949, Owen Lattimore, a State Department official, had said that the only thing to do was to let South Korea fall but not to let it look as if the U.S. had pushed it to fall. Calling into question Lattimore's loyalty and priorities, Alexander wanted to know what kind of message that was sending to the North Koreans and the Soviets, who were arming and training them.

"I'll tell you what kind of message," Richter said. "Come any time, take what you want. Take what you think is yours. Reunite— please. We won't stop you and, more important, we don't want to stop you."

Alexander had just read the military intel reports from General Charles Willoughby, who said that the North Koreans, despite their firm denials were already amassing on the 38th parallel.

"We're pulling out our troops, and they're arming the DMZ?" Richter said. "Do you see a small problem with this?"

Alexander saw.

"Come spring, they're going to invade," said Richter, "be in Seoul a month later and then we won't be able to stop them even if we wanted to."

"If our troops are getting pulled out, Tom, maybe we won't have to go?" Vikki said expectantly, taking his hand.

"Bite your tongue, woman," Richter said, pulling his hand away. "We're shipping out to Seoul, even if you and I and Willoughby are the only Americans left in the entire fucking Korean peninsula."

"Well, that's just great, Lieutenant-husband," said a deflated Vikki. "That's just fucking great."

Pouring her wine and lighting her cigarettes, Richter said, "Stop sulking." He turned her to him. "That's an order, Viktoria."

"That's an order, Viktoria," she mimicked.

And then they kissed for five minutes, wine glasses in hand, right at the table, while Alexander turned his gaze politely away to Tatiana, who did not turn politely away, her expression affectionate and unwithering. He didn't have to even ask for a seal of approval on Tom Richter—from the first moment she met him. "Richter could take your Vikki right on the table," Alexander whispered into Tatiana's ear, his forehead pressed to her temple, "and it would be just dandy with you, but my poor buddy Steve tells one tasteless joke and gets nothing but scorn."

During dessert Vikki finally managed to edge in one complaint. "It was our first anniversary last month," she said, "and do you know what my newlywed besotted husband bought me? A food processor! *Me*—a food processor!"

"It was a hint, Viktoria."

Vikki theatrically rolled her eyes. Richter just rolled his.

Trying not to smile, Alexander glanced at Tania, who was loving on her death by-chocolate cake and hardly paying attention. She embraced electric gadgets with all her heart. There was not an electric can opener, a blender, a coffee maker that did not get his wife wildly enthusiastic. She window shopped for these items every Saturday, read their manuals in the store and then at night regaled Alexander with their technical attributes, as if the manuals she was reciting were Pushkin's poetry.

"Tania, darling, my closest friend," said Vikki, "please tell me you agree. Don't you think a food processor is extremely unromantic?"

After thinking carefully, her mouth full, Tatiana said, "What kind of food processor?"

For Christmas, Alexander bought Tatiana a Kitchen-Aid food processor, top of the line, the best on the market. Inside it she found a gold necklace. Despite a very full house, and Anthony right outside on the couch, she made love to Alexander that Christmas night in candlelight wearing nothing but the necklace, perched and posted on top of him, her soft silken hair floating in a mane and her warm breasts swinging into his chest.

The Roofer

She had gotten herself dressed up, a yellow flowing dress with a short jacket; her hair was loosely braided and her face was scrubbed. She'd brought Alexander lunch but he was nowhere to be seen on the site—just the roofers, who were busy in the open loft space of the new structure. She stood by the car and while she waited, she thought about her dear Vikki, who had just left, and how uncomfortable she made her son Anthony, who wasn't himself for the week Vikki and Tom had stayed with them. And Vikki wasn't her usual self either. She married Richter after a whirlwind romance a year ago, but now he was about to leave for Korea, and she didn't want to go, but what was a married young gal to do while her husband was across the world? Vikki had witnessed first hand how Tatiana lived by herself in New York. "I don't want to live like Tania did, being a flippin' widow," Vikki complained, even to Alexander.

"Tell me," Alexander said to Vikki, who looked puzzled by the suddenly pleased look on his face, "exactly how bereaved was she? And spare me no macabre detail." Tatiana had to rescue her friend, drag away her trouble-making husband and end the conversation.

Tatiana's thoughts were interrupted by the roofers, who had stopped their work and were staring at her. Feeling self-conscious, she got back in the car and no sooner than she did that—

"Hello, Tania." Steve Balkman was knocking on the window, opening the sedan's door. "Alexander's not here. He must have forgotten you were coming."

"Unlikely," said Tatiana, reluctantly getting out.

"He had to run back to Pop's office to get some forms for the damn inspectors. I had the wrong forms on hand. He'll be back soon."

Tatiana debated not waiting.

Steve cleared his throat.

"Please," she said. "The less said the better."

"If I offended you in the hospital that time, I apologize," he said.

"No offense taken." Which time?

"You know I never would've said anything to you had I known Alexander."

Tell that to the former foreman with a girlfriend.

"I was just fooling with you. I'm very happy with Amanda."

A man can be perfectly happy with any woman, as long as he does not love her, Tatiana thought, in memory of the immortal Oscar Wilde. She said nothing, moving a step away from him. Where was that husband of hers? She didn't like the way the roofers were staring at her. They'd never act like that if Alexander were here.

Steve smiled. "You look very pretty today," he said, looking her up and down. "Come, I'll introduce you to our crew."

Shaking her head, Tatiana said, "I'm not the queen, Stevie. I'm Alexander's wife. Do yourself a *big* favor, don't introduce me to other men."

Steve's smile barely faltered. "Oh, we're all friendly around here. Believe me, your husband knows very well how it is."

"No," Tatiana said coldly. "I don't think my husband does."

It was to the frozen smile on Steve's face that Alexander returned, and Tatiana and Steve did not get to have a fuller discussion about Alexander's understanding nature. Alexander handed the signature forms to Steve and took Tatiana and the food basket in his truck to a lot nearby, where they had their lunch away from everyone.

"You're dressed too nicely, Tania," he said. "I don't need it, and those animals certainly don't."

She didn't want to say what she was thinking—I can't get dressed up for you because the people you work with can't show a little basic respect?

He leaned over. "They're just assholes, ignore them. I have to go back. Kiss me."

She was all pulpy-lipped and slightly dishevelled from having his hands in her hair and under her petticoat when they returned to the construction site. As Alexander was walking her to her car, there was a wolf whistle. Alexander glared at the pack of roofers who were finishing their lunch. "Are you out of your minds?"

No one acknowledged his speaking to them.

Tatiana drove away without comment.

Alexander walked away without comment.

He didn't get far before the head roofer gave Alexander a knowing smile.

Where did Balkman get these people from? But the worker must have been from a country that did not know the ancient code of man. With raised eyebrows, the roofer looked down the road where her sedan had disappeared and said, "She is somethin' else, that one. Must keep you up—"

"You must be fucking kidding me," said Alexander.

The roofer was also missing the faintest sense of self-preservation. He opened his mouth again to speak. Alexander grabbed the man by the shirt lapels and hurled him to the ground. In an offended huff (*he* was offended!) the roofer quit and took his whole crew with him.

Bill Balkman was not happy.

"You work for me," Balkman said to Alexander. "You represent my company. This reflects badly on our business, people quitting left and right. And you know these people don't mean anything by it. It's just men talking."

"That's bullshit," said Alexander. "I've been around, I've been in the army, for fuck's sake, and nowhere did men talk like that about another man's wife—not unless they wanted to lose their teeth."

"Oh, come on, it's just good old fun. Amanda, Margaret, they don't mind."

Margaret was Bill's girlfriend. Alexander said pointedly, "Tania is my *wife*. Marriage is her protection." Maybe it wasn't in the Soviet Union, where it was her death sentence. But they weren't in the Soviet Union. "She is completely off limits," he said. "There is no discussion on this issue. Bill, we're going to have a major problem over this if I'm going to have to explain it again"—Alexander glared at Balkman—"to anybody."

"Calm down, calm down," Balkman said quickly. "You're right, of course. He was out of line. I'm glad he's gone. He was terrible, anyway. But in the meantime, what are we going to do without even a terrible roofer?"

Alexander hired a few extra guys and spent the spring hauling heavy glazed blocks and concrete and sitting under the hot sun spackling the mortar undercoating and then laying ceramic roof tile on top of it, which Balkman showed him how to do. He was diligent, hard-working, fast. "Good work, man," Balkman called from below, in full hearing of Steve, and gave Alexander a raise.

From hauling thousands of pounds of roof tiles and cement bags, day in and day out, Alexander's arms and chest started to look like they were carved out of stone, by Roman sculptors. He became massive. None of his shirts and jackets fit; he had to buy a new everything.

In the summer Tatiana hosted her first Tupperware party. She did it for her friend Carolyn Kaminsky, who was always doing something extra besides nursing. This month it was Tupperware. Tatiana invited a few nurses, Francesca—who declined, having recently given birth—and reluctantly, on a plea from Alexander, Amanda and Cindy, Jeff's girl. Despite the social gatherings they all went to, the dinner parties, the barbecues, and the occasional all-girl lunches, Tatiana's friendship with Amanda was proceeding slowly, much like the vaunted wedding—that did not happen in spring.

Twelve women came over on a Sunday afternoon. Anthony went over Sergio's. Alexander promised to stay in the work shed and not come out until the women left.

The party was a success. Tatiana had prepared little *pirozhki* and finger sandwiches with homemade bread. They drank black tea like Russians. The ladies, always taking an opportunity to look attractive, were all well turned out, comely and tall Carolyn especially, teased, tweezed, back combed, sprayed, swing skirts, petticoats, full panty girdles, high collar pressed shirts all. A pint of black liquid eye liner was used among them. Only Tatiana wore little makeup, her freckles uncovered by pancake powder. She had on a dress Alexander liked, sans petticoat, a soft floral raw silk dress with bow ties for sleeves, and was bare-legged (he liked that too), her hair plaited and swirled into a bun to maintain appearance with the rest of the ladies.

They were nearly at the end of the gathering, the girls deciding on their plastic container orders. They'd been chattering about the latest in *Ladies Home Journal*—"Frozen Foods that Will Send Shivers Down his Spine," "Two Novel Ways to Use Mirrors," "Faking Flawless Skin"—when one of the women looked out the window and said, "Tania, you have workmen here on a Sunday? One of them is coming to your house." All the girls peeked out.

Tatiana bit her lip. He was supposed to stay in the shed!

"Oh, that's not a workman," said Amanda. "That's her husband."

Slowly, the nurses turned their heads to Tatiana.

The back kitchen door opened and Alexander stepped in. He was wearing his torn, faded Lees and large brown work boots, in which he must have stood six-five. He was perspiring, and his enormous browned bare arms were covered with dirt and wood particles. The short sleeves of his black T-shirt were rolled up to his shoulders, and the slices of gray scars and blue tattoos were clearly visible. "Hello, ladies," he said, standing in the doorway, grinning white teeth at them through his black stubble, a day unshaven. He brought with him heat from the outside, cigarette smoke, sweat—and clammy confusion among the decorous women. "Hi, Carolyn, how's it going? Sorry to interrupt. Tania, can you get me my cigarettes and something to drink, please? I've run out."

Quickly Tatiana got up.

"Aren't you going to introduce us?" said Melissa in a stilted voice.

"Oh, yes, sorry. Um, girls, this is Alexander, my husband."

He tipped his invisible hat; she hurried to get him his things.

Carolyn said, "Alexander, why don't you sit down right here and have a drink with us. We're almost done, aren't we, girls?"

"Oh, yes! It's so hot out, by all means, do please sit. And we're almost done anyway."

Promptly bringing him his lemonade and cigarettes, Tatiana said, "Alexander has a lot of work to do in the shed, don't you?" She pushed him to the door.

"Oh. Yes. As it turns out, yes, yes, I do."

He drank straight from the pitcher and didn't stop until half the lemonade was gone. "It is *hot* out there. Well, nice to meet you, ladies." He took his cigarettes from her, with a wink, and was gone. When the door had shut, a smiling Carolyn said, "Tania, where did you find him?"

"Loose on the street," said Tatiana, starting to clear off the table.

"Was he loose for long? Where did his scars and tattoos come from?"

"Scars, where did those arms come from?" said Melissa.

"Scars and tattoos from war, arms from roofing." She busied herself with cleaning up.

"He's a roofer? He has a tattoo of a cross. Is he religious?"

"He has another one, of a hammer or something. Is that a roofing thing, too?"

Oh, bless them. It was if the Iron Curtain had not descended all over Europe.

"When'd you get married?"

"In 1942."

The girls fortunately did not pick up on 1942 being in the middle of some silly war somewhere. Time really did mute many things.

Amanda said, "He works for my fiancé, Steve, of Balkman Custom Homes. Steve and his dad own the business. Steve and I are getting married soon ourselves. He and Alex are best friends."

Cindy, a pixie girl with short dark hair, said, "He works with my fiancé, Jeff, too. We're getting married soon."

The nurses listened politely and then turned to Tatiana. "So tell us, what kind of a husband is he?" Melissa asked. "Is he grumpy? Is he moody? Is he demanding?"

Tatiana tried hard not to compress her mouth. Her husband was all those things, and then some. "He's the reason you punch the clock and pop the clutch as soon as your shift is over," said Carolyn, pinching Tatiana.

"Doesn't she just," said Erin. She was the receptionist. "She won't even wait for the next shift nurse to come in. Seven o'clock comes and she's in her car at seven oh one."

"Girls, are you quite done?" Tatiana said, and Carolyn and Erin laughed.

They wanted to know what he did for a living, how many hours he worked, whether he had to get dressed up to go to work, or if he looked like that all day long, whether he came home tired. He was a soldier, for how long? What was his rank? Was he still a captain? How long was he at the front? Did he bring some of the war home? Giggling accompanied that question.

"He brought all of the war home," said Tatiana, not giggling.

Another thirty minutes of rampant and largely unanswered curiosity passed before she waved goodbye to the last of them and came around the house to the back deck, where she found Alexander sitting on the deck rail, smoking. He had taken off his T-shirt in the heat.

"What are you doing coming in, especially so messy?" Tatiana said, walking up the deck steps. "You promised to stay away. They talked about nothing else but you the rest of the party."

"Oh?" he grinned. "What did they want to know?"

She shook her head and laughed.

"So what did you tell them?" His smile was from ear to ear. "Anything *good*?"

"Stop that. Go get clean. Ant will be home soon."

"Did you tell them at least," he asked, lowering his voice, "how much you like me messy?"

He was impossible. Yet seeing him sitting on top of the railing, his legs dangling in her favorite jeans of his, his happy crème brûlée eyes melting at her, the whites of his teeth beaming through the stubble, his spiky black hair, his gorgeous muscled arms and smooth bare chest glistening, Tatiana had to hold on to the deck chair because she didn't want him to see her legs start to tremble. But Alexander was smiling at her so widely, he must have already known. He put down his lemonade, put out his cigarette, and jumped down.

She put up her hands. "Shura, please," she said hoarsely.

"All right," he purred. "Since you asked so nicely."

Picking her up into his arms, he carried her to his work shed, kicking the door shut behind them and setting her down. It was scorching inside. The shed was organized, cleaned up, but it still smelled of saw and wood and metal and large power tools, oiled with grease. Reaching out, he moved one strap of her sundress down, then the other. He pulled the dress off, unhooked her bra, pulled off her underwear, and left her standing bare in front of him.

She tried to keep her breath from quickening, as she stood naked under his man's gaze, her legs from trembling, her nipples from hardening. She failed on all counts.

Finally he spoke. "Tania," he said calmly, his hands circling her waist, pulling her against his jeans and his belt buckle. "I'm not even going to get undressed. I'm going to leave my jeans on and my boots on, but you're going to be naked like this"—he lifted her and set her down on his work counter—"on the potato counter I built for you." Standing between her legs he rubbed his perspired chest against her impossible erect nipples. This time there was nothing suppressed about her moan. She leaned back on her unsteady arms. He scoured his stubble over her mouth, her neck, her breasts. "You like a bit of this," Alexander whispered, less calm. "Did you tell *that* to your Tupperware friends?" He tugged her nipples. "Did you?"

She moaned into his mouth in response. They kissed hotly. Her arms wrapped around his neck. His arms wrapped around her back.

"Of course not," he said, unbuckling his belt, unzipping his jeans. "You're all prim and proper and buttoned up with them." He laid her flat on his work surface, bringing her hips to the edge. Her hands grasped the counter.

"What do you want me to do next, Tatia?" he said, standing over her, his hands gripping her thighs. "Tell me."

She couldn't even mouth an *oh Shura*, crying out.

She came instantly upon his entering her.

Sunday by the Pool

The summers are broiling, no question about it.

But during winter in Scottsdale, as they try to live a regular life, they wear long sleeve shirts and light jackets and still sit outside and drink their tea and have a smoke, looking at the valley and the mountains and the sunset over the desert. After their first spring on the hill, Alexander says that perhaps Tatiana is right, perhaps there is nothing quite like the Sonoran Desert covered by brittlebush, like sunflowers in vivid bloom, with the red ocotillo and the white saguaro and the pale rose palo-de-fierro reflecting in the relentless sunglow.

It never rains except during the short monsoon season, every day is sunny, every night is warm and the stars are out. There is no snow. "It's good there is no snow," they say obliquely to each other. Aunt Esther caught a virulent cold in the blizzard of 1951, barely made it out alive. Tatiana wonders if there is snow in Korea where Vikki and Richter are. North Korea crossed the 38th parallel in June 1950, just as Richter had predicted, and surrounded Seoul in South Korea in weeks, and it was another two months before the United Nations finally got their act together and let MacArthur fight back.

Alexander and Tatiana drive 200 miles to Tucson and back at least one weekend a month for his intel work at Fort Huachuca. She and Ant sightsee while Alexander sifts through reams of classified, top secret, unanalyzed Russian data about weapons and satellites—space and European—and activities—space and worldwide. He also reads many of General Willoughby's reports. Yuma Test Station is reopened during the course of the war and Alexander gets reassigned there, where to satisfy his additional seventeen days a year of active duty he tests and trains other young reservists on new ground-combat weapons—munitions, artillery, armored vehicles. Yuma is larger in size than Rhode Island. It tests weapons for all four branches of the U.S. military and Alexander's assignment orders start coming only to Yuma. Tania is not as happy. Tucson is historical and beautiful and full of Catholic missions for her and Anthony to tour, while Yuma is in the middle of nowhere, and has nothing in it but Alexander. She grumbles only slightly. She always goes. Anthony never grumbles. It's his favorite part of the month, because every once in a while, if his father is not preoccupied or busy, he takes Anthony for a ride in a WWII armored Jeep.

At home, Tatiana never stops cooking. Thanks to Francesca, she now knows how to make tacos and enchiladas, burritos and tostadas, fajitas and killer beergaritas. Infrequently she makes Russian food—pirozhki, blinchiki, chicken soup, salad Olivier. She wishes she could make borsht, but borsht has cabbage. All Russian food does something to them, like Russian language. They still speak Russian at the dinner table, so that Anthony will continue to know Russian, but they're Americans now; they have gotten so used to speaking English in front of other people that some-times even in bed, they speak it. After all, the things Alexander whispers to her in the swelter of night have always been in English.

But Tatiana hears Alexander humming Soviet war songs as he works around the house. He hums them quietly so she doesn't hear, but she hears. The days she hears them, she speaks Russian to him, and as if understanding, he speaks Russian back. But Russian hurts them both. He tries to stop humming, they hang their heads and continue with their outer life, in English, except for the vestiges of the past they can't burn down.

Tatiana makes bread dough on the days she doesn't work, so that there is always enough; all Alexander has to do is put it in the oven. "Even you can turn an oven on, can't you, commander of a battalion?" There is no talking her out of the bread-making and he has stopped trying and helps her now, seeing that with his help she gets done quicker. Kneading the dough, they chat qui-etly. They talk of work, his—not hers—she tells him jokes, they talk of Sundays—they are always together on Sundays—of Anthony's school, of how he's doing, what he's doing, the friends he's made. They talk of Alexander's architecture courses, of his heavy workload, of whether he needs a degree, whether it's worth it to continue—it seems too much, with work, college, reserve. He asks her once if she thinks he should resign the reserve when his commission is up, and she stares him down and replies that it's not the commission he should resign. He does not bring it up again.

Sometimes they try to iron out their few small difficulties—him working too much and too late, him going out with Steve, which Tatiana never likes. Alexander doesn't want to hear it. He says he accepts that there are some people she is just not going to like, and that's fine with him. But because of her muted antipathy to the people Alexander works with, certain things that should be easy are made slightly more difficult: social gatherings, parties, days at carnival fairs, work dinners, encounters at construction sites.

The undercurrent of her solemn, barely hidden disapproval is further sustained by their mutual inability to talk to his home building friends or to her hospital friends about the things that brought them here: courtships, engagements, families at weddings, things that for other people are fairly straightforward. They don't admit even to each other they have a little trouble navigating the waters of the life of the magazine quizzes that everyone else around them seems to be sailing through. They do their best—they go to parties, they mingle—and then they come home and cook and clean and play with Anthony and build things, and make caramel (her burnt sugar, his condensed milk) and every once in a while even play war hide-and-seek in the saguaros.

Bill Balkman loves Alexander, and Alexander knows it and needs it, and Bill is the main reason why Tatiana says much less than she wants to about the cannibalistic lobsters her perfect husband is in a live tank with. Alexander is never home because of Bill's love for him. He has been put in charge of nearly everything in the home building process, from the pouring of the foundation to the landscaping. He is so competent and swift that Balkman begins to give Alexander small bonuses for houses built ahead of schedule. While Alexander is thrilled at the bonus, Tatiana wants to emphasize the small—but of course doesn't.

Alexander and Tatiana talk of Truman, of McCarthy, of Sam Gulotta thinking about premature retirement, of Korea and Richter, of the French fighting in Indochina against Stalin's guerrillas, and how Southeast Asia will most likely be the next stop on Richter's military train through life. They speak of many things.

What they never talk about in their *Ladies Home Journal* life: Mothers and fathers, sisters and brothers. The rivers in which they swam, the rivers they fought across, their blood trail that runs across continents. Sisters with warm hands. Grandfathers in hammocks. Bare linden trees in Germany. And frozen lakes with ice holes.

In the early spring of 1952, Alexander said to Tatiana, "Let's build a swimming pool."

She said no. "We can go to the public pools."

"Like you'd let mothers and small children look at my body. I want a pool so I can swim any time I want. Naked with you."

"How much?"

"Three thousand dollars."

"Too much! Our whole trailer cost that much."

"It's not a trailer, it's a mobile home. How many times do you have to be told?"

"But we're saving for a house!"

It was time to light another cigarette and stare blinklessly at her for a second. "Tania," he said, "let's build a fucking pool."

It was something else. At twelve feet wide and fifty feet long, the lap pool had a diving board and an outdoor hot tub on a raised platform. It took seven weeks to build, and there were one or two hidden costs: like the large intricate meandering stone deck, the wrought-iron fence, the desert landscaping and the decorative lighting. Also the heating equipment to keep it at eighty degrees all year round. The total came to over six thousand dollars. Alexander just paid the surplus out of his bonus account with Bill and didn't tell Tatiana.

In early May, Bill Balkman, his girlfriend, Margaret, Steve and Amanda came over for a Sunday afternoon pool party. The sun was, as always, out; it was in the high eighties, a fine Sunday. Tatiana had bought a fashionable new yellow polka-dot bikini, but Alexander took one look at her and forbid her to wear it.

Steve didn't look her way in any case. He had a gash on his cheek with three black stitches. He hadn't come to Phoenix Memorial, and since it was the only hospital in the city, Tatiana had to wonder where Bill Balkman was now taking his son to get sewn up so that he wouldn't come to a place where Tatiana would know what happened. Uncharacteristically silent, Steve didn't explain and no one asked. He didn't swim, hardly ate, cracked no jokes, barely talked to his father, and his father barely talked to him. His father did, however, talk to Alexander—non-stop. "Great place you got here, Alexander," Balkman said as they sat out on the patio after swimming. "But I don't understand, why don't you build yourself a real house? I hear you know a good builder." He chuckled. "Why live in a hut?"

Alexander avoided meeting Tatiana's eye, for he hated other people to see what was inside him: a small hut in the pine woods on pine needle river banks where freshly spawned sturgeon swam past on their way to life in the Caspian Sea. Or—holes in the woods, his weapons around him, waiting at dawn for the enemy to come from below. All that was in his laconic reply to Bill: "It's plenty for us right now."

Sunbathing in a pleated satin and wired-bust maroon Marilyn

Monroe one-piece, Amanda said, "Tania, the maillot you're wearing is so forties. Alexander, you should buy your wife a nice new bikini to celebrate that pool of yours and to show off her little figure."

"You think?" said Alexander, glancing at Tatiana.

"But you're a very good diver," Amanda continued, looking Tatiana over with a puzzled brow. "That back flip was hopping, and that cartwheel off the board! Where did you learn to dive like that? I thought you grew up in New York City."

"Oh, you know, here and there, Mand." Mostly there.

"Tania, can you go get us some more potato salad, please?" That was Alexander, running interference.

Balkman, when she returned, was saying, "Alexander, good boy you've got there."

Anthony was showing off in the water.

"Thanks, Bill."

Tatiana found it fascinating the way Bill hardly ever addressed her.

"Anthony!" Balkman called. "Come here for a sec."

Anthony came out of the pool, long, lean, dark, dripping, and stood shyly by Balkman.

"You're a good swimmer," Balkman said.

"Thank you. My dad taught me."

"How old are you?"

"I'm nine on June 30."

"You're going to be tall like your father."

Tatiana watched Alexander sitting smoking, his calm eyes appraising his son.

"So what do you want to be when you grow up?" Balkman asked. "My son, Stevie over here is a builder like me. What do you think? Are you going to come build houses with me and your dad?"

"Maybe," said Anthony, deflecting with the best of them. Tatiana smiled at her son's skills. "But my dad's been lots of things. He was a lobster man. He made wine. And he drove boats. I drove a boat with him. He was a fisherman, too. He can make all kinds of furniture. What's that called?"

"A furniture maker," said Tatiana helpfully, her own eyes adoring her son.

"Yes. Oh, and he is also a captain in the United States Army, and was," said Anthony, "a soldier in the Second World War. He went up the mountains carrying—how many pounds of gear, Mom? I forgot. Like a hundred and fifty."

"Sixty, Ant," said Tatiana, glancing at Alexander, shaking his head at *her*.

"Sixty," said Anthony. "He was in a POW camp, and in a real castle, and he led battalions of men across—"

"Anthony!" That was both Tatiana and Alexander, who got up and took Anthony by the hand. "Come," he said. "Show me that reverse pike dive your impossible mother's been teaching you." As they walked past, Tatiana heard Alexander quietly saying, "Ant, how many damn times do I have to tell you?" And Anthony in a distressed voice replying, "But, Dad, you said don't speak about you to *strangers*!"

Brown-haired Margaret, tall and angular, in her forties but trying to look younger, was clearly trying to make up for Bill ignoring Tatiana. She said, "Tania, you do know that Bill loves Alexander? We both do."

"Of course. Alexander is lucky to have found Bill." Tatiana didn't like Margaret much. She kissed Alexander hello and good-bye too close to his mouth.

"No, no. Bill's lucky to have *him*. He couldn't do without him." She lowered her voice. "Stevie is . . . don't get me wrong, he's the son, he'll inherit the business, but he is just not cut out for . . . for hard work. Not like Alexander."

Tatiana agreed.

And then Margaret said, louder, "Why do you still work? Your husband makes a very good living—and will make even a better one as soon as he resigns his commission."

"I didn't know my husband was resigning his commission," Tatiana said, her eyebrows tensing. Nearby, Alexander shook his head slightly and rolled his eyes.

Margaret went on. "You know Bill and I have been seeing each other for a couple of years, but I'm already not working." She smiled proudly. "Bill likes to take care of everything."

Tatiana did not say, oh, congratulations, doesn't that make you a concubine?

The sun was setting. They were sitting on their brand new deck, around their patio tables, smoking, listening to jazz and blues. Tatiana made some more margaritas, poured them for everyone, for her husband first. "Tania," he said, "you didn't want to make beergaritas?" He smiled. "From her friend from Mexico, Tania got a recipe for margaritas with beer that . . ."

"Let's just say, we'd have four overnight guests after a pitcher

of those," finished Tatiana. Which is why she didn't make them.
"They light you up." Alexander's eyes twinkled at her.

"I bet they're good for drinking games," said Stevie. It was practically the only thing he said all afternoon.

"Steve, there you go, always with the naughty," said Amanda,
somehow seeming less happy about it. She turned to Tatiana. "So,
Tania, when are you and Alex having another baby? Anthony
needs a little brother or sister to play with in that pool."

"It's definitely time, Mand," Tatiana agreed pleasantly. "When
are you and Steve going to get married?"

"It's definitely time, Stevie," said Margaret, and laughed, and
Bill laughed. Amanda didn't laugh, but she did stop asking Tatiana
about babies.

They were enjoying the evening, listening to Louis Armstrong,
finishing the margaritas before dessert was put out, when Balkman
said thoughtfully, "Wonder if this land is worth anything."

They had been lounging near the swimming pool they had built
in the frontier country, in the setting sun, near the mountains,
overlooking the dimming mulberry desert under a violet sky. There
was no one around. After Balkman's question, Tatiana sat up
straighter. "There's nothing to buy here," she said. "The U.S.
Government owns everything to the left, including the mountains.
Down below us, it's already been bought by Berk Land
Development. There's nothing available."

Balkman pointed. "What about this right here, the land to the
mountains?"

After a marital pause, Alexander said, "We own that."

Balkman turned his head away from the saguaros. "Own what?"

Tatiana turned her head away from the saguaros and to
Alexander. She made her gaze calm, her face inscrutable, but with
her eyes it was as if she were putting a staying hand on him saying,
Pride, soldier, it's your pride talking. Don't do it.

But she saw he couldn't help himself. He must have really wanted
to impress Bill Balkman. "Two hundred feet to the left, two hundred
to the right, and fifty acres straight to the mountains," said Alexander.

No one at the table spoke. They were in a silent picture, just
moving without words.

Tatiana got up abruptly and began clearing the table. Loud
sounds erupted—of her clearing the dishes and of Balkman
exclaiming, "You own all this land? How much altogether?"

"Ninety-seven acres," said Alexander.

Tatiana shook her head. The smile of pride was still on Alexander's face when Balkman said, "Do you have any idea what a gold mine you're sitting on? How much damn money we can make?"

Tatiana brusquely moved Alexander's hand out of the way to get his plate and stared hard at him, wondering with frustration why it was so difficult for him sometimes to see even *one* chess move ahead. He saw it now, though; saw it nice and clear. The smile wiped off his face, he cast her a resentful glare—as if it was her fault!—and yelled for Anthony. "Ant, get out of the pool and help your mother." Turning to Balkman, he said, "Bill, the land's not for sale."

"What do you mean?" Balkman boomed. "Everything is for sale."

"Not this land."

Tatiana laid her hand on Alexander's shoulder. "What my husband is trying to say, Bill"—her voice was genial—"is that this land belongs to his family."

"Well, surely you don't need ninety-seven acres! You live in a trailer on a postage stamp lot. A bomb shelter would take up more room than where you're living. Even with the pool and the work shed you've barely used up a quarter of an acre. You can keep seven acres." He wasn't even addressing Tatiana, who had spoken to him. He was talking directly to Alexander, his gestures all twitchy. "You sell ninety acres to the business, make a shitload— pardon my French—of money, and then we parcel out the rest into quarter-acre units. I will split the profit on the land with you fifty-fifty. Your wife here will be covered in diamonds by the time we're through. She won't be able to see the desert for all the rocks you'll buy her." He was feverishly calculating on a napkin—using one of *her* napkins to calculate his nefarious little math!

"Bill," Tatiana said, still genially, "first of all, it's not a trailer, it's a mobile home. And second of all, the land is not for sale."

"Sweetheart, please," said Balkman, not even looking up, "let the men take care of business, all right?"

Tatiana took her hand off Alexander's shoulder.

"Bill," Alexander said, "the land is not for sale."

Balkman wasn't listening. "We can have a whole community here. We'll call it Paradise Hills, Love Hills, Tatiana Hills, whatever you want. Ninety acres will parcel out to 300 units. We can even have a community pool, a clubhouse, charge annual fees. Three hundred units at a thousand dollars a pop just for the land, that's one hundred and fifty thousand dollars for your end, Alexander. And the 300 houses on these lots will be twenty-five bucks a square foot, plus an extra fifty a square foot for the concrete bomb shelters we'll sell for each one. If we cap the size of the houses at 4000 square feet—I don't have a napkin big enough to calculate those profits!"

Tatiana stood up straight with the dirty trays in her hands. "Bill," she said calmly, "even without the bomb shelters you'll make twenty-six million dollars, but we won't have our land. What would be the point of that?"

"Twenty-six million? How did you?—Well, there you have it! What's the point? Sweetheart, because you'll never have to work again. Alexander, she can just stay home and make you babies all day. Now where were we?"

Tatiana dropped her stack of dirty trays onto the new sandstone patio. The trays were metal and didn't break, but what a clang they made, and all the food she had made that the Balkmans did not finish fell onto the weathered concrete tiles. "Excuse me," she said. "Accident." She crouched to clean it. Alexander crouched beside her. "Tell me," she said through her teeth, "will you be resigning your commission before or after you give him our land?"

"Stop it."

"You either tell him to leave my house, Shura," she whispered, "or I'm going to tell him a few things he won't want to hear."

"What did I say?" he whispered. "Go inside and calm down."

Of course he was right—dessert had not been served. Apple pie, blueberry muffins, chocolate chip cookies, strawberry shortcake that Tatiana made to show hospitality to her guests, to Alexander's boss, to his boss's family. Snatching the trays from him she squalled into the house.

Balkman opened his mouth and Alexander said, "Let's talk about this tomorrow."

"Oh, come on—"

"Tomorrow, Bill."

"You know, Alexander," Bill said in a wise voice, "sometimes women get a little upset by things. They don't understand the ways of men. All you have to do is show them who's boss—they're quick learners." Bill smacked Margaret's rump. "Aren't they, hon?"

* * *

The next morning at eight, Balkman said, "Have you talked some sense into that wife of yours?"

Now nearly three years with Balkman, Alexander remained convinced that this was the right job for him, the right place for him. He was so convinced of this that he tried yesterday, after everyone had left, to convince Tatiana. That perhaps they could consider, just consider, Balkman's offer. He was met with such uncommon, unusual and unwelcome hostility from his normally mild wife that he had to drop the subject before he said some things himself he would later regret.

This morning Alexander stood in front of Bill, his eyes cold, his arms crossed, trying to forget the sight of Tatiana yesterday, her eyes cold, her arms crossed. "This has nothing to do with my wife, Bill," he said. "We've been offered quite a lot of money for that land. Ever since Scottsdale incorporated two years ago, the land's value has gone out of control. It's now worth $5000 an acre. That's a return of nearly half a million dollars on our original invest-ment. Believe me, if we wanted to sell it, we would sell it. We're not interested."

"But there's so much money to be made!"

"It's not about the money. It's about the land," Alexander said. "You've seen our life. We live simply. I realize it's not for everyone. There's much to be said for making more and spending more, but as long as we have enough for our small things, that's plenty for us. And we have enough for our small things. The home is paid for. The cars are paid for. We want for nothing."

"What about—"

Alexander stopped him. "Enough. Please. Let's talk about our present business. Have you put together a budget proposal for the Schreiner house, or do you want me to do that? They're eager to get financing and get started. And they're willing to spend thirty a square foot to get the marble in all the bathrooms, not just the master."

"Stop changing the subject. 50-50 profit on three hundred land parcels, Alexander! I tell you what, to sweeten the pot, I'll split the builder's commission on the houses with you, 75-25. You're only getting a three percent commission now. Think how much twenty-five percent is going to be on—what did your wife say yes-terday? Twenty-six million dollars? She was right, by the way."

Alexander sighed. Of course she was right. And yes, the money was incredible.

Balkman must have seen his conflict. "Your wife is advising you poorly," he said, "You should not listen to her. You should do what you feel is right. This is for your future and the future of your family."

Bill was a fine one to talk about a family—not marrying Margaret so he could keep his options open. Well, Alexander thought, that's right, why buy the cow when you can have the milk—

And suddenly his mind cleared. He remembered something. "Bill," he said, "do you know how much cows were worth in Soviet villages?"

"What?" Bill said dumbly. He looked as if he had misheard. "In what villages?"

"Cows. In Soviet villages. Do you know how much you could sell your cow for, if you had one?"

"No—but—"

"Fifteen hundred rubles," Alexander said. "Now, fifteen hundred rubles is a colossal amount of money to a Russian peasant, who makes maybe twenty rubles a month selling his fish to the collective. But if you sold the cow, your money would be gone in three months, while the cow would feed you for seven years." He smiled. "I'm not selling my cow, Bill."

Visibly aggravated, Balkman hit the desk with his fist. "Fucking cows. What are you talking about? I've taken very good care of you, Alexander."

"I know. And I have taken very good care of you."

"Yes, but what's good for the business is by definition good for you." Balkman paused. "The reverse is also true. How would that wife of yours feel about that?"

Alexander stood straight up in silence. To the left of Bill was a larger, more graphic picture of a naked Miss Viva Las Vegas. Something regretfully boiled up inside him. "Bill, if you don't want me to work for you, fire me. Don't threaten me, just do what you have to. But the land is not for sale. And do me a favor, leave my wife out of it."

Balkman growled something in reply. Alexander waited, his arms crossed. He knew Bill couldn't fire him—he needed Alexander to run the business. They didn't talk about it again, but Balkman made it clear that he felt Alexander's intransigence in matters of the ninety-seven acres was all Tatiana's doing, just like Alexander's not playing with the boys in Vegas.

The Boys and the Girls

"Dad really wants you to come to Vegas with us next month," Steve said to Alexander, as they were having a drink after work with Jeff. "The International Builders' Show is coming up. You must go. He's going to have to insist."

They had just been talking about their girls, who had had lunch earlier that day. What do *you* think they talk about? the boys wondered. Do you think they complain about us? Oh, sure they complain. We ask them to do things they don't want to do, said Jeff. We won't marry them, said Steve. Alexander wanted to say that his wife did not complain about him—but what if she did? What if she told the girls he thought he was always right? That he had to have almost everything his way? That occasionally he came home late and not sober and took his fill of whatever he wanted?

Now they were back to Vegas. "Something tells me you don't get a lot of work done when you go." Alexander grinned. "And what are you, your father's fucking secretary? Bill wants to tell me something, he can tell me himself."

"Come on, Alex, aren't you the least bit curious about the bestial cauldron of libertine decadence?" asked Jeff. "I was."

Alexander palmed his beer glass. His whole life in the Leningrad garrison before Tania was a bestial cauldron of proletarian decadence—with weekends off, officer duds, drinks and perks, and hot and cold running ladies.

"Boys, I have something to tell you," Jeff announced solemnly. "I fear my Las Vegas days are over. I'm going to marry Cindy."

"Oh, *no*," said Alexander. "Not marry Cindy."

"Cut the shit. Yes. She has informed me that there are other interested parties."

"She's lying," said Steve. "Amanda tells me that once a month, like clockwork. I set my watch by it. Don't fall for it; it's a mantrap." And laughed loudly at his double-entendre: mantrap had cruder meanings. "Don't do it, Jeff, save yourself, don't do it."

Jeff turned to Alexander. "What do you think I should do?"

"Cindy will make a fine wife," said Alexander.

Jeff lowered his voice. "I like her. I love her. I guess I'll marry her." He sighed. "But Alex, there are some things Cindy just won't do. Is it unreasonable to expect your wife to do some of the things the ladies in Vegas do?"

"Amanda does them," Steve said with a grin. "She does what I tell her. But her heart's not in it. She does them just so I'll marry her. It's a mantrap."

They all laughed. "Man, are you fucked up," Alexander said. "She does what you want, mantrap and all, and you're still not happy?"

"What do you think, Alex?" Jeff said. "Wives one thing, Vegas girls another?"

"Our boy hasn't been corrupted by the Vegas girls yet," said Steve with a shoulder shove at Alexander.

Yet? Steve had drunk too much too fast, and was now loose-lipped. "Jeff, man," said Alexander, "you better pray this is not the kind of thing the girls talk about—how Cindy's other boyfriend compares with you. What if you don't stack up?"

"Hey, Alex, is it true?" Steve asked suddenly. "Manda told me the other day that Tania's never had another boyfriend?"

Jeff laughed. "Oh, man, you're so fucking lucky! No wonder you're so cocky. You're not stacking up to nothin'."

Alexander jumped off the bar stool. His beer glass swilled on the counter unfinished.

"What, have to run home already?" said Steve. "It's early."

"It's not early, it's late," said Alexander.

This is what Amanda, Cindy and Tatiana talked about at lunch: What was wrong with their bodies. Their feet were too big, their nipples too little, their ears stuck out, their behinds not enough. They were too big, too small, too flat, too tall. It was a Dr. Seuss book for nitpicking women. Staying out of it, Tatiana ate her fettuccine and thought about making it for dinner, with a little garlic bread and lemon chicken, or lime garlic chicken with salsa? Or . . .

"Tania, did you hear us?"

"Sorry, what?" She had forty-five minutes before Anthony's bus and wanted to order a slice of cherry pie before she had to run. She continued eating. The bodily analysis was singularly uninter-esting to her—she had moved far beyond the magazines and their counseling quizzes. "The Real Secret to a Long and Happy Marriage," "A Thousand Things You Are Doing Wrong." "Five Hundred Things You Can Do to Please Your Husband." Alexander said and showed he was pleased, and she didn't think about it beyond that. She and Francesca never talked about this. They talked about sons and cooking—and beergaritas. Tatiana smiled. *That* was the real secret to a long and happy marriage. She wanted to counsel the girls regarding wasting valuable time on things they could not change—but what if they listened to her? Then what would they have to talk about?

"Tania, Cindy thinks Jeff is finally going to take the plunge."

"Oh, that's great, Cind," said Tatiana.

"But what do you think I should do?" Amanda said. "War is over, and it's been not two war days, like you and Alexander, not three years like Jeff and Cindy here, but seven years! I'm twenty-five, still live at home, and despite all his promises and a ring, he just won't marry me."

"So why don't you tell him to fish or cut bait, Mand?" asked Tatiana.

Amanda was quiet. "Because what if he cuts bait, Tania?"

Tatiana hoped that what she was thinking was not plain on her face, which was, *Hallelujah*. She placed her hand on Amanda's hand. "You want me to give you a secret way to get Steve to marry you? I don't have it. I didn't have it for me. I don't have it for you."

"Well, Alexander married *you*, didn't he?" Amanda said. "You must have done something."

"Alexander and I are not you and Steve," said Tatiana, and when she saw Amanda's fallen face, she added quickly, "Cindy and Jeff aren't you and Steve either. Everybody is different. You have to do what's right for you."

"You know what I did? I told my Jeff there was someone else," Cindy giggled. "That got him really worked up."

Amanda waved her off. "I've been telling that to Steve for five years. You know what he says? The more the merrier, Mand. Let's bring him to Vegas with us for a little threeway."

Oh, he is such a prize, Tatiana wanted to say. Please let *that* not show on my face.

"Tania, tell me what to do," Amanda said. "Please."

"Manda," said Tatiana, "I don't know why you keep thinking I have all the answers."

"Because look at what you and Alexander have," Amanda said resentfully.

"You don't want my life, trust me," said Tatiana. "You don't want to know what it took for him and me to claw our way up that hill off Pima. You won't believe it if I ever told you. And we're still finding our way. I'm a terrible example. I was lucky in this—

he loved me. But had he not, I would've had to move on. I would've had no choice, right?"

"Tatiana!" That was Amanda raising her genteel voice in a restaurant. "Are you saying Steve doesn't love me?"

How did she get drawn into this inane conversation? "He doesn't want to marry you," Tatiana said quietly. "That much is clear."

Amanda got up sharply from the table. "He does love me," she said, her voice shaking. "He does. You don't know. He's a good man. He does love me." She stormed out of the restaurant.

Across the table Cindy stared perplexed at Tatiana, who shrugged and said, "Why does she ask for advice, if she doesn't want the advice?" and motioned the waitress for the bill. No cherry pie today.

After coming home from the bar that night, in bed, as Alexander was rubbing Tatiana's back, he said, his mouth moving down her spine, "Tania, stop talking to Amanda about me."

"I don't talk to Amanda about you."

"You told her you'd never been with anyone else, didn't you?"

"First of all, I didn't say that. They were having quite a conversation last week at lunch—these lunches, by the way, that you keep insisting I go to—about whether Cindy was an actual virgin or a technical virgin when she got together with Jeff. I, for one, was having some trouble with the differences. Apparently Cindy has read in one of her magazines that in some parts of the world, in some countries, she would have been considered a technical virgin. So I asked," said Tatiana, "if they stamped that sort of thing on her passport when she traveled."

Alexander laughed; even his caressing hands on her buttocks laughed.

"Amanda joked that on her passport, the words 'was born not a virgin' would be printed—at least I hope that was a joke," said Tatiana. "At this point, I ordered dessert and excused myself from the conversation. However, they pursued me like lions running after a frail zebra. I simply said you were my actual first and gave no other information. What was I going to say? What did you want me to say? That you were my technical twentieth?"

Alexander wasn't laughing anymore. "What I want you to do is change the subject." He held her in place with his open palms, his mouth moving over her tailbone.

"I do change the subject!" With uncharacteristic irritation,

Tatiana moved away from him and sat up. "I'm the queen of the changed subject, Alexander. Including that burning question. Whether there were some small technicalities that I perhaps over-looked. But eventually I have to say something, no?"

He sat up himself. "What the hell is wrong with you?"

"Nothing. Answer me—did you want me to lie?"

"Just tell them it's none of their fucking business, Tatiana. Leave the table. But what happens is, you tell it to Amanda, and she goes and tells it to Steve who then tells Jeff, and suddenly I find myself being snickered at by two drinking men at a bar at night. It's too much information for them, you understand that part, right?"

"What kind of screwed-up friendship, screwed-up universe is that," Tatiana exclaimed, "where I can't reply to a simple question from two girlfriends because of the way it's going to be interpreted among the animals you call your friends? Vikki knows this about me, and I'm sure she's told Richter—Richter, who fought with Patton and MacArthur! Do you see him snickering?"

"This is how it is in *this* universe," Alexander retorted. "In this one, keep quiet."

Tatiana cleared her throat. "Really?" she said, "Well, let me ask you, do you think I should be hearing from Amanda that you wish I weren't working and that you want to have a baby and I don't?"

Alexander sat up against the brass rails. "I didn't say that." He paused. "But surely it's no surprise to you that I want you to stop working."

"Oh that's not the surprise," said Tatiana. "What is a surprise, however, is hearing Amanda talk to me about my private life that you discuss with Steve, of all people!" Her voice was raised.

"I don't discuss it with Steve," said Alexander, keeping his quieter. "He casually asked me if I liked your job and I casually told him less than you. That was all. I wasn't complaining." He broke off, not looking at her.

"You were just being pretend casual?"

Now he raised his eyes. "It's not a surprise to you, Tania, that I was being pretend casual, is it?"

Tatiana took a breath. "You know what?" she said, "I can't believe you haven't quit *your* job yet," she said. "But if you insist on staying with Balkman, please do me a favor and stop talking about my personal business to your buddy Steve. Just like you asked me not to discuss the simplest things with my friend Amanda.

All right? Not even pretend casual."

Alexander did not resume caressing her lower back.

The Bachelor Party

Jeff and Cindy were getting married! Jeff was thirty-five and a bachelor all his life. He had started working with Steve four years ago, kept going to Vegas with Steve, got engaged to Cindy, dragged his feet like Steve, set several dates, like Steve, but now really was getting married—and not postponing! Amanda was swollen with indignation. Over dinner Tatiana asked Alexander what he thought about it. They had just finished eating. "I think nothing about it. I stay out of their business." He cleared his throat. "But the groom and his friends are having a bachelor party."

Tatiana sat like a stone. Stirring her tea pretend casual. "I've heard about bachelor parties. Sort of a last hurrah before marriage? You get drunk, offer him marriage advice." She smiled thinly. "Sounds like fun."

"Yes, something like that," said Alexander, not taking his eyes off her. "Every once in a while . . ."

Tatiana got up abruptly and started clearing the table.

". . . once in a while, the men go to a place where women dance."

Tatiana stacked dishes in silence.

"Is this . . . upsetting you?" he asked.

"Is this upsetting me?" she said incredulously. "I don't understand the question. Are the women dressed?"

"Not entirely dressed."

"So you have the answer to your own question built in."

"I go, I drink, I sit, I talk, somewhere the girls dance, I come home. What's the problem? You have no trouble with me going out for a drink. This is a drink with some pool—"

"And naked women."

"I deserve your trust. I've been exemplary."

"Oh, I'm sorry," said Tatiana, "I must have forgotten, in your slew of medals, I can't remember—did you get one for being exemplary?"

"What's with the sarcasm? I didn't say I deserved a medal. I said I deserved your trust."

"Exemplary is not a favor to me, Alexander. It's a condition."

"How can I not go?" Alexander said cajolingly, standing up. "I have to go. It's Jeff. You and I are in the wedding party. I mean, be serious. They'll laugh me out of town. It's for Jeff."

"Naked girls for you on Jeff's behalf?" Tatiana raised her hand to stop him. "Look, don't use that voice of yours with me and don't insult me with your I-just-don't-understand-why-you'd-be-upset attitude. I may not have had as much experience as you in this area—as if such a thing is even possible—but I'm not stupid."

"I didn't say you were—"

"I know what goes on. Carolyn told me that at her fiancé Brian's bachelor party, the girls not only got naked but performed personal dances for the men. When Carolyn found out she postponed the wedding for a year."

"Brian? I thought her husband's name was Dan," said Alexander.

"It is," Tatiana said pointedly. "I'm using the word postpone loosely. A year later she married Dan, who did not have naked women at his bachelor party."

"Tania," he said, lowering his voice, "give me a fucking break."

"Naked girls dancing in front of you—real close. Am I just too naïve to get why this is okay? Explain it to me. I'm just a peasant girl from Luga. Explain it to me slowly and declaratively so I understand."

His bemused expression didn't change as he opened his arms to her. She backed all the way to the other side of the kitchen, raising her hands to stop herself and him. "I can't talk about this anymore. That Steve . . . I can't talk about it."

His eyebrows puzzled. "Steve? What does this have to do with him?"

"Everything, I'm sure. He's the one arranging the entertainment? He's got you so that even you now think I'm too prudish. The damn ironies just pile up, don't they?" She glared at him. "You keep saying to me, this is the modern world, this isn't the Soviet village. You say that's how it's done in America. Fine. That's how men behave. Great. If you think it's okay, that's enough for me. I don't know anything but you," Tatiana said, trying not to let her voice break. "Now you tell me that you want to go get drunk and have naked women flap their boobs in your face. Go ahead, make your wife okay with that one, too."

"It's a bachelor party!"

"It's naked women!"

"Just looking," he said, opening his hands.

"At naked women!"

They were getting too loud.

Anthony came out. His radio show was over. He observed his mother, tight-lipped, panting, at one end of the counter, and his father, standing tensely at the other, looked at one, the other, then turned around and walked back to his room.

They forced themselves to stop for Anthony's sake. Alexander stepped away, Tatiana turned to the sink. He went outside to smoke. She followed him in a little while and stood on the deck in front of him holding on to the railing behind her. "Shura, I'm going to make it nice and simple for you," she said. "I'm going to tell you what I think."

"Please. Because I just don't know."

"You are my husband," she said. "I trust you explicitly. I believe in you completely. But the thought of you going to this little shindig profoundly upsets me. I see no good that can come from it. I question Steve's motives. You caring what Steve or Jeff or Bill Balkman will think of you if you don't go disappoints me. You should care what I will think if you do."

Alexander was sitting on the bench, not looking up at her at the rail.

"I'm asking you please not to go," said Tatiana. "I can't imagine you thought I'd be all right with it."

"I thought you'd see it for what it is," he said, "which is nothing."

"You going to see naked women dance while you're drunk is not nothing, Shura. It's a difference of degree, not kind, from here to the girls of Las Vegas."

"Come on," he said. "You're—"

"Overreacting? Not understanding? Being too naïve? You're right, I wish I could be more understanding—like, say, Amanda. I know that at times like these, you wish perhaps you were married to someone like her. But you're not. Though I hear she is available."

Groaning, Alexander shook his head, not looking at her.

"I'm going to tell you something," Tatiana said. "I didn't want to say anything, because I had no intention of going. But . . . I've been invited to a party, too."

Now he looked up at her.

"That's right. Saturday night," she said. "The girls are having a hen night. Cindy invited me."

"A hen night?"

"Yes. We all get dolled up and go out. They want to go to this place called the Golden Corral. Have you heard of it?"

Now he stood up. Even his cigarette was put out. "Yes, I've heard of it," he said. "Servicemen go there to party with the party girls."

"Oh, servicemen. You mean like soldiers? And it's rowdy? Ah, well. See, that's the kind of place I thought it was," Tatiana said. "And I don't go out without you at night. I don't go drinking and playing cards like you do. And so when Cindy asked me, I said no. Because I didn't think you'd like me in a place like that."

"And you'd be right."

"Well, I," she said, looking across at him, "don't like you in a place like *that*."

"All the men are going!" he exclaimed. "It's a normal thing. Normal, remember?"

"You can't sell me your double standard on this one," said Tatiana, shaking her head. "Not buying it—I already got plenty, thanks." She paused and waited, and when there was nothing from him, she folded her hands and said, "You know, I thought you had no interest in that anymore. But you're telling me I'm wrong. I didn't know that. You live and learn. So since you don't want to do this for me to be kind to me, and since the rules are changing in our marriage, then why don't we not talk about it anymore. I don't want to be a party pooper. You go to your naked party, and I will go to the Golden Corral, and we'll leave it at that. Now, if you'll excuse me, I have to go put Ant to bed." She turned to go.

He came up to her and put his hand over her mouth. "Stop it, you impossible Russian wife," he said. "Just stop it. I won't go." Tatiana's hands glided over his arms. "I don't want to upset you. I thought you might've been all right with it. What was I thinking?" He shook his head. "I'll go, have a few drinks, play some pool, give marital advice, but I won't go to the club. Fair enough?"

She muttered a muffled assent.

He kissed the top of her head and took his hand away from her face with a great sigh.

Friday night, Alexander, in black slacks, a black collared shirt and black shiny shoes, shaven, showered, spiky-haired, strapping, sparkling, sober, left for the bachelor party at eight, saying he'd be home by one, which was later than he'd ever gotten home. He kissed her when he left. He smelled great and looked fantastic.

One o'clock came.

In her silk robe, bare underneath, Tatiana waited. When he came home late and not sober, he liked to breathe his beer-laden breath on her, liked to lay his intoxicated hands on her.

Two o'clock came—and went.

She waited with increasing anxiety until 2:30, thinking that was enough time to get home from practically anywhere in Phoenix, but when 2:45 came and went, suddenly the anxiety turned into frantic fear. Forget the naked dancers, she imagined only the mangled car accident victims she saw die nearly every day in ER. He would be drunk and driving home for many miles with other Friday-night revelers. She paced the trailer up and down, she changed into jeans and his old army shirt, she sat by the phone, and suddenly became afraid that it was possible, just possible, that these years were all they were going to have together. All of it, gone on this Friday night.

The minutes dripped one into another. She looked at the kitchen clock. 2:55. Only ten minutes had passed since the last time she'd looked, since her irregular heart slipped and hammered in her chest, whiling away the seconds, drip drip drip, beat beat beat, sixty nine drops of her blood draining into a minute of an open infected wound in his back, one hundred and fifty beats of her heart into a minute of his life. Gripping her stomach, her chest, she turned off the AC and paced the house, paced outside, listened in the night air for him. It was the beginning of June. Just last week Alexander had turned thirty-three. They had a pool party with many of the same friends he was out with tonight.

Was that her fate—and his? After all they had been through, beginning in one June, ending in another? In three weeks, they were supposed to be celebrating their tenth wedding anniversary. She shouted "Alexander!" into the night. An echo came back to her, a faint *Alexander* . . . They lived so far out, in such deathly silence near the mountains, that Tatiana could usually hear his truck when he was still three miles down on Pima. She could see his lights. She would sit outside other nights listening for the sound of his truck engine rolling down the highway and making the right onto Jomax. She looked at the clock.

2:58. Was it only three minutes since she last looked?

Oh my God.

3:00.

3:30.

3:53.

4:17.

Tatiana called Phoenix Memorial emergency room and spoke to Erin, who told her that no, Alexander had not been brought in bleeding and dead.

4:47.

She lay on the floor prone, motionless.

At eight minutes past five (5:08!!) she heard the truck in the drive. It was lurching forward.

She jumped up and ran outside, and was nearly run over by the Chevy. It crashed into a cinder block in the drive; the door was flung open. Tatiana saw instantly he was all right and very drunk. She had never seen him this drunk. It was useless to scream at him now, but what was she going to do with all her anger? He looked at her completely unfocused and mouthed, "Hey, babe."

"My God, Alexander," she whispered, shaking. "It's *five* in the morning."

He stumbled out of the truck, his keys falling on the pebbled ground, leaned into her, smelling aggressively of alcohol and smoke, but also of . . .

The sick pit inside Tatiana opened up. The sick pit she had before she started thinking he was dead. He smelled of cheap perfume.

Rocking from side to side, he staggered past her into the house, fell on the bed and was unconscious in all his clothes, in his shoes, everything. Tatiana undressed him and somehow got him under the covers. She searched through his clothes, she didn't know for what, and then through his wallet. She went outside and searched his entire truck and his glove compartment—for condoms maybe? It was horrible. Nothing. But the smell of cheap perfume lingered, and now was in their bed.

She lay down next to him, keeping her hand on him. It was nearing seven when she managed to fall asleep herself.

Anthony woke her up at ten, whispering, Mom, Mom.

Alexander was still unconscious.

Tatiana got up, showered, made Anthony breakfast; she herself could not eat. The phone rang; it was Margaret, one of the last people Tatiana wanted to talk to. "How is he this morning?" Margaret asked cheerily. "Did you hear what they were up to?"

"No." Tatiana sat down. "Margaret, I really have to go—"

"They rented out a two-bedroom suite at the Westward Ho downtown, I heard they had a blast," she said with a giggle. "Had some kind of a wild girl show. You should ask Alexander about it, if and when he sobers up. Bill and Stevie are still pretty tanked."

Tatiana hung up. It was all she could do to not retch.

She and Anthony went shopping. She didn't even leave a note for Alexander.

When they got home around four, Alexander came outside to meet them in the driveway, looking hung over but almost sober. "Hey," he said, and luckily before she could answer, Anthony started talking to him and he got distracted.

Tatiana silently unpacked the groceries while Alexander and Anthony carried them in. Alexander came up to her in the kitchen and again said, "Hey," nudging her with his body.

She said, "Hey," and turned to the refrigerator.

"Kiss me, Tania," he said.

She lifted her face without looking at him. He kissed her and then said, "Look at me."

She opened her eyes and glared at him.

"Ah," he said. "You're upset."

"I'm beyond upset," she said, slamming the refrigerator door.

Anthony was pulling on his dad to show him the fishing-boat-gunship-destroyer he had been making in the shed.

Tatiana went into the bedroom and got ready to go out. She put on the new Jonathan Logan violet silk dress she just bought, with gathered chiffon around the full swing skirt and velvet piping. Tonight she put on black mascara and black liner, rouge and even painted her lips red. The only time she put on that lipstick for Alexander was when she was a nurse attending to his ill humors. The memory of their Friday nights hurt her stomach. She put on earrings, a choker string of pearls and expensive perfume (to weaken the smell of the cheap one still lingering in their bedroom, on her beautiful quilt!), and threw on her new mauve high-heeled patent leather pumps. She was finishing brushing out her hair when Alexander walked into the bedroom. For a few moments he stood watching her at the dressing table. Glaring at him through the mirror, Tatiana said, "There is some beef stew from yesterday and plenty of bread and butter—"

"I know where the food is." He kicked the door closed behind him. She heard that sound only when he was carrying her into the bedroom for love. That sound hurt her stomach, too. "Where are you going?"

"Tonight's the hen party, remember?"

Quietly Alexander said, "You told me you weren't going."

"And you told me," she said, "you'd be home at one." She was doing all she could to keep her voice down.

"I got drunk. I forgot to call. The bars close at two."

"What about the Westward Ho suite, what time does that close?"

There was silence behind her, and a sigh. She couldn't look into the mirror to see his face. "It's that damn Steve," Alexander said. "He couldn't walk and asked me to help him upstairs."

"Well, isn't that the blind leading the blind."

"I left soon after, but it took me forever to get home."

"It sure did. For a whole night you acted as if you didn't have a home."

"What are you talking about?"

"Alexander!" she said, spinning around to face him. "Enough from you."

He stepped in front of her. "Did you see me last night?"

"No," she snapped, "but you were quite a sight at five this morning. Can you get out of my way?"

"It took me three hours to get home from downtown. I had to stop every mile and close my eyes. I must have fallen asleep by the side of the road. I couldn't drive. I was trying to be safe. I thought you'd want that."

"Very good. Did you wear a French letter, too, just to be safe?"

"Oh, for God's sake!"

"Don't shout—Anthony," she said through her teeth.

"He's in the shed."

"Five in the morning!" she yelled. "That's not coming home late, that's coming home early! Where is your decency? Can you even imagine what I was going through? I thought you had crashed the truck . . ." She wasn't going to cry. No. "And when you finally disgraced this house with your presence, I smelled perfume all over you!"

"Perfume?" He sounded dumbfounded. "Well, you undressed me," he said loudly. "You took off my clothes. Why didn't you smell me to see if I'd had a condom on me?"

She inhaled sharply, stunned at his callousness. To think she could ever say to him, did you smell me to smell the rubber of a diaphragm I put in to have sex with another man? She started to shake. "Who says I didn't?" she said, trying to move past him to the door.

Alexander stood in her way. "This is ridiculous."

"I'm going to be late."

"You told me you weren't going."

"You told me you weren't going to see any women! You told me you were coming home at one!"

"We were drinking! I was drunk."

"Love your excuses. So why didn't you call me?"

"I. Was. Drunk," he repeated slowly as if speaking to a child.

"I. Am. Leaving." She tried to move past him again.

He took her by the arms. "Babe, I'm sorry. I promise—"

"You and your stupid promises!" she cried, pulling his hands off her. "You get drunk and forget all about me!"

"I don't forget all about you," he said. "Stop shouting. My skull is splitting in four pieces."

"How thoughtless of me. Let's not say another word. We'll talk about this tomorrow when I'm less upset and perhaps less sober myself." She made to go around him. He wouldn't let her, locking the door behind him.

"Alexander, stop it," she said, trying to push him away, but he stood in front of her like a block of cement.

"I went yesterday for my friend, not because I was angry," he said quietly and slowly, but not kindly and slowly.

"I'm also going for my friend," she said, shoving him, "and not because I'm angry. Did you get a naked dance for your friend, too?"

Alexander took her by the arms and sat her down on the bed. "You're not going."

Tatiana jumped up. He seized her by the arms and set her back down on the bed.

As soon as he let go of her, she jumped up again. He grabbed her by the arms and brought her to him very close. "Tania," he said, in a low voice. "Stop it."

This time she couldn't lift her arms.

"Let go of me. What are you worried about? I'll be very good. As good as you."

"Oh, for fuck's sake!" His fingers tightened around her. "You are not going, so calm down and then we can talk about this like adults."

"Let go of me," she breathed out. "You can't do this."

"I can't?" he said. "So stop me, Tania."

Desperately trying not to squirm from the gripping discomfort of his hands, she struggled against him, losing her breath.

"You're just doing this to upset me," said Alexander. "And it's working. Consider me upset." The more she struggled, the harder he held her. She bit down on her lip, trying not to groan in pain—not wanting to give him the satisfaction. Switching his grasp on her, Alexander held her against him with just one arm, while his free hand went under her silk dress and up her stockings to the horizontal line of her naked flesh. "You're going to a poontang palace dressed like this, wearing a lacy open girdle, and black seamed stockings, going with your thighs all bare, are you?" he said, breathing out hard, touching her underwear. "Why even bother with the panties, Tania?"

"Alexander! Let go of me."

"Stop fighting me and I'll let go." He was so enormous and upset, he was forgetting himself too, forgetting his strength, he was going to bruise her.

"Let go, and I'll stop fighting."

"Tania." His fingers clenched, on her arm, on her thigh. And she cried out.

There was no actual way she could leave the bedroom unless he let her leave. She could not get free of him unless he freed her. Perhaps at another time this might have made her calmer, but at the moment it made Tatiana only more upset. She started struggling against him again, her small frame heaving, wringing herself out of his vise-like arms. "You can't win this," he said, and he wasn't even panting. "So stop right now."

To add to her humiliation, she was going to lose her footing in her high heels and fall backwards on the bed. "You stop right now," she mouthed. Even the strength to yell was leaving her, the words came out almost soundless. His hands were hurting her, his belt buckle was hurting her, his words were hurting her, and she was already hurting from yesterday. "Tell me," she croaked, "did you do this to your naked whore, too? Did she like it?"

"Not as much as you," Alexander retorted, and Tatiana burst into tears and then started to scream.

And Anthony was knocking on the door, shouting on the other side. "Mommy! Mom! MOM!"

Alexander pushed her onto the bed, and she scrambled up, and she ran into the bathroom, slamming and locking the door. He kicked the door open, she backed away, stumbling against the bathtub, crying loudly *stop, please stop*, putting up her hands as he came for her. He grabbed her face, squeezing her mouth shut and through his teeth said, "Stop yelling. Your son is outside. You want to go? Go ahead. Go. I don't give a fuck what you do." Roughly releasing her, he left the bathroom, and she slammed the broken door that wouldn't slam. The bedroom went quiet, only Tatiana was crying inside, and Anthony was crying outside, his plain whimper sounding through the walls. "Mama, please, please . . ."

After a few minutes she heard Alexander unlocking and opening the bedroom door. "Everything's okay, Ant," he said. "Go outside for a minute. It's okay. Let Mom and Dad—just go outside."

Anthony said no.

"What did you just say? Go outside!"

Cleaned up, red-eyed, moist in the face, Tatiana came out of the bathroom. "Leave him alone, he did nothing wrong." Her hands were shaking as she walked past Alexander and touched Anthony's face, kissing his head.

"Are you all right, Mama?" he asked, himself crying.

"I'm fine, honey," she said, trying to make her voice not break. "Don't worry about a thing. Your dad will take care of you this evening. Mommy is going out."

She left the house, got into her car and drove away.

Alexander and Anthony didn't speak during dinner, but as they were cleaning up, Alexander said, "Bud, sometimes grown-ups have arguments. It's okay. Don't you and Sergio have arguments?"

"Not like that."

"Well, there's more at stake between grown-ups."

"I never heard Mom yell like that before." He started to cry again.

"Shh. Sometimes even your mom gets upset."

"Not like that."

"Sometimes."

"Never before."

"Not often, that's true. But sometimes."

"Where did she go?"

"Out with her friends."

"Is she coming back?"

"Of course!" Alexander took a deep breath, staring at his son. "Of course, Ant. Look, everything will be fine. Let's just . . . hey, you want to go to a movie?"

A movie at night alone with his always working father was an unprecedented treat for the boy. Anthony cheered up. They drove

to Scottsdale's only picture house to see *The Greatest Show on Earth.*
Alexander sat with unseeing eyes and smoked. He didn't hear a
word of the movie. He had no idea what happened in it. Something
about trapeze artists. All he was thinking about was Tatiana at the
Golden Corral. Images of her there were making him deaf and
blind. Tatiana may not have known the ways of men, but Alexander
knew the ways of men very well.

After the movie, he took Anthony to get some ice cream at the
soda shop; they talked about baseball, football, basketball; they
even talked a little about the woods in Poland. Anthony, having
heard some of the story from Tatiana, wanted to hear more about
it from his father. "Mommy told me you stormed Poland practically by yourself, without weapons, with just one tank, with prisoners as soldiers, and the men never fought before but you taught
them all how, and you never stayed in the rear despite the protests
from your lieutenant."

"Did you ever ask your mother how she knows this?"

Anthony shrugged. "I find it's better not to know how Mommy
knows many of the things she knows."

"I couldn't agree more."

Walking back to the truck from the soda shop, Anthony took
Alexander's hand.

Tatiana was still not home.

After putting Ant to bed, Alexander debated going to the Golden
Corral but couldn't leave his son alone in the house.

This was ridiculous!

His Tania was with a bunch of raving, joking girls, all of them
drinking, dancing . . . army men coming up to his wife—

He wasn't going to think about it.

—drunk men propositioning her, their hands on her, in a smoke-
filled club—and what was she going to do to stop them, even if
she wanted to?

He wasn't going to think about it!

Alexander got into the truck and started the engine, and then
turned it off, knowing he couldn't leave. He went back inside,
paced, smoked, drank, smoked, looked at the clock. It was eleven.
He went to the work shed and made a new frame for the broken
bathroom door.

When he turned off his circular saw, he heard her car in the
drive. After cleaning the wood shavings off himself as best he could,
he slowly returned to the house.

The door was open to the dimly lit bedroom. Tatiana was in front of her dresser mirror, taking off her earrings. Alexander stood in the doorway and then came in. He had been so tense he thought he would have to get control of himself before he could deal with her, but when he saw her, the fight went out of him. All he wanted was the peace of her, the comfort of her, the relief of her. He stepped in without closing the door and came up behind her. Silently he stood, looking at her blonde hair falling down her back, glancing through the mirror at her face, tilted down. Her hands went up to remove her pearls; she was having trouble with the clasp. He took a breath and moved her hair out of the way. "Here, let me." Slowly he undid the clasp and lay the necklace on the dresser.

"How is Ant?" she asked.

"He's fine."

"Did you feed him?"

"Yes, I fed him. Took him to the movies, too."

"He must have enjoyed that. Spending time with you."

Tatiana did not smell remotely of alcohol or smoke, or other people. Not remotely. She smelled of the same musk oil perfume she had put on earlier. She was not crumpled, she was not touched, she didn't have the breath of other people on her. Alexander was standing very close to her, right behind her; his stomach was pressing into her back, her strawberry-scented head was deep under his chin, and her hair was in his hands.

"Can you help me with the dress?" she asked quietly. "I can't get the hooks undone."

Alexander undid her dress, leaving his hands on her bare arms. Leaning down he kissed her shoulder. She moved away. "Don't, all right."

"Tania . . ."

"Just don't, all right."

He turned her to him. She wouldn't look up. The dress was loose, falling down. She let it drop to the floor and was left in a new one-piece purple lace corselet and black stockings. He wanted to mention the purple lace bought for a night out without him but didn't think now was the time. She still wouldn't look at him. He cupped her face, lifting it to him, bent, and kissed her reluctant lips. Her hands came up to push him away, and didn't.

"Where've you been?" he asked.

"I went to the hospital. I kept Erin company on nightwatch."

He exhaled heavily out. Her face was still in his hands.

Turning away from his mouth, from his eyes, she stood pressed against him. They were so quiet now, as if the fight had left them, the way they should've been when Anthony was outside their door. They stared mutely at each other. Her eyes filled with tears.

"No, no, come on, shh," Alexander said. He went to close and lock the door and took the phone off the hook. Fully undressing her and himself, he lay her down on the bed, and caressed her as slowly as his impatient roving hands would let him. "Shh . . . look how warm and soft you are . . . I'm sorry I hurt you earlier. I'll make it better, I'll make it up to you." With a groan, he lightly fondled her breasts. "Don't be upset with me, all right?"

"I'm *so* upset with you. How could I not be?"

"I don't know." He stared into her wet, unsmiling, disconcertingly made-up eyes. "Just don't be. You know I can't take it when you're upset with me." He kissed her pouty lips until they opened and kissed him back, he kissed her until she lay a little flatter and more relaxed on the bed, and all the while his palm caressed her small patch of downy hair.

"Shura . . . don't . . ."

"Don't what?" Alexander bent open-mouthed to her breasts.

"I don't want you to . . ." she moaned, trying to lie still, not squirm.

"No?" Bending below her navel, Alexander rubbed his lips back and forth against her blonde silken mound, his hand nudging her thighs. "Come on . . ." he whispered. "Spread your thighs for me . . . like I love." With his fingertips he stroked her lightly. "Tell me, whisper to me what else I can do to make you happy with me . . ." She said nothing. "Come on . . . something nice? . . . something gentle . . . ?"

She held her breath, not speaking. But now she lay like he loved. He kissed her. "Tania . . . look, your softest lips, your lovely pink tender lips, so moist, so parted, look, they're not upset with me . . ." Alexander whispered soothingly, his tongue slipping in and out of her mouth while his fingers slipped in and out of her. She grasped the sheets, bare and open under his hands.

From his years with her, from the thousand beats of their common time, there were few things Alexander knew better than her body's response to him. He stopped touching her. A breathless "Ah," escaped her mouth.

He waited a few moments, and then resumed his caresses,

increasing the pressure ever so slightly, and when she moaned in a peaking tremor, he pulled away again. A barely stifled heave left her hips. When Tania was happy she pleaded with him in two languages at this juncture to do all sorts of things to her.

But not tonight. She wasn't even touching him. Tonight she pleaded nothing, spoke in no tongues, her eyes closed, her lips parted, even as her curving body began to shudder.

"Tatia . . ." Alexander murmured, looking at her, "please tell me, anything at all you want me to do to make you happy?"

She turned her face away, in a deep moan, her head back, her throat elongated, her hips rising up to him. She was glistening, but she wasn't pleading.

He shook his head, kneeling between her splayed legs. She was so stubborn—and so blonde and bloomy.

There were so many things he liked to do to her, but tonight there was barely time for her penchant weakness—his fingertips caressing her nipples while he softly sucked her—before she cried out, clutching his head, and became neither reluctant nor unforgiving, nor stubborn. Alexander didn't pull away. He kept his heated mouth over her, his hand on her, his insistent fingers on her, and she didn't—and couldn't—stop crying out or quivering or grasping onto his head until he thoroughly released her and then and only then did she unclench slightly and lie panting with her feet still tapping out a rasping drumbeat on his back.

Oh Shura, she whispered. Oh Shura was certainly better than Shura, don't.

Yes, babe? Climbing up and kneeling over her, Alexander put himself into her moaning mouth, but he was so aroused he didn't need another thrust, another squeeze of her hands. He needed only one thing.

Getting off the bed, he pulled her forward to lie in front of him and leaned between her legs to kiss her. She reached for him, taking him, pulling him in; her eyes open, her lips open.

His hands gripping the backs of her thighs, Alexander thrust once, twice, then stopped. Straightening out, he moved shallow and slow, and then as deep deep deep as he thought she could take. Tatiana's mouth was in an O, she couldn't breathe. *Tania . . . too much?* he whispered. She couldn't speak, not even a yes. He waited a moment, he would have liked a yes, waited, pulled fully out, thrust fully in, and then she was suffocating and crying out. Holding her as steady as he could, he pulsed shallowly to prolong her moaning spasms and then stopped for a few moments, to catch a breath, to let her catch a breath, to kiss her, to nuzzle her breasts, to whisper how sweet she was like this as he stood over her, his hands on her folded thighs, bearing down on her, seeing her, seeing himself; he resumed the asymmetry of his jagged motion while continuing to whisper about his desire and her sweetness until she cried out, her stretched arms trying to grasp onto anything, and melted out again, moaning helplessly . . . and now it really was too much for her. Alexander knew he should stop. He knew he needed to stop. But he didn't stop. Too soon she began to sound close to agony instead of ecstasy, and then she was convulsing and crying out.

Okay, okay, shh, he said, stroking her, watching her as she lay gasping, her eyes closed, her thighs open, her body in a shiver. *Tania, you're beyond lovely,* he whispered, caressing her, touching her lightly, with his hands, with his mouth, until she was soothed, until she was softened and her time was lengthened.

When he came back on the bed and climbed on her, holding her legs up against his rigid arms, she started to shake—her head from side to side. *It's too much like this, please,* she whispered. *I can't take it.* He released her legs—but couldn't help himself, the ratchet of her plea too much for *him*—released her legs but not before two deep full slow agonizing thrusts and her two deep full slow agonizing cries. Leaving her raised legs live and loose, he took her like she loved, on his upright arms in what she called his arc of conjugal perfection, fitted into her slender thighs, her lips, her milling hips reaching for him, her fingers desperately clasping into his chest and neck and head as if to navigate him, in spondaic sync, in iambic rhythm. *Come on, Shura . . . come on, Shura . . . come on, come on, come on, come on.* After she quivered out, he didn't even wait before he came on, he took it the way he wanted it, placing her trembling legs straight up onto his shoulders. But she shook again and whispered, *I can't take it, you're too much for me like this, please, please.* This time he was implacable, undeterred and unreleasing, whispering back, *yes, but you're so good for me like this,* and was steady and slow and unceasing through her rattling body and grasping arms, eventually lying flush on top of her, his arms encircling her, his body overwhelming her, confining and surrounding her, confined and surrounded by her, completely consuming her so that when she came again, it was like an earthquake inside him. And during her impassioned cries, having forgotten herself, she recklessly whispered a rash *I love you.*

Now that is what I *call a whisper,* said Alexander, rubbing his lips against her eyebrows.

Oh, Shura . . . She lay slack underneath him, softly weeping, her face in his neck. Her arms and legs wrapped around his back.

Are you still upset with me?

Less upset, honey, husband, she moaned. *Less upset.*

Lifting off her, he whispered, *Get on your hands and knees, Tatia.*

She turned over on her hands and knees. Lowering her head into the sheets, her arms stretching out, she raised her hips to him. *Come on, Shura. Come on. Come on.* Everything was prone but her hips.

His hands covering her buttocks and the small of her back, eventually he had to close his eyes and hold his breath because *it was so fucking good . . .* until she, in her tumult, in her gasping abandon, tried to crawl away from him. A drenched Alexander leaned over her quivering weakening body, his chest on her back, his face in her satin hair, fondling her breasts, threading his taut hard fingers through her taut soft ones, slipping slowly out and slowly in. *You're so good, Tatia,* he whispered. *Just a little more. You're so beautiful . . . you're so lovely . . .*

He finished married, stressed and stark, on top of her and in her arms, and after stroking her to calm her down while she begged him for mercy in two languages even as she was coming down, Alexander, propped up on his elbow, lay beside her soaked, racked body and kissed her face, gazing at her all freshly loved and parched and breathless. "Why do you get so frantic?" he asked. "I swear, there are times you act as if you're married to someone else. What's the matter with you?"

Her eyes were closed as she received his kisses, her hand stroking the back of his head. She moved to cradle into him. He pulled the quilts over them. "I'm sorry I was late coming home," he said. "I won't come home that late again, I won't upset you. But what are you worried about?"

"You told me you weren't going to see any girls . . . "

"Come on," he whispered. "Shh."

Her damp face became tight.

"I took Steve up to the suite," Alexander said, wiping her forehead and speaking with reluctance, "and fell into a chair. There were, I don't know, thirty of us, it was loud, there was music, and commotion, and I was still sitting there trying to sober up a little when two or three girls were brought in—complete with their bodyguards."

She looked up at him.

"What? Tania, you have to get that drunk just once in your life, to understand what it's like. There is nothing but stupor in the chair. You saw me at five, after sleeping in the car for hours. Can you imagine what I was like at two? I couldn't walk. I was a disgrace." Alexander laughed lightly.

Tatiana didn't laugh. "What were they doing?"

"Who?"

"The girls, Alexander."

"I don't know." He didn't want to upset her.

"Were they dancing?"

"I don't know." He paused. "I think so." They had been naked and dancing. "You are such a good girl," Alexander whispered. "You're such a good girl." He kissed her lips. "It's all right. They might have been dancing, but I don't think you can call what I did watching, I was so out of it. But I shouldn't have come up."

"So where did the perfume on you come from?"

"As I was trying to get out of the chair, one of the girls came by and said something like, you need help getting up, cowboy? Wait! Where are you going? You're in my arms, I just made love to you." He held her in place. "Tania, I just made love to you," he whispered, looking down into her face. "You're in our bed, this is the final destination, last stop, all alight here, there's nowhere else to go."

Her lips were trembling.

"Let me finish telling you. I don't want you to hear this thirdhand from Amanda who might hear a more slimy version from Steve."

"Oh, so now your best friend is slimy? I can't listen to one more thing."

"One more. And you are my best friend. Listen."

"I can't listen. I can't."

"She came by, said some stupid things, Steve was standing right by me the whole time. I got up, I'm almost sure without her help. I left. And that's it." He stroked her unhappy face. "I promise, I swear."

"Did you . . . kiss her?" Tatiana started to cry.

"Tania!" He pressed her head to him. "Holy God. Of course not. She stood next to me, grabbing my sleeve. She must have reeked for her perfume to still be on my clothes. Steve thought I was too drunk to drive. I didn't want to hear it. He may've been right. I left anyway."

"That Steve." Tatiana shook her head. "Was the girl . . . naked?"

The girl had been barely clad. "I don't think so. I think they only get undressed for the dancing," said Alexander, not letting Tatiana move away an inch. He saw such misery on her face. "Look, this is the thing—I went up to the suite, I sat in the chair, I didn't leave right away." His hand was gliding over her breasts, her stomach, her legs, like he knew she loved; she was like a cat, she adored to be caressed, slow and light, from her shins up to the face, to the hair, and back down, through everything. If his words couldn't soothe her, perhaps his hands could. "I shouldn't have gone, that was my mistake, but I did nothing wrong." Alexander paused. "I'm going to tell you something—do you remember that night in Leningrad when I came drunk to see you at the hospital?"

"Oh, I don't want to talk about that now."

"I do. That night, I was in Sadko, and Marazov had women with him, and one of them, very flirtatious, sat on my lap. I was drunk, and young, and full of myself, as you remember—and I barely knew you then. We had behind us only the Sunday bus ride, the Kirov walks, and burning Luga. And we were at a complete dead end. It would've been so easy. I could have taken that girl in ten minutes in the back alley and still come to see you at the hospital and you would have never known. But I didn't— even then. I came to you in the middle of the night, despite everything stacked against us, despite Dimitri, despite your sister, who thought she loved me."

"She did love you. Dasha did love you."

"Yes. She thought she did."

"Oh . . . help me," she whispered.

"I came to you because you were the only one I wanted. Do you remember how we kissed that night?" he whispered, cupping her breast. "You, sitting topless in front of me, you who had never been touched—oh God! I go insane *now* remembering the state of myself then. You know what it had meant to me, and you know what it means to me still. Don't you remember anything?"

Tatiana was shuddering in her own memories. "I remember . . . But . . ."

"Look at me, feel my body, touch me, touch my heart, I'm right here. It's me," said Alexander. "I stayed away from whores even when I thought you were gone from my life and I was at war. I shouldn't have gone to the Ho, but, honestly, what would I want with anyone when I have you? Who are you talking to? Who are you being angry with?"

"Oh, Shura . . ." she whispered, clinging to him.

"You know all this like you know my name," said Alexander. "I come every night and kneel at your altar. Why do you worry about nonsense?"

And with his voice and his hands, with his lips and eyes, his kisses and caresses, and deathless ways about him to bring her and himself divine ecstasy, he soothed her and found peace and bliss in her, for his promises were strong but his love was stronger, and when they, wrapped around one another, finally fell asleep, made up, relieved, beloved, they believed the worst of the Balkman world was behind them.

A Day at a Wedding

Jeff and Cindy's wedding was the following Saturday afternoon, at the First Presbyterian Church with reception at the Scottsdale Country Club, filled with white lilies and beautiful people dressed in spring colors.

Standing at the side of the altar in her strapless peach taffeta ballgown with a circle ruffled petticoat, Tatiana stared at Alexander in his black tuxedo, trying not to remember their own altar, their small Russian church, their Lazarevo sun over their heads filtering through the stained-glass windows almost ten years ago.

She saw his face, his eyes staring at her. Outside the church he found her and very carefully—so as not to disturb her peach bows and silk pleats and petticoats—lifted her into the air for a moment without saying a word.

There was good food and good music, the girls had flowers in their hair, someone caught the bouquet—not Amanda—steak was good, shrimp even better, the speeches slurred and funny. Cindy was a good-looking bride, even with her too-short hair, and Jeff in a white tux looked like he belonged on a wedding cake. Ten of them sat together at the bridal table, and Steve kept alluding to the bachelor party, and Alexander kept humoring him, but the one who wasn't laughing was Amanda. Rather she was laughing fakely and every time she laughed she cast furtive glances at Alexander and then at Tatiana. After the nineteenth or twentieth furtive glance, Tatiana couldn't help but notice.

The Anniversary Waltz began to play—for Jeff and Cindy. Tatiana searched for Alexander; he was talking to people three tables away and didn't look up. She resumed her own conversation, but in a moment, when she turned, he was standing at her chair. He stretched out his hand to her.

Alexander and Tatiana danced to their wedding song, unable this once to hide their intimacy from prying, idly curious eyes; their hands entwined, their bodies pressed together, they waltzed by the banks of the Kama in their Lazarevo clearing under the crimson moon, an officer in his Red Army uniform, a peasant girl in her wedding dress—her white dress with red roses—and when Tatiana lifted her glistening eyes to him, Alexander was looking down at her with his I'll-get-on-the-bus-for-you-anytime face. She couldn't believe it—he bent his head and kissed her, openly and deeply, as they continued to swirl away the minutes of someone else's wedding.

As they walked back to the table, Tatiana saw Amanda's cold, judging stare on Alexander and a pitying glance on herself. "Why is she looking at me like that?" Tatiana whispered to him. "What's wrong with her today?"

"She must stop giving him milk. Tell her that."

Her elbow went in his ribs.

Steve and Jeff were getting quite drunk, even though it was still the afternoon. Their comments about the upcoming wedding night started getting cruder. Jeff plonked down and said, "Alexander, you've been married a century. Do you have any advice for the newly married?"

Another glance from Amanda.

Alexander said, "It's probably too late for advice, Jeffrey-boy. Wedding night's in three hours."

"Come on, give me the wealth of your experience. What did you do on your wedding night?"

"Drank a little less than you," said Alexander, and Tatiana laughed.

"Come on, man, don't hold out. Tania, tell me, is there anything I should know? From a woman's point of view?"

Oh, how loudly Steve laughed.

"Jeff, all right, enough, man," Alexander said, getting up and helping Jeff straighten out, pushing him away from the table.

"If I were Jeff," whispered Tatiana to Alexander, "I'd spend some time doing the thing that Cindy says he almost never does—but that's just from a woman's point of view." Oh how loudly Alexander now laughed, and Steve, who must have thought it was at his expense, glared at Tatiana.

She got up to go to the ladies' room. Amanda got up to go with her. As they were walking around the dance floor, Tatiana said, "What's the matter with you today? You don't seem very happy."

"No, I am, I am."

"What is it? Cindy's wedding making you blue?" Tatiana stayed dry through her own irony.

"No, no. I mean, a little, yes, but . . ." She took Tatiana by the arm. "Can I talk to you?"

"Seriously talk to me?"

"I need your advice."

Last time the advice giving didn't go so well. They went into one of the small quiet rooms off the main banquet hall and sat down on the couch. "What's going on?" said Tatiana.

Amanda looked distressed. "Tania, I don't know what a good friend is supposed to do. I want to ask you—if you knew something about Steve, something you thought I should know, would you tell me?"

Tatiana's face flushed hot red. Oh, no. Amanda found out about the hospital! No wonder she's upset. What to do now, I must own up. I should've told her straight away, but how could I have—and Tatiana said, "Oh, look, Mand, I'm sorry—"

"What I want to know is: would a good friend tell her friend something unpleasant, something hurtful, something that could ruin their friendship? Does a good friend keep her mouth shut or is she obligated to say something? Is the mark of a good friend to tell or not to tell?" Amanda lifted her conflicted eyes to Tatiana.

You weren't my good friend! Tatiana cried to herself. It's not fair, I didn't know you, and he apologized and it was in the past. I should never have kept my mouth shut.

"I think a good friend should tell, Amanda," said Tatiana. "I'm sorry—"

Amanda grabbed Tatiana's hands. "I'm sorry, Tania. I don't want to tell you this. I really don't. I just think you should know, that's all."

Very slowly Tatiana pulled her hands away from Amanda and stared hard at her cringing. "You have something to tell *me*?"

"It's about that cursed bachelor party. I wish they'd never had it."

"I know about the bachelor party," Tatiana said.

Amanda waved her off. "Oh, the girls, that's meaningless."

"Oh? Well, if it's not about the meaningless naked girls, then what is it?"

She lowered her voice. "Alexander went into the bedroom with one of them."

Tatiana shook her head.

Amanda shook her head. "The drunk was later, Tania," she said. "That was for your benefit. As in, later the excuse was he got so drunk he couldn't think straight. He was apparently fine when the girls were there. A number of people saw him go in, not just Stevie, please don't be upset with me, you promise?"

"I think it's too late for that promise," said Tatiana, standing up.

Amanda covered her face.

Tatiana, because her legs wouldn't hold her, sat back down. She took Amanda's hands away. "Amanda," she said, "did Steve tell you this?"

Amanda nodded.

Tatiana tried to keep it together. "Did it ever occur to you that Steve might be lying?"

"What?"

"Lying, Mand. Not telling the truth. Shuckstering. Deceiving. Lying."

"Why would Steve lie about this?"

"There are a thousand reasons, none of them I can go into now. Why would you repeat something like this to me on Cindy's wedding day? Why wouldn't you wait at least until the day after?"

"You asked me to tell you!"

Tatiana patted her. "Well, I walked into a trap there. But now I have two options. Either I believe my husband, or I believe your fiancé. My Alexander or your Steve. You'll forgive me if I choose to believe my husband. And you know what, let's not talk about this—ever again. If that's all right with you."

"Tania, you're being willfully blind, but that's your choice."

"You think I'm being blind? There is only one way to settle this. We can bring Steve and Alexander in here—is that what you want? How do you think that's going to end?"

"One of them is going to lie," Amanda said pointedly.

"Exactly, but unlike you," Tatiana said, plenty pointed herself, "I am married to the man who sleeps next to me every night, who wakes up next to me every morning." She paused to let that sink in. "How often do you think he can lie before I know the truth?

Especially that kind of truth—that he goes into rooms for twenty minutes and has it off with unclean whores who have it off with hundreds of men? You think that truth is easy to hide?"

"Some men are very good at hiding their true selves."

"Some women are very good at not seeing their men's true selves."

Amanda narrowed her eyes. "Are you making some kind of aspersions on Steve?"

"No. But if we bring Alexander and Stevie in here—how many more stitches can Steve get in his face, how many more broken arms? And Cindy's wedding will be ruined. You've already ruined my day. But I'm not the bride, I don't have to recall this as my wedding day, which was blissfully unmarred by idiocy." She took a deep breath. "So we're just going to pretend that you never said a word to me."

"But it's true, Tania! I know you don't want to believe it about Alexander—"

"No! You don't want to believe this about Steve."

"Tell me what you know about Steve."

"In this case, that he is a malicious liar. Is that enough? The rest is more than I have the decency to share with you on this beautiful day. And you, Amanda, should open your eyes to your life. Now, if you'll excuse me . . ." Tatiana walked out of the room in her peach high heels and her taffeta dress.

Amanda came back to the table, without glancing at Alexander, who sat patiently, drank his wine, and finally asked Amanda where Tatiana was. Amanda said she didn't know. Alexander waited a little longer and went to look for her. He walked the corridors and looked into every small room. He went outside to the back gardens where the photographers were setting up for the final photo of the bride and groom. Around the corner of the country club, he found her standing against the back wall, her arms by her side, her fists pressed into the stone behind her. Her eyes were closed, and she was hyperventilating.

"Tania?" he said with worry. She opened her eyes and stared cold and hard at him. She didn't speak, not even when he touched her. "What happened?"

She said in a low dull voice, "What have you done to us, Alexander? What have you let into our house?" She couldn't step away from the wall. Her knees were shaking. "I don't know what to do anymore. How to help you, how to stop their subterfuge. I thought I gave you what you needed most from me."

"What are you *talking* about?"

"But when are you going to give me what I need from you?"

"What are you talking about?"

"What I need from you," she said, "is not to be blind. Can you do that?"

"Yes," he said. "I can do that. What's going on?"

Shaking her head, she took his arm and stepped away from the wall. "I can't stay here another minute. Call me a cab and I'll go home. You stay as long as you want."

"You can't leave in the middle of a wedding! What a scandal. We have to stay for the cake."

"I can't stay here another minute." Tatiana put her face in her hands. She couldn't look at him. "I need to go home. Tell them I wasn't feeling well. It's not a lie."

She refused to go inside even to say good-bye. Alexander went back to make his apologies to Jeff, and they went home. What was happening?

She kept saying, I'm doing the best I can. She kept repeating it like a mantra. But she wouldn't tell him anything. He felt things start to slip away from him, invisible things, threads unraveling on a blanket he didn't know was covering him.

No, he knew.

The blanket of his new calling, his new father, his new friends, his new brother. He chose them. They chose him. He chose them despite her tight-lipped reservations, because he believed she was naïve and her worries were unfounded. He still believed that. Days now since the wedding, and she still wasn't talking.

Eventually he asked her silent stoic back, "Who are you trying to protect?"

And she replied through her back: "You." She was washing the dishes.

"Turn around." She turned. "I need protecting?"

"I can't believe I'm saying it, but yes, as much as ever."

"Tania, do you think it's possible for you not to speak in code? When you talk can you speak either Russian or English, but not gibberish?"

She said nothing, turning to the sink again.

"Okay, that's it," he said, striding to her. "Don't you shake your plummy little tail at me." Picking her up from the sink, he carried her over and dropped her on the couch, stomach down. Falling on top of her, he pinned her legs between his, and clasped her wrists over her head. Her face was in the couch pillow. "Are you going to tell me, or am I going to have to *take* the truth from you?"

"Shh!"

He stuck his chin into her neck, into her cheek, into her shoulder blades. He was tickling her and whispering to her as she kept laughing. "I'm trying to figure out if I should get it out of you by making love to you until you tell me, or by not making love to you until you tell me . . ."

"Tough one," she said. "But if the choice is mine, I might as well have the former."

"I think," Alexander whispered into her ear, squeezing her wrists tighter, "the choice is mine, tadpole . . ."

There was coughing behind them. They turned their heads and Anthony was standing at the foot of the couch, looking puzzled. "What are you doing?" he asked quietly.

"Mommy won't tell me something, and I'm trying to tickle it out of her."

"Dad's trying to stubble it out of me," Tatiana said, her head out of the sofa pillow. Alexander got off her, pulled her up; they sat primly on the couch and looked at their son, who stared at them with solemnity and finally said, "Whatever it is you were doing, Dad, it wasn't working."

"Tell me about it."

In the heat of the night, near the mountains, Alexander sat outside with a cigarette on the rocking bench he had built for them, and she came out and climbed into his lap. It was sunset over the saguaro desert valley, and he rocked them back and forth, while she nuzzled him and murmured love in his ear, cooing pidgin English into him, through his skin. But nothing she said or did could erase the image of her in a peach taffeta dress, standing against the wall, her fists to the stone, saying, "What have you let into our house, Alexander?"

What did that mean?

What had he let in?

But finally even the densest, most wrapped-up-in-himself husband in all of Scottsdale figured out that something wasn't right when Tatiana brought him lunch, and Steve came by with inspection papers to sign, and Tatiana wouldn't look at him. He said, "Hi,

Tania," and Tatiana didn't even mutter a "Hey." It was like Steve didn't exist.

Even blind Alexander noticed.

Steve said, "Mand and I haven't seen much of you guys lately. We should go out."

"Been busy, Stevie," Alexander said slowly, staring at Tatiana, whose head was down. "Been in Yuma four days in the last two weeks. That little Korean conflict."

"Oh, yeah. Well, how about this Saturday?"

"We're busy." That was Tatiana, eyes to the ground.

"Next Saturday?"

"It's our tenth anniversary," she said.

"The following weekend?"

"Anthony's birthday."

"Well, we're having a Fourth of July party—you guys are coming to that, right?"

"If it's on a Friday, I have to work. In fact, I have to go now." She never raised her eyes to him.

At the car, Alexander opened the door for her and she got in without looking at him either! "Whoa," he said, reaching for her through the open window. His fingers under her chin lifted her face. "What's going on?"

"Nothing. You have to get back to work. Look, the homeowners are here. Everything is fine."

"Tania."

"What do you want to do? Have it out on your construction site while a nice married couple waits for you to show them their plaster walls? You've got work to do. I'm going home to make dinner. What would you like? I was thinking of chili and corn bread."

"Yes, fine," he said. "Tania, did Steve say something to you at the wedding?"

"No," she said.

"What then?"

"In the middle of the construction site?"

"When I get home."

"Anthony and Sergio are having dinner with us."

"Tonight in bed."

"I've got to get up early for work tomorrow."

He opened the car door and pulled her out. "Come on, babe. Don't play fucking games with *me*."

"You don't want to know, Alexander. Believe me, you haven't wanted the truth for three years, you aren't going to want it now."

Frustrated, he let her go. Clearly now was not the time. And later at home was not the time—with Anthony and Sergio in the next room, and quiet music, and the sound of running water from the dishes and the laundry, and the laughter of two boys playing ball outside and Monopoly inside, there was no place for *Sturm und Drang*, which is why they both hated having any. Their quiet life worked in small decibels, or in higher decibels in their great bed behind locked doors, with Anthony long asleep or at his friend's house. But not in bed, not together in a hot bath, not outside in the pool, or running around together, or watching the sunset and smoking, or during their divine Sundays, not during the most convivial moments, the most comfortable moments, the most conjugal moments was there a good time for these storms. Alexander realized unhappily that the only harsh words they'd had in the three years they'd lived in Phoenix had been over something to do with Steve or his father.

Turned out that after the chili and corn bread, and a game of basketball, Anthony walked Sergio back down the road and Alexander and Tatiana had thirty minutes to themselves. He took her by the hand outside to their deck, placed her in front of him, sat down on the bench, lit a cigarette, and said, "Let's have it."

She wasted no time. She had a lot to get out. "Alexander," she said, "I've kept quiet for three years because I wanted to give you what you wanted. I know how you feel about Bill. You wanted to work with him, you wanted to be friends with Steve, you wanted me to keep quiet—so I did. After I have seen you be so unhappy, I wanted to do nothing to upset you. So I kept my mouth shut. But I can't keep quiet any longer. Stevie—and his dad—they're no good, Shura. They're no good as friends, they're no good as employers, and they're no good as people. That's the bad news. The good news is: the beautiful thing about living here, in Phoenix, is that they don't matter. There's somewhere else to go, something else to do, somewhere else to work. You are free, and you now have indispensable skills. Carolyn had her house built by a man named G.G. Cain, and she said he was the nicest man—"

"Tatiana, wait, what are you talking about? I know G.G. But I'm not going to work for someone else. I'm not leaving Bill."

"Shura, you have to leave him. You do know that Stevie beat a man nearly to death?"

Alexander shrugged. "What's that got to do with me? Or Bill?"

"Everything. How far do you think that fruit has fallen from the tree? Did you hear what I said? He beat a man nearly to death."

"It was a long time ago. I did some things too, a long time ago." His face darkened.

"You know what was a long time ago? Your birth," Tatiana snapped. "As in, you weren't born yesterday."

"Yes, because you know the way of male drunken bar fights. The guy had been making awful remarks about Amanda."

"Stevie says this to you and you believe him? Stevie, the man who tells anyone who will listen, including you, what Amanda does and does not do, is suddenly going to step up for her honor?" Tatiana laughed before turning grave. "Stevie, whose father buys his son's freedom with the money he makes off your back?"

Alexander rubbed his eyes.

"Before he knew I was married to you, Steve was coming to the hospital pretending to be taken up with me. Would you like to know the kinds of things he said to me?"

"I can imagine. But he didn't know me."

"He knew Amanda, didn't he? He knew he was engaged, didn't he? He knew I was married!"

"All right, so he doesn't treat his women very well."

"I'm not his woman. I'm your woman. And I'm telling you loud and clear that you need to protect your family."

"What the hell are you talking about?" Alexander said, his voice rising. "Protect my family? What the fuck does that mean? I work all day six days a week for my family."

"I'm not impugning how hard you work. I'm impugning who you work for."

"That's it. I've heard enough."

"No," said Tatiana, shaking her head, "I don't think you have." She took a breath. "Do you know that to this day, Steve says suggestive things to me when I come to see you and you're not there? 'You must be used to men looking at you, Tania,' he says in his smarmy voice. 'Even Walter said you looked pretty the other day, Tania, and I always thought Walter was a pansy,' he says. 'I like that dress, it really shows off your figure.' And, 'Don't wear that dress again in front of Dudley, Tania. He's going to go crazy.'"

"Who the fuck is Dudley?" said Alexander.

"How should I know?" replied Tatiana. "He says to Amanda, 'How about a threeway, Amanda?' instead of 'Let's get married in June, Amanda.' And you, as they try to buy your land and take your wife, you don't want to hear it so you can continue to pretend that the naked picture in Balkman's office is just an anomaly, and that the wolf whistling, ogling, leering men building his houses are normal, too!"

"Take my wife? They're just men on roofs! What, New York didn't have wolf whistling?"

"Nothing like this. Never like this—so that I can't come have lunch with my husband? Even a soldier, a warrior husband, is not enough anymore to make them stop? They ask you to go to Las Vegas, they invite you to strip clubs, and finally they get you out on a stag night." Tatiana took a very deep breath. "To all this you keep shaking your blind head—"

"Look, I'm not blind! I know it all. Why do you think I don't go to Vegas? I know exactly what's going on, but it's just bullshit," he said. "I'm inured to bullshit. You should've heard how the men in my penal battalion talked. Steve is a monk compared to them."

"Your men talked about me?"

"Steve doesn't talk to me about you!"

"Not to you, but to others! Go ask Walter what Steve says about me. Recently Walter's been so embarrassed, he won't look at me anymore, not even to say hello."

She saw Alexander taken aback by that. Finally. Something got in. He frowned. "That's it, you're not coming to the construction sites anymore," he said.

Tatiana looked at him, opened her palms to him. When all she saw was his closed face, she crossed her arms on her chest. "That seems a normal way to live? Hiding your wife from the people you work with, as if you're still with the soldiers who buy or take women when they pass through foreign towns? This is your solution? Live like we're in a penal battalion? Live like we're in the Gulag?"

"Stop your overreacting. Stevie's all right. And he is my friend."

"Like Dimitri was your friend? Like Ouspensky was your friend?"

"No! Are you really comparing Stevie with Dimitri?"

"Even here, this is not how people are, Shura. They weren't like this at Ellis, at NYU. They're not like this at my hospital, they're not like this at the market, at the gas stations. Sure, some try to get friendly. But there is something else going on here. Can't you see—Bill Balkman hires *only* these kinds of people. You don't see something wrong with that?"

"No!"

"Everything is raunchy and grody. Nothing is sacred. Nothing. You don't think it rubs off on you? Weren't you the one who told me you breathe oxen, you live oxen?"

"Stop using my own words against me. This isn't it."

"Is that what you're doing? Recreating the Red Army for yourself on your little construction sites?"

"Tania!" exclaimed Alexander. "You better stop right now. I'm not going to get into what you're trying to recreate in your little emergency room, so don't start a fight that you can't finish and can't win." He raised his hand before she said another word. "Look, I don't want to quit my job," he said, "and I'm not going to. Bill treats me very well. I have seven houses I'm building, he gives me a three percent bonus for each one. Who else is going to do that for me?"

"He charges twice as much for his builder's commission as G.G. Cain does, which is why all your houses are so expensive and many are built like cardboard boxes. That seems normal to you, a low-quality custom home and a thirty percent commission? Bill should give you twenty-five percent of his damn commission, not three, seeing he couldn't finish one house on time if it weren't for you."

"Oh, now you're a regular Milton Friedman, too?"

"Who?"

"Balkman is talking of making me partner soon. If I go somewhere else, I'd have to start at the bottom and make no money again. That's your idea of a happy Alexander? Here, I do well, Bill trusts me, and no one bothers me."

"They bother *me*."

"Don't come there!" Alexander broke off. Lowering his voice, breathing hard, he said, "I'm done—done—talking about this. Anything else?"

"There is."

"If you don't get to it in exactly one fucking second—"

"Oh." Tatiana clasped her hands together. "I see. Well, in that case, let me get to it in exactly one second. Steve is all right, you say. He's your friend. Fine. So when your unassailable buddy Steve tells Amanda who tells me—at Cindy's wedding—that at the Westward Ho, you"—She grasped the sides of the rail—"that you took one of the girls into one of the rooms—"

Alexander stood up abruptly. Tatiana stopped speaking. He didn't blink, but something happened to his face—it fell and hardened at the same time. Something crumbled and cemented. He said nothing, just continued to stare at her.

"Shura . . ."

"Tania, I need a second."

"You need a second? I've managed to live carrying those words inside me since last week."

"You know how you did it. You did it because you know they're not true." He lit another cigarette. His fingers were stiff.

"It's your word against his, husband," Tatiana whispered. "That's all I got. Your word against his. And you just spent fifteen minutes telling me that his word is good. You're working with a man who says these things so that your wife hears, so that your wife believes they could be true. You're good friends with someone who wants your wife to think those words are true."

"Leave me alone." He backed away from her. "I need to—just leave me alone."

He spent the rest of the evening outside, in his shed and swimming. Tatiana put Anthony to bed, made bread, looked at a coffee table book of the Grand Canyon. She made him tea and brought it out to him with a fresh sweet bun with blackberry jam, but didn't speak. There was nothing to say. She had told him—the days of ignorance, of innocence, as always, were so short-lived, which is why she cherished and relished them.

Tatiana couldn't fall asleep in their bed without him. She fell asleep on the couch and woke up, naked and under the covers, feeling his hands on her, Alexander leaning over her, whispering comfort—and then it was five thirty in the morning, and she had to go to work. He got up with her, made coffee while she got herself ready, and brought her a cup in the bedroom. They touched lightly. They kissed lightly. As she was leaving, he said, sitting on the bed, "What am I supposed to do now?"

"You leave them behind, darling," she said. "All of them. You are not going to change them. Leave them behind and never look back."

Alexander worked that Friday and Saturday, and on Sunday they went to a Catholic Mass and took a long drive with Anthony up to Sedona to walk amid the Red Rock hills. They had lunch at their favorite Mexican restaurant, they talked about the Grand Canyon, they bought a Spanish vase. At night when they came home and put Ant to sleep, they swam in their pool and made love in the heated whirlpool tub. In bed, Alexander told her there was no way he could be without work for their anniversary, and Tatiana turned away and didn't say anything, and Monday came and she went to the hospital and he went to work, just as if nothing had changed.

But Alexander found himself like Tatiana—unable to look Steve in the eye. All communication between them ceased except for the professional kind. What's the status of the Schreiner house? What's the status of the Kilmer house? What's the status of . . .

He didn't know what to do. Their tenth anniversary weekend was in four days! He bought Tatiana a very expensive ring, though he had just spent all of his bonus account and some of their savings on the extravagant pool. He couldn't be without work. He decided that he would figure out a way to part company with Stevie while still continuing to work for his father. He also decided not to share his plan with Tania. For some odd reason, he didn't think she'd agree.

The day before they left for the Grand Canyon, Alexander met Dudley.

Walter, the framer, had told Alexander a little about Dudley, the itinerant worker Stevie had hired a few weeks ago. He was a johnny-come-lately, Walter said, a jack of all trades. Walter said he was a wastrel, that something was not right with him. "Rumor is he's on the run." The framer lowered his voice. "Rumor is he's wanted for murder in Montana."

Really, Alexander said. For murder in Montana.

"Yeah. But Stevie says that on the plus side, he works cheap, does everything, doesn't complain." Walter laughed.

Dudley was a tall man, as tall as Alexander. He was wearing cowboy boots and a cowboy hat, which he took off for a mock bow, and underneath it he had messy light ash hair pulled back in a stringy ponytail. His scraggly beard covered most of his face. He was chewing tobacco and then obnoxiously spitting it on the ground too close to everyone's feet.

Steve said, "You two should have a lot to talk about. Dudley served in Europe, too, on the Eastern front, right, Dud?"

He was unkempt, which was a peculiar thing for a soldier, as Alexander knew, but soldiers came in all kinds and some could not be retrained. Dudley's handshake was strong and he didn't look away. He said, "Fuckin'a. Two hundred and eightieth division. We crossed the Oder in April '45." He spat.

"Alexander was there, on the Oder. He was south in Poland, though, POW camp there, Catowice, isn't that right, Alex?"

"Catowice? How the hell did you get so far out east?" Dudley asked.

"I don't ask questions when I'm in German hands," said Alexander. "I've got to get going. I'll see you."

"Hey, you want to come out for a drink with us tonight?" Steve asked.

"Can't. We're going away tomorrow."

Dudley said with an insinuating smile, "You and the little lady?"

Alexander's hands fisted up involuntarily. That was just a little too much insolence thrown down as a gauntlet in front of him in the middle of a sunny working afternoon. "What's the smirk for, Dudley?" said Alexander in a voice that was so quiet, he could barely hear it himself.

"It's ten years for you, isn't it, Alex?" Steve interjected.

"Ten, huh?" said Dudley. "You know if this was a prison sentence, you'd be out by now." He and Steve laughed. Then Dudley said, "How'd you get spliced in '42, stuck in Catowice and all?"

"I wasn't in Catowice in '42," Alexander said. "But two eightieth, that was an infantry unit, wasn't it?"

"Uh-huh."

"You were what, a corporal?"

"Sergeant first grade."

"Sergeant. I see."

"Alexander here was a captain," Steve said.

Alexander smiled coldly. "Still am a captain, even as we speak," he said. "Officer Reserve Corps, combat support services in Yuma." Dudley didn't smile even coldly. With the ranking order thus clearly established, now Alexander could unclench. "See you Tuesday. Steve, Dudley." He started to walk away.

"You two have fun now," said Dudley.

Alexander stopped walking and slowly turned around. Steve elbowed Dudley.

Alexander knew that in one moment everything he had worked for could be gone. In one moment, Tatiana and Alexander wouldn't be going anywhere for their anniversary because Alexander would be talking to the police. It was only for her that he gritted his teeth and took control of himself but still couldn't let it go completely.

"Dudley," he said, stepping back to the two men, "I never met you before two minutes ago, but I'm going to give you a friendly word of advice. Don't have that tone in your voice when you talk about my wife. In fact, better for you not to speak of her at all. Understood?"

Dudley laughed, chewing his tobacco with an open mouth. "Hey, man, I said nothing, why is your cage rattled?"

"As long as we're clear, my cage is not rattled."

But the cage was clattering.

The Germans in the Grand Canyon

Early Friday morning, they left Anthony with Francesca and drove two hundred and forty miles to the Grand Canyon, where they trekked in the blinding heat six winding hours down the Bright Angel Trail, down the Redwall and the Tonto, to the Archean granite, to the boiling Colorado. They set up their tent and stayed the weekend on the desert shores of another thousand-mile river, this one carving its way through two-billion-year-old igneous rock. Their three days was an oasis in the middle of their life. Alexander himself tried very hard to forget what was outside their tent.

They weren't allowed to build a fire, but they swam and ate Tatiana's bread, and Spam out of cans, and drank vodka straight from the bottle and had chocolate out of tinfoil. He gave her a white gold one-carat diamond ring, and she gave him a U.S. Army military watch, because his Red Army one had broken, and new leather boots before they had left home, because his had gotten worn. They played railroad tracks, railroad tracks (Russian-style *and* American-style), strip poker and even dominos. He lay in her lap and she told him jokes. ("A very sick man comes down from his deathbed, smelling something delicious in the kitchen, where he finds that his wife has baked him a batch of his favorite cookies. Gratefully he reaches for one, and she slaps his hand away and says, 'They're not for you! They're for the funeral.'") She read to him—as if in a Shakespearean soliloquy—the entire manual for a prototype of a color television, and in a much more Gracie Allen tone an article from *Ladies Home Journal*: "Are You a Match Made in Heaven, Crabby Cancer Girl and Chatty Gemini Guy?" ("They got us all wrong, Shura, didn't they? It's so the other way around.");

she explained to him what an algorithm was (a precise set of logical rules for solving a problem), asked him if he wanted to know what a divide-and-conquer algorithm was and when he groaned and said, God no, she bent and kissed him as if she were raising the dead.

She asked him to tell her one non-bedroom thing about her he loved, and he pretended he couldn't think of one. He asked her to tell him one bedroom thing about him she loved and she pretended she couldn't think of one.

Touché indeed.

He liked the way she laughed, he said, like choral music.

She liked the way he moved, she purred, like poetry, in song and sonnetry—in major scales and intervals and sympathetic strings, in undiminished chords and canons and compound meter rhythms, in passion rhyme, in tango time, in great ionic verse, in pyrrhics and dispondees when he was not so lyrical, in anapests and dactyls when he was.

Alexander, ever the poet *and* a scientist, immediately tested the law of gravitational physics: The force of attraction between two bodies being directly proportional to the product of their masses and inversely proportional to the square of the distance between them. And then lying in pitch black, at the end of radioactive choriambic love, Tatiana in her first soprano murmured, "I really don't know what you think the classical sciences will teach you."

He laughed and said, "That you are the funniest girl a man could marry."

Very nearly asleep, they were lying quietly bare against each other.

"Shura," she whispered, "please don't worry. We'll get pregnant. We haven't been lucky, that's all. We'll get there." She cleared her throat. "Though . . . don't you wonder sometimes if maybe we're meant to have just our one Antman?"

"He's enough boy for anyone," said Alexander. "But why do you want him to remain an only child? *I* was an only child."

"Yes, and you're enough boy for anyone." She squeezed him.

"No, no, I'm tapped. Closed for the evening. Please come again tomorrow."

Choral laughter. "I do nothing to stop us from having a baby, darling. I know my husband thinks I occasionally have divine powers, but he is not right in this case."

And all Alexander said by way of drowsy reply was "Occasionally?"

She fell silent.

"Remember Luga?" he whispered. "Before I ever kissed you, remember lying naked in my arms?"

Tatiana started to cry.

"Did you ever imagine then, on the verge of our Armageddon, that we would be eleven years down the pike, across the million mystic miles, lying here in the Grand Canyon where the winter never comes, and you're still naked in my arms, and I'm still rubbing my lips across your hair?"

"No." She was kissing his bare clavicles. "The Germans aren't across the river, Shura."

"That's true. Many things are forever behind us." Alexander closed his eyes in the blackness.

"Yes. There's plenty around us, too," she said. "We must be strong." She shimmered and whispered. "When I left you for dead, I thought nothing would ever touch me again. But you're with me now. Nothing can touch us, my husband."

For three days they remained in the eternal space where there was nothing else in the world but them.

And then they came home.

The rock Alexander bought her was a one-carat VVS diamond set in four smaller diamonds in beveled white gold. It was a remarkable ring, and she showed it off to everyone in the hospital until Carolyn said, "Do you have any idea how much he must have spent on that?"

The military watch and the new boots Tatiana had bought him cost her fifty-one dollars. She thought she was a bit reckless and had spent too much. When she got the ring appraised during lunch, she found out it was valued at twenty-two hundred dollars. She burst into tears right at the jeweler's.

Back home she begged Alexander to take it back. "We're saving for a house," Tatiana said. "We lived through Leningrad. You may be leaving your job. We can't spend twenty-two hundred dollars on a ring!"

"It's a diamond for you, for our tenth wedding anniversary. And I'm not leaving my job."

"I don't need diamonds, Shura, you know that. But you have to leave Balkman."

"We're not talking about this! I don't understand—did I actually marry a woman who thinks the ice her husband bought for her is too big? It's a gift, Tatiana. I will remind you again, eleven years later, that in this country, when you get a gift, you open it and say thank you. Take the fucking thing back if you want, but don't speak about it again to me."

"Don't be upset with me. Don't take your stress out on me!"

"Too late."

The oasis was gone, the life was back.

Dudley of Montana

On Wednesday, the day after they returned, Alexander was nailing down the subflooring in the Schreiner house. The boards were warped and had come loose. His mouth was full of nails, and the hammer was in his hands. He needed to get new floor guys. This subflooring was so subpar. It would usually warp right before the final inspection. Where did Balkman get these crews from?

Steve came to see the progress of the house with Dudley by his side. "How was your time off?" he asked. "Where did you go?"

Alexander glanced back, his mouth full of nails.

Dudley was scrutinizing his bare arms. It was over a hundred degrees and Alexander was wearing only a sleeveless football tank; all the people he worked with had long seen and gotten used to his scars and his tattoos. Alexander spit the nails out of his mouth, right next to Dudley's feet. He stood up, his hand gripping the hammer. "Grand Canyon," he said. He certainly wasn't going to tell them he spent three days in a tent with her. Silently he raised his eyes to Dudley, who raised his eyes to Alexander.

"Nice tattoos you got there, Captain," Dudley said quietly.

"Steve," Alexander said, "did you bring the glass for the window like I asked?"

After lunch Steve came by with the glass for the window. Dudley wasn't with him.

"Are you coming to our Fourth of July party?"

"I don't know. Tania is working." He was eating his sandwich and trying to read the paper.

"What's wrong, man?"

But Alexander knew what Tatiana had known: once said, things could not be unsaid. "Nothing."

Steve persisted. "What's up? You've been acting very odd these last few weeks. What did I do?"

"You know what, I'm having my lunch. I don't want to talk about it now."

"Is there anything to talk about?"

"Yes."

"Well, come on then, let's clear the air."

Alexander threw out the rest of his sandwich. "Steve, did you tell Amanda I had it off with one of the flossies you invited to the Ho?"

Steve laughed. "No, no, she misunderstood. Is that what this is all about?"

"She misunderstood?"

"Yeah, it was just a joke. Manda has no sense of humor."

"Amanda thought it was pretty serious when she told a pretty serious Tatiana."

"Sorry about that. It was a joke. I didn't mean to upset Tania." He shrugged. "But I know she saw right through it, she couldn't have been upset for long."

"What kind of fucking joke is that?"

"Remember that tootsy? She told you for twenty bucks she would go into the room with you? And I told you for twenty more she'd take it up the—"

"Stevie, we were drunk, but that's no misunderstanding. Amanda told Tania I went into that room."

"I must have not made myself clear."

"You think?"

Steve laughed. "What are you getting in a twist about? You want me to talk to Tania? Bring her by. I'll tell her it was just a gag."

"No." Alexander threw the newspaper in the trash, and stood up from the wooden plank. "And you know what else, Steve-o— I don't give a shit about the friends you make with out-of-state prison freaks, but I better never find out you're talking to one of them about my wife. If you want to talk to them about available women, talk about your girlfriend."

"What did you just say?" said Steve, squinting. "I think I must have misheard."

Alexander stepped closer. "Don't ever speak to him—or anyone—about my wife. Do you understand what I'm telling you? Am I making myself clear now?"

"Oh, come on, Dudley's a good guy."

Obviously still not clear.

"He's a soldier like us," Steve went on. "He fought in a war, just like you, used to plenty of women—just like you. He doesn't know Tania from Eve, or care. Come for a drink with us, get to know him. He's a lot of fun."

Alexander was walking away when he said, "No." And never again, he wanted to add. It might take a while for Steve to get it, but finally he'd get it. And then he'd leave Alexander alone and Alexander could keep his job. That's what he kept hoping for.

Waiting For Tatiana. It was like a play. He was once again waiting for Tatiana—this time at Balkman's barbecue-and-fireworks Fourth of July party.

Margaret, Bill's girlfriend, who tried to kiss Alexander hello on the lips, asked where Tania was. Amanda asked where Tania was. Cindy asked where Tania was. Alexander himself wanted to know where Tania was. They took Ant to Francesca's early that morning and Alexander drove her to work so they would have only his truck after the party. She "promised" him with a smile as she got out that she would be at Balkman's by eight, "the latest," and here it was, 8:45 and she was still not there. He drank a bit, picked on some chips, had a beer. The food had been served buffet-style in aluminum trays over sterno heaters, but he didn't want to eat until she got there. He was impatient and irritable. He meandered around the backyard, finally getting into a conversation with Jeff about the Korean War.

"Alexander!" It was Margaret, leading Tatiana across the lawn. "Look who finally graced us with her presence! Party's almost over, darling. Food's nearly all gone. See, if you weren't working, you could've had it all hot."

Tatiana nodded hello to their friends. "Hey," she said to Alexander. "Erin couldn't get off work, and she was giving me a ride. Sorry I'm late."

"You're always sorry," he said without smiling. Of course she wasn't wearing a watch. It was like asking her to wear a weapon.

She had on a tank sundress with a swing skirt and wide straps with satin ties at the shoulders. The dress was pale green with pale yellow flowers. The skirt was flouncy, she must have had a petticoat under it. The unusual thing was that her hair was down, flowing loose on her back. Alexander frowned. "Let's go. I'll get you a drink," he said, leading her away, and when they were at a sufficient distance from everyone, he said quietly, "Why's your hair down like that?"

"Well, look." Turning her back to him, Tatiana lifted the hair away from her neck to show him his nocturnal obsessions spilling over into their daytime life. There were four or five fresh scarlet-purple suck marks on the back of her neck and down the rear slope of her shoulders. "Don't have much choice but to leave my hair down, do I?" She turned to face him. "What would you rather have, everybody see my hair or see those and imagine what you must have been doing to me?" Slightly blushing, she lowered her head. Alexander was silent, recalling what he had been doing to her. Sighing, he kissed her hands.

Suddenly Margaret was upon them. "No, no, no. No spousal privileges at parties. You can do that at home." She was carrying a tray of crudités. "Tania, you don't know what a treasure you have in your husband—he didn't flirt with anyone. He is very good when you're not around."

"And that would be quite frequently," Alexander whispered to Tatiana, standing slightly behind her. She suppressed a laugh.

Margaret took Tatiana by the hand. "Come, let me introduce you to someone. I have a friend here, Joan—she worked once, too. I want you to talk to her about it. She got it out of her system. Alexander, now that your wife is here, go flirt. It's bad manners for spouses to talk to each other at a party."

Tatiana left to mingle. Alexander, too, but every once in a while he looked for her amid the talkers. He discussed with Jeff the prospects for the mediocre Boston Red Sox this season and then became embroiled in a conversation with Bill Balkman over Truman's firing of Douglas MacArthur, who had retaken *all* of Korea from the Chinese-led Communists in mere months and had wanted to push over the Yalu River right into China against Truman's wishes; hence the sacking. Balkman said, "No, no. I agree with Truman. Moderation is key. Truman said, 'Let's be calm, let's do nothing.' MacArthur was out of line. I agree with the President."

Alexander said, "You don't think MacArthur was right when he said that moderation in this instance was like advising a man whose family is about to be killed not to take hasty action for fear of alienating the affection of the murderers?"

Balkman laughed, slapping Alexander on the shoulder. "Alexander, you're hilarious. Look, much more pertinently, did Steve tell you our fabulous news?"

"What news?"

Balkman was beaming. "We got the contract for the Hayes house."

Alexander was pleased. Dee and Mike Hayes bought three acres of land on a freshly made lake in Scottsdale, north of Dynamite, and had been for months shopping around for a builder for their proposed 7000 square foot home. It was great news for the company and great exposure, since the house was going to be photographed for the *Phoenix Sun* newspaper and for *Modern Home* magazine. They toasted their success.

"We're breaking ground in three weeks. Alex, I want you to foreman the whole op—as they say in the army."

"Well, they don't use the word foreman," said Alexander.

"Ha! Get all the help you need. Mike Hayes told me he needs the house by early spring so we have our work cut out for us. Jeff and Steve have their hands full, but you're going to finish the Schreiners ahead of schedule." He patted Alexander affectionately. "I heard you actually put in new subflooring yourself to get it ready earlier. We'll get a bonus for early delivery, you know. You'll get half of five thousand dollars."

"Thanks, Bill." They shook hands.

"Borrow Dudley from Steve-o," said Balkman. "He works hard. He'll help you. Have you met him yet?"

"Yes." Alexander's fingers tensed around his beer glass.

"I see Tania's met him, too." Balkman smiled. "He's been flirting with your wife for the last half-hour."

The smile faded from Alexander's face. Tatiana was walking toward him, a plate in her hands. By her side was Dudley, swaying from the free booze.

He had his hand on her back—on her hair!

"Dudley-boy, I see you've met our Tania," said Balkman, shaking Dudley's hand. "Dudley's another one, Alexander, who'll do anything. You're a fine worker, Dud; good to have you on board. How are you enjoying our little party?"

Tatiana went to stand next to Alexander, not meeting his gaze.

"You okay?" he said in a low voice.

"I'm just dandy," she said. "He's been following me around for forty minutes. What, you haven't noticed? Ah, but then, you don't notice anything anymore."

Before Alexander could defend his observational skills, she walked away from him. Taking a deep breath he followed her.

They went to get a drink, away from other ears for a moment. "Tania, I don't want you to talk to him. Don't go near him. He is fucked up—can't you see it?"

"Who? Dudley? Oh, come on. He's harmless," she said in her little mocking voice. "All men are like that. Don't worry, he's fine."

Alexander was in no mood to be mocked. "Excuse me," he said, "if I don't want to have this argument with you in the middle of my boss's party."

"I don't want to talk another second about this," she said. "You've made it very clear you're not listening. Oh, and about the other thing—I'll try not to talk to Dudley, but he's very persistent. But so what? Just men being men, right? I heard," Tatiana said, widening her eyes, "it's much worse in the army."

"Tania!"

"Yes?"

His back stiff, he opened himself a beer. She poured herself a little wine. They stood and drank without talking.

Balkman caught up with them.

"Tania, did Alexander tell you about our great coup?"

"No," she said curtly.

Balkman himself told her about the Hayes house, and about his plans for Alexander for the next year. Tatiana listened—like a stone might listen—and then said, "That's great," but didn't muster the sincerity or the fake smile.

"What's the matter?" Balkman said. "Everything all right? Another long day at work?"

"Everything is just fine," she replied to him, in a voice that said, you jerk, can't you see how bad it is? "Will you two excuse me?" Her crisp skirt flounced as she swirled away.

Alexander excused himself and went after her. "Are you kidding me," he said, "acting that way in front of my employer? You want a fight, let's take it home, and I'll give you a fight good and proper but don't bark at me and turn up your nose at my boss when he talks to you." They were across the lawn standing tensely near the landscaped azaleas.

"Alexander," said Tatiana, "I am through pretending."

"No, you're not," he said. "You're going to pretend to be gracious in his house."

"Like he was gracious to me in my house, telling you to put me in my place?"

"The way you're acting," he snapped, "it's obvious you don't know it."

She sharply turned to walk away from him. With great difficulty, he did not grab her arm. Stepping in front of her, he said through his closed mouth, "Stop it. Right now. Do you hear me?"

"I don't want to be here."

"That much is clear. But don't walk away from me." He did not grab her arm, he took her by the arm, and because the arm was bare, he didn't squeeze her, he just circled it in his hands. "Now come on. Let's go sit. The fireworks will come on soon, and then we'll go."

"Oh, yes, please. Let's go sit by your friend, Stevie. Maybe we can talk to him about services at the Ho. I hear it's a fine hotel. Very accommodating."

It was all he could do not to *fling* her arm away from him. They went to sit in a circle of chairs on the edge of the lawn by Jeff and Cindy, Steve and Amanda.

Cindy had been married a month. She was telling Amanda and Tatiana what her first month of marriage was like. Alexander's face involuntarily turned to Tatiana, sitting to his right. Ten years ago, they had been living their first month together, too. Here under the blackening Phoenix sky, they had almost forgotten. But then she turned her face to him, and in her supplicating expression, he saw that she had not forgotten. Just a glance, a blink, a short nod of the head as a toast to the everlasting Ural Mountains and the everflowing Kama.

"We have news," said Cindy. "Jeff doesn't want me to say anything, but you're my closest friends, I can't not tell you."

Jeff rolled his eyes.

"We're having a baby!" she exclaimed.

There was exultation and congratulations. The men shook Jeff's hand. The women hugged Cindy. Nobody could believe it. "Already?" Amanda said.

"Well done, man," Steve said. "Well done! Quick work of it."

"Why dawdle, I say. If you're going to do something, do it right."

Alexander was very careful not to look at Tatiana as they both maintained their smiles for Jeff and Cindy.

Dudley angled by, saw them, and pulled up an empty lawn chair next to Tatiana. Everyone stopped talking about babies. Dudley asked Tatiana if she wanted another glass of *wiiiine*, seeing that hers was empty; called her Tania. Said that he knew some Russian soldiers when he was in Europe, and heard that Russian girls named Tania were sometimes called Tanechka. "Does anyone call you Tanechka, like you are a Russian girl?" chuckled Dudley, his mouth curled up in a seedy smile.

"Tania is not Russian, Dudley," said Amanda. "She is from New York."

"Look at that hair," said Dudley. "That's not New York hair. That's Russian peasant hair." He grinned and raised his coarse eyebrows. "*Before* the emancipation of the serfs," he added suggestively.

Alexander got up, eased a paling Tatiana out of her chair, and switched places with her. "So you and Amanda are not talking over me," he said, sitting down next to Dudley without glancing at him. But suddenly the conversation sagged.

"I saw your tattoos the other day when you were doing the subflooring," Dudley said to Alexander. "You got some nifty ones. A hammer and sickle on your arm?"

"Yeah, what of it?"

"Where'd you get it?"

"Catowice."

"Voluntary or forced?"

"Forced."

"How'd they get you to sit still for that? I would have fought until I was bled out before I had that on my arm."

Tatiana reached over and put her hand on Alexander's leg—her way of comfort, and of warning. He ignored it, turning to silently stare down Dudley with his back to her. "You've got tattoos from your neck down to your back," Alexander said. "The other day at the Schreiners', I saw on your forearm a tattoo of a dragon doing unspeakable things to a damsel in distress. You've got knives plunged into people's hearts, beheadings, disembowelings. All that is better than a hammer and sickle?"

"Better than a Red brand? Where are you living? Absolutely!" said Dudley. "And I got those willingly, not held down in chains. The choice was mine."

"Did you get them at the big house?"

"Yeah. So what?"

"Ah. Prison was your choice?"

The other people in the chairs looked uncomfortably into the green grass.

"Prison was not my choice," said Dudley slowly. "But tell me, is a SchutzStaffel Eagle on your other arm your choice? A hammer and sickle on one arm, a swastika on the other? Where the fuck did you come from?"

"Dud, come on, there are ladies present," said Jeff.

Dudley continued as if not spoken to. "The Nazis didn't brand POW with SS Eagles. You know who did?"

"*I* know who did," said Alexander grimly.

"The Sovietskis. In Germany, when they took over the Nazi camps. I know it because we were in one of them watching the Soviet guards with one of their own prisoners. They did it as a sign of respect after the man didn't confess despite severe torture. They beat him, tortured him, tattooed him and then shot him anyway."

A groan of pain came from Tatiana behind him.

"What's your point?" Alexander said, stretching his hand back, to touch her, to say, it's all right. I'm here. It wasn't me they shot.

"My point is," Dudley said too loudly, "you may be in the Reserve now, but you were never in our army during the war."

Alexander said nothing.

"Who were you fighting for?"

"Against Hitler. Who were *you* fighting for?"

"You and I, we never fought on the same side, buddy. I know it. No one has tattoos like you. The SS Eagle is a badge of blind honor for the Nazis, a sign of ultimate respect—they would saw off their own dicks before they gave one to an American POW—even in a fuckhole like Catowice. No, you were captured too far east to have fought for us. Americans never got to where you were."

"Dudley, what the hell are you saying?" asked Steve, getting up out of his chair and walking over to stand near him.

"This man is an impostor," said Dudley. "He is in hiding here. This man was in the Red Army. The Germans branded the Soviet officers with the hammer and sickles—before they shot them. The Soviets branded the Soviet expat soldiers with the SS Eagles—before they shot them."

There was silence in the circle. Everyone gaped at Alexander, who said nothing, his mouth clenched, his eyes dark. Tatiana squeezed his leg. They exchanged a glance. She said quietly, "You think we should go now?"

"No, no, don't be silly, stay for the fireworks," Amanda said

quickly. The girls tittered uncomfortably. Jeff said, "I'm sure
Dudley's mistaken. It's some kind of mistake, that's all." Raising
his eyebrows, he looked over at Cindy. "Cin, you know what? This
is a very good time to go dance."

Everybody got up except Tatiana and Alexander. Even Dudley
managed to hoist himself off the chair. "What a great idea," he
said, crossing Alexander's path heading to Tatiana. "Want to dance,
Tanechka?"

Alexander stood up suddenly and body-checked Dudley, who
lost his balance and fell to the ground.

"Dudley," said Alexander, having already pulled Tatiana out of
the chair and away, "if you're right about me, then you must know
what I will do if you touch her again."

Before Dudley, back on his feet, could even open his mouth,
Jeff and Steve were already between them. "Guys, guys, come on,"
said Jeff, pushing Alexander away, while Steve pushed Dudley
away. "Alex, what's wrong with you? It's a party. At my *father's*
house. Dud, forget it, come with me, let me introduce you to Theo.
Come, you'll like *him*." With a sharp stare at Alexander, to say,
cool it, can't you see he's just wasted? Steve led Dudley away, and
Amanda was about to lead Tatiana away, but Tatiana went to
Alexander, placed her hand on his chest and said, "Do you want
to go home? We can go right now."

Jeff said not to go. "He's drunk. It's nothing. Alexander, forget
about him. He's not worth it, man."

Tatiana was not moving. She pressed against him and looked
up. He brushed the hair out of her face, stroked her cheek briefly
and then disengaged from her. "We'll wait for the fireworks. Look,
Margaret is looking for you again. Go. Just remember what I told
you."

Casting him a nervous look, she left, flanked by Margaret and
Amanda, and Alexander remained with Jeff. Balkman came over,
and they got caught up discussing breaking ground on the Hayes
house and whose palms needed to be greased in order to get
the inspectors to the site in two weeks and not in two over-
booked months. Suddenly Alexander wasn't paying any attention. The Balkmans had a large lawn, with a pool, a gazebo,
landscaped bushes and trees. Across the lawn through the bushes
he spotted a plaid shirt and a ponytail. From beyond the man's
jeans, Alexander saw the floral print of Tatiana's green dress.

His gaze briefly losing its focus, Alexander barely excused himself as he made his way across. Tatiana was pressed against the wood fence and he was leaning over her. Alexander didn't acknowledge Dudley as he pushed between them to separate them, his eyes on Tatiana's distressed face. He pulled her away from the fence and only then did he turn. Behind him, Tatiana was grasping his shirt.

"You are completely fucked up," Alexander said quietly to Dudley. "What are you doing? I'm telling you, walk away. Turn around, walk away, stay away from my wife."

"What is your *problem*, man? This is a free country, unlike that red country you came from. And your wife, for your information, was talking to me. Weren't you, Tania?"

Tatiana, her mouth tight and skin pale, took Alexander's hand and said, "Come on, Shura. The fireworks are about to start."

But Alexander could not walk away. He could not turn his back.

It was dark; there was much commotion. They were near the edge of the lawn slightly away from other people. The first burst of fireworks whistled into the sky and exploded. Over the whistling of the rockets, Alexander heard Dudley's voice.

"You didn't answer me," said Dudley. "I said, what in the world is your fucking problem?"

"What in the world is *your* fucking problem?" said Alexander, turning square to him. "Tania, go wait for me across the grass."

Tatiana squeezed his hand. "No. Please. Come on, Shura," she said, trying to pull him away. "Let's go home."

But Alexander wasn't moving. He and Dudley faced off, eye to eye.

"You've had a problem with me from the very beginning," said Dudley, spitting out a black chunk of chewed tobacco.

"You've been out of fucking line from the very beginning."

"Oh, really?" Dudley said. "Well, you want to take it outside?"

"We are outside, asshole."

"Shura, please!" She walked between them, taking hold of both of Alexander's hands.

"Tania!" Alexander ripped his hands from her, not for a second taking his eyes off Dudley. "I *said* go wait for me across the grass."

"Let's go home, darling," she said, still in front of him, looking up at him, still trying to take hold of him. "Please."

"Yes, let's go home, darling," mimicked Dudley. "*Please*. And I'll get on my knees and suck your cock."

"Shura, no!"

Alexander moved Tatiana forcibly out of the way with one hand and punched Dudley so savagely and swiftly in the face with the other that if Dudley hadn't fallen backward, no one would have known that anything at all had transpired between them. The fireworks continued to burst in the sky. People were clapping, cheering. There was music playing. Harry James and his orchestra were finally beginning to see the light.

But fall Dudley did into the corner of the lawn, in the dark, near the bushes. Tatiana, ever the nurse, peered at him. He was bleeding profusely from the mouth. His front teeth were dangling by their bloodied roots. Alexander—who had been methodically trained and then baptized by fire in vicious hand-to-hand combat through the Byelorussian villages, fighting the Germans with knives and bayonets and with single fatal blows up through the nose—thought that Dudley got off easy. Without breathing out, he took Tatiana by the hand. "Now we can go," he said. Nothing in his face moved.

Speechlessly she stared at him.

He walked across the lawn to the back gate. Margaret and Bill were standing on the patio watching the fireworks. Alexander, barely even stopping, came up to Balkman and said into the man's initially smiling and then sinking face, "That's it. I've had it up to here with you and your fucking business. I quit—for good. Don't pay me for last week, don't give me any of the money you owe me. I'm done with you. Don't ever call me again."

"Alexander! Wait! What's happened?"

Balkman ran after him.

"Alexander! Please wait! Steve! What the hell happened?"

Alexander was moving quickly, pulling Tatiana behind him; she had to run to keep up. Outside on the front walkway, Steve intercepted them, running around to face them, panting, red, fists clenched. "How dare you! How dare you—after all we did for you—"

Alexander jerked his head back but not before Steve jabbed him hard in the chin, knocking him into Tatiana, who lost her footing and fell.

Alexander, without straightening out, punched Steve, smashing his jaw. Steve doubled over. Alexander uppercut him again but harder. He would have hit him a third time, but crumbling onto himself, Steve fell on the stone walkway. "Let's see how well you lie your way through your miserable life now, you sack of shit,"

Alexander said, kicking him hard, and then turning to a frightened and panicked Tatiana to help her off the ground.

They were driving in a matter of minutes. They were utterly silent for several miles.

"Are you all right?" Tatiana asked.

"I'm fine." He wiped his mouth.

"You could've broken your knuckles."

"They're fine." He clenched and unclenched his fist.

She was watching him. "Shura . . . ?"

"Tania," he said calmly, "I don't want to talk about a single thing, a single fucking thing. So just—sit very quietly and say nothing."

She fell instantly mute. In a few minutes, he stopped his truck on an empty Shea Boulevard by the side of the road. Somewhere far away fireworks were going off. Inside the truck his unsteady hands were gripping the wheel.

"Darling . . ." she said soothingly.

"I have been such a fucking idiot. I don't even know what to do with myself."

"Please, it'll be all right. Do you want me to drive?"

His head was on the wheel. She scooted over to him on the bench seat, sat by him. When he looked up, she took a napkin and dabbed his lip. He moved her hand away, and soon began driving again. "Are *you* okay?" he asked. "That bastard hit me knowing you were behind me, knowing you could get hurt. I didn't even have a chance to move you out of the way."

"Are you surprised he wasn't more of a gentleman?" asked Tatiana.

"Did you not hear me when I said I don't want you to say a single fucking thing?"

After a while she spoke. "Dudley asked me if I had heard the rumor about him. That he *keeled* a man in Montana. I said that he'd been at war, he must have seen plenty of death. And he said, 'War isn't real. Montana, now that's real.'"

"I've seen Montana," said Alexander, his hands grim around the wheel. "I don't think it's so real."

Tatiana couldn't sleep. He slept. She made out the hands of the clock. Ten to two. The house was quiet, outside was quiet, it was the deep of night by the mountains. Nothing was moving, except Tatiana's anxiety, freely roaming around in her chest. She couldn't sleep at all. She was unsettled and anxious.

Quietly reaching over him, she replaced the phone back on the cradle. He always took it off the hook at night before he made love to her.

Anthony was sleeping over at Sergio's. She wished Ant were home, so she could go and check on him and feel a bit of comfort. Instead, Tatiana placed her hand on Alexander's chest and listened to his heart. All her adult life this is what she did—listened to his heart. What was it telling her now? It was rhythmic, subdued, whooshing. Lightly she rubbed her lips back and forth against his stubble, kissed him softly, brought her hand down, cupped him, caressed him. He was deeply sleeping, but sometimes, if he felt her like this through sleep, he would roll on his side and throw his arm over her. Tonight he did not wake, remaining on his back. His lip was swollen. His right hand was swollen, iced over, bandaged. He barely let her bandage it. He hated to be pampered over his injuries. He liked to be pampered over other things, bathed, fed, fussed over, kissed—all that he took gladly—but he never liked any fussing over his wounds. It was like he was remembering himself incapacitated in Morozovo where he lay helpless in a hospital bed for two months until he was arrested and she was gone.

Tatiana tossed and tossed, and finally got up, threw on her cream camisole and went out to the living room. She got herself a glass of water, sat on a high stool near the kitchen counter; she didn't move, she tried not to breathe. The air conditioner was off, there was no noise at all, and it was then, at two thirty in the morning, that Tatiana thought she heard the sound of a distant engine. Slightly opening the front door, she listened. Nothing. Outside was black dread, and there was no moon. After bolting and locking the front door, she went to quietly close the bedroom door, so as not to disturb Alexander and then from the kitchen dialed the hospital.

Erin, her friend and the night receptionist answered, and the first words out of her mouth were, "Tania! Why was your phone off the hook? I've been calling and calling you!"

"Why? What's the matter?" Tatiana asked quietly.

"Steve Balkman was brought in here again with some other guy. Balkman is still unconscious, but the other one was a wild animal. They had to subdue him with tranquilizers. He was drunk and bleeding. He kept yelling, threatening unbelievable things, and before they shot him up full of drugs, he kept saying your husband's name, cursing! Do you know anything about that?"

"I do. Is Sergeant Miller there?"

"He went out on his break. Who *is* that man? And how do you know him? We've been trying to call you for three hours!"

"Let me talk to Sergeant Miller. That man needs to be detained."

"Tania! He can't be, he left already."

"He what?"

"Yes, that's what I'm trying to tell you! At one thirty he stormed out of here without a doctor, without a discharge, without anything. Just pulled out his IV, put on his clothes and left."

Tatiana's voice was a whisper when she said, "Erin, tell Miller to send a car to my house."

"What's going—"

Tatiana hung up. But now her heart was thudding so hard that she couldn't hear the quiet, the outside, the inside. Was it a car she had heard? Or was it a fever? A delusion?

She was standing at the kitchen counter. The shades weren't drawn in the living room. They never drew the shades. There was no one around. Was there wind? She couldn't tell, but the black-and-blue shadows kept moving in long strides through the windows. She couldn't hear anything outside. She was paralyzed with deafening fear on the inside. She needed to walk across the living room into the bedroom and wake Alexander, but she couldn't move. It would mean walking across the house, past two unshaded windows, past two doors.

She was still in the kitchen when the shadow in her window rose in the darkness into the shape of a man moving slowly up the steps of her front deck. She always left that window open so she could see Alexander walking up the steps to his home. This wasn't the wind!

She moved, she took three steps away from the counter, past the front door, and before she could take another, the door crashed open, and before she had a chance to scream, Dudley, his mouth full of black holes, his eyes filled with black rage, was in front of her. He grabbed her around the mouth and throat so she couldn't make a sound and twisted her head back so hard she thought her neck would break. There was a pistol in his hand. And she had so solicitously closed the bedroom door to let Alexander sleep!

But the front door, the door! It was such a loud crash. Maybe he would hear.

He heard.

The bedroom door slowly opened, and Alexander appeared and

stood naked in the doorway. Dudley showed him Tatiana. "Here I am, motherfucker," Dudley said, lisping through the missing incisors. "And here she is. We're going to finish this in your house." He was holding Tatiana around the throat. The cocked pistol was pointed at Alexander. "You pigging Red, don't move. You think you can break my fucking face and get away with it? You don't know soldiers for shit. I've brought it right back home to you." Dudley's hand around Tatiana's throat fanned out over her breast. She exhaled piercingly, her eyes wildly pleading to Alexander, who stood like a tomb, not blinking, not breathing, looking only at Dudley. "Stevie told me she never had another cock but yours," Dudley said. "Oh, we said, how *sweet* that must've been for you— with tiny little her. Well, guess what? I'm going to find out if she's still like candy"—he smacked his lips—"find out right in front of you, and then you can have my sloppy seconds. Now step away from the door"—Dudley steadied his cocked weapon—"but slowly."

Alexander did as he was told. He slowly stepped away from the door, and without anything else moving on him and without another instant of time ticking by, he raised his left arm that had been hidden behind the door jamb, pointed the Colt M1911 pistol straight at Tatiana's face and fired in the dark.

The reverberating thudding impact of the .45 caliber round travelling a distance of 20 feet at a speed of 830 feet per second and breaking apart a skull was so loud and shocking that it felt as if Alexander had shot her. Dudley's head exploded six inches away from Tatiana's face. With Dudley still clutching her, they were both thrown back; he hit the wall behind him and slumped forward to the floor in a heap on top of her. She was blinded, she couldn't see, she didn't even know if she was screaming, or crying, or dying. His arm remained around her throat.

Alexander was pulling her from under him, untangling her, lifting her. That's when she heard herself screaming. She started flailing at him, hitting him, trying to get away from him. He said nothing, did nothing but held her to him; he held her to his chest while she thrashed and screamed in terror. His heart was just inches away through his breastplate. It was beating steady, it was pounding on, and he was saying, *shh*, and his heart was saying shh, and staying sanguine. But she couldn't calm down. She thought she had been hit. Her skin was cold, her own heartbeat at two hundred. Alexander sat her down, held her firmly around the shoulders, pressed her to him, and put his hand over her mouth. "Shh," he said. "Calm down." His hand remained over her as she breathed in out carbon dioxide. "Shh. Shh," he kept saying. He took his hand away, opened her mouth and exhaled into it. "Feel my calm breath? Now slow down, it's all right. Slow down."

Her eyes gazed at him in horror. "You *shot* me?" she mouthed.

He rocked his head, rocked his body, rocked her. "No. You're fine. Shh."

"I'm covered in—is that my blood? Is that my skull?"

He held her as she continued to shake. They were still on the couch when the lights of the police cars flashed outside. The silk camisole she was wearing was blood slick and sheer, and he was still naked. The police officers walked in through the open door. Alexander left Tatiana on the couch and went to put on jeans and a T-shirt, bringing her a terry cloth robe. She remembered about the blood on her. She struggled to her feet to go get cleaned up, but the police said no, Alexander said no.

She knew two of the police officers. One of them was Miller. More police came. A reporter from the *Phoenix Sun* came. He was shooed away, but not before he took pictures.

The police began to ask her questions and took Alexander from her, to ask him questions in the bedroom. When he stood up to walk away, she started to cry.

He sat back down. She clutched him. "Don't—don't go—please."

"Just in the bedroom, Tatiasha, just in our bedroom."

Sitting, covered in blood, she talked to the police, her head down, while in the bedroom, away from her, Alexander, his head up, standing, talked to the police.

Why were you up, they asked her. Why did you call the hospital? Why were you in the kitchen? Why didn't you run to the bedroom? Did you hear him come up the steps? Why did he come? Is it true he and your husband had a fight? We got a report of an assault, of two assaults. That man wanted to press charges against your husband. What happened? The man was badly hurt. The other man is badly hurt. Sergeant Miller intervened. The other man is Steve Balkman, he said. All the policemen nodded. Not again, someone said. Were they drunk, was your husband drunk? What was the fight over? Were there two separate fights or was it the same fight? Alexander shattered a man's face, broke another man's teeth, why? Was it true that there already was bad blood? His father, Bill Balkman, a long-time member of this community, said he didn't know what had happened. It was a complete surprise. He said it was just a fight between boys. Boys will be boys, he said. He told them all to take it easy. His son was going to be fine. It would all be just fine. Yet a man was lying in her house dead.

Where did your husband shoot from? He didn't know Dudley had a pistol, how did he know to take a gun to the bedroom door? Why did he use deadly force? Was there a way to get the man to release you without lethal violence? Was it breaking and entering? Attempted assault, attempted rape, attempted murder? Was it excessive force on the part of your husband to hit another man at a party simply for making a rude comment about you? And was Dudley overreacting to Alexander's overreacting? And what did Steve Balkman do *this* time?

Two more reporters came from the *Phoenix Sun*, standing in the living room with their spiral notebooks and their whooshing camera flashes, writing it all down, recording it for the morning papers. Did he touch you? Did he hit you? Did he cut you? Is any of this your blood?

Was Tatiana hurt? No one could say for sure, not even Tatiana. Only Alexander said, no, she's not hurt, she's in shock. They were worried about her. They called for a doctor. Sergeant Miller said he wanted her to go to the hospital. She refused. Alexander thought she should go. She refused. She was fine, she said. She was a nurse, she knew about these things.

Hours went by. Alexander remained in the bedroom with the police. She would catch glimpses of him, pacing, smoking, sitting on the bed. Then they closed the door, and she cried again. Dudley's body remained limp on the floor behind the bloodied couch where she sat.

Finally Alexander came out of the bedroom. She clutched at him desperately, she buried her face in him. He kept repeating, *shh, shh*. His arms were around her. Suddenly his presence terrified her. She began to cry again, push him away. The police, the medical emergency workers, the reporters, stood silently watching while Alexander, pressing her bloodied head to him, kept soothing her. *Tania*, he kept whispering, *shh, shh. Come on.* She might need a shot, he finally said, getting up to get her nurse's bag. She is clammy. I'm fine, she said, but couldn't stop shaking. She looked at Alexander standing smoking. He was calm. He wasn't agitated, his hands were steady, his movements normal. He was in control of himself. She remembered him near Berlin on the hillside, strapped with machine guns, grenades, semi-automatic pistols, automatic weapons, alone in a trench, systematically mowing down the battalion of soldiers who were crawling, running, charging up the hill to kill him, to kill her.

A man came up the hill to hurt my wife, Alexander said to the police without emotion, a cigarette in his mouth. Look at the door. The front door lock is busted, one of the hinges broken. The police were going to check out the Montana prison escape story. They were going to talk to Bill Balkman about hiring a man suspected of escaping prison, suspected of murder. It was a federal offense to hire a man suspected of a felony.

How did Dudley know where Alexander lived? Who would have given Dudley Alexander's address? And if it was Steve Balkman, wouldn't he have had to give him the address *before* the party, since after the party, he wasn't talking? Why would Steve do that— give Dudley Alexander's address? That Steve Balkman, Miller said, shaking his head. Loved trouble, caused trouble, always been trouble. Well, that's it, he said. This time we're not keeping it out of the papers, no matter what his father does.

It was six in the morning. The light was barely steel blue over the mountains. Someone brought coffee, rolls. Alexander gave Tatiana a cup, tried to get her to eat.

A drunk, belligerent man was dead in the middle of the night after breaking and entering a mobile home in the McDowell Hills a mile up a dirt road from Pima Boulevard in the middle of nowhere. Those were the undisputed facts. Neither Tatiana nor Alexander shared with the police the three years of disputed facts. Or the lifetime of disputed facts.

Sun came up, more police came, took more pictures. At eight in the morning Alexander called Francesca and asked her to keep Anthony the rest of the day. Tatiana continued to sit on the couch. She leaned back at one point, fell back and thought she passed out. When she opened her eyes, she was in the crook of Alexander's arm, and Dudley's body was still behind her. The chalkline was on their black and white linoleum floor. In the light of merciless day, the blood was now drying and browning, chips of bone were over the living room carpet, in the hall in front of Anthony's bedroom, on the counters, on the door, on the walls. Tatiana looked back only once. Dudley was still all over Tatiana. Nothing anybody could do about that until the police left.

The phone did not stop ringing.

The police asked Alexander if he knew Dudley's next of kin. Who did they notify of his death? Alexander and Tatiana exchanged a disbelieving glance. Were they really being asked about Dudley's next of kin?

A doctor finally arrived to examine her. She was fine, she said, shaking; she didn't need a doctor. Alexander got her a blanket, covered her with it. Carefully the doctor removed the blanket and took off her robe. He asked if she'd been assaulted, if she'd been beaten, hurt, penetrated. She watched Alexander watching her from across the room in her stained see-through camisole. He walked over and pulled the terry robe back over her. The doctor pulled it off again, looked at her arms, her legs, her red throat where Dudley had grabbed her. Pulling her hair back, he noticed the suck marks on the back of her neck. He asked about them. She didn't reply. Normally she would have blushed, but not this morning. "Are you hurt?" he asked.

"No."

"What are those?"

She didn't reply, just raised her eyes at him. The doctor was the one who became deeply flustered. "You're covered with blood, with some bruises. It's hard to tell where you're actually hurt from this particular incident. I apologize."

"I'm a nurse at Phoenix Memorial Hospital," she said. "I know if I'm hurt."

The doctor was David Bradley. She'd never met him. He was one of the attending physicians in ER, but he worked nights and she worked days. After seeing the marks on the back of her neck, he was unable to meet her eyes. She closed hers anyway.

Ten, eleven in the morning. Finally the coroner came and pronounced the body—dead! What would we do without coroners? Alexander quietly said to Tatiana.

The medical examiner's assistants examined the body to determine cause of death. Gunshot wound to the head, Alexander said evenly.

Gunshot wound to the head, they wrote.

Who was Alexander, the police asked, to shoot a man in the head when his wife was only inches away? Who are you? They said something about reckless endangerment. Couldn't you have waited until he wasn't so close to your wife before you shot him?

He didn't think he could have waited, no. For the thirtieth time he told them that once he came fully out of that doorway, he would have had to drop his weapon, and there would have been no other time, and his wife would have been assaulted in front of him, and then they both would have been killed. Impatiently he pointed to Dudley's loaded pistol, reminded them that they were policemen. They reminded him *he* wasn't a policeman. He said that surely they knew it was all about snap judgment in a pitched battle. You lost your life, or he his. That was the only choice. There was no later.

They said it wasn't war. But Alexander disagreed. He said it was. A man came up the hill to his house wanting to kill him and hurt his wife. The man brought war to his house. Now he lay dead. These were the facts and they were not in dispute. Only the degree of force, and Alexander's snap judgment, and Steve Balkman's broken face were in dispute.

The police examined the Colt, the rounds. Did he always keep a loaded gun in his house? Yes, all his weapons were always loaded, said Alexander. They lived by themselves up in the mountains. He had to be prepared for anything. They examined the weapons he kept in the bedroom: two models of the M-1 carbine, and an M4 submachine gun in a locked cabinet with the ammunition. He kept the German Walther, the Colt Commando, the M1911, and a .22 caliber Ruger with their extra magazines and all his knives in his nightstand, which he locked during the day and unlocked at night. They asked why he chose the M1911 out of all his handguns. The Ruger was supposed to be more accurate. Alexander said he chose the weapon that would inflict the maximum damage. He chose the M1911, the handcannon of pistols, he said because he knew he would get only one chance to kill Dudley.

Who *was* he? the police asked. Where did he learn to shoot? Did he have marksman qualifications?

Alexander looked at Tatiana. She sat numbly. Yes, he said. He had marksman qualifications. He was a captain in the U.S. Officer Reserve Corps. Funny how one little sentence could change things. They looked at Alexander differently then. Treated him differently. A captain in the U.S. Army. Did he fight in the Second World War? Yes, he said. He fought in the Second World War.

And no one asked him anything after that.

At noon, the hospital arrived with a body bag.

The police told them not to touch anything. This was a crime scene. On Monday, a cleaning crew would come to break it down and clear the room of the detritus of death. Until Monday the captain and his wife and child had to stay elsewhere.

Sergeant Miller said there would be a public inquest into a wrongful death, but privately Miller told Tatiana and Alexander he didn't know how the Balkman kid made it as long as he had without getting killed. Rumor was, Miller said, that his army injury while stationed in England had not been just friendly fire.

Everyone left—and finally they were alone.

Alexander closed the door after Miller and came to sit next to her on the couch. She raised her eyes to him. They stared at each other. Perhaps he stared. She glared.

"You call this normal, Alexander?" said Tatiana.

Without saying a word he got up and disappeared into the bedroom. She heard the shower go on in the ensuite bath. "Let's go," he said when he came out. But she couldn't walk, couldn't move. Lifting her into his arms, he carried her inside. "I can't stand up," she said. "Let me have a bath."

"No," he said. "I can't have you sitting in his bloody water. Just stand for five minutes, and when you're clean, I'll run you a bath."

Alexander took off her terry robe, her bloodied camisole, threw them both in the trash. He held her hand as she stepped into the tub. He took off his clothes, got under the shower with her. The water was so hot, and yet she shivered uncontrollably while he carefully washed the brown dried blood from her face, her neck, her hair. He shampooed her hair twice, three times. Bit by bit, Alexander pulled Dudley out of Tatiana's hair. When she saw the bony chunks he was pulling out, she started to sink into the tub and, slippery and scared, couldn't stand, no matter how much he implored her. Crouching beside her, he continued to clean her hair. "It's useless," she said, reaching into the cabinet near the sink for the scissors. "I can't touch it anymore. I can't have you touch it anymore."

"No," he said, stopping her, taking the scissors away. "You've cut off your hair once before, but now I'm here. I'll get it clean. If you cut it, you'll be upsetting only me."

She stared hard at him. He said, "Ah. Is that the point?" And handed her back the scissors.

But she didn't cut it. She leaned over the tub and threw up in the toilet.

He waited, his head down. He cleaned himself with the soapy

washcloth, and afterwards silently washed her face and scrubbed her entire body, holding her up with one wet arm.

"How many times in my life will you be cleaning blood off me?" Tatiana asked, too weak to stand.

"By my count, it's only twice," Alexander replied. "And both times, the blood is not yours. So we can be thankful for the mercies we're given."

"My leg isn't broken this time, or my ribs." But this violence in her little house. The Germans with their tanks across the River Luga, from their Luftwaffe plane formations raining down warning leaflets before the machine gun rounds, punctually from nine to eleven. *Surrender or die*, the leaflets said.

Alexander didn't speak to her through the subsequent bath, which he ran for her, didn't speak as he dried her and laid her on the bed, covering her, bringing her coffee, holding her head while she drank. He asked if there was anything else she needed, because he had to go outside to clear his head. She pleaded with him not to go. She closed her eyes. When she opened them again, he was sitting and watching her from the armchair, all his weapons, including the automatic rifles, between his legs.

"Why did you come out? What did you hear?" Tatiana asked.

"The crashing door. First I reach for my weapon, then I open my eyes."

"The Colt has come in quite useful." She stared at him. "The Fritzes, the Soviets, Karolich, and now even in America, we're recreating our old life. We just can't seem to get away from it."

"We're not recreating our old life. Every once in a while, we simply can't hide who we are. But he is the dregs found everywhere, even in America. You know what's come in useful? My U.S. Army commission. Richter had said I'd never know when it would come in handy. He's been proven quite right." Alexander paused. "Why did you get up? Why were you out there?"

"I couldn't sleep."

"Why?"

"I felt something. I was frightened."

"Why didn't you wake me?"

"Why would I?"

"Because you felt something. Because you were frightened."

"You didn't give a damn about my feelings and fears for three years," she said. "Now suddenly I've got to wake you in the middle of the night for them?"

He shot up off the armchair.

"Please, please don't go," she said. "I didn't mean it."

He left anyway.

Tatiana heard the back door opening, closing. She wanted to get up, go to him. But she was crashing. She slept.

The phone kept ringing, or was that just a dream? She kept hearing his voice. Was that just a dream, too? For some reason she started being afraid she was alone again, without him, she began to whimper in her sleep, to cry for him. "Alexander, please help me, please . . . Alexander . . ." She couldn't shake herself awake. It was his hands that woke her, holding her firmly, lifting her to sit.

They looked at each other. "We have to leave here," he said.

"We have to get Anthony." She started to cry. "My God, what if he'd been here with us?"

"Well, he wasn't. And Francesca said she'd keep him till Sunday."

"Let's stay here. I don't want to leave my bed."

"I can't be in this house with his blood and brains everywhere."

Her tears spilling, she stretched out her arms to him. He got into bed with her. She curled up inside his body.

"How do you do it?" she whispered. "Such frenzy, and you stay calm."

"Well, somebody has to stay calm, Tania." He patted her behind.

"But it's almost like you get calmer. Were you like this always?"

"I guess."

"Were you like this at war? In Finland? Over the Neva in your pontoon boat? Crossing Polish rivers? In all your battles? From the beginning?" She peered into his cool bronze eyes.

"I guess," he said.

"I want to be like you." She stroked his face. "It's a survival thing. That's how you did it, stayed alive. You're never rattled."

"Obviously," said Alexander, "I'm sometimes rattled."

They got dressed and left their house. Dudley's insides remained on their walls.

She went into shaking distress when they passed the old beat-up truck parked a mile down by the side of the road.

"Which hotel?" he asked her, grim but not in shaking distress.

"Don't care. As long as it's not the Ho," she said, her head back.

They went to the Arizona Biltmore Resort, designed by another of Phoenix's adopted sons, the architect Frank Lloyd Wright. They took a penthouse suite and were in the steaming bath together when the room service came. They ordered it, Alexander went to get it, but they didn't eat it. Barely dry, they crawled out into a starched hotel bed and slept dead till Sunday morning.

When they got Anthony, they told him there had been a burglar at the house, a small problem, they couldn't go back for a while. They stayed a luxurious two days at the Biltmore, had Sunday brunch, swam in the pool. On Monday morning the clean-up squad came from the coroner's office, and by Tuesday morning when they returned, it was as if Dudley had never existed.

They replaced the rug, the linoleum. Alexander built two new kitchen cabinets. They repainted the house, they bought a new couch.

But Alexander became wretched again. The house had become soiled for him. Arizona had become soiled for him. He told her if everything went all right at the inquest, they would sell the land and leave. He made his choice, chose Bill Balkman, and look what happened. "And you know, Tania, it all began with that picture of the naked girl."

Tatiana was silent.

"I couldn't place my finger on what was wrong with it, but now I know. It was a test for everyone who came in, every painter, every roofer, every framer Balkman hired. They all had to walk past that topless gate. They said something about it, they smiled knowingly, they exchanged a glance that told Bill they were on the same page. It's not a coincidence that every crew he hired behaved exactly the same way. He hired them based on their reaction to that picture. That's how he managed to weed them out. Now I know."

"What did my husband do to make Bill Balkman think he was one of them?" Tatiana asked quietly.

Alexander sighed. "I did nothing. I said nothing. And that's how he knew I would be okay with it. And he was right. I was willing to overlook it."

Tatiana disagreed. She said that perhaps Balkman wanted some of what Alexander was to rub off on his son. Perhaps a better example than himself was what Balkman wanted for his son Stevie.

Alexander said nothing.

Tatiana couldn't fall asleep in her own house without a tranquilizer, couldn't fall asleep without the P-38 by her side of the bed.

Even with the tranquilizer and the Walther, she woke up every night, perspiring, screaming, seeing before her sleeping eyes an image she could not shake down, not even during daylight—her husband, her Alexander standing like a black knight, looking straight at her with his deadly unwavering gaze, pointing a .45 caliber weapon at her face—and firing. The deafening sound of that shot reverberated through all the chambers of Tatiana's heart.

She needed nearly the whole bottle of champagne before she would let him touch her again. After a pained and underwhelming coupling, she lay in his arms, the alcohol making her woozy and light-headed.

"Tatiasha," he whispered, "you know, don't you, that if it weren't for women like you who love their men, the soldiers who come back from war would all be a little like Dudley. Cast out, afflicted, completely alone, unable to relate to other human beings, hating what they know, yet wanting what they hate."

"You mean," Tatiana said, looking into his face, "what you were like when you came back?

"Yes," Alexander said, closing his eyes. "Like that."

She cried in his arms. "You're still like that, walking around with the war this close."

"Yes, I'm pretending I'm civilized. What did you tell me in Berlin under the linden tree? *Live as if you have faith, and faith shall be given to you.* So that's what I keep trying to do."

"How could you have shot him when I was just inches away? And shot him with your left hand, too. God! Your marksman rating is for your right hand, soldier. You don't know how to shoot with your left."

"Um—"

"What if you missed?"

"I didn't miss."

"I'm asking you—what if you did?"

"There was a lot at stake. I tried not to miss. But Tania, you threw in your lot with mine. You knew what you were getting into. Who better than you knows what I am?" Suddenly he let go of her and moved away.

"What?" Tatiana said, reaching for him. "What?"

He shook her arm off him. "Stop talking to me. I can hear you loud and clear through all the pores of your skin. You're so hostile. I know what you're thinking."

"No, you don't. What?"

"That because I had forgotten what you are, look what I've let into our house," Alexander said coldly. "Isn't that what you said to me?"

In their bed, under the white quilt, Tatiana pulled him back to her, held him close, pressed him to her heart, to her breasts. "That's not what I'm thinking, darling," she said. "When did I ever expect you to be perfect? You pick yourself up and you try to do better. You fix what you can, you move on, you hope you can learn. The struggle doesn't end just because you know the way. That's when it's only beginning."

"So what are you thinking then, if not that? The things Dudley said?" He shuddered and his fists clenched. "The things he threatened?"

She shook her head. "Shh. No. He was saying the things he knew were the most vicious for you to hear because he was declaring war. He was taking what is most sacred to you and degrading it to debase you, and us. I know something about this. And you do, too—Steve's been doing that for three years." She paused. "But I'm not thinking of that. I'm thinking of me, not you this time," Tatiana said. "And of what Blanca Davidovna once said to me. I wish she never said it. I wish I never knew. I saved her from the burning house and this is the thanks I get. She said to me, God has a plan for each of us. And both the crown and the cross are in your tea cup, Tatiana."

"Yes," said Alexander. "And my father said to me, here's my plan for you, son. I'm taking you to the Soviet Union because I want it to make you into the man you are meant to be. And so what you and I have been doing, when there's been a little too much cross for us, is raging against our fate. And believe me, we're not done. Because, despite Dudley's best efforts, our life is not over yet."

Second Interlude

The Queen of
Spades

Beware the Queen of Spades for she bears ill will.
Aleksandr Pushkin

Cousin Marina

Mama, bless her, went back to Leningrad, and Marina came to Luga.

The exhausted Mama never lifted her eyes to Tatiana, but cousin Marina, who usually did, this time lifted them to Saika. Tatiana hid behind the trees with Oleg, watching them laugh and parry. Marina was a dark, short-haired round girl with round eyes, round arms, round hips, round black birthmarks all over.

"Can you believe what's happening in Abyssinia, Tania?"

Oh, Oleg. Can you believe what's happening under your nose? My own flesh and blood Marina is choosing not to play with me!

"What the Japanese are doing in Nanking is unconscionable. Isn't anyone going to stop them?"

How Saika is stealing Marina's attention is unconscionable. Isn't anyone going to stop her?

"Someone has to give Chamberlain an ultimatum. My country now or your country in a year."

Someone has to give Marina an ultimatum. Choose to play with me now, or be sorry later.

Pasha sat on Tatiana, pressed down her arms, tickled her with his chin and sang, "Tania is jealous, Tania is jealous."

And Tatiana throwing him off and pinning him to the ground, sang back, "Pasha is ridiculous, Pasha is ridiculous."

But it was Marina who now sat in the trees and Marina who swam in the river, and went to the fields to eat clover. Like Marina even knew how to eat clover until Tatiana taught her. The cheek of it.

Saika and Marina whispered and giggled; they had girlish secrets, they were full of youthful delights. They lay on the grass with their feet up on the trunks of trees while the boys played football with Tania. Before Marina came, Saika had been at Tatiana's window morning, noon, and night, asking to go somewhere, to do something. And worse, to divulge, to sit in the trees, to have midnight confessions. Tatiana revealed nothing, but that didn't stop Saika, who tried to tell Tatiana secrets of a kind that Tatiana had less than no interest in keeping. So on the one hand Tatiana was grateful that someone finally came along to divert Saika's attentions, but on the other hand—it was her Marinka! A mixed blessing, if ever there was one.

Since Saika was otherwise occupied, Oleg started talking to Tatiana again—a mixed blessing, if ever there was one.

"Oleg," Tatiana said, goading him, "please tell me Sir Neville hasn't appeased you, too, now that he has embraced Franco in Spain and said that the new Anglo-Italian agreement removes clouds of mistrust and paves the way for peace."

"You are either ironic or so naïve," said Oleg solemnly. "Almost as naïve as Chamberlain. The rest of the world is going to Fascism in a handbasket, while we stand and watch, but you just go ahead and laugh and tease and play your little games. Europe will be the battlefield and the battle in Europe will be for world order. The Fascist order or the Communist order. Hitler against Stalin."

"And the Fascists will lose," said Tatiana.

"Certainly doesn't look like Fascism is losing now, does it, Tanechka?" said Oleg acidly.

At home her grandfather still played chess with her. Which didn't make up for anything since Marina didn't know how to play chess. To Tatiana Deda said, "In two moves it's checkmate." And Tatiana replied, emitting an exuberant giggle, "Maybe in two moves it's checkmate, but right now it's check."

Three Ducks in a Row

Oh, so finally she was invited into their games. Tatiana, Marina and Saika went swimming in the river. The Luga water was afternoon-warm, soft on the body, easy on the limbs. They played splashing games where they could still touch bottom, but Saika jumped farther out, and Marina eagerly followed, splashing back, and Tatiana reluctantly followed, splashing no one. Saika jumped farther still. Tatiana called out, "Marina, don't swim so deep into the current, stay near the shore," and Marina called her a wet blanket. Three in a row the girls swam, Marina, then Saika, then Tatiana, letting the current pull them along—when suddenly Marina disappeared under the water.

She resurfaced, choking with water in her lungs. She tried to swim but couldn't. She was trapped in a vortex—an eddy, where the water tripled and quadrupled to form a swirl too powerful for Marina, who flailed in a panic, only letting more water into her mouth. The choking panicked her and the water was deep; Marina was being spinned and dragged helplessly downstream. Tatiana swam all out, trying to get around Saika to catch up with her cousin, but she knew that in a moment Marina would disappear under again. She also knew that she was not strong enough to help her by herself. "Saika, quick!" she yelled. "Help me!"

Panting and not responding, Saika swam a little faster, in Tatiana's way, keeping up with Marina.

"We can both do it!" Tatiana repeated, still trying to get around Saika. "Come on, just grab her arm and pull."

Saika acted as if she didn't hear. Marina went under, bobbed up, tried to scream, her arms splashing wildly.

Tatiana could barely hear Marina through her own panic, but she heard her name being sputtered. "Oh, Tania . . . please, oh, Tania, please . . . . . . help me."

Taking a deep breath, Tatiana shoved Saika out of the way and grabbed one of Marina's arms, and before the girl had a chance to pull her down like an anchor, Tatiana yanked her cousin with all her strength, once and again and then . . .

You'd think there would be a word of thanks after that, but no.

The next day when Tatiana came to the clearing, Anton was whispering to Natasha who was whispering to Marina, who was whispering to Oleg who was whispering to Saika, who glanced at Tatiana and stopped whispering.

"What's the matter with you?" she asked. No one replied.

Even Pasha was looking at her askance.

And no one would play football with her! Not even Pasha and Anton!

Tatiana threw up her hands and left. Later Pasha came and sat by her bed but Tatiana was buried in her book and ignored him. "So what happened in the river yesterday?" he finally asked.

"Marina was sucked into a vortex and I pulled her out."

Pasha sat. "It's not what we heard. We heard you pushed Saika out of the way."

Tatiana laughed.

Pasha was silent. "Did you push Saika out of the way?"

"I did."

"Why?"

"Because she wouldn't help Marina, Pasha!"

"She said she was just about to."

"It's hard for me to tell what she might've done. All I know is what she wasn't doing."

"She said she was about to."

"Convenient. However, no matter how Saika twists it, there's only one truth about what happened."

"Why would Saika need to twist it? Stop picking on her."

"All right, fine," said Tatiana. "All I know is that Saika did not raise a finger to help Marina." Tatiana put her face back into her book.

"Well, you better talk to Marina," said Pasha, "because she is seeing it very differently."

"The ingrate," Tatiana said without rancor.

The Palms and the Rowan Trees

Later, on the hammock where the children usually collected after dark, Tatiana wanting to rattle things up a bit, said, "So what are these stories you're telling everyone about what happened in the river, Saika?"

"Oh, how silly, let's not do this," Saika said carelessly with a wave of her arm. "It's water under the bridge."

"Really, Tania," Marina said. "It was hard to know what was going on in that river. I'm fine now, that's the important thing." She changed the subject. "Tonight, Saika invited me to her mother's, who is going to read my fortune. Did you want to come? You don't have to. But Pasha is coming. Even Dasha is coming."

"Saika," Tatiana said evenly, "your mother, then, will be available tonight?"

Pasha kicked her on one side, Dasha on the other.

"My mother was a *kockek* in the old country, Tania," Saika said with pride. "Do you know what that is? It's a soothsayer. It's an *ecstatic.* She tells the future. And an ecstatic is someone who is prone to very strong emotion. That's my mother. No shame in that."

Before Tatiana could say a word, Dasha hissed, "You're going to be prone to very strong emotion in a minute—intense pain. Keep quiet and come." She dragged her by the hand.

When they walked in, Shavtala was chanting dirges. She had a mane of tangled black hair, was wearing a long dark kaftan and smoking unfiltered cigarettes in a room where all the windows were closed. "The cigarettes are my incense," she said. Tatiana guessed it was supposed to be a joke.

Marina was first. Indifferently Shavtala took Marina's hands, turned the palms over for a second or two, observed them (cursorily, thought Tatiana), told Marina that she would find satisfying proletarian educational pursuits and that she would be an asset to her country. "But cold weather is your enemy. Dress warm. Wear galoshes."

"What?"

"I'm just telling you what I see. Also—you're practical but lack imagination. Try to see old things in a new way. Work on that. Next."

"How specific *are* these palms?" muttered Tatiana, pushing Dasha forward.

With great apathy, Shavtala turned Dasha's palms over. "Interesting," she said. "Very very interesting," in a voice that said, "Boring. Very very boring." To Dasha, after telling her about the satisfying proletarian work she would be useful for, Shavtala added, "Your heart line shows some ill health. Some unhealthy eyesight. Do you wear glasses?"

"What?"

"I might get a pair. Next."

"Wait, what about love?" asked Dasha.

"I don't know," replied Shavtala. "Your cousin Marina is a worrier. Has many worry lines. You on the other hand don't worry enough."

"I didn't say worry. I said love."

"Yes, well. I'd worry a little more. And watch out for the ice. I see ice in your future."

"Ice?"

"Ice, galoshes," Tatiana whispered. "This woman has obviously been to Leningrad from October to April."

"Shh!"

"But will there be love?" repeated Dasha to Shavtala. "It's the only thing I want to know."

Shavtala raised her lifeless black eyes to Dasha. "Yes," she said. "There will be love."

And to Pasha she said, "Rust is not your friend."

"Well," said Pasha philosophically, exchanging a dry glance with Tatiana, "whose friend is it really? And how come I don't get any useful work?"

"Because," said Shavtala, "you are not going to be a very good proletarian. Your heart is fickle. You next, Tania."

"Me not next, no," said Tatiana. "I don't do it. I'm not interested. Ask anybody. I didn't realize the time. Oh, my, it's getting late."

Standing up, Shavtala took a step forward and grabbed Tatiana's hands, forcibly turning her palms over. Emitting a short unhappy sound, Tatiana tried to pull her hands away, but Shavtala was much bigger and stronger and didn't let her, staring deep into Tatiana's palms. "Whew, what a Saturn fate line, Tania." She whistled. "I've never seen anything like it. Why, it cleaves both your palms in two!"

"Come on," Tatiana muttered, pulling on her hands, trying to turn her palms inward. "Please stop. It's not nice."

Shavtala did not hear her or did not care. She stared into one palm, then the other. No indifference on Shavtala's face now. She was flushed, she was panting. "Look. Heart, head, and life lines all connected, all flowing from the same source. Means grave trauma for you up ahead, girly."

Whimpering, Tatiana squeezed Shavtala's hands hard between her own. "Please stop!" she exclaimed, holding on to Shavtala and scowling at her. "Can't you see I don't like it?"

Suddenly Shavtala yanked away with a sharp cry. She dropped Tatiana's hands, pushed them far from herself and stood looking at Tatiana with panicked eyes. Tatiana was still pale but now she was calm.

"What did you see, Mama?" said Saika.

Shavtala fell back in her armchair. "Nothing. But . . . Tania . . ." She stared at her intensely. "Did you just . . . see inside me?"

"No!" Tatiana backed away into her brother, nearly knocking him over.

Shavtala nodded. "You did. I know you did."

"No." Tatiana hid behind Pasha, who was dodging out of her way, pushing her forward, tickling her.

Tatiana did not look at Shavtala again. "Come on, we have to go."

"What did you see, Tania?" Shavtala asked again.

Tatiana did not return the gaze, nor reply, nor lift her head.

Saika crouched by her mother's side. "Mama, what is it?"

"Daughter," Shavtala said dully, "don't come near her. Stay away from her."

"Pasha, are you a pod of salt? Let's go!" Tatiana pulled at her gawking brother.

When they were outside on the village road, Tania said, "Now do you see why these things are stupid? What a fraud. *And* unhelpful. I mean, Pasha, what are you supposed to do with the warning about rust?"

"Or me with the glasses!" said Dasha. "I can see perfectly well."

"Like I said. Be like me and not want to know."

"Yes, but Tania, Madame Kantorova said there will be love!" Dasha glowed.

"Yes, and she told Marina to wear galoshes."

When the Metanov children and Marina were on the porch of their own house, Pasha asked, "Tania, Saika's mother was wrong about what she said about you, wasn't she? You didn't actually see—"

"Did she seem a reliable source of information to you, Pasha?" muttered Tatiana, not looking at her brother. "Of course she was wrong."

Pasha and Dasha studied her curiously.

"Oh, the both of you!" She went to bed.

Applied Physics on the Hill

The next afternoon Saika proposed a bike race. Tatiana didn't want to but didn't want to be a spoil sport either. She wanted to race down with Pasha, but Saika said, you always race him. Race me instead.

The race worked like this: in pairs, the entire group navigated the steep narrow dirt hill leading from the town of Luga to the huts by the river where they lived. By itself it was child's play; what made it worthy of Newton himself was the part played by

the Soviet distribution trucks, which passed almost empty downhill into the chambers of the cucumber beds and the liters of freshly
drawn milk, to return uphill full of labors of the Luga villagers.
The children waited for just the right moment when the truck was
nearly upon them at the top of the slope, and then frantically pedaled downhill, with the truck a few meters behind them, blaring
the horn and trying in vain to slow down. The mass and velocity
of the 10-ton truck careening 30 kilometers per hour down a 40°
hill was pitted against the mass and velocity of the 10-kilo rusted
bikes at 20 kilometers per hour.

The trick was to know two things: how close to let the truck
come to make it interesting and when to pitch your bike to the
grass before another law of physics came into play: the well-tested
one that said that two objects could not occupy the same space at
the same time. When they beat the truck to the bottom and didn't
get killed, now *that* was a race.

There was obviously a degree of experimental uncertainty, there
were some independent variables they could not foresee, and a
small chance for random error. To sum up: the race was educational and enlightening, with high stakes.

The group drew straws; Pasha and Marina were first. They had
waited much too long for a truck to appear and when one finally
did, they were so impatient and eager that they started down too
soon. "Cowards!" Tatiana yelled into their backs. Tatiana and Saika
remained stopped.

"Tania, now?"

But Tatiana never went too soon. She knew the speed of her
bike. She knew what it could do. They waited, poised to take off,
perched on their seats, glancing back at the approaching truck.
Saika asked again, "Now?" and Tatiana said, "In just a—" and Saika
said, "Now!" and Tatiana said calmly, "All right, now."

The girls pushed off and pedaled downhill. The truck's horn was
honking madly behind them, their bikes rattled. Pasha and Marina,
already at the bottom, were jumping and screaming, and Tatiana
suddenly felt the truck accelerating instead of decelerating. This
made her glance over her shoulder at Saika and say, "Quicker, come
on!" At the very instant of Tatiana's impromptu glance, Saika seemed
to have lost control of her bike—because she swerved sharply into
Tatiana's front wheel. The next instant Tatiana was on the ground,
her foot caught in the rim spokes. She was dragged downhill by
the force of the fall. The truck driver slammed his brake, but that

was like two owls trying to stop a byplane from plummeting down. The truck continued to skid toward her. Tatiana dimly heard Pasha now agonizingly screaming, and somehow she managed to stand up, leg still caught in the spokes of the wheel and hurl herself onto the grass. She freed herself from the bike as she leapt. The truck swerved—its back door coming unhinged and flying open—the bike got caught in its tires and was dragged under the chassis until the truck came to a slow, lumbering stop at the bottom.

The truck driver jumped out of the cabin and started running uphill to Tatiana screaming, "I'm going to kill you! I'm going to kill you!"

Tatiana was on the ground, covered with dust, heart pounding, the gash on her knee bleeding. Pasha was already at her side, Marina was behind the running truck driver, who got to Tatiana, crouched down and with an angry and concerned face said, "You're crazy! You could've been killed, you know that?"

"I'm sorry I scared you," Tatiana said, holding her bleeding knee. "Is your truck all right?"

Pasha took off his shirt and wrapped it around Tatiana's leg. Saika stood silently near her bike, and when Pasha said, glaring at her, "What the hell happened?" Saika sheepishly replied, "I don't know. I just lost control of my bike. Sorry, Tania."

Tatiana struggled up with Pasha's help. "It's okay. Just an accident."

"Yeah, Tania," said Marina with a nervous giggle. "Just a crazy game. Lucky for us no one got really hurt."

Tatiana didn't say anything else and Pasha said nothing else, but when they had hobbled back home, he asked, "Were my eyes deceiving me, or did she ram your bike?"

"I'm sure your eyes were deceiving you," replied Tatiana.

The Sack of Sugar

"Children!" exclaimed Babushka, dragging a heavy burlap bag onto the porch. "Look what I found lying in the grass by the side of the road. Sugar!" No one was more excited than Babushka. "It's incredible! My children will have sweet pie—oh, what happened to you, Tania?"

While Dasha was bandaging Tatiana's leg, Pasha told Babushka what happened. Marina added, "It was an accident, though."

"As opposed to what?" snapped Pasha. Tatiana kicked him with her good leg.

Babushka was unconcerned. "Oh, so that was *your* mangled bike I saw where I found the sugar. I should've known, you urchin. Serves you right. Won't do that again, will you? Still, look what we have! Nice consolation prize, no?"

"No." Deda came in from the garden. "Woman, what are you thinking? The children can't have it. It's not ours."

"So? It's nobody's. We don't know whose it is."

"That's true." He nodded. "We don't know whose it is. But there is one thing we know for absolute certain . . ." Here he raised his voice. "It's not *ours*!"

Babushka had quite a lot to say to that in response.

"What are you railing at me for, Anna?" Deda was inflexible. "Read the bag. Clearly it says: Property of the U.S.S.R. Collective Administration."

"Like I said. Nobody's," Babushka repeated stubbornly.

"Deda," Tatiana cajoled, her leg hurting, "because we didn't steal it, maybe we could have just a cupful out of that large sack, and the rest we'll give to the orphanage in Luga and to the Staretskys down the road? They haven't had sugar since Tsarist times."

Quietly Deda sat with the bag of sugar on the floor in front of him. Dasha said, "Deda, let's just keep the stupid bag," and Pasha whole-heartedly agreed, but Deda shook his head. "Tanechka, you know we can't."

"What—you won't give even your own grandchildren a cupful?" Anna shouted. "I'm not listening to you. I'm giving it to them."

"You *are* listening to me! We have to return the bag to the local *Soviet* in Luga, and when we do, they will weigh it, and what do you think they'll say when they see that we've taken a kilo for ourselves?"

"That's why we can't return it to them," exclaimed Babushka. "We keep it, we cook with it, we eat it, we throw the burlap out. The truck driver will never know it's gone."

"You don't think they count their bags of sugar, Anna?"

"Oh, cut it out. You think you know everything. What are you worried about? Trust me, no one will know. Now, Tania, are you going to sit around all night or can you hobble over Blanca's to get us our evening milk? Dinner's in an hour."

On the way to Blanca's, Marina ran to Saika's house to ask her if she wanted to come, too. Murmuring more apologies about Tatiana's leg, Saika came.

Melek Taus

Gray, tiny, extremely wrinkled Blanca Davidovna looked warily at Saika when the children were at her door. "Come in," she said unhappily. "Who's coming for the tea leaves?"

"Not me," said Tatiana.

"Tea leaves for me, Blanca Davidovna," said Marina. "The other day Saika's mother read my fortune. She told me I would go far. I'd like to know what my tea leaves say this year."

The children settled around the small parlor in the hut, and Pasha told Blanca Davidovna what happened to Tatiana's leg. "But I'm fine," Tatiana quickly added, seeing Blanca's critical scrutiny of Saika.

Marina must have seen it too, because she said, "Come on, it's all water under the bridge now. Tania, why don't you have Blanca Davidovna read your tea leaves this year? She hasn't read yours in ages."

"Our Tania here doesn't like the ancient arts," said Saika. "Tea leaves, palms, rowan trees. Why not, Tania? Palmistry *is* an art. The ancient Greeks, the Chinese, the Indians learned much about fate by the reading of palms. And my mother, by the way, is a very good *kochek*. Very accurate."

"It's not helpful," said Tatiana. "Blanca Davidovna knows that better than anyone." She nodded to the old woman. "Other things are helpful. Not that."

Saika wanted to know what was helpful.

Tatiana demurred from answering. Blanca Davidovna took her by the hand, gently pulling on her. "Darling . . . come here."

"No tea, no palms, Blanca Davidovna," Tatiana said firmly. "You promised."

"I know, dear child. I don't go back on my promise. You are right, of course. I should know better than anyone—" she crossed herself. "That fatal curiosity is so pointless—and dangerous. The future is not to be fooled with, not to be trifled with. You can have warm milk from my cow. I don't read milk. I just want you to sit on my lap, Tanechka."

"I'm too heavy for you."

"You're a wisp, baby girl. Sit. Does your leg hurt?"

"It's fine." Tatiana sat on Blanca's lap. "Don't touch my hands," she said. "I know you."

But Blanca did. She took them—and kissed them. "I know you don't want to know your future," she whispered.

Saika perched on the floor, her legs crossed, palms out, watching them intently. "Oh, so, you *do* believe in the ancient arts, Tania! And there I was, misunderstanding you. So what are you afraid of? Blanca Davidovna, what is Tania afraid of?"

"She simply doesn't want to know," replied the old woman. "She hates all this talk about fate."

"I don't hate it," Tatiana said, on Blanca's lap. "It's unnecessary. Just live your life. Because what else have you got, really?"

"But what is Tania afraid of?" said Saika. "Will you read my hands, my leaves, Blanca Davidovna? I'm not afraid of the future. I'm not afraid of anything."

"You're so brave, Saika!" Marina exclaimed.

Blanca was quiet. "You seem to me like the kind of girl," she said to Saika, "who's had her fortune read a few times."

"You're so right about that," Saika said with a laugh.

Barely paying attention, Tatiana was purring as the old woman caressed her back. The kids in the village always played such rough games, Pasha especially; gentleness was not in his repetoire. Dasha touched her gently when she brushed her hair, but otherwise, Tatiana had to have a nightmare for Dasha to touch her gently, to whisper love to her.

"Did you say your mother was a *kochek*, girl?" said Blanca to Saika, her voice like gravel. Her wrinkled brow got more wrinkled. "Aren't kocheks part of the Yezidi clergy?"

"Not necessarily," said Saika, herself frowning. "You know about the Yezidi?"

Tatiana explained to Blanca that Saika's family was Yezidi.

"*Are* they?" Blanca exclaimed, peering with great interest into Saika's face.

Saika jumped up. "Were. *Were*. Can we just have the tea, or are we going to talk all night with dry throats?"

"What are the Yezidi?" The ever-curious Pasha.

"Recall Bluebeard's nosy wife, Pasha," whispered Tatiana.

"Shut up, Tania."

Blanca Davidovna was pretending to be busy with serving tea and did not answer Pasha. But Pasha was not a let-it-go kind of boy. And since this afternoon's bike race, he had lost his good cheer. Pasha lost his good cheer! Tatiana went to sit next to her brother cross-legged on the floor. Pasha sat, sat, and then said, "Saika does the large painting of a blue peacock in your living room have anything to do with the Yezidi?"

"What?"

"The other night, while your mother was in ecstasy over the lack of my rusty proletarian future," Pasha said, "I couldn't help but notice the bright blue bird prominently displayed on your mantel. I've been meaning to ask you about it. Is that a Yezidi thing?"

"Just a bird, Pasha. Why such interest?"

"Just making conversation, Saika."

"All right, I'll tell you, if you tell me something about Tania."

"Why is it always about me?" Tatiana exclaimed. "Pasha, tell her something about Marina instead."

"I know everything about Marina," said Saika. "Well? You want to play or not, Pasha?"

"Okay, you're on," said Pasha. "You first. Tell me about the peacock."

Tatiana poked him, as if to say, stop making trouble.

"Pasha, do you know what the word Yezidi means?" asked Saika as Marina listened raptly, sitting close. "It means angels in Arabic. The Yezidi is a Kurdish religion of angels." She smiled. "The peacock is the main angel. He is called the peacock angel."

Tatiana's breath was short in her chest. Blanca Davidovna opened her mouth to say, all right, enough now, but of course Tatiana's brother, with less sense than God gave a goose, was unstoppable. "Does this peacock have a name?" asked Pasha.

"Melek Taus," Saika replied.

"Blanca Davidovna," Pasha asked, "does that name translate into our language?"

Tania very slowly moved her hand to rest on Pasha's leg, and pinched him hard through his trousers. She thought he was trying to provoke Saika. He had that intense look about him. Hell-bent was the word.

Blanca didn't answer. She was swirling the children's empty tea cups, seeing how the leaves settled. She did this to three cups, and then put the cups down, her wary eyes on the young people. Her shrewd gaze finished and stayed on Tatiana.

"Lucifer," Blanca finally replied in her raspy voice.

"Lucifer?" Pasha mouthed.

Shaking her head, Tatiana closed her eyes. Well, there you have it. Enough provocation for a whole darn summer.

"How does a village woman know so much about the ancient religions?" asked Saika, staring hard at Blanca.

"You live long enough, you pick up a few things," replied Blanca. "And I'm a hundred and one."

Pasha finally found his voice. "LU-CI-FER?" he repeated loudly.

Calmly Saika stared at Pasha and Blanca and Tatiana. "Yes. So?"

Three blank faces stared back at her. Where. To. Start. Pasha tried. "Lucifer, the peacock, is the main symbol of your church, Saika?"

"Yes. What's your point? Lucifer is the angel of light," Saika said. "Everybody knows that. Even his name means light."

Pasha coughed as if he had the croup. Even Tatiana's pinching didn't deter him. "Ahem, excuse me, Saika," Pasha said. "I've read a few things about Lucifer."

"Pasha, don't lie, you don't know how to read," Tatiana said.

He elbowed her. "And while you may call him what you like," he went on to Saika, "the rest of the world distinctly thinks of Lucifer as something just a *touch* different than an angel of light."

"The world misunderstands him, as it misunderstands much," said Saika. "Enlightenment is possible."

"Enlighten *me*," said Pasha. "Wasn't Lucifer an archangel who believed he was wiser than God, and then fell from grace?"

"I know where you're going with this," said Saika. "You want me to admit that while our small religious sect of a few lousy thousand hangs pictures of angels on our walls, the rest of the world thinks we worship the devil."

"You know," said Pasha, "I never looked at it like that. Ouch! Tania, leave me alone! But now that you brought it to my attention, Saika, let me say this—if we're going to be correcting one another and all—worship not just the devil but Satan himself."

Oh, what got into her brother tonight!

"It is simply not true," said Saika. "There is no such thing as Satan. Our religion accepts evil as a natural part of creation—"

"It doesn't embrace it?" Pasha asked tauntingly.

"No." Saika was unflappable. "We give it the respect it deserves. We put it in its proper context. Take your little Garden of Eden story for example. All the serpent was saying to Adam and Eve in the Garden of Eden was know both fully—good and evil—and then decide. So actually," Saika continued pleasantly, "if what *you* believe is true, then the serpent was doing your religion a favor by giving it the knowledge to decide between right and wrong. In other words, the serpent gave you free will."

Blanca Davidovna shook her head.

"Oh, Saika!" Marina cried. "You're so smart. You know so much."

"Thank you, Marina. I take great pride in it."

Tatiana and Pasha exchanged a glance. "Marina," said Pasha slowly, "did you ever hear the expression, *the devil dances in an empty pocket*?"

"No."

"Pasha," Tatiana said, speaking about Marina as if the girl weren't in the room, "I think the expression is, *the devil dances in an empty heart*." She turned to Saika. "You do know quite a bit—but I don't agree with you about the serpent."

"Of course not," said Saika. "You love to argue, Tania. You have an opposite opinion on everything."

Unflappable herself, Tatiana went on. "Well, in my humble opinion, by choosing to follow the serpent, Adam and Eve were already choosing—just unwisely. God commanded, they *chose* not to listen to Him. The serpent sibilated, and they chose to listen to him. The free will came before, not after."

Saika laughed dismissively. "What's this obsession with free will? The ancient Greeks and Romans, believed in fate."

"The pagan Greeks and Romans, you mean?"

Saika widened her eyes and laughed. "Oh, I just got it! That's why you don't like this talk about fate! That's at the root of your troubles with it! You're not afraid of it, you just don't believe in it."

"This isn't about me," Tatiana said evenly.

"The *pagans* believed in fate! That's what you just said with such derision."

"There was no derision," said Pasha. "And Saika—leave Tania alone." He was clearly unforgiving over the biking incident. "Tania, I know you know about Lucifer. If Saika won't enlighten me, tell me what you've read in your little books about the peacock angel."

"I don't know much," said Tatiana. "But in one book Blanca Davidovna lent me, Lucifer spends eternity in the center of the earth in the deepest circle of hell while three traitors are submerged in his three open mouths, Judas in the middle, head first." Tatiana shrugged. "That's all I know."

"You've been poisoned by lies," declared Saika. "Lucifer has been blatantly misrepresented by your overzealous singing baptizing village women and your overwrought medieval writers. Our religion is called angel-worship, because that's what it is. Unlike you, we don't even recognize that demons exist. Circles of hell! Bah!"

The children stared at Saika. Even Pasha was speechless. A withered Blanca Davidovna, her head involuntarily nodding, studied Tatiana.

"Wait," Tatiana said, grasping to understand. "What do you mean, you don't recognize demons? What about the devil? What about Satan?"

"No, no—and no."

"You mean you think there are only angels?"

"That's right."

"*Everybody* is an angel?"

"Yes!"

Tatiana and Pasha glanced pleadingly at Blanca Davidovna for guidance. Blanca remained mute staring into the tea cups.

Tatiana quietly asked, "No right, no wrong then for the Yezidi, Saika? No light, no dark? No Newtonian laws?"

"Different principles, Tania. Why is it so hard to understand? Lucifer is an angel who is reconciled—and one—with everything in the universe. In Lucifer's universe, everything is good and everything is in balance. Our religion believes that since he was forgiven for his perceived transgressions, those who worship him are forgiven for theirs."

A question hung in the air that Tatiana didn't hear an answer to—though she suspected it was a rhetorical question. She opened her mouth. "Forgiven by who?" asked Tatiana.

"By who? Those who worship Lucifer are forgiven for their transgressions by Lucifer," Saika replied.

"Yes," Tatiana said quietly, "but who is Lucifer forgiven by?"

She heard her thudding heartbeat in the gathering silence.

Saika jumped to her feet. "Your question, as you well know, has no answer," she said. "Why don't you stand under the rowan tree to ward off the evil spirits you're so worried about."

Blanca Davidovna spoke at last. "Why in the world would we need the rowan tree," she asked, "when we have the cross?"

"Well, tell that to the Ukranian Catholics, tell that to the Romanovs," snapped Saika. "The cross didn't save them, did it?"

"Then it didn't save Peter. Or Paul. Or Luke. Or Matthew—"

"I don't want to talk about this nonsense anymore. I'm going home. Coming, Marina?"

Marina jumped to her feet.

"Want your tea leaves read, Marina?" said Blanca Davidovna. "Because they're ready."

"Maybe later, Blanca Davidovna."

Tatiana got up herself. "Pasha, don't just sit there. Babushka will kill us, we're so late. I still have to milk the cow. Come help."

Saika called after him, "Wait, Pasha! I told you about the peacock, but you haven't told me something about Tatiana!"

"I changed my mind," said Pasha, striding away. "I have a fickle heart. Your own ecstatic mother said so."

Back near their dacha, Pasha dragged Tatiana away from Marina and said, "Tania, I don't care what Marina does, but you're not allowed to play with Saika anymore."

"What?"

"I'm serious. You're not allowed to play with her. Not at her house, not in the hammock, not in the river, not on the bikes."

"Well, I don't have a bike now," said Tatiana.

"Talk to Dasha, talk to Deda, but I think they will agree that you should not play with anyone who doesn't believe there are demons."

"I've been telling you about her, Pasha. From the very beginning. You didn't want to listen."

"I'm listening now."

A Knock on the Door

Late that evening, well after dinner, there was a knock on the door. Murak Kantorov stood on their porch. The Metanovs didn't know he was back from Kolpino. They weren't sure what he wanted, but they invited him in and offered him some vodka. At first it seemed as if he wanted to be neighborly. He sat with them a while; the vodka flowed, the talk soon followed. Even Deda was politely fascinated by Murak's travels, and Murak was only too happy to regale. "Two years ago when we were picking cotton near Alma-Ata . . ."

Tatiana listened carefully.

"And a few years ago when we were in the oilfields in Tash-kent . . ."

"We stayed in Yerevan just a few months . . ."

"In Saki we lived the longest of any stretch, two years. Saika started to call it home and then we came here. No, thank you," Murak said to the black caviar offered by Babushka. "In Baku on the Caspian Sea we ate so much sturgeon caviar, we never want to see caviar again. Sturgeon are bottom dwellers, you know."

"Where haven't you lived!" exclaimed Babushka.

"We've lived everywhere," Murak said boastfully. "In the Kara-Kum desert like nomads in tents, and in the mountains of Turkmenistan. On collective farms, in collective fishing villages, in collective concerns all across the Soviet Union. Saika has lived in twenty different places in her fifteen years."

Deda was quiet. "Where is the place you call home?" he asked.

"The place I am at the moment," Murak replied, downing a large glass of pepper vodka without even a pickle to chase it down. "I'm home everywhere. Everywhere is my home."

Pasha and Tatiana exchanged a glance. "Saika told me only about a few places," she said. "Three maybe."

"Yes, Stefan, too," seconded Dasha.

"Oh, they don't like to brag." Murak had another long drink of vodka. "By the way, Saika told me that earlier today she saw Anna Lvovna dragging a heavy burlap bag." He smiled politely. "What was that?"

Everyone fell silent. It was Dasha who came forward. "It was a bag of sugar, comrade Kantorov. What's your interest in it?"

"My interest in it," said Murak, and his tone was mild, "is that my daughter said it had a hammer and sickle on the canvas."

"Haven't answered the question though," said Dasha. Tatiana was proud of her.

Deda stood up, his hand raised. "My granddaughter is forward for her age. She is learning to have more tact, but you know youth." He came closer to Kantorov. "What do you want, Murak Vlasovich?"

"The bag belongs to the State and must be returned to the State." Kantorov got up and headed toward the door. Turning around, he said, "I don't have to tell you—you're a smart man—that every seed of grain, every grain of sugar, every potato goes toward ful-filling our Five-Year Plan production quota. This is the last year of the second plan. It is therefore even more imperative that the quotas be met. Make sure it's returned tomorrow."

After he had gone, the Metanovs stared at each other in confounded apprehension. Babushka placed her arm on Deda. "You were right, Vasili."

"When am I ever *not* right? And had you not taken what didn't belong to you, we wouldn't be in this predicament! How many times have I told you? Don't touch what isn't yours!"

"Oh, look at him, raising his voice!" yelled Babushka.

They stormed off to their room.

Tatiana's head was shaking. Deda and Babushka were *arguing*? She went and knocked on Deda's door. The sharp voices behind the door had no choice but to stop. She came in, gently pulled Deda to sit, climbed into his lap and pressed herself against him. "Shh," she said.

"You see? Even your child is telling you to shh," said Babushka loudly. "Heed her at least."

"I told you not to touch a grain of that sugar! Did you heed me? I don't think so. Didn't you hear? It's for the Five-Year-Plan."

They laughed, and then stopped shouting.

Still on Deda's lap, Tatiana said, "Deda, what do you think Murak Kantorov does for a living, moving so often from collective to collective?"

Her grandfather thoughtfully stroked her hair, wrestling with himself, looking at Babushka, glancing down at her. Finally he spoke.

"Tanechka, Murak Kantorov is a weeder."

"What's a weeder, Deda?"

The First Five-Year Plan

During the First Five-Year Plan, the farms in the Ukraine fell short of yearly goals. The Politburo had set the goals based not on demand, or capital costs or labor costs—the fixed capital—or operating costs or any practical concerns. It set its goals in 1927, based only on one thing: what they thought the farms needed to produce for one hundred and fifty million people over the next five years. There were convex hull formulas, divide and conquer algorithms, statistical probabilities, logical assumptions. The plan was faultless, the triumph of tortuously long meetings of the Politburo's most brilliant economic minds. All it required was execution.

But a few things happened that the Party had not foreseen despite its wisdom and its plan. For one, the people turned out to be hungrier than anticipated. They needed more wheat and more rye, more potatoes, more milk. So in 1928 the demand had spiked up. And in 1928 there was a terrible drought in the Ukraine. Supply went down. *And* in 1928 there was a typhus epidemic in the Ukraine. Labor went down. *And* millions of Ukrainians, who had owned big productive profitable farms, had been taken into "protective custody," tried as "kulaks" and "enemies of the people" and shot, and their farms brought under government control. So means of production *and* supply went down, and the farms in the agrarian republic of Kazakhstan were unable to make up the shortage. The prices remained static—set in 1927.

And so it began.

To feed the hungry in the industrialized cities, the *Soviet* councils—men and women armed with rifles and under orders to shoot to kill—came and requisitioned the food in the farms, without compensation. In Central Asia, there had been little protest. But in the Ukraine—ninety percent of Soviet agriculture—the farmers protested. They were shot, exacerbating the paucity of labor.

And so it continued.

The new collectivized farms could not produce enough; the workers were in the fields from sunup to sundown, and their entire harvest went on trucks to the cities, while the farmers remained with their families in the Ukraine—one of the most fertile regions in the world—without income and without food. To everyone's surprise, the farmers, their wives gone, their children dying, their parents long dead, started working less. They were shot for idleness. The orphaned children were promptly sent off to the Siberian collectives, and those who survived the transit trains worked there.

Despite these minor setbacks, the Ukraine continued with the Five-Year Plan, into 1929, 1930, and 1931. While 1930 and 1931 were better harvest years, they were no better for the farmers, who had fallen so far behind the five-year grain requirement that all the produce from the farms continued to be forcibly removed by the Party apparatchiks.

The farmers did the only thing they could. They started stealing.

For this they were shot, further narrowing the human capital.

Those still alive during the famine of 1933—the last, and worst, year of the first Plan—had finally had their fill, and in an act of futile protest, slaughtered their cattle before they could be taken away and ate the remains on the village streets. They burned down their own collectives and their carriages and their huts; and then they scorched the fields they refused to harvest.

All across the Ukraine they were hanged on the streets, shot in public, burned with their cattle; all silage, seed stock, farm stock and grain was confiscated. All rail lines and roads were closed by the Red Army and the OGPU. Labor—the fixed capital—became unfixed at a rate of ten thousand executions a week, with hunger and disease swelling the numbers of the dead to several million in the Ukraine alone between 1932 and 1933.

Comrade Stalin vowed to do better in the next Five-Year Plan.

Doing Better in the Next Five-Year Plan

For the second Five-Year Plan from 1933-1938, the Politburo set the production goals a little lower and the prices a little higher. Impatiently they waited out the drought in 1933 and the government-sponsored famine in 1933 and 1934, but in 1934, Stalin had had quite enough. When he received a letter from the Nobel prize-winning author Mikhail Sholokhov accusing him, the Great Leader and Teacher, of destroying the Ukrainian countryside and starving its people, his brisk reply was, "No, Comrade Sholokhov. *They* are starving *me*."

Reconstruction and industrialization of the country was proceeding apace, but Stalin recognized that labor—the most expensive part of production—was going to be the hardest to come by in the next few years, for reasons, he felt, that were completely outside his control. Fortunately he had conceived a plan in the 1920s that he believed solved the fledgling state's early problems. He expanded his solution in the 1930s.

An organized system of government work camps!

An organized system of government farms!

Against all reason, the Ukrainian farmers allowed themselves to be starved and hanged and shot! rather than give up their grain, their cattle, and their farms. The wealth of the country and therefore the future of the Soviet Union rested in the hands of the Ukrainian farmers.

Suddenly a firm believer in free will, Stalin changed policy. He gave the farmers in the Soviet Union a choice: Work on the collective farm or work in the Gulag.

This reorganization of social structure of a vast country required massive help at the lowest levels. The OGPU hired and paid regular folk to help them. Young men, women, and children who had the stomach, the disposition and the inclination for this kind of work, stood with rifles in the fields from dawn till night, making sure the farmers continued to choose to toil on the volunteer collectives and not steal.

These people were called weeders.

The Future

The next morning, when Deda and Babushka went to the *Soviet* to return the bag of sugar, Tatiana and Pasha came with them. They sat on the bench outside the open window of a two-room wooden council house, where they could hear what was happening. Inside, councilman Viktor Rodinko, said, "Comrade Metanov, we've been expecting you. Where is the sugar?"

The councilman and his two assistants weighed the bag—three times. And then Rodinko stood in front of Deda and Babushka and asked them why it took so long to return it. "Why didn't you return it immediately, comrade?"

"It was late in the day. We were about to have dinner. The *Soviet* was closing."

"Look at it from our point of view. It's almost as if you weren't planning on returning the bag until Comrade Kantorov came to see you."

Deda and Babushka were quiet. Deda said, "I do not need Comrade Kantorov to tell me to return what isn't mine," in a voice so neutral Comrade Kantorov had no place in it. "Will there be anything else?"

"There will be," said Rodinko. "Have a seat."

And so it began.

The bag of sugar, Comrade Metanov, belongs to our soldiers, our factory workers, our proletarian farmers. As you very well know, we are fighting for our existence. We don't have enough to feed our soldiers, our factory workers, our proletarian farmers . . .

"That's why we returned it."

"When you take as much as a spoonful for yourself, you are stealing from the people who are building our country."

"I understand."

"We have many enemies who would like to see us fail. The fascists in Europe, the capitalists in America, they're all waiting for our collapse. We import the sugar from China, but there is not enough for a hundred and fifty million people, of which you and your family are just seven."

And so it continued.

What about the workers who build the tanks? The doctors who treat the wounded? The farmers who reap the grain? The Red Army soldier, who will lay down his life to protect you . . . "Get in line, Comrade Metanov."

"I've been in line since 1917, Comrade Rodinko. I'm well aware of my place," said Deda. "My intentions were always to return the bag."

The councilman nodded. "But one hundred and twenty five grams lighter, no?"

Deda and Babushka said nothing.

"Comrade Metanov, as a nation we need to trust our people. But we are also realistic. There are some people who will think of their families first. I'm not saying you are such a man, what I'm saying is that such men exist. Even during the noble French Revolution, despite fighting for liberty, fraternity and equality, men resorted to all kinds of criminal behavior to provide for their families."

The councilman fell quiet. Tatiana and Pasha, listening outside the window, waited. Rodinko wanted something from Deda. After many minutes of silence, Deda spoke. "That is criminal, you're right," he said with resignation. "Placing your family before the survival of the state."

Rodinko smiled. "Absolutely. I am *so* glad we understand each other. For taking the sugar, you and your wife are to spend two weeks without pay at a *kholhoz* in Pelkino, helping with the summer harvest. Let that be part of your rehabilitation and re-education. And from now on, there will be no more bags of sugar falling at the feet of your family, no matter how accidental, no matter how providential. Am I making myself clear?"

"Very clear."

"Have a good day, Comrade Metanov. You and your wife leave for Pelkino tomorrow morning at eight. Come here first for your papers."

Deda's Burning Questions

That night after dinner, Tania was gently swinging in the hammock with Deda, his arm around her. She knew Pasha was waiting for her, but she didn't want to go just yet. Her heart was unusually heavy.

"What's wrong, Tanechka?" Deda asked. "We got off easy. Just two weeks on a collective. Better than five years in Siberia. And I don't mind doing my part to feed the people in the cities. After all, we are those people. The day may come when we need food, too." He smiled at her.

But Tatiana wasn't worried about Deda or Babushka, two weeks and they would be back; no, there was something more ominous that troubled her. She asked, "Deda, do you think Saika knows about her parents?"

"Probably not. Children blessedly know little about their parents. Why do you ask?"

Murak coming to their house because Saika told him about the bag of sugar. Wasn't that reason enough? She didn't want to tell her grandfather about Marina's river "incident," or the biking "incident." Or Saika coming by with Stefan just when Dasha's Mark was visiting. Or glimpsing the black malevolence inside Shavtala.

She chewed her lip.

"I'm going to tell you something about me, Tania," Deda said. "Did you know I was asked to become a Party member? Yes, at the university. They offered to make me a full professor and to double my salary. They promised me that Pasha will be kept out of active combat when he reaches draft age. And some other benefits too." He smiled. "Now see what I mean? Even *you* didn't know that, did you?"

Tatiana was silent. Breathlessly she asked, "What kind of benefits?"

Deda laughed. "Vacation villas in Batumi on the Black Sea. Triple meat rations. Our very own five room apartment."

"When did they offer you this?"

"Last year. I would also get a good pension, and that's something I must think about since I'll be retiring soon."

Tatiana was still breathless. "Did you tell them no?"

Deda smiled. "Did you want me to tell them yes?"

That stumped her. "Do they ask you for things in return?"

"What do you think?"

She mulled. "Maybe they just ask you to wear a little hammer and sickle pin."

"Yes, first. Then your son is expected to become a Party member. And your grandchildren are required to become Comsomols. And then they ask you why the son refused, and why the insubordinate, impossible youngest granddaughter refused, and why the people down the stairs have been meeting with foreigners in secret and I, as a diligent Party member, never said a word about it."

"What people down the stairs?"

"Precisely. Everything comes at a price, Tatiana. Everything in your life. The question you have to ask yourself is, what price are you willing to pay?"

Tatiana felt a cold shiver. "I think it's right to keep away if your heart tells you to keep away," she said.

"Yes, you're a great believer in that. Well, my heart told me to keep away." Deda paused. "What is your heart telling you about the girl next door?"

"I think . . ." she drew out her words, "it's telling me to keep away."

Deda nodded. "Pasha certainly seems to think you should."

"But really, Deda, I'm not sure of anything anymore. Everything seems so muddled this summer." She heaved a sigh out of her shoulders.

Deda nodded again. "And what did I tell you to do to unmuddle? Whenever you're unsure of yourself, whenever you're in doubt, ask yourself three questions. What do you believe in? What do you hope for? But most important, ask yourself, what do you love?" His arm was around her. "And when you answer, Tania, you will know who you are. And more important—if you ask this question of the people around you, you will know who they are, too." He paused. "Here, I'll give you an example. I believe in my word. I don't give it lightly, but when I give it, I keep it. I hope for my grandchildren. I hope you will grow up to have love. And I love your grandmother. That's who I love most of all." He smiled. "I think she's listening to me just inside the porch."

Tatiana, barely breathing, listened to her grandfather, looking up at him. "I love my family," she said. "Since that's all I know, that's all I can answer."

She didn't want to lose this moment with her grandfather. He kissed her head and embracing her, whispered, "Tania, you're making your grandfather want to cry. It's the first time you've come and sat and wanted my advice. Please don't tell me you're growing up, my little baby."

Tatiana had hoped that things would return to normal, but right after her grandparents left for Pelkino, poor Dasha for some mysterious, grown-up, tear-stained reason had to quickly return to Leningrad. She didn't say how long she'd be gone, but because there was now no one to take care of Pasha and Tatiana, Dasha arranged for Pasha to be sent a week early to the boys camp in Tolmachevo, and for Tatiana to be sent fifty kilometers east to Novgorod to stay with Marina's parents on their dacha on Lake Ilmen.

Though Tatiana loved going with Marina to Lake Ilmen, her joy was short-lived indeed when Marina said, "Tania, my mother said I could bring Saika, too! Isn't that great?"

Everything was so fine in Luga once, but recently there had been nothing but unbounded chaos. What did Blanca Davidovna rasp to Marina, just before the girls left? "He will wile away, and he will chip away, and he will erode your goodwill and your strength, gram by gram, grain by grain, and the glass that was once round will become jagged with his ministrations. He will not rest until he has you in his clutches, because you are susceptible, because you can be swayed." Marina said she didn't know whose tea leaves Blanca was talking about, because while she was saying this to Marina, Blanca was gripping Tatiana's hands. But Tatiana knew. And she knew because of only one thing. Tatiana knew that like Deda, she could not be swayed.

Swimming on a Summer Afternoon

Lake Ilmen is an immense twenty-seven-mile-long lake, shaped like a dolphin and surrounded by flat shores and tall elms. The lake is shallow, thirty feet deep at most, its many low-lying areas silt and swamp. Because of this, the lake is warm to swim in. A hundred rivers and streams feed into Lake Ilmen, but only one flows out—the Volkhov River, which flows north to Lake Ladoga. On the shores of the Volkhov River and Lake Ilmen stands a nine-hundred-year-old city: Novgorod, or "New City," the oldest city in Russia. Novgorod was ideally placed along the trade route from the East to the West, and flourished and grew in its wattle and daub splendor until Moscow overtook it in importance in the fifteenth century and St. Petersburg, the new capital of Russia, further diminished its glory from 1703 onward.

But the ancient ruins in the town remain on full display, and the myriad white onion-domed churches are magnificent even without the gold crosses on the crests. The river runs through the center of town, connected to Rurik's wall and St. Sophia's church by a stone footbridge.

Tatiana loved to walk with Pasha and Marina through Novgorod's cobbled streets, and on top of Rurik's wall. This time, however, there were no excursions to the city from the dacha, just a short bus ride away. Pasha was not here, and Marina and Saika didn't want to go. All they wanted to do was lie indolently near the lake and talk in lurid whispers, and if Tatiana came too close, they would say, go away, Tania, this conversation is not for you.

So Tatiana went away. Aunt Rita and Uncle Boris's small dacha was nestled on a gentle slope leading to the lake, covered by a canopy of elms, blissfully isolated. Tatiana read, swam, and even went to Novgorod by herself once. Upon returning, she found the girls as she had left them, on their stomachs on the blanket, legs up at the knees, heads together, eyes toward the lake.

Tatiana noticed Aunt Rita and Uncle Boris were fighting more than usual. They had always clashed, but there had not been this constant stream of hostility through the sap-covered house. It wasn't the fighting she didn't understand. Her family fought too. It was the lack of loving that troubled her.

While inside Aunt Rita and Uncle Boris argued and outside Marina and Saika conspired, what Tatiana did was daydream. She sat with her back against the trees and daydreamed of Queen Margot and La Môle. What if Margot weren't queen, married to a king? What if La Môle had been tortured but not beheaded? What if they escaped, ran away to the south of France perhaps, found an unnamed cobblestoned village and became lost? They married. They were alive. They were together. What bliss. What happiness. But what would a queen and a commoner's grand passion look like in the everyday? Would it all be like this? Did even the most soaring love affair turn into Aunt Rita and Uncle Boris after a while?

That was so distasteful to Tatiana that the daydream instantly ended—as if the reel in the film broke. How intolerable. Better for La Môle to sweat blood and die on the rack. And as she climbed into her creaking cot and closed her eyes, the images in her head darkening, the images outside darkening, she thought, not another day like this one, please not one more day like this one.

The next day was not quite like this one.

"Tania, why don't you come swim with us?"

"I already swam. See? My hair is wet."

"Tania doesn't want to swim!"

"She's afraid of the lake."

"She doesn't like warm water."

"No, Marina," said Saika, "you know what it is, don't you? She is embarrassed. She doesn't want to get naked. Do you, Tania?"

"Tania, you're not embarrassed, are you, that you have smaller breasts than Pasha?" And this was from Marina!

Tatiana didn't look up her book. Suddenly she found two naked, tittering, dripping girls, standing over her and Queen Margot.

"Come on, Tania," said Saika, hands on her hips. "Want us to help you get undressed?"

"Yes, we'll help." Marina pulled on Tatiana's vest.

Tatiana jumped up. "Don't touch me," she said, pressing her book to her chest.

"Tania is a chicken!"

"Tania, have you considered the possibility that you will never grow breasts, or hips or hair?"

"Tania," Saika said, putting on a serious face. "Have you ever been kissed? I really want to know."

Marina laughed. "You know she's never been anythinged, Saika. She's saving herself for some of that Queen Margot loooove."

"Unlike you, Marina? Unlike you, Saika?" said Tatiana.

"Oooh! She's in a fighting mood today," Marina said merrily.

"This brings me to my point," said Saika to Tatiana. "No boy is going to love you if you don't grow some boobies. And even more important, and you and I talked about this, no one is going to want your unbloomed unopened flower, Tania."

"Come in the water, Tania," said Marina, tugging at her.

"Marina," said Tatiana, yanking her arm away, "what do you think Pasha would say if he heard you?"

"Oh, like your brother doesn't tease you!"

Tatiana cast her disapproving eyes on her cousin. She did not look at Saika at all. "Why didn't you do this in front of him then?" she asked. "You waited until you got me where you think no one can see or hear you. But you're forgetting—*I* can see and hear you."

"Tania," Saika said mock-seriously, "do you know what I heard in Azerbaijan? That if you're unbloomed but touch the hair and breasts of a developed young woman, you will grow hair and breasts yourself."

Tatiana kept stepping away and they kept following her, two wet girls stalking her through the clearing.

"Saika, is that true?" Marina said. "I never heard that."

"Oh, yes. It's true." Saika paused. "Well?"

"Well, what?" Tatiana snapped. "Just go back in your water and continue whatever it was you were doing there."

"Also the reverse is true," Saika said quietly. "You don't believe me. But it's true. You will bloom if you're touched by someone with a little bit of . . . savvy. It's for your own good. Do you *want* to remain breastless and unloved? In the interest of helping you, I'm willing to break, how shall I put it, um, your . . . *cover.*"

Tatiana nearly tripped and fell on the ground, staggering backwards.

"It won't hurt," Saika whispered. "I promise you, it won't hurt."

"Listen to Saika, Tania," said Marina. "She is wise beyond her years."

"Come on," said Saika, reaching for her. "It'll be so much better later. Let me touch you."

Tatiana swiped Saika's hand with the *Queen Margot* book, swirled around and ran away while the girls bounded back into the water, their laughing voices carrying in an echo across the lake.

"Tania, come swim with us," Marina called. "We're just joking with you."

Tatiana sat under a pine and pined for her summer. That's it, I'm going back to Luga, she decided. Blanca Davidovna can take care of me until Dasha comes back.

Marina and Saika were splashing each other, diving and giggling as Tatiana sat far away, grimly watching.

Marina was on the shore reaching for a towel when Tatiana heard Saika's voice from the lake. The voice sounded not quite panicked but not quite calm either. Saika said, "Marina," and there was a tense timbre that made Tatiana get up off her haunches to better see Saika, who remained in the lake up to her waist, muddy and covered with what looked like weeds.

"Marina!" Saika said once again.

Marina, who was bent over a towel, said, what, then turned around—and started to scream.

When Tatiana heard the screaming, she ran to the lake.

It wasn't weeds on Saika's body. It was leeches.

Tatiana knew the leeches that lived in the silt of Lake Ilmen—long, fat, black, with hundreds of minute teeth in their two circular jaws that sawed through the skin of the host. Painlessly they attached themselves with one clamp at their mouth and another at their anus. Then they relaxed their bodies and began to suck, emitting an enzyme that prevented the two wounds from clotting. The blood suckers were four to eight millimeters in length and another seven millimeters in their ringed diameter. Dozens, hundreds of these, covered Saika's body. Each of them could drink twice their body weight in blood before it fell away bloated.

"AHHHHHH! AHHHHHHH!"

That was Marina—who knew something about the Ilmen leeches, having once been bitten by one so badly that she required a week in the hospital and intravenous sulfa drugs to battle the infection that had spread into her abdomen.

"Marina, could you . . . *stop*." That was Tatiana. She took another step to the shore. The leeches were all over Saika. One was on her face. Tatiana had no doubt they were in Saika's matted black hair. She didn't want to think about it, but she was sure they were in *all* of Saika's hair, the hair Saika not ten minutes ago had asked Tatiana to touch. Tatiana stood in her white vest and white underwear, wanting only to turn and run back to the house and put on more clothes to cover herself, while Marina in a palpitating panic was running up and down the clearing, shrieking, "Oh, no! Oh, no! MAMA!!! MAMA!!! What are we going to do?"

"God, Marina!" Tatiana said quietly.

"Tatiana," Saika said quietly. "Can you help me?" She smiled. "Help me, Tania, please. I'm sorry about everything."

Aunt Rita, having heard Marina's screams—who hadn't?—came running from the house, her eyes as panicked as Marina's voice. But once Rita saw that Marina was all right, not only did she not offer help, she didn't offer much sympathy either. Her face a mask of disgust, Aunt Rita backed away, and her expression did not escape Tatiana—or Saika.

To make matters worse, Marina used that moment to start retching and throwing up her lunch of eggs and fish. Aunt Rita did not make matters better by flying to Marina and crying, "Darling, are you all right? Poor thing, look at you, oh, darling, let me—"

"Aunt Rita," Tatiana said, walking toward Saika, "I need some salt and matches right away. Also some iodine." She did not ask for a response nor invite any. Aunt Rita hurried to the house with Marina securely in tow.

"Tatiana," Saika whispered. "Will you please fucking hurry before they suck me dry?" She pulled one of them off her stomach. The worm hung on and when she threw it away, it left a pair of bleeding circles.

"Don't pull them off like that," Tatiana said. "You'll scar." For a moment, the girls' eyes met on the word *scar*.

Tatiana took another step toward Saika. "Come out of the water and lie on the ground." Saika did as she was told.

Opening the bag of salt as soon as Rita brought it to her, Tatiana poured the coarse crystals over Saika's body. The girl twitched; the reaction of the slugs was also instantaneous. They jerked and shriveled, attempting to crawl away, crawling through more salt as they did so. In their death agony, their black elongated bodies began to drip out their slimy entrails onto Saika's naked flesh, mixing with her blood and their own anti-coagulant protein, hirudin, a whitish, pus-like liquid. Where they had been sucking her, small, coin-like wounds remained, trickling blood.

Making Saika turn on her stomach, Tatiana poured the salt over her hair and back and buttocks and legs. There were many leeches that did not let go. For them, Tatiana needed matches. She had to burn them off.

Saika was quietly howling.

Tatiana lit a match and lowered it to a leech that was oozing from the salt, yet remained alive and vampirous. Lighting a wet, salted slick worm was harder than one imagined, the leech in damp self-preservation refusing to self-immolate. Saika twitched. "Tania, wait—"

But Tatiana couldn't wait. She knew that the blood sucking did not stop until the teeth of the parasite were no longer in the host's body. With a good few dozen of them still attached to Saika, the girl's ability to remain conscious was diminishing, as was her blood supply. If each leech could drink twenty milliliters of blood every ten minutes, then . . .

Tatiana hurried. One leech would not come off Saika's back; the match was burning Tatiana's fingers. She threw it to the side and lit another one, bringing it even closer to Saika's skin. Finally, the worm fell off, leaving an ashen singe behind. After taking twenty more leeches off the legs, Tatiana turned Saika over.

"Hurry up," whispered Saika, "but stop burning my skin with your fingers."

"It's the fire."

"Stop touching me. Press the match to the thing and then move on. Don't touch my skin with your fingers."

Unnerved but calm, her hands steady, Tatiana slowly burned off the leeches that refused to fall away; swollen, turning gray and writhing, they continued to feed on Saika. There had been only a few on Saika's back. Must be because of the scars, thought Tatiana. Even leeches can't attach themselves to dead skin. With so much salt in her open wounds, Saika's body was beginning to swell, turn gray itself. She had stopped howling.

"Tania . . ." Saika's mouth was sluggish, saturated with salt and water. "Between my legs, Tania . . ."

Tatiana was glad that Saika's eyes were closed and the girl couldn't see her revulsion. She would have liked to call Marina, Saika's best friend, or Aunt Rita, an adult. She would have liked to call Uncle—

"Tania!" It was Uncle Boris. He was behind her, leaning over her. "What's happened?"

"Leeches, Uncle Boris," Tatiana breathed out. "I think I got most of them—"

"Look," said Boris, pointing to Saika's pubic hair.

"I know," said Tatiana. "Those are the only ones left." Tatiana didn't know what to say or do next. Was it indelicate to ask her uncle for help? To do it herself was impossible. Tatiana couldn't and, more importantly, wouldn't touch Saika there. "I poured salt on her, but they're just not releasing."

"Tania, do something." This was from Saika. "Don't just sit and have a fucking conversation."

"Well, what am I supposed to do, Saika? I can't light a match to you, can I?"

"Oh, for fuck's sake," said Saika. "Help me sit up, will you?"

Uncle Boris and Tatiana helped her. Saika reached between her legs, grabbed a leech and yanked. The leech came out with a chunkful of hair. She did it again to another one, wedged in a little further down, a little deeper. Tatiana looked away. She couldn't help but notice that her uncle did not. Unlike the sickened eyes of his wife, Tatiana saw that in Uncle Boris, revulsion and sympathy mixed with something else, something even kindly Uncle Boris could not hide. A naked girl sat in front of him on the grass, covered with welts, leeches between her legs, bloodied and swollen and swampfilthy. But she was naked.

Intensely uncomfortable, Tatiana stood up and backed away, matches in hand. "Well, if you're all right now, I think I'll go inside," she muttered. "Would you like some soap? Some iodine?"

"I'll be fine," Saika said, not moving.

Tatiana didn't pursue it. Without iodine, the wounds would get infected, but it wasn't her problem.

Aunt Rita was standing by the window. "What's your uncle doing?" she demanded of Tatiana.

"I don't know." Tatiana went to the basin and picked up the industrial soap. It was neither a lie nor an equivocation. She really did not know what her uncle was doing.

The answer did not satisfy Aunt Rita, who went to the screen door and screamed, "Boris! What are you doing?"

She had to scream it three times, and still he did not come. Opening the door, Rita descended down the steps. "Boris!"

When Rita was ten meters away, Boris stood up. Marina and Tatiana watched them from the window.

"Tania, I don't know how you did that," Marina said. "I would've thought you'd faint."

"Why would you think that, Marinka?"

"Because *I* would've."

"Am I you?"

"I've never seen so many leeches in one place," said Marina, lowering her voice. "How could she have not known they were on her? I was bitten by one leech, I noticed right away."

"They're supposed to be painless," said Tatiana. "Otherwise they'd be extinct. Also I think, her threshold for pain has been raised because of her back."

They watched Saika limp to the lake to wash the blood off herself.

"I can't believe she is going in again," Marina said. "I'd never go in the water after something like that."

"I have a feeling that if Saika applied that sentiment to her life," Tatiana said, "there would be many things she would never do again, don't you think?"

"I don't know what you're talking about, Tania," replied Marina, averting her gaze and moving away.

Tatiana went to the door to close it because she didn't want to hear the bitter words that were being exchanged between an incensed Aunt Rita and a quieter but defenseless Uncle Boris.

"The child is fifteen and was just attacked by leeches!" he said.

"What does that have to do with anything? What does that have to do with you not walking away?"

"I was trying to help her."

"I bet you were!"

"She couldn't get up."

"Why would she need to when her favorite position seems to be on her back!"

"Rita!"

Tatiana closed the door with a sigh.

Strife followed the girl wherever she went. Into the village, into the woods, into the road, into the river, into the lake. Tea leaves, palms, rowan trees, sugar, bicycles, old, young, willing, reluctant, every step she walked on this earth, strife walked with her.

The Weeder's Daughter

And then it rained, and it kept coming down.

The three of them were sitting on the porch. The rain was pounding. "I heard you go every year after it rains across the lake to pick mushrooms and blueberries in the woods," said Saika. "Can we go this year?" Her face was swollen; her body she covered in Marina's clothes and blankets.

"If you want," said Marina.

"I want, I want." Saika looked across the expanse of the lake. "How do we get there?"

Marina said with a tinge of pride, "Tania rows us."

"Not all the way there? It looks like two kilometers across."

"Two and a half to the densest part of the forest, which is where the best mushrooms are. She rows the whole way. She is the Queen of Lake Ilmen, aren't you, Tanechka?"

Tatiana usually blushed with pride at her rowing, but today she had lost her happy thoughts. "It's only two lousy kilometers," she said.

"One time I had to walk almost seventy kilometers," Saika said. "You rowed two, I walked seventy."

"That's a long way, Saika," Tatiana said. "Where were you going?"

"I was running away."

"By yourself?"

Saika was quiet. "How do you do that?" she said at last. "Out of all the damn questions to ask me, how is it you always manage to ask the one I don't want to answer? Is it your special gift?"

They were sitting on two small porch couches, all played out.

"You ask too many questions," Saika said. "Rather, you ask the wrong kinds of questions."

"I don't know what you're talking about." But Tatiana didn't look puzzled. "Where were you headed? Is *that* a better question?"

"Iran," Saika replied. "We lived only a hundred kilometers from the border then."

Tatiana was listening to the nuance of her voice, between the lines, trying to catch, hoping to catch, failing to catch. "When was this?"

"A few years ago."

Saika was fifteen now.

"We were doomed, Tania. If you knew what I was talking about, you'd understand. I can't explain it to you. Marina understands."

"I understand," said Marina. "I want to feel that doomed."

Doomed at thirteen? "So what happened?"

"Well, you know what happened," Saika said. "My father caught us."

Marina rubbed Saika's arm. "Let's not talk about it, Saika, dear. Let's talk about something happy instead—like going across Lake Ilmen!"

"Yes, yes, let's talk about that," said Saika. "Do Aunt Rita and Uncle Boris come, too?"

"Of course," said Marina. "Nobody lets children go into the woods alone."

"Hmm," Saika said. "We're not children anymore. Even Tania is fourteen. She's practically a young woman." Saika cleared her throat. "And your parents, Marina, they've been getting along so poorly. Perhaps they'd enjoy one day by themselves. Without us kids around. To do adult things." She smiled.

"Oh, they'll never let us go by ourselves!" said Marina, her face lighting up. "But how delightful that would be!"

"Let's ask them," Saika said. "The worst they'll do is say no. Right, Tania?"

"I have no idea," Tatiana said indifferently. "Because I'm going home tomorrow. So you girls do what you like."

"You're going home? Why?" Marina said, all high-pitched. "Does Mama know?"

"She'll know tomorrow," said Tatiana.

"No, no. Don't go. Why are you going?"

Tatiana stared at Marina and said nothing.

"Oh, come on!" Marina exclaimed. "We were just playing with you, right Saika? It's all water under the bridge now."

"That water under the bridge is getting quite full," said Tatiana. "It's rising above the banks."

"It's me," Saika said suddenly and coldly. "She's never liked me, Marina. I told you that and you didn't believe me. I tried to be her friend, I tried to talk, to play. Nothing I ever did was right."

"Tania, tell Saika that's not true!"

"This isn't about me," said Tatiana, deflecting with the best of them.

"Admit it—you've never liked me," said Saika.

"It has nothing to do with you either," Tatiana said. "I'm going home because I want to be with my family."

"No, you're judging me," said Saika.

"This is getting *so* tiresome."

"You've judged me from the beginning," Saika went on, her voice rising. "You judged me for my scars, you judged me for my forward manner. You even judge me for my developed body! You judge me now for taking up with a boy too young. You. Just. Judge. Me."

Tatiana said nothing at first. Then, "Well, tell me, what happened to the boy you took up with? We know what you got, but what did *he* get?" She was so quiet when she spoke, yet her words were like clanging cymbals on the quiet porch as the rain kept falling.

"I told you about Azeri justice," said Saika. "And I don't want to talk about it with you. Because everything I say, you use against me."

There was almost no sound from Tatiana, just an inflective breathing out. "Out of the abundance of the heart, the mouth speaks," she whispered.

"You see, Marina!" Saika jumped up, blankets off, shoulders heaving, eyes blazing, face red. Tatiana, smaller, unheaving, face pale, slowly stood up. Her hands were at her sides.

"Tatiana, honestly, what's got into you?" Marina exclaimed, rising herself. "Saika is our guest!"

"Oh, shut up, Marina," said Tatiana. "She's not *my* guest. I haven't invited her in."

Saika stepped away. "Tania, Tania, Tania," she said. "How simple-minded your view of the world. The world is such a complex place, so many wants and needs and desires all crashing against one another. We try to make sense of it, we all do the best we can, and then comes along a primitive like you." She shook her black head. "Who knows nothing. Who understands nothing."

Tatiana was quiet. She could have walked away right then and there. She would have walked away right then and there. But she felt this wasn't an entirely pointless discussion. Not when Marina was involved, Marina with her good but weak heart.

"Okay, I know nothing," Tatiana said. "So what do you care what I think? Even if I don't like you, so what? For the sake of argument, let's say I don't. Just for the sake of argument. Let's say I don't want to play with you or talk to you. I don't like your secrets, I don't like your world of twisted soothsaying fraud—this is all hypothetical, Saika. I'm just laying it on to make my point. So what, even if I don't? In Luga you got all the other kids to play with you. And here you have Marina. My point is, you can't win over everybody," Tatiana said. "What do you care what *I* think of you?"

"I *don't* care what you think of me," said Saika. "You're just jealous your friends played with me instead of you, jealous your brother played with me. That's why you don't like me. Maybe if you were more interesting, Tania, you'd be able to keep your friends."

"Maybe. But there you go again, pretending it's about me. Why aren't you thrilled you got them all to play with *you*? Why isn't that enough? Why isn't Marina enough?"

"Girls, stop it," Marina said, going to Tatiana. "Tania, stop it."

Tatiana put out her arm to stop Marina from getting any closer.

"You have no right to judge me, Tatiana," said Saika.

"That was never my intention," Tatiana said. "My point was always this and remains this: it is your choice whether or not you come and play with me. It has always been your choice. But if you choose to play with me, you play with me on my terms, not on yours. That's all."

"And what are those terms, Tatiana?"

"You know them well," Tatiana said. "First of all, I don't like to be mocked or ridiculed. I don't like to be told things I don't want to hear, or things that aren't true. I don't like to be constantly and underhandedly subverted."

"This is what I mean! You're judging me even now!"

Tatiana didn't reply to that, saying instead, "I've never bothered you in any way. I didn't seek you out, I never called on you. I didn't come to your door. I helped you when I could—and you're welcome by the way."

"Oh, like I'm going to thank you for that!" Saika exclaimed. "You think I deserved those leeches. I know how you think, you and your fucking Newton. You think I was mean to you and got what was coming to me."

At this point Tatiana could have protested. A feeble denial perhaps.

But what a calm Tatiana said was, "And by what mechanism do the Yezidi think the universe rights itself in this manner?"

Marina gasped. "Tania!"

"What do you want with me, Saika?" asked Tatiana. "As you keep telling Marina and anyone who will listen, I'm just a barely educated simpleton. Why is your struggle for my approval so overwrought? Why are you always tugging on me to come join your circle? Not content to leave me alone, are you?"

Saika stepped suddenly closer.

Without backing away, without taking her eyes off the girl, and without opening her hands, Tatiana said, coldly quiet, "Be grateful."

"Grateful for what?"

"Be grateful it was just the leeches that got you in the lake."

"What are you talking about?"

"It could have been worse," said Tatiana in a low voice. "It could have been the *bloodworms*."

"The what?" Now Saika backed away, her eyes darkening.

"Haven't heard of them? Oh, yes. They're the real bottom dwellers in this lake. Red bloodworms. Glycera species of the segmented worm. The worm's nose is twenty percent the length of its body. It's got four fangs at the tip of it. Each fang is attached to a venom gland. And the bloodworm bites. Imagine thousands of them on you."

"You're sick," said Saika, paling, backing away another step until she was nearly at the door.

"I'm sick and tired of you," said Tatiana, stepping forward and whispering, "I know who you are."

"Get your hands away from me!" Saika cried. "Being touched by you is worse than being sucked dry by those leeches. Don't touch me again. You're like a bloodworm."

It had stopped raining when Tatiana told Aunt Rita she was leaving.

Uncle Boris stared wearily at his wife, at his daughter. "Marina, why does Tania want to go home? What are you doing to make Tania want to leave us?"

"She is not going!" cried Rita. "My brother will never forgive me if I don't take care of his daughter the way he takes care of ours every August. We might need him to take care of Marina again in the future. What if we need his help? Tania's not going!"

"Why don't you treat her a little better," Boris yelled, "and maybe she won't want to leave your house! How many times do I have to tell you?"

"Another thousand before I listen to you!" cried Rita, and off they went, slamming screen doors, into dark trees, screaming through the echoes of the damp night that carried their voices across the water, their shouting returned to them unsoftened even by the serenity of the lake amid the tinny din of the mosquitoes that were too displeased by the racket to sting them.

Late that night, Marina crept to Tatiana's cot in the hall. "Tanechka," she whispered, putting her hands on Tatiana. "Saika says she is sorry. I'm sorry, too. Please don't go back to Luga. Please. Come with us tomorrow. It rained so well today, the mushrooms will cover the forest. Come on. It's our annual Lake Ilmen trip. We always go, you, me, Pasha."

"You don't notice my brother here, do you?"

"Mama wants our blueberries and mushrooms. Yours too. We'll have the best soup, the best pie. Your Dasha is waiting for the mushrooms. You know how she loves them. Come on, think of her. I'm sorry if I upset you."

"You did upset me," said Tatiana.

"I'm just playing. You know that. Stop being so sensitive. Please come. I won't do it again, I promise. Come on, you'll be happy to row without Pasha."

"I'm not happy doing anything without Pasha," said Tatiana. "Look, what do you need from me? I'm tired."

Marina touched Tania's hand. "I just don't understand why you don't like Saika, Tania. She's so funny and worldly—"

"How can she be worldly, Marina? She grew up on collectives in the middle of Transcaucasus. She's been with unclean goats her whole life. Even her pores smell of goat. Where did she get her worldliness from, you think? And why does she talk to me like that, say those unbelievable things to me and you stand and snicker?"

"She is just being funny. You don't understand her." Marina chuckled. "It's child's play."

"The children are sure growing up fast under Saika's eye," said Tatiana. "She would've touched me if I let her," she whispered, shuddering. "That's child's play? Have you seen her back? Is that child's play?" She fell back on her bed. "And mark my words, there is something she's not telling us."

"Forget it, it's got nothing to do with us," said Marina.

"All right, so go with her. What do you need me for? Go with her, go into the woods, pick your mushrooms, pick your berries."

"I don't want to go without you. Please, Tania."

Tatiana rubbed her eyes, lying in bed, wanting to be asleep, or back home, or somewhere else, unattainable.

"Please don't be angry with me," Marina said. "Please come. It'll be such fun! Mama and Papa are letting the three of us go alone! Isn't that incredible?"

Tatiana grunted.

"So you'll come? And you'll be nice?"

Tatiana crossed her arms on her chest. "I'll come," she said. "But I'm not going to be nice."

Flying through the Stars

Tatiana slept. And before the next morning when they set off just the three of them for the woods across Lake Ilmen, she dreamt of lying on her back, looking out onto the sky, and the stars kept coming closer and shining brighter and she wanted to close her eyes and look away but could not, and suddenly she realized that it wasn't the stars that were coming closer to her, it was she who was flying to them, right under them, arms stretched out over her head, her face light and her heart full under every star of night, and all the while Blanca Davidovna's whispering voice echoed inside her head. "The crown and the cross are in your tea cup, Tatiana."

Book Three

Dissonance

Take but degree away, untune that string,
And, hark, what discord follows!

William Shakespeare, Troilus and Cressida. *I. iii.*

CHAPTER NINE

The Five-Year Plan

Pushkin's Book

It is August 1952, scorching afternoon, and they are in the pool. Alexander is sitting on the diving board, swinging his legs, while Tatiana and Anthony are standing ready to jump into the shallow end. This is their fourth race.

"Tania, give the boy a break," says Alexander.

Onetwothree. They dive in. Anthony, who's been taking swimming lessons, courtesy of Aunt Esther (what isn't courtesy of Aunt Esther concerning Anthony?), is using the breast stroke to keep up with his languid mother, who, in her yellow polka dot bikini is using—Alexander doesn't even know what. Wings maybe? She is merrily gliding through the water, and this time Anthony reaches Alexander's foot half a second before her and shrieks with glee. Tatiana grabs on to Alexander's other foot. Anthony takes one look at his father's skeptical face and says, "What? She didn't let me win. I beat her fair and square."

"Yes, son."

"Oh," says Anthony. "Well, let's see if you can do better."

"Don't challenge your father, Anthony," says Tatiana. "You know he doesn't like to be challenged." Her eyes are twinkling.

"I'll show you challenged," he says.

Alexander and Tatiana stand together at the edge of their fifty-foot-long pool, their own half a width of a prehistoric river. She is slim and white and freckled from the sun. He is chocolate with long gray ridges. His man's body is hard and muscular and looks unbeatable by an elfin woman who barely comes up to the hammer and sickle tattoo on his upper arm.

Onetwothree, they dive in, Alexander and his Tatiana, man and woman, husband and wife, lovers.

Anthony sits on the diving board and cheers wildly—for his mother! The mother he has just wanted his father to race and beat.

Alexander slows down, turns his head and says, "What's the matter, tadpole? Feet made of molasses?" But he speaks too soon; she's already in front of him, kicking him in the face for good measure as she swims ahead. With him she is not gliding; she is using all her wings and things. He lunges forward and falls on her in the deep end, pushing her under and then hoists her up, turns her to him, treading water, and says, *you cheater!* that's how you play dominoes, too. Tatiana is squealing, and he is gripping her kicking body, and his face is in her wet gleaming neck, and Anthony, that boy, jumps from the diving board, right onto his mother and father, and says, all right, break it up, and then wrests the mother from the arms of the father. He lets him.

Alexander shows Anthony how he crouches and she climbs on his shoulders; he straightens up, holding on to her hands and then lets go, and she also straightens up and balances, standing on top of his shoulders for a long moment before pushing off his trapezoid in a nearly perfect, splashless forward dive. Mom, says Anthony, looking impressed, where did you and Dad learn to do that? And Dad, glancing at Mom in the water, says, *Lazarevo.*

Mom teaches Anthony the racing dive, the backward pike, the reverse pike—and then Alexander brings the diving lesson to a screeching halt when he sees her show Anthony the reverse flip dive, facing away from the pool, springing into the air, somersaulting and nearly hitting her head on the board. He orders them both out, though not before throwing her on his back, holding her upside down by her feet and jumping in the pool with her—for his own version of the flip dive.

They've eaten, he's smoked, they've played basketball—her against Anthony, and then facing off against him in a comical one on one—they're back in the pool gliding about—not diving, not racing—digesting, and it's broiling out though nearing evening. It's been an average of a hundred and ten for forty days.

Tatiana says to him as she swims by, "Shura, do you have a plan?"

"Like a five-year plan?" Alexander says, smiling, floating on his back.

"Like in—how long do you *plan* to be out of work?"

"Who's out of work?" he replies. "Somebody's got to take care of the boy. It's his summer vacation. He and Sergio need supervision. Someone has to be the sheriff to their cops and robbers, someone has to make them lunch while they chase lizards, read the comics and swim all day. I've become a modern housewife. My day is not complete unless I wipe my hands on a dishrag."

Tatiana says fondly, "I don't care. Stay home as long as you want."

Alexander doesn't tell her that he interviewed with G.G. Cain two weeks ago. He met his wife, Amoret, met his grown kids. He told G.G. everything upfront, told him about the war and the Red Army and Tatiana. They talked about the Balkmans. The things in the papers about Stevie had been devastating. Bill Balkman had no choice but to sell his business to a competitor, take his son, who was barely out of the hospital, and leave Phoenix, no one knew for where. Amanda had tearfully come by Phoenix Memorial and told Tatiana that Steve, his jaw wired shut, demanded his engagement ring back. Tatiana tried to make her feel better. "You'll find someone else, Mand. You'll see."

"Easy for you to say, Tania. I'm twenty-six next month. Who's going to want an old maid of twenty-six?"

Alexander told G.G. everything, then waited. G.G. called him back, took him to lunch, and said that he and Amoret considered him very seriously, but in the end just couldn't hire him. "I wish you would've come to work for me three years ago when we first talked. You would've been invaluable to my business." But now . . . yes, the inquest concluded it was self-defense and extreme provocation under duress—a justifiable homicide. Yes, Alexander was an army captain. But it was bad publicity. His was a small family-run company, G.G. said, it built only five homes a year. No room for mistakes, and this sort of thing could potentially be very bad for business. He was sorry. He paid for lunch.

Alexander doesn't tell Tatiana any of this. He has another plan. He watches her swim away and calls after her, "I want to sell the land. I want to move."

She is pretending she doesn't hear. She swims back. "What did you say?" she says. "I didn't hear."

Alexander chases her across the pool. God, she is fast. He's never seen a stronger woman swimmer. After he catches her and swirls her around and gets the breath out of her, he says, "Ignore me at your own peril."

"Ignore *me*," she says, panting, "at your own peril. I told you we're not selling it and I don't want to talk about it anymore."

His fingers are in her ribs. She squirms. "I have only one word for you," he says. "Six hundred *thousand* dollars."

Tatiana is trying to wriggle away from him. "My genius mathematician grandfather taught *me* well, but even your nine-year-old son can tell you that's four words—ow!"

Back under the water she goes. While she is under she pulls the hair on his legs.

He yanks her up. "We can go to Napa Valley, open that winery you wanted."

Tatiana is still spluttering. "No, thank you. In fact, a little less champagne these days would do me good. I can barely walk." She smiles, breathless.

Lifting her high, Alexander throws her into the deep end. "All right, but this is my final offer," he says, panting when he catches her again. "I will go to New York for you. You can get your stupid job back at NYU, be close to Vikki."

Now she jumps on *him*, tries to push him under. "Oh, you," Tatiana says, her hands around his neck, rocking him into falling over. "You'll say anything, won't you?"

"Vikki needs you," Alexander tells her solemnly, throwing her off, then dodging her. "She's so distraught at leaving Richter out in Korea. For the sake of our nation, I hope he's a better soldier than he is a husband. But what's a girl like Vikki to do all alone in New York City? She needs you. Oh, and did I mention six hundred thousand dollars?"

Getting out of the pool, Tatiana stands on the stone deck, dripping and panting, her hands on her hips. "Stop this. We're not moving," she says. She's got a tiny waist out of which her hips extend like two halves of a golden delicious apple. Her flat stomach glistens, her breasts are heaving. He is looking up at her. She is golden delicious.

"In the words of our Great Leader and Teacher, Comrade Stalin," says Alexander, "what is this slavish attachment to a small plot of land?"

"Shura, for three years they tried to buy it from us, tried to take it from us. They didn't succeed, but you're telling me they're going to take it from us anyway?"

"Um, do you not remember what happened," asks Alexander, "in our house? In *our* house, Tania."

"Yes. Every day I try to forget. But you're going to let a crazy man from Montana take away your ninety-seven acres? Your *mother* bought this for you," says Tatiana. "She kept the money secret from your father to give to you, so someday you might make your way back home and build yourself a new life. This land was in the *Bronze Horseman* book you gave me eleven years ago when we walked through the Summer Garden."

"What's this Summer Garden?"

Her hands remain unbaited at her hips. "Did you forget that I didn't let Dasha burn that book when we needed fuel during the blockade? She and I carried it on the truck across the Road of Life." She pauses just briefly in the blazing Arizona sun. "And then by myself I carried it halfway across the Soviet Union. You came to Lazarevo to get this money—"

"Is *that* why I came to Lazarevo?"

"That money," she continues unperturbed, "bought me safe passage to Sweden, to England, and to America. And now, every morning when you go outside to smoke and see the Phoenix valley, your mother is reminding you what she thought about the life of her only son. This is what you want to sell out to buy a houseboat in Coconut Grove?"

After a minute's pause, Alexander says, "In all fairness, my mother also loved boats."

Tatiana takes a long jump off the deck right into his arms. Strapping her legs around him, she wraps her arms around him and making her voice deep like his, she says, "That's it, ho ho ho, and I don't want to talk about it anymore."

Alexander laughs. They kiss exuberantly.

"Now—much more seriously," she says, "what would you like to play, Captain? Marco Polo?"

"How about Little Red Riding Tania?" he says, all teeth.

"Okey-dokey." Making her voice high high high, she says gamely, batting her eyes, "Oh, Captain, what big *arms* you have . . ."

"All the better to hold you with, my dear." He squeezes her wet body to him.

"Oh, Captain, what big *hands* you have . . ."

"All the better to grab you with, my dear." He grabs her behind and presses into her.

"Oh, my, Captain! What a—"

Anthony takes a running jump, right into the pool, right into his mother and father.

Alexander pushes his son underwater and when he releases him, Tatiana pushes her son underwater, and when she releases him they both embrace him and kiss his face.

"Ant, want to play Marco Polo?"

"Yes, Dad," says Anthony. "You're it. And no chasing only Mommy this time."

Alexander has one more plan. He is a little afraid to talk to Tatiana about it, because after this one, he's all out. But the deed to the land has both their names on it. To mortgage it, he needs her signature. He has to talk to her, but he is afraid she won't give in; she hates all loans, all borrowing. He knows how she feels about touching any part of the land. She won't mortgage even ten acres to build herself her own dream house!

It takes Alexander two hours of stilted beginnings and many cigarettes to get his idea for himself out to Tatiana.

To his surprise, she doesn't just approve. She joyously, wholeheartedly, completely approves. They take out a mortgage on twenty acres, a fifth of their land, for eighty thousand dollars. He rents a tiny storefront on Scottsdale's Main Street, gets community association approvals to build in several upscale Scottsdale subdivisions, advertises in the paper, incorporates as Barrington Custom Homes and starts his own business. This is what Pushkin's *Bronze Horseman* buys for Alexander.

In between working at the hospital, Tatiana consumes herself with helping him. She combs through the finances, organizes the books, pays the bills, buys the office supplies, the furniture, the phones, the drafting table. Both she and Anthony help him paint, decorate.

"With no offending pictures anywhere," Tatiana says happily.

"Oh, I take them down before you come," says Alexander.

Free Market Forces

They both thought the business would start slow. They prepared for that. In the beginning Alexander planned to do everything himself because there would be only one or two houses to build. He would continue going to school to finish his degree, and meanwhile they would be looking to hire and train the right people and adjust to the demands of owning a small business. She would keep the books, he would do everything else.

But what happened was not in their plan. Alexander got two phone calls the first week, seventeen the second, fifty-four the third.

"Are you *the* Alexander Barrington, the army captain who was all over the papers a few months ago?"

"I am, yes."

When they came, the wives gaped, and the men, after talking for a few minutes about building the house, would say, "So tell us what really happened that night. What a story!"

News of Alexander's feat had swept the cities of Phoenix, Tempe and Scottsdale like brushfire.

In Scottsdale every person knew about him.

Here goes Alexander, who, to protect his wife, *keeled* a man and got away with it, they whispered, as Alexander, Tatiana, and Anthony strolled down Main Street. They studied Tatiana surreptitiously, but no man so much as openly *glanced* at her. She became invisible to most men. Her invisibility was in inverse proportion to Alexander's visibility. All the girls—single, married, widowed—in Maricopa County came past his office to take a look at the architect, home builder, prisoner of war, commissioned officer, a man who loved his wife so much he *keeled* for her.

After advertising for staff, Alexander received five hundred applications, nearly all from women. He made Tatiana interview them. To say that the girls were disappointed in being interviewed by the rescued wife would have been an understatement. Tatiana recommended Linda Collier as an office manager, the most proficient, organized and brisk woman—in her early fifties—she could find, and gave Francesca the cleaning account.

Both Alexander and Tatiana—and G.G. Cain, much to his detriment—grossly underestimated the free market phenomenon known as "a temporary demand spike," brought on by forces outside the control of the marketplace, such as umbrella sales during rain, lumber sales during tornado season—or shooting a man dead for your wife's honor in your own mobile home.

Alexander had to hire an architect and a foreman right away. Skip was his architect, Phil his foreman. Skip was doughy and sparkless, but Alexander had seen Skip's portfolio; his work was good. Phil, in his late forties, wiry like a winter twig, always in his jeans and plaid shirts, didn't say much, but he played guitar—which Anthony liked—had been living with the same woman for twenty years—which Tatiana liked—and boy, did he know a remarkable amount about building—which Alexander liked. Alexander couldn't have built more than one house a year without Phil's unflappable efficiency. With his new title as project manager, Phil took on four houses, while Alexander kept his hands firmly on two, and ran the rest of his business: hired contractors, met with clients—which took up a tremendous amount of his time—and helped Skip with home design. Linda scheduled him. Tatiana counted his money.

The subcontractors and suppliers whom he hired talked about their kids and wives, about birthdays and holidays, about the money they were making and spending, about sports and politics. It was a different world, but even with monks for roofers, with one hand on the rosary, the other on the clay tiles, Tatiana no longer came to his construction sites. Instead, on the days she was off, Alexander went home for lunch. He was the boss now, he could do as he pleased. It worked out much better. They were home, they were alone, and lunch often included some sweet afternoon love for Alexander, after which he wanted nothing but a nap. He returned to work as happy as if he had his senses. The smile never left his face.

Richter called Thanksgiving of 1952 from Korea, mutely listened to the story of Dudley from Montana. When Alexander finished telling him, he said, "Tom, it's what any man would do for his wife, right?"

And Tom Richter said after a beat, "Well, I think that depends on the wife."

He asked Alexander for a small favor. One of his young sergeants had been wounded and was coming back stateside; he was originally from San Diego, but was willing to work anywhere; would Alexander have a position for him? As it happened, Alexander had signed contracts to build four more homes, and even before that he'd known Phil had too much work, with all the houses going up nearly simultaneously. He readily agreed to help his friend, and that's how he met Shannon Clay.

Shannon, barely twenty-two, went into combat in Korea on May 9, 1952 and went MIA three days later. His recon patrol team was ambushed, they lost contact with headquarters, and while waiting for a helicopter extraction were engaged in a firefight that left all of Shannon's team dead and him with a round in his leg. He was in enemy territory for four weeks, living in the woods, before he was picked up by another chopper passing through the area. Alexander and Tatiana thought any man who could be wounded and survive by himself for a month in the mountains of Korea would do well in anything. Shannon walked with a slight limp from the round that was still lodged in his thigh, but was mild-faced, well-presented, polite to a fault, eager to please, and incredibly hard-working.

Alexander liked Shannon instantly, and liked him even more after Tatiana said, "He is *wonderful*," when they came home after having a drink with him. "But lonely. Do we know any single girls?"

A smiling Alexander wanted to know if Tatiana was really asking him if he knew any single girls.

"I said we, Shura. *We*."

One afternoon when Alexander and Shannon were both in the office, Tatiana stopped by to say hello. She had just run into Amanda while shopping in Scottsdale.

No sooner had she walked through Alexander's office door, than Shannon stood up and said, "Tania, aren't you going to introduce me to your friend?"

With unsuppressed reluctance, Tatiana introduced a smiling Shannon to a smiling Amanda. Two days later, the four of them went out to dinner to Bobo's. Amanda *quite* liked Shannon—who wouldn't like him, said Tatiana, with his polite face and innocent blue eyes—but Shannon *extremely* liked Amanda.

"So what do you think of our adorable Shannon with her?" Tatiana asked Alexander that night as they were brushing their teeth before bed.

"Hmm," he said, rinsing his mouth.

"What, you have reservations, too?"

He spat into the sink. "I have none. But I think Amanda does. *He* seemed quite taken with her. She less so with him." He shrugged. "Women."

Tatiana studied her face in the bathroom mirror. "Where's the surprise? Shannon is a decent young man. And Amanda likes bad boys."

"Does she indeed?" Alexander looked at Tatiana sideways. "And what kind does my own wife like?"

"I like," she said, grinning back through the mirror, "the baddest boy of all."

Shannon and Amanda didn't need Tatiana and Alexander after the first outing. They got engaged two months later, in March

1953, right around the time of Stalin's death (though Shannon maintained the events were concomitant, not consequent—unlike, say, the arrest and execution of Lavrenti Beria), married in June and the following March had their first baby.

Baby Baby Baby

And it wasn't just Amanda who was having a baby.

What in heaven's name was going on in Phoenix? Alexander could not walk through the Indian School Road market, to the drive-in, for ice cream, to the Apache Trail in the Superstitions without seeing strollers, babies, twins, toddlers everywhere. He played ball with Anthony in the Scottsdale Commons—babies all over, arrayed like lilies in the fields, baby boys, baby girls, pink blue yellow green, chubby, white, dark, brown, and all the colors in between. The Yuma married barracks, where they stayed once a month, had twelve carriages all in a row on the decks outside. Ghost towns in the Superstitions? Babies. Pueblo Grande Museum? Babies. Why did babies need to go to the Indian Museum? Or the Sonoran Desert National Monument? Alexander couldn't see the giant saguaros for all the tiny babies in his way. It was the first topic of every conversation, and the last. Who was pregnant again? Who just had a baby, who was having a third? When were they moving to a bigger house, and how many more children were they planning on having? Alexander even made it a motto of his business efficiency. He told all the crews he hired and all the prospective homeowners he talked to that his goal was to have their house built to the same high standards but in less time than it took one woman to grow one human being.

To the one unpregnant woman, he said, "That's it. I'm taking charge. I obviously need to take matters into my own hands."

She smiled. "Hands? Perhaps it's this small mistake in anatomy that's been the problem all along."

He applied himself to the business of making a baby the same way he applied himself to everything—dutifully, tirelessly, and conscientiously. For a year his spawn went nowhere but over the redd. He even stopped smoking in the house, saying the nicotine was not good for her once tubercular lungs.

"It's your house," Tatiana said. "You smoke where you want. And I'm not growing the baby in my lungs."

They waited noisily; Alexander held his breath around the days when they would know, and when one more month brought no baby, he breathed out and went on and worked and built another month. There were no babies, but there was swimming in December! Plunging into the heated pool at night under the desert stars. And sometimes not heating it, and plunging in stark naked—oh, the ice, the numbing squealing joy of it.

There were no babies, but there was Rosemary Clooney *wanting a piece of his heart*, and the Andrews Sisters, who *wanted to be loved*, and Alexander making love to Tatiana in the night on one of their deck lounge chairs and humming, "If I Knew You Were Coming, I Would Have Baked You a Cake," and Tatiana, holding his head, murmuring, "Shh. Shh!"

Humming "The Song of the Volga Boatmen" he had sung when he plowed through Byelorussia, Alexander put in a pebbled driveway for the house, poured a cement basketball court for him and Anthony, and built a flat roof sun cover for their cars.

Armed with "The Russian Sailors' Dance" he had hummed on the approach to Majdanek death camp in Poland, he tried to get rid of the cholla. The cholla cactus penetrates anything that comes near it—leather, rubber, gloves, the soles of Alexander's boots—penetrates to pollinate; jumps and germinates; imbued with evil spirits, cholla.

"Dad," said Anthony, who was helping him, "you're in America now. You're an officer. Here we sing 'The Battle Hymn of the Republic' when we conquer cholla. You don't know the words to it? Want me to teach you?"

With "Varshavyanka" at his lips, Alexander planted palm trees and agaves, built masonry walls for Tatiana's flower garden—which she found "endearing *and* symbolic"—and laid terra cotta winding walkways around the yuccas and the palo verdes. After dinner they would amble down the paths Alexander set down amid lush desert foliage. The ocotillos, the prickly pears, the velvet mesquites, the purple lupines, the desert poppies all bloomed in their landscaped summer garden by the mountains. And below them through the towering saguaros, the lights in the valley twinkled and multiplied, the farmland was long gone, the communities sprang up, and had streetlights and residential associations and pools and golf courses and baby carriages, and homes Alexander built for the newly pregnant women and their anxiously waiting husbands.

Tatiana had her arm through his, gazing up at him when he

talked about building houses, about Shannon, about Richter still in Korea, and the French fighting to their death in Dien Bien Phu—and sometimes Alexander could swear she wasn't listening to a word he was saying, her mouth was just dropping open and her eyes were unblinking, as if . . . almost as if . . . he was in uniform and she was in factory clothes, and the rifle was slung on his shoulder, and her hair was down, and they were ambling through Leningrad, through the streets and the boulevards, past the canals and the train stations in the first summer of their life when the war first cleaved them together before it rent them apart.

Meanwhile, the one great boy they managed to have played his guitar on the deck, learning Francesca's Mexican songs, and his own mother's Russian ones. Tatiana would hum them, and Anthony would strum them, and she would cry when she heard them. And he serenaded his father and mother with "Corazon Magico" and "Moscow Nights," as they strolled and smoked and chatted in the fond falling evening.

And then at night—love.

And then—another month.

Anthony sees Mommy Kissing Santa Claus

Tatiana had just come out of the bath, and was perched on their bed, brushing out her hair and leaning in as Alexander spread out the final version of the blueprints for their new house. With a pencil in his hand, he led her down the driveway, showing her the plan: first the elevation, then the inside of the house, then the back elevation, and then the artist's rendering of the kitchen.

"It's so sprawling," said Tatiana.

"Yes. Our sprawling adobe house is in the shape of a crescent Lazarevo moon," said Alexander, "curving out to the meandering driveway, the basketball courts and the garages."

"I love how that looks."

"You walk in through faux-gilded gates"—Alexander lifted his eyes to Tatiana, hoping she'd remember the reference to the other—not faux—gilded gates, ones that opened a certain elm-filled garden onto a certain white night river. By the dreamy look of her on his bed, she remembered. The blueprints as foreplay. Nodding his head in tacit approval at himself, Alexander continued.

"Through these gates you walk into a tumbled travertine square courtyard with palo de fierros around a circular fountain, and then proceed into the heart of the house—the kitchen, gallery, family room, playroom, library, and the long, wide dining room through the butler's pantry. Nice, right?"

"How *big* is this dining room?" She peered closer.

"Twenty-four feet by fifteen. With a fireplace."

"That's *big*," she said.

"I'm thinking generationally," he said cheerfully. "As in, three generations down, there will be a *lot* of children. Look—the kitchen connects to the den by a gallery, with wall to ceiling windows for plants and the long wall across for photographs and memories. And here on the left are the children's bedrooms. And here on the right wing is our secluded master suite . . ."

"Is that what you call it? A *master* suite?"

"*I* don't call it that. That's what it is. Are you listening, or are you being saucy?"

"Why can't I listen *and* be saucy? All right, all right, I'm listening." Tatiana made a serious face. "What's this?"

"A fireplace that faces both the bedroom *and* the *en suite* bath," said Alexander. "And this just outside is a private stone garden that faces both the mountains *and* the valley. I'm going to build us an enclosure for an outside fire."

"I like the fireplace in the bedroom," she said quietly, still brushing out her hair, but quicker. "I'd love to have one here."

"Yes, well. They don't put fireplaces in trailers," Alexander said. "The house is all limestone and flagstone and terra cotta, and hardwood plank floors. Except our bedroom—that's wall-to-wall carpet." He grinned from ear to ear. "Where was I? Oh, yes. A covered porch runs the length of the inward curve of the back of the house. Over here is a patio and a walkway that leads to the pool."

"It's all extraordinary," she said.

"The bathrooms are white," he said, "just like you like. The kitchen is white. But look here, see this island? This is one of the most important features of the whole place."

"Even more important than the fireplace between the bed and the whirlpool tub?"

"Almost," Alexander said. "Imagine this black granite island, like Vishnu schist, in the middle of *your* kitchen as the heartbeat of your house. On this island you prepare food and make your dough.

It's where your children and your husband sit on cushioned barstools and eat your bread and drink your coffee and shout and argue and read the paper and talk about their day, and move earth and heaven. It's the beginning and middle and end of every day. The music plays and your kitchen is never quiet."

"All isolated and alone in the mountains," Tatiana murmured.

"Yes," Alexander said. "Privacy to yell, to weep, to swim, to sleep. Privacy for everything."

"Shura," Tatiana said caressingly. "It's a beautiful dream. I see it. I see it all. I feel it. As soon as I get pregnant, we'll build our house."

Pointing out the increasing need for *privacy* now, with Anthony growing up and becoming more aware of things in their little home, Alexander, who had spent *four* years changing and adjusting and tinkering with the blueprints, carefully suggested building the house anyway. Tatiana gently declined.

"Who is going to manage the floorboards and the crown molding and the paint colors and the door handles? It's a full time job. Amanda can do it, but she doesn't work. I can't. My two plates are full."

Alexander was quiet, it seemed to him for, like, an hour, staring into the blueprints lying on their cream-and-crimson bedspread. "So make one of your plates less full," he finally said, raising his eyes to her.

From across the bed she gazed mildly and affectionately at him. "Shura," she said, "as soon as I get pregnant, I'll leave work. We'll build our house. What's the hurry?" She smiled. "We have everything we need for now. *Everything*," she whispered. "And we have plenty of privacy." Putting the hairbrush down, Tatiana took off her robe and flung herself onto the bed, right on top of the house plans. Tilting her head back and stretching out her arms, she murmured, "Here on your bed, on her back, lies a naked young woman with her hair down, just as you like it, just as you like her. And to this you say . . ."

"Um, can you just ease up off the blueprints, please."

Another year passed. They paid off the note on the land, gave everyone raises, hired new people, for the holidays flew in Esther and Rosa, a miserable Vikki and a sullen Richter, just back from Korea, gave lavish Christmas gifts and parties, had loud Sunday barbecues, went out to dinner every Saturday night, and traveled far and wide on their Sundays together, transsecting Arizona, riding horses in the mountains.

They remodeled the kitchen, bought new appliances. Alexander finished his degree, became an architect.

In the winter of 1954 they started watching television. Tatiana allowed Alexander to spare no expense in buying her one of the new color sets, on which they watched *The Singing Cowboy* and *Death Valley Days*, *I Love Lucy* and *The Honeymooners*. Sometimes when they watched TV Alexander lay down in her lap—as if they were still in front of the fire in Lazarevo. Sometimes Tatiana lay down in his lap.

And sometimes . . . as Marlene Dietrich would say, *she had, mmm, mmm, kisses sweeter than wine.*

Around Christmas season 1955, they forgot to lock their bedroom door and Anthony opened it late one night. He came in perhaps because of a nightmare, perhaps because the Christmas music was too loud on their radio, and so while *"I Saw Mommy Kissing Santa Claus,"* played on, twelve-year-old Anthony saw his naked mother underneath his upraised naked father, he saw gripped legs and small white hands clutching large arms, and he saw *unspeakable* motion, and he heard his mother making noises as if she were in pain but yet not in pain. He made a noise himself, and Alexander, without even turning around, stopped moving, lay down on top of Tatiana to cover her, and said, "Anthony—"

The boy was out, vanished, the door open wide.

They tried to imagine the things he may have seen. They tried to feel grateful for the other—completely unexplainable—things that he could have seen and blessedly had not.

"Should we build a house *now*?" Alexander asked.

"Why?" Tatiana said, "You can leave the door unlocked in a brand new house just as well as in our mobile home. But now you better go talk to your son, Shura."

"Oh suddenly it's a mobile home, not a trailer—and what am I supposed to say to him?"

"I don't know, Alexander Barrington, but you're going to have to think of something, or do you want *me* to talk to him the way your mother talked to you?"

"All right, let's just take one small step back toward reality," said Alexander. "My family and I were living in a communal apartment where the man in the next room kept bringing in whores he picked up at the train station. My mother had a responsibility. She was trying to scare me off with nightmarish stories of French disease. I don't need to scare my boy off; I think what he's seen tonight will put him off sex for life."

The next day Anthony squirreled away in his room with the door closed instead of sitting at the kitchen table doing his homework and chatting with Alexander. Tatiana came home; they ate. Unable to look at his mother, Anthony disappeared into his bedroom immediately after cleaning up; he didn't even want to play basketball, despite Tatiana's offer of a ten-point handicap.

"Has this been the order of things this morning and evening?" she asked.

"Oh yes," Alexander replied. "He wouldn't speak to me at breakfast either. And I'm beginning to understand my own father's predicament. My mother pushed him on me: go talk to him, go talk to him. At the time I thought it was hilarious. Why don't I think so anymore?"

Tatiana pushed him toward Anthony's bedroom. "I still think it's hilarious. Go talk to him, go talk to him."

Alexander didn't budge "It occurs to me—suddenly—that *I* didn't need the talk from my parents. Why does Ant?"

"Because he does. Stop with your excuses. You keep telling me how you're the one in charge of him. So go be in charge. Go."

Reluctantly Alexander knocked on the door. After coming in, he sat by a quiet Anthony on the bed, and taking a deep breath asked, "Bud, is there anything you want to talk to me about?"

"NO!" Anthony said.

"Hmm. You sure?" He patted his leg, prodded him.

Anthony didn't say anything.

Alexander talked to him anyway. He explained that adults every once in a while wanted to have a baby. The men had *this*, and the women had *that*, and to make a baby there needed to be some conjoining, much like a tight connection of mortice and tenon between two pieces of wood. For the conjoining to be effective, there needed to be movement (which is where the mortise and tenon analogy broke down but Anthony thankfully didn't question it), which is probably the thing that frightened Anthony, but really it was nothing to be afraid of, it was just the essence of the grand design.

To reward Alexander's valiant efforts, Anthony stared at his father as if he had just been told his parents drank the cold blood of vampires every night before bed. "You were doing *what*?" And then he said, after a considerable pause, "You and Mom were trying to have a—*baby*?"

"Um—yes."

"Did you have to do that once before—to make me?"

"Um—yes."

"This is what all adults have to do to make a baby?"

"Yes."

"So, Sergio's mom has three children. Does that mean his parents had to do that . . . *three* times?"

Alexander bit his lip. "Yes," he said.

"Dad," said Anthony, "I don't think Mom wants to have any more children. Didn't you hear her?"

"Son . . ."

"Didn't you hear her? Please, Dad."

Alexander stood up. "All righty then. Well, I'm glad we had this talk."

"Not me."

When he came outside, Tatiana was waiting at the table. "How did it go?"

"Pretty much," said Alexander, "like my father's conversation went with me."

Tatiana laughed. "You better hope it went better than that. Your father wasn't very effective."

"Your son *is* reading *Wonder Woman* comics, Tatia," said Alexander. "I don't know how effective anything I say is going to be very shortly."

"*Wonder Woman*?"

"Have you seen Wonder Woman?" Alexander shook his head and went to get his cigarettes. "Never mind. Soon it'll all become clear. So yes for building the house, or no?"

"No, Shura. Just lock the door next time."

So the house went unbuilt. *Wonder Woman* got read, Anthony's voice changed, he started barricading his bedroom door at night, while across the mobile home, across the kitchen and the living room, behind a locked door, "I Saw Mommy Kissing Santa Claus" played on and on and on.

Though Alexander was almost certain that every once in a while he heard Rosemary Clooney croon to him that his mother was right, there were blues in the night.

* * *

Tatiana and Alexander were sitting by their pool. The transistor radio was playing, he was smoking, she was sipping her tea, the dim yellow lights by the pool were on. They had been quietly chatting. There is rarely any wind in the desert at night and there wasn't any now. A song came on that Alexander loved, a slow sad favorite song of his, and he stood and took a step to her. Tatiana looked up at him uncertainly, put her tea down. He pulled her up, he pulled her close. His hand went around her back, their fingers entwined, and on the stone deck they swirled to Nat King Cole's *"Nature Boy,"* and Tatiana pressed into him as they glided in slow rivulets, in small circles by the blue ripples of their lit-up pool under the December southwestern stars. She put her head on his chest while Nat King Cole and Alexander sang to her about *the magic day he passed her way*, and when Alexander looked up toward the house, he saw himself, a fourteen-year-old, standing in adolescent embarrassment, watching his own father dance close with his mother near a hammock in Krasnaya Polyana, twenty years ago, in 1935—at the beginning of the end. It had been *the last time* he saw his parents touching gently, touching in love, and when Alexander blinked himself away, he saw his son, Anthony, standing on the deck of the house, in adolescent embarrassment watching his father dance close with his mother.

For the last time?

No matter how close Alexander and Tatiana danced—and they danced pretty darn close—there was still no child, and the relentless tick tock of the clock was heard louder and louder in all the rooms of their home, in the expanse of the plans for a pueblo mansion lying on their table. It lived with them—this white elephant in their just the right size double wide trailer—the white elephant that pored over the blueprints with them and whispered, *why do we need a custom-made castle with courtyards and fountains and dining rooms and playrooms and six bedrooms if there are going to be no more children?*

CHAPTER TEN

Blockade Girl

The Nurse Is In, Flip Side

On a Friday night that December, 1955, Alexander came home from work with Anthony, and lo and behold Tatiana was already home! Not only was she home, but she was wearing a clingy cotton-knit cream-colored top over a black pencil skirt. The table was set, the candles were lit, the music was playing, and the wine was poured.

"What is that unbelievable smell?" Alexander said, walking in confounded.

"Leek and bacon stuffing!" she exclaimed.

Standing close, she pressed intimately against him as she served him. They had a roast with oven potatoes, with leek and bacon crunchy stuffing, which Alexander declared was the best. "What's in it?"

"Leeks. Bacon." Tatiana laughed. "Also cubed and toasted bread, made by yours truly."

"Of course."

"A few diced carrots, some garlic, some butter, chicken broth, a little milk, all cooked for about an hour. I'm so glad you like it, darling."

Darling?

For dessert she made him cream puffs with chocolate sauce and black Russian tea. Alexander was so full he couldn't move from the table.

"Whatever it is you did, Dad, you have to do more of it. Mom, this was great."

"Thank you, son."

Tatiana and Ant were clearing the dishes when Alexander said, "So what exactly did I do that was so wonderful?"

With the plates in her hands, Tatiana said, "I have great news, you two. Guess what?"

Alexander's breath stopped in his chest. Please, *please*, let it be—

"I've been promoted!"

The breath was let out.

"You *what*?"

"Shura, they made me head ER nurse!"

Alexander sat quietly. Anthony stood quietly. "That's great, Mom," he said, glancing at his father. "Congratulations."

Alexander said nothing. Now he understood the clingy sweater and the leek stuffing.

"Aren't you happy for me?" she asked, frowning slightly. "I got a raise."

"Have you accepted yet?"

Tatiana stammered. "I said I was going to talk to my husband, but—"

Nodding, Alexander said, "Good, let's talk about it," cutting her off, glancing at Anthony. "Later."

Anthony looked away.

Later, on the deck, it went like this:

"Honey, a raise, isn't that great?"

"Yes, wonderful." Alexander said, smoking and not looking at her. "Seven thousand dollars. Tania, our profit from the business last year after paying all labor and operating costs was $92,000. The business is booming. We can't keep up with the work. Our land is now worth $10,000 an acre. That's nearly a million dollars, in case you forgot your math skills. So I'm pleased for your raise, but . . . let's just put it into a little bit of perspective." Alexander paused. "This raise," he said, "does it come with a raise in hours?"

"Just one more shift, honey."

He waited to hear.

"Just four days a week. You work six days."

"I know how many days I work, Tatiana," he said. "When is this extra shift going to be?"

She coughed and stopped looking at him. "I would work Monday, Wednesday, Thursday—and then Friday seven to seven . . ." Tatiana stopped, adding very quietly, "Graveyard."

"I didn't hear," Alexander said. "What?"

"The graveyard shift. Seven in the evening till seven on Saturday morning." She must have seen the expression on his face because she said quickly, "But I'll be here for Ant on Saturdays, like always. And I know you have to go to Yuma, but you and Ant can just pick me up from the hospital on Saturday morning and we'll drive straight out. I'll sleep in the truck. I'll be fine. Really. We'll work everything out. I'm sorry, but as head ER nurse I have to work on the busiest night of the week. It's such a big responsibility."

He was smoking and said nothing.

She came closer to him. "I'll have off Tuesdays, and Saturdays and Sundays. All the other nurses have work at least one weekend day . . ."

"*Already* gone from the house," Alexander interrupted, "gone from your family fourteen hours a day three days a week. Forty-two hours not in this house. On Wednesday you came home at almost eight-thirty."

"Iris was late," Tatiana said apologetically.

"Now you want to be gone all night," Alexander continued, "gone from the house *at night*. I didn't go to Las Vegas once without you. I didn't go to DC for Richter. I don't go to Yuma, I don't go anywhere that will take me from your bed for an *occasional* overnight, and you want to work overnight in the fucking hospital, every week, times fifty-two, times forever?"

"Darling," Tatiana said pleadingly, "what can I do?" She touched his arm; he yanked away. She stood up to face him. "I know you don't like my work," she said. "You've never liked it. But this is what I do. This is what I am. I have to work—"

"Bullshit. You choose to work."

"For us!"

"No, Tatiana, for you."

"Well, who do *you* work for? Don't you work for you?"

"No," said Alexander. "I work for *you*. I work so that I can build you a house that will please you. I work very hard so you don't have to, because your life has been hard enough. I work so you can get pregnant; so you can cook and putter and pick Anthony up from school and drive him to baseball and chess club and guitar lessons and let him have a rock band in our new garage with Serge and Mary, and grow desert flowers in our backyard. I work so you can buy yourself whatever you want, all your stiletto heels and clingy clothes and pastry mixers. So you can have Tupperware parties and bake cakes and wear white gloves to lunch with your friends. So you can make bread every day for your family. So you

will have nothing to do but cook and make love to your husband.
I work so you can have an ice cream life. From my first lobster
on Deer Isle, to every boat trip in Coconut Grove, to the last brick
in Scottsdale, this is what I do. What do you do, Tatiana?"

The wind taken out of her sails, she took one step to him, then
stopped and opened her palms when Alexander turned his face
from her. "Darling," she said. "Please. I can't leave my job."

"Why not? People leave their jobs every day."

"Yes, other people," she said. "But too many people depend on
me. You *know* that."

"Your son and husband depend on you too, Tania. The babies
you're not having depend on you, too."

"I'm sorry," she whispered, clenching her fists against her
stomach. "I know—but we'll get pregnant, we will, it's just a matter
of time."

"I've been back nearly ten years," said Alexander. "Tick tock."

Her legs shaking, Tatiana stepped away. Alexander stood from
the bench. "Okay, I'm going to tell you what I think. It's like this,"
he said grimly. "Quit or don't quit. Take the promotion or not take
it. *But,* if you take the graveyard shift, mark my words, we will
eventually—I don't know how, and I don't know when—live to
regret it." Without saying another word he walked inside.

In bed Alexander let her kiss his hands. He was on his back, and
Tatiana sidled up to him naked, kneeling by his side. Taking his
hands, she kissed them slowly, digit by digit, knuckle by knuckle,
pressing them to her trembling breasts, but when she opened her
mouth to speak, Alexander took his hands away.

"I know what you're about to do," he said. "I've been there a
thousand times. Go ahead. Touch me. Caress me. Whisper to me.
Tell me first you don't see my scars anymore, then make it all right.
You always do, you always manage to convince me that whatever
crazy plan you have is really the best for you and me," he said.
"Returning to blockaded Leningrad, escaping to Sweden, Finland,
running to Berlin, the graveyard shift. I know what's coming. Go
ahead, I'll be good to you right back. You're going to try to make
me all right with you staying in Leningrad when I tell you that to
save your hard-headed skull you *must* return to Lazarevo? You want
to convince me that escaping through enemy territory across
Finland's iced-over marsh while pregnant is the only way for us?
Please. You want to tell me that working all Friday night and not
sleeping in my bed is the best thing for our family? Try. I know

eventually you'll succeed." He was staring at her blonde and lowered head. "Even if you don't," he continued, "I know eventually, you'll do what you want anyway. I don't want you to do it. You know you should be resigning, not working graveyard—nomenclature, by the way, that I find ironic for more reasons that I care to go into. I'm telling you here and now, the path you're taking us on is going to lead to chaos and discord not order and accord. It's your choice, though. This defines you—as a nurse, as a woman, as a wife—pretend servitude. But you can't fool me. You and I both know what you're made of underneath the velvet glove: cast iron."

When Tatiana said nothing, Alexander brought her to him and laid her on his chest. "You gave me too much leeway with Balkman," he said, kissing her forehead. "You kept your mouth shut too long, but I've learned from your mistake. I'm not keeping mine shut—I'm telling you right from the start: you're choosing unwisely. You are not seeing the future. But you do what you want."

Kneeling next to him, she cupped him below the groin into one palm, kneading him gently, and caressed him back and forth with the other.

"Yes," he said, putting his arms under his head and closing his eyes. "You know I love that, your healing stroke. I'm in your hands."

She kissed him and whispered to him, and told him she didn't see his scars anymore, and made it if not all right then at least forgotten for the next few hours of darkness.

Tatiana accepted her new position, and Alexander's money went to the bank. They lived on her salary and had plenty left over. They had nothing to spend money on. Alexander did buy Tatiana a new car. She wanted something sporty, so he bought her a red Ford Thunderbird—just out on the market and all the rage—so his wife could have the wind blowing through her nurse's cap as she flew to the hospital to work her Friday night graveyard shift.

They spent money on clothes and shoes. Quite a fashion plate, she bought designer dresses and the latest capri slacks and stiletto heels and silk slips. She bought Alexander fatigues and rayon shirts and long johns and jerseys, and suits that were not drab flannel but linen and cotton, so when Alexander went out for a drink without her on Friday nights, he could look smashing.

Anthony was the best dressed boy in school. Smartest, tallest, strongest, most athletic, most beautiful boy in all of Phoenix. There was nothing that Anthony could not do. Having learned from his own experience, Alexander tried to instill in his distressingly good-natured and open son a sense of the circumspect, a slight reserve, some conservation of the confident gleam when it came to the opposite sex. He was slightly anxious for Anthony's future: the playing field was so unlevel.

Alexander's family strolled out into the Commons, starched, shined, slick. The husband and son: tanned and dark and broad, one a miniature of the other, pressed without a wrinkle, and *she!* petite but high-heeled, freckled still, blonde and buxomy, bedazzling still, her arm always through his. Families with children, for whom Alexander had built houses, stopped them on Main Street, near the Little Red School House, shook his hand, offered him cigars, a drink, small gifts, as they told him how much they liked their new homes, appreciated the craftsmanship that went into them.

And once an old man fell on his knees—but not in front of Alexander—and cried and said I know you. I'd know you anywhere. Thank you for saving my little girl.

It had been months since Alexander and Tatiana talked about building the house. Maybe months was too kind.

It had been months since they talked about having a baby. Maybe months was too kind.

They were busy, busy, busy.

Alexander didn't know when the change happened, because it was so gradual, like the slight ebbing away of the shoreline, like dune erosion; years went by unnoticed, and suddenly you looked and the dunes were gone, but one day when he glimpsed in her closet her crisp white nurse's uniform, not only did he not feel one solitary beat of arousal, but distinctly what he felt in his chest was a cold gnashing of the metaphoric teeth.

The Russian Cook

On Friday nights Alexander took care of Anthony, but the boy got older, became more self-sufficient and often wanted to stay out with his friends. Alexander started to stay out with his friends himself, drinking or going over Johnny's to play poker.

Young and single, the high-wired stud Johnny was his latest foreman. The business was hopping and after working hard, Johnny really liked to unwind. Shannon and Skip, who played poker with them, had to go home at midnight. But Johnny didn't have anywhere to be at any time and so he and Alexander went out with a bunch of his derelict friends.

On Fridays, Alexander could come home at midnight, at two, at three, and once, he went to a strip club downtown with Johnny-boy and his friend Tyrone and came home at 4:30—not 5:08!! but plenty late, and plenty drunk. The house was quiet. Anthony was at Francesca's. No one knew when Alexander came home. No one cared. It was all okay. There wasn't a single voice in the wilderness to cry, to be upset, to say, darling, do you know what time it is? Where have you been? Please don't stay out so late. I'm waiting for you warm in our bed. I waited for you in Coconut Grove, and on Bethel Island, and I waited for you in this house, too, leaning over the table for you in my little silk robe, all delicious and bare underneath. But that was then. Now what Alexander got instead every Saturday morning at eight was Tatiana's small hand on his head, her kissing lips on his cheek, and her murmur: "Husband, woo-hoo, it's eight, you've got to go to work. Wake up, sleepy head. Did you have fun last night with your wild friends?"

In the early summer of 1956, Shannon and Alexander were drinking by themselves at Maloney's on Stetson. Skip had had a fight with his pregnant wife Karen, and they were making up. Phil never went out drinking without Sharon. Johnny was pursuing new female pastures. Alexander and Shannon talked about the Red Sox's terrible year, about the plutonium bomb, about possibly including bomb shelters with the new construction, and about Israel and Egypt and the Suez War. They talked about the upcoming Presidential election, and whether Adlai Stevenson had a chance of beating Eisenhower. They talked about the civil war raging in Indochina after the defeat of France—but Alexander noticed that Shannon was bothered by something. When he asked if everything was all right, Shannon avoided the issue but finally, around midnight, when he had to be home, blurted out that he simply didn't know how he was going to remain monogamous for the rest of his life.

"Oh, man," Shannon said, "I don't know about you, but you won't *believe* the kinds of crazy excuses I'm hearing not to get it on—and this after just three years of marriage. I swear, Alexander, some of them I've never heard before. She says it keeps her awake afterward and she can't do her daily work the next day! Do you believe it? You hire me a cleaning lady, she says to me, and I'll have sex with you. I said to her, why don't I just have sex with the cleaning lady?"

"Good," said Alexander, nodding. "I'm sure that went over well."

Shannon continued like he was on fire. "Or, she says, how can you think about sex, didn't you read about what's happening in the Suez? Alexander! I can't have a pop because there's trouble in the Middle East? If peace in that region were a criteria for sex, all civilization would come to a grinding halt!"

Alexander laughed.

Shannon, with a lot to get off his chest, and unable to do it in front of other men, in a torrent told Alexander that not only had his marital relations become more sporadic, but what remained of them was so rudimentary as to be comparable to self-abuse. "She says to me, I have to get up early tomorrow to take care of *your* children. Can you just get it over and done with? Don't worry about me, she says. Just take care of yourself. I'll be all right. I don't need anything."

"Oh, so Amanda is a thoughtful wife," said Alexander. "I don't know why you're complaining."

Shannon said he found himself more and more attracted to other women, aroused by complete strangers in the street. He couldn't stop fantasizing about the wives who came to house meetings, whom he met at construction sites. He dreamed of make-up girls, librarians, other mothers with young babies. "Basically anyone in a skirt," said Shannon, and then added quickly and gravely, "But not nurses. Not at all. They're an absolute turn off. Ugh. They might as well be a man."

"Very good, sergeant." With an approving grin, Alexander patted Shannon on the back and bought him another drink. "But I don't know what to tell you, man. You're fucked."

"Would that I were. But I'm warning you, you're going to be without a foreman soon, because I'll be arrested for the graphic thoughts I have about other women. All of them with their pointy bras and tight sweaters, their swing skirts, their stockinged ankles. I dream all day of girdles and petticoats." Shannon paused, lowering his voice. "Even the full long-leg panty girdles."

"No, please," said Alexander. "Not those. Never has anything worse been invented in the history of women's fashion." The open girdle, with its nylon stockings, satin garters, slivers of thighs, peeking panties and promise of heaven was set on a royal plinth, but the panty girdle was hideous. Tania did not own one.

"Really, you think so?" said Shannon, rubbing his flushed face. "I find them quite attractive. Do you see what kind of trouble I'm in?"

"I do, I do, man. *Desperate* trouble."

"How do *you* do it, Alexander—stay sane? You have a swarm of women constantly around you. You always act a bit aloof, but I see them trying to flirt with you. Don't you notice them? Don't you find them attractive?"

"You can't help but notice," said Alexander. "But it's not the same with me, Shan. I did it smart, you see, I went out with all the girls—without girdles—before I got married. Now that I'm married, I don't need sex." He grinned.

Shannon's drunk mouth fell open. "You're *joking*?"

"Yes," Alexander said, making a serious face, and they laughed and clinked glasses and drank.

Shannon said he could no longer ignore the chore that his marriage bed had become. "Is this going to be it? Forever? That's all I'm going to get? Straight up once a week?"

"Why didn't you think about this before you married her?"

"Amanda was so hot before we got married! She lured me in, and then said, Hah, little fishy, joke's on you."

"Indeed, my good friend, indeed." Steve Balkman did nail that one, didn't he, Alexander thought. He did say Amanda was only putting out to get him to marry her. To think that that bastard was right about anything.

"Alexander . . ." Shannon asked cautiously, "Tania didn't trick you?"

Alexander debated answering. "Not yet," he said at last. "But some women are a complete mystery. Who knows what's next?"

"Is she a mystery?"

"Yes," Alexander said. "She is a complete mystery."

"How do you work through the other stuff?"

"Through what?"

"You know . . . the one woman stuff." Shannon struggled with his words. "I mean . . . I know you like steak. Who doesn't? Filet mignon is great—but every night? Don't you once in a while crave a plain old cheeseburger out?"

Alexander was thoughtfully rubbing his beer glass. "I think the trick is," he finally said, "you've got to marry yourself a girl that can cook across a broad range of menu options, so you don't have to go out. Because you're right. Every once in a while, a small American snack is all that's required. But sometimes you want a full course Russian meal with dessert."

"Exactly!" said Shannon. "And I've been to your house. Tania is a very good cook."

Alexander nodded, lighting a cigarette.

"And she makes everything. She's made us fajitas, and lasagna, and some Russian food—oh, those blinchiki were incredible."

"Yes, blinchiki are her Russian specialty," Alexander agreed. "She only makes them on extra special occasions. But what about the unbelievable sweet potatoes with rum and marshmallows she made last Thanksgiving? Oh, and let's not forget plantain. When we lived in Coconut Grove, all she served me was plantain. I had nothing but plantain every day, every way, for months." Alexander smiled. He took a long happy inhale of his cigarette. "Also she bakes."

"Yes, she makes the most delicious cream pies, lemon meringue, cream puffs."

"Shannon, stop thinking about my wife's cooking."

They stared into their beers.

"I think I'm just hungry," Shannon said. "We've drunk aplenty but haven't eaten anything. You want to order some bar food?" They looked around. There were only a few patrons settled in the chairs, mostly male.

"I'll just wait till I get home," said Alexander, turning to his drink. "I know she left me a small something in the coldest part of the ice box while she works."

Shannon stared at Alexander. "Hey, man," he said, "why don't you just tell her you don't want her working anymore? It's so simple."

Not looking up from his glass, Alexander didn't answer for some time. "Shannon," he finally said, "the three-dimensional, divide-and-conquer algorithm of why Tatiana continues to work is too fucking complicated for me to explain to you after six beers. Let's just leave it."

"Um—yes, I think that would be best," mumbled a dazed and drunk Shannon.

That Sunday when everyone was gathered at their house for a

barbecue, Tatiana brought out a tray of food to the pool patio and said, "Shannon, what would you like? I've got some tenderloin here, but there are also cheeseburgers on the grill if you prefer."

Shannon's horrified eyes flared from Tatiana to Alexander, who held his mouth closed to keep from laughing. Nothing on her face moved.

Alexander followed her to the grill and whispered, bending to her neck, "You're a very naughty girl. He's never going to tell me anything again."

Tatiana turned to him, handing him a tray of cheeseburgers and toasted buns. "I'm a very good girl," she said. "Tell him when you're hungry, I feed you."

Shannon Fed

A few months later, Amanda called Tatiana at the hospital and asked to see her. Tatiana would have said no: she was too nerve-racked at work to idly chit chat, and the forty-five minutes in the middle of the day she had to herself she reserved for solitude, or to sit with the other nurses or with the attending physicians. But Amanda sounded so forlorn that Tatiana could not say no. They met at a small luncheonette outside the hospital on Buckeye. The sleeping baby was with Amanda. The toddler was with grandma. Amanda ordered nothing except coffee. Tatiana ordered a BLT, eyeing Amanda's swollen eyes, her unmade-up face, her barely brushed hair.

"If I tell you, you won't believe it."

"Tell me."

"Shannon is seeing someone." Amanda started to cry.

"No, not Shannon!"

"Yes. I found a receipt from a hotel room in his pants pocket when I was doing his laundry. During the day, Tatiana! Do you understand?"

Tatiana was quiet. "You were doing his laundry during the day?"

"During *work* hours. He is supposed to be on construction sites, and instead—look!" Amanda flung a receipt from the Westward Ho across the table.

"That Ho is trouble," said Tatiana, shaking her head. "What did I tell you? I thought so from the beginning. It's haunted by evil spirits."

"You'd think he'd be more careful." Amanda sniffled. "But I

think he wanted me to find out, I really do. He wanted me to know."

Tatiana took Amanda's hand.

Amanda was not eating. Tatiana was hungry, but Amanda was sniffling! Tatiana thought it was bad form to dig into her appetizing BLT when her friend was having such a crisis. She kept murmuring, "Mmm," for comfort, all the while glancing at the bacon, lettuce and tomato on white toast.

"I don't know what to do," said Amanda, wiping her face. "What would you do?"

"What does Shannon want to do?" asked an evasive Tatiana. She didn't think Amanda was ready to hear what Tatiana would do. "What did he say when you confronted him?"

"Can you believe it," said Amanda, "he asked if I had taken a good look at our marriage lately. He said I take him for granted, I never get dressed up, or made up anymore, and how I never want to, you *know* . . . do it anymore, and when I do it's just no good!"

"Oh God," said Tatiana. "He didn't say that. Well, did you tell him it's not true?"

"No!" Amanda cried. "Because it *is* true! I *don't* get dressed up or made up. I *don't* want to have sex anymore. I'm tired, I'm busy, I want to read my book, I have a thousand things I'm thinking of that I can't turn off. But he wants to have sex all the time—like every weekend! Every single one! For God's sake, I'm not a whore, Tania. I can't do it every weekend. I've got responsibilities now. I'm a mother, a wife. I've got a house to maintain, to clean, two babies to raise. I told him he was unreasonable and demanding. He told me it was my fault he went to the Ho because I wear pajamas to bed. Can you even believe it?"

"I can't believe it," Tatiana said. "You wear pajamas to bed?"

"I need you to tell me. You and Alexander . . . you have a perfect marriage. Is Shannon being unreasonable?"

Tatiana coughed. "Look, I told you before, all relationships are different. What's right for one isn't right for another. You have to find your own comfort zone."

"Shannon says sex is part of the marriage contract. He says I *owe* him sex! Is he being ridiculous or what?"

Tatiana didn't answer.

"Tania?"

She deflected slightly. "You're upset now. Figure it out slow, see what you can live with. Then go from there." She paused. "But, Amanda," said Tatiana, "Shannon is right. How much and what kind and when, that you have to work out, but there is no question that marriage must provide the one thing nothing else provides."

"You think so?" Amanda frowned skeptically.

"It's indisputable."

"Oh—but every cursed week!"

"Like I said, you have to figure out what's reasonable."

"But what do you think? Is it reasonable for him to be so demanding?"

"I really don't know, Mandy, honey," Tatiana said. "And don't fool yourself, my marriage isn't perfect. It is what it is. Like life. It's true, my cup has been very full. It has also been very bitter." She looked away for a moment. "But we do happen to be well-matched in many areas."

"Is once a week too much?"

Tatiana averted her gaze and her reply. "I don't know what to tell you. Obviously for you it is." Once a week! She could hear Alexander's voice in her head: "*Pajamas to bed, straight up and once a week! What mortal man would put up with that?*" "But it's also obvious that for Shannon it isn't."

Tatiana and Amanda didn't speak for a few moments. "What do I do, Tania?" Amanda asked quietly. "I don't want to lose my marriage. I wanted to get married for so long."

"I know that. Let me talk to . . . let's just take this one day at a time."

"What do *you* think I should do?"

"I wouldn't wear pajamas to bed, Mand."

A Christening Conversation

Shannon did not leave Amanda. Somehow they worked it out, she put on a nightgown instead of pajamas, got pregnant right away and had another baby.

Tatiana, Alexander, and Anthony were invited to the christening in June 1957. Anthony, much to his dismay, was put in charge of seven children under five. His father advised strict order.

Amanda asked Alexander if he wanted to hold her newly christened month-old baby girl. He politely declined.

"Don't be afraid," said Amanda. "She won't break."

Touching the baby's head, Alexander again declined.

Tatiana ran quick interference, moving him away, diverting his attention to a small thing at the buffet counter. Amanda could not know that Tatiana's husband had never held a baby in his life.

After dinner, the adults were sitting in Shannon's dining room having coffee and cake when Skip's wife, Karen, commented, "Do you know that besides our Tania, I don't know any other women who work outside the home?"

The women at the table seconded with murmurs. The men glanced at Alexander and then at their dirty forks. Tatiana stared at Alexander sitting across from her, and he gave her a look that said, *You want to handle this one?*

All right, Shura, I'll handle it. "Well, Karen," said Tatiana, putting down her fork and folding her hands, "I know I'm not the only nurse in my hospital. There are 194 other nurses, all women. And Anthony's teachers—all women. The librarians—women. Oh, and the tall ladies selling you makeup at the cosmetics counter at Macy's, women, too. Maybe," Tatiana said, "you don't know any women working outside the home, because they're too busy working."

There was tittering, followed by an uncomfortable silence. Everyone was pretending to nibble at their cake—including Alexander!

"Yes, but how many of them are married like you?"

"No one is married like me," said Tatiana, her eyes on her husband. "It's true, most of the women are widows, or unmarried. Some are older. Some are younger. But, Karen, they're still all *women*."

"Oh, I know, I know, but I'd never want to be a nurse. It seems so yucky," said Karen with distaste in her voice and on her face. "Are you a triage nurse? Or a receptionist nurse?"

"I'm an acute care nurse. A critical care nurse." Alexander did not look up, palming his hands. Right, Shura? Tatiana wanted to say. You remember, no, when I was a critical care nurse, running out onto the Neva River ice in the middle of the battle for Leningrad to carry your body back to shore? And then I became your terminal care nurse?

"You must see some wicked bad things," Karen said.

"In my life," said Tatiana, "I have seen many things I wish I had not seen." She looked down at her hands still folded on the table.

"So how many hours do you work?"

"Fifty."

"Fifty!" No one at the table could believe it. "I can't imagine there is any time left for all the other work," said Karen. "Who cooks in your house?"

"I do."

"Who cleans?"

"I do."

"Laundry?"

"Still me."

The girls whistled. There was a silence.

And then Amanda said, "Yes, but who has the *children*, Tania?"

Tatiana didn't say anything; she looked at Alexander, who kept his steady gaze on his own steady hands.

It was Anthony who leapt inside the dining room and in a loud upset voice exclaimed, "Leave my mother alone! She works harder than any of you—at everything. While you're having your little lunches, she heals sick people and dying people. That's what *she* does while you're sipping ice cream sodas, passing judgment on her. That's what she is—a critical care nurse *and* a mother."

Tatiana pointed to Anthony. "Amanda, here is my child. You remember him, don't you?"

Anthony whirled on his father. "And if she wasn't a Red Cross *nurse*, you," he said, shaking, pointing his finger at Alexander, "you know where you would be."

"Anthony! That's enough." That was Tatiana.

"It's not enough!"

Alexander stood from the table and fixed Anthony with such a grim and deadly stare that the boy fell mute and ran from the room. Tatiana excused herself. They left soon after.

In the truck, they managed to remain quiet, but at home, Anthony did not remain quiet. They had barely got in the door, still standing in the open space in front of the kitchen where Dudley had been shot when Anthony said, trying to keep his voice low, "Dad, I simply don't understand how you could've sat there and said nothing."

"Anthony!" Tatiana yelled. "Go to your room!"

"No!" Anthony yelled back.

Alexander slapped Anthony square in the mouth with the flat of his hand. "Do not *ever*," he said, "raise your voice to your mother."

"Why not—*you* do!"

Coming between them, Tatiana grabbed Alexander by his fore-arms and said very quietly, "No. Stop right *now*."

"You're telling *me* to stop right now?" Alexander said. "Are you listening to him?"

And behind her, a suddenly empowered Anthony said, "It's all your fault, Mom. It's because everything he does is fine with you—*everything*! He yells at you, that's fine. He doesn't say one syllable when people are *attacking* you—that's fine, too!"

"Anthony!" yelled Alexander. Tatiana dug her nails into his arms, knowing that he wouldn't be able to dislodge her without vio-lently dislodging her, and she was hoping he would stop himself in front of his son.

He did. The tension in his body slightly receding, Alexander lifted his arms up and away from her, took her by the shoulders, looked down into her face and said quietly, "He speaks that way because *you* let him. You've been letting him get away with every-thing his entire life. I'm not going to let him. Now let go of me."

Anthony was standing panting.

"What the hell is wrong with you?" Alexander said to Anthony. "How many times does your mother tell you, stay out of our busi-ness. You want to try your luck with me, fine, be upset with me, but what are you even thinking, talking that way to your *mother*?"

With tears of pride pinching his face, Anthony said in a much quieter voice, "Oh, I get it now, so against *me*, my mother needs defending!"

This time, Tatiana wasn't holding on to Alexander anymore. She whirled on Anthony herself. "Your father is right, you are com-pletely out of line," she said as she pushed him down the hallway and into his room, mouthing, "Stop it!" before she slammed the door.

Anthony didn't hear his parents argue. He was sure he would hear loud voices, shouting, but he heard nothing. A half-hour later he walked out of his room into silence. Their bedroom door was open. Quietly opening the back door, he glimpsed his father sitting on the deck bench. His mother was in his lap, her arms around him. Their faces were pressed together. They were rocking. Anthony coughed. His father stopped rocking; his mother with her back to Anthony fixed her blouse. Anthony started to say he needed a permission slip signed for a school trip.

"Your mother will be right there. Go." Alexander didn't even turn his head when he spoke. Anthony went inside.

In a little while his door opened. He was expecting—and hoping—for his mother, but it was his father who came in. He signed the note, and then sat on the edge of the bed. Anthony's mouth was twisted. He couldn't speak to him. He could barely speak about it to his mother, but at least he could cry with her, yell at her, say cruel things to her. He was free to be anything with her. But with his father, he knew he could not be. Still, Anthony was so upset, so angry.

"What's the matter with you?" Alexander said. "Go ahead. Speak your mind."

Trying to keep his voice straight, Anthony said, "I don't understand how you could have not defended her, Dad. They were being so mean to her. Isn't Amanda supposed to be Mommy's friend?"

"She's a foul-weather friend," said Alexander. "Mommy doesn't expect much from Amanda, who never disappoints her." He fell silent for a moment. "But Ant," he said, "you know that our life is not a parade for acquaintances at the dessert table. You *know* that. You are my son, but you're fourteen. Mommy and I are not fourteen. And we are going through adult things that we are not going to explain, either to our casual friends or to you." Alexander leaned to his son and said quietly, "But you know that when your mother needs real defending, I'm her man."

Anthony looked up at his father. "I thought tonight was such a time."

Alexander brushed the hair from Anthony's forehead. "No," he said. "Tonight, the mother lion managed fine by herself. Now stop being so overwrought. You're a boy, and the son of a soldier. Emotions in check, buddy."

But then his mother came to see him. And he closed his eyes, turning in to her, while she kneeled by his bed and held his head and whispered words to him he barely heard and did not need to. *You are a good boy, Antman. You have always been a lovely, protective, open, beautiful boy.* And he cried in her arms, and she was all right with it.

Outside Tatiana climbed into Alexander's lap once more, kissing away the evening from his heart.

Alexander sat cradled in her, smoking, breathing in the night air. "Let me ask you . . ." he finally said, trying to keep his voice even, keep it from cracking. "Can *you* explain to me, in a way I can understand, why you and I, of all the people in this world, after all the love that we have made, can't make one little baby?"

Tatiana groaned, her eyes deeply averted from him, her body shrinking down, curling around herself. "Shura, darling . . ." Her voice was defeated. "I'm very sorry. Something must be wrong."

"That much is clear," said Alexander, his eyes deeply averted from her.

Tatiana stared at Alexander after he said that. And then she got off his lap.

The Soviet Union Baby Boom

It was another Friday night.

Tonight was not a poker night, or a drink with the buddies night, or a downtown with Tyrone and Johnny night. Alexander kept Anthony home with him. They played basketball, had pot roast Tatiana left for them, went to the pictures, had ice cream, came home, played dominoes to hone their skills against her. Anthony was long asleep.

It was three in the morning.

In his black BVDs Alexander was sitting on the couch in the dark living room, his long legs stretched out nearly to the TV, his head thrown back, arms dangling by his sides, a burned down cigarette between his fingers, eyes open, staring at the ceiling.

They weren't having another baby because they both weren't here. Alexander Belov wasn't in America, he was decaying where they didn't have children after the war that killed fifty million people.

In the United States, two million babies were born in 1946. Three million in 1947 and in 1948, and four million every single year from 1948 to 1956. Women were being sneezed at and they were getting pregnant. Not Alexander's Soviet woman. Because her husband was a Soviet man, and he was logging in Siberia where he and two million other repatriates were sent after being handed over by the Allies. The soldiers who weren't killed in the war were sent to Kolyma, to Perm-35, to Aykhal, to Archangelsk. Who else was going to rebuild the Soviet Union?

So while in the decade after the war, England, France, Germany, Japan, Italy, Austria and, most of all, the United States enjoyed a population explosion unheard of in history, the Soviet Union had a population *decrease*. How could that be? Where were the men?

Well, the young, the old, the healthy, the sick were in Magadan. Twenty-five percent of all able-bodied Soviet men were in the camps. The maimed were dead. Unlike the United States, where veterans without arms could come home and still sire children, most of the Soviet one-armed veterans were in the earth, because there had not been enough penicillin to save them.

To increase the birth rate, the Soviet government gave periodic amnesty to the Gulag male prisoners. When that was not enough, it abolished abortion. There never had been another form of contraception for women in Soviet Russia, and without abortion available every afternoon from three to five at every hospital clinic in every city, surely there would be a baby boom.

There wasn't. So condoms were removed from the command production line. Black market condoms became exorbitantly priced. You went to prison for buying them and for selling them. When that was not enough, the government practically abolished marriage. The one woman, one man union clearly wasn't working in the Soviet Union. There weren't enough men left for Christian marriage.

Married women, whose husbands' whereabouts were— ahem— unknown, were given instant, no questions asked, no reasons needed divorce dispensation so they wouldn't waste valuable time waiting around for their missing spouses. The women became divorced with flourishing ease and then were given bonuses, raises, prizes, medals, time off work, cash in hand for having children by absolutely anyone. Proof of paternity was not necessary. Marriage was not essential—and not encouraged. Cohabitation was not essential—and not encouraged. Not only not encouraged, it was not even possible. There was nowhere for married couples to live. The women lived banded together in communal apartments where the men had once been. One amnestied Gulag man among thirteen desperate women, and suddenly there was a chance at repopulation. Once his business was done, the man could move on to the next communal apartment. It seemed so foolproof: both sexes got exactly what they most wanted. Men got absolute sexual freedom and women got financial security.

Yet even with these enticing procreation stimulus packages, ten years after the war, the population growth was zero! Worse than zero—there were fewer people in Russia in 1955 than there had been in 1945. More people were dying than were being born. Why? Sex wasn't abolished; *where* were the children?

It was the women's fault. They were having sex, all right, but they weren't idiots. They worked all day, they lived in tight quarters with other women, and those unfortunate enough to become pregnant went to doctors and paid vast sums to get under-the-table abortions. When this was discovered, both the doctors and the women got ten years' hard labor. To save their skins, the doctors refused to perform abortions. In their unrepentant desperation, the women started performing their own. The women's mortality rates soared. At the later stages of pregnancy, at five, six, seven months, the babies were delivered by midwives and then aborted right in the communal apartments and thrown out with the communal trash.

The Soviet Government solemnly proclaimed the population was stagnating because of a soaring infant mortality rate.

The women were dying, the babies were dying, and meanwhile the dying men were where Nikolai Ouspensky now was, where Alexander should have been, five thousand kilometers across the tundra, out in the forests from dawn to dusk, building forts and fences, cutting down the pines. That's where his spirit was, but his strong, healthy body was in Arizona, building a house for every house he had destroyed when he was a tank commander, a penal battalion commander, a leader of wretched men who burned down the towns they vanquished, burned the bridges and the huts and the marketplaces. No more apples or cabbages, no more watches or whorehouses. Alexander had a lifetime of villages to rebuild before he was done. And alongside Ouspensky, he had a lifetime of fences to put up before he was done, fences so the men couldn't get to the imprisoned women (who got ten years for illegal abortions), who were on their hands and knees lifting up their skirts, presenting themselves through the rusty barbed wire.

In America, Alexander worked for himself building houses so that American men could live in them with their American women and have the children he couldn't with his Soviet factory-girl wisp of a wife who still got up every morning when it was dark in the winter to go get her family their daily bread, their cardboard bread so that they might live. Dasha, Papa, Mama, Marina, Babushka slept while the bombs fell on the emaciated girl in a white dress as she made her way down the empty snowdrift streets where the dead lay wrapped in sheets. Alexander warned Tatiana to walk only on the left side of the avenues and to wait out the bombing, and Tatiana listened to him, waiting impatiently in doorways in her overcoat and hat, and then, her face to the howling wind, making her way in the blizzard to the store—that was all out.

She was still waiting out the bombing, tubercular, starving, twisting her exhausted body like a vine on which nothing could grow. Alexander could build a lifetime of adobe houses, but no matter how many hours Tatiana put in at Phoenix Memorial, she would never be able to save her grandfather, her mother, her father, her sister, her brother. Who could make babies in this barren landscape of her Soviet womb when sired by the sterile landscape of his Soviet seed?

CHAPTER ELEVEN

Blue Christmas

Merry Merry Merry

In early November 1957, Alexander was checking out a new marble and granite quarry down on West Yuma and thought he'd stop by to see Tatiana at the hospital. The receptionist told him she was in the cafeteria. Through the glass door he saw her sitting with—who was that? He looked slightly familiar—a doctor. Usually he found her having lunch with one of the other nurses, but here she was sitting with a doctor—ah yes, it was Dr. Bradley. Alexander vaguely remembered him from the Christmas parties. Fair-haired Bradley looked fit for a doctor.

What struck Alexander about Tania having lunch with Bradley was the casual ease of her body while she sat with him. She was relaxed, elbows on the table, legs carelessly crossed. Sucking her drink through a straw like a little girl, she was listening animatedly while he talked animatedly. Alexander was just about to come in when she threw back her head and laughed at something the doctor said.

Perplexed, Alexander watched her, his eyes and solar plexus opening to something he had not expected to see. He was used to seeing the eyes of men on her—though Bradley's were perhaps a little more keen than most—but this was new. Tatiana laughed long and with joy at this regular Bob Hope of a doctor while she blithely rearranged and tightened her hair bun.

Alexander didn't go in. He stood a moment by the door and then turned around.

"You didn't find her?" Cassandra called after him.

"No." He was walking out.

"Want me to page her?"

"No. Got to get back to work. Thanks, though."

That night after she came home, Alexander was quiet, observing her. She made him meatball soup and fajitas. Anthony was at basketball practice.

"Shura, Cassandra told me you came by today, is that true?"

"I did, but I didn't realize what time it was. I had to run."

"You didn't even page me to say hello?"

"I was ten minutes late to my one thirty." Alexander took a spoonful of the soup, weighed his words. "What did you do for lunch?"

"Oh, it was so quick today—we had four code blues," she said. "I had it with Dr. Bradley. You remember him?"

"I do." Alexander didn't say anymore. What was interesting to him was that she didn't say anymore.

"You like the fajitas, Shura?"

"Yes. Francesca has taught you well."

After dinner, Alexander was lying on the couch, not going outside for his smoke, still watching her. He had to go pick up Ant in a little while.

"Are you okay?" she asked.

"Fine." But Alexander wasn't fine.

Was it his imagination? Could he be wrong?

No, he saw her happiness. He wasn't imagining that.

"Come here," he said, sitting up.

She was drying the dishes.

"Put the rag down and come here."

"Shura . . . you have to go pick up Ant in fifteen minutes."

"Why so much discussion? Come."

She came and stood in front of him, her eyes soft, fond.

Taking the rag out of her hands, Alexander drew her close between his legs, his hands going underneath her wool jersey skirt to the bare space above her stockings. The girdle was open and satin, the underwear sheer nylon mesh. Pulling up her sweater, he pressed his mouth into the top of her warm stomach and silently rubbed the backs of her thighs, his fingers circling, circling, becoming more insistent when he felt her skin flush and get warmer.

After her hands went around his head and her breath became shallow, Alexander lay her down on the couch and opening her legs slightly so he could see her, caressed her thighs in steady circles. She was *very* flushed, very warm. He watched her face, her elongated neck, her white thighs, her barely there underwear. He unhooked the front clasp of her bra and her breasts fell out, the nipples up and coral.

"Shura, please . . ."

"Okay, babe." He bent to her breasts, continuing to rub her. A quivering unquiet minute went by. And another. Straightening up, Alexander whispered, "Look at you. Your nipples are *so* wet, so hard, and you are so warm, and my fingers are *so* close, rubbing you gently, round and round and round . . . right on the seam of your underwear . . . Tania, can you feel me?"

She barely moved, barely breathed.

"I can pull back your underwear, like this, just a little, move it over an inch with my fingers . . ."

She moaned. His fingers circled.

"Come on, Shura, *please* . . ." She clutched his forearms.

"Please what? Tell me. Please what?"

". . . Put your fingers on me, *please* . . ."

"Tatia," he whispered, "my fingers . . . or my lips?"

Tatiana moaned so loud, and when she did, Alexander took his hands off her. She opened her eyes, opened her mouth. "Oh my God, Shura, what—"

"I gotta run," he said, helping her sit up, giving her a slight push off the couch. "Have to pick up Ant."

She fell back into his arms.

"Mommy . . . your son needs to be picked up from practice."

"Oh God. I can't wait, Shura" she said, kissing him hungrily. "I can't wait another *second*."

She had to wait another few hours, but that night Alexander made love to her as if it weren't a Wednesday and they had to be up again at five. Completely in command, he made love to her so thoroughly, so relentlessly and by the end so desperately that after he was done, there was not a pod or a wedge or a hollow on Tatiana's body that had not been kissed, licked, stroked, sucked, confined, filled, restrained and released. He devoured her. He made love to her until she was limp, until she was hobbled by love. Until there was not a single weeping inaudible *Oh Shura* left in her throat, not a single breath even to beg for mercy. She couldn't move after he was done with her. He came inside her while kneeling upright on their bed, holding her upright too, under her buttocks. She was pressed up to him and over him and around him, while their mouths were agape against each other. His climax was so intense he nearly dropped her.

The next morning at five thirty, Tatiana made him potato pancakes with bacon on the side.

"So *this* is what I have to do to get potato pancakes around here?" Alexander said, his mouth full.

She was too embarrassed to lift her gaze to him. Her fingers trembled when she touched him, her raw, tender lips trembled when she raised her face to say good-bye to him. "Shura, darling, what got into you?" she murmured, blushing, averting her eyes. "It's a school night."

"You got into me," replied Alexander. "Like a hand grenade."

But it didn't last. That night was just a moment in time. Tatiana didn't run home that evening, didn't especially fuss around him; she simply went on as she always was and so nothing erased for Alexander the image of her sitting comfortably across from the comedian doctor.

Tatiana's laughing was another girl's disrobing.

Alexander did what he always did when he carried too many things that were too heavy for him: from the effort of dragging them around, he withdrew. He became sullen, moody. He snapped at her for the little things, unable to snap at her for the big things. He constantly showed his irritation with her for being late, for being tired, absent-minded, for falling asleep during TV shows, for forgetting to buy things. In his silence he went on and took care of what he had to take care of. He put on his suit and had meetings with husbands and wives, he paid his crews. He put on fatigues and got his hands dirty when he had to. He played poker with Johnny, he went out with Shannon, he played basketball with Anthony, he swam. He came home and warmed up what she had made for him when she wasn't home, he sat at her table and ate her food hot when she was, and when he needed her, he took what he needed.

Alexander wanted to ask her about the doctor but couldn't. The man who fought the world wasn't strong enough to ask if his maiden wife had a flicker of feeling in her heart for someone else.

Holy Mother, Hear My Prayer

Thanksgiving 1957 quietly came and went. Vikki and Richter had separated. Now *he* was miserable and she was in Italy with her new "friend," also an Italian. Vikki said she would come for Christmas, and in her unfathomable world, Tom Richter would be coming with her. "He is still my husband," Vikki said indignantly to Tatiana. "Why the shock?"

Aunt Esther was not feeling well and remained in Barrington. She too was going to come for Christmas with Rosa. Now that there was no war, Alexander's Yuma duty was reduced to a small sporadic amount of classified intel. Last year, around the time of the Hungarian revolt, it got busy, but this year he satisfied his annual duty back in July when there was a ton of stuff for him to translate. Alexander always made sure his twenty-four days of service were finished by November because there were never enough days between Thanksgiving and Christmas for all the things Tatiana had to do.

Friday night after Thanksgiving, Tatiana was working, and Anthony and Alexander were together. They had pizza and Cokes, went to see *Around the World in Eighty Days*, and were on their way home in Alexander's truck. It was after ten.

Though Anthony may have wanted to be like his mother—and it was a certainly a fine thing to aspire to—he was often silent and inward with his father. Tonight they were by each other without speaking, one lost here, the other there.

Tatiana always tried to engage the boy, to draw him out, so Alexander tried—like her. "What'ya thinkin' about, bud?"

Anthony shrugged. "I was just wondering . . . if you had a mother."

"That's what you're thinking about? My mother? Not girls your own age?"

"I'm not talking about that with you, Dad."

A smiling Alexander said, "Of course I had a mother. You know I did. You saw pictures of her at Aunt Esther's house."

"Do you remember her?"

"I do."

"Mommy says you don't like to talk about her."

"She's right." Alexander didn't like to talk about his mother most of all, Dennis Burck from the State Department still a stain, a stab in his heart, reminding him of the things he could not fix. "But Mommy doesn't talk about her family either, does she?"

"Are you joking? She never stops. All she talks about is Luga. I've heard the stories so many times, it's almost become *my* childhood."

Alexander nodded in agreement. "Mommy does like to talk about Luga, doesn't she?"

Anthony stared ahead at the road. "She told me about Leningrad, too."

"She did?" Inside the truck got quiet.

"I didn't say she told it to me easy. I said she told me." Anthony's fingers twitched. "She even told me about you and her brother."

"She *did*?" Alexander nearly stopped driving.

"I didn't say she told it to me easy," Anthony repeated. They stopped speaking. Alexander's chest started to hurt.

"I'll talk to you," Alexander said. "What do you want to know?"

Anthony was looking at his father. "Was *your* mother pretty?"

"*I* thought so. She was very Italian. Dark curly hair, tall."

"What about your father?"

"He wasn't pretty," Alexander said dryly. "He was a Mayflower Pilgrim. Very New England."

"Did you love him?"

"Anthony, he was my father." Alexander tightened his hands around the wheel, frowning, glancing at his son. "Of course I did."

"No, no, Dad, I—I meant—" Anthony stammered, got flustered. "I meant, did you love him even though he was a Communist?"

"Yes, even though he was a Communist."

"But how?"

"He was infectiously idealistic," said Alexander. "He thought it would work; I think to the end he didn't understand why it didn't. On the surface it seemed so right! Everyone working only for the common good, everyone sharing the fruits of their labors. Suddenly there was no fruit. No one could understand why, least of all him."

"What about your mother?"

"She wasn't an idealist," Alexander said. "She was a romantic. She did it for him, believed in it for him."

"What about you—were you on his side or hers?"

"Initially his . . . he had a way about him. He could convince you of anything. He was a bit like your mother in that respect," said Alexander. "I wanted to be like him. But when I got to be about your age, I couldn't ignore the realities as well as he could. My mother and I both couldn't ignore them. So my father and I, you know, we butted heads."

Alexander and Anthony fell silent again, staring at the night road. They were coming down Shea to Pima, just desert around them. Alexander knew what Anthony was thinking—that in their house there was only one rule of law, and it wasn't Anthony's. Head butting was not allowed in their house. Thinking back, Alexander couldn't believe some of the things Harold Barrington allowed an adolescent Alexander to get away with. "My father was a civilian, not a soldier, Ant," Alexander said finally. "There's a world of difference."

"Did I say anything?" said Anthony. "And then they were arrested?"

"Then they were arrested."

"Mommy said you were arrested, too."

"Bud, I was arrested so many times, I lost count." Alexander smiled.

"She said you saw your father in prison right before he died?"

"Yes." They made a left on Pima. Soon they'd be home.

"Did you see your mother?" Anthony was looking at him intensely.

"No." And here it was. Here was the infernal moment of the burnt-out cigarette, singeing another hole in the soul. *Alexander had walked out of his house one morning to go to school, and when he came out, the mother was gone, the father was gone, the family was gone. He never saw or spoke to his mother again after that morning when he left so casually without even a "catch you later."*

"Your mom is once again unfortunately right about me," Alexander said. "This is the one thing I really *can't* talk about. Ask her if you want. Sorry, bud." Alexander tightened his hands around the wheel.

They retreated back into their corners of the bench.

"So how did you escape?" Anthony asked.

"Which time?"

"When you were seventeen."

"I jumped off a train off a bridge into the River Volga."

"A long way down?"

"A *long* way down." A hundred feet into the great unknown.

"And then you met Mommy?"

Alexander laughed. "Yes," he said. "I jumped into the river, details details details, typhus, army, war with Finland, and then I met Mommy."

"Typhus . . . is that why you're always telling me to shower?"

"I'm telling you to shower," Alexander said, "so you don't repel the girls when you're older." Though perhaps less showering and more repelling might level that field a little.

"Dad, please," said Anthony, "we're not having another one of your talks, are we?"

"No, son, no."

"Tell me how you met her." Anthony's eyes warmed in anticipation. His whole body turned on the bench seat to his father.

"I was walking down a Leningrad street, on patrol," said Alexander, "and she was sitting across the road on a bench eating ice cream."

"That's not how Mommy tells it," Anthony said teasingly. "She says you got on the bus for her and stalked her practically to Finland."

"The stalking was second. First she sat on a bench." Alexander smiled. "She was *really* enjoying her ice cream."

"What else?"

"That's it. She was singing. Humming. 'We'll Meet Again in Lvov, My Love and I.'" Alexander breathed in the distant melody of that song. He could barely remember how it went.

"And what did you do?"

"I crossed the street."

Anthony was staring at him. "But why?"

"You *have* seen your mother, Anthony, right?"

"Was she pretty at sixteen, too?"

"You could say that." Alexander blinked her away from his eyes so he could see the road.

"But there were other pretty girls in Leningrad, weren't there? Mommy says you had other lady friends before her."

Alexander shrugged, to convey what he couldn't say to his son, which was: there was a nightly parade, a pleasant buffet of girlsgirlsgirlsgirlsgirls—and then there was your mother.

Anthony was thoughtful. "I once heard you say to Mommy that you had been born twice. Once in 1919 and once with her. Was it on that street in Leningrad?"

"*I* said this?" Alexander did not remember. "When did I say that?"

"On Bethel Island. I was lying next to her. And you were whispering."

"You remember Bethel Island?" Alexander smiled with piercing nostalgia.

"Yes," Anthony said, not smiling. "You two were so happy then." He turned to the passenger window.

And Alexander stopped smiling.

After getting home, he walked in and sat on Anthony's bed. "Listen," he said, "are you going to be okay alone for a few hours if I go see Mommy at the hospital?"

"Why, what's wrong?"

"Nothing."

"Oh."

"I just . . . You're such a big guy now, fourteen and a half."

"I'll be fine, Dad. Go. Leave the pistol by my bed."

Alexander gave his son a poke. "Don't ever tell your mother I taught you how to shoot, or there will be no joy for either of us."

"You don't think she knows what we do when she is away?"

"Anthony."

"All right, all right."

"Be good. Call the hospital if there's a problem."

An hour later Alexander was at the reception desk at ER. Erin's face lit up. "Hi, Alexander," she said. "This is a surprise. Hold on, I'll page Tania. She's in surgery. She has a spleen rupture and a five-car accident."

In a moment the phone rang. "Your husband is here to see you," Erin said into the phone. She paused with a smile. "Yes, *your* husband."

Alexander saw an old man in rags shuffle limply and stop next to him. "Is she coming soon?" the man said, looking at Erin expectantly.

"I told you, she'll be here in a few minutes, Charlie," replied the nurse. "Take a seat."

Alexander looked inquisitively at Erin.

"Without her," she whispered, "he can't stay sober."

A mother walked up carrying in a boy not much older than nine. "We've been waiting so long," the mother said in a strident voice. "He needs her."

"She'll be here in a minute," Erin said, whispering to Alexander, "I should say, take a number, shouldn't I?"

Alexander thought of leaving.

But the next minute through the latched double doors came Tatiana, and her eyes were on him and for him and there was a smile on her face. If he'd had a cap, he would have taken it off and held it in his hands.

"Hey," she said, coming close.

"Hey."

She pressed against him briefly. "What's wrong? You okay?"

"I am now." Alexander nearly shuddered. "You busy?"

"Swamped as usual. What's the matter?" She peered at him, her palm on his chest.

"Nothing."

"Oh." Tatiana paused, chewed her lip. "I have maybe a half-hour before the next surgery. Want to go get a cup of coffee?"

What I want is to meander eight kilometers down the canals with you from Kirov to your Fifth Soviet door. I want to get on the tram with you, the bus with you, sit in the Italian Gardens with you. That is what I want. I will take the cup of coffee in your hospital cafeteria.

Erin cleared her throat and motioned with her eyes over to the seats. Tatiana glanced over. "Who's first?"

"Husband first"—Erin smiled—"then Charlie."

"I'll be right back," she said to Alexander and walked over to Charlie.

Alexander watched Charlie's face. It softened, the smile curled up on his dried, scabbed lips. She sat next to him and took his hand. "Charlie, what's bothering you today?" she said solemnly in her sing song voice.

"Want a drink so bad, Nurse Tania," he stammered.

"Yes, but you don't want to be unconscious under the cars again, do you? You don't want to be brought here on a stretcher with your leg broken again, do you?"

Charlie's mouth mulled. "You'd take care of me."

"Charlie, I'm not here every day, you know that. And you see how many people I have to take care of," said Tatiana. "Now you can do this. Have you been going to your meetings?"

After spending five minutes with him, she walked three seats over to the patiently waiting boy and the impatiently waiting mother. The boy was having spasms again in his legs, crippled by muscular dystrophy. Tatiana rubbed his legs and talked to him, and Alexander watched the boy's stricken face and the mother's resentful face.

When Tatiana came back to him, Alexander said, "Twenty minutes left."

But as they were walking past examination room Number 7 on the way to the cafeteria, a young girl inside was crying for her mother. Apparently the girl had been found in an empty apartment down on Baseline, the mother gone, the apartment filthy. Social Services and the police were trying to locate another living relative.

"We're all trying to find our mothers," Alexander whispered before Tatiana went into the exam room, replaced the glucose IV bag and sat by the four-year-old until she stopped crying.

In the cafeteria, they got coffee and sat side by side, their arms touching. He took her hand under the table. "Five-car accident, huh?"

"I'm telling you, this drinking and driving business is nasty." Tatiana shook her head. "People don't know the laws of motion. They should be required to take a physics course before they set foot in a bar or inside a car."

"But of course they should." Alexander smiled. "Which laws of motion are these now?" With his thumb he wiped a piece of who knew what off her eyebrow.

"Objects in motion—say, blood in the veins—will stay in motion even when suddenly compelled to stop by an outside force. You won't believe how tough sudden deceleration is on the veins."

"You and your physics. You're not racing bikes in the hospital, are you?"

"We did that yesterday," Tatiana said, smiling lightly, "but the unwitting ambulance driver we were racing got *real* upset."

"I bet." Alexander was staring at her. Her Russian moon face was drawn tonight, her eyes were opaque and her mouth was pale, as if she'd been breathing too much through it while running from critical tent to terminal tent. He adjusted the strands of her hair back under her cap.

"What's the matter, darling?" she said softly, placing her hand on his face. "What's wrong with my husband that I need to fix?"

Alexander lowered his head. But before he could tell her all the things that were wrong with her husband—one of the minor ones being that he could not sleep alone one more Friday night, not *one* more—a male voice from behind them said, "Tania?" It was Dr. Bradley. Alexander let go of Tatiana. "Sorry to interrupt, but it's time," Bradley said, glancing at Alexander. "We're due in scrubs in three minutes."

They got up. "Yes, I'll be right there," said Tatiana, taking a last sip of coffee. "Dr. Bradley, you remember Alexander, my husband?"

Alexander shook hands with the doctor, who went to wait by the door.

Tatiana patted Alexander on the chest. "I'll see you tomorrow morning, honey," she said, and made to go. He didn't move and said nothing. She stopped, studied him, this way, that, considered him. Then she stepped in and lifted her face.

Blocking her with his body so she was hidden from Bob Hope's view, Alexander bent to her upturned face, and kissed her soft pale pink parted lips.

"I'll see you, babe," he said.

And then he watched her rush out, talking about surgeries and sutures. Dr. Bradley opened the door for her and prodded her out with his hand on her back. Alexander emphatically threw their coffee cups away. Before he left, he sat in the waiting room next to Charlie, who reeked something terrible. Alexander had to move two seats over. Charlie turned to him, gummed toothlessly, nodded his head, and said, "That's right. If you sit long enough, sometimes she comes again."

"Does she?"

"If she has time. Sometimes I sit all night. I fall asleep, I wake up and she is sitting by me. I go when she goes."

Alexander remained in the chair another thirty minutes, watching the doors. But Tatiana didn't come again, and he went home.

That Saturday morning he said to her as he was getting ready for work and she was in bed, getting ready for sleep, "Tania, is Bradley the doctor in charge of ER?"

"Just the night shift."

"He works only at night?"

"No. He does work the Friday graveyard. Why?"

"No reason," said Alexander. "I didn't remember until last night, but is my memory wrong or is David Bradley the same doctor who came to see you five years ago when Dudley was killed?"

"*Was* killed? I note with irony your use of the passive voice," said a smiling Tatiana from the bed. "Yes, I think Bradley was. Why?"

"No reason." Alexander was thoughtful as he fixed his tie. "Is he the one who looked at the marks on the back of your neck and then got all flustered like a schoolgirl?"

"Shura, I don't know," said Tatiana. "How do you remember that?"

"I didn't remember it. Until just now."

"Why are you remembering it just now?"

"No reason."

"That's the third time you said that."

"Is it? I gotta go. I have a meeting at nine. Don't forget we're getting the Christmas tree this afternoon." It was the end of November. The Christmas season was just beginning, but they liked to have their tree up for as long as possible. Had Bradley been carrying a torch for his wife for five years? Alexander wouldn't have thought about it again, wouldn't have cared, except that he couldn't get her laughing head out of his chest, her throwing back her head, her hair, and heartily, throatily, lustily laughing.

Winter Wonderland

Two days later on Monday, Alexander and Anthony were once again impatiently waiting for Tatiana to come home. Alexander was bubbling inside. Anthony wouldn't eat without her, and so Alexander sat like a stone on the couch and read the paper. Those lights in the desert valley sure were twinkling. And every one of them was another damn roadblock in the thirty-seven miles separating the hospital from their front door. Anthony had set the table, the bread was ready, the butter had been taken out of the ice box, the beef bourguignon she had made was heated up.

Tatiana walked in the door at *nine thirty*. "Sorry, I'm late," she said.

Alexander got up from the couch—and said nothing. He did glare at her until he saw how wiped out she was. "Iris was late again," said Tatiana, taking off her coat, putting her bag down. Yes, Alexander thought. But there was once a time when you punched the card and popped the clutch at 7:01, and didn't care how late Iris was. "I have more responsibilities now," she said.

"Did I say a word?" snapped Alexander.

The tips of her fingers were trembling. She barely ate. There was a small problem with Anthony at school, but Alexander didn't know how to bring it up seeing how she was.

"Ant, Shura, you guys really should eat before I get home," Tatiana said. "This is too late for you to have dinner. Please. Don't wait. It makes me feel too bad, thinking of you sitting here waiting for me. Just eat in the future."

"You want your family to eat without you three nights a week?" Alexander said quietly.

And she, *nodding!* said, "I'd rather you eat without me than eat this late. This is terrible."

"Yes, it is," Alexander said.

She didn't lift her eyes.

Anthony came to his usual Phyrric rescue. Clearing his throat, he said, "Mom, don't be angry, okay?"

"Great introduction." Tatiana lifted her eyes to her son. "What did you do?"

"The principal wants to see you first thing tomorrow."

Tatiana leveled her gaze on him. "And there I was," she said, "going to go Christmas shopping for you first thing tomorrow, Anthony Alexander Barrington."

"Sorry," he said sheepishly. "I got into a fight, Mom."

She did a double take. "You what?"

"I'm fine, thank you," said Anthony. "But the other kid has a broken nose."

Tatiana glared at Alexander.

"What are you giving *me* dirty looks for?" Alexander said. "I didn't break the kid's nose."

"Is his name Damian Mesker, by any chance?" asked Tatiana.

"Yes! God, how did you know?"

"Because we set his nose at ER this afternoon. Anthony, I thought you two were friends."

"Mom, I didn't mean to break his nose. We just got into a fight."

"Where are your marks?"

"Well . . ." Anthony said, "I didn't get hit. He went for me but I ducked."

"I see." Once again she glared at Alexander.

"What?" he said, shrugging. "You want your only child to stand there and take it?"

"It's all my fault," Anthony said quickly. "Don't be upset with Dad."

"Clean up, Ant." Tatiana got up from the table. "Alexander, would you like to have your cigarette outside—now?"

Alexander gave his son a shove as he went out. "See what you did?" he whispered.

On the deck, Tatiana said, "Shura, what are you thinking teaching your boy to fight but not to have sense? He'll break somebody's nose now, but you know better than anyone that tomorrow it'll be front teeth. And he did not use equal force. The other boy just pushed Ant."

"Anthony has to know how to defend himself," said Alexander. "The broken nose was an accident."

"You're impossible, that's what you are," said Tatiana. "Now I have to call the boy's family. That's another hour gone by, and it's already after ten."

"Yes," said Alexander, sitting back against the bench, smoking, looking out onto the dark desert. "It is very late, isn't it?"

After Anthony was made to call Damien and apologize, Tatiana talked a long time to Damien's mother.

When Alexander came inside the bedroom, he found Tatiana asleep on top of the quilt in her uniform. He sat on the edge of the bed and watched her. In the cauldron inside his chest, tenderness swirled around, jumbled and swallowed by hostility. He shook her leg.

"Oh God," she muttered, waking up. "I'm not alive tonight."

"As always," said Alexander. "At least tomorrow you have a day off."

Quickly she undressed, stumbled to the bathroom, stumbled out, and fell into bed, her hair still in a bun, turning her face to him for a kiss, eyes closed.

"Do you want me to rub you?" Alexander whispered. She smelled faintly of musk oil that seemed to have permanently soaked into her skin, of lilac soap, of mint on her breath. His hand crept down her spine. Tatiana muttered something, groaned and was asleep. Alexander lay behind her, against her warmth, caressing her up and down, her soft round buttocks that fit so nicely into his hands, her soft thighs. Her skin was like a baby's. This is what he imagined baby's skin might feel like. He fondled her breasts that fit so nicely into his hands, gently pulled on her nipples, making her stir even in sleep, glided into the slope of her waist, rubbed her smooth stomach, stroked her fine fair hair. His hand prodded . . . but then he stopped. Leaning over her, his hand fanning her face, Alexander kissed her temple. Eventually he fell unhappily asleep.

In the morning he reached for her but she had to be at the principal's office first thing. "Tania," he said, sitting down to breakfast,

"I'll be home around twelve thirty for lunch." He raised his eyebrows.

"Oh, Shura," Tatiana said, pouring him a cup of coffee and placing a croissant on his plate. "I . . . did I forget to tell you?" She laughed a little. "I'm not going to be here in the afternoon. After meeting with the principal, I was going to buy groceries, Christmas decorations, and then . . . um, I have to run to the hospital for a few hours."

Alexander stopped drinking his coffee, stopped looking at her. For a few seconds he did not speak. Finally he said, "Anthony, can you wait outside for your mother? She'll be right there."

"Mom, we have to go. Mrs. Larkin is waiting."

"Wait outside for your mother, I said."

Casting an anxious look at Tatiana, Anthony left.

As soon as the door closed, Alexander turned to her. He was still sitting at the table. "What are you doing? Tell me, because I have no idea."

"Honey," Tatiana said softly, "you're working anyway. What difference does it make?"

"All the fucking difference in the world, Tatiana," said Alexander. "You're not sitting in an architect's office, say mine, answering phones. Don't tell me you're working on your only day off till the weekend."

"Well, I didn't know you wanted to come for lunch," she said apologetically. "You don't usually come to have lunch with me anymore."

They stared at each other for a short moment. "So?" he said. "I wanted to come today."

"Anthony is going to be late for school," said Tatiana. "And the principal is waiting."

"Why are you going to the hospital? Are you picking up someone's shift?"

"No," she said, clearing her throat, her hands fidgeting. "It's the children's clinic at St. Monica's Mission. They don't have enough people to run it. They asked me to help, just for the Christmas season. They're paying me double for four hours—"

"I don't give a fuck if they give you ten thousand dollars!" exclaimed Alexander. "How many times am I going to have to say it, we don't need the money—" Suddenly he broke off, narrowing his eyes on her. "But you already know that," he said slowly. "Let me ask you, who's running this clinic with you?"

"What do you mean?"

"I mean, is there an attending doctor? Or is it just you by your lonesome?"

"Yes, it's mostly me. When I need extra help, sometimes Dr. Bradley—"

Alexander had heard all he needed to. He raised his hand and got up from the table.

"I run that clinic, Shura. Only when I need extra help . . ."

"You're unbelievable."

"We can't . . . we can't do this now," Tatiana said faintly. "Anthony is waiting."

"He certainly is," said Alexander. "I'm waiting, too. You know what I'm waiting for? To have a full-time wife. You know how long I've been waiting? Since 1949. When—if ever—do you think I'm going to get that?"

"You're not being fair," Tatiana whispered, lowering her head so he wouldn't see tears in her eyes. But Alexander saw. And he also saw Charlie's eyes, and Erin's eyes, and the boy's and his mother's eyes, and Dr. Bradley's hand, and small Anthony jumping up and down for her when they were on the boat coming back from Berlin, and he saw her raised, naked hips in his fanned-out hands, and he lowered his own eyes and turned away from her.

Alexander turned his gaze, his head, his heart away from her.

Swinging his hand across the table, he flung his cup of coffee down onto the floor, where it shattered and spilled. Grabbing his wallet, he left with a great satisfying slam of the trailer door.

When he came home at six, Tatiana was home, the house was decorated comfortingly for Christmas, dinner was made, and the candles were burning. She made beef stroganoff, one of his favorites. She served him, poured his drink, served Anthony. They sat and broke their bread.

"Mom," said Anthony, "how did you manage to put up all our decorations so quickly? The fake snow around the windowsills is an especially nice touch. Doesn't it look great, Dad?"

"It does." Alexander's eyes were on his plate.

"How's the stroganoff, Shura?"

"Good." His eyes were on his plate.

"How was your day today?"

"Good." His eyes were on his plate.

"I love Christmas," Anthony said, bursting into song, *It's my favorite time of the year!* Are we going to trim the tree this weekend?"

They ate with their son as their buffer, talking with him and through him. She made them bananas with rum and vanilla ice cream for dessert. Afterward Tatiana and Anthony cleaned up, while Alexander disappeared in the bedroom. He came out twenty minutes later, dressed in clean gray slacks, a clean white shirt, a gray tie. He was showered and clean shaven. He put on his jacket.

Tatiana wiped her hands on the dishtowel.

"I'm going out," Alexander said.

"Where are you going?"

"Out."

"On a Tuesday?"

"That's right."

Tatiana opened her mouth, but Anthony was on the couch pretending to watch TV, and so she turned on her heels and gave him the back of her head.

Alexander met up at Maloney's with duck-billed, rockabillied Johnny-boy, who was on a desperate prowl. Problem was, as Johnny put it, he was looking for a "week-long wife." He had no interest in getting married, but all the girls, of which there weren't enough, wanted nothing *but* to get married. All the servicemen had come home long ago, and now it was a buyer's market—unfortunately for Johnny—with one girl for every five boys who wanted her. The girl didn't have to put out until she was sure of Johnny's seriousness of purpose, which he faked as best he could, being cocky and wily and a fast talker, but the conflict never went away, and Johnny never tired of talking about it. So this Tuesday night, he and Alexander talked and talked about it, and about their houses and their crews, and their customers, and then Johnny said, "Is everything all right, man?"

"Yes, fine."

"You're never out on a Tuesday night. Is Mrs. Barrington working or something?"

"No, no." Alexander stared into his drink.

"Well, don't look," said Johnny, "but there are two young ladies eyeballing who I'm hoping is me."

Alexander glanced over. Johnny smiled at the girls, who smiled back and then ignored him. He sighed. "It seems so easy. They smile. Why is the rest so hard?"

"Because you're overthinking it," said Alexander. "The hard part is getting them to look at you in the first place. If they're eyeing you from the next table, the hard part's done."

"Hard part's done?"

"Absofuckinglutely," said Alexander. "Call the bartender, ask him to send them a round of drinks."

"And then?"

"You'll see."

Johnny did. A few minutes later, drinks in hand, the two women sauntered over to Johnny and Alexander.

"Thanks for the drinks, gentlemen," they said, all smiles.

"You're welcome," said Johnny, glancing approvingly at Alexander. "But don't give *him* any credit; he sent no drinks."

"No?" said one of them. He glanced at her, then at his beer. "You're Alexander Barrington, aren't you?" she said.

"I am. Who wants to know?"

She stuck out her hand. "I'm Carmen Rosario. Remember, me and my husband talked to you last month about building in Glendale?"

"Oh, yeah." Alexander didn't remember. "So what happened with that?"

"We're still thinking about it. Actually, I wanted to make an appointment to meet with you again, perhaps see some of your spec homes. We're now thinking of building in Paradise Valley instead. We've got some land down in Chandler we've been trying to sell so we can build a little more centrally."

"Call the office." Alexander gave her his card. "I'll be glad to sit down with you and . . ."

"Cubert."

"Cubert." He and Johnny exchanged a glance. *Cubert?*

"So, girls, where are your husbands?" asked Johnny. He was so out of control. He just said the first thing that came into his head.

The younger girl, whose name was Emily, tittered and said she wasn't married. Carmen said her husband was in Las Vegas. Alexander smirked into his beer. Las Vegas! But no, Cubert apparently was a corporate real estate agent and had a lot of business there. "He's also an EMT trainee at PMH. Where are *your* wives, gentlemen?"

"Alexander's is home, and *I* don't have one," said Johnny, pseudo-plaintively. He had had too much to drink and wasn't thinking even one pathetic move ahead because he said, "But I'm *loooking* for one."

Emily immediately backed off—as in, took two steps back.

Carmen didn't. "So are you Tuesday night regulars at this dive?"

"No, we're Friday night regulars," said Johnny.

"Oh, yeah?" said Carmen, smiling at Alexander. She was statuesque, dark-haired, put-together, coiffed, made-up, well-dressed, extremely large-breasted. "Where do you two live?"

"I live far," said Alexander, putting down his empty glass on the bar. "And I've got to be going."

Johnny pulled him aside. "You can't leave yet!" he whispered. "I think I said something wrong, scared Emily off."

"You *think*?" said Alexander. "Probably telling her you're trawling for a wife was not the smartest thing you could've said. Oh, well, slick, better luck next time. Try the other one—she seems more friendly. After all, Cubert's in *Las Vegas*."

They laughed quietly. "Friendly to you, maybe," Johnny said. "You're indifferent and yet she is being flirty with you, why?"

"That's why."

Johnny convinced Alexander to stay for another drink.

They all went to sit at a darkened table in the corner. Carmen sat next to Alexander. Quickly he drank his beer, his fifth of the night. Carmen volunteered a lot of information about herself. She asked him questions about building a house, designing it, about stone or stucco, flat roofs or pitched. She heard flat roofs were more energy-efficient; was that true?

"That may be true," said Alexander. "But there are only two kinds of flat roofs. Ones that leak and ones that don't leak *yet*."

Oh, how merrily Carmen laughed, jiggling her backcombed head, as if *Alexander* were Bob Hope! "You're an architect, a home builder. You're a jack of many trades, aren't you?"

"And you don't know the half of it, girls," Johnny said, grinning. "Tell them about all the other things you were, man."

Alexander got up. "I *really* have to go. Thanks for the drink, Johnny. Nice to meet you, ladies."

Carmen got up, too. "So I'll call you then, and we'll arrange something?"

"Not me," said Alexander. "Call Linda. She is my arranger."

"Well, it was *very* nice to meet you, Alexander." Nodding her breasts at him and smiling, she gave him her red-nailed hand.

Alexander drove home carefully. He'd had a little too much to drink.

At the house, the porch light shone for him. The door was locked. Tatiana didn't like to lock the doors when he wasn't home; she said it seemed like locking him out, but after Dudley, Alexander instilled in her the importance of dead bolt locking both doors at all times and drawing the shades while she was by herself in the middle of the desert wilderness.

When he came in, she was sitting at the kitchen table waiting for him, drumming her fingers. The house was dark, just the stove light was on. Alexander didn't say anything as he shut and locked the door and took off his jacket. When he went to get some water from the fridge, she said, "Why are you going out drinking on a Tuesday night?"

"Why not?"

"What are you doing, Alexander?"

"What are *you* doing, Tatiana?" His voice was raised. It was the liquor.

She kept hers quieter. "Why are you fighting with me?"

"I'm not fighting with you. I walked in the door. I said nothing."

"I know you're upset. But you think the reasonable way to deal with it is for you to be away from me drinking at a bar?"

"Oh, is that what we'd be doing if I was home?" said Alexander. "Dealing with it?"

"Away from me drinking on a Tuesday!"

"And why not? You're away from me sixty hours a week."

"I work!" she yelled.

In two strides Alexander loomed over her. "First of all," he said, "do I seem to you like I'm in the mood to be yelled at? How many times have I told you—don't raise your fucking voice to me. And second of all—I don't want to hear about your work *ever* again. Got that?"

Looking up at him from the chair, Tatiana pulled his hand away from her face. Her short silk robe was coming loose. "Soldier, what are you doing?" she said tremulously. "Stand down."

"You don't tell *me* to stand down," Alexander said loudly. "I'll stand down when I want. Since you do whatever the fuck you want." He turned and walked into the bedroom.

Slowly Tatiana followed him. "Can we just talk about this reasonably—"

"We're not going to talk about it at all." He was at his closet. "Tell me—have you been so out of it, you haven't noticed our days have been getting harder? Our minutes have been getting harder?"

"If they're getting harder it's because you're making them harder," said Tatiana.

"Oh, I'm doing that, am I?" Alexander ripped off his tie.

Tatiana sat tensely on the edge of the bed. The sashes of her robe had come half-undone; he could see a glimpse of her breasts, her navel, her blonde mound, her white thighs. "Yes," she said. "You going out drinking, coming home late and not sober, acting like this, that's making it harder."

He unhooked his cuff links, took off his white shirt, his white tank, and stood before her bare to the waist. "Well, you know something?" Alexander said. "I'm done being nice. Completely done."

"It's just for December," Tatiana said. "One month, and then—"

"What did I say?" he yelled. "I don't want to talk about it!"

"Stop yelling! God!"

"Are you angry? Want to take it out on me?" Alexander tapped his chest. "Come on, babe. You want a fight? You've come to the right place."

She blinked. "I don't want to fight with you, what are you talking about?"

He unbuckled his belt, pulled it out of the loops.

"You can't be this upset with me, Shura," said Tatiana, "for four hours at a children's clinic. Is it something else—"

Not letting her finish, Alexander raised his hand and swung the belt down. She gasped as it whistled through the air and hit the bed in a thud next to her bare thigh. "Tania!" he said, bent over her. "I said I *didn't* want to talk about it. Which part of that didn't you understand?"

"Oh, what's *wrong* with you?" Tatiana said in a frightened voice, nearly falling back on the bed, her hands barely supporting her.

"Did I say, don't rattle me?" Her robe had come open.

"Yes." Quietly.

"Did I say, don't speak about your fucking work to me?"

"Yes." Quieter and quieter. "Shh."

"Don't tell me to shh. You shh. Because the *very* next time you open your mouth," he said through his teeth, "I'm going to lose my temper." He was still standing enormous over her, half naked himself.

Tatiana edged her way off the bed. "Excuse me," she said in a small voice. "I need to get past."

As always, her tiny, naked vulnerability with her trembling erect nipples pointing up at him brought out the worst in him when his temper was this hot at his throat. Her surrender didn't quell him; just the opposite, it incensed him; and incensed his concupiscence also. She was afraid? She had every right to be. Sometimes he was just plain not nice, and knew it, and didn't care. Unable to restrain himself, Alexander did not let her go past.

Her robe flung off, his clothes off, blankets and pillows off the bed, he laid her on her back in front of him, straddling her, holding her wrists tight above her head. Squirming slightly, she said nothing, raising her face to him, raising her breasts to him. "Shura," she whispered.

"Don't Shura me." He flipped her by her legs onto her stomach, pressing her into the bed, pressing her lower back, her hips, her upper thighs into the bed.

"Shura," Tatiana repeated, muffled in the sheets.

Restraining her with one hand, Alexander unwrapped her braid with the other, fingers pulling through the strands, letting her hair spill out. "Are you too tired tonight, Tania? Barely awake? Would you like to put on some pajamas? Are you not in the mood?" he whispered into her neck, slipping his fingers between her legs, and groaning.

After a few moments, she moaned in return. "Let me turn around."

"No." The flat palms that had been spanning her back were now spanning the backs of her thighs. "I want it my way, not your way." He spread her legs and knelt between them, leaning over her prone body, gripping her hair, sliding inside her. It felt so good that he stayed a while, but then withdrew, opened her up a little more, and pressed himself between her buttocks.

Oh dear God . . . wait, Shura, wait . . . Tatiana whispered hoarsely. *Let me touch you.*

"No," whispered Alexander as he guided himself into her, slowly, but not that slowly. "I'm going to touch *you*. Lie still."

Her hands grasped the sheets, the edge of the mattress, the rattling brass rails of the headboard. He continued to push himself in.

Shura . . . wait . . . I'll—let me turn around and you can—

"No." He was fully inside. He took a breath, still so upset with her. His face was in her neck. She smelled of vanilla . . . of burnt caramel sugar . . . of cream . . . of rum.

Both his hands moved up to grip her forearms. He pulled out and thrust back in.

The brass rails nearly came apart as she cried out.

He pulled out and thrust back in.

In out, in out, his every thrust punctuated by her jagged cries.

He didn't stop moving, or whispering to her.

She was panting, perspiring, her neck, her face wet from the great tension.

Pressing her head into the sheets, sucking the rear slope of her shoulders, his body over her, *don't move, Tania,* oh but he moved.

He had to stop. He couldn't believe it, but he was about to come—unheard of this fast, especially after drinking. She was always too much for him like this, in such exquisite distress, on her stomach, face in sheets, blonde mane all over, gasping, grasping. Slowing down, taking shallow breaths, propping up, Alexander tried to get control of himself, but it was no use. He was done for.

Panting he lay collapsed on top of her afterward as she continued to heave underneath him in small whimpers. His face was in her hair.

The next morning when Alexander opened his eyes, Tatiana was already up and in uniform. They didn't speak for a few minutes. She wasn't smiling as she eyed him. "Do you ever intend to tell me where you were last night," she finally asked, "or should I stop asking and draw my own conclusions?"

He stretched. "I had a drink with Johnny."

"Ah. Your nice, ever-searching, ever single, bar-hopping, doll-hunting friend Johnny-boy. You're teaching him a few things you know?"

Alexander rubbed his eyes. "Um—isn't it a little early for this?"

"Last night you weren't interested in talking."

He got a hot leap in his stomach as he sense-remembered her last night. All his five senses remembered her. He didn't feel just a *beat* of arousal, he felt a pounding.

Tatiana left the room and Alexander got up to go wash. She came back with a cup of coffee for him. "Don't forget about the party tonight."

"What party?" He took the coffee from her hands.

"The Christmas party at the hospital," Tatiana said slowly, frowning.

"Oh. Yeah." Now Alexander remembered. "I don't want to go."

"We have to."

"Perhaps you haven't noticed," said Alexander, "but I'm not in a party mood."

"I can't help but notice." Tatiana lowered her gaze. "Still, we have to go."

"We don't."

"Alexander," she said, staring up at him, "are you telling me that you don't want to go to the Christmas party at my hospital, to which all the spouses come?"

"Finally I'm making myself clear."

"Fine, suit yourself," she said, grabbing her bag and walking away. "But I'm going."

"Great, go," Alexander said into her white-uniformed back. "You do all sorts of things I don't want you to, why stop at a party?"

Tatiana stopped at the bedroom door. After watching him warily, with a great sigh she slowly came back to him. Alexander stood in front of her, angry and naked, and morning-and-Tatiana-inflamed. She put down her nurse's bag.

"Shh," she said softly, lifting her face to him, as her hands lowered and took hold of him. "Shh. Come on." She stroked him. "Come on . . . out of the battle zone. Weapons down, soldier."

He wanted her on her knees in front of him. His palm nearly went on top of her head. On the one hand, such gratification. But on the other hand—"It's after six. You're going to be late for work." Alexander with inhuman effort forced himself to pull her hands off him. "Run along now."

"You're going to come, right?" She kissed his chest.

"Under protest."

"Of course."

As soon as Alexander walked into the common room on the third floor of the hospital and took one look at his wife, he knew the night was going to lead to no good. Tatiana had this uncanny ability: be exhausted and raw like twine when she came home, but when she was at a hospital party, surrounded by her friends, it was as if she had done nothing all day but soak in a hot bath. She was refreshed and flushed, and as Alexander walked in, she was standing with a group of people, one of them Dr. Bradley, and she was throwing her head back in delight.

He must be quite a joker, quite the wit, Alexander thought, making his way to her, something ugly twitching inside his heart. She just can't stop the pealing when she's around him.

Her hair was loosely braided, there was a long curled tuft at the back that bobbed when she laughed and the red velvet ribbons that barely held the braid together bobbed and shook, too. Gold hair strands fell around her face. She was wearing makeup and her mouth was glossy red. To match the mouth, she was wearing a show-stopping new dress in flaming Christmas red—Alexander guessed trying to get as far away as she could from nursing white. The dress had a fitted bodice stacked with breasts and taffeta, taffeta that zigzagged into a swing skirt full of gathered tulle and netting layers. Underneath she wore a starched crinoline petticoat he could hear crinkle every time she moved. He bet he wasn't the only one who could hear it. The dress had puffed bolero sleeves—as though she were a flamenco dancer, about to dance the salsa and sing "*La Bruja*". The boned corset made her waist even more tiny and her breasts even more prominent than usual. Her four-inch-high red slingbacks were satin and her legs, in seamed nylon stockings, were lovely.

She was lovely.

Alexander said nothing about the unbelievable dress, not a word. While he shook hands all around, Tatiana got him a drink and some food. He joined in the ongoing conversation regarding the future of the medical profession in the United States. There was heavy overcrowding at hospitals because of the baby boom. The hospitals couldn't cope, the maternity clinics couldn't cope. Somebody asked why, if the building industry could cope with the demand for more housing, couldn't more hospitals be built with larger maternity wings? Alexander said that in the eight years they had lived in Arizona, a million new houses went up, while Phoenix still only had the one hospital.

"Well, perhaps you should design and build us a new hospital, Alexander," said Carolyn. "To help with the baby overcrowding. And then your wife could run it."

"A hospital just for Tania!" said Bradley with a laugh, looking at Tatiana. "What an idea!"

"Yes, but did you know," said Carolyn, "that more and more women are choosing to have their babies at home with the help of a midwife? I decided to take a course and I'm now a registered midwife, thank you very much." She smiled. "No more Tupperware for me. Tania," she said, "you won't *believe* how much money I make in my spare time. You should become a midwife. You'd be very good at it, you know."

"Of course she would," said Bradley. "Tania is good at everything."

Tatiana demurred from an answer; Alexander demurred from

so much as glancing at her, curtly excusing himself out of the idiotic conversation and going to get another drink.

"Well, hello there, Alexander!"

He turned. It was the woman from yesterday—Carmen.

"Oh, hello," he said coolly, stepping away and glancing across the room. Tatiana was otherwise engaged and hadn't looked his way. "What are you doing here?"

"I told you, Cubert, my husband, is training to be an EMT here in his spare time." She tutted. "Because he's got so much of it. But more important, what are *you* doing here?"

"My wife works here."

"Your wife works? Which one is she?"

"Which one's Cubert?" he asked, not pointing out Tatiana.

"Right over there." Cubert was a little skinny nervous thing, motioning for Carmen from the other side of the room. Tutting, she ignored him, taking out a cigarette. "Have you got a light?"

Flicking on his lighter, Alexander brought it to Carmen's cigarette. She cupped his hand as she lit up, as if there were an Arizona supercell tornado swirling through the common room at Phoenix Memorial Hospital.

Of course it was at this very moment that Alexander lifted his eyes and saw Tatiana across the floor, her darkening gaze on him.

"So I called your secretary," Carmen said, puffing, smiling, "but she said you're busy until after the New Year. Is there anything you can do about that?"

"If Linda says I'm booked, I'm booked." Alexander stepped away. "I have to go. Excuse me—Carmen, right?"

Cubert was getting more insistent in calling for her, and an exasperated Carmen rushed off.

And then Tatiana wouldn't speak to him. Alexander asked her if she wanted a drink. She said no. He asked her if she wanted some more food. She said no. He stopped asking and she moved away, going to stand next to Bradley, Carolyn, and Erin. She drank, ebbed, flowed, and then said something and they burst into laughter, and Bradley took Tatiana's hand, bowed before her theatrically, and kissed it.

He did it as a joke, everyone smiled and went on talking as if it were nothing, everyone except Alexander, that is, who walked over to Tatiana, took her carefully by her arm, pulled her slightly away with an "excuse me" and said, "I'm leaving."

"It's only eleven."

"Seems *plenty* late, don't you think?"

She wasn't looking at him. "All right, go," she said. "I'll be home a little later."

"You're not coming?"

"I am . . . later."

His hand on her bolero sleeve squeezed harder.

"It's fine. You go." Tatiana pulled herself away. "This way you'll still have time to make your bar rounds." Her mouth was tight. And then she looked up at him. "When you need to stay and talk to me, you run out for a drink with your boys who go to meet the girls. If you had any decency you would stay with your wife for thirty more minutes at her Christmas party." The starched crinoline crackling, she turned to walk away, making a little dismissing motion with her hand. "But you go to it, little barfly, fly away. Shoo."

Alexander stared hard at *her*!—her loose blonde hair swirling in a wild wind inside his heart.

He left.

Trouble waited for her at home, Tatiana knew.

The porch light was on. Alexander was sitting out back. Well, at least they would have this one dressed. Tatiana was helpless during the naked arguments in the bedroom. She always lost the fight and had to plead for understanding, agree to anything, acquiesce to anything, to everything. It wasn't even acquiescing, it was just complete submission. Like yesterday. She was never right in the bedroom, which was why he liked to fight in it so much.

The house was unlocked—because the man of the house was home. She came in, dropped her purse on the shelf, and went to check on Anthony. He was sleeping deeply.

After taking off her cashmere ivory coat and red heels, Tatiana made herself a cup of tea but couldn't go out back. She went on the front deck instead and sipped her tea, shivering in her Christmas dress.

Alexander was on the rear deck with his back to the house, and Tatiana was on the front deck with her back to the house.

Finally, her tea long finished, she walked through, opened the back door and stepped out. Only a small yellow light shone over the door. Alexander was smoking, drinking a beer, and didn't turn her way. She debated going to sit at the table in the corner across from him. He didn't like her close when he was upset. But she knew he needed her close when he was upset, and so she sat by him on the rocking bench, not touching him, but close enough to smell the leather of his WWII bomber jacket and the cigarettes and beer on his breath. He looked so handsome tonight when he came to the party, his short black hair in a clean sheen, face freshly shaven, dark suit pressed, white shirt crisp. And now he was in his black long johns that he knew she loved and his bomber jacket that he knew she loved, his long limbs spread out on the bench, his body so wide, and so grim tonight.

"It's cold out, no?" Tatiana said. "The desert in the winter is not always hospitable."

"Yes, it's ice everywhere."

"No, it isn't, Alexander." So he wasn't wasting time. "Come on, what's been the matter with you?"

"Nothing's been the matter with *me*."

"How in the world do you know Cubert's wife?"

"She and her husband came to look at some spec homes last month. But what does *she* have to do with anything? Tania, women have been dressing up, coming close, flirting, asking me for a light, for a house, for a job for years. They were on the boat in Coconut Grove, they are here in Scottsdale. Who cares?"

"Shura, where are we going wrong?" Tatiana whispered. "You and I are not allowed to go wrong anywhere—what are we doing that's not right?"

"I'm going to tell you what," Alexander replied, finally turning to face her. "Because obviously I have *not* been making myself clear the last eight years. What's not right in our house," he said, "is you putting your work, your hospital, the things you do, the *other* things you do before me and our marriage."

"Alexander, I don't put anything before you," she said. "I put up with everything—"

"*Put up* with me? Are you fucking kidding me?"

"Wait, wait, I misspoke," she said, her hands fanning out, trying to steady him. "I meant I never cease to be what I've always been for you. And as you know," she said, with slight color coming to her cheeks, "I never deny you."

"Tania, you're not home for sixty to sixty-five hours in your week!" said Alexander. "You deny me those hours, don't you? The hours you *are* home you are no fucking good to anybody. Have you seen yourself lately? You're worse than ever."

"No good to anybody, are you *joking*?" she exclaimed, and suddenly her hands went down as she became less interested in steadying him, needing to steady herself instead. "What's not done for you? Is your house not clean? Are your shirts not pressed? Is your dinner not on the table? Is your bread not fresh? Do you ever have to move to pick up your own plate, to pour your own coffee, make your own bed? For God's sake, Alexander," Tatiana said, "I'm your maid and your *milk*-maid." She paused to let the army words sink in. "What is it that I *don't* do for you?"

Alexander said nothing.

All Tatiana heard in the silent chasm was his internal screaming.

"Oh, what's happening?" she whispered, and her hands went up to him again. "Shura, angel, come on, look at all we have . . . I know you're sad about . . . but look at the rest of our beautiful life. Look at our perfect Ant. We have him. And so many bad things are behind us."

"Obviously not all bad things," said Alexander. His elbows were on his knees as he lit another cigarette.

"No, they are, they are."

He pulled away from her reaching hands. "Lazarevo is behind us, too, Tania," he said. "Lazarevo, Deer Isle, Coconut Grove, Napa, Bethel Island. They're all behind us. You know what's *not* behind us? Leningrad." He blew out smoke from his mouth. "That's not behind us."

Tatiana, despite her great effort at self-control, started to shake. Addressing only what she could of his comment, she said, her teeth clattering, her face in her chest, "Yes, but every day when I drive home, I think of running out of Kirov, turning my face to you. Every night when I come in your arms, it's a bit of Lazarevo for me—every day in Arizona."

And what did her loving husband say to that? "Oh, give me a fucking break," he said. "Frankly the amount of time I spend on you, I could make a chair come."

Gasping, she jumped up. She whirled to go.

"That's right, go," he said, taking a drag on his cigarette. "Can't even finish it, can you?"

"Finish what?" Her voice was raised. "You say things like that, and you want me to finish? Fine, I'll finish." She felt herself getting hot in the neck. "You spend *time* on me? Yesterday you spent time on me? Yes, you're right, because that *was* effective and satisfying."

"Yes," said Alexander, smoking, staring at her with his brazen eyes. "It was both."

Tatiana had to back away and grasp the deck railing behind her. "It's late," she said quietly, her eyes to the ground. And this is so pointless. "It's very late, and I'm exhausted. I have to work tomorrow. I can't be without sleep and then be on my feet for twelve hours. Why don't you hang in there until the weekend and then we can talk some more about this."

Alexander made a mirthless sound. "Oh, you're good. To show me how much you want to solve our problems, you're telling me to wait till the weekend?"

"And what problems would you like to solve tonight?" Tatiana asked tiredly.

"This very fucking thing in your voice," he said. "You're with me right now and look, you're already thinking of tomorrow, of flying to your work; you're already glazed over. I've become the annoying thing you do while you can't wait to get to the thing you *really* want to do. I'm now Kirov instead of Alexander. You say you remember Kirov? When you slogged twelve dogged hours to have five flurry minutes with me—and not the other way around?"

"God, is it possible for you just *once*," exclaimed Tatiana, "to keep yourself from saying every nasty thing you can think of?"

"I'm not saying every nasty thing I can think of."

She twisted away to give him the back of her head, to face the desert.

She heard him light another cigarette. They didn't speak for a few minutes. Then Alexander spoke. "Who are you putting on a red dress for, Tatiana?" he asked quietly, inhaling his nicotine. "I know it can't be for me."

That made her spin back to him. He was sitting casually, a foot crossed over a knee, an arm stretched out across the back of the bench, smoking, but his eyes on her were black and anything but casual. Tatiana walked across the deck, her hands in supplication. She wasn't angry at him anymore and she wasn't afraid. She didn't care what he did. Moving his foot off his knee, she kneeled between his open legs, her swing skirt ballooning out in a red parachute on the deck. "Husband," she whispered, "what are you talking about?" Looking up into his ominous face, she slid her hands up his quads until they rested on him.

Alexander continued to smoke, his other arm draped over the bench. He didn't touch her himself, but he let her touch him. "What's happened to my wife?" he asked. "Where are her hands to bless me?"

"Here they are, darling," she whispered, caressing him. "Here they are."

"Who are you wearing *red* for, Tatiana?"

"You, Shura . . . only you—what are you worrying yourself over?"

"Where's that burka to cover you completely?" He took a breath. "Are you dressing up for Dr. Bradley?"

"No!"

"Do you think I'm blind?" Nothing was casual or relaxed anymore about his tense body. The arm came off the bench. "That I have no idea what good old Dr. Ha-ha-so-fucking-funny Bradley is thinking when he touches your back? When he kisses your hand, pretending it's just a joke, you think I don't know what he's thinking? When he stands close to you, looks into your nice red lips as you talk, when his eyes shimmer at the mention of your name? He's gone soft in the head, you think *I* don't know? I was the one with the hat in my hands, standing for hours waiting for you to get out of Kirov. What," said Alexander, "you've moved on from me? You want to bring Bradley to his knees now?" He paused. "You don't have to wear red for that." Here it came. His face darkened and he grabbed her caressing arm and pushed her so hard away that she fell on the deck. "Well, go to it, little one," said Alexander. "Because, personally, I'm broken from being on my knees so long."

"Oh, Shura," Tatiana whispered, creeping back to him. "I *beg* you, please stop. Please. You're getting yourself crazy over nothing." She came between his legs again, pulling up on him, clinging to his leather jacket, to his neck, looking up into his face, into his eyes, pulling him down to herself, to her soft and quivering mouth. They kissed, her hands surrendering up to him, his cigarette thrown down. His hands gripping her face, he was bent to her, kissing her helplessly as she was on her knees in front of him in her red bolero dress.

"Go—go twirl your hair in his face, Tania," whispered Alexander into her mouth. "Like you once did for me. Maybe he's unblemished. Not me. I'm fucking scarred from the inside out."

"Yes!" Tatiana cried in a temper, pulling away from his hands. "Mostly on your damned heart!" Pushing him in the chest, she jumped up. She was panting. "I know what it is," she said. "This is absurd of you, and deliberately cruel. This is our life *here*, our *real* life, with real things going on. I know this isn't Kirov or

Lazarevo. What *ever* is." Her voice cracked. "What *ever* is. I know you want it back, but it's gone, Alexander! It's gone and we will never have it again, no matter how much you want it."

Alexander stood from the bench. "You think it's Lazarevo I want from you?" he said in a stunned voice.

"Yes," Tatiana said loudly, taking half a step back. "You want that young girl back. Look at her, how beautiful she was, how young, and how much she loved me!"

"No!" Tatiana saw he was struggling to restrain himself from taking one step to her. "I don't need your 18-year-old self to love me. I can get that any second of any day." He was breathing hard to keep in control. "I don't even have to close my eyes." He broke off to take another breath.

Oh Shura.

"I'd settle not for Lazarevo but for Napa," he said. "I'd settle for our first months here in Scottsdale. I'd settle for a week in Coconut Grove, for one *hour* on Bethel Island. I'd settle for anything other than what I'm getting from you lately," he said, "which is a whole lot of fucking nothing."

"Oh God, I honestly don't know what you're accusing me of," she whispered, unable to look at him, lowering her stricken head. Tatiana's hands were clenched at her chest. Alexander's hands were clenched at his sides. He was on one side of the wooden deck railing, she on the other, the potted yellow prickly pears between them, their hands knotted, their mouths twisted.

Black silence passed crashingly between them.

"You're glad we don't have a baby," Alexander finally said. "Because you don't ever want to leave your work."

"I'm not glad we don't have a baby!" she said, her voice breaking. "But you're right, I don't want to leave my work. Leave work and do what? Stare at the walls all day?" She squeezed her hands together, trying to keep herself from emitting a cry. "Shura, we've been through this and through this. When I get . . ." She couldn't continue.

"That's right, do *please* stop yourself," he said, shaking his head. "Words are so fucking cheap. But don't you find it ironic," he went on in a voice that was anything but ironic, "that we made Anthony in Leningrad? In complete desperation, when the bombs were whistling by, when we were both at death's open door, the besieged and starving Leningrad begat our only child. You'd think that here, in the land of plenty—" He broke off, his gaze fixed on the planks of the deck, and stepped further away from her. "You don't want to hear it. You've never wanted to hear it, but I'm telling you once again," Alexander said, "it's because you've put that place between us in our bed—you with your trembling fingers and visions of death—and you've put it between us and our hope of *ever* having another baby—yes! Don't shake your head at me!"

"What you're saying is not true!" Tatiana cried, fighting the impulse to put her hands over her ears.

"Oh, it's true and you know it! You've got *nothing* left for a baby, nothing! Everything you have goes to that fucking hospital."

"Please stop, please," she whispered. "I'm begging you . . ."

Alexander stopped. When he spoke again, every breath out of him was exhaled with alkaloid poison anguish. "I *won't* make peace with it," he said. "I know you want me to, but I can't and I won't. I know you think we've been dealt a fine hand here, but very soon Ant will be grown and gone—and then what?"

"Shura, *please*!"

"Don't you *see*," said Alexander, "that unless an infant comes to this house, we are forever in the ice in Lake Ladoga with your dead sister and sunk under the winter tree with your brother? We are against the wall with my mother and father with blindfolds over our faces, and I'm digging coal in Kolyma. The *baby*," he whispered wrenchingly, "is the American thing. The baby is the new house and the new life. The baby is the power that sustains the stars. Don't *you* see that?"

Her head shuddering in sorrow, Tatiana's hands were clasped in a suffocating prayer—at her throat.

Everything she had she gave to him. Everything—except the one thing he desperately wanted. Except the one thing he desperately needed.

"Our house is divided against itself," said Alexander.

She shook her head. "Please don't say that," she whispered. "God, please."

Waving his hand to flag the finish, Alexander collected his beer can, his ash tray. "There's no use talking any more about it," he said, walking past Tatiana to the house. "We've talked it now to *death*."

These were the snapshots of their brief and unspeakably silent love that night: Tatiana with her legs draped over the bedroom chair, her white crinoline and red flowing skirt spread around and near and over Alexander's lowered *black black* head. And this:

Alexander standing, not touching, and Tatiana kneeling on the floor in front of him. And this: Tatiana on her hands and knees in her red bolero dress, Alexander behind her. And finally the afterglow: he's gone back outside and is sitting on the deck, smoking, and she is alone in the armchair, in her red bolero dress. The ticks of time, the fractions of an hour, four bars of a rhyme. There was no whispering, no sighing, no crying out, not a single *oh Shura*. The only muted sounds coming out of her throat were as if she had been suffocating.

And the next morning Tatiana got up and flew to work in the red Ford Thunderbird rag-top Alexander bought her so she would love him.

Faith Noël

Tatiana and Bradley were sitting across from each other having lunch that afternoon, a Thursday. Tatiana kept the conversation flowing, shop talk, other nurses, and patients, Red Cross blood drive, which she organized every year for the city of Phoenix. Did you hear about the woman who refused a Cesarian section for her twins?" Tatiana asked.

"This isn't one of your little jokes, is it?" He grinned.

"No, no joke," she said seriously, now wishing it were. "One of the babies was stillborn."

Bradley stopped smiling and nodded. "I know. The other one is okay, though. He's already been adopted. But sometimes this happens with twins."

"Yes," said Tatiana. "I was one of those too-small, non-Cesarian twins. But that was in a Soviet peasant village. This is going on in your maternity clinic, David. The woman refused the op because she said the doctor looked shifty."

"I'm not responsible for the choices Cesarian mothers make in my clinic."

"Mmm," she said. "You mean non-Cesarian mothers. Are you responsible for Dr. Culkin?"

Bradley rolled his eyes. "Unfortunately for him, yes. Shifty, she said? Dr. Culkin, a pediatric *surgeon* who came to work drunk?"

Tatiana nodded. "Perhaps that woman was right to express reservations about his services, don't you think? He could've cut out her lungs by mistake."

They both smiled.

She looked away.

"By the way," Bradley said, "you looked very beautiful yesterday."

"Thank you." She wasn't looking at him.

"You were the loveliest woman in that room."

"Very specific, but thank you."

Suddenly Bradley reached over and placed his hand over hers. It was not the hand that had her wedding ring on it. She took her hand away. Reaching for her again, he opened his mouth, and she shook her head.

"David," she said, in a very low voice. "Don't say anything."

"Tania . . ."

"No. I beg you."

"Tania . . ."

"Please," she said, her eyes lowered.

He leaned to her, halfway across the narrow table.

"David!" she cut him off, too loudly, then lowered her voice in supplication. "Please . . ."

"Tania, I have to tell you—"

"If you speak another word to me, one more word, I won't be able to have lunch with you again," said Tatiana. "I won't be able to talk to you again or work with you again. Do you understand?"

He stopped, silently staring at her.

"If you break the unspoken barrier between us, you'll stop being like everyone else I sit down to have lunch with. We've been good friends, it's no secret." She blinked. "There will be no fooling anymore if you open your mouth. Because then I won't be able to come home and look my husband in the face and say you and I are just co-workers."

"Is that what you say to him when he asks?"

"Of course."

"Does he . . . ask?"

She blinked again, swallowing the lump in her throat. "Yes. Even then he doesn't believe me. I'm not doing anything wrong by sitting down having lunch with you twice a week, as we chat about all sorts of nonsense. But I *would* be doing something wrong if I sat down with you after hearing what you cannot say to another man's wife." Tatiana could see Bradley was deeply conflicted. "What you cannot say," she repeated intensely, "to another man's wife."

"Tania, if you only knew . . ."

"Now I know."

"You have *no* idea."

"Now I do."

"No, Tania," Bradley said, shaking his head with sadness. "You really don't."

"We were friends," she said weakly. "We are still friends."

"Did you know how I felt?"

"I'm married, David," said Tatiana. "Married in a church, sworn before God, promised for life to someone else." She winced as she said it. Her Alexander was now *someone else*? Tatiana's head was deeply down. She was ashamed. She sat with Bradley because he was calm and didn't blame her for unfathomable sorrows she could not fix; because he made her laugh; she sat with him because he made her a little bit happy. Isn't that what friends did? This is what Vikki did.

But Tatiana *had* known very well how he felt.

"Tania, what if . . ." Bradley broke off. "What if you weren't married?"

"But I am."

"But what if . . . he never came back from war? What if you were still alone, like before, in New York? When it was just you and Ant."

"State your question," Tatiana said quietly.

"What about you and me, Tania?" His blue eyes were so emotional. "If you weren't married?"

"But I am," she whispered.

"Oh God. Is there no chance for us? No chance at all?"

Reaching out, Tatiana put her hand on his face. "No, David," she replied. "Not in this life."

Bradley looked across at her. For a moment he did not speak, and she did not take her palm away. Then he whispered, "Thank you. Thank you for giving me my answer." He kissed her hand. "You are a very good wife," he said. "And perhaps in another life, I might have known that."

"I really have to go," Tatiana said, hastily getting up. "Please don't mention this again." As steadily as she could, Tatiana walked out of the cafeteria, leaving Dr. Bradley alone at the table.

Jingle Bell Swing

A day later, on Friday night, Tatiana was working, Anthony was overnight with Sergio, and Alexander was at Maloney's with Shannon, Skip and Johnny. Johnny was regaling everyone with stories of how Emily went out with him for dinner earlier in the week, how Emily agreed to go to Scottsdale Commons with him on Sunday, how Emily was planning to invite him over for Christmas to meet the folks.

"The problem is, you see, she is looking at it like a courtship, when courtship is the *last* thing I need. Why am I spending so long getting her to do what I want her to do?"

"A *week* is too long?" Alexander laughed. "Oh, man. They have places for people like you, Johnny-boy. Special darkened places that don't require courtship."

Johnny waved him off. He was a young hard kid in good duds with a hot rod, a biker, a strapper. "I'm not paying for it, no way. Who do you think I am?"

Shannon, Skip, Alexander exchanged glances, and shook their collective married heads. Alexander said, "Johnny, how much have you spent so far on dinner, drinks, pictures, flowers?"

You could tell Johnny had never thought about it like that. "It's not the same," he said, downing his drink. "It's the conquest, the chase that's interesting. The pro-cre-ative process."

"Oh, the pro-cre-ative process," mimicked Shannon. "You're such an asshole."

Skip and Shannon branched off to talk about their new babies. Alexander and Johnny branched off to talk about Emily and whether she was worth pursuing further.

"Don't you think," said Johnny, "it's too much effort to expend on a little fly-cage?"

Alexander was thoughtful. "Depends how much you like her," he replied. "If you like her, it's not too much effort."

"Well, how would I know? I haven't—"

"If you liked her," said Alexander, "no effort would be too much."

"You know something about that?"

"I know something about that," said Alexander.

A hand went on Alexander's shoulder. "Well, hello!" It was

Carmen and Emily. They had gotten all gussied up and sprayed. Johnny suavely kissed Emily's cheek.

"Alexander, we really must stop meeting like this," said Carmen. "It's our third time in a week."

Soon Shannon and Skip left to go home to their waiting wives, who cared what time they came home.

Emily, Johnny, Carmen, and Alexander went to a corner booth and ordered drinks. Carmen sat next to him on the bench. Her perfume was unfamiliar and a little strong but not terrible. She herself wasn't terrible. Her dark eyes flashed, she had some vim. She had a good laugh, she was a flirt, a talker. She was not shy, she was not afraid. During their conversation she moved her leg and it touched his. And at one in the morning, Alexander didn't move it away.

"So, Alexander," Carmen said, "is my memory failing me, or are you the same Alexander Barrington who killed a man that broke into your house late one night a few years ago? I recall reading something in the paper about that."

"He's one and the same man, Carmen," said Johnny. "So don't get on his bad side."

"Oh, how positively *frightening*!" squealed Carmen, moving an inch closer. "So you have a bad side?"

"I might," said Alexander.

"How bad?" she asked in a low voice.

Alexander could have said nothing. Certainly he should have said nothing. But it was late Friday night and he'd been drinking, and his head was swimming, and so what he said instead of keeping silent was, "Very very bad, Carmen."

And Carmen went red, and tittered, and moved even closer to him on the bench seat.

She told Alexander that she and Cubert, married for two years, wanted a bigger place because they were trying for a baby. The truth was, though, that Cubert was not home *so* often, she needed the building of the house to occupy herself because she was becoming "awfully bored."

Johnny was busy talking to Emily, and so Alexander quietly said, "With him away so often, it might be difficult to have that baby." He didn't want to add that blinding proximity still guaranteed nothing.

Carmen laughed. "That's why I said, *trying*. Not succeeding. But I am late this month, so we'll see." She looked slightly sheepish when she said it.

Alexander actually asked, "Do you, um, *want* children?"

"Oh, yes, very much," Carmen said. "All my friends are having children at nineteen, twenty. I'm starting to feel old at twenty-four." She smiled, raising her eyebrows. "But I'm doing what I can to keep myself youthful." She pinched his arm. "Do you have any children?"

"Yes," said Alexander. "A son. He's fourteen."

"Fourteen!" said Carmen. "He's practically a grown up. Does he look like you?"

"A little."

"He'll be a lucky boy," she said, giving him a diffused stare, "if he looks like you."

Alexander took a sip of his cold drink and a long inhale of his burning cigarette. "Carmen," he said, "how in the world did you get together with Cubert?" What Alexander was really saying is he thought Cubert was too pale and small for vivid Carmen, and she must have known it because she threw back her head.

"Why, thank you, Alexander! Coming from you, that's *quite* a compliment, you are a very reticent fellow."

He smiled. "I'm not reticent. I'm thoughtful."

"Oh, is there a difference?" She chuckled. "Cubert, though he doesn't look it, has a few things going for him that I really liked when we were courting."

"Like what?"

"Are you being insinuating and naughty, Alexander? How delightful!"

"Not at all." He kept a straight face. "I'm asking a polite question."

"Well," she said, "first of all, he is quite enamored of me."

"And second of all?"

"He is quite enamored of me." When she laughed her breasts rose up and down. The more Alexander drank, the more he noticed the breasts.

"So tell me," said Carmen, "how does a married man get to stay out until all hours on a Friday night? My Cubert is away," she said, "but where's your wife?"

"My wife is also away," said Alexander. "She works Friday nights."

Carmen's eyes went wide. "The fact that your wife works is shocking enough. But at *night*? In the name of all that is gracious, *why*?"

"You are not the only one who asks this question, Carmen."

She laughed. She sat close, swelling, laughing at any stupid thing he said. When he lit her cigarette, as gallant men do for ladies, she cupped his hand and, raising her eyes to him, breathed out, "Thank you." For a moment their eyes met.

And Alexander, suddenly finding himself mental years away, in a uniform, at Sadko, in a different time, in a different life, as a different man, said to Carmen, "Did you girls come in one car?" Though at Sadko he would have said something else. Do you want to go for a walk, he would've said. For a walk by the river parapets, for a smoke in the alley?

"Yes," said Carmen throatily. "We came in Emily's car."

"I have to go home, Carmen," said Emily. "My parents will kill me for staying out this late. It's absolutely ghastly—why, it's nearly last call."

Carmen grazed Alexander's hand. "Do you think you can give me a ride so Emily can go home now? I'm only half an hour south from here, in Chandler."

He glanced over at Johnny, who was staring at him with an expression that said, I don't know what the hell you think *you're* doing.

Alexander himself didn't know. But even at two in the morning on a Friday night after five hours of drinking, Alexander knew this: no woman other than his wife could get into his truck. Another woman could not sit in his truck, where Tatiana sat, where his son sat, in which he took his family out. Even when not sober, when youthfully stirred up by an attractive, well-built young woman, all decked out and ready to party, this was something that a 38-year-old Alexander could not do. He also could not explain it to Carmen.

"I can't drive you," he said. "I've got to go home. My son is waiting."

"So? He's likely asleep. You can drop me off on the way."

"I'm not on the way to anything," he said. "But Emily is on the way, and she's leaving. You might as well go with her."

Reluctantly Carmen stood up, while Alexander paid, remaining behind, as the other three got ready to leave.

"Aren't you coming?"

"In a minute. Good night now."

Carmen shooed Johnny and Emily away and sat down again. "I'll wait with you while you finish your drink."

He stared at her, wondering if she was worth it. She didn't seem bright, though somehow that wasn't so important. "Carmen," he finally said when minutes passed and she couldn't figure it out, "I come to this bar every Friday. This is my local joint. People know me here. I come here with my friends, with people I work with. I come here with my wife. Do you understand why I can't leave this bar with you?"

Why did she look so pleased by that? She left by herself, and Alexander waited a few minutes, and then left, too.

In the parking lot she was waiting, coming up to him to say good-bye. "So will you be here on Tuesday?"

"No, not likely."

"What about next Friday?"

He shrugged. "That I might."

"So maybe I'll see you then." She smiled. "Have you had any cancellations in your schedule so we can meet some evening, have dinner, talk about the house perhaps?"

"I'll have to check," he said, "I might have a cancellation."

"I hope so." She planted a slow moist kiss on his cheek. "Well, good night, now." Her breasts pressed into his shirt.

After she left, Alexander sat in his truck, his hands on the wheel. He didn't go home.

He went to the hospital.

He lurched and lurched, scraping away what was left of his clutch, trying to put the transmission in gear, and after parking— badly—meandered his way into ER. There was no one at the reception desk, the unit nurse was out, no one received him. He staggered instead to the waiting room, where half a dozen people were arrayed like sacks in chairs. One of those people was Charlie. Alexander fell into a chair one away from him. "Has there been a sighting?"

"Not yet," said Charlie. "That just means there might be one soon."

They waited.

And soon and summarily she appeared in their view. Small, round-faced, freckled, pale, her lips unadorned by lipstick, her neck by perfume, her breath by wine, her hair tied up in a bun inside the nurse's cap, her legs in white stockings, slender and subdued, Tatiana came, and yet her lips were full and pulpy, her breasts swayed, and Alexander could see them, could feel them warm. She might as well have stood in front of him naked, lay in front of him naked, so clearly could he see all of her, see her, smell her, taste her.

Her white uniform covered with eight hours of a Friday night, her high forehead glistening, her freckles diminished by winter, Tatiana's green-spoked eyes stared sad and despondent on Alexander. Sitting between them, she took their hands, Alexander's in one, Charlie's in the other. "Now, Charlie," Tatiana said. "Now, Alexander. I've told you and told you not to drink so much. It leads to no good. It's leading you to a bad place. It's leading you to darkness." She looked from one to the other as they sat and nodded. "You both have made promises to me. Charlie, you swore that you would not drink this Friday night."

"And what did I promise you, Tatiana?" Alexander said, slurring his words.

She turned to him and said nothing. A small tear trickled down her cheek. She let go of Charlie's hand but held on to Alexander's. "I'm going to go get you some coffees, a little ice for your head. Wait here." As if either had anywhere else to go.

She came back with two coffees. Charlie said he wanted whisky in his. Alexander put his down on the floor and, taking Tatiana's wrist, pulled her to him to stand between his splayed legs. "Smell my breath," he said huskily, breathing on her. "So good, right?" He entwined her in his large, intoxicated arms. "Babe, come home with me," he muttered. "Come home and I'll"—he still had the sense to lower his voice to a whisper—"give you some of that drunk true love you like."

Staring down at him, Tatiana brushed his hair away, and bending, kissed his forehead. "That drunk love is sometimes a little rough on your wife," she said quietly. "Finish the coffee, put some ice on your head, sober up a little, go home. Anthony is home alone."

"Ant is with Sergio," muttered Alexander. "*He* is not alone."

Gently she wrested herself away from him. "I've got broken bones in the tent, a busted median artery, a perforated stomach, and an unstable heart. I have to go."

As she was walking away Tatiana turned her head. "Next time you come," she said, "wipe the lipstick off your face first, Alexander."

O Come, All Ye Faithful

The following Friday night at Maloney's, Johnny happily and unexpectedly admitted he was no longer pursuing Emily. Apparently at last week's Saturday night Christmas party, Emily, nicely drunk and relaxed, had given him some milk for free in one of the upstairs bedrooms, and his thirst thus slaked, Johnny met another girl at the party and was now "courting" her.

"So needless to say Emily won't be coming here tonight?" Alexander asked, palming his glass of beer.

They all agreed with a hearty laugh that she probably wouldn't be.

At midnight, Shannon and Skip left; at one Johnny left.

Alexander had two more drinks alone, and then left himself.

He was about to get into his truck when a voice said, "Alexander."

It was Carmen. She got out of the sedan parked next to his truck. She was wearing a circle skirt, a button-down blouse, a cardigan. Her hair was all teased and prepared. Her lips were painted. Alexander remembered wiping her lipstick off his cheek in the hospital last week. A pang of something hit him.

But just a small pang.

"Well, hello there." He smiled. "What are you doing here?"

She smiled happily back. "As I'm sure you found out, your slimy friend Johnny did not do right by my nice friend Emily, so now we can't come here anymore. And I don't have other unmarried friends that I can drag to bars with me while my husband is on his little trips. So . . ."

"So . . ." He looked her up and down. "I like your blouse," he said.

"Do you? Well, thank you . . . ." She appraised him herself. "Are you done for the night? Do you have to run?"

Alexander chewed his lip.

"Because I brought some wine and beer," Carmen said quickly. "I have glasses. We can have a drink in your truck if you want. Listen to some music." She smiled.

"I tell you what," he said, coming close to her. "Why don't we have a drink in *your* car where the wine is?"

"Oh, sure. You don't want to go into your truck? Is it messy?" She glanced in. The truck was spotless. He didn't elaborate or answer her, but took off his bomber jacket and threw it on the bench in his truck. He didn't want unfamiliar smells on it he would not be able to explain.

They fit into her front seat, turned on the engine, turned up the radio. Alexander poured her a glass of wine, himself a beer. They clinked. "What do you want to drink to?" she asked.

"To Friday nights," he replied.

"Amen," she said, adding cheerfully, "it's tough when the spouses are away, isn't it?"

"Hmm." He lit his cigarette, and hers, too.

"But you know what," Carmen said, "I'm so used to Cubert not being here, that when he *is* here, I almost don't know what to do. We're always fighting over something or other. Is it the same with you and your wife?"

"No."

"Oh? What's it like?"

"Carmen, you're sitting in the car with me, drinking, your hair all coiffed, your lipstick bright. You can't think of anything else to talk to me about other than my wife?"

"Oh, all right, when you put it like that." She tittered. "What do *you* like to talk to girls about?"

"I don't know," said Alexander. "I don't talk to girls other than my wife."

She laughed.

The music played.

"Winter Wonderland."

"Santa Baby."

They sat in her car, they smoked, he drank, she drank, she became tipsier, and with every swallow of the wine, she moved closer to him on the bench seat, touching his shirt sleeves, his jeans leg, his hand.

"So . . . do you *want* to talk about your wife?"

"I can," said Alexander, "but then I'll have to leave." She really wasn't very bright. But she smelled pretty good. And her boobs were huge.

"I told you about Cubert. Tell me at least what I'm up against. What's her name?"

What she was up against? What did that mean? He didn't reply.

"All right, all right. How many years were you married?"

"I'm still married. Fifteen."

She whistled. "Wow." She took his hand and sighed. "Me just

two, and already I'm not sure if I'm in love with Cubert. Do you know what I mean?"

"No, I don't know Cubert at all," said Alexander.

Carmen held his hand, placing it against her own. Her hand was long. "What about you and your wife?"

"I'm still in love with my wife," Alexander said, taking his hand away.

"So what are you doing in my car, Alexander?"

"Drinking," he said. "Smoking."

She picked up his hand again. "You've got such large hands," she said huskily.

"Well," he said, "I am a man."

She looked at him through lowered lids. "Are you comfortable behind that wheel?"

Alexander palmed the steering column. "I'm fine. Nice car you've got." It was a Ford sedan like Tania used to drive.

"What I mean is . . . would you be more comfortable in the back seat?"

He didn't reply, his male blood flowing, his excitement bubbling. The music played on. "Only You Can Bring Me Cheer."

They got out of the car, switched to the back seat.

"It's getting very late," Carmen said, stretching. She smiled. "Isn't it?" She moved across the back seat to him.

Without putting down his drink, Alexander leaned over and kissed her. She smelled of smoke, of liquor, the tastes were unfamiliar, the feel mushy, all was so foreign and not entirely pleasing, but not entirely unpleasing either after the drink. He lowered his lips to her neck, where the perfume was better, and with his one free hand unbuttoned her blouse. Carmen readily helped him. Her long-line bra was like armor over her breasts. It had eight or ten hooks and she had to dislodge the bra herself, but when the breasts were out, they were very large indeed. His face must have shown his surprise.

"Nice, huh?" Carmen said proudly. "Come on," she said, "put your big hands on them." He put his drink carefully on the car floor, and fondled her. He felt he could have used an extra pair of hands. Carmen pushed his head down, pressing his face flush into her breasts. Alexander had to push away a little, take a breath before moving over her nipples. They took a while to harden. She didn't stir at his mouth. "Mmm," she said, holding his head. "You *like* them, don't you?"

"I like them." What Alexander liked best though was the women's response to him. Even in the days of the Leningrad garrison, when the flow of girls was like a three-ring circus, coming and going in all shapes and sizes, and he liked them all. Aside from his purely personal esthetic preferences—that happened to be met by the one woman he had married—his sexual preferences had always been about one thing only: the girls' reaction to his action. "Do *you* like my mouth on you?"

"I like that you like it," Carmen said, placing her hand on his jeans. "And I feel that you do *like* it . . ."

Still at her breasts, Alexander looked at her. "Where are you going with this, Carmen?"

"I don't know." She smiled, giving him a squeeze. "Where are *you* going with it? Where do you *want* to go with it?"

"Oh, it's like that, is it?" He dragged his hand underneath her petticoat, up her fleshy legs.

"Hey," she said, trying to push his hand away. "I'm not going to be that easy for you. I want you to come back next week for some more. I'm not going to repeat Emily's mistake."

As if not hearing her, Alexander moved his hand up her stocking and found her closed panty girdle that came down to the middle of her thighs. His excitement morphed slightly into dismay. He couldn't imagine how they would get this thing off in the car—it would require his army knife, which was in the nightstand by his bed. When he thought of the nightstand, he thought of the bed, when he thought of the bed, he thought of Tania buying the quilts and the pillows and the sheets for it over eight years ago, making the bed and then happily calling him in. Alexander took his hands away from under Carmen's skirt.

She pressed his head back into her breasts. "Go ahead," she murmured. "This will have to be enough for now. I love your face in them. Go ahead. *Feast.*"

When he touched her nipples, she didn't move. Alexander was not used to that and decided he wasn't trying hard enough. He rubbed them, kneaded them, squeezed them, sucked them, pulled on them, twisted them harder than he thought was conscionable. Carmen sat, her eyes closed, her body still, her hands on his head, looking extremely contented. "That feels so good," she said. "Doesn't it feel good?"

"Carmen, is there, um, anything else you want me to do for you?" Alexander said.

She opened her eyes. "Oh, baby, what are you offering me?"

"I got a little of everything. What do you want?"

"I really like you touching my breasts." She put her hands on him. "What do *you* like? Is there something you want me to do for you? Or are my breasts enough?"

"They're certainly plenty," said Alexander. "But I might need a *touch* more." He smiled.

Carmen touched him, rubbing him to attention, and was soon unbuckling him and he wasn't stopping her.

"Get out of that girdle, Carmen," said Alexander.

"The breasts are out," she said joyously. "But who said I'm getting out of the girdle? Boy, you grown men. You don't waste any time, do you?" She was smiling. "I like that, though. So forward. Always know what you want."

Alexander said nothing. His hands and mouth on her breasts were getting more insistent as her hand on him was getting more insistent. They were both panting.

She stopped touching him. "Wait. I don't want to get into something we'll have to cut in a hour."

Alexander paused, considering her briefly, trying to figure out the polite thing to say under the circumstances. What did she think this was? And was this really the best time to be pointing out to her what it was? "Um—so—what would you like?" he asked.

"I don't know." She smiled, unbuttoning him. "What would *you* like? When does your wife get home?"

Carmen broke the cardinal rule—the taboo against talking about a man's wife while she was taking his joint out of his jeans. Alexander pushed her hands away and said, "You know what? I think you're right. It's getting late."

But Carmen had gotten a feel of a bare Alexander, and she said, "Oh, wait just a second. Wait." Her breath quickening, she rubbed him and said in a low voice, "Do you think you might have that cancellation for me next week? Perhaps we can get together, have dinner, talk about that house?" She squeezed him tightly. "Go somewhere a little more comfortable?"

"Perhaps," said Alexander, closing his eyes.

She continued to stroke him. "How does that feel?"

"Good."

"Will you come next week?"

"I'd like to come now."

"Oh! You are funny! You are—something."

"Am I?" He let her rub him another moment or two, and then his hand went in her hair. "Carmen . . . ?" said Alexander, pushing her head down slightly.

"Oh, you are something else," she said. Chuckling, she adjusted herself on the seat, bent her head, and took him into her mouth. He sat with a drink in one hand, eyes closed, while she struggled up and down on him.

Alexander knew himself very well: she would have had to be magic mouth—and she clearly wasn't—to get him off this way when he'd had so much to drink. Knowing this, he still let her persevere to see if maybe he would surprise himself. He steadied her head, tried to get her to move more rhythmically, told her to hold him a little tighter. She tried to do what she was told, but couldn't seem to do it all at once. Finally Carmen pulled her mouth away, looked up and said, "You're getting close, I can tell."

He smiled politely. He wasn't anywhere near close.

"Because I just want to warn you, I don't do any of that . . ." she waved her hand, "you know . . . milt in the mouth stuff. I know some men really go for that."

"*Some* men?" Sighing into his last sip of beer, Alexander put down the glass. "Look," he said, "I'm going to have to get going."

"Get going? What do you mean? You're so . . . unbelievably hard." She was still yanking at him.

He put his hand on her hand. "Carmen, shh," he said. "Steady on."

"But don't you need to finish?"

"I've been drinking," said Alexander. "I need something else."

"I have something else." Carmen straightened out, showing him her breasts. "I'll lie down on the seat, you climb over me and put yourself between them, and do what you have to. As hard as you want. Honestly, as hard as you want. It's the best way. All the boys love it."

His hand moved inside her formidable cleavage. "Won't work for me after the drink. But thank you."

Carmen smiled, taking hold of him again. "So what will work then?"

He didn't answer.

"Fine," she said, squeezing him. "To feel *that* inside me, I'll break my own cardinal rule, I'll take off my girdle here and now. I only put it on for a little extra protection, if you know what I mean. Come on, help me take it off. Then you finish how you want."

He played with her breasts. But Alexander had brought nothing with him.

She saw his hesitation. "What? Don't worry. I have a pessary."

"Oh yeah? Filled with acacia?" In the olden days that's what the women used. Plastic rings filled with tropical flowers. Still got pregnant.

"What?"

Alexander moved her hands off him. "No. I need a condom."

"Why? I told you. I'm safe." She put her hands back.

"Yes, but I'm not."

"What do you mean? Come on, look at you. Let me . . ."

"Can't do it, Carmen." He moved away from her on the seat, buttoning himself up, fixing his belt.

She scooted close to him, looking up at him with dreamy eyes. "What about next week? You can bring what you need then."

"Yes, next week I'll bring what I need."

"I can't wait," she said. "I won't be able to think of anything else. Mmm. Me, on top of *you*, with these babies over your face." She actually made a sound of pleasure at the anticipation. "Doesn't that sound good?"

"Very good." Alexander helped her hook her bra in the back.

"So did you like them?" Carmen asked. "Cubert is *crazy* for them."

Not so crazy that he stays home, Alexander thought. When she was dressed, he helped her out of the backseat and behind the wheel.

"He's in town next weekend, unfortunately," said Carmen. "He's going away Monday to Thursday, though. You want to meet Wednesday night?"

They agreed to meet in a restaurant in Chandler where she lived. The restaurant was next to a Westin Hotel. He told her he wouldn't be able to stay out too late and Carmen said with a smile that that was okay; they would have to get right down to business. She turned up her face to him from the car window. "Well? Aren't you going to kiss me good night?"

Alexander gave her a kiss on the cheek.

"I'll see you Wednesday," she said.

"See you Wednesday," he said, got into his truck and drove away.

It was five thirty in the morning, and for some reason, as Alexander was coming up Pima, he became afraid that Tatiana was already home, that she got off work early and came home and found him not there. His heart started beating so violently that he had to pull over to get a grip on himself. It was another twenty minutes before he could get back on the road.

Tatiana wasn't home. Yet the relief wasn't there. Alexander smelled like all kinds of bad news. He unlocked the door stealthily. Anthony's door was closed. When he opened it, he saw his sleeping son in the bed. Why was Ant home? He was supposed to be at Sergio's!

Alexander took off his clothes, ran them through the wash, and had a long shower, as hot as he could stand it, where he scrubbed himself raw. When he smelled like himself again, he put his clothes in the dryer and went to bed. It was light out, nearly seven.

No sooner had he closed his eyes that he felt Tatiana's small hand on his face and her soft lips on his forehead. "Hey," she said. "Woo-hoo. Wake up, sleepy head. You've got to go to work. Did you have fun last night with your friends?"

Rolling over, he muttered he wasn't going to his morning appointments. A truck had run him over, he said; he could not open his eyes.

"What time did you get back?"

"I don't know," he muttered. "Around two, three, maybe."

"A little hung over, are we?" Tatiana said, kissing him on the back of the head. He heard her switch on the shower, and that's all he heard. But in bed she lay close to him, still slightly damp. He turned away from her. She pressed her bare breasts into his back, nuzzled his shoulder blades, rubbed against him, murmured that it was nice to have him so big and warm next to her on a Saturday morning, put her arms around him and fell asleep.

At eleven Alexander dragged his sorry self out of bed, showered again, dressed and went out into the kitchen. While he was making coffee and fixing some rolls, Anthony came out, fresh from sleep, and Tatiana, who heard their voices, came out, too. Anthony and Sergio apparently had had a fight, which was why Anthony had stormed home.

"I hope no broken noses, Ant," said Tatiana.

"No, Mom, Serge is my best friend. I'd never hit him. Dad, how come you're not at work?"

Tatiana smiled sleepily. "Daddy had a late night last night."

"You can say that again," said Anthony.

"Tania," said Alexander, "you want a cup of coffee?"

"Oh, yes, please."

"Because," Anthony continued, "I got up around six to use the bathroom and your truck wasn't outside."

Alexander's back was to Tatiana as he poured cream into her coffee and studiously stirred the sugar. "No, I'm sure it was," he said.

"Well, I don't know then. Because you weren't in your bed."

And then silence dripped through their just the right size double wide trailer, through their little home.

Turning around, Alexander extended his hand to her with the coffee but couldn't look up. Tatiana stood for a few moments holding on to the back of the kitchen chair, and then turned and slowly walked back into the bedroom without taking the cup from his proffered hands.

Alexander sat down with Anthony but the roll kept getting stuck in his throat. He needed to go to work, but how could he walk into that bedroom to say good-bye? How could he *not* walk into that bedroom?

His mouth tight, his coffee drunk, Alexander stood at the open bedroom door. Tatiana was in the bathroom with the door shut.

"Tania," he called out, "I have to go."

There was a gathering of silence and then her barely audible voice. "All right, see you later."

Alexander left.

When he came home Saturday night, Anthony was watching TV alone and the door to the bedroom was closed. Alexander dropped his keys on the table, took off his jacket and sat by Anthony. "What's Mommy doing?"

"She said she wasn't feeling well."

The house didn't smell like Saturday usual—like it had been cooked in. "What, there's no food?"

"Mom and I had leftovers. She said you would have had your dinner out."

"She said I would have had my dinner *out*?"

"Yes."

After fixing himself a plate of cold stuffed peppers and bread, Alexander sat back down on the couch. "Did you go grocery shopping? There's no milk."

"We didn't go. She said we weren't going today."

"What'ya watching?"

"*Gunsmoke*."

"Um—so you didn't go grocery shopping, what did you do?"

The Christmas tree stood in the corner of the living room unlit. "No one turned on the tree?"

Anthony looked. "Guess not."

Alexander went to turn it on. "So what did you do?" he repeated.

"Spent all day at the mission orphanage."

"Where?"

"Dad, remember? We go every Christmas. We bring our old clothes, I do crafts with the kids, Mom reads to them."

"Oh. Yeah. So . . . how was your mother today?"

"Silent. I thought I'd done something wrong."

"Did you?"

"I asked her, she said no."

Alexander finished his food and waited until *Gunsmoke* was over. "Ant, you shouldn't have said anything about me coming home so late. I had told Mommy I came home earlier because I didn't want her to worry. Now she thinks I was lying."

"Well . . ." Anthony was weighing his thoughts. "Weren't you?"

"Technically. Because I didn't want to upset your mother for nothing."

Anthony clammed up.

They sat.

"She didn't seem upset, like angry, Dad, if that's what you're worried about," said Anthony at last. "She just seemed extra tired. She said she hadn't been feeling well."

Unable to go into his bedroom, Alexander asked the boy if he wanted to go to the pictures. Anthony jumped up, they threw on their jackets and went out. They saw *Attack of the Crab Monsters* and *Aztec Mummy*, and when they came home, the bedroom door was still closed.

Alexander couldn't face her. He didn't know how he was going to get into bed with her. After Anthony went to sleep, Alexander had three shots of vodka and half a pack of cigarettes and thought about all the things he could say when she would inevitably ask him why he had lied to her. He decided he would blame it all on poker-playing Johnny.

Poker with Johnny, till six in the morning—stayed out too late, didn't want to tell you, when I was half dead, in bed, upset you for nothing, I'm sorry I'm sorry, was going to come clean—Poker with Johnny, till six in the morning.

Were they going to see Johnny any time soon? He'd need to give Johnny-boy a heads-up on that one. Thus fortified with poetic lies and prosaic vodka, Alexander opened the bedroom door. Tatiana was sleeping in a fetal position on top of the covers. The room was dark. Not wanting to accidentally wake her—God forbid—Alexander covered her with a couch blanket and crawled into bed. He was unconscious in seconds, having barely slept the night before.

In the morning when he finally woke up, he heard noises of her and Anthony making breakfast outside.

"Good morning, Dad," said Anthony when Alexander staggered out. "Today is cookie day."

He had forgotten that, too. Five friends of Tatiana's from the hospital were coming over to bake cookies for St. Monica's Mission. In the evening they were going to Shannon and Amanda's Christmas party. Would Johnny be there?

"They'll be here soon," Tatiana said, not addressing him. Meaning, he was nearly naked, wearing only his snug-fitting BVDs, reminiscent of his Red Army skivvies. He wore them because Tatiana liked the way he looked in them. Not today perhaps, because her back was to him. When he turned to go, he heard her voice. "I found your clothes in the dryer," Tatiana said. "I didn't know you knew how to use the washer and dryer. Imagine my surprise. I folded them for you and put them on your dresser." Slowly Alexander turned to her. She was facing the stove.

"I spilled beer on them," he said lamely.

Poker with Johnny, till six in the morning—stayed out too late, didn't want to tell you, when I was half dead, in bed, upset you for nothing I'm sorry I'm sorry, was going to come clean, I spilled beer on my jeans—Poker with Johnny, till six in the morning.

She didn't bring him any coffee. He poured his own. But since she made eggs and bacon for herself and Ant, she did put some on a plate for him, and she did put the plate in front of him. They didn't speak, not even through Anthony. Alexander was incapable of speaking to her about bullshit when an African elephant was sitting on top of their breakfast eggs.

At noon the girls came and started baking, eating, laughing, reading recipe books. Christmas music went on, there was cheer. Anthony helped part of the time, Alexander disappeared in the woodshed, and then he and Ant went out to shoot some baskets. It was a mild December Sunday in Arizona, sixty degrees. *Tatia, would you like to live in Arizona, the land of the small spring?"*

Alexander was outside picking the ball out of the bushes, and he was careless for a moment—careless because he was consumed with the impossible and trying not to think of the impossible—and was not paying attention, and didn't see two rolled-up cholla clusters that had separated and drifted over to the basketball. The germinating cholla plant pollinated by jumping and attaching itself to whatever was near. Alexander was near. He grabbed the ball, and the cholla instantly attached itself to his palms. Hundreds of needle-like fine teeth penetrated his skin, pierced it, broke in and dug in, burrowing inside like malignant animals. The palms immediately started to swell. The ball game was over.

Anthony ran to the house. "Mom! Mom! Look what Dad did. Mom!"

Her hands were covered in flour. "What did he do now?" she said to Anthony, turning to look.

"It's nothing," Alexander said.

"Alexander," said Tatiana, "you have blood on your hands."

They stood. "Just a little cholla," he said. "Nothing to worry about."

The girls, all nurses, gasped and twittered, fussed and fretted, dispensing anxious, *extremely* high-pitched advice. "Oh, no, not cholla!" "The needles will fall out after seven to ten days." "Oh yes, but there will be such an infection!" "Oh, yes, but to pull them out is impossible!" "It will positively *shred* him!" "The cholla is like barbed wire!"

There was so much lamentation. Only Tatiana remained silent.

"Well, what do you want to do?" she said, looking into his face, the first time this Sunday. Her eyes were green ocean water, frozen over. "You want to leave the needles in? They'll get infected, but they will fall out in a week. Or I can pull them out. It'll rip your palms up. But they'll be out."

Anthony was patting him on the back. "You're between a rock and a hard place, Dad," he said. "As you say, either way, you're—"

"Anthony!"

"What?" Anthony was all innocence.

"Rip them out," Alexander said to Tatiana.

He sat at her table; she took out her anesthetic needle. He declined. The anesthetic he needed was not for his palms. "If you want me to do this for you," Tatiana said, "let me numb your hands."

"Tania," said Alexander, "you stitched a gash in my shoulder, a shrapnel wound, without anesthetic. I'll be fine."

Without discussing it further, Tatiana put the needle away and started to take off her surgical gloves.

"All right, all right." He sighed. "Numb the hands."

"Mom," said Anthony, "how come you're wearing gloves?" He chuckled. "Are you afraid Dad will infect you?"

Tatiana paused a little too long before she said, "The needles penetrate. I'll need two pairs of gloves, to protect myself, and it still won't be enough."

Alexander's gaze was on his unfeeling bloodied hands. Anthony stood by Alexander's side, his supportive patting arm on his father's shoulder, and five women stood watching, over Tatiana's back, over Alexander's, while she with surgical pliers *wrenched* the barbed-wire cholla glochids out of his upturned palms, leaving oozing wounds.

Anthony, not flinching and never taking his hand off Alexander's back, said to the women, "Want to know what my dad says about cholla?"

"Anthony!"

"What? No, no, this is the mild version." Anthony grinned. "When we first came here, Dad didn't know what cholla was. But he learned quick, though he's never gotten hit like this. So he started saying, 'I know there is no hell, because they keep telling me it's hot down there. Well, don't give me hot, because I do hot every day. Now if they told me there was cholla in hell, then I'd believe them.' Isn't that right?"

"Well," said Alexander, "they don't call it the devil cholla for nothing."

"Mom says," said Anthony, smiling at his mother, "that the cholla is possessed by evil spirits."

"Well, Antman, they don't call it the devil cholla for nothing," said Tatiana.

The ladies clucked as Tatiana continued to twist the needles out of Alexander's palms. She had to stop at one point to staunch the copious bleeding by pressing a cloth to his hands for a minute before continuing. They sat during this minute, with him looking down at her blonde braided head and her looking down at his palm in her hands.

"I would *not*, could not, be so calm," said Carolyn, with an impressed chuckle. "I'd be a wreck with my Dan. Tania, how do you stay so calm with your own husband?"

Tatiana's head was bent. "I really don't know," she said without glancing up.

Alexander flinched.

"Dad," said Anthony, "your hands are numb. Why are you flinching? Mom, maybe you should give him another shot."

"Your father needs a shot of whiskey, is what he needs," said Carolyn, going to get the bottle from the cabinet. "Tania, do you think if his hands were smaller, less cholla would have gotten in?"

"Cholla is cholla," Tatiana said, leveling her frigid stare away from Alexander. "What does it know about hands?" After she was done, she disinfected his wounds with iodine, cauterized them with silver nitrate, bandaged them tightly, and said, *oh, and you're welcome by the way.* And Alexander flinched again.

Poker with Johnny, till six in the morning—stayed out too late, didn't want to tell you, when I was half dead, in bed, upset you for nothing, I'm sorry I'm sorry, was going to come clean, I spilled beer on my jeans, the cholla knows nothing—Poker with Johnny, till six in the morning.

Deck the halls with boughs of holly . . .

She is so beautiful his heart hurts. Her skin is porcelain cream and to match it she is wearing an ivory pencil skirt, ivory stockings, and a tight ivory cashmere cropped sweater with a shelf top. She is a sweater girl bar none. Her gold hair is pinned but down, flaxen and soft. She must be the only woman in the United States whose hair remains long and unteased, uncurled and unsprayed. She smells like musk and cinnamon and burnt sugar—from the cookies she's been making—and her lips have gloss.

'Tis the season to be jolly . . .

Alexander imagines the ivory cream skin above her lace stockings. Tonight, despite that they haven't talked—despite everything—when stopped at a light, he slips his bandaged hand under her skirt and glides it up under her open girdle to touch the adored bare sliver of her thigh with the tips of his fingers. Her skin is cold. They're in his truck. She and Anthony are sharing the passenger seat. Tatiana was going to get in after Ant, but the boy said, no, no, I don't get into any vehicle before my mother, you first, Mom, like always. So now she is next to Alexander, motionless like a block of ice. There are so many things crashing against Alexander's chest that he *has* to take his hand away.

He drives in silence.

"How do I look?" she asks. They are on their way to Shannon and Amanda's party. The season is full of them, joyful parties, one after another. Alexander wonders if Johnny is going to be there; he needs him for perfidy. He wasn't able to reach him by telephone during the day. He wonders if he would get some points for keeping his *truck* chaste. Look, I didn't let a floozy sit in my *truck* in which I take my family out on nights like tonight, that's good, right? Keeping a *truck* faithful? Because that's what you want to keep faithful.

"Fine," he manages to reply, his hands like clamps around the wheel.

"Don't listen to Dad," says Anthony. "He never knows the right thing to say. You're going to be the prettiest mom at the party."

"Thank you, son."

Alexander speaks. "Anthony, I'm going to tell you something. In 1941, when I met your mother, she had turned seventeen and was working at the Kirov factory, the largest weapons production facility in the Soviet Union. Do you know what she wore? A ratty brown cardigan that belonged to her grandmother. It was tattered and patched and two sizes too big for her. Even though it was June, she wore her much larger sister's black skirt that was scratchy wool. The skirt came down to her shins. Her too-big thick black cotton stockings bunched up around her brown work boots. Her hands were covered in black grime she couldn't scrub off. She smelled of gasoline and nitrocellulose because she had been making bombs and flamethrowers all day. And still I came every day to walk her home."

Anthony laughs. "Well, you were smitten with Mommy back then, and I don't think you want her to wear black stockings bunched at her ankles and to smell of nitrocellulose *now*, do you, Dad?"

"I'm saying it doesn't matter, son."

Tatiana wrapped her arms around herself and stared straight ahead.

Anthony suddenly peered at his mother, glanced at his father—and turned his face away. They all fell quiet. Alexander laid a patch on the road. What choice did they have?

Tra-la-la-la-LAA-la-la-la-LAAAAA.

At Shannon and Amanda's house Tatiana went straight to the kitchen to help the girls, carrying out food trays, wine glasses, finger foods. There was some general oohing and ahhing over a stoic wife pulling needles out of her husband's palms. "Are they shredded?" asked Shannon. "Are they *absolutely* shredded? Johnny-boy, come here and see what our Alexander has done. Oh, man, he won't be able to hold a glass of beer for weeks!"

"Oh, come on," said Johnny, drinking and grinning. "Not even a glass of beer? What's he going to do on Friday nights?"

Alexander holding a glass of beer at that very moment, said nothing. Johnny turned to Tatiana. "Um—how are you, Mrs. Barrington?" he said with grave solemnity. "May I just say, you're looking especially fine this evening." Johnny was always insipidly stilted when he talked to Tatiana. He told Alexander once that he was terrified of her because despite all the charming, polite, nice things he tried to say, she seemed to somehow see right through to the bone, to the asshole that was buried deep underneath.

Alexander had laughed. "She doesn't think you're an asshole," he said. "I couldn't have hired you if she thought so. She just thinks you're a bit wild."

"Yes," said Johnny. "Wild in that asshole kind of way."

And so, tonight after he paid her a compliment, she eyed him with spectacular detachment and said, "Thank you, Johnny-boy. Have a late night Friday night?"

"No, no, ma'am, it wasn't too bad," said Johnny, glancing frightened at Alexander as if already sensing that he was once again being set up and shown up for being exactly the asshole that he was, not knowing that it wasn't him who was being set up.

Well. That was that. And that was too bad, because the poker poetry was good poetry and would have gone over well. And she would have believed it. She would have believed it because she wanted to believe it.

Your move, Alexander.

His next move was Tyrone, Johnny-boy's *really* wild friend. Alexander would say he went with Tyrone to a strip club downtown. Very very very sorry. No poetry this time. Strip club and Tyrone were bad enough.

Tatiana didn't dance with Alexander, didn't talk to him, didn't look at him.

He watched her from afar. When she wasn't putting on a smiling face for the mingling Christmas crowd, Anthony was right, there was something vanquished in her demeanor. She didn't look quite herself.

The music was plenty loud, Elvis Presley gyrated on the radio, exhorting the partygoers to be true, to love him tender, be his teddy bear, to not be cruel to a heart that was true . . .

Nat King Cole sang some Christmas music, played "Unforgettable," played "Auld Lang Syne."

Nat King Cole played "Nature Boy."

Alexander was standing in one cluster in the living room, talking to a group of friends. Tatiana, with Anthony by her side, was standing nearby. "Oh, listen, Dad," Anthony called over grimly. "Your favorite song." In front of them was a patch of floor where couples were dancing pressed together. The tree was twinkling, the Christmas candles burned. And Nat King Cole sang of loving and being loved in return.

Alexander made his way over to her and said, "Let's go home."

He held the coat for her in front of Shannon and Amanda, who asked if everything was all right, and Shannon gave Alexander a tense non-glance into the plants. "Everything is wonderful," Tatiana said to her hosts without a glimmer of a smile.

On the way home, it was Anthony who broke the searing silence by starting to sing . . . *it's lovely weather/for a sleigh ride together with you* . . . Alexander leaned forward and shot Anthony a side look that said you better stop this second. Anthony stopped that second but not before he whispered, *it'll be the perfect ending/to a perfect day* . . .

Alexander stayed outside, read the paper and smoked, and sat so long, he fell asleep on the bench. Waking up freezing and cramped, he went to bed and lay down beside her. He remembered them in Lazarevo, lying clamped together near the fire under the stars, searching for Perseus up in the galaxy. Her family was gone. His was gone. And fifteen and a half years later, in a miracle, in a dream, with divine grace, they lay unclamped in a home they had made for themselves after all they had been through, while she was in a nightgown, possibly wore underwear and a bra, possibly even a steel helmet and flak jacket, and he couldn't come near her to find out, thinking of all the possible lies for last Friday and all the possible lies for the coming Wednesday.

> Poker with Johnny
> Till six in the morning—
> Stayed out too late
> Didn't want to tell you
> When I was half dead

In bed
Upset you for nothing
I'm sorry, I'm sorry
Was going to come clean
Spilled beer on my jeans
The cholla knows nothing
I'm sorry I'm sorry
But Carmen is waiting
For me at the Westin
—Poker with Johnny
Till six in the morning.

CHAPTER TWELVE

Gone Astray

So Blue Thinking About You

Wednesday night after work Alexander sat in front of an obscure bar-restaurant all the way south in Chandler. He sat in his truck, the engine still running, his unbandaged, barely scabbed-over hands on the wheel. He was in his best suit. He had driven miles from his usual haunts to meet Carmen.

It was past eight, past the time he was supposed to meet her and he—who was never late unless Tatiana made him late—was sitting in the truck. All he had to do was turn off the engine and go inside. What was the problem?

Tatiana was still making him late.

It took something out of Alexander to prepare for this, to prevent questions in case any arose, to think of contingencies. "Can Ant go to Francesca's after school? I'm working late," he had said to Tatiana that morning. They hadn't been speaking, except through and about Anthony. Alexander had been counting—depending—on more unbearable silence, but instead this morning, Tatiana had said, "Oh, I'm sorry. Another late meeting? Like you don't work hard enough. Will you eat?"

Alexander promised her he would eat.

And now it was eating him up inside.

He said to her as they were getting ready, "I don't know how late I'll be. It's way down south."

And Tatiana said, "Don't worry. Just go do what you have to do. I'll be waiting. How are your hands? Are they feeling better? You want me to rebandage them?"

This after four days of barely speaking!

So now Alexander was sitting here, about to go do what he had to do. And he couldn't leave the truck.

"Do you want me to call?" he asked just before she left for work, when she was already at the door, cap on, nurse bag in her hands.

"If you're going to be very late, call," said Tatiana. "Otherwise just come home." She did not, however, look at him when she said these things, nor raise her eyes to him.

The engine hummed. The whirling dervish inside him was so unstill and so merciless that he found himself shaking the wheel in a hellish attempt to get control of himself.

It was all right. It would be all right. She would never know—about this. Alexander did not tell her his prepared lies about Tyrone because she had not asked, and he was certainly not going to volunteer. Saturday, Sunday, Monday, Tuesday, she never looked at him and said, "Where were you till six in the morning?"

Yet things were happening in his tranquil house that he could hardly ignore. Tatiana had not cooked for him since Friday; had not made fresh *bread*! She had not washed his clothes. She had not made his side of the bed, or picked up his cigarette butts, or thrown away his newspapers, or brought him coffee. Tatiana had not gone grocery shopping. Both Monday and Tuesday, Alexander had to bring milk home.

"You haven't bought milk," he said on Monday.

"I forgot," she said.

Tuesday she said nothing and he didn't ask. Both days she worked, and at night the lamps had not gone on, the candles had not been lit. Both evenings Alexander had to light the Christmas tree himself when he got home. And despite their civil words this Wednesday morning—a fact remained as stark and foreign as the Japanese in Normandy: they had not kissed since Saturday, had not *touched* in bed since Saturday. These were uncharted waters in their marriage. Since they had been together, they had not spent a single day without touching; it was as certain as the moontides; and now they—who slept at night as if they were still on the ground in his tent in Luga—had not touched for four days!

What did Alexander think was going on with her?

He wasn't thinking about her. He was thinking only about himself and all the lies he could tell her so that she would never find out.

Carmen's sedan was in the lot. She was already inside waiting. He turned off the engine. He had to go in. They would have a

drink, maybe a quick—very quick—bite to eat. Afterward—
Alexander had brought cash for the Westin hotel, condoms for
himself, he was ready. He'd go with her, spend an hour, maybe
two, shower, get dressed, leave.

And here's where the trouble was: right at the point of showering with hotel soap and leaving Carmen to go home to an "I'll
be waiting" Tatiana. When he came home after having sex with
another woman, would he have to look Tatiana in the face, or
could he count on her eyes being turned away from him? Or would
he have to *not* look her in the face? She would smell the hotel
soap. He'd have to shower without soap. She'd smell the wet hair.
She would know by the look in his eyes. She would know by his
averted eyes. She'd know by touching him. She would know
instantly.

Carmen was waiting for him. Shouldn't he have decided not to
go through with it *before* the moment he was nattily dressed and
freshly showered and had condoms in his pocket?

Condoms.

Alexander's heart closed in around itself. That's how deliberate
he was, how prepared, how set for betrayal. This wasn't an out of
control moment, like last Friday night. Oh, honey, I'm sorry, I
didn't mean to. I just got drunk and lost control. It doesn't mean
anything, honey, honey, honey.

No. This was premeditated betrayal. This was betrayal in cold
blood.

Alexander wasn't drunk, he wasn't out of control, and he had
bought condoms in advance.

He could barely convince even himself about the out of control
moment last Friday night. He did, after all, sit at the bar alone,
waiting for Carmen to show up. Would that sound out of control
to Tatiana's ears? On the one hand, Tania, my faithful truck, on
the other sitting in a bar for an hour waiting for the party girl. It
all evens out, right?

It was dark in the lot. The lights of the bar were twinkling.
Through the decorated-for-Christmas windows, Alexander could
see people moving about inside, couples talking.

She is so sanguine and *so* busy. She works sixty hours a week.
She'll never find out. Even if she finds out, she'll forgive me. She
forgives me for everything. We will go on as before.

Yet his house was not cleaned and his clothes were not
washed. There was no food on his table, nor lips on his face.

Alexander was breathing hard, trying to wade through his mire. Having dinner with another woman! He had never done it, not even in the years before Tatiana when he was in the army—especially when he was in the army. When he was a garrison soldier, he bought the girls drinks, and thirty minutes later, their skirts were hitched up at the parapets. Those were his courtships. Alexander was thirty-eight-years old and he had never taken anyone out for dinner before he had sex with them, except Tatiana.

The imagining himself in the awkwardness, in the stilted conversation, in the pretend flirtation was paralyzing his hands behind the wheel, was tamping out his desire for someone new, his excitement for a bit of strange. And then the coming home, showered— or perhaps *not* showered? It was unimaginable. Tamping out with a talon of steel.

And suddenly—*He is lying on dirty straw. He has been beaten so many times, his body is one bloodied bruise; he is filthy, he is hideous, he is a sinner and he is utterly unloved. At any moment, at any instant, he will be put on a train in his shackles and taken through Cerberus's mouth to Hades for the rest of his wretched life. And it is at that precise moment that the light shines from the door of his dark cell #7, and in front of him Tatiana stands, tiny, determined, disbelieving, having returned for him. Having abandoned the infant boy who needs her most to go find the broken beast who needs her most. She stands mutely in front of him, and doesn't see the blood, doesn't see the filth, sees only the man, and then he knows: he is not cast out. He is loved.*

What a blithering idiot.

Alexander started up the engine, put the truck into reverse, peeled out of the parking lot and drove home, leaving Carmen waiting for him inside the restaurant. On the way home, he remembered—just in time—pulled into a gas station, and threw out the condoms he bought into the public trash.

He got home after ninethirty.

After parking the truck next to her Thunderbird, Alexander walked quietly up the deck stairs and watched Tatiana from the unshaded window. She was in her short silk robe, her hair was down. She hadn't seen him yet, hadn't heard him pull up; the music must be playing. She was sitting at the kitchen table, her back to the door, her head lowered, her shoulders slumped. She was holding her stomach and she was crying.

On the table there was fresh bread. One candle was lit. The

Christmas tree was bright, the table lamps were on, the lights around the windows sparkled.

Anthony was nowhere to be seen.

Unable to watch her anymore, Alexander took a deep breath, and with his heart as heavy as a rock, opened the door. Please, *please,* let me keep my brave and indifferent face.

Tatiana wiped her eyes first and then turned to him. "Hey," she said. She pressed her lips together to keep them from trembling.

"I was done early," Alexander said, taking off his suit jacket, looking around.

"Oh."

"Where's Ant?"

"With Sergio. I'm letting him stay over."

Alexander frowned, his troubled mind reeling. "You're letting him stay overnight on a Wednesday?" This was incongruous.

"As a treat for him."

His heart was hammering in his chest.

"Are you hungry?" she asked. "I made a little food."

Alexander dumbly nodded.

"Well, go wash then. I made some . . . blinchiki. Meatball soup. Soda bread."

Without washing, he sank into the chair. She made *blinchiki?* It's a good thing she wasn't close to him because she would've heard the repentant pounding of his wanton black heart. "Aren't you going to eat?" Alexander asked.

"I'm not hungry," she replied. "But I'll sit with you—if you want." Tatiana put food on his plate, poured him a beer, water, brought him the day's newspaper. The music was on, the candle was burning at his table!

Comfort and joy . . . o tidings of comfort and joy . . .

God rest ye merry gentlemen, let nothing ye dismay,

Remember, Christ, our Savior, was born on Christmas day . . .

The sash of her robe had gotten loose. As she stood to pour him another beer, Alexander glimpsed an ivory lace camisole, through which he could see her body, nude except for the white suspender belt and lace stockings. He felt sick. Looking down, he read the paper, and ate—and did not lift his eyes to her. The only things they said to each other during dinner were, hers, "How do you like the blinchiki?" and his, "They're excellent, we haven't had them in years."

When he was done and Tatiana stepped close to take his plate, Alexander put down the paper and stopped her with his hands on her waist, slowly turning her to him. Opening the robe, he pulled it off her shoulders.

"Hmm," he said. "Chemise new?"

"For you," she said. "You like?"

"I like." But he couldn't look up. He did manage to pull the camisole down, to bare her heavy milky breasts to his wounded hands. Fondling her, cupping her, he put his lips on her nipples, as she quaked and moaned under his mouth, quivering uncontrollably like a violin, alive, soft, perfect. "Why so sensitive?" Alexander whispered, one torn half of him still clambering up from the abyss. Suddenly he became afraid—almost certain—that Tatiana was reading his thoughts. Putting his hand under the camisole and patting her bottom, Alexander let go of her and quickly stood from the table.

He *may* have been able to hide his thoughts from her, but what he could not hide in their bed was the ravening lead gravity of guilt pulling all his organs down into the earth. There was simply no love tonight. "I don't know what's wrong with me," he said.

"No?" she said, and turned away.

He offered her something for herself. Tatia, remember our fifth wedding anniversary? he whispered achingly to her. Anthony was napping in the trailer and we were in Naples on a deserted Gulf beach in the late afternoon, on a blanket on white sand. We had been swimming and you were briny and wet. I lay stretched out on my back and you kneeled over my mouth. You couldn't keep yourself upright; you pitched forward and remained on your sandy elbows and knees. My head was thrown back, my face buried in you, and I held your hips in place with my hands. We were in a straight line, you and I, you above me. Happy birthday, happy anniversary, happy napping Anthony, and on *joyful wing/cleaving the sky/sun, moon and stars forgot,/upward I fly*. Everything was forgot for that one hour of honeysuckle bliss on a white sand beach on the Gulf of Mexico. Please, Tatiasha. Kneel over me. Keel forward, let me touch you. Give me honey, give me bliss, cleave the sky, and forget everything.

Her back to him was still, as if she had not heard, as if he had not whispered.

After she was asleep, Alexander spooned her to him, into the crook of his arm, against his chest. Her hair tickled his ribs. It took him hours to fall asleep. Was it his imagination, or was there a promise of future agony that he heard in her clipped voice all evening? She kept trying to say something to him—and failing. He certainly wasn't going to ask, but how did she go from lying in bed in a fetal position Saturday night to making him his favorite meal and crashing her naked body through his hit parade?

"Lay your sleeping head, on my faithless arm," he inaudibly whispered, trying to remember Auden, suffocating on the poison cocktail of his self-hatred and his conscience.

Baby, Please Come Home

The following morning, Alexander walked into the office to get his messages, to see his appointments for the day, and to make sure Linda had taken care of the hundreds of Christmas bonuses. Efficient to a fault, she said she had done it weeks ago when he first asked. She said to him, "Were you a bad boy and forget about your appointment last night?"

"What appointment?"

"What appointment? With Mrs. Rosario, Alexander! *You* made it. She was in your book."

"Oh. I must've forgotten," he said carefully. "Why do you ask?"

"Well, you weren't home either," said Linda. "Because she came here last night around nine looking for you."

"Who?"

"Mrs. Rosario."

Alexander was quiet. "Linda, what's wrong with you that you were still here at nine?"

"Don't you know I have no life?" she said. "I live to manage yours. She came by and asked if she could call your house. I didn't know what to do. I was *very* worried myself. We thought maybe something had happened. You never forget your appointments."

"Did she"— Alexander spoke with difficulty— "call my house?"

"Uh-huh. Spoke to Tania."

"Mrs. Rosario spoke to Tatiana?"

"Uh-huh. She was pretty upset."

"Who?" Alexander said in a dull voice.

"The client, of course," said Linda. "You know your wife is constitutionally incapable of getting angry at you."

Unsteadily Alexander walked outside and sat in his truck. He was doing that a lot these days. Sitting in his truck. Soon it was going to become his home.

Fucking Carmen called his house! Well, that was one scenario he did not imagine—the married woman calling his house, asking for him. That's the permutation Alexander had not seen, and he thought he had prepared for every quadratic contingency.

He couldn't think straight. But why *didn't* bad things go down? Why didn't they have it out yesterday? They were alone, they had all night. He would have thought of something to say that sounded like the truth. Why did Tania dress down to a see-through che- mise for him? Why the food, the candles? What in the name of heaven was going on at his house? Alexander's mind was baffled and bewildered.

He had to go check on the status of three of his houses. The electricians were coming to one, the foundation was being poured on another, and the Certificate of Occupancy inspector was coming to the third. But at lunch Alexander went to the hospital. Even though he knew Tatiana never had a break long enough to have a cup of coffee, much less a brief calm talk about another woman calling their house asking for him, how could he not go?

He found her sitting by herself in the cafeteria, drinking milk; she looked grim and white. "Hey," she said, barely glancing at him. "What are you doing here?"

"Come outside for a minute," he said.

When they were out in the sun-filled parking lot, Alexander stopped walking and said, his teeth grinding, his eyes to the ground, "Why didn't you tell me Carmen Rosario called you last night?"

"Did you come to the hospital to ask me this? She didn't call me," said Tatiana. "She called our house looking for *you*." She laughed lightly. "She asked to speak to you and when I said you weren't home, she said, well, where *is* he? in a tone that you can imagine *I* for one found peculiar. I told her you were working late. She said yes, and she was the one you were supposed to be working late with. I'll tell you," Tatiana continued, folding her hands together, "she seemed *quite* upset. I didn't know what to say, since I didn't know where you were, so I apologized for you. I thought you would want me to do that, right, Alexander? Apologize to Carmen Rosario for you?" She paused. "I told her you must've forgotten. It must have slipped your mind. Sometimes your mind does that, plays tricks on you, I told her. Where you forget cer- tain things."

If Alexander's head were any lower, it would be hitting the fucking ground. He took a shaky step back. "Why are you doing this?" he said quietly. "Why didn't you tell me this yesterday? Why did you play this charade with me, make me dinner, put music on? What for?" He could not lift his eyes to her.

"I don't understand the question," said Tatiana.

Alexander examined the cracks in the pavement.

"You have a hundred appointments like this throughout the year," said Tatiana. "You told me you were working late. You've told me that many times when you met with clients in the past. Yes, you didn't show up for your appointment, but I don't know why. You could have gotten busy with other things. You could have not had her number handy. You could have made a mistake and gone to the wrong restaurant. It's your business, I don't get that closely involved in it. You didn't tell me it was Carmen you were meeting, but so what? You don't submit to me the names of the clients who are interested in building a home with you. That's never been our marriage." Tatiana stopped. Alexander couldn't even hear her inhale and exhale, that's how quiet she was while speaking and breathing. "The woman you were meeting to talk about building a house called and said you never showed up. She seemed perfectly within her rights to be irritated. I would think most of your clients would not look kindly on being left waiting in some bar/restaurant down south in Chandler and would prob-ably call our house demanding, 'Well, where *is* he?'"

They could not continue this conversation in the parking lot. "Tatiana . . ." he repeated. "Why didn't you tell me this yesterday?"

"What's the matter? Why are you getting yourself all worked up?" Tatiana said. Only the tips of her fingers trembled. It was the only part of her, besides her white-stockinged legs and the hem of her white uniform, Alexander could see.

"If you thought I was having dinner out," Alexander said, because he could think of nothing else—nothing else at all—to say, "why did you make me food then?"

"When does my husband ever refuse blinchiki?" said Tatiana in a straight voice, staring directly at him, "even when he has his dinner out?"

Oh God! "Tania . . ." he let out in a hoarse breath.

She backed away and said, "Well, listen, if there is nothing else, I have to go back to work."

Yes, go back to the root of all evil. He didn't say it, just in case she told him *he* was the root of all evil. "Wait," Alexander said. His reeling mind couldn't see through the fog in the clear-blue-sky, broad-daylight, crisp winter day. Should he now lie and say, I really truly was just going to meet up for a drink with Carmen? We really truly *were* going to talk about the house—condoms in my pocket notwithstanding? Should he say, I did *almost* nothing wrong—this Wednesday—aside from premeditating my lascivious and traitorous plans. As opposed perhaps to last Friday, when things really truly were much more murky and tawdry, but I'm hoping you'll forget about last Friday altogether. And I know it seems bad, me going to meet another woman to take her to a hotel to have sex with her, but I didn't let her go in my truck on Friday. My truck is pristine. Don't I get *some* points for that? Isn't that at least like moving my pawn one square forward on the board?

Alexander couldn't see one move ahead, one step ahead, one word ahead. He would be damned if he opened his mouth. So he said to her, *wait*, but what he meant was, *I got nothing*.

"I really must fly," said Tatiana. "But you have to go back to work, too, no? Have you rescheduled your appointment with Mrs. Rosario? Will you be working late in Chandler tonight?"

"Tania, no," Alexander said in a defeated voice.

"Ah," she said, walking away.

If Alexander didn't have to meet with the electricians at a 7000-square-foot River Crossing house for a family who needed the house delivered yesterday, he never would have gotten out of his truck. But he had to meet with the electricians, and he was still with them in the late afternoon when Carmen's sedan pulled up and she got out, all flashy earrings, flashy makeup, flashy tight black and white sweater. Don Joly, the electrician, watching her from the window, whistled softly under his breath. "Va-va-voom," he said.

Alexander turned his back.

She walked in, found him. "Hello, Alexander."

"You might want to get out of the house," he said without facing her. "It's not safe here. A construction site. I'm not insured for accidents to unauthorized visitors."

"Um, can I speak to you a moment?"

"Speak at your own peril," Alexander said, without looking up from the framing, where thirty feet of electrical wire lay tangled. He was measuring the distance between the outlets; according to code they had to be no more than six feet apart and he was afraid the one in front of him was more than six feet from the one on the left, which meant it would have to be redone, which meant, like dominoes, all the rest in a room would have to be redone. He had to measure it out six hundred times in a house this size, and all before Christmas next week.

"Alexander, can you turn around?"

Slowly he stood up and turned around. "What?" he said. "I'm busy."

"I see that. Were you busy last night, too, when I waited like a fool alone in that restaurant?"

"I was busy last night, too." Every single thing inside him had shut off to her. He couldn't believe he was speaking to her.

"I don't understand anything," Carmen said. "I thought we had agreed to meet. Did you forget?"

"That's right," he said. "I forgot."

Sharply inhaling, she said, "I don't believe you. We made plans. You couldn't forget."

"Except I did, Carmen, I *completely* forgot."

"You're trying to humiliate me! Why?"

"Why?" He took a breath to calm himself. "Why did you call my wife?"

"I didn't call her! I was calling *you*."

"At my fucking *house*?" Alexander's voice was too loud. He was disgusted by her. And by himself. Don Joly amid planks on the second floor must have been listening, and how could he not, Don Joly and all his merry men, listening to Alexander fighting with a woman not his wife. This was crossing the border into another country, and it was going to get around to everyone, all because of his own indecency.

"Yes, at your fucking house!" Carmen said, just as loudly.

Alexander had enough. He took her by the elbow and led her out into the street. "Look," he said. "I work here. Work. Do you understand? Also I'm married. Do you understand *that*? Unlike you I don't have a pretend marriage, I have an actual marriage. You were calling my home, where I live with my wife, to ask her why I didn't show up for our rendezvous! Have you got no fucking sense at all?"

"That's not what I did," Carmen said defensively. "I was very professional."

"Professional? Screeching into the phone, 'Where *is* he?' That's professional?"

"Your wife was very composed," Carmen said. "More than you are right now. But if you didn't want me to call, then why didn't you just show up like you promised?"

They were standing on the sidewalk in the middle of a new street, in the middle of a new community, Alexander and a woman, arguing!

"Carmen, I never thought about it again after Friday," said Alexander. "That's why. But besides that, first priority to my wife, second to everything else."

"You weren't thinking about your wife last Friday," she said, raising her voice, sticking out her ridiculous chest. "She was quite far from your thoughts then."

"Not as far as you flatter yourself into thinking," Alexander retorted. "But are you even fucking kidding coming here and raising your voice to me?"

"Stop talking trash!" she yelled. "I'm not your wife. You better show *me* some respect."

"Who the fuck do you think you are, lady?" said Alexander, stepping closer to her and speaking quieter. "Respect? You get into a car with a complete stranger and you think because I let you suck my dick for two minutes you deserve *respect*?"

She gasped. "*Let* me?" She turned red in the face.

"As opposed to *what*? Not only did I let you, Carmen, but you didn't get as much as a free drink from me."

"Oh!" She was flushed and wheezing. "Oh—oh—you'll be sorry, Alexander!"

"I'm already plenty sorry."

"Because of your deplorable conduct, your wife—"

"You know what," Alexander said, cutting her off, coming up close, too close, and leaning into her face. "Before you say another word, this is what you're going to do. You are going to get into your car and drive the fuck away from here. You obviously haven't read the papers carefully about me, and you might want to go do that, but I'm warning you right now, don't threaten me, don't insult me, don't rail at me, just get quietly into your car and drive away—while you still can—and don't ever come near me or my houses again."

She opened her mouth but Alexander shook his head, taking one more half step until he was inches away from her face. "Not near me, or my houses, or my wife, ever again."

She opened her mouth.

He shook his head. "No, Carmen. When I said, not another fucking word, I meant—not another fucking word. Just get into your car and drive away." He was talking so menacingly that she finally shut up, hearing him loud and clear.

Her stockinged knees shaking, chest heaving in her va-va-voom sweater, Carmen managed to open the car door, get in, and drive away.

Having a fight with a woman not his wife! It was so unseemly, it was so scandalously wrong.

"Where is my mother?" Anthony said at ten o'clock that evening.

That was a good question indeed. Where *was* his mother? When Alexander called the hospital, Erin told him Tatiana was working a double shift.

"She is *what*?" Alexander put his hand on the counter to steady himself. "Erin, let me speak to her."

"I can't, she's in major trauma, she can't come to the phone. I'll ask her to call you when she gets out."

Anthony didn't believe his mother was working a double shift. Alexander didn't believe it himself. They didn't know what to do as they sat numbly at the kitchen table. Earlier they had eaten the remains of yesterday's blinchiki, and Anthony—still happy then, his mouth full—said, "Oh, Dad, thank you, what did you do so right that we have blinchiki tonight?"

What *did* he do that they had blinchiki? Certainly nothing right.

But at ten thirty in the evening, with the food long gone, Anthony said, "Something's happening, isn't it? Mom shuffled me off to Sergio's in the middle of the week as if another Dudley is lying dead in our house."

Alexander thought his son's association was quite apropos.

An unquenchably upset boy was Alexander's ostensible reason for driving forty miles at midnight on Thursday to see Tatiana. They sat in the waiting room with two drunks, a man with a broken leg, a woman with a hacking cough, and a feverish tiny baby.

They paged her again, and again. They had to wait another thirty-five minutes before she rushed out through the double doors. The son ran to her. The husband stayed put in his seat, grimly studying his scabbed palms.

"What's wrong, what's happened?" she said, extremely stressed.

"Nothing," Anthony said. "Mom, why are you here? Why are

you working a double shift? You never work a double shift. And why didn't you call us back? We were so worried. Why didn't you tell us you were working tonight? Why aren't you coming home?"

Alexander thought the boy did pretty well with the questions. He forgot these: What do you suspect that I can instantly deny so I can make you feel better and touch you again, and never have to think or talk about this in my life? What have I done? What lies can I spin out now to undo it? And when is the coroner's crew coming to clean our house of Carmen, Tatiana? That's the question Alexander thought Anthony should ask.

Tatiana sat down in the chair. They tried to keep their voices low. The drunks were listening. "I'm working a double shift, bud, that's all," she said. "It's Christmas. We're short-staffed, and very busy. Everybody is getting hurt. Everybody," she said, "is getting very very hurt."

"Please," said Anthony. "You threw me out of the house yesterday. You think I'm a child? Yesterday Dad said he was working and not coming home. Tonight you're working and not coming home. You've been fighting since last week. You think I don't see things going on?" He was near tears. "Please."

Tatiana took his face into her hands. He was already seven inches taller than she, and fifty pounds heavier, and yet he stayed in the space where she held him, his head pressed into her neck, as if he were three. Alexander sat with his elbows on his knees, looking at the floor. He knew that space himself.

"There is a Christmas concert in my school tomorrow," said Anthony.

Tatiana nodded. "I know. I'm coming."

"Mom!" Anthony exclaimed. "Are you upset with Dad? Please don't be upset with Dad about the other—"

"Anthony!" That was Alexander. "Not another word."

"Yes, Anthony," said Tatiana. "Not another word."

She was paged. Another ambulance came in. She tried to disengage herself. "Bud, I'm sorry. I'll be home soon. But right now I really have to run."

The triage nurse called for her. One of the drunks crept up to her. Anthony was still pressed to her. Someone was wheeled fast and bloodied on a stretcher. Alexander couldn't look at her. He knew she needed his help with Anthony, but he wasn't giving it to her until she called him by name. "Anthony," said Tatiana, "tell your father I *have* to go."

"He's sitting right here, Mom," said Anthony. "Tell him your-self."

Alexander got up. Very quietly he said to her, "As always—you can do without all of us sinners, can't you?" And then physically dragged Anthony away from his mother. "Come on, bud," he said. "Mommy is busy. Let's go home. Look what I bought today." He took out a bag of peanut M&Ms. "Have you seen these? M&Ms with peanuts in them. What a country. Want one?"

David Bradley flung open the double doors, in scrubs. "God, where *is* she?" Then he saw her. "Tatiana, *please!*" he called. "Now!"

"Don't worry, son," Tatiana said to Anthony, standing up. "Your father will take care of you. Go home." She didn't even glance at the father before she rushed away.

At eight in the morning on Friday, Tatiana was not home. Alexander waited until nine. Anthony's concert was at 9:30. He drove to the school, watching for her car coming up Jomax. He found her in the packed auditorium, still in her nurse's uniform, and she hadn't even saved him a seat! He had to stand in the back. The principal came out, the piano played, the children sang, the band performed. He watched her clap clap clap for their son, she stood up, took pictures, and even talked to the other parents about what a nice job the children had done of rendering the Christmas classics. The children went back to their classrooms, and she vanished in the departing crowd. By the time Alexander caught up with her, she was already at her Thunderbird. His hand slammed shut the car door. "Tania!"

Her head was down. "Can you let me open my car, please?" she said.

"No. Can we do this like adults?"

"Do what?"

He leaned in to her. "What are you doing?"

"Nothing, what are you doing?" They stared at each other for a moment before he looked away. She looked immensely tired. She couldn't stand straight.

"Did you get off work at seven?" he asked quietly, standing close, wanting to touch the pallid cheek, the blonde eyebrows.

"Yes."

"Why didn't you come home?"

"Why didn't *you* come home?"

"I did come home," Alexander said, his fingers reaching for her face. "Come on. Let's go. I took the morning off work."

"You did? Great!" Tatiana said, moving away from his hands. "One thing though—I don't want to talk to you."

"I know," said Alexander. It was no longer a question of what lie to spin that she would believe. It was becoming in a whirlwind a question of how much truth to give her so that she would ever believe him again. "I know you don't want to, but you *have* to talk to me." He took her upper arm. "Come on, let's not do this in the middle of the school parking lot. All these people . . ." The other parents were ambling to their cars, chatting happily about Christmas plans, gifts for the kids, the lovely weather, the sleigh rides together. Alexander and Tatiana stood mutely to let them pass.

"I know you're upset with me—"

She raised her hand to stop him.

"What do you want to do?" Alexander said, opening his hands. "Go on like this? Not speaking? Eventually you'll have to talk to me, no?"

"No," said Tatiana, barely shaking her head and opening the car door. "I'm all talked out."

How can you be talked out, you haven't spoken three words to me since Saturday! Alexander wanted to say. "Let's go home," he said cajolingly. "You can yell, you can do whatever—"

"Do I look to you like I can yell or do whatever?" Tatiana stood at the open car door. "And do I *need* to yell?" She looked like she would fall down or faint if she didn't sit down. Alexander reached out to hold her steady, to touch her, but she put her hands up as if she wanted him to disappear from her sight. "No." She leaned against the car, crossing her arms, and shut her eyes.

"Open your eyes," said Alexander. She opened them. They were almost obsidian, the color of the Black Sea. "Tania . . ." he said, keeping his voice from breaking—just. "Babe, please. Let's go home. Let me explain, let me talk to you."

She shook her head. "No," she said. "No more talking for us. Besides, I have to go to the mission."

"The mission?" he said, frowning. "You just worked twenty-four straight hours. You have to go home and sleep, no?"

"No. The little children don't know and don't care about my sleep. The children are waiting."

"Yes, they certainly are," Alexander said, his fists clenching, finally stepping away from her. She always knew how to say just the thing to make him step away. "Your son—who is your actual child—has been waiting and waiting."

"His father is taking care of him, no?"

"He needs his mother."

She clenched her own fists, and stepped *toward* him. Alexander opened his arms. "Right here," he said. "Here I stand."

"Indeed you do," said Tatiana. She took a breath. "Alexander, when you asked me to marry you, did you realize our marriage might last longer than one moon cycle?"

"I was hoping."

"No, I don't think you were. Yes, you said, we were only going to do this once and we might as well do it right, but you were thinking do it right for a month. A year between furloughs, perhaps. While you were trying to get into Germany from Russia. I'm not saying the quest for me wasn't real, but what else, after all, did you have to live for? You could try to find me, try to stay alive for me, or you could smoke away your life in a Soviet onion field. So you chose me. How ennobling! But this isn't briefest Lazarevo, is it? This is days and days and months and years, and all the minutes in between, just you and me, one man and one woman in one marriage."

"I know very well what this is, Tatiana," said Alexander, her fragile voice like concrete pressing on his heart.

"Do you? A *marriage* isn't as easy as taking a drink of water. This is not pretend life during war, or pretend Soviet marriage, the two of us against the NKVD, with pretend Soviet choices. This is real American life. Full of choices, full of freedoms, full of opportunities, money, conflicts, constant pressures. There is suffering—when we cannot have what we think we deserve and it torments us." She paused. "And there is temptation."

"Tania, stop. Not in the parking lot. I want to go home."

"You want to have this conversation at home?" Her eyes had dulled again. "In the home I worked so hard to make as a sanctuary for you from the rest of your life? A haven I made for you where you could go and have peace?" She shook her head. "I don't think you want to have this conversation there."

"I do."

"Alexander Barrington," Tatiana said, "my friend, my husband, I don't think you have been paying attention. I'm not talking about *love*. Richter thinks he loves Vikki, too. Vikki thinks she loves each of the boys she is with. Love *is* like taking a drink of water. You have the nerve to whisper to me about Naples. *Strangers* could love in Naples on a white sand beach!" she cried.

"Dogs could love in Napa. Fruitflies mate in Lazarevo. Love is *so* easy!"

He stood breathless and blinking, listening to her wash away the colors his life was painted with.

"I'm not talking about love," she repeated.

"Clearly," he said. "Can you *not* talk about it in a parking lot? Can we go home? The house is empty. Ant is in school."

"There is no peace in that house."

"Oh, I know. You've taken it with you. I want to go there anyway."

Tatiana stared him down, which was quite a feat considering she came up to his elbow. "You think you can do as you please, and then take me home?"

"Tania, if you will let me talk to you, it will be fine," said Alexander. "I will make it fine. Because I did nothing wrong."

"No?"

"No," he said, his brave and indifferent face on like a stone mask. "But *please* let's go home so I can explain."

Tatiana stepped close, in her white uniform, and she lifted her earnest face to him, her yearning eyes to him, in the sunlit parking lot of Anthony's school, in the middle of the cold December morning, and she put her hands on his chest. "Alexander," she whispered, "*kiss* me."

An involuntary gasp left Alexander's throat.

Her fists were clenched on his shirt, near his heart, her questioning, hoping, hurting eyes filling with tears were gazing up at him. "You heard me," she breathed out. "My husband, the father of my baby, my horse and cart, my life, my soul, with your truest lips, *kiss* me."

The coroner's crew wasn't coming anytime soon to clean Carmen off the walls of their house. Alexander's choice was before him. Either he kissed her or he stepped away. But either way, whichever way, he was finished.

Because it was checkmate.

Alexander stepped away. "Tatiana, this is ridiculous. I'm asking and asking, let's go home and finish this. I refuse to do this with you in public." He could not look at her.

Tatiana got into her Thunderbird and screeched out of the empty parking lot.

Baby, it's Cold Outside

Tatiana didn't come home any time that Friday. Next Wednesday was Christmas. On *Monday,* Vikki, Richter, Esther, Rosa were all flying in from snowy East to spend Christmas with them. What were they going to do?

Alexander called her at the mission, called her at the hospital, but she didn't come to the phone or return his call. "I'm sorry, Alexander," said Erin, said Cassandra. "She's busy, she's in surgery, she's in trauma one, trauma two, one accident after another, one heart attack after another, there's even been a knifing! she can't come to the phone."

He and Anthony couldn't stay in their empty house. They went out to dinner and to the pictures. They saw *The Invasion of the Body Snatchers.* They barely spoke.

The Christmas tree remained unlit, and Alexander had forgotten to put the outside lights on. Coming back at eleven at night, they couldn't see their house at all at the top of the Jomax hill. The little beacon was pitch black from the inside and out.

Alexander called her again. He thought of going to see her, but they'd already had three fruitless discussions in parking lots and waiting rooms. For the second night he couldn't sleep in their bed. He smoked until he couldn't see straight from the poison and remained on the couch until Saturday morning.

After the ER receptionist told him that Tatiana had left the hospital at seven, Alexander waited for her, but when she wasn't home by nine, he went to work, taking Ant with him, not wanting the boy to stay by himself in the house.

Anthony was so dismally mute sitting in the corner of the reception area, that Alexander could barely attend to his appointments. Go shopping, Ant, get an ice cream; here, take some cash, buy yourself anything. But Anthony wouldn't move.

Tonight the Barrington Custom Homes Christmas party was being held at the new spectacular model home they had just finished. Alexander and Tatiana were hosting, as they had every year for the last six. A hundred and fifty people were invited. There was a lot at stake, for instance, a coveted invitation to build a house for the prestigious Parade of Homes builders' competition of 1959.

At four in the afternoon, Alexander returned home with Anthony to get ready. Tatiana was not home.

She had *been* home, however, because all the dishes that were once in the cupboards and cabinets were lying shattered on the linoleum floor. *All* the dishes. And the cups and bowls, too. Dudley, Carmen, their marriage on the floor of their house.

Alexander and Anthony stood grim, gaping at the chaos, at the madness.

"Tania, will you forgive me for going to prison?"

"Yes."

"Will you forgive me for dying?"

"Yes."

"Will you forgive me . . ."

"Shura, I will forgive you for everything."

"Somebody's been home," said Anthony, throwing his jacket on the coathook. "But I don't think it was my mother."

It took them over an hour to clean up the broken shards.

When Alexander came inside the bedroom to change, he emitted a wretched groan. On their quilt, on their cream blanket with crimson buds, lay spread out in long sad bitter strands the remains of Tatiana's blonde hair. All chopped up and chopped off, the hair lay in a tangled mess. Alexander's sharpest army knife with the gun-blue steel blade was thrown on the floor nearby.

For a long time Alexander sat on the bed, his hands on his knees, while on the bedroom radio Vivaldi's *Sposa Son Disprezzata* played. He was simply astonished at the reaction of the serene woman he thought he knew so well to the man-made battle he had brought into their quiet house. He had thought that like everything else it would be at worst a skirmish. But this was war. *Fida son oltraggiata . . .*

And inside his head, he kept hearing Tatiana's soft voice, hard as nails, saying, *"Alexander Barrington, my friend, my husband, I don't think you have been paying attention."*

It wasn't possible that this was happening! Alexander's heart cried. It wasn't possible! Real life couldn't grind them down, too. They were beyond this, weren't they? They were Alexander and Tatiana. They had crawled on their bellies across frozen oceans, across continents on jagged rusted spikes, they were flayed for their sins, were beaten and bled dry, to get to each other again. This could *not* be happening.

When Alexander came out of the bedroom, showered and ready, Tatiana's fifteen years of hair cleaned up and on his dresser, he said to his son, "Ant, something tells me that Mommy isn't going to be coming to our party this evening. What do you want to do? I *have* to go."

The affair was being catered while in the house there was nothing to eat except Spam—the American Lend-Lease gift to the starving war-torn Soviet Union—which Tatiana always kept on hand, Spam which Anthony was now eating with a fork, right out of the metal can. Sunk down in the couch, Anthony looked up at his father and said, "She's left us, hasn't she?" He started to cry.

His throat closing up, Alexander sat down next to his son. "She hasn't left us," he said. "She hasn't left *you*." Somebody give me a fucking tracheotomy.

"So where is she?"

"You think if I knew, I wouldn't be there right now, party or no party?" said Alexander. "I don't know."

"Oh, Dad."

"Ant, I'm sorry. Your dad behaved badly and Mommy is very upset. I'm not going to sugarcoat it for you. But don't worry, she'll return, you'll see."

"Like she returned for you?"

Alexander attempted to stay casual. "Something like that." He ruffled his son's hair. "Now come on. There's actual food at the party."

"Spam *is* actual food," said Anthony, looking inside the can. "That was the last one. I've been eating them since last week. That and her dry stale bread in the breadbin."

"It's good we can buy more Spam and bread," Alexander said as he locked up. This time he left the tree on, the Christmas lights on, the porch light on, in case she came back before they did. What had happened yesterday to cause the mad emotion he just saw in their house? Anthony was right—the woman who smashed the dishes and hacked off her hair with his army knife was not Tatiana. Something must have happened.

Or rather—something *else* must have happened. But what?

In the truck, Anthony said, "Why can't you just tell Mom you're sorry? That's what *I* do."

Alexander smiled bleakly. "What do *you* have to be sorry for, Antman? You know you can do no wrong in your mother's eyes."

"I do things that upset her sometimes," Anthony said with a shrug. "Like fighting with that Mesker kid. But you know how she is. She just wants to hear you say you're sorry, and she'll forgive you."

"I think this one time," said Alexander, "she might need more than I'm sorry."

Of course she didn't show up at the party. Alexander, broiling, defeated, outraged, exhausted, was losing his mind. Without her by his side, he walked around, drinking, pretending to be social, to be hospitable, yes, the house, and yes, the food, and yes, the son is quite handsome, and the son sat on the couch and didn't touch the food, and every other question was, "Where is Tania?" and meanwhile, every five minutes, Alexander would go to a small private office and dial everybody he knew who wasn't at the party. No, Carolyn and Cassandra told him, we don't know where she is. No, Erin and Helena told him, we don't know where she is. No, Francesca told him, but with a pause, I don't know where she is. He kept her on the phone longer because of the pause, but she maintained she knew nothing. He even called Vikki in New York, where it was one in the morning. Vikki was obviously indisposed—but also uninformed. "Have you lost our Tania?" Vikki asked. "Don't worry. She's never far. Try to find her before I come on Monday."

Where was she? She could be collapsed somewhere, fainted on the road. How could she subject her son to this? The boy had done nothing; why make *him* suffer?

The party wound down, by eleven everyone had gone. The caterers cleaned up. Linda helped close up. When she said goodnight to Alexander, sympathy and pity were in her eyes.

He and Anthony didn't speak on the way home. Alexander was chewing over what he could possibly say or do if she was home—feeling the way he was feeling, which was coming off his hinges—while Anthony was within earshot. So when they got home and saw her car not there, Anthony became distraught, but Alexander was relieved. He didn't want to see her in front of their son.

A stiff and withdrawn Anthony turned on the TV, but there was nothing on. It was late. He stared at the color bars and numbers flashing on the screen. Alexander sat on the couch with him. Their shoulders were pressed into each other.

"Ant, go to bed."

"I'm going to wait for her."

"I'll wait. You go on to bed."

"I'll wait, too."

"No."

Anthony opened his mouth to speak.

Alexander got up. "Go to bed, Anthony. I'm not asking you."

Anthony too got up. "You're going to be waiting a long time," he said emptily, walking past his father. "I know something about that. And just like before, she won't be coming back." What he didn't say, but what he clearly wanted to say, and what Alexander heard and felt was, *she won't be coming back—just like last time, and it's all your fault—just like last time.*

When Anthony was in bed, Alexander came in and sat by him, patting his back, his shoulders, his legs. He leaned over, touched Anthony's black hair. The boy was on his stomach facing away.

"What time is it?" Anthony asked in a muffled voice.

"Twelve-thirty."

They both groaned.

"Anthony," said Alexander, "you want your mom and dad to try and make it better? Then I'm warning you, if your mom comes back tonight, don't come out of your room. The adults need to have it out their own way. You have to stay inside, put a pillow over your head, go to sleep, do whatever you need to, but under no circumstances do I want to see you open your door. You got it?"

"Why?" Anthony said. "There are no dishes left to break."

Alexander pressed his mouth to Anthony's head. "You're a good kid, bud," he whispered. "Just stay in your room."

He called the hospital. "Erin, please," he said, choking over his rasping words. "Tell me where she is."

"Alexander, I don't know. I'm sorry. I would tell you. I promise you, I would tell you. I honest to God don't know."

One in the morning, and she was still not home.

He went outside, and in near dark, by feel alone, with just the small yellow light on the deck, he chopped wood. They didn't have a fireplace, but he chopped wood for the fireplaces in houses he built, to make them more pleasing at finish-out stage. Wood logs in the fireplace on move-in day. Just a little personal touch from Barrington Custom Homes at no extra charge.

He kept hearing her voice inside his head. *"Alexander, I know you've lost everyone you ever loved, but you're not going to lose me. I swear to you on my wedding band, and on my maiden ring that you broke, I will forever be your faithful wife."*

She had said this to him once, in Lazarevo.

It was cold in the desert in the December night. Alexander wore nothing but fatigues and a black army T-shirt and it was just what he needed. The labor got rid of some of the fury, the grinding anxiety, the debilitating fear.

What if this was one of the things they couldn't fix?

What if she didn't come home again tonight?

Alexander had no sanity left, none.

Faster and faster the axe came down. He wanted to be weak from the physical exertion; he did not trust himself. Groaning in his agony, he brought the axe down on withered stump until there was no oxygen left in his lungs.

He heard a noise. Oh God—the pebbles! That was her car in the driveway. He threw down the axe and ran, coming around the house and under the covered carport just as she was getting out, and Tatiana didn't even have a chance to gasp before he was on her. He grabbed her and shook her. He was so out of breath, he could not speak, and she did not speak.

"Where the *fuck* have you been?" he groaned, shaking her limp in his arms. "Do you have *any* idea what—Anthony has been going through? My God—couldn't you have thought one fucking *second*— at least about him?" He was shaking her but weaker and weaker, and then his hands went around her, his arms clasped around her. He pressed her to his chest. "My God, where have you been?" he said. He was trembling.

"Let go of me," she said, in a voice he did not recognize. "Get your hands *off* me."

Alexander didn't just let go. He staggered away.

With Leningrad ice and a blockaded face, with her bitter condemning eyes on him, Tatiana stood, her back to the red Thunderbird. She was wearing pink capris and a short pink sweater. She looked shattered like she hadn't slept in days; the raccoon-like rings, the ashen mouth, the sunken cheeks, and the hair! Her hair . . . it was gone, cut off, sheared to her neck. It curled up now, was tousled. Alexander had been afraid she had given herself a military cut, but she had merely changed her life and become a different woman. This new woman looked barely able to stand. Perhaps it was the pink stilettos. That was his other thought after the shock of her hair. Having been gone for three days, having vanished, disappeared, she was coming back home at one thirty on a Sunday morning, wearing pink capris and pink stilettos.

Tatiana stood by her car. Alexander was panting a few feet away. It was cold; he was burning hot.

"Where the *fuck* have you been?" he repeated. "Answer me."

"Where have *you* been?" she said. "Did you answer *me*?"

"You didn't ask me a single thing."

"I didn't have to, did I?"

Blinking, he took a step back. "Since Thursday gone from our house," Alexander said. "Where were you?"

"I owe you no explanation," she said in a barely controlled voice. "So stop talking to me like I do. I owe you nothing."

"You owe *me* nothing?" His head shuddered, his body shuddered from the effort to control his emotion. "Who are you talking to, Tatiana?" Alexander said, deathly quiet.

"You, Alexander," she said, her acrid voice in her eyes. "I'm talking to you. Because it's very obvious that you owe *me* nothing."

He tried not to look away. Tried and failed. "That's not true."

"Stop speaking! Stop. Stop." Her voice got lower and lower. "I can't do this," she said just above a whisper, pressed against the car, her fists at her sides. "I don't know what's happening, what's happened to us. I understand *nothing*! But I can't do this anymore." She started to shake like he was shaking. "You have to leave this house."

"*What*?"

"You heard me."

"You haven't been home for three days," said Alexander. "You're coming home at one thirty in the morning, wearing fuck-me heels, and you're telling me *I* have to pack my bags? Where have you *been*?" His voice rose decibel by decibel. He took a step toward her, and one more.

"I'm done answering your questions."

"You haven't answered a single fucking one!"

Tatiana's fists were pressed to her chest. She was leaning against the car, and it was a good thing, because she was falling down. Holding herself up by the door handle, she reached down and threw the stilettos off. Now she was minute. Alexander's heart, burned, scarred, furious, raw, was helpless before her.

"Yesterday in ER—" she began to say, but he cut her off.

"No," he said. "Not until you tell me where you were *tonight*."

"I had dinner with David Bradley."

The sails, the boat, the rudders, the anchor were pulled out from under Alexander. "You had *dinner* with David Bradley?" he repeated slowly.

"That's right."

He was quiet. "Must have been a long dinner," he said at last.

"It was," said Tatiana. "And now that we have *that* out of the way, let me tell you about last night. Last night your friend Carmen Rosario and her husband were brought in, accompanied by police, amid charges of a knifing. They had a domestic dispute that escalated out of control. Apparently Cubert stabbed Carmen, and she retaliated by stabbing him back. He got a shoulder wound, nothing too serious. We managed to save him—so unfortunately for you, she's not a widow."

All Alexander said was, "She is not my friend."

"No?"

"No."

Tatiana was supported by the car. "Apparently Carmen—" She broke off. "I know this," she said in her fake calm voice, "because I chose *not* to take care of Carmen's wound—I'm sure *you* understand the delicacy of the situation—and took care of Cubert's wound instead, and he, in his emotional state, told me more than I think he intended to. According to Cubert, his wife has been addicted to the lustful desire that men have for her rather, um, substantial breasts." Tatiana paused.

Alexander stepped three feet back. He would have liked to step three countries back.

"Carmen could not keep the boobs in her shirt since before they were married. They had been having this trouble since the start. Cubert had hoped that marriage would cure her, but alas, it had not, resulting in his year-long bout with impotence and his frequent trips away from home. Yes, I agree with your shaking head. I also thought he was telling me too much. And I wouldn't tell you this," Tatiana said, "except as it relates to my larger story. Imagine Cubert's surprise then, when upon his return from Las Vegas yesterday, Carmen informed him that she was pregnant."

Alexander listened intently, frowning, sensing more trouble for him blowing in just around the next breath—as if he already didn't have plenty. His hand went up. "I'm going to stop you *right* there," he said.

Tatiana continued as if he had not spoken. "Cubert and Carmen had some words about this," she said in her infuriating, fraudulently collected voice. "Cubert, as any normal husband would—when informed of his wife's pregnancy—naturally tried to stab her in the chest." Tatiana paused, for maximum effect, Alexander thought, though no pause was necessary: everything was already to the fucking hilt. "Then and only then, as she was bleeding from her mammary, did Cubert inquire of his wife whose child it was. Since he knew, you see, that it couldn't be his. And just guess, Alexander," said Tatiana, less collected, less fraudulent, her hand gripping the door handle behind her, "what Carmen told Cubert?"

Alexander was mute. He wished he were deaf. So that's why all the dishes were broken. So that's why the hair was cut. Now he understood. Madness indeed. Fucking Carmen. In war, men lost their lives for less than this. Dudley lost his life for threatening his family. What was Alexander supposed to do now? "Why didn't you walk over to exam room number two," he finally asked, "and talk to Carmen? One question and you would've known she was lying."

"Oh, I would have," said Tatiana, "but having been stabbed in her ample bosom, Carmen was unconscious, so it was difficult to extract information from her, other than science confirming her positive bloodwork." She uttered a sound of such anger and despair that Alexander himself wished he had something to hold on to.

"Tania," he said, taking one of the deepest breaths of his life. There was nothing left for him to do but stand up, but he simply could not believe what he was about to say to his wife. "Last Friday I was with her, but I didn't have sex with her."

Tatiana broke down.

Alexander stood helplessly, and then went to her, trying to take her by the arms. She hit him, straight up into his chin, and staggered from the car, barefoot on the pebbles. Seeing double for a moment, he went after her, catching her by the front deck, trying to hold her, to calm her down, the way he had done so many times when she was upset and he held her to make her better.

This time he did not make her better.

Tatiana didn't say, "Let go of me," which he could take. She said, "Don't *touch* me!" Which he could not.

He stopped touching her. "Let me tell you what happened."

"Do I look to you like I want to hear anything?" she yelled, hobbling back to the car.

"Had you come home with me yesterday," Alexander said, following her, "I would've told you what happened. I would have told you the truth before you got to fucking Cubert, who doesn't know the truth. How many times did I ask you to come home?"

She whirled to him. "You haven't lifted your lying eyes to me all week! You have been *screaming* to me for the last seven days! I'm going deaf from your *screaming!* What more do you think I need to hear? The details? Oh, yes, do, please—*regale!*"

In a low voice he said, "Babe, I'm *so* sorry." They were standing feet apart. His chin was at his chest.

"And what about Wednesday?" she asked. Her hands covered her face.

He could barely look at the periphery of her convulsing body. "On Wednesday, I was going to meet up with her again, but you know I didn't. I came home."

"Meet up with her again for what?" Tatiana said into her hands. "Tell your wife, Alexander—meet up with her again for what?"

In one large step, Alexander came and took her in his arms. "Please, Tania," he whispered. She didn't just struggle with him; she pushed him away like he was burning her. Her emotion made her frantic and stronger, whereas his remorse made him quiet and weaker. To hold her required more from him than he was able to give and talk at the same time, to explain what he could not explain, to say what he could not say. He lost his breath trying to keep her still. She was hyperventilating from the struggle to twist away. "Let *go* of me! Let go!"

"No!" he said, spinning her around and getting behind her. He pinned her forearms in front of her, to keep her from hurting either herself or him. "Slow down, or you're going to faint. Come on—just a bit of reason—"

Tatiana flailed her head from side to side, her body in spasms. "I'll show you fucking reason," she said, fighting desperately to get out of his hold.

It was the first time in his life Alexander heard Tatiana swear. He held her arms tighter, standing pressed behind her, his face lowered into her neck. She was against the side of the Thunderbird. "Tania, I'm trying very hard to tell you what happened," he said, "but you won't let me get two words out."

"Oh, I'm listening," she panted. "I'm just not believing my fucking ears. Now let *go* of me, I said!" Heaving sideways, she hit him in the jaw with her head and tore away from him. They were both speechless. He tried to get his breath back, and she wasn't even trying. She couldn't breathe at all.

"Tania, please," Alexander said, stretching out his hand.

She reeled away. "Tell me," she said, "how does it work? Do you take your wedding ring off beforehand? Or during?"

"Ring doesn't come off," said Alexander. "Carmen is lying."

"Oh, *she's* the one who is lying, is she!"

"She is. I know this for a fact because I didn't have sex with her." He took a step to her. Her fist flew out and struck him. "Oh, for fuck's sake!" he yelled, remorse gone, quiet gone, temper here, anger here. "What are you doing? Stop fighting me!"

She squared off against him—yes, that's right, *she* squared off against *him*—feet away, half his size, chest to chest, fists to fists. "Don't come near me, Alexander," said Tatiana, clenched and blazing. "Don't *ever* touch me again."

"Stop fucking saying that!"

"No." She jabbed her fist at him so fast, he barely jerked away. "Get out of my house."

"Fuck you," Alexander said, grabbing her fists. "This is my house, too. I'm not going anywhere." She tried to pull away, but he bore down on her, grinding her fists in his hands. "You didn't come back at one thirty in the morning to tell me to go. If you didn't want to see me, you could've just stayed with your fucking doctor, stayed all night with him, and not bothered me with your bullshit." Alexander shook his head like a black Lab, and perspiration flew at her from his hair. "You don't want to hear it from me, you don't want to have it out, so what'd you come back for, Tatiana? Just to tell me not to touch you?" He squeezed her fists furiously and then pushed her away. "I wasn't fucking touching you when you weren't here! Why didn't you just stay where you were?"

"I was three days in the hospital, working!" she yelled, hitting him against his raised and parrying hands. "I wasn't fucking Carmen!"

"I wasn't fucking Carmen either!"

"She says you were!"

"She's a lying cunt!"

"Well, *you* should know, Alexander," said Tatiana. "You were fucking her."

Alexander shoved her away from him. He was unbearably hot. From his intense effort to control himself and her, cold sweat was covering him, soaking his T-shirt, soaking his body. He stepped away, and she, grabbing her stomach, bent over, breathing shallow, trying to stop herself from retching. There was no comfort, not for her, not for him.

"Tatiana, I'm going to repeat *again*," he said, panting, "I didn't have sex with her."

"I'm going to repeat again, I don't believe a word you say—so stop speaking! She's lying is she? Are you often accused of knocking up women you have no business with? So what were you doing with her last Friday until six in the morning? Just having a drink? A little smoke? Getting her up the stick with your cigarette?" She exhaled her misery, still bent over, clutching her stomach, unable to look up or straighten up. When he said nothing was when she lifted her eyes. "Those were not rhetorical questions," she said scathingly. "I would like an answer."

"What the fuck am I supposed to say to that?"

"That's right! How about, you've been banging her for months. Her, anyone, everyone, every Friday night. So convenient for you—Ant's away, I'm away. You never would have told me about this either. Just happened to be caught this time, weren't you?"

"Stop it!" Alexander didn't know how to calm her down, he didn't know how to calm himself down. "This is crazy! I didn't have sex with her. And you know she is lying because you know she can't be pregnant by me."

"I don't know it at all," said Tatiana. "Your lies are what I know."

"You *know* it!" Alexander yelled. "I can't believe I even have to tell you this, for *fuck's* sake! For fuck's sake!"

"Oh, yes, scream at me, good!" she screamed, holding on to the car and pointing to the house. "Your son is inside. What, he isn't traumatized enough?"

"Oh, plenty traumatized," Alexander said, lower and through his teeth. "And why not? His mother never comes home. He must think he's an orphan again."

Gasping, she came at him with violence on her face and hands. There was no getting away from her jabbing fists, from her frenzied arms. "I can't *believe*," she said, her face streaming, "I left my baby to go and find *you*. I can't believe I chose such a heartless bastard over my boy. I wish to God I had never gone. You with your ugly fucked-up *faithless* heart, you should be rotting in Kolyma, gang raping the *male* loggers there—that should be your fate, instead of coming here to betray *me*!"

Alexander rammed her against the car, his hand on her throat. A red veil covered his sight. He wasn't just hot anymore, smoke was coming out of his pores. "Oh my God," he said, gripping her neck. "Will you never fucking stop?"

"Will *you* never fucking stop? Get away from me," she said hoarsely, choking, trying to pull away from his hands. He let go. She was coughing.

"Why are you still here? Quick. Go to your Carmen. She and her tits are waiting for you." Insane she came for him again, and Alexander didn't know how to stop her when he himself was so close to the void. He moved his face away slightly, put his hands up slightly. His only advantage was his height because she was unstoppable. She seized his T-shirt; he yanked away, and the shirt ripped, tore from top to bottom. She hit him in the chest, in the stomach. He'd had enough.

"Tania," he said, grabbing her wrists, "that's it. Stop it."

"No!"

He squeezed her wrists harder and harder but she didn't cry out. Instead she stood like she was numb and without flinching said, "*Break* them. Go ahead. Everything else I got, you broke."

He pushed her away but she was right back on him. "I'm warning you," he said, pushing her away again, keeping her literally at arm's length. "Get away from me—"

"*You* get away from me," she said, choking on her tears and her words. "That's what you want, isn't it? Nothing I ever gave you was enough. All *we* had, all I gave you, all that *I* gave you was not enough!" She went to strike him with her right fist, he half-blocked her and she struck him with her left, and he took it because he deserved it.

"There is no hope for us," said Tatiana. "I will not live like this. I will *never* live like this. Loyalty was your *only* condition for a life with me, and you knew it when you went and fucked another woman, degraded me, and showed me exactly what I'm worth, which is *nothing*—and what you're worth, which is *nothing*. So now pack your bags and go where you want, go where you belong. It's not with me. I don't care what you do anymore."

Alexander *had* to get away from her—she wasn't the only one whose judgment was about to be vanquished by her anger. She, having lost all reason, was saying things to deprive him of all reason. "*Listen* to me! Are you fucking deaf? I will repeat—*once again*—I didn't have sex with her! I didn't have sex with her!"

"Repeat ad nauseam—but it's her word against yours, Alexander," Tatiana said, her face distorted, her body shaking. "That's all I got. Your word against hers. And we now know what your word is worth, don't we? Not even a breath on which it's uttered. Unholy lies on your side, and she says she is pregnant—do you understand—*pregnant*!" She was overcome, devastated; she couldn't continue.

"Well, at least someone around here is getting pregnant," Alexander said through clenched teeth, bending in his own stricken fury. "And it didn't take fifteen fucking years."

"Like I'd keep any baby that was yours!" cried Tatiana. "I'd take a coat hanger to it before I kept one of your babies!"

Alexander hit her so hard across the face that she reeled sideways and fell to the ground.

Blinded he stood over her. Guttural sounds were coming from his throat. Her arms covered her head. "You have stepped out of all bounds, all decency," he said, yanking her up. "I can't believe how much you hate me." When he flung her away from him, Tatiana couldn't get her balance and fell again on the pebbled stones, shaking her head, mouthing something, trying to stand up, crawl away. But Alexander had lost his mind. Growling in his helpless rage, he came after her, bent over her, shoved her back down onto the ground, swung out his open hand—

And from behind Anthony came running up to him, knocking him away. "Don't touch my mother!" he yelled.

Alexander pushed his son aside. Fleetingly he remembered himself fighting with his own father, just like this, over his own mother, just like this, twenty-five years earlier in Leningrad, on the very edge of their deaths. There was only one difference. Alexander was not Harold Barrington.

"Anthony," he said, grabbing the boy and nearly lifting him in the air as he pushed him toward the deck, "what the fuck are you doing? What did I tell you?"

Anthony ripped away from Alexander. "Don't you dare hurt my mother," he said, clenching his fists.

"Oh, for fuck's sake!" Alexander yelled. "How many times do I have to say it? Can we have one minute of privacy? One fucking minute! I told you to stay inside! GO!" Grabbing Anthony, he pushed him through the door, down the corridor and into his room, where he shoved him on the bed, and said, "Who do you think you're dealing with? Stay in your fucking room."

"Don't hurt my mother," whispered Anthony, crying into Alexander's back. "*Please.*"

Alexander somehow managed not to go out front to her.

Blinded, he groped his way to the back door, and stormed panting outside.

Tatiana got herself off the ground and, holding on to the deck railing, stumbled her way to the bathroom. She wanted to go comfort Anthony but she didn't want him to see her like this. She remained alone for many minutes, trying to pull herself together. Alexander had hit her very hard. She cleaned the blood from her mouth as best she could. From her temple down to her jaw, her eye, her nose, her mouth, nothing was uninjured. Her ear was ringing deafening bells in her head. Her whole body was throbbing.

Finally she went to see her son. Tatiana knew very well his conflicted dual allegiance to his parents. Tonight it was tearing Anthony up; he was inconsolable. Tatiana listened to him, nodded, said, I know, and yes, it's like this and like that. "You're a child. Let the grown-ups try to solve their messes. Dad told you—why did you disobey? Stay in your room, he said."

"Mom, don't go near him again, stay away from him. Leave him alone. For God's sake, he shot a man *dead*."

"Anthony, he shot more than one man dead. Every one of the marks on his body is nothing compared to what he has seen and done in his short life, in the rivers, in the lakes, house to house, door to door, and yes, hand to hand. You know about your father. I've told you enough times. He saved you and me, we left him behind, and he was nearly destroyed. This is what's left."

"Stop making excuses for him."

"Don't you want me to make excuses for him?" she asked in a breath.

"I don't know anymore," Anthony whispered.

Me neither, Ant, Tatiana thought. Me neither. She caressed her son's face. She was not in control, she was doing what she could for the boy. "Your dad's lived a brutal life. He's doing the best he can. I'm making no excuses. I'm telling you once again to stay out of our business."

He turned away from her, his shoulders heaving.

"All your life, Anthony, from the time you were small, you've tried to get between our grown-up words, our fights, as if it's your responsibility to moderate us. Well, it isn't. It's ours."

"Mama, are you . . . very upset with him?"

"I'm not going to speak about it to you. You're young. When I was fourteen, I also knew so little. But believe me, one day you'll understand." She swallowed. "The power you have over someone who loves you," said Tatiana, "is greater than any other power you'll ever have." She fought to continue. "You know—you've known all your life—that your father has that power over me." She lowered her head. "But yes, Anthony, yes, darling. I am very upset with him."

Anthony continued to cry. From the outside, Tatiana heard breaking booming noises. They were piercing her.

She left the son and walked unsteadily outside to the father.

Alexander was taking the deck table to the stump. Holding on to the railing, she watched the axe go up and down. He didn't stop until the table was shattered into splintered fragments.

"Alexander . . ."

"Don't come near me."

He walked up the deck, picked up the wooden rocking bench he had built for them, raised it above his head and hurled it crashing to the ground. Jumping over the railing, he grabbed his dropped axe and hacked the bench on which they had sat and rocked every night, his axe flying like a scythe up and down through the night air, slicing apart their life.

Then he came for her, gasping, panting.

Seeing his wild eyes, Tatiana backed away but, tripping over her own hasty feet, slipped to the floor of the deck. "Alexander, stop it!" she cried, her hands up. "I can't finish this with you when you're like this."

"You want to finish it with me, do you?" he said. "Well, come on then, I'm your man, finish it." His black shirt was hanging in matted shreds on him, his fatigues were soiled, his fists clenched, his arms raised. "Here I am—go ahead, Tatiana, stand up and fucking finish it."

"Please! You're *scaring* me . . ." She was having trouble getting the words out through her numb jaw. She was down on the deck, trembling, her hands at her face. "*Please*, get hold of yourself."

"I was telling and telling you—you have to get hold of *your*self," he said, towering over her, utterly unrepentant. "Did you fucking listen? I don't think so. And believe me, this *is* hold of myself. Now stand up." He took a menacing step toward her; his boots were at her bare feet. "Stand up, I said."

"Okay. Okay. Just—" He needed her to stand up, she struggled up, grabbing on to the railing and managing to pull herself to her feet. Tiny she stood, terrified and shaking in front of drenched heaving enormous unhinged him, and did the only thing she ever did when she didn't know how to make things better but when she wanted to calm, to comfort, to bring impossible things down to a possible level. Slowly she opened her hands. "Here I am, Shura," Tatiana whispered, her face up, her palms up. "Here I am. Okay? I'm not shouting anymore."

"Yes, you're a paragon of virtue," Alexander said, looking away from her face. "Calm and you, like birds of a feather." But he withdrew, one step, two. His hand gripped the railing. "Why are you here?" he asked. "You can't possibly have anything else to say. You've said it all, every last fucking thing you could think of. Hope you're proud of yourself. Hope you're happy with yourself."

Tatiana didn't know what to say. *The thing I said, you know I didn't mean it*, she whispered inaudibly, only her mouth moving. *I'm just in pain.* He didn't hear. She couldn't speak and stand at the same time, barely having the strength for one. Hoping it wouldn't upset him again, she whispered, *Shh, shh* as she sank to the deck. Alexander panted, struggling for breath, and she tried to find the voice in her chest.

At last she found it. "This is your house," said Tatiana. "I won't tell you to leave your house again. Don't break the furniture you built with your hands." It was too late for that. All the wood furniture he had made for the deck was gone, except for one lonely chair in the corner. "*I'll* go," she said. "I'll take Ant and we'll go. Then I'll figure out what to do." Her mouth twisted, she lowered her head.

His mouth twisted, Alexander lowered his. Both his hands now gripped the railing. "I see. So you weren't *quite* finished. You still have some evil left." He nodded. "Quite a bottomless pit inside you, isn't there?" He paused. "What's next? Are you about to tell me you'll take Anthony and go stay with your fucking doctor until you figure out what to do?" His liquid eyes pools of despair, Alexander stood looking at her as if waiting for her to answer. But she remained silent. Not a sound came from Tatiana.

After a short disbelieving gasp, he said, "So what are you waiting for? Would you like me to help you pack?" His voice trembled. "Or first give you my hand to help you off the ground?"

Tatiana wanted to stand up on her own to go, without silently beseeching him, but couldn't. She didn't know what to do. She couldn't stand up without Alexander's help. And that's when she knew she was finished. That's when she knew she was power-less against him, that she didn't even have her anger as a weapon anymore. She might as well have been naked. She sat and counted out the beats of her heart.

"I left you on Fridays in all my trust and love," Tatiana said at last, utterly broken, "believing you would know the way even if I didn't stand over you every admonishing minute."

"I knew the fucking way," said Alexander. "I was blind drunk when I found my way to your hospital—to you—because I needed saving, and what did you do?" He pitched his voice to mimic her. "I have to go, Shura; I have to attend to someone else with *real* needs, Shura; can't you be more understanding, Shura; I'm working, working, working, so go to hell, Shura."

Tatiana, shivering hot, was glad she was on the floor of the deck and didn't have far to fall, her head hung low, her jaw not moving, her lip swelling, trickling blood. "Was it the Friday when you had her lipstick all over your face?" she asked. "Is that the Friday you're talking about? My mentioning it wasn't enough? You wanted me to wipe it off for you, too?"

Alexander backed away from her, to the farthest corner and sank in the solitary chair. Tatiana heard the lighter flick on, once, twice, as he unsuccessfully tried to light a cigarette. Finally she smelled the burning nicotine. She wasn't looking up. But she listened to him inhale, hold, inhale, hold, smoking it down. After he smoked down one, he lit another.

"What did you think would happen?" Tatiana asked. "Did you think I wouldn't know?"

At first he didn't answer. "Obviously," he finally replied. "This is what I thought, and wanted, and hoped for. That you would never know."

"You thought you could keep this a secret from me?" she asked. "Of all the secrets you could keep, you thought you could keep this one? You, with the truest eyes, all you had to do was lift them to me after you got caught in a little white lie, lift them to me and say I didn't want you to worry; sorry. That's all you would have had to do when passing me that coffee cup last Saturday—just look me in the eye and lie." Shaking her head, she stared into her palms. "And when you touched me, you couldn't tremble, and when I asked your lips to kiss me, you had to kiss me instead of step away. You think you can love me and betray me? You think you can *kiss* me and betray me?" whispered Tatiana. "You couldn't a day ago, but that's all you would have had to do—then you could've kept your secret."

Alexander smoked and said nothing.

"It also would've been helpful if your lovers didn't call my house."

Alexander smoked and said nothing.

"To say you were transparent would not be doing justice to how clearly you were telling me in a dozen different ways you were up to no good." Tatiana didn't even want to feel the shadow of his presence fifteen feet away. "So I'll ask differently—what did you think was going to happen when I knew?"

Alexander smoked down his cigarette before he answered her. "I thought you wouldn't really care," he said. "I know that once you might have cared, but I thought that now you would go on with your consuming work, having your little secret lunches, pretending you're chaste. I thought we might have words, and then you'd pat me gently on the back, kiss me fondly on the head, but in your heart of hearts not give a rat's ass."

Tatiana flattened over her knees. "Oh, Alexander," she whispered. She couldn't speak. "What did I ever do to you that you can say that to me." She gasped it out through the throat and chest.

A desperate sound came from his smoke-filled mouth.

"I can't *take* it," she said, holding her stomach. "I can't *bear* it. Come here." She stretched out her arms. "Beat me unconscious and then I won't care." A choking Tatiana felt for the deck under her knees. He and his Carmen were like cholla in her eyes. She couldn't see in front of her. She opened her hands. "Oh, my God, but who is going to help *me* . . . ?" she whispered in a suffocating voice. "I need help, who is going to help *me*?" She had to leave the deck immediately, *immediately*, or she would lose what little sense she had left, the smooth glass of her center already so jagged with his ministrations. *Please help me. Please.* One ounce of pride to lift me off my feet. One stale gram of sawdust and cardboard pride.

"Tania," Alexander said into her back. "I know you give yourself to the dying and the afflicted." He groaned. "But I'm dying and afflicted, too."

"I can't help you anymore, Alexander" said Tatiana. "I can't even help myself." She was weeping on her hands and knees. "You turned your back on me despite everything. Well, I'm turning my back on you, despite more things than you know. There. Those are my words. Fond enough for you?" Groping for the deck, she started crawling away from him to the house, crawling away from the only love she had ever known.

She heard him get up and come toward her where she was tilting, spilling over. She lifted her face. Motionless he stood, and then fell on his knees before her.

"Afflicted, Tania," he said in a ruptured voice. "Look at me. I'm not the drunk in the ER waiting room. I'm your husband. Have mercy on me, too." He had to stop speaking for a moment. "I come to you every single day of the life that you've given me", said Alexander, "hoping you will touch me—and I stand in line—and you touch me, and I'm good to go for just a few more hours until I need your comfort again. I can't do without you." His hands were gripped in front of him, his words barely carrying. "I can't make it without you, and you know it."

Tatiana couldn't turn from him, both of them feeble with fear and sadness.

"Please believe me," he said. "I didn't have sex with her. All the things you think I forgot, I remembered them last Wednesday. I haven't been blameless—" He lowered his head in defeat. "You're blinded and can't see straight, I know, but just think for one second and you'll see through her lies."

"I can't even see through yours," said Tatiana. "I don't know her at all."

Alexander tilted his head to stare into her face. Their wretched anguished eyes blinked miserably at each other.

"You know I can't make her pregnant," he said. "You know she is lying at least about *that*, right? After what I'd seen in Moscow, after what my mother taught me, and all during my years as a garrison soldier, think—what did I tell you about myself and the women I'd been with? Have I ever had it off bareback with anyone? Ever, even *once* in my whole fucking life?"

"Yes," she said faintly. "With me."

"Yes," Alexander said, sinking down. "Only with you." His shoulders slumped. "Because you are holy." He looked at his hands. "And a fat load of good it's done me."

Tatiana clutched her arms over her stomach, bending over. She couldn't speak, couldn't find her voice. When she looked up at him, she found him leaning forward, the copper champagne seeping out of his eyes. "Shura," she whispered. "I'm going to have a baby."

At first she didn't think Alexander heard her, he was mute so long. "You *what*?" he said in horror.

"I'm going to have a baby," she mouthed, her shoulders quaking, her swollen lips quivering.

On his haunches Alexander staggered away. Everything became silent except for her low crying, and the terrible sounds that were coming from his throat. "Oh my God," he breathed out, pressing his back against the wall like a wounded animal. "*When* were you going to tell me this? God, please, *please* don't say—"

"On blinchiki Wednesday," whispered Tatiana. "When you went to have sex with another woman."

Alexander groaned as if he were being flayed. He turned away into the wall of the house. His body was in a shudder.

Time passed, and Alexander said nothing, his head in his knees.

And Tatiana said nothing, her head in her knees.

Indeed now it felt as if they had said everything.

She had been feeling so poorly for weeks, and had been throwing up since Saturday. She attributed the sickness to the unfathomable things that had been going on inside her house, things that she found herself completely unable to deal with. She almost wished her husband *could* look her in the face and lie, like he did in the Soviet Union when he had to save her life, look her in the face and lie, so she wouldn't have to live with the ghastly truth—and her life would be saved. She was a month late, but in the stress of the last few weeks, no one noticed, not him, and not even her. Last Tuesday night she was having a bath when she ran a soapy washcloth over her nipples, and she yelped so loudly that Alexander came in from the living room, knocked on the door and asked if she was all right.

And so on Wednesday Tatiana went and got herself a blood test.

Afterward she left work early, bought some food, bought a nice thing to wear for him. Came home, made a little bread, cooked. Alexander was working late, but he would never say no to blinchiki, no matter what time he came home. He would come in, and he would know she had something to tell him, because that is how she always told him things that were too big for regular clothes, for regular food. She lit the candles, put on the music. Tatiana thought that after she would tell Alexander the *only* thing he had wanted to hear every single month for ten years, that somehow they would make better whatever impossible thing had happened last Friday night. She thought somehow they would pull through it. Maybe he could pretend he was telling the truth and she could pretend to believe him.

But then at nine o'clock, the phone rang, and it was Carmen. Carmen saying, "Well, where *is* he?" in a tone no woman was allowed to use about someone else's husband. That's when Tatiana realized that maybe they wouldn't pull through it.

And thirty minutes later, someone else's husband walked through the door. Alexander looked so guilty, so repentant, so threatened, and so bewildered, that not only could he not look at Tatiana, not only could he not kiss her, or speak to her, or make love to her, he couldn't even see through the blinchiki and the see-through camisole for what they really were: Shura, I have something *fantastic* to tell you. Sit down, because you simply won't believe it. And that's when she knew how blinding the black vile visions in his eyes must have been.

Tatiana lifted her head from her knees, and Alexander was standing in front of her, eyes full of black vile visions. She hadn't even heard him come near. Once a soldier, always a soldier, in stealth, even in life.

"Come on," he said quietly, bending to her and lifting her whole into his arms. He carried her inside. After setting her down next to the sink, he crushed five trays of ice into it and filled it with cold water. Tatiana thought he was going to tell her to put her face into it, and was about to meekly impotently protest—when Alexander submerged his own head into the ice.

After five seconds of watching him, *her* face ached. "Alexander," she whispered. "Alexander . . ." Her hand went on his back. He was still under. How long had it been? She got a little worried, and pulled on his soaked shredded T-shirt, tried to pull him up, but he stood like he had turned to stone, his hands gripping the edge of the porcelain sink, his body bent forward, his entire head up to his neck sunk downward into the freezing slush.

"Alexander, *please*," she whispered. Oh, he was good. She was now begging *him*. She yanked on him. "Come on, please." It must have been well over a minute, possibly two, when he finally lifted his head, gasping for breath.

"I'm burning up," was all he said, crossing himself.

Panting, not drying off, he put some ice into a dish towel dipped in the freezing water, and took her by the shoulders. Setting her down on the couch, settling her deep into the crook of his arm, he held the towel to her face, his molten eyes blinking at her from inches away, wet, icy, inflamed, in silent remorse. Her head tipping back onto his shoulder, Tatiana closed her eyes. Soon her face was numb. The heart wasn't numb, though. Maybe he could submerge her heart in ice for two, three years, and when he pulled it out, she'd be as good as new.

"The swelling has gone down a little," Alexander said. "I know it hurts. Ice, no ice, you're going to be black and blue tomorrow. I'm sorry."

"For this you're sorry?"

In their bed, Tatiana couldn't stop sobbing, turned away from him, rolled into a fetal ball. But she was naked. He was naked. He had removed the blankets off the bed and left them uncovered. He was on his back, with both arms over his face. She kept wiping her uninjured cheek; the salt was eating her lip. It was dark.

An excruciating sound came from his throat. "You have no right to say such vicious things to me, no right to incite me intentionally and deliberately when you know I'm at the end of my fucking rope. How could you not have had the slightest sense to protect yourself, especially knowing that you're—" Alexander couldn't continue.

"What, *you* of all people can't understand why I'd be completely crazed? Completely beyond the sanity pale?"

He was breathing heavily. "I honestly don't understand what's wrong with you," he said. "You're telling me to pack my bags, to leave our house, knowing you're going to have a baby?"

"And this surprises you why? Have you seen what's been happening in our house?"

"Stop talking to me like this in our bed, Tatiana. My white flag is up," said Alexander. "I have no more."

"My white flag is up, too, Shura," she said. "You know when mine went up? June 22, 1941."

They lay. He struggled for his words. "Did you . . . sleep with that man?"

Tatiana coiled around herself, pressing her face into the pillow. "I can't talk to you," she said, her voice muffled. "I had dinner with him in a public place. Unlike you I never forget what I am. I can't believe you're shameless enough to ask about him."

Alexander started to ask something else and broke off. Tatiana knew, there were some things her warrior husband had no strength for, and this was one of them. There were some things Alexander could not ask. But she would be damned before she let him turn it around to her. Damned. This time she wasn't going to help him with a single word.

Tatiana wanted to ask him about Carmen, but she herself was so afraid. She knew he would lie to save them—especially now. He would look her in the face and with his velvet voice and his velvet eyes lie, and she would never know the truth, and would never understand, and would walk around with lies *and* betrayal for the rest of her life, and never again know what Alexander's word was worth.

She couldn't not ask.

Yet she couldn't ask.

She felt him creep up behind her. She felt his warm pained breath as he pressed his face into the nape of her neck, into what was left of her hair.

"Tatia, I didn't sleep with her," he said. "Please believe me."

Lies? Truth?

"Turn to me," he whispered.

"I am your one wife," she said without turning.

"Please turn to me, my one wife."

"Except for this—anything you do is fine with me," Tatiana said, and started to cry. "Our son is right. *Anything* you do is fine with me. Every day I *love* the ground on which you walk, Alexander," she whispered. "From the beginning, this was so. So if you raise your voice or your hand to me, I bow my head and take it. And if you need me, any way you need me, any time you need me, I give you my body and take it. You have ruled over me with your scepter. And if you're shut away and can't find your heart, I walk beside you up and down the Stonington hills, walk beside you through our entire America, waiting until you love me again. And when you raise your weapon, your .45 caliber cannon and fire into my face, and I am now served *that* up too without fail as I close my eyes each night—that and Leningrad and Stockholm and Berlin—I say, this is the hand that I have been dealt. I say as I say to everything, this is my cross." Tatiana's already cracked voice broke, and broke again. "And for that—I have *you*."

Alexander brought himself closer to her, to fit behind her in a spoon, in a crescent moon. His face remained in her hair. His hand slipped around her hip and over her stomach. His body was shaking. "Please . . . turn to me."

"No," Tatiana said. "Can't you see how afraid I am to face you? I made you a promise in that Lazarevo church. I gave you my hand, I promised you, no matter how you treat me, what you do to me, I am steadfast by you, I am resolute, I am always with you."

He turned her around himself.

Tatiana closed her crying eyes so she wouldn't see his lying eyes.

"I followed you a thousand miles to the front," she said brokenly. "I would've followed you to hell. And did."

"I know," he said.

"I would have lived out the rest of my days with you in one room on Fifth Soviet, making you kasha and stepping over crazy Slavin as I ran to get you your daily bread." Her shoulders rose and fell. "My whole life, I have been nothing but good to you, why are you hurting me like this?"

His trembling arms went around her. "Please . . ." Alexander whispered, his voice, his body breaking down. "I can't take it. I'm running on empty seeing you like this—please—" He exhaled in raw shallow breaths.

They lay not speaking until he was a little calmer, and she was a little calmer, smelling his familiar scent, being held by him. "Shh," Alexander whispered soothingly. "Shh. Come on. Please don't cry. Please." He moved to lie on her pillow, his lips touching where he had hit her, his hands stroking her hair. "Tania, my wife, I didn't sleep with her," he said. "Open your eyes and look at what I am. Look inside me. I didn't sleep with her."

She stared at him in the dark, intensely mining his face. "You're doing this deliberately," she said after a minute. "You'll tell me *anything* I want to hear, because you know how desperately I want to believe you. You'll make your eyes *anything*, because you know how desperately I want them to be true."

"They are true." His hand glided over her, from the crown of her hair, down her back, slow and soft and soothing to her calves . . . and up again. Her eyes involuntarily closed. His velvet hands, too, would lie, to save them.

"I'm working late, Tania, you said. I have a meeting, Tania. I spilled beer on my jeans. You laid out your lies for me like a buffet at Christmas. What were you covering up for if not . . ." She squeezed her eyes to stop the tears from springing to them again. "I don't want to know."

"I don't want to tell you."

"What am I going to do? I can't have her name mentioned in our bed. But I don't know what to do with the black hole where my faith in you has been."

His arms stretched unyielding around her. "Have faith," he said. "I will fix it."

She took a frail breath. "Did you . . . touch her?"

He stopped caressing her. "Tatiana, *please* forgive me." Alexander breathed out, crestfallen. "I did." He wouldn't let her gasping body turn away. "Look at me, here I am," he whispered, his face weak from shame. "Don't turn away. I'm yours. I am only yours. I belong to you. I just fucked up, babe."

Hours passed in darkness.

Over it, under it, across it, through it, passed torrents of grisly words and storms of shattered confessions. Everything was out, everything was in their bed, everything was said, and felt.

Tatiana watched Alexander's face when he spoke to her, watched it for truth, for meaning. She listened to him, her hands on him when she asked him things over and over, her hands on him when he answered her over and over. She placed her cheek on his chest when he spoke to her, to hear his voice through his heart. Her mouth was over his mouth, inhaling for the truth on his breath that came from inside him. Lies? Truth?

But the truth was merciless. Completely uncircumspect, weighing no consequence, he planned, talked, sat, bought drinks, flirted with another woman, fully aware, fully receptive, week in, week out, as if he were not married. He lay in wait and went into a car with another woman, remembering to take off his jacket, but leaving his wedding ring on. What odd lines of right and wrong he marked inside his head. And if that grave matter weren't enough, four days later, amid blatant lies, with full knowledge of his actions and deliberate consent of his mind, he bought condoms to take another woman to bed while his wife sat at home waiting to tell him they were going to have a desperately wanted baby. Alexander kissed another woman. He touched another woman. And she touched him. Tatiana simply didn't have the necessary armor around her untainted, unprotected heart to bear this.

She lay stunned and numb, lay quietly and stared at him in the dark, wondering if this was indeed unfixable and if it wasn't, why did it feel so unfixable, while Alexander kneeled at the bottom of the bed and kissed her feet, and whispered, Please Tania, please forgive me.

She knocked, yes, but how could you let her in, Shura. How could you let her in.

He faced away from her, his scarred back to her.

She crept to him and touched his wounds, his tattoos, his hammer and sickles his SS Eagles, she put her face lower on his back where his kidney had been ruptured, vividly seeing him lying gray on the crimson ice, knowing that if she didn't do something instantly, he was going to die. Tonight she wanted all his scars, his tattoos, his body, his soul to tell her what to do, how to set it right.

She tried to set it right by touching him. She stroked the knotted muscles in his arms, in his shoulders, she kissed his stomach, though kissing was difficult with her swollen lip, but to touch him she did it. She tried to move lower, down the line of his black hair, but couldn't after what he had told her.

Please, Tania, please forgive me. And touch me.

In a little while, she tried again. With her unsteady hands, she took hold of him. He was so familiar, so true. She knew him so well, what he liked, what he loved, what he needed. She was like his own hands: anytime anywhere she knew how to give it to him in a dozen different ways. And tonight when he responded to her sad and milking hands, she put her swelling mouth on swelling him. But it hurt too much. She pressed her wet face against him, rubbing salt into him, her hands falling away, her body falling away. How could you let her touch you.

I'm sorry, Tania, I'm so sorry.

I guess even we can be broken.

"We cannot be broken," he said. "We cannot be broken by fucking Carmen. She was *nothing*. She meant nothing. It meant nothing."

"Alexander, you and I have been through too much to have this kind of compound fraud in our bed. You're right in this sense—it's not any of the other things we have borne. It's not death. It's not our lost families or your butchered body. It's not starvation, or Leningrad. It's not war, or life in the Soviet Union." She paused. "You know what it is though, Shura?"

His head was hung. He didn't look at her. "I'm sorry, Tania. Please."

"I'm your only family. The only allegiance you have in this world is to me. You selling *me* out for meaningless milt-market—not even for love—that's not nothing, is it? Meanwhile I'm *shackled* to you." She started to cry again. "I'm holding all your open wounds together. I'm on the train to Kolyma with you, I'm in the filth of the Gulag with you. I'm lashed with you and burned with you, I eat out of the same bowl with you, and when you die I'll be the one to stick the helmet over your rifle into that shallow ground."

"Oh dear God, Tania, please." He was astride her, threading his arms around her. His shoulders were shaking. *Please*. I'm sorry."

She turned her head and closed her eyes and tried to fly away from bitter life.

He held her hands apart and put his face between her breasts. He was kissing her chest and he was whispering, but what she couldn't hear. Because she was crying. He whispered inaudible unheard truths into her mouth, kissed her bruised lips, kissed her breasts, cupping them, caressing them, whispering again, kissed her achingly sensitive nipples until she pleaded no more no more, and he whispered, just a little more, his wet contrite lips kissing her wet vulnerable nipples.

Oh, Shura . . .

When she could heave her body up from the bed, she tried again. Sitting next to him, she took hold of him, caressing him, and when her soft hands made him hard, she put her bloodied lips on him and kissed all of him, from his groin up to his head that was cupped into her kneading palm, kissed him and lightly rubbed him, smooth and straight into her lips and into her tears. You are so beautiful, she whispered, crying. Without knowing anything but you, I always thought so.

"And I *have* known," he said. "I have come to you knowing. No one is like you. You are more than I have ever deserved. I was so afraid you didn't love me like you used to. I was terrified you felt for someone else. You were always working, and I was felled by our other struggle"—he choked—"and I wasn't thinking. But those are just words, nothing more. I'm sorry." Pledging, repenting, promising, pleading.

She listened to him, she nodded. They *were* all just words. What good were his promises to her? He couldn't explain, she didn't understand. She tried to fix it by letting him touch her.

With her tiny hand, she took his big hands, all ripped up and raw from the cholla, and placed them on her breasts. You have the strongest hands, she whispered. He pulled away. With her slender hand she took his long, thick fingers, tense and trembling, and put them between her thighs. He pulled away. Look at me, she whispered, crying, lying on her back, opening her legs. I'm defenseless before you. Please touch me. I'm like you love, Shura. Like you love.

Kissing her mound, pressing his palm over her, covering her, he shook his head and crawled away.

"Please touch me," she said. "Why won't you touch me?"

"Don't you understand what I come to you for?" said Alexander. "I can't have communion with you until you forgive me."

He was right.

He pressed his forehead to her forehead, his damp stubbled face to her face. He pressed his lips into her heart, his wet black hair tickling her clavicles. Please forgive me. *White gold is the color of my true love's hair.*

All that love, and it still was not enough. She was weeping in her despair.

"How can I forgive you?" she said. "This is the one thing I don't know how to forgive."

"I'm damned," Alexander said, falling on his back. "I was blinded by stupidity for a brief moment in our life, for a flicker in the eternity in which you and I live, and I stumbled. I fucked up. I am sick and *completely* wrong. I am low and revolted. I promise I will do everything I can to fix it, to make it better." He took a breath. "But—what do you mean, you don't know how to forgive me?"

In her weakest whisper, Tatiana spoke. "Alexander Barrington," she said, "tell me, would you know how to forgive *me*?"

They both knew the inconceivable answer to that inconceivable question.

The answer was no.

He stared at her mutely and then covered his face with his arm. "Well, what are you and I going to do, Tatiana?" he said in a desperate voice. "We can't live like we've been living."

She started to speak, to present him with a number of choices, and that's when he opened her legs and climbed on her to comfort her shaking body from its monumental distress of the unbearable endless night.

"Listen to me," Alexander said, holding her head between his forearms. His hands were clamped on top of her head. "Understand this one thing and then everything else will become easier. You and I have only one life. There *is* no other choice. A long time ago we went to war together, went into one trench together, lived through Leningrad together. Remind yourself of all we have been through. Did we think we would get even a Lazarevo? And after Lazarevo that we would have Napa, or Bethel Island—or here? I know that sometimes the things we carry become too much for us.

We are burned down, but somehow we have to pick ourselves up and keep going. Sometimes I come back from war, and I'm dead, and sometimes I hear your voice and ignore it, and sometimes the impossible happens, I don't know how, and I don't know why. I have no defense for myself," he said. "I know you want one, but I have no excuse. I don't have a single justification. This one time in my life when I need more than just I'm sorry, I have nothing but my profound regret. I don't want justice from you," said Alexander. "I want mercy." He groaned. "I made a terrible mistake, and I'm begging you to forgive me. Tatiana, I'm *begging* you," he said in a collapsing breath, "to forgive me. But there is no separate life for you and me. There is no other bunker, no packed bags, there is no leaving, there are no other wives. There is nothing else ever, but you and me." He held down her hands, his body was over her, covering her, his face was above hers and she was tiny underneath him, looking up at him, under the black moon. "Do you really think I would let you leave me?" he whispered. "Don't you remember what I said to you in Berlin? When we were lost in the woods, raging against our fate?"

"Yes," Tatiana whispered back, her hands going around his neck, closing her eyes. "You said, I let you go once. This time we live together, or we die together."

"That's right," said Alexander. "And this time, we live together."

Tears rolled from her eyes.

He bent and kissed the sorrow from her face. *Milaya, rodnaya moya, kolybel i mogila moya . . . zhena moya luybimaya, zhizn moya, lyubov moya . . . prosti menya. Prosti menya, Tania . . . prosti menya i pomilui . . .* he whispered into her broken face, into her broken mouth.

What? I can't hear, what are you saying?

In two languages, whispered Alexander, I am singing for my marriage.

Prostrate, he knelt between her legs. "Babe, Tatiasha, my whole life," said Alexander, pressing his forehead into her heart. "My cradle and my grave, my wife, the only woman I have ever loved— I'm *sorry*. Please, Tania, help me. Have mercy on me. Please *forgive* me."

He lay down next to her, his left hand threading under her head. His right hand caressed her. He kissed her body, from the top of her short hair to the tips of her feet, and all within her. His gentle fingers touched her. His big hands held her. And it was sometime when his warm, repentant mouth was on her without relief that Tatiana, desperately moaning, exquisitely aroused in all her sorrow, said, "I will forgive you."

"You'll say anything right now, won't you?"

"Yes, right now, anything." She lifted herself up, folded her body over him, took hold of his black sad head, and cried.

Alexander, you broke my heart. But for carrying me on your back, for pulling my dying sled, for giving me your last bread, for the body you destroyed for me, for the son you have given me, for the twenty-nine days we lived like Red Birds of Paradise, for all our Naples sands and Napa wines, for all the days you have been my first and last breath, for Orbeli—I will forgive you.

And then, at last, he was inside her. There was communion.

Oh, Shura.

Oh, Tania.

And so it was.

Afterward they lay nestled, tangled, breast to breast, belly to belly, still conjoined, welded, smelted, soldered to each other, their mouths barely touching, barely breathing, flush together, side by side, soul to soul. Her arms were around him. His arms were around her. Their eyes were closing. They hadn't slept in three days and it was light on Sunday morning. She kissed his pulsing throat, touched his damp back. His scarred warm hands cupping her bruised face, he said, his voice breaking, "O merciful God, are we really going to have a . . . *baby*?"

"Yes, Shura, yes, my husband, yes. We are really going to have a baby."

Tonight was a night of many firsts. Alexander did something he had not done since 1943 when he found out whose blood was coursing through his bloodless veins.

He wept.

Tatiana resigned from Phoenix Memorial Hospital.

CHAPTER THIRTEEN

The Summer Garden

Red Wings

Bobo was very happy to see Alexander. "Señor!" he exclaimed. "I haven't seen you in so long! How have you been?" They shook hands.

"Busy, Bobo, very very busy."

"Business is good then?"

"More business than I can handle. You heard we got that Parade of Homes slot? Very good indeed."

"And your bellissima senora? Also good?"

"Splendidly good. Wait till you see her, Bobo."

"I'm looking forward to it. She is working late again?"

"She is shopping late again. But look, it's a special day. It's our anniversary."

Bobo beamed—as though it were *his* anniversary.

Alexander brought in from the truck two large bouquets of white roses and white lilies. "Bobo, I'm going to need your help. It's also señora's birthday today."

"Anniversary and birthday on the same day?"

Alexander smiled. "I told her that way she'd never forget me."

"Very good planning, señor. Leave it to me. Would you like some champagne?"

"The best. Cristal."

"Of course. When will the señora be arriving?"

"Who can tell with her?" Alexander said. "She'll be late for her own funeral."

He had some bread, some water and a smoke. He was thinking

of calling the house when he heard Bobo's exultations from the host's podium. As Alexander had expected, when Bobo saw Tatiana in a peach halter dress, fantastically pregnant, flamboyantly freckled, summery, shiny, smiling, resplendent, extending her hand to him, he cried. Literally cried. Tears dripped from his eyes onto her hands, and then with his arm around her, he walked her gingerly across the restaurant to a standing Alexander. "Señor! You told me nothing!" cried Bobo, his face wet. "Why, this is one of the happiest days of my life to finally see our señora so big with child."

"Bobo," said Alexander, kissing Tatiana's hands, "your joy is of some concern to me."

"Oh, no, why?"

"Fine, rejoice now, but I'm warning you, if, when the baby is born, he looks like you—bald and wrinkled and cries all the time— I'm coming for you, Bobo." Alexander grinned, pointing a finger at him. "Coming for *you.*"

Just the implication of such delectable impropriety sent Bobo into peals of excruciating mortification. Finally he left to go get the menus.

Tatiana lifted her face to Alexander. "What are you doing to poor Bobo?" she murmured.

His hands fanning her pregnant belly, he leaned down to kiss her. "You're only twenty minutes late," he said, appraising her, patting the soft peach fabric. "And without a watch, too. Well done. The dress new?"

"For you." Her round face was up. "You like?"

"I like." He sat her down, adjusted her chair, sat across from her, and took in her golden freckles, her red lips, her sparkling eyes, her lavish glorious breasts. After a minute he got up and went around to sit in the chair next to her. "Are you hungry," he said, "or would you like to go straight home?"

"Are you joking?" She giggled. "Oh. Because I am very hungry."

"You're very delicious-looking is what you are."

"I am?" she said, beaming with pleasure. "Shura, I feel *enormous.*"

"Yes," said Alexander. "Enormously *delicious.*"

"Shura!"

"What?" he said, blinking mischievously and not so innocently at her. He poured her a little champagne and they raised their glasses to their anniversary, to her birthday. Usually they went away just the two of them, but not with her being nearly eight months pregnant and the house so close to completion.

Alexander's chair was pulled right next to hers. His suited-up shoulders were pressing against her alabaster bare skin, his arm was around the back of her chair as he fingered the looms of her slowly growing-out gold-silk hair. The champagne glass was in his other hand. She was talking, her lips were moving, her white teeth gleamed, but there was no sound coming from her mouth, just a slight whooshing in Alexander's head, whoosh . . . whoosh . . . rustling leaves, and the lapping Neva waves against the granite carapace . . .

"You were so right, Shura," Tatiana was saying, "I don't know how I *ever* had time to work. I had a thousand things to do today. But honestly, how do you think our house is going to be finished next month?"

"What?" Alexander came out of his reverie. "Don't worry," he said. "It'll be finished."

"The baby is going to be finished in August whether or not the house is ready." She grinned. "I'm doing my part."

"Yes," Alexander said. "And I'm doing mine. The house will be ready." He leaned in. "You might have to sleep with the builder to get him to move a little faster."

"Oh, well . . ." she said with a shrug. "Only if I absolutely *have* to." Her beryl eyes squinted up cat-like. "So, do you know what I did today?"

"No, babe," said Alexander, his hand on her bare shoulder blades. "What did you do today?"

"I spent nearly all day at the *appliance* store."

"Ah," he said. "You must have thought it was your birthday."

"Well . . . yes." She laughed. "It *is* my birthday."

"I *know*. So, stressful . . . but perfect?"

"Yes! So many decisions. The sinks, the faucets, the refrigerators, the freezers, the breadwarmer—we're going to have warm bread even when it's stale—my *two* ovens, the bathtubs, wait till you see the bathtub I picked out for our master! It has the most wonderful whirlpool—" She suddenly stopped with a small puzzled furrow. "Shura, what are you doing? You haven't listened to a word I said. Why are you looking at me like that?"

"Like what?" Alexander said softly, roaming all over her face for youth, for love, for beauty, for white nights in the Summer Garden. All was there, and all the Coconut Grove years in between, all the lupine lilac Deer Isle Napa years in between, fired up by the furnace inside her, warming her an extra two degrees and all his memories along with her. His heart was throbbing, doubling him over.

"Shura . . . are you listening to me? I was telling you about the ovens . . ."

"Go ahead. The ovens. Were they warm? Hot? Too hot? I'm listening." He could smell the champagne on her breath as she spoke. He could smell her musk perfume, her strawberry shampoo, faint chocolate, coconut suntan lotion. She had new freckles, just above her eyelids. Must be spending a lot of time by the pool. Moving closer to her neck, he breathed in for the coconut again; the smell always took him to the summer ocean in Miami. He hoped she wasn't doing any of her running jump reverse pike half-twist flips with that immense belly of hers. As she was speaking, his hand drifted down and rested on it.

The appetizers came.

". . . And the cabinet man called today to say he could not do a distressed finish on the cabinets near the oven because the glaze would catch fire. What does that mean? I said to him, glaze them— and I'm not asking you. And the tile man told me this morning his entire shipment was cracked, *cracked*! And if we wanted delivery on new travertine tiles before August we would have to pay ten percent extra. I told him he would have to explain that one directly to you. I think he's giving you the business. Shura? Are you *listening*?"

"I'm listening," he said in a most unlistening tone. "Don't worry about the travertine man. He is delivering all new tiles in ten days and giving us a discount on the price. Do you remember your seventeenth birthday?" Alexander asked, his body turned to her, champagne in his hands.

"Yes," she whispered.

"We had eaten caviar and chocolates and drank vodka straight from the bottle because I had forgotten the glasses, and then went for a walk by the sunlit Neva. It was so late, yet so light. I spread out all my limbs on the bench, and still somehow you managed not to touch me or even glance at me. You were so *breathtakingly* shy. But river, no river, Pushkin's lucent dusk, white nights, a city like we've never seen—I could not take my eyes off of you." Alexander paused. "Why are you crying?"

"Why are you speaking of things that make me weep?"

"How desperately I wanted to kiss you." Wiping her cheek, Alexander leaned to her, a breath away from her mouth, lowering his voice to a whisper. "To this day, when I think of it, I feel that ache—in my throat, in my stomach, in my heart. I don't know how I kept myself from *ravishing* you."

"Me neither," Tatiana said. "Because nowadays"—she lowered her own voice—"you can't keep from ravishing me any time you feel that ache."

"How lucky for me that your day job finally consists of nothing more than being ravished by your husband."

"Lucky indeed," Tatiana whispered, "but for me, for *me*, my soldier Summer Garden lover." Their tilted heads leaned in one more inch, their lips parted, touched softly. She moved decorously away. Alexander offered her one of his shrimp and then a sip of his champagne. "I don't know why you order prosciutto," he said. "All you eat is what's on my plate."

"Hey, don't be greedy with your shrimp," she said. "Do you want me to tell you the parable of the shrimp cocktail and marriage?"

"If you wish," Alexander said. "Don't expect me to listen. My mind is in Leningrad."

"Please," Tatiana whispered. "Don't make me cry."

"Tell me about the shrimp cocktail and marriage. Is it a joke?"

"You tell me. When a man is first courting a woman," Tatiana began, "he orders a shrimp cocktail for himself and offers her one of the shrimp, but she is too shy and demure to accept—so she declines." She smiled. "When they're first married, he offers her the shrimp and she *gladly gladly* accepts." She grinned. "When they've been married for five years, he doesn't offer anymore, but when she asks for one, he graciously gives her one. After fifteen years, she doesn't ask, she just takes one, and he resents her for taking it. Why doesn't she just order her own damn shrimp cocktail if she likes his so much, he thinks." She poked Alexander's arm. "After twenty-five years of marriage, he still doesn't offer, and she has stopped taking it. After fifty years, not only does he not offer her his shrimp, but even if he did, she would not accept."

Alexander stared at her blankly.

Tatiana threw back her head and laughed, her happy eyes like slits.

"On our sixteenth wedding anniversary," said Alexander, "and after seventeen years together, I tell you about your golden hair in Leningrad, and you tell me *that*?"

Her cream cleavage rising and falling with delight, Tatiana pulled him down to herself so she could rub her lips against his slightly stubbled face. Their dinner came, filet mignon, cooked medium-rare for him, filet mignon, cooked rare for her. "I'm going to tell you something more shocking," Tatiana said as they ate. "Vikki is moving here."

"Moving *where*?"

"Ha! Here. Phoenix."

"Oh, thank goodness," said Alexander. "I thought for a second you meant our house."

"To make it like a communal apartment?" Tatiana grinned. "No, she is fed up with New York, fed up with that Tom Richter of yours, fed up. She says she's going to get a job at Phoenix Memorial, that way I can live vicariously through her."

"Do you . . . need to live vicariously through her?" asked Alexander.

"Nope. It'll be nice to have my friend here, though."

"Yes. But don't tell Ant. He'll leave us for good," said Alexander. "You know how he gets when she's around." They drank, they ate, they listened to Bobo's serenading big band music. Bobo always found good bands to play in his popular restaurant. "I'm glad for you your Vikki is moving here," Alexander said, "but your flip mention of that bane of my existence place you worked in reminds me of something more important. You were supposed to talk to your doctor today. Did you?"

"Um, yes." Tatiana put down her fork. "Shura, he knows how you feel," she said, rubbing his suit sleeve. "But what is he supposed to do? He says it's hospital policy. He can't change it. Husbands are simply *not* allowed in the delivery room. It's just not done."

Alexander put down his fork. "Tania, did I not make myself clear last time we went to see him?"

"You did," she said. "That's why you are not allowed to come to the doctor with me anymore. You're getting all upset with him, but it's not his fault. It's just policy."

Having finished his food, Alexander filled his flute full, filled hers halfway. "Policy, fault, procedure, hospital rules, blah blah blah. I don't care. Did you tell him that your husband doesn't give a shit about his hospital policy?"

"Perhaps not in those *exact* words," said Tatiana, "but I did tell him—"

"That either I'm going to be in the delivery room," said Alexander, "at the birth of my own child, or you're not having the baby in his fucking hospital."

"Something along those lines, yes."

"God, I was right to hate that place. It's still torturing me."

"Shh." Tatiana took a sip of champagne and turned to him. Her hand went over his. "The doctor is a civilian. He doesn't understand the firefight in the woods mentality. He just knows the rules. Now shh," she murmured, her elongated peach-polished nails lightly scratching the back of his hand. "Don't worry. I'll figure out something. I'm thinking of a plan."

"Oh, no." Alexander laughed. "Oh, no! Please, no, not another plan."

"Shura!"

His shoulders heaved up and down. "Honestly, I don't know if we can survive another one of your plans, Tatiasha," he said. "We are just not the strength that we once were."

Her shoulders heaved up and down as she laughed herself.

Alexander gazed down the plunging neckline of her halter dress. He didn't understand how her always remarkable breasts could have gotten this mouth-wateringly enlarged, this milky, this creamy—her whole full-up, pulsing, pregnant body had gotten stunningly sexy. She was like extravagant Napa Valley Tania but squared. Maybe cubed. Alexander couldn't *think* of her without embarrassing himself. The other day he drove by a fruit stand and found himself inexplicably thickening. A fruit stand! Turned out it was the word STRAWBERRIES on the sign. She washed her hair with strawberry shampoo. No, the things that roamed and rambled in his crazed head these last few months . . . "Stop laughing," he said. "Stop, or I'm going to bend down in this restaurant, in front of everyone . . ." He couldn't help himself. He lowered his head and put his mouth into her soft swelling cleavage.

Blushing, embarrassed, exceedingly pleased, Tatiana said hoarsely, "Husband, it's unseemly for you to be this excited by a pregnant woman."

Alexander smiled, his arm going around her. "Why? You think making love to a pregnant woman is redundant?"

Her hands resting on his forearm, they stared at each other, blinking, twinkling, at a loss for words.

"What?" she asked.

"Nothing." He roamed her face. "Still can't take my eyes off of you." Holding her head to him, caressing her stomach, he kissed the freckles near her nose, kissed her lightly pulsing lips. "How is our potato pancake baby today?" Referring to the desperate November spawning that finally produced a fry, a fingerling.

"Moving, marching, shoving, kicking," she replied. "A true warrior like his father."

Alexander remembered helping her out of the bath last night, watching her dry herself, and when he couldn't take it anymore, kneeling in front of her, his hands spanning her great, taut, still damp, naked belly, and pressing his mouth against her navel. "If it's a boy," said Alexander at Bobo's, "I want to name him Charles Gordon—after the warrior-saint defender of Khartoum. To the Sudanese he was the Gordon King, or as they called him, the Gordon Pasha. And we can call him *Pasha*."

Tatiana blinked, once, twice. "Anything you want, my love," she said.

"If it's a girl, I want to name her Janie."

"Anything you want," Tatiana whispered, "my love." She took a small sip of champagne and placed his obeisant cheek into the palm of her hand. "The white night I left you in the Summer Garden I sailed home on wings through azure skies. I grew red wings—I fell in love with you—that summer night when I was barely seventeen and you were twenty-two . . ."

With all the flowers and the gifts, Alexander took Tatiana home in his faithful 1947 Chevy truck that had 194,000 miles on it. They left her car in Bobo's lot.

The midsummer night had a thousand burning stars, the Queen of the Night, the orchid cactus, opened, and at lilac dawn the swallows sang.

The Second Coming

One sweltering August night, two weeks in their brand new magnificent adobe pueblo house with a red-rust tile roof, a home that smelled like new wood and fresh paint and cut flowers, on top of their great bed where they slept and loved and fought and bled, with the blankets off and clean sheets on, in the blue light of night, under a waxing gibbous moon, Tatiana was almost at the very end. They had propped her up at the lower part of the bed. The curtains over the French doors to their secluded garden were open and the moon shined through, otherwise there was no other light in the bedroom, just darkness to soothe her. Anthony was in his wing on the other side of the house.

Their good friend, the registered midwife, Carolyn Kaminski, was sitting on a stool at the foot of the bed, and Alexander, who was supposed to be sitting on his own stool up near Tatiana's head, kept jumping up every few minutes and going to stand next to Carolyn. The central air was off; the room was the temperature of the womb. Alexander was so hot that he had to excuse himself to Carolyn and take off his T-shirt, and now stood bare to the waist, in his long johns, saying, when, when, when, she can't do this much longer.

I can do this as long as I need to, Shura, whispered Tatiana from the bed.

Alexander, go sit next to your wife. Hold her hand. Give her a drink. There is nothing to see here, folks, nothing yet.

Alexander would go, give Tatiana a drink, sit for a fidgety second, rub, stroke, hold, wipe, whisper, kiss, and then, as soon as he felt the belly tighten, up he was again, by her legs, crowding Carolyn.

Tania, your husband is impossible. Is he always this impossible?

Yes, Tatiana breathed out. He is always this impossible.

He is crowding me. He is making me nervous. Alexander, go. Give me some room, your wife needs you when she bears down. I've never had a husband present at the birth, said Carolyn, and now I see why. This is very stressful. I don't think this is for men. Tania, tell him to go sit. Alexander, you obviously won't listen to me, but you'll do what your wife tells you, won't you?

I will do what my wife tells me, said Alexander, standing like a post at the foot of the bed.

Tatiana smiled. Carolyn, let me push my foot into his hand. My feet keep slipping off the bed when I bear down. Shura, sit on the stool, or however you're comfortable, and hold my foot steady while Carolyn holds the other, okay?

He went on one knee on the floor and held her foot steady, while Carolyn sat on the stool and held the other. The belly spasmed, Tatiana bore down, and Alexander breathed out. Carolyn, *look*—is that the crown?

Yes—and now even Carolyn smiled. Almost here. That is the crown. Alexander had thirty seconds to get up, to lean over, to put his lips on Tatiana's wet face, to whisper, you're doing great, babe. The crown, Tatiasha, almost, oh God, almost.

Hurts, Tania? asked Carolyn. You are being so brave. Alexander, your wife is being so brave.

She always does quite well.

Yes, Tatiana said. After all, my threshold for pain has been set so high. I can walk under that limbo stick.

The span of Alexander's arms was wide enough that he was able to, while kneeling, hold Tatiana's hand with one hand and her foot with the other. The next time she bore down was the worst time for her, she might have even been screaming, but Alexander could barely hear, seeing only the baby's head appear in slow motion. Tatiana's stiff body relaxed for a few panting seconds, and Alexander, letting go of her foot, reached past Carolyn to put his hand on the sticky soft grapefuit-sized head.

Alexander, don't touch, said Carolyn.

Carolyn, let him touch, said Tatiana.

Alexander, calm down, this is it, said Carolyn. The baby will be here in half a minute. I'll clean him up, I'll wrap him in a blanket, I'll give him to you to hold, but please, for the love of God, let me do my business now. Go sit by your wife.

Where's the rest of him? said Alexander, hand on the baby's head, moving slightly to the center instead of to the side.

Be patient, Alexander, the rest is next. Go sit, I tell you.

A panting Tatiana said nothing, her eyes barely open. She motioned for him. Not surrendering his new position a millimeter, Alexander pulled up, and propping himself on one arm, leaned fully over a naked Tatiana—his other hand still between her legs on the baby's head—and kissed her. He was so hot, he was drenched, almost like she was drenched. When he straightened up, he refused to move out of Carolyn's way, and she kept saying, move, Alexander, move just a foot over, move to the side where you were. Tania! Your husband is not letting me do my job.

Alexander's intense eyes were only on Tatiana, who smiled and said, Carolyn, can't you see? He is pushing you out of the way.

I see. Tell him to stop.

Let him, Carolyn, Tatiana whispered. Let him. Show him how to catch that baby.

Tania, no!

What are you afraid of? Just look at him. Let him catch his baby.

Thank you, Tatiana. And Alexander went on one knee between

her legs, as Carolyn was anxiously bent by his side, her hands next to his. The order of the universe, Alexander felt, was restored.

The belly tightened, Tatiana clenched up, one soft slippery push, and the purple baby glided out, swam out face down, front down into the waiting, grasping, open hands of his father. It's a boy, Tania, Alexander breathed out without turning his son over. Hold him, just like that, don't move, Carolyn was saying as she cleaned out his mouth and Alexander finally heard his first sound all night.

"Wah . . . Wah . . . Wah . . . Wah . . ." Like a little wailing warble. And with his first breath he became pink not purple.

Alexander let the boy be placed front down on Tatiana's stomach, keeping his hand over him and over her, and after Carolyn tied up the cord, he picked up his warm sticky infant, holding him in his palms, and brought him close to Tatiana's face, whispering, Tania, our boy. Look how small he is.

He pressed his wet forehead into her wet cheek.

Look at him flailing, squirming, wailing. Buddy, what? Been cooped up too long?

He held the boy in his fanned-out palms.

Oh God, how can he be so blessedly tiny? He is smaller than my hands.

Yes, my love, said Tatiana, one hand on her husband, one hand on her child. But then you do have very big hands.

Standing up, Alexander walked over to the open French doors so he could take a better look at the baby in the moonbeam light. Charles Gordon Pasha, he whispered. *Pasha.*

The baby stopped squirming, moving, crying; he relaxed all his limbs and lay sticky and small and completely still in Alexander's open palms, blinking, clearing his eyes, blinking, clearing his eyes, trying to focus on his father's face so close.

Tania, whispered Alexander, pressing his damp son to his bare chest, to his heart. Look, Tania, look, what a small, little, lovely, tiny baby.

Book Four

Moon Lai

Then I heard the voice of the Lord saying,
"Whom shall I send? And who will go for us?"
And I said, "Here am I. Send me."
                                    Isaiah 6:8

CHAPTER FOURTEEN

The Man
on the Moon

The Wages of Harold Barrington, 1965

Tatiana and Alexander are watching Anthony. It's just the three of them in their kitchen this morning, just like before, when there were just the three of them. The babies are still asleep. The morning is Tatiana's favorite time of the day in her favorite room of the house. The kitchen—just as they had dreamed it—is sparkling white, with off-white limestone floors, white glazed cabinets, white appliances, pale yellow curtains, and every morning sunlight rises in the kitchen and moves through the house room by room. In the mornings they gather here to make their cereal and their coffee, to eat the croissants and the jam she's made.

But early this morning, at seven thirty, only Anthony is eating, sitting on a high stool at the island while his mother and father stand at attention, across from him. Alexander, like a pillar, just stands. Tatiana clutches the back of the bar stool. As if oblivious to them, Anthony drinks his coffee and picks up his second croissant.

"Guys, at ease," he says. "My food is getting stuck in my throat."

They don't move.

"Mom, the jam is unbelievable. What is it, blueberry/raspberry?"

Anthony! Tatiana wants to cry. Anthony. She is speechless before her firstborn son. Twenty-two in three weeks! Tatiana has a twenty-month-old baby girl, still in diapers, whom she is still nursing; she has two primary-school-age boys. And two days ago Anthony graduated from West Point.

The whole family flew out east to see him throw his white cap in the air. A frail Aunt Esther came down with Rosa from

Barrington and cried through nearly the entire ceremony. Sam Gulotta and his wife came up from Washington. Tom Richter and Vikki came, estranged yet together. Richter gave the commencement address. Richter, in full military dress with bars and stripes and a lieutenant-colonel's insignia, standing tall at the podium, speaking to five hundred men and their families, all in oppressive, melting June heat on the open fields, speaking loud and clear to Tatiana and Alexander, speaking to Anthony Barrington.

"You walk in the footsteps of Eisenhower and MacArthur, Patton and Bradley, the commanders that saved a civilization. The eyes of the world are upon you."

Richter has been in Southeast Asia since 1959, an officer in a military advisory group, training the South Vietnamese to fight the North, but he is a big wig now in MACV—Military Assistance Command, Vietnam—the brain that controls the entire body that is American involvement in Southeast Asia. Rosa was so impressed by him, she asked to be seated next to him at dinner. The boys demanded to sit next to their cadet brother, but so did Aunt Esther. They wouldn't budge. Neither would she. They ended up, sulkily, sitting between their parents, while Anthony was flanked by Aunt Esther on one side and Vikki and Richter on the other.

Tatiana and Alexander rented the Pool Terrace Room at the modern and opulent Four Seasons restaurant in New York City, where they spent a raucous evening. Even Aunt Esther was raucous. At eighty-six, nearly deaf, sitting *very* close to Anthony—ostensibly to hear him better—all she wanted to hear was his cadet stories. Anthony tried to stay circumspect just like his father had taught him. He behaved well, he said; played football, Army against Navy, won finally, Army's first win in six years. He played pick-up basketball games on the open courts—"Basketball," Anthony told his aunt, "that was more like rugby." He played tennis, and his coach was Lieutenant Arthur Ashe, and Esther said, "Who's Arthur Ashe?" and, before Ant could reply, stated firmly that she wasn't in the least interested in Anthony's athletic escapades (and this is where Tatiana wanted to concur) but was "most interested" in his romantic ones. Anthony smiled and said nothing (the good boy), but Richter, always ready to stir some trouble, said, "Lieutenant, why don't you tell your great aunt about your two demerits in Chicago." And when Anthony flat-out refused, Richter happily regaled Aunt Esther with the story of how, when the West

Point Firsties came to Chicago, Mayor Daley's wife arranged for all the cadets to have dates with the good local girls from fine families. "Some great times for the cadets," Richter said with a grin.

"Yes, and a mess for the Daleys," Anthony added dryly.

"Details, Anthony, details!" cried Aunt Esther.

Tatiana smiled while feeding Janie sweet potatoes, glancing at Alexander, who was also smiling, though tensely, while telling Pasha and Harry to pipe down and stop flicking their peas and shooting bread balls out of their straws. Vikki wanted to know if there was more drink. Aunt Esther asked Anthony if he was going to follow the honored West Point cadet tradition and get married right after graduation at the academy chapel, and Rosa said only if it was a Catholic chapel, and Richter said only if he got married "to a good local Chicago girl," and Anthony deadpan replied that he couldn't find one. "Despite his best efforts," piped up Richter, and oh, how everyone laughed, and Vikki said where *is* that wine already, and Tatiana said, "Harry, you fire one more bread ball at Anthony . . ." And Harry said, "Mom, they're not bread balls, they're buckshot." And Alexander said, "Tom, how are the South Vietnamese holding up—Harry, *what* did your mother tell you!"

They talked about everything and anything, except the one thing they needed and *had* to talk about—Anthony's future. That was the burning question on everyone's mind, and has been the *only* thing on the minds of Tatiana and Alexander since August 1964 when the Tonkin Gulf Resolution was passed by Congress, authorizing the use of any and all appropriate force to keep South Vietnam free from North Vietnam, the way South Korea had been kept and was still being kept free from North Korea. Tom Richter had been with MacArthur in Bataan and in the dense jungles of New Guinea during WWII, he'd been with MacArthur in Japan after the war, and then leading MacArthur's men from Port Inchon to the Yalu River in Korea, and now MacArthur had heard the bugle call and crossed his own river, and Richter was with Westmoreland (West Point, '36) in Vietnam. He didn't speak much about what went on there, but Tatiana knew from Alexander that Richter ran clandestine special ops units. Obviously letting the South Vietnamese defend themselves with only a small U.S. presence had not done the trick. They were not holding up. They were getting run over. The North Vietnamese, the Viet Cong, the Viet Cong Self-Defense Forces, the Viet Cong Secret Self-Defense Forces were better supplied.

Something more was needed.

"You think you are entering a world far different from the one your fathers entered, but you're not. I graduated in June 1941, and six months later, on December 7th, our Naval officers saw something so out of line on their radar screens that they ignored it. It must be friendly planes, they said. And thirty minutes later, nearly our entire Naval fleet was destroyed. I'm telling you now, in the face of imperial communism, our greatest threat is complacency. During the American Civil War, Union General Sedgwick looked over a parapet toward Confederate lines and said that they couldn't hit an elephant at this distance. Those were his last words. At that moment a sharpshooter took his life. For the last twenty years, the East and West have engaged in stand-offs, in proxy wars, all against a backdrop of a nuclear Armageddon. Soon the time for pretend will be over. That is the world you are entering as West Point men."

This bright Arizona morning Tatiana and Alexander are waiting for Anthony to tell them how he intends to enter that world. Tatiana feels Alexander so tense behind her that she backs away from the island, squeezes his arm, looks up into his stone-like face and whispers, "Shh," and then says, "Darling, do you hear Harry in the front yard? Why is he up already?"

"He's convinced he can catch a Gila monster in the early morning," says Alexander, not taking his eyes off Anthony. "He thinks it's like fishing." He pulls his arm away from Tatiana. "Ant, do you want to talk later? I have to save Harry from himself."

"If you have to go, then go, Dad," says Anthony, not looking up from the paper. "I have a reception at Luke Air Force base at ten."

"I don't have to go, but once the kids come in, talking as you know will become impossible," Alexander says. The kids are noisy, especially the boys. Like wild dogs, they never stop moving. The girl is marginally quieter—but attention must be on her at all times. Once they get her up, there will be no adult conversation until her nap time.

Anthony! Do you see what you're doing to your father's heart, to your mother's heart? We can't speak, our throats are so full of our pride, of our love, of our fears for you.

"Let's talk later then," Anthony says, his head in the paper. "I just got here. My first morning back. I'll be here two months. Can we just *please* ease up . . ."

"Anthony." That's Tatiana. Finally she speaks. His name is all she says.

He sighs, wipes his mouth, closes the paper. And then he too stands up. So now, Anthony is standing at one side of the island, Tatiana and Alexander at another. All are stiff as boards.

"You're about to man the walls of democracy and freedom. We hope to see a world transformed by your presence in it."

In full white military dress, Anthony picks up his white cap off the black granite and puts it on. He is a West Point graduate, a commissioned lieutenant. In return for a first class education at the most prestigious military training academy in the United States, Anthony owes the U.S. Government four more years of active service. He knows it. His mother and father know it.

And the Tonkin Gulf Resolution had been unanimously passed. U.S. troops, little by little, are filling the planes that are heading en masse for Southeast Asia.

For the last nine months, Alexander has been talking to every person he knows in Military Intelligence and in the newly formed Defense Intelligence Agency, trying to get Anthony a position that would be equal to his talents, that would satisfy his active duty requirement, and that—most importantly—would be stateside. Finally, four weeks ago, the Director of DIA said he would hire Anthony to work on his Special Staff. He would be reporting directly to the head of the department that is the primary producer of foreign military intelligence for the United States. The formal written offer had gone out to Anthony two weeks ago.

"Duty, Honor, Country—those are the words you walk with. Douglas MacArthur, the liberator of the Philippines, of Japan, the man who in one night reversed the course of the Korean War and saved South Korea, the Supreme Commander of the Allied Powers, stood before you three years ago at this very lectern and told you that all his adult life he listened for the witching melody of faint bugles, of far drums beating the long roll, but when he crossed the river, his last thought would be the Corps, and the Corps, and the Corps. Duty, Honor, Country. Let that be your first thought as well as your last."

Anthony stands so tall, so wide, so black-haired and dark-eyed. He is his father's son in every physical way but one: he has his mother's mouth. Men do not need full mouths like hers to draw the bees to the nectar—but Anthony has it. He is young, idealistic, beautiful. He is heartbreaking.

Both Tatiana and Alexander lower their heads. Though the child is now nearly the size of her outsized husband, her larger-than-life Alexander, what Tatiana sees in front of her is fifteen-month-old Anthony, a chubby dark little boy, sitting in their New York apartment, eating her croissants, his pudgy little hands covered with crumbs and glistening with butter. He is smiling at her with his four milk teeth, sitting in their lonely apartment without his daddy, who is in the mud and blood of the River Vistula with his penal battalion. She wonders what Alexander sees.

Alexander says, "Ant, so what have you decided?"

Anthony looks only at his warily blinking mother. "It's a great offer from the DIA, Dad," he says. "I know you're trying to help. I appreciate it. But I'm not going to take it."

"In 1903, the Secretary of War told the West Point graduating class, of which Douglas MacArthur was first, 'Before you leave the Army, you will be engaged in another war. Prepare your country.' And that is what I am saying to you today."

Taking a breath, Anthony stops looking at either of his parents. "I'm going to Vietnam."

"Today in our ears ring the ominous words of Plato—Only the dead have seen the end of war."

Silence drips through the white kitchen. Somewhere on the other side of the house a door slams. Two children are running, running. Tatiana can hear the thump of their creature feet.

Tatiana says nothing, Alexander says nothing, but she can feel him behind her, coiling up.

"Come on, guys," says Anthony. "After surviving Beast Barracks cadet training and my drill sergeant, the King of Beasts, did you really think I was going to sit behind a desk at DIA?" He is so blasé, so casual. He can be. He is only twenty-one. They were twenty- one once, too.

"Anthony, don't be ridiculous," says Alexander. "You won't be sitting behind a desk. It's Military Intelligence, for God's sake. It's active combat support."

"That's just the thing, Dad—I don't want combat support. I want combat."

"Don't be"—Alexander stops to keep his voice low—"Don't be stupid, Anthony—"

"Look, it's decided. I talked to Tom Richter. It's done."

"Oh, to *Richter* you talked about this!" No keeping voice low.

"He's going to recommend me for the 2nd Airborne Division in Company A," Anthony says. "One tour with them, and he might be able to get me a Special Forces spot with him for the next round."

"The *next* round?" Tatiana repeats incredulously.

No one moves.

"Mom, Dad, you do know we're at war, right?"

Tatiana sinks into a chair, puts her arms out on the kitchen table, palms down. Alexander's arm goes on her back, on her shoulder.

"Mom, come on," says Anthony.

"Too fucking late to comfort your mother now," says Alexander. "Why the theater, Ant? Why not just tell us at graduation, at Four Seasons? Obviously Richter already knew—why not tell us, too?" Alexander's voice is distraught, but he places his steady hands on Tatiana. She knows she needs to get up to calm *him* down, but she can't calm herself down. She needs his hands.

"Anthony, please," Tatiana whispers. "You don't have to prove anything to anybody."

He is so tall with his brown sparkling eyes, with his thick black hair. So full of impossible youth. "I'm not proving anything to anybody," he says. "This is about me."

Tatiana and Alexander stare blackly at their son, and he, unable to take their dual agonized gaze, looks away.

"I graduated from *West Point*," Anthony says. "Eisenhower, Grant, Stonewall Jackson, Patton—*MacArthur*, for God's sake! I graduated from the school that makes warriors. What do you want me to do? What did you think I was going to a military academy for?"

"To get a first-rate education," Alexander returns to Anthony's rhetorical question. "Military intel for strategy and planning, for weapons acquisition in Southeast Asia. You speak fluent Russian. Bilingual backing for Soviet documents outlining the extent of their massive support for the NVA, for Pathet Lao. You'd be working for the director of Command Central for all U.S. military intelligence. It's an incredible opportunity."

"They already have *you* for that," rejoins Anthony. "Take the spot since one is available. *I'm* not going to sit and analyze data."

"You are fucking unbelievable, you know that."

"Shh!" Tatiana says. And Alexander's hands come off her shoulders.

"I'm not going to argue with you again," Anthony says to Alexander. "I'm not going to do it. I'm not going to spend the next two months in this house fighting with you. I'll leave right now and go back to New York if that's what my life is going to be like around here."

"Anthony!" Tatiana yells.

"So go!" yells Alexander. "Get the fuck out of here! Who's keeping you?"

"Alexander!" Tatiana yells. "Both of you, *please*!" They're panting, she's panting. "This is insane," she says. "Ant, you have a great opportunity to stay in the U.S. Why won't you take it?"

"Because I don't want it!"

"How can you say that when you know how hard your father worked to help you?"

"Did I ask him to help me? Who asked for his help?"

"That's exactly right," says Alexander. "That's exactly fucking right. So go, Ant, what are you waiting for? A ride?"

"Alexander, no!" yells Tatiana, whirling to him.

"Tania, stay out of it!"

Anthony lowers his head.

Suddenly Tatiana is facing Alexander's tormented eyes, and she realizes, falling mute, this is how many of these arguments have been going the last seven years. She cajoles one man, then the other, she gets between them, she tries to make it better, they stand their ground, one argues thick-headed, the other argues thick-headed, Anthony raises his voice, Alexander loses his temper, and suddenly it's Tatiana whirling on her husband, asking him to have reason, and suddenly what was between father and son is between husband and wife. Since Anthony was fourteen this has been so.

Alexander is right. Contrite in her face and body, she puts her palms on his forearms. *Sorry*, she mouths but stands her ground. Because this one is different. This isn't just between father and son. This is for the life of her family. This is the Sonoran Desert artillery fire.

Before another harsh word is spoken, two white-blond boys roll like shrieking tumbleweeds into the kitchen. Gordon Pasha is six,

Harry is five. Joyously slapping Anthony, they run past him to their father; one hangs on one arm, one on the other. Tatiana steps away as Alexander jacks them up into the air and holds them both. Alexander wore Pasha for the first sixteen months of the boy's life, first on his chest, then on his back. And then he wore Harry. He barely surrendered them to their mother for nursings. They may be blond like her, but they stride and swagger like their dad, they talk like him, they hold their plastic hammers and drive their plastic trucks like him, they wear their hair short, they bang the table, and sometimes, when they need to get their mother's attention, they say, "Ta-TIA-na!" in their father's tone. They roll and play over him fearlessly, they worship him unconditionally and without any baggage.

"Antman," says Harry, "why are you wearing your ice cream man clothes again?"

"Going to an air force base in a little while, bud."

"Can I come?"

"Can I come?"

Not replying to his brothers, Anthony says to Alexander, pointing to the older boy, "When you name my brother *Charles Gordon*, what do you *think* he is going to grow up to be?"

And Pasha replies, "A doctor, Ant. So I can heal people like Mommy. And my name is Pasha."

And Harry says, his arm around Alexander's neck, "And I'm gonna make weapons like Daddy, Ant. You should see the spear I caught a lizard with."

Tatiana nearly cries, seeing Anthony chasing lizards on their empty land when he was four.

"You *fool*," says Pasha, reaching across Alexander and pulling his brother's hair. "You absolute *fool*. Daddy doesn't make weapons. Except wood spears, but they don't count."

"Mommy, I'm hungry," wails Harry.

"Me, too, Mommy," says Pasha.

From a distant place in the house, they hear the demanding squeal of a small girl.

"You know what, Ant?" Alexander says loudly. "This is not about Pasha, or even about you and me. This is just about you."

"You got *that* right," Anthony says loudly.

Pasha and Harry stare with surprise at their father, at their brother, and then at their mother, who mouths to them, *Get down and get on out of here. Now.*

A grim Alexander, still holding his sons, says, trying to soften his voice, "Guys, hear Jane yell? Hear Jane call? Go see your sister, will you. I'm right behind you. We'll get her ready, and then Mommy will feed us."

They leap down, their palms knocking into Anthony on their way out.

"Ant," says Harry, "come swimming with us. I want to show you my forward pike."

"Later, bud. And I'll show you my reverse pike." His hand goes over Harry's head.

"Ant," says Pasha, "you promised you would play 'Do Wah Diddy.'"

"Absolutely. When I come back from Luke."

They roll out of the kitchen and bound down the gallery, singing *Do Wah Diddy . . . .*

"You think you're so smart doing what you want?" Alexander says to Anthony as soon as they've gone. Tatiana wants to touch him but can't. "You didn't talk to us before you took the spot at West Point, you know how upset your mother was—"

"I thought you would try to talk me out of it," Anthony retorts, "and I was right, wasn't I? Look at you now."

"And now you don't talk to us before you volunteer for *combat*? For fuck's sake, Anthony! You think it's just you doing the opposite of what I want, of what your mother wants? You're not fifteen any more, coming home too late. This isn't you trying to mouth off to me. This is about the irreversible path of your life." Alexander takes a deep breath. "Why don't you think of yourself first for once, instead of thinking first of upsetting *me*?"

"Oh God, this isn't about *you*!" Anthony yells.

Tatiana bites her lip and closes her eyes because next—

"Don't raise your fucking voice to me in my house," says Alexander, stepping forward.

Anthony steps back. Not another word comes out of him.

"Why tell us at all?" asks Alexander. "Why not just send a letter from Kontum? Guess where I am, folks. That's what you're doing now anyway. Why even come here?" Alexander flings his arm out. "Go—train at Yuma. Your mother promises she'll send you a care package. She'll send you one to Yuma, she'll send you one to Saigon." He turns, taking Tatiana by the arm. "Let's go."

Glaring at Anthony and trying to peel Alexander's fingers off her, Tatiana says, "I'll be right there, darling. Give me a minute."

Alexander pulls her. "No, Tania. Let's go. No more talking to him. Can't you see it's useless?"

She looks up at him, placing her hand on his chest. "Just . . . one minute, Shura. *Please.*"

He lets go of her arm, storms out, and no sooner does he disappear than Tatiana whirls on Anthony. "What is *with* you?" she says furiously.

She can see that her being upset with him is more than he can take. Funny how he can take his father's anger, but from her—one cross word, and he falls quiet and uncertain. "Mom, this country is at war. I know they're not calling it war; conflict, disagreement, whatnot. But it's war! There will be a draft any minute. If I don't put in a request for a spot now, Richter soon won't be able to get me into 2nd Airborne."

She comes close to him. He is a head and a half taller than she, twice as wide, but when she comes near, he sinks into a chair, so she can stand over him. "Anthony, please," she says. "You are not going to be drafted if you're working for the Director of DIA. Dad promised you that."

"Mom, I went to *West Point*, not Harvard. My future is in the U.S. Army. I go where they need me. They don't need me in MI. They need me in Vietnam."

She grabs his hands and presses them to her, propping herself on the edge of the kitchen table. "Ant, you know what your father went through, you know better than anyone, you of all people! You know where your mom and dad have been. War, Anthony. We didn't read about the war. We lived through it, and you did, too. You do know that boys die in war, no? And those are the lucky ones. The unlucky ones come back like Nick Moore. Remember him? Or they come back somewhere in between, like your father. You do remember your father, no? Is that what you want?"

Not pulling his hands away from her, Anthony says, "First and foremost, I'm not him."

Pushing him away, Tatiana steps away. "You know what?" she says coldly. "You would do well to aspire to be half the man your father is. Why don't you learn to walk with grace and valor."

"Ah, yes, of course," Anthony says, nodding. "How could I forget? If only I could live up to his impossible standards." He glares pointedly at his mother. "And he certainly has some high ones."

"Well, surely that's not why you enlisted in Vietnam, is it?" she cries. "What is that going to prove?"

"I know you're finding it hard to believe, Mom," Anthony says, shaking his head, "but this really does have *nothing* to do with you. Or him."

Tatiana just stares at him with bleak eyes.

Shaking his head, he says, "It doesn't! Can't you see, this is *my* life I'm living!"

"What kind of a rebellion is that?" she snaps. "Following your father's footsteps?"

"Clearly in your eyes no one can ever follow his footsteps."

"Not like this, no." She comes to him, to touch him, to embrace him; she is so sad for him, and he puts up his hands against her, almost as if protecting himself.

"He has always said to me, you choose what you want to be. Well, this is what I choose. This is what I want." Anthony blinks.

"Your father," Tatiana whispers, "didn't *want* to go to war. He had no choice. You think he went through what he went through, to save us, to save himself, so his first born son could go fight the Viet Cong?" She is so upset, she can't stand in front of him any-more; she turns to leave her kitchen. She doesn't want Anthony to see her cry for him.

Taking her hand, Anthony doesn't let her leave. Bringing her back, he looks at her contritely. "I'm sorry, Mom. Don't be upset with me, please," he says. "West Point *was* my choice, that's true, but this isn't. Now I *have* to go. Just like *he* had to, *I* have to. I don't know why Dad is wasting his time fighting the inevitable."

"Your mission remains fixed, determined, inviolable. It is to win our wars. You are this nation's gladiators in the arena of battle."

Somewhere in her house, three small children are shrieking. Even Alexander can't get the two boys to quieten down for long. One time he yelled at Harry in a booming voice, "Calm down!" And Harry, in the same booming voice, yelled right back at Alexander, "I'll calm down when I'm dead!" Though he has never since raised his voice to his father, he also hasn't calmed down.

Tatiana bends to Anthony, her hand on his cropped head. "Don't be upset with your father, darling," she whispers, kissing his hair. "He is just trying to save his son, any way he knows how." She rushes out of the kitchen, unable to tell Anthony why his father always fights the inevitable.

"Let others debate the issues that divide men's minds. Not you. May you, West Point soldiers, always be worthy of the long gray line that stretches two centuries before you."

She cannot show Anthony how afraid she is, seeing nothing but flocks of ravens flying over the heads of all the people in her lovely desert house.

The Long Gray Line

Anthony spent the summer at home, playing wild, out-of-control war and pool games with his siblings, and left for Vietnam in August 1965. Pasha, Harry and Janie missed him when he went.

Every day when Alexander came home, the first thing he said after kissing Tatiana was, "Any news?" Meaning, *any letters? Any phone calls?*

He'd call during the day and say, "Did the mail come?"

And if the mail did come and bring tidings from La Chu, from Laos, from Dakto, from Quang Tri, Alexander took his smokes to the garden outside their bedroom and sat by himself and read his son's letters.

Alexander was slightly graying. The fierce Arizona sun had darkened his face. Lines came to his eyes. But the genes were good from his Italian mother and his Pilgrim father. Though he had gained a little weight, Alexander worked too hard and trained too hard at Yuma to feel the years. Upright, wide-shouldered, watchful like always, he carried his large frame with the unspoken but clear, *don't even think of messing with me* air. No one could mistake him for anything but a military man.

As they had during the Korean War, his combat support duties increased. He often spent more than seventeen active duty days a year at Yuma—still the largest weapons testing facility in the world. In the late fifties and early sixties, when the boys were infants and toddlers, and Anthony came to help, Tatiana still went with Alexander once a month, and their baby carriages were arrayed in a row with the others outside the married barracks. But once the boys got too big for carriages, and Anthony went to West Point, and Janie was born, vast Yuma became too small for her two untamed sons and their baby sister who thought she was a male cub herself. It was either rein themselves in or stay home with Mom, while their father went alone, translating volumes of raw data coming in from Russian services and conducting extensive training drills and weapons tests.

The children reined themselves in.

In 1966, after his widely read translation of the criticism the Soviets were heaping on the first generation of the M-16—the U.S. version of the Kalashnikov rifle—which tended to jam if you didn't clean it, Alexander was finally promoted to major, having served twenty years as captain. Richter telegraphed him congratulations from Saigon with the words—"YOU INSUFFERABLE BASTARD. STILL, I'M A LIEUTENANT-COLONEL."

Alexander telegraphed him back. "YOU INSUFFERABLE BASTARD. WHEN IS MY SON COMING HOME?"

After a successful twelve-month tour with the 2nd Airborne, Anthony signed on for a second tour and moved over to train under Richter, who ran the Special Forces central command post out of Kontum under a quaint and harmless moniker of Studies and Observation Group. Anthony joined an unconventional warfare special ops ground unit. He led a recon team, he led a Search, Locate, Annihilate Mission (SLAM) team, he led a Hatchet force. He became a Green Beret. He re-upped for a third tour and lived through a bloody 1968, through Tet, and re-upped again, and lived through the 1969 Viet Cong spring offensive. During one of his recon missions in early July 1969, he captured Viet Cong documents that showed that the enemy was much larger and better equipped than the U.S. high command pretended, and that the NVA were wildly inflating the numbers of the American casualties, claiming 45,000 armed U.S. troops had been killed in the spring offensive when the actual number was 1718, against 24,361 enemy dead. He was promoted to captain.

Copies of Anthony's seven citations came home. Two Purple Hearts for a shoulder wound and a leg shrapnel, two Silver Stars, two Bronze Stars, and a Distinguished Service Cross for heroism during an assault in Laos on his long-range recon platoon. After he was promoted to captain, the letter from Richter said, "RHIP—RANK HAS ITS PRIVILEGES: AT LEAST NOW OUR BOY IS SUPERVISING GROUND STUDIES GROUPS, NOT LEADING AMBUSHES DOWN THE HO CHI MINH TRAIL."

What was amazing to Alexander during those years was that his life went on. His three blond children grew like saplings, Christmas trees were bought, large custom homes kept going up, new people were hired. Johnny-boy left, got married—twice. Amanda abandoned Shannon and her three kids for a migrant construction worker from Wyoming, and disappeared across state lines. The Barringtons went on vacation to Coconut Grove, and to Vail, Colorado so that the children could see something called "snow."

They went out with friends, they played cards, they went dancing, they swam. They celebrated their twenty-fifth wedding anniversary in 1967 with a seven-hour mule ride to Phantom Ranch by the Colorado River, celebrated with advanced married love, and his whispering words and her tears.

Every night when he came home, the house smelled of warm bread and dinner, and Tania was nicely dressed and smiling, and walking to the door to greet him, to kiss him, with her hallowed hair down her shoulders, and he would say, "Tania, I'm home!" and she would laugh, just like she had when she was seventeen in Leningrad, on Fifth Soviet. She took care of him, of his children, of his house, of his life, like she had in Coconut Grove, like she had on Bethel Island.

They lived—while their firstborn son was in the mountains of Dakto in the mud. They lived while he was in Cambodia and Khammouan and forcing the Viet Cong from Khe Sahn. They lived while he fought on the Perfume River in Hué. They lived and felt guilty, they sent carepackages and felt better, they heard from him and felt better still. During these years, he never did come back stateside, but he would call Christmas Day and talk to his mother, and at the end say quietly, "Say hi to Dad," and Dad was on the other extension listening in, and he would say quietly, "I'm here, son." And they would chat for a few brief minutes.

"So how's it going over there?"

"Oh, fine, fine. A lot of hurry up and wait."

"Yes, sometimes it's like that."

"I hate it."

"Yeah. I did too."

"No fields of Verdun here, no tank battle of Kursk. We're always in the jungle. And it's damnably wet. Must be what Holy Cross, Swietocryzt, was like for you."

"Swietocryzt was ice cold," says Alexander. "Well, watch your back."

"I will, Dad. I am, Dad."

Gordon Pasha was nearly 11, Harry was 9, Janie almost 6. Tatiana was 45. Alexander was 50.

On Sunday evening, July 20, 1969, they all sat with their eyes riveted on the television. Tatiana had been thinking that she wished Anthony were here with them, watching, and Pasha said, as if reading her mind, "Ant would love this." And Tatiana asked Alexander, "What time is it now in Kontum?" And Alexander replied, "In Kontum it is tomorrow," as Neil Armstrong took a small step for man, a giant leap for mankind, and set foot on the moon.

And the phone rang.

When the phone rang, Tatiana and Alexander turned their heads away from the TV to stare at one another. Their gazes darkened. It could not be anyone from the United States. Because in the United States everyone was watching Neil Armstrong.

Tatiana couldn't go pick it up; Alexander went.

When he came back his face was gray.

What would her kids remember about their mother from July 20, 1969?

She struggled off the couch and went to stand with Alexander in the archway to the den. She opened her mouth to speak but nothing came out. *What?* she wanted to say. *What?*

Ant's missing, he mouthed inaudibly back. She had to cover her face from them, she had to cover her face from Alexander most of all. She didn't want him to see her like this. She knew her impassable weakness would frighten her husband. With her faith shaken, his would positively crumble down like his bombed-out village huts. But how does she hide from him that Pushkin's Queen of Spades, *bearing ill will,* has entered their house? She is blinded by the ravens, their horny beaks in her eyes.

She was going to ask him not to touch her, but, true to himself, he wasn't coming anywhere near her.

She had a terrible fifteen minutes by herself in the bedroom. Maybe twenty. Then she flung open the bedroom door.

"What do you mean missing?" Tatiana said when she found Alexander outside. "Missing where?"

Alexander, less able to fling open any doors, sat mutely on the deck watching his sons in the right-time, lit-up pool. Janie was in front of him, adjusting her mask and fins. Tatiana fell silent until he finished helping the girl. No one was interested in the man on the moon anymore.

When Jane plopped away in her fins to jump in the water, Alexander turned to Tatiana.

After his successful recon mission earlier in the month, Anthony had been given a seven-day leave. He was supposed to report back for duty on the 18th of July. He had not.

"Maybe he just forgot when he was supposed to come back," said Tatiana.

"Yeah. Maybe."

"Are they looking for him?"

"Of course they're looking for him, Tatiana."

"How many days has it been?"

"Three."

Vanished with him were his weapons and his MACV-SOG special pass card, which allowed him unrestricted privileges across all South Vietnamese roads and towns. All he had to do was flash the pass and he could get into any plane, any truck, any slick and be taken anywhere he wanted to go. The pass had not been flashed; he had not gotten into anything; had not been taken anywhere.

"Who did he go on leave with?"

"Alone. He signed out to go to Pleiku." Pleiku was a town fifty kilometers from the Kontum base. Lieutenant Dan Elkins, Anthony's friend and recon leader, told Richter that the only odd thing in retrospect was Anthony going on leave by himself. He was doing that a lot in the past year. Normally, Dan and Ant, friends since '66, traveled together to unwind; they would go way down south to Vung Tau, hit the bars, the officers' clubs, get a little R&R.

The other thing that was odd in retrospect was that Anthony had not yet re-upped for another tour. His current year was ending in August, and he had not yet said he would be renewing his commission. As if perhaps he wouldn't be.

Tatiana and Alexander were silent, their stares on the splashing kids. "So what does Richter think?"

"I don't know. I'm not Richter, am I?"

"Alexander!"

"What are you yelling at me for?" He pointed to the nearby children.

She lowered her voice. "What are you all clipped with me for? What does Richter think happened to him?"

"I don't know!"

"What are you yelling at me for?" Tatiana took a breath. "Did they list him as MIA?"

Motionless at first, Alexander finally shook his head. "He wasn't in action."

They stared at each other.

"Where is he?" Alexander asked Tatiana in a faint voice. "Aren't in you the answers to all things?"

She opened her hands. "Darling, let's just wait and see. Maybe . . ."

"Yeah," said Alexander, abruptly getting up. "Maybe." Both of them couldn't speak about it anymore. Thank God for the three wet puppies in the pool, thank God for their irreducible, incontrovertible needs.

But at night after the kids were asleep, they went through Anthony's letters. They sat on the floor of their bedroom and obsessively read and reread every one, looking for clues, for a *single word*.

"*Situation here worse than we realized . . . Communist will to persist very strong . . . U.S. measures will not deter the Vietnamese . . . Mom, I'm just gathering intel, don't worry about me . . . Most of the indigenous mountain men we train, the Montagnards, speak no English . . . good guys, the Yards, but no English! Except for one, and I'm always with him because of it. Ha Si knows English better than me. Dad would like him; he is some warrior . . . Devastating storms . . . Torrential rains . . . Oppressive wet heat . . . Loneliness in the jungle . . . Sometimes I dream of the lupines in the desert. I must be mistaken. I've never seen them in Arizona. Where were we, Mom, where I could've seen fields of purple lupines?*"

Anthony asked after his brothers and sister, talked a little about his mates: Dan Elkins, Charlie Mercer; about Tom Richter and what a fine commander he was. He did not write about girls. He never mentioned girls, not in his Vietnam letters, not in his conversations from West Point. He had not brought anyone home since his high school prom. He did not talk about his injuries. He did not talk about his battles, or about the men he had lost or saved. Those things they heard about from Richter and from copies of Anthony's citations.

There was nothing that raised a flag for a numb Tatiana. "He'll turn up any second," she said bloodlessly to Alexander. "You'll see."

Alexander said nothing, still holding the letters in his hands, grim, mute, white-faced. Tatiana brought him to her on the floor and they sat with Anthony's letters between them. She held his head and whispered, *Shh* and *It'll be all right* and *There's a simple explanation.* He was so crushed in her arms that she stopped talking.

They waited to hear.

A day went by.

And then another.

Richter's men combed the woods and the trails and the rice paddies in the flat distance between Pleiku and Kontum, searched the hooches, the rivers, the mud, looking for a *trace* of Anthony, or his weapons, or his ID. He must have stepped on a mine, Richter finally, resignedly, said to Alexander. He must have been booby-trapped. He must have walked into an ambush. The dirt road between Pleiku and Kontum was relatively safe and full of American troops traveling back and forth, but perhaps he veered off course for some reason, perhaps . . .

But without a trace of evidence, the command could not firmly declare anything.

Tatiana kept praying they wouldn't find a *trace* of him.

"He's not MIA," she said to Alexander after another three days had passed. "So what are they calling him?" She had followed him into his shed and now stood near him, staring at him.

"Nothing. Just missing." He didn't look up from his work table.

"Missing? There's a designation called missing?"

"Yes."

"What's the official name for that designation?"

There was a long pause. "AWOL."

Tatiana stumbled out of the shed and stopped asking him things.

Three days became a week.

A week turned into two.

She began to step over the stones, to gnaw over all the sticks on the paths of her life, lamenting, exalting, breathing over them, examining them, as if by raking up the limbs of memory she could find the ones that had broken and repair them perhaps, mend them, or yank them away and destroy them, do anything so that on July 20, 1969, Tom Richter would not call them from Vietnam. Maybe if she had died in the blockade. Maybe if she had died on Lake Ladoga, on the Volga, from TB, from her collapsed lung. Maybe if she had not fallen for Alexander's damnable lies. *Go, Tatiana. I'm dead, Tatiana. Leave me dead and go—oh, and remember Orbeli.* Maybe if she had stayed in Stockholm when she was seven months pregnant. She would be a Swedish citizen now. Anthony would be a Swedish citizen. No Vietnam War for the Swedes. She knew she mustn't think like that, knotting herself up inside. If only, if only, if only.

While Tatiana was busy with knots, Alexander was on the phone. He talked to the commander at Yuma, to the commander at Fort Huachuca, to the Director of DIA. He talked to the Chairman of the Joint Chiefs of Staff, he talked to the President of the Defense Military School. He talked to Tom Richter nearly every day. Richter who ran MACV-SOG Command Control Central out of Kontum interviewed three hundred people who knew Anthony, who had seen him, here, there, everywhere. He had four RT teams looking for Anthony from Vang Tau to Khe Sahn. No one had seen him.

Part of the difficulty was that SOG soldiers fought secret missions with no dog tags, no identification, no bars or stripes, no whistles of any kind, fighting and falling in complete anonymity. But Anthony had not been on a secret mission. He was on official leave. And now he was absent.

Alexander sat stretched out on the floor of the living room. Janie was on his lap, Harry was on one side, Pasha on the other. Tatiana was lying on her side on the couch behind them, her hand lightly caressing the back of Alexander's head and neck as they watched *Mission:Impossible*. The kids sat raptly until the commercial break, during which Janie stood on her head, Pasha bent one of Alexander's knees over the other and started hitting it with a metal hammer to see if he could get a knee-jerk response and Harry straddled him, hands on his face, asking if Dad could help him make a timer to a balloon water bomb.

"*Make* a timer?" said Alexander, "You mean, *rig* a timer, Harry?"

"No, Dad, I want to make a custom timer first, then rig it."

"Dad, look, I'm standing on my head. Mommy taught me. How am I doing?"

"Dad, do you feel that in your knee?"

"Yes, Pasha, I feel the metal hammering at my knee."

Alexander tilted his head up and back. Tatiana was gazing at him. She leaned over and kissed his forehead.

"What's with the forehead?" he said to her. "What is this, Deer Isle?" The commercial break was over—and then the phone rang. In two seconds, all the kids off him, Tatiana's lips off him, Alexander was up and in the gallery by the receiver, talking quietly, talking low, having forgotten about everything.

"I don't understand," Tatiana said to Alexander later that night.

"Why are you talking to the Director of Military Intelligence? What would *he* know about Anthony?"

"I'm just trying all the options," he said. "I'm doing everything I can."

"That's good, but why are you calling the commander at Arizona's military installation? Why would a nice man, who has not left the base in thirty years, know anything about Anthony in Pleiku?"

"Just trying all the options, Tania." And Alexander turned his back to her.

And so Tatiana turned her back to him, turned her back to the fortress they had built around the two of them, the fortress around which the moat was wide, and the gates were shut, and there was no entry for anyone but them. The things that had brought them together, that had kept them together—no one knew those stories, only they knew them—and Anthony, the boy who had lived Deer Isle with them, who had lived through being orphaned for Berlin with them. Their later children, their later friends, none of them knew. The stories fell into the forested chasms of the past.

The weeks passed.

"Please—let's just wait and see." Tatiana kept reciting the hollow words to her increasingly despondent husband. She paced around him every feverish night, never still, not when she cooked, or read to the kids, or lay in bed with him. Some part of her was always moving, always pacing around her pride. "Let's just . . . we don't know anything. Let's just wait until they find him."

"Find him where?" Alexander was sitting outside in his chair, smoking. He was not pacing.

"Let's just see, okay?" she said, back and forth in front of him.

"You're saying let's just see if something of him will be found? Let's see if he stepped on a mine, or if an RPG-7 hit him?" Alexander was loud. "Or if he was in a freak explosion coming back to Kontum? Well, I'm not waiting for that! Are *you* waiting for that?"

"Stop it," she whispered. Her voice shook. "I'm just telling you to have a little faith, soldier. A little faith, that's all." Tatiana's hands were twisted in front of her.

Alexander stopped speaking. "How do I regain my faith," he whispered at last, "when there seems to be so little cause for faith?"

She would have wept if she didn't see him in such desperate need of her comfort. It was the only thing that stopped her from disintegrating on the travertine tile, from turning to ashes. "Please,"

Tatiana whispered in an unconvincing voice. "Maybe they're right, maybe he's gone AWOL —"

"Yes, let's hope for that. Maybe he is AWOL," Alexander said. "Perhaps he is addicted. Perhaps his own opiate of a girl smoked up his head and then some, and now he is in the Ural Mountains with her."

"I'd rather he be AWOL than dead!"

"If he is AWOL, he'll be court-martialed," said Alexander. "After thirty days, there is little difference between AWOL and desertion. Do you really want Ant to be court-martialed for desertion during wartime? He won't be alive for long, Tania."

And then her tears came down. No comfort for Alexander. He jumped up and went inside. Tatiana was left alone on the travertine tile.

Thirty days passed.

Their life stopped.

They sat and watched Pasha, Harry, and Janie make joy because they were children and couldn't help it. They made joy and their parents sat with frozen smiles upon their faces, while the young ones frolicked in the pool and rough-housed with one another and watched *Mission:Impossible*. The children did their level best to buck up their mother and father. Pasha never stopped reading and talking to them about the things he'd read. Janie never stopped baking with Tatiana, baking meringue pies and puff pastry that she knew her father loved. Harry always felt he had to try harder because he was the third son. ("Anthony may have been first," Gordon Pasha—the philosopher king, not warrior king—would explain to his younger brother from whom he was inseparable, "but *I* was the most wanted. Mom and Dad tried fifteen years for me. You Harry-boy, you were just a seven-month-old afterthought. You were supposed to be Janie.") So Harry tried harder. He made things that he thought would most please his unsmiling but revered father. Out of wood, out of stone, out of blocks of ice, out of branches and cacti and metal, Harry did nothing but whittle, carve, bend, shape and make weapons. He made pistols from soap, he made knives from sticks, and papier-mâché gray tanks. Dozens of his etched and scored and perfect ice hand grenades were in all three freezers. One evening they found him in front of Alexander's closet, putting on his father's grenade bandolier stuffed with ice grenades that were dripping all over their bedroom carpet.

Forty days.

They couldn't sleep. They tossed and turned, and made fractured love, praying for oblivion that wouldn't come.

"I have to know what you're thinking," Tatiana finally said after sleepless hours one impossible night. "I don't *want* to know. But I *have* to know. Because you can't carry it alone. Look at you. Harry made you a beautiful replica of a Claymore mine today—at least I hope it was a replica—and you couldn't even say thank you. Just tell me—be out with it. Don't tell me what Richter thinks, or what Dan Elkins thinks. Tell me what *you* think. You are the only one I listen to." She sat up in bed.

Alexander was lying on his back, his eyes closed. "Stop looking at me," he said. "I'm exhausted."

"Shura, what are you so afraid of? Tell me. Look at me." She knew he wouldn't look at her because he didn't want her to see inside him. And Tatiana had let him turn away because she didn't want to see inside him either.

Tonight he turned from her, but she climbed over him to face him; she sat on him and poked and prodded him and breathed on him and kept on at him until his choice was to get out of bed or tell her. Alexander did what he always did when he couldn't talk to her about impossible things. He made love to her.

He had barely dismounted when Tatiana said, "You've called every MI man you know. What are you searching for?"

"Holy God! Stop!" Throwing on his BVDs, he went outside into their garden. She threw on her robe and followed him. It was the end of August.

"It's not obvious?" he said, smoking, pacing around the narrow paths, through the desert flowers.

"No!"

"I'm looking for Ant, Tania."

"In MI?" She stood in front of him.

He lifted his eyes to her. "Now that so much time has passed," said a worn-out Alexander, "and there has been no sign of him, and they haven't found a trace of him, I think—" he paused "—that Anthony might have been taken prisoner."

Prisoner! Tatiana scrutinized him. Why did he say that so wretchedly? Wasn't that better than the alternative?

"That's what I've been looking for all along," he admitted. "Any classfied intel of him in a POW camp."

They stared at each other, Tatiana becoming grimmer with each breath she took as she tried to absorb the gravity of what he was telling her. She couldn't touch him, she felt him from across the path so afraid.

"Why are you trying to invent more trouble?" she said, trying to sound casual. "Don't we have enough? I keep telling you, let's just wait and see." She reached for his hand. "Come on, let's go back to bed."

"After hammering at me for half the night you now don't want to hear it?" Alexander said with disbelief.

Letting go of him, Tatiana said nothing.

"Tell me," Alexander said, "if Ant is taken prisoner by the NVA, do you think the KGB might be interested in the fate of an American soldier whose name is Anthony Alexander Barrington?"

"Shura, what did I say? Don't tell me anymore." Her hands were at her heart.

"If he was captured—"

"Please don't speak! I'm begging you."

She backed away but he came after her, taking her by her arms, his eyes in a blaze. "In Romania," Alexander said, "they just picked up a 68-year-old man and brought him to Kolyma. Gave him ten years. The man had escaped from a Kazakhstan collective in 1934. In 1934, Tania, and they *just* picked him up. He was a nobody— a nobody who hopped on a train and kept going."

"Please stop speaking!"

But Alexander wouldn't stop. "What do you think—is my meter-thick file open or closed with the KGB?"

"This is absurd, what you're thinking," Tatiana said breathlessly. "They're not—"

"Anthony had three tours in Vietnam without incident and disappeared a month before his fourth was over. You don't think his luck has run out? You don't think Pushkin's Queen of Spades is bearing ill will?"

"No," she whispered, her body shaking.

"Really? Do you remember Dennis Burck at State? *He* knew of me, of you, of my parents; he knew *everything*! If the NVA captured Ant, how many weeks would it be before a lackey behind a desk connected my KGB file with his name? Our old friend the French national Germanovsky managed to get through eleven checkpoints in Belgium before he was finally stopped. That's how long it took them to find his name in their books. How many checkpoints do you think it will take them to find an Anthony

Alexander Barrington?" Alexander let go of her, and stepped away, peering into his hands as if hoping to find different answers to his questions.

Tatiana stepped away too, hurriedly. "You're worrying yourself unnecessarily." Her voice was very small. "There are millions of troops and there is so much chaos."

"Not like in Belgium after a world war, no," he said.

"Millions of Vietnamese troops. They're not looking for American troops who were once Red Army soldiers. Besides, Anthony is twenty-six and obviously not you. It's 1969. Even if he were . . . captured, no one would piece anything together. Better for him to be taken prisoner but be alive, Shura. Believe me," said Tatiana, taking another step away from him, and another, "*I* know something about this."

"And I too," said Alexander, stepping away from her with his torture wounds and torture tattoos from the German camps and the Soviet camps, "know something about this."

The days ticked by.

The ill will penetrated even their white immaculate kitchen, where not a single unkind word had crossed the island in eleven years. Now they stood at opposite ends of the black granite block, not touching, not speaking. It was night; the babies, as they still called their giant children, were asleep. Tatiana had just finished making dough for tomorrow's breakfast bread. Alexander had just finished closing up for the night. They were pretending to drink tea.

"I don't know what you want me to do," Alexander said at last. "Tell me where he is, and I will go find him."

"I don't *know* where he is, I'm not a clairvoyant— and what are you talking about? I don't want you to go anywhere. It was then— *then*!—I wanted you to tell *him* not to go."

"I did tell him not to go."

"You should've stopped him."

"He is a commissioned lieutenant! Should I have called Richter and told him daddy was forbidding a twenty-two-year-old to go to war?"

"Stop making fun of me."

"I'm not making fun of you. But honestly, what do you think I should have done?"

"More. Less. Something else."

"Oh, why didn't *I* think of that?"

"I wish we had done something sooner!" Tatiana exclaimed. "We had been so proud, so casual."

"Who was casual?" said Alexander. "*You*?" He shook his head. "Not me. I didn't want this for him, and he knew it. He could have gone anywhere." His voice cracked. "He could have been *anything*. He was the one who wanted this for himself."

"And why do you think *that* was?" Tatiana said acidly.

Alexander's hands slammed flat down on the island. "And how would you have liked me to fix *that*?"

"You should have convinced him not to go," she said. "Eventually he would've listened to you."

"He would have listened to me least of all! He would have done the opposite of anything I advised him. That's why I tried to keep my mouth shut—"

"You should've tried harder not to. You knew what was at stake."

"Tania, this country is at war! And not only are we at war, but we're at war to keep Vietnam from going the way of the Soviet Union, of China, of Korea, of Cuba. Who better than you and me knows what that means? Who better than Ant knows what that means? How could *I* have kept him from *that*?"

"Oh, we certainly all know," said Tatiana. "Aren't we so smart. Now look at us. We should've seen this coming: the future. We should've seen the whole thing."

"And prevented it?"

"Yes!" she cried. "You knew what he was risking! You knew!"

"Come on, now you're just being . . . unreasonable," Alexander said. "And that's the *kindest* thing I can think of."

Tatiana was shaking her head. "I don't think I'm unreasonable. Not at all. You should have stopped it."

"How?" he yelled.

"Maybe if you hadn't come back from Berlin in your military dress greens, he wouldn't have become so enamored of them. Maybe if you stopped wearing your battle fatigues every chance you got, but no! Maybe if you stopped handing him your officer's cap in Deer Isle, like I asked!"

"Well, maybe *you* should have stopped telling him I had been a soldier every chance you got, but no!" said Alexander. "Maybe you should have paraded my wounds to him less. I wasn't the one flaunting my stupid *Hero of the Soviet Union* medal in front of him!"

"Oh? And teaching him how to load your weapon when he was five?" Tatiana yelled right back. "Teaching him how to shoot when he was twelve? What, you think I couldn't smell sulfur, potassium nitrate on your clothes when I'd come back from work? When you teach your twelve-year-old how to fire your weapons, when you take your sixteen-year-old to Yuma to test new missile launchers with you, what do you think he's going to do with his life?"

"I don't know, Tania," Alexander said, rubbing his face, closing his eyes. "You mean, maybe if you and I had been two completely different people, this wouldn't be happening?"

"Oh, so clever. Well, look at him now, wearing his dress whites, Purple Hearts, Bronze Stars, Silver Stars, carrying all his Claymore mines and M-16 rifles, and missing. What good are those medals to him, your cap to him, your rifle to him?" Tatiana cried. "He's missing!"

"I know he's missing!"

"Where is he? You've been in MI for twenty years—has that been good for nothing?"

"I know very well what weapons the Soviets are developing. But no, they don't seem to be sending me dossiers with Anthony's location on them."

"That's great, Alexander, charming," Tatiana said, crossing her arms. "Despite your sarcasm, you still don't know anything. We should have known better and been smarter. Made better decisions."

"Holy Mother of God!" Alexander ran his hands through his hair. "Are we analyzing *all* our decisions? How far back are we going? Every minuscule decision we had made over the years that might have led to Anthony's frame of mind at the moment of his choosing West Point among six universities, at the moment of his choosing to extend his tour for the fourth time? Do you really want to do this?"

"He did not become what he became in a vacuum," Tatiana said. "And, as you well know, those decisions were not so minuscule." She stared at him pointedly. "And yes, they *all* affected him."

"Yes!" Alexander yelled. "Starting with the very first one."

They fell silent. Tatiana held her breath. Alexander held his breath.

"I'm not talking about the decision to have him," he said, not even trying to keep his voice down. "He didn't begin with himself. He began with us. And believe it or not, we began *before* the moment you went crawling in the snow and bleeding in a truck across Finland and Sweden with him in your womb."

"Yes," she snapped. "We certainly did begin before that, didn't we? But how far back do you want to go, to change *your* fate, Alexander Belov?"

"All the way, Tatiana Metanova," Alexander said, his fists on the granite, swiping their china cups of tea across the island onto the limestone floor and storming out of the kitchen. "All the way to crossing that fucking street."

There was nothing to say after that. There was just nothing to say. Anthony was gone. Alexander *had* crossed the street, and now his son was lost, and there was nothing to do but run to the ringing phone, play with three babies, work, go to Yuma. Look at each other. Go to sleep with each other, back against back staring into walls, trying to find the answers there, or belly to belly, trying to find the answers there, too.

They walked around with gritted teeth, they slammed doors against their life.

The weeks became months, and like days they passed, the long gray line becoming longer and grayer with each passing day.

Add another lash onto Alexander's back. Add another lowering of Tatiana's head as she took care of her children and her house and ran the Phoenix Red Cross Chapter, barely raising her eyes to Alexander. The Sonoran Desert with lowered eyes, with fears so deep, each thought just another hammer upon the heart, each memory another sickle on the back, until there was almost nothing left under the scar tissue, neither Alexander nor Tatiana.

Just the boy climbing into the bed with them at three in the morning, crushed by his nightmares, in which his mother left him to go find his father, knowing she might never come back, and in his dreams never did.

Just the boy's mother, sixteen years old with her family in the small Fifth Soviet room, her feet up on the wall, on the morning war started for Soviet Russia, on June 22, 1941, hearing the voice of her beloved Deda saying to her, *"What are you thinking Tania? The life you know is over. From this day forward nothing will be as you imagined."*

How right he was. Not two hours later, Tatiana was sitting eating ice cream in her white dress and red sandals, her hair blowing all around her face.

Leningrad is still with them, everywhere they turn. Anthony missing is their continuing eternal struggle against their fate.

Their sweet boy, his brown body in Coconut Grove, walking the line, behind his mother, his hands apart, laughing, trying to keep his balance, imitating her. Swinging upside down like a monkey on the bars, like her. Sitting on top of his father's shoulders, tapping him on his scarred and sheared head, saying, faster, faster, and Alexander, not knowing babies, or children, or boys, running faster, faster, trying to forget he was Harold Barrington's son as he tried to become Anthony Barrington's father.

And Harold Barrington saying to a young Alexander, *"We're going to the Soviet Union because I want it to make you into the man you are meant to be."*

And it did.

And Alexander Barrington saying to a young Anthony, *"You decide what kind of man you want to grow up to be."*

And he did.

The sins, the scars, the wishes, the desires, the dreams of the fathers, all in that one small boy on Bethel Island learning how to fish, sitting patiently waiting for the prehistoric sturgeon that wasn't coming, now lost. Now gone.

Oh my God, Tatiana thought, is this what my father and mother went through when our Pasha went missing? How little I understood.

Tatiana and Alexander lost their way. After Anthony went missing, they all went missing, all went lost in the woods of the wretched imaginings of the things that could have befallen him.

One evening Alexander came home late from work to find Tatiana lying fetal in the bedroom on top of the bed while the small ones were by themselves in the playroom.

"Come on, Tania," he said quietly, giving her his hand. "We still have three other children. They can't find their way either. You have to help them. Without you, they've got nothing."

"I keep waiting for the next stage," Tatiana whispered, struggling up. "What is it? When will it come?"

"Don't wish for it, babe," said Alexander. "It'll be here soon enough."

It came with a visit from Vikki.

Many people called with sympathy, with misgiving. Many people called with advice, with consolation. Francesca cooked dinner for Alexander and the children for weeks. Shannon, Phil, Skip, Linda all took care of Alexander's business. After Amanda had left him, Shannon thought he would never rebuild his life,

but soon he had found a woman named Sheila with two kids of
her own, who'd been left by her husband. She moved in, they
combined their families, were given a wholehearted seal of
approval by Tatiana, who thought Sheila was almost the woman
Francesca was, and now Sheila helped Tatiana by picking her
kids up from school, driving them to dance, to baseball, taking
them to her house to play. Everyone was solicitous; they all
helped out.

Vikki didn't do any of that.

Ordo Amoris

Vikki had been out of touch for months, traveling in Europe.
She flew in from Leonardo DaVinci in Rome to Sky Harbor in
Phoenix by way of JFK in New York. Vikki rented a car, and drove
north on Pima and made a right on Jomax. Vikki stormed through
the faux-gilded gates, through the large square stone courtyard
with the paths and the trees and the fountains, sank down at their
white kitchen table, threw her arms down, threw her head down,
and wept.

Alexander, in his suit, having just come home from work, and
Tatiana, in a short fashionable checkered silk dress—the modern
fad having finally caught up with her clean look and long,
unsprayed hair—both stood and watched Vikki's inexplicable
sorrow, staring first at her and then at each other in such troubled apprehension that Tatiana could not even go and put her arm
around her closest friend. It was Alexander who patted Vikki's back
and got Vikki a cup of coffee and a smoke, and stood by her until
the slow motion deafening moment ended. Vikki calmed down
enough to speak. She said she had called Tom to wish him a happy
birthday, and heard what happened. In a strident voice, over and
over, she kept repeating that her husband would help Anthony,
would find Anthony. . .

"He's trying Vikki," said Alexander pacifically. "He's doing all he
can."

"Tom is CCC, Alexander, he knows everything."

"He doesn't know *this*."

"They have men crawling through that jungle. If anyone can
find him, Tom can."

"I suppose. He's had men looking for him for four months."

Four months!

It was dinner time. The children ran in, climbed all over Aunt Vikki, who calmed down, even smiled. Tatiana fed everyone, Alexander liberally poured the wine. After the children went to play, the adults discussed the possibilities.

A bald fact remained: Anthony wasn't on assignment when he vanished. He was on leave. Unless foul play or AWOL was involved, men didn't vanish while signed out on leave thirty miles away down a straight road in a safe town filled with U.S. servicemen.

Vikki looked like she had something to say about that.

She looked like she had something to say about a whole manner of things. But not looking at Tatiana, she said nothing, and they, not looking at her, asked her nothing.

They didn't speak to each other as they got ready for bed. Tatiana read, Alexander went outside their patio for his last smoke of the night. In bed they stayed quiet. Her tight mouth told him more than he wanted to know. Sidling toward her, Alexander bumped his head against her arm.

"Shh. I'm trying to read." She leaned over and kissed his hair. Didn't look at him, though. Alexander thoughtfully rubbed his face, remaining at her shoulder. Vikki's reaction to Anthony's disappearance was not Francesca's reaction to Anthony's disappearance, and Francesca had spent fifteen years feeding Anthony and driving Anthony and watching Anthony play with Sergio—who had enlisted to fight in Southeast Asia himself, until he found out he was sick with lymphoma and couldn't go. (Now he was in remission—and *home*.)

Alexander bumped his head against Tatiana's arm again.

"I'm. Trying. To. Read."

Pulling down the sheet covering her, Alexander gathered her nipple into his fingers, nuzzling his face against her breast.

Tatiana put down her book.

After he made love to her, after her last *oh Shura*, after turning off the lights, Tatiana said quietly into the hollow of his throat, "It's because Vikki doesn't have a child of her own. That's why she's so overwrought. Think how far back she and Ant go. She's known him his whole life, from the moment he was born at Ellis."

"I know that," said Alexander, rubbing her back. He could not have this conversation with Tania. He didn't know if he could have it with Vikki.

Alexander waited until he was sure Tatiana was asleep; she still fell asleep in the crook of his arm—either facing him like now as a vestige of their long-ago Luga tent, or spooned by him as a vestige of their long-ago Deer Isle twin bed—and then quietly disengaged, threw on his long johns and went outside.

Alexander found Vikki on the covered patio in the back, smoking.

Vikki Sabatella Richter, at nearly forty-seven, remained what she had always been—a remarkable, striking woman. Dark, tanned, lean, with long hair, long neck, long arms, *long* graceful coltish legs that tonight were crossed and bare. Her ankles were tapered, her toe-nails painted red like her fingernails. She wore lots of makeup, lots of jewelry, she smelled of heady perfume and operas and late nights out. She was the dramatic, full-breasted, dark-haired, dark-eyed friend that was too attractive for most girls to be friends with. Most girls were always in Vikki's tall shadow.

Alexander had known Vikki for nearly a quarter-century. They were old friends. But now for the first time Alexander looked at Vikki as he had not looked at her before. He looked at her as a man might look at a woman. And this woman was sitting on his porch, sunken and shrunk into her drink and her cigarette, and her hair was unbrushed and her makeup smeared around her eyes. To the man in him this arresting woman looked as if she were fracturing from her broken heart.

"It's so nice, here, Alexander," she said in her smoky voice. Even the mournful voice was redolent of drink and too many late cigarettes. "I've always loved it here. It really is like magic."

"Yes, it's good." He lit his own late cigarette. They smoked and listened to the wind. The lights were always on in the twinkling valley, as if it were Christmas every night. There was great comfort in the big house, in the taupe and azure desert, in the silence of the mystic mountains.

"Are you fretting?" Vikki asked. "Can't sleep? I'm not surprised. I have something, if you want. I can't go sleep myself when I'm frantic. I took one earlier. I've got maybe thirty not so good minutes left."

"No, I don't need anything," Alexander said. "It's been months for us. This is fresh only for you."

She was quiet, and then she was crying again, crying like her heart was being cut out. Alexander wanted to say *shh* but his throat failed him for a moment. "What's going on, Vikki?" he whispered.

"Oh, Alexander," she said.

Oh, Alexander?

Minutes passed.

With a great inhale of breath, he spoke. "Vikki," he said. "I talk to your husband three times a week to find out if he has any news about Ant. I need you to tell me"—Alexander drew another breath—"is there anything Richter suspects that might prevent him from helping me fully and with his whole heart?"

Through her barest mouth, Vikki whispered, "No. Not a thing."

"You said earlier, my husband knows everything."

"Not this."

Teary minutes dripped by. "I'm very sorry, Alexander. I can't look at you in my shame. Please don't hate me."

"Vikki, the day I judge you will be a sorry day for me at the gates of hell." He tried not to show his disapproval, his displeasure.

"Do you think Tania saw through me?"

"Now there's a judge for you. But I think in this one instance, she didn't."

They sat.

Crying again, Vikki said, "For so many years I pretended so well."

"You certainly did." Alexander shook his head in dismay. "You both did. How in the world did you do it?"

When she was silent, Alexander, distressed by her non-answer, turned to her, only to be even more distressed by the sight of Vikki sitting with her long arms draped in a cross supporting her rocking body. Alexander knew something about this pose of anguish. He turned his whole chair to face her. "All right. Calm down." He paused, lightly patting her. "Vikki, what were you thinking? I don't understand how *you* of all people could have let it happen."

Vikki collected herself, carefully chose her words. "I didn't let it happen. I fought against him since he turned seventeen."

"Seventeen? Oh my God, Vikki."

"He simply wouldn't take no for an answer. I said to him from the very beginning, Ant, what the hell are you thinking? Have you completely lost your mind? And he said—*yes*."

Alexander closed his eyes. Seventeen! Vikki stopped speaking.

"Don't be afraid of me," Alexander said, with a miserable sigh, squeezing Vikki's hands. "I'm not Tania. I was once a teenage boy myself, and I'm still a man. As a man, I understand. As a teenage boy, I understand. Just—tell me what happened."

"For over a year I steadfastly fought against him, is what happened." Vikki spoke in a voice so low as if the mountains should not hear. "At first I was shocked—like you; when I realized how serious he was, I tried to talk him out of it. I didn't even know why I had to point out to him the reasons against it, they were so numerous and insurmountable. Certainly I don't have to point them out to you or to the woman who is going to feel like I've committed an unspeakable sin. However, Anthony saw nothing, understood nothing, cared about nothing. To say that he was persistent and utterly indifferent to each and every one of my persuasive arguments would be a flagrant understatement. He was relentless."

"Shh," said Alexander. "Slow, and quieter, Vikki."

"I surrendered right after his high school graduation, the summer before he left for West Point. You bought him his truck, and a brand new guitar that year, remember? Oh, he liked his truck and he played a fine guitar. Played the guitar like he was ringing a bell, as they say. He sang a fine tune—"Jailhouse Rock" performed Anthony style. He sang me songs in English, Russian, Spanish and even my Italian!" Tears falling down her face, Vikki sang for Alexander the way Anthony once sang for her. "'*O Sole Mio/sta 'nfronte a te/the Sun, my own sun/is in your face.*' He sang me, '*I will give my very soul/just to kiss you.*' He sang me '*Cupido, cupido prego*' ... and your very own 'Dark Eyes'—yes, 'Ochi Chernye' was his specialty!" Vikki exclaimed. "'*Ochi chernye/ ochi strastnye/ ochi zhguchie/ i prekrasnye ...*'" She faded off. "He was so *multi-lingual.*" She broke a piece off her smoky singing voice and choked on it. "Yes," she said, nodding, "he had quite an arsenal, your son. And for a year he kept bringing *all* his weapons. No harm, he said. He was going away in a few months. He was not a child, he was almost eighteen—as if that were the only problem—and now we were two adults! We knew what we wanted—one long weekend at the Biltmore to sate his hunger and appease my curiosity. I said to him surely he didn't need a whole weekend and he replied that yes—he did." She shook her head. "On *fire*, I tell you," she whispered. "He became impossible to refuse, to refute, to resist. And so ... "

Alexander remembered Anthony from that summer before he left for West Point sitting alone outside on the moon deck, strumming his guitar, nearly naked in the Arizona 115-degree *heat*, singing "Ochi Chernye" over and over. Alexander and Tatiana had said quietly to each other that the girl must have been something else.

Tonight he shook his incredulous head. "You stopped resisting," he said to Vikki, lighting another cigarette. "Feel free to move forward through this part."

Vikki nodded. "I stopped resisting. Queen Victoria would have stopped resisting." Seeking relief from visceral memory, her arms crossed over her torso, her body folded over her crossed legs. "Do you want to hear what happened with us after?"

Alexander shuddered. "No. The rest I know."

"Do you?" But Vikki didn't say it with surprise. She said it as in, *no, you don't.*

Alexander said he did. "Many years ago," he said, "when I was even younger than Ant, I found myself in a similar situation with one of my mother's friends, who was about the same age as you had been—thirty-nine. I was barely sixteen. She was my first, and she was great, but once I got a taste of it, I wanted all the girls. Needless to say it lasted just one summer with her."

Vikki studied her hands. "Well, I wasn't Anthony's first." They both didn't know what to say.

Alexander stared at her, realizing something. "Vik, you moved here in '58 and then suddenly moved back to New York in '61. That August, as I remember. When Ant went to West Point."

"Yes."

"You didn't—you didn't move back . . . for him, did you?"

"I thought you knew the rest?"

"Obviously—less well than I thought."

"Alexander!" Vikki whispered. "No one could lay a hand on that boy without falling *completely* under his spell. Certainly not a thirty-eight-year-old woman who had traveled the world over, who had seen and loved and endured she thought everything. He made me lose all reason." Vikki shuddered. "He didn't win my heart. He took my heart." She lowered her chin into her chest. "But he was *eighteen.*"

"Not answering my question, Vik."

"I am," she replied. "I am answering your question."

Alexander shook his head. His own Svetlana had been heartbroken but not as brave. She had wanted something more from him that he did not have and could not give. When he moved on, she didn't persist. He could only imagine how his own son treated the woman in front of him. He didn't know what to ask next. "Did you . . . see him again?"

"Yes," she replied. "When he had his weekend pass, he would come to New York and stay with me."

"Until when?"

"Until he left for Vietnam," said Vikki.

That was the jaw-dropping thing.

"You continued to see each other for *four* years?" Alexander said, astonished.

"Yes. Don't know everything, do you? Our casual weekend at the Biltmore lasted a little longer than we expected. I don't know how we kept it hidden from you, from Tania. From Tania particularly."

Alexander asked (*having* to ask!), "Ant didn't end it?"

"He didn't end it," said Vikki, her voice cracking, her demeanor crushed, "because I acted like there was nothing to end. I was just a freewheeling gal. Anytime he wanted to get together, we got together. When he didn't, we didn't. No pressure either way. No promises, not a single pledge for tomorrow. Just fun with us. From beginning to end, nothing else but fun."

Alexander's chair was no longer facing Vikki. He certainly wasn't. His elbows were on his knees, his head was down. The cigarette dangled out of his mouth.

"I won't lie to you," Vikki said. "There was some fun. New York in the 1960s for a fledgling man and his tour guide. New York is a city for all seasons, for all lovers. Even dead end lovers like us. And, I didn't fool myself for a second, Alexander," she said. "No one knew better than I what a dead end we were. I'm 20 years older than him!" she cried. "When he would be 40, still a young man, I would be 60! When he would be your age now, still virile and strong, I would be 70! I'm older than his mother, for God's sake! His mother and I—I can't look her in the face. This is shameful. It's degrading for me to explain to you."

"No need to explain anymore."

"I didn't want him to think anything he could do would hurt me," Vikki went on. "I know how frightening that is for a young boy just starting out. Last thing he needed. So I pretended I was casual toward him, to let him have his young life, the life he needed to have and deserved to have, knowing that eventually he would find someone to marry, someone to have children with. He could not have that with me."

"After all," said Alexander, "you are already married."

"That's right. To his commanding officer." She didn't look at Alexander when she spoke.

"What did Ant want, Vikki?" Alexander asked quietly.

"What do you think, Alexander?" said Vikki. "He wants what you have. What you've had your whole life." She looked like she was in a suffering haze. "He could not have that with me. I am many things, but I know my limitations—and he knows them, too." Her hands were trembling. "And—my sham marriage gives me a permanent air of respectability so I don't have these complications in my life. It's much simpler that way. Never any explanation for the lack of anything on my part. Life for weekends at the Biltmore is all Vikki is capable of."

Alexander was listening and wished he weren't. "Answer me," he said. "What did Anthony want?"

"Oh, look," Vikki said, with fake dismissiveness, "you know how the young are. He wanted his cake, he wanted his fun, his Biltmores, his strolls down the Hudson. Sure, he said he wanted me. He wanted *all* the girls. He wanted everything. And why not? He had everything." She wept. "*Everything.*"

Every stone tile in the deck flooring was being examined by Alexander.

"I thought for sure he'd be finished with me after a month, after six months, a year. But, no, he kept coming back," Vikki said, wiping her face. "Until he graduated—and then without a backward glance left for Vietnam. I said to him, it's a good thing we were just having fun, Antman. Makes it easier for you to go. Thank you for having a good time with me. Thank you for the moonlight waltzes you and I have never had, thank you for the promises we never made, for the sun that didn't shine above our heads. Aren't you glad you're not breaking my heart? Aren't you glad now, when you are leaving, that you're not in love with me?" Vikki's face was in her hands.

Alexander sat with her a while. But there was really nothing more to say.

When he got up, he said, "Vikki, you might think this one over a little more carefully. The parents may be forgiven for being blind fools, but I'm telling you, this kind of thing is *very* difficult to hide from a husband."

Vikki waved him off. "Alexander, you know better than anyone that, unlike you, Tom has been a terrible husband. A good man, a bad husband."

"Even terrible husbands see things like this."

"Yes, well, when the husband is in Vietnam since 1959, coming back stateside only twice a year, and bleeding U.S. Army since 1941, I know he can't see anything. I haven't seen Tom in two years. I hadn't spoken to him in six months. Had it not been his birthday, I never would've called. Certainly he didn't call me to tell me about Ant; and why would he? I wouldn't worry about it. He knows nothing." She paused. "Are you going to tell Tania?"

"I don't know," Alexander replied. "I don't *want* to tell her. But for twenty-eight years I've had a hard time keeping anything from my wife." Vikki looked away and Alexander looked away, collecting the glasses, throwing out their butts. "You think now is the time to improve my game?"

He said good night to her.

In stealth, with calm breath, he came back to bed, listening for Tatiana's breathing.

"I'm awake," she said.

He sighed. "Of course you are."

She turned to him and they lay silently, their arms intermingling.

"You went to talk to her?"

He nodded, searching her face for a frame of mind.

"Does she know where Ant is?"

"No." Alexander brought her closer. "I didn't ask."

Tatiana lay her ear on his chest, listening minutely to his heart. "Did you ask her . . . did she tell you things you didn't want to hear?"

"She told me things I didn't want to hear."

Alexander told Tatiana about Vikki and Anthony.

After he was done, Tatiana was silent and when she spoke, she spoke very slowly. "Suddenly, Dasha not seeing what was right in front of her nose is easier to understand, isn't it? And they didn't hide it—like we didn't. They left it everywhere for us to see—and I see it everywhere now." She put her hands over her face for a moment. "My friend Vikki has always been a spirited gal," she said then. "When I first met her she was crying because her first husband was coming back from war and she didn't know how to tell her lover, whom she had not even told she had a husband. She was unfaithful to her first, she was unfaithful to her last, and to all the boyfriends in between. She fell for Richter—she always wanted to fall for a war hero—and married him despite all sense and reason. Certainly he has not done right by her in return, and I won't speculate on the chicken or the egg question. My opinion is," said Tatiana, "that she chose him to marry exactly because she knew she was always going to be the mistress and not the wife with him. The role suits her." Tatiana paused. "And here's my small solace to us: Vikki has had beaus in Africa, in Europe, in Asia, in Australia. She has traveled far and wide, having fun with the boys." Tatiana blinked unhappily. "It wasn't until she cried at my table today that I knew—of all the parasailing, passing fancies that have come and gone, Anthony is the one boy she cannot forget."

Facing each other, they lay in their bed. Quietly nodding, Tatiana cupped her hand over Alexander's face. "I know well the spell of those songs of love," she whispered.

He moved closer to her, spooling his arm under her neck, so he could feel her large warm breasts press soft against his bare chest, for comfort, for compassion.

The next morning over breakfast, the first thing an ashen-faced, tear-streaked Vikki said to them, after the children had gone to school, was, "Alexander, did you tell her?"

Alexander and Tatiana exchanged a look. "I told her," he said.

Vikki nodded. "Well, *now*, there is something I have to tell the two of you that I don't know how to tell Tom. As you can imagine, there are a couple of reasons why he might not be as understanding as you, Alexander."

"*I'm* not as understanding as Alexander," Tatiana said grimly.

"I know you are not," said Vikki. "Because you're not a sinner. I'm sorry. It's inexcusable and I don't know what to say to you. We will spend the next decade fixing this and figuring it out, and I know we'll be all right—because you have forgiven worse than this." All three of them lowered their heads into their coffees. "But right now," Vikki said, "we have to find our boy."

They agreed. They had to find their boy.

From her pocket Vikki pulled out a letter. "I got this four months ago from Anthony. This is partly why I've been hiding out in Europe. I wasn't about to share it with anyone, and I don't want to share it with you now. This is going to be hard for you to hear, this is going to be hard for me to read. If Anthony is ever found, this is going to be hard for him to know you've heard. And it is absolutely *impossible* for my husband—who loves Ant—to ever see, to ever know about. Unfortunately, now that Anthony is missing, there are some things in this letter you must know." With her shaking hands she unfolded it. "I'm going to cry. Can you take it?"

"We *can't* take it," said Tatiana, grasping Alexander's forearm. "Read your letter, Vikki."

Vikki flinched as she started to read, flinched as if were being slapped—with the very first word.

> *Gelsomina!*
>
> *In the hope of quieting your worries about me, worries I know you've carried for years, I'm writing you now. Vietnam is not the place to do much soul-searching (is Italy?), which is perfect for me since as you know I don't like to trouble myself with that, and here, who's got the time? I like to drink and smoke and party with the girls, as you say. No one was more surprised than me when north in Hué, near the Perfume River, I had unexpectedly found what I had been searching for. And now you're the first and the only to know—I got married. My Vietnamese bride speaks a little English, which is good because I do not speak Vietnamese. She is young, she is a white swan on her bike and we are expecting a baby.*

Vikki had to stop reading. Tatiana and Alexander had to stop listening. While Vikki tried to calm herself, Alexander scrutinized an intense and intently concentrating Tatiana. He saw by her motionless face, by her slightly parted, barely breathing mouth and her unblinking, completely transparent stare that she was not listening for heartbreak, or Grand Guignol, but for some other vapors to pass through.

Barely composed, her voice already breaking ahead of the remains of the letter she obviously knew by heart, Vikki resumed:

> *I thought you might like to know this—you were always so anxious about my life and my choices, where I was and wasn't going, what I was and wasn't doing. I kept telling you I already had a mother, but you just weren't satisfied in the role you had. You wanted expanded duties. So in the interest of full disclosure, that's why I'm telling you what's happened to me here, so far away from you.*
>
> *It's been four years since I last played guitar for you, sang "Malaguene Salerosa" for you—"Perhaps, Perhaps, Perhaps" you sometimes think of me when the radio plays "The Rain, The Park & Other Things."*
>
> *"Traces."*
>
> *"Grazing in the Grass."*
>
> *And "Jean."*

We had our blissful years, you and I, but it's all over now, Baby Blue. You were a "Spooky Wild Thing" and I'd been a fool—and so young—intoxicated with the Central Park troika rides under the big yellow moon and the palo verdes outside our fogged-up Biltmore windows. You kept telling me we never had a future—and you were right. I had been dreaming about "la luna ché non c'e." Remember we talked about St. Augustine? About something he called "Ordo Amoris." The "order of love," or "just sentiment." He said true virtue and true love for human beings were defined as every object being accorded the precise degree of love that was appropriate to it, that it deserved.

You and I were always out of balance on that one. I'm lucky to have found it with Moon Lai. I now have what you always wanted for me—what you kept saying I wanted for myself: to be married, to have a child, to have real love.

But I'm still in the heart of darkness, my time here is not over until August, and just in case this is the last letter I ever write you, know this: There was once a time I believed that what I felt for you was real, no matter how imperfect. There was once a time I believed what I felt for you was Love. "Vy sgubili menya/ochi chernye." Now I find myself grateful that you always knew the difference, being so much wiser. Thanks for steering me clear of the lie of you and me that had felt so much like truth.

Ti amavo e tremo.
Anthony

Not Vikki, not Tatiana, not Alexander were able to lift their eyes. Vikki cried as she kissed Anthony's letter and pressed it to her chest. Tatiana was so deeply chin down, she looked as if she could've fallen asleep. And Alexander, his eyes blackened with the impossible permutations of what he had just heard, was trying to make sense of the nonsensical. When Tatiana's eyes looked up at him, they were no longer crystal, but *chernye* with *stradania*, occluded with suffering.

He had a day's work and an evening full of his children to live through but at night in their garden, in the back, in private, Alexander and Tatiana *both* paced like caged tigers. Frantically they tried to piece together the fragments of a puzzle they could not understand.

Anthony had gotten married! Anthony married a Vietnamese girl who was pregnant. And then Anthony disappeared. Could he have gotten his head so crazed that he ran into the Ural Mountains with his pregnant wife and abandoned his men, his commander, his duty, his Military Code of honor, his country?

Could Anthony have betrayed the United States for a Vietnamese girl named Moon Lai?

"No," said Anthony's adamant feral mother, a vehement *Panthera leo*. "His whole life that child has had only one example of how to be a man, and that has been yours. He is your son, Alexander," said Tatiana. "We did not stay in Lazarevo in 1942, we did not stay on Bethel Island in 1948, both times when we had *everything* to lose. Anthony did not run into the Ural Mountains with her. Something else happened to him."

How deeply Alexander and Tatiana bowed their heads. That's what he had been afraid of. Anthony was a West Point graduate. He was a captain in Special Forces, in MACV-SOG, the elite of the elite. SOG operated separately from regular operations and in secrecy, both commando and long-range recon, reporting straight to the top. SOG was the tip of the sword. There were 500,000 U.S. troops in Southeast Asia, of which 2000 were Special Ops soldiers, of which Ant was one of only 200 strike-force ground troops. This West Point man, this soldier, their son could not have gone AWOL. It was simply impossible.

"You sometimes call Vikki *Gelsomina*," Alexander said, hoping she did not hear the resignation in his voice.

"Her sainted grandmother Isabella, who raised her, called her that. It means jasmine," Tatiana said. "Only people who love her call her that. But what's that in your voice?"

"Oh God." Mystified, Alexander raised his eyes to her. "Well, why would Ant marry someone else then?"

"Because Vikki is married to Tom Richter," Tatiana said. "And Anthony knows his place. But a long time ago, your one word to me was *Orbeli*. I had asked you not to leave me without a word, and you didn't. You gave me Orbeli. *Moon Lai* is Anthony's one word to us. Across the miles, to another woman, it's as inscrutable as Orbeli, as infuriating, as meaningless—and as fraught with meaning as Orbeli. It's unforgivable—just like what you had done to me, since you knew I didn't know what Orbeli meant because I did not know the Hermitage director's name. That cursed curator with his crates of art."

"Yes," said Alexander. "The art was Orbeli's sole passion. He sent it away to save it."

"All very well and good. It wasn't exactly," said Tatiana, "co-ordinates to your location in Special Camp Number 7 in Sachsenhausen." She smiled lightly. "Well, Moon Lai is Anthony's voice from the wilderness. Moon Lai is Anthony's Orbeli."

Alexander couldn't smoke enough cigarettes in their stone garden. "And what are we going to do with this one cryptic word?" he asked. "The only person who can help us is the husband of a woman who got a letter from our son that the husband can never read." He paused. "If I tell Richter what we know, he's not going to help us, he's going to find and kill Anthony himself."

"Well, obviously, you don't tell him everything you know," said Tatiana. Then: "What are you looking all skeptical and forlorn for— *now* suddenly you've lost your ability to say whatever you have to? This is for your son. Call Richter, put on your brave and indifferent face and lie with all your heart."

Alexander had stopped pacing and from afar was standing and staring at her.

She shook her head, looked away, fervently shook her head again, and said, "No. Absolutely not. Not under any circumstances. No." She came to him, he came to her. Their arms wrapped around each other. She was still so small, so slender, pressed into his chest, under his chin, his arms still swallowed her.

"Oh, Tatia."

"No, Shura."

They were in their secluded nighttime garden. It was October 1969, it was cool. Alexander made a fire in a stone enclosure, and when it was blazing, they undressed and he laid her down in front of it on a thick quilted blanket. They were barricaded by flowers, the fire, a low adobe wall. This was their private Lazarevo place under the Perseus galaxy stars in Arizona. They made love; in tandem and in unison they used their lips on each other, and then Alexander sat against the low wall, his legs drawn up, and Tatiana poured herself into his lap, her legs drawn up, too, her arms around his neck, her bare navel against his bare navel, her heart against his heart, her mouth on his mouth. He held her flush to him, his hands on her hips, on her back, in her hair.

Afterward, he put on his army bottoms and she his army crew. She sat in front of the fire, and he lay down, his head in her lap. They sat without moving, without speaking while the fire burned down in the little garden.

"Babe, please," Alexander said, "why are your tears falling on me?"

She stroked his forehead, his eyes, his stubble. "Oh my God," said Tatiana. "Because I realize what you've been thinking. It's *not* what I'm thinking. You want to go to Vietnam to find him. Please, no. No. I can't make it, Shura. I can't make it without you, too. I can't." A hollow cry followed her words. "I wish I had died in the Lake Ilmen woods! I should have died. No one could believe I had made it. Had I died, none of this would be happening!"

"Tania," Alexander said, furling with unhappiness, "you've been telling your husband, your family, the Lake Ilmen story for thirty years—to give us strength, to give us hope, to give us faith. The two most important life lessons Anthony will ever learn are in that story. And now you're telling me the life lesson in it was that you should have *died*?"

"Do you think Ant remembers the story of me in the Lake Ilmen woods?"

"How could he forget? He can't forget." He reached up to wipe her face. "Help me. *Oh, give strong drink unto him that is ready to perish*," he whispered. "Tell *me*."

Tatiana bent down, pressing her wet face to him, her wet lips to him, she kissed him, holding his head to her breasts. "*The song of songs, which is ours*," she whispered. "*Let him kiss me with the kisses of his mouth, for his love is better than wine . . .* " She straightened up. He lit a cigarette, not taking his eyes off her face, watching her lips move, her eyes glisten, inhaling nicotine, and through it her sweet breath, listening to her murmur to him about ravens and brothers.

CHAPTER FIFTEEN

The Queen of Lake Ilmen

Ravens and Brothers

Tatiana rowed the boat across the lake. She wasn't talking much to either Saika or Marina, concentrating on the rowing, listening to them chatting.

It was overcast. Yesterday's heavy rain did not clear the sky, the clouds hung close over the lake as if threatening rain again at any capricious minute. It was seasonably cool, perhaps 25°C. The girls wore long-sleeved shirts and long trousers to protect their arms and legs from burning nettles and biting mosquitoes. Saika had wanted to wear a dress, but one word of advice from Tatiana and she was changing into trousers and thanking her. Saika didn't want to rub stinky and stinging alcohol all over her body, still covered with swollen red wounds from the leech attack the other day, but again, Tatiana convinced her that the bug bites would be worse than the smell and almost as bad as the leech bites. Saika listened and was grateful. In the boat under Tatiana's legs were two wicker baskets, one for the blueberries, one for the mushrooms. She brought a small paring knife, so as not to frighten the mushrooms with a big blade.

Her grandfather—a big believer in the just in case—always counseled her to bring a watch and a compass into the woods. The compass hung around her neck, but truthfully, Tatiana had doubts about it: A fledgling scientist in a Jules Verne mode, she had been experimenting with it a little. The watch, borrowed from Dasha, Tatiana was convinced was running two minutes slow—an hour. Tatiana herself did not own a watch, because she did not keep time.

Perspiring slightly, Tatiana was lost in thought and only

belatedly saw a black fast-moving cloud over her head; she looked up and instinctively raised her oar in defense. The cloud was black crows, in a formation of hundreds, swooping too close to the girls' heads. The birds screeched, flapped in a frenzy and flew away, leaving Tatiana puzzled and troubled. She was already breathing hard from the rowing.

"Hmm," she said through her panting. "What do you think of *that*?"

"Is that a superstition, Tanechka?" Saika said with a wide smile. "The birds?"

"Tania is right, I've never seen so many either. And *so* close," Marina said.

With a laugh, Saika said, "Oh, come on, you sillies. They're just birds. If they were pigeons or seagulls you wouldn't be sitting motionless in the middle of a lake, would you?"

"But they weren't pigeons," Marina said, with a peculiar glance toward Saika.

"And seagulls over an inland lake might as well be polar bears in Africa." Tatiana thoughtfully lowered her oars into the water.

"Tania, are you too tired to row the rest of the way?" Saika asked. "Want me to row? I'll be glad to."

"What did I tell you, Saika? Tania doesn't let anyone touch the oars," said Marina, grinning, when Tatiana shook her head. "That's just complete defeat, isn't it, Tania?"

"Complete," agreed Tatiana. "Good thing Pasha's not here." She was still looking up at the sky where the birds had flown. She resumed rowing and Saika resumed her conversation with Marina. They were discussing a place Saika had lived in.

"You think I wanted to leave Oral?" Saika was saying to Marina. "I didn't. Kazakhstan was very good to us. But we were forced to leave." Saika spat right into the boat. Her demeanor suddenly changed from affable to angry. "It was those *bastards*. Late one night, you see, they tried to kill my father."

Tatiana strained to listen.

"Who? Why did they do that?" Marina asked.

"I don't know. I was young. Maybe ten. My brother told me Papa was doing his job too well. He was doing what he was paid to do, working very hard, and the sloths, the slackers, the swine he was watching didn't like it. So they dragged him from his bed in the middle of the night and nearly beat him to death. They had wooden boards and spades and coal in their grimy thieving hands."

"Oh, that's terrible! So what happened?"

"What do you mean, what happened? They didn't kill him, did they?" Saika was agitated. "They didn't kill him, but they opened up his head and broke three of his teeth. They broke his ribs on both sides and crushed his kneecap. They even cracked his breast-bone, can you believe it? Do you know how hard you have to hit someone to crack their breastbone? I think it's the strongest bone in the body, isn't it, Tanechka?"

"I don't know," Tatiana said. "One of them."

"Why did they stop? Did they think he was dead?" Marina asked.

"No! My father wasn't lying down, he wasn't dead. He was an ox and he fought like an ox." Saika took a stormy breath while remembering. "Then my brother rushed out with a lead pipe and helped him."

Tatiana stopped rowing. She had been unable to concentrate on the rowing and Saika's story.

"Stefan and I were yelling for him not to get hurt but he didn't listen. He wielded that lead pipe as if he meant to kill them all."

"*Who* wielded the lead pipe?" Tatiana asked, confused.

"I told you! My *brother*," exclaimed Saika. "Sabir, we were yelling to him," she continued, her eyes glazed as if entranced. "Sabir, get out of the mêlée, save yourself, Sabir! Papa can take care of him-self."

"*Who* was yelling?" Tatiana said, uncomprehending.

"Me and Stefan! Are you paying attention?" Saika paused.

And then—she blinked, and glanced at Tatiana.

They did not speak. For several minutes there was silence.

"Yes. So? There *was* another brother," Saika finally said. "He's dead now."

Tatiana's only response was starting to row again, while Marina, failing to catch Tatiana's uncatchable eye, haltingly continued the conversation with Saika.

A weakened Tatiana, after sucking in her breath, turned around to see how far it was to the shore. Her arms were tired, and there was no sail and no wind, just Tatiana and her small wooden oars, doing the best she could, rowing as fast as she was able. *So how come you didn't tell us you had another brother, Saika?*

Why was that so frightening to think about?

They arrived on the eastern forest shore of Lake Ilmen at eleven. The girls had promised Aunt Rita that they would pick mushrooms and berries until four at the latest, and then start for home to be

back by six. That gave them about five hours in the woods. Tatiana
had on the only watch, and Marina asked for it to see if she could
coordinate the time with the position of the peeking sun. Tatiana
kept teaching her how to do it, but Marina was a slow learner. Saika
had brought a flask of water and some bread and eggs. Was anyone
hungry, she asked as they got out of the boat. Eager to get started,
the girls wolfed down the food and then Marina and Saika helped
Tatiana pull the boat halfway onto the sandy bank and Tatiana tied
it with rope to a fallen tree trunk. She wore Uncle Boris's high
galoshes over her shoes. After wading in the water and pulling the
boat onto the shore, she took off the galoshes and laid them back in
the boat. Looking up at the sky, she wondered if it was going to rain.

"So what if it does?" said Saika.

"I don't want the boat to get filled with water," replied Tatiana,
frowning, not remembering if she wondered about the rain out
loud. "It'll be hard to row back. I suppose we can always ladle it
out with this bucket."

"Good thinking, Tanechka," said Saika. "You're always thinking.
But it won't rain. Should we take the extra rain bucket in case
we find lots of mushrooms?"

"I think we shouldn't pick more than we can carry," said Tatiana.
"One bucket of mushrooms, one of blueberries will be plenty."

"Oh, you're right, of course," said Saika merrily. "Whatever you
say, Tania. You lead. Which way?"

The swampy woods began right at the lake. There was a short
sandy bank full of conifer needles, some sap, some fallen branches,
pebbles, larger rocks, dessicated fish—and the forest. Tatiana
grabbed a few large handfuls of pebbles and put them into her
pants pockets.

It was peaceful in the forest, it was restful and pleasant.

Saika asked for Tatiana's compass. What do you need that for,
Tatiana wanted to know, but the question might have involved
eye contact. After the story on the boat, Tatiana didn't want to be
making any eye contact with Saika. She decided to just give it to
the girl, careful not to touch any part of Saika's hand as she handed
the compass over.

"Thank you, Tanechka." Saika smiled. "I'll give it right back. I
love compasses. Marina, has Tania always been so organized? She's
brought everything."

"Yes, Tania always prepares for contingencies. She is so much
like Deda."

Tatiana liked that. She strived to be like Deda most of all.

"I wish I were like that," said Saika. "It's such a good way to be. Don't you think, Marina? Better than me. I never know where I put anything. I'm never prepared for a single thing. Everything I do, I do on the spur of the moment. Tania, look, I found a mushroom, and I don't even have a knife. I'm just plain silly. Can you tell I've never done this before? Teach me, Tania. Like, what are you doing? Why are you throwing little pebbles down on the ground?"

"So we know which way we came," replied Tatiana.

"But we have a compass."

"It's always good to throw down the stones. They never make a mistake."

"Oh, so true." Saika giggled. "You must have done this many times. Marina, isn't it good to have a guide?"

"I'm hardly a guide," Tatiana muttered.

"Yes," said Marina. "She *is* good, but it's also just common sense, a lot of what Tania knows."

"So true," agreed Saika heartily. "Common sense is key. Tania seems to have a surplus. I'm sorry I'm so silly and forgot to bring my own, but, Tanechka, may I borrow your knife to cut this *podberyozovik* mushroom?"

"Of course," Tatiana said, staring at Saika with incredulity. A small twinge of remorse prickled her chest, but then she blinked again, a small styptic blink, and saw the scars and the lies, and the steady hands, and the faintly foul odor, and the unmentioned brother, and the twinge was gone.

They looked and peeked and picked and wandered. The mushroom bucket was getting filled up, but as they were walking in the dense forest, Tatiana realized that it was not getting filled up by her. She was better at the blueberries, but she hadn't found a single mushroom. And what was worse, she wasn't even wondering why she hadn't found one. She'd been mindlessly picking the blueberries, but for mushrooms you needed steady focus and her mind wasn't steady. It wasn't seeing the mushrooms. She couldn't stop thinking about Saika and the words that came out of her mouth, all sounding like lies or fraud, Tatiana didn't know which. Did Saika herself know? Lived in one place, Tatiana muttered to herself, or five dozen places? Was she a shepherd's daughter, a farmer's daughter, a field hand's daughter, or an engineer's daughter? Or just a weeder's daughter? Saika once told Tatiana she rode horses in Kazakhstan to herd the sheep, yet when Marina talked about a horse chomping at the bit, Saika asked what a bit was. Despite having lived on farms all her life, when she came to Berta's house, she didn't know how to shear a sheep or milk a cow. She was a peasant who should barely be able to read, yet she knew everything. She had been so belligerent lately, yet this fine morning was nicer than ice cream. What was Tatiana supposed to believe?

Why had she never mentioned Sabir, her other brother? Why were there no pictures of him in their house, no words about him on her family's lips? And here was the thing—the effort Tatiana was expending on *not* thinking about why the brother was dead and why the family never mentioned him made it impossible for her to also concentrate on hidden fungus. Don't raise your eyes, Tatiana told herself. Bend to the leaves, look for mushrooms, find them and avoid at all costs the dark shape behind you. Soon she was successful and didn't notice Saika in her peripheral vision anymore.

Tatiana's thoughts must have spilled out of the pores in her body, because Saika stayed meters behind. Marina and Saika chatted quietly. It was better this way, Tatiana thought, bending to pick off the blueberries. But where were those mushrooms?

In the thick deciduous coniferous forest, Tatiana was crouched next to what she thought were good mushrooms. She was close to the ground, being small, but still she needed to use her magnifying glass, for the difference between a white mushroom and a *white* mushroom was in the stem only. They both grew under oaks, they were both squat, they were both grey white—only one was a delicacy and one was deadly poison. She was crouching, trying to ascertain whether it was one or the other—since there was no trial by error, she thought with amusement—and as the magnifying glass was pressed against the mushroom with her nose on the other side, she called out, "Marina, what do you think, is this one good?"

The forest was quiet. It occurred to Tatiana just then that it had been quiet for some time. She was concentrating too hard on finding mushrooms and hadn't noticed.

"Marina?"

She called a third time. And then she looked up.

"Marina!" she called, raising her voice another octave.

There was no answer.

Now Tatiana stood up. Her legs were aching from crouching so long. Everything was quiet and still. She yelled again, good and loud this time.

Her high voice carried through the birches and above the underbrush. It echoed off rock somewhere, off the water maybe, and returned to her, fainter and gone, like a stone skipping on the water, hard, then softer, softer, and sinking.

Yes, there was no answer. But there was something more than that.

Tatiana did not *feel* their presence nearby. She did not *feel* another soul even out of earshot, she did not feel Marina bending over her own mushrooms, not responding. She felt Marina not near. But how not near? Could Tatiana have walked so far that she left the girls behind? She spun around once, twice. Which way did she come from?

She had been hearing their voices as they walked, softly laughing, softly talking, softly whispering, softer, muter, mute.

Gone.

"Marina!"

Where were the pebbles she threw down on their trail from the boat? Why couldn't she find them? How long had she been this absorbed? That was the thing with absorption—it was by definition consuming. Tatiana could not tell how long it had been since she last heard the girls' voices, and when she looked at her wrist, she remembered with a quiver of frustration that she had lent her watch to Marina when they were still in the boat.

And now she remembered giving her compass to Saika, who had asked and been freely given.

No watch, no compass, and the pebbles were gone. Tatiana looked up at the sky. It was cast with cover. The sun was gone, too.

At a complete loss as to what to do next, she did the only thing she could to prove to herself she was in control. She crouched back down and pressed the magnifying loop to the mushroom to figure out once and for all if it was the Beluga caviar or the black adder of the fungal forest.

She concluded it was the former.

She went to cut it and . . . *"Tanechka, please may I borrow your knife so I can cut this podberyozovik mushroom?"*

Tatiana had lent Saika her knife, and hadn't asked for it back, and was not given it back.

"Marina," Tatiana called, feebly this time, and then tore the white mushroom from the ground. She tossed it on top of the blueberries in the bucket, and took a deep unrelaxed breath. Saika had the mushroom bucket.

What now?

She decided to stay put until Marina and Saika came looking for her. Otherwise, they'd be looking for her, she'd be looking for them, and they would all get lost.

So she stayed in the small clearing. She found three more mushrooms. Minutes went by? She couldn't tell. She counted once—to sixty, but it was interminable, so she stopped.

"Marina!" Tatiana kept shouting. "Marina!"

Sabir

Marina and Saika were sitting on the ground, hidden by bushes, behind two boulders. Marina said nothing at first, still heavily panting. She had gotten very out of breath as they ran. A fully relaxed Saika giggled. "Don't you just wish you could be two places at once?"

Marina grumbled something in return, something like, "Yes, if one of those places was dry." The ground was waterlogged after continual rain. While walking you couldn't tell you were in a swamp, but planting down your behind notified you with all deliberate speed. Your trousers, and then your underwear were soon damp like the raw cold earth. This did not make Marina relaxed *or* giggly.

"Saika, I'm uncomfortable."

"So crouch. Just make sure you stay hidden. Crouching will make your legs fall asleep, though. I hate that feeling."

"I hate the feeling of being wet," Marina said, pulling up to crouching.

"I'm not uncomfortable. I've got plastic in my trousers. Just in case."

Marina glanced sideways at Saika, and something bitter rose up in her throat. "You put plastic in your trousers?"

"Well, doesn't our Tanechka say prepare for every contingency?"

Marina winced from irritation. She wasn't brave enough to say: you knew we might get wet, why didn't you tell *me* to put plastic in my seat? She said nothing, wondering how long it would take for Tatiana to come looking for them. They had run fairly fast.

Marina didn't know how far they had got from her cousin, but she did know that once Tatiana was absorbed in something, she could remain in a trance indefinitely.

"So how long are we planning to sit here?"

"Till she comes looking for us."

"That could be forever!" Marina was petulant. "Come on, how long? Let's just do it for five more minutes."

Saika didn't reply.

Time crawled by.

Then Saika spoke. "Did you see her on the boat? How she couldn't stop herself from judging me when I was telling the story about my father?"

Marina shrugged. "I don't think she was judging. I think she was just listening."

"I tell you, Marinka," said Saika, "there is a world out there that Tania will never understand. She is very narrow-minded and has such a small view of the universe."

Marina nodded with a sigh. Where *was* her narrow-minded, judging cousin?

"She thinks that just because she can't see herself doing something, that it's wrong for someone else to do it. Well, I *hate* to be judged. Simply hate it!" Saika's voice rose. "She doesn't do a whole mess of things that the rest of the world does, what does that prove?"

They were supposed to be *quietly* hiding. Marina held her breath. Then: "*I* don't judge you, Saika," she said.

"Oh, I know," Saika said dismissively and quieter.

Marina thought Saika did not care a whit for her approval. Marina could have cursed her, and Saika wouldn't have cared.

Carefully Marina said, "I think Tania was surprised you had another brother. You never mentioned him. That's why she got quiet."

"He's dead. We don't talk about the dead. They're gone, as if they never existed. What's to keep going over?" Saika said, her eyes blinking coldly into the distance.

She said it so casually. Her brother was dead. "Well, I know," Marina said slowly. Could Tania be so cavalier about her brother? "But the dead leave something of themselves behind, no? A trace? The people who loved them talk about them, remember them, tell stories about them. Their photographs are on the walls. They live on."

Dismissively, Saika waved her off. "Maybe in your world. But
. . . my parents weren't happy with Sabir. He disappointed them.
They weren't going to be keeping his pictures on walls."

"What did he do?"

"You really want to know?"

And suddenly Marina said, "You know, I really don't."

"It's all right, Marina. No secrets between us." Saika paused.
"What can I tell you? I didn't think things through. My brother
and I played some childhood games that got a little out of hand."

Her breath stopping in her chest, Marina wanted to stop this
conversation, hiding out behind boulders. Shuddering, she tried to
shut her mind to the imagining. Had Tatiana already intuited as
much? Is that why she—Oh my God. "Please," Marina said, "don't
tell me anymore. We should go."

"Sit down. We'll wait a little longer for her. Where was I? Oh,
yes. I know Tania, who thinks she knows everything, thinks my
father had dealt with me too harshly. But what do *you* think?
Harshly, or not harshly enough?"

"I don't know," Marina said faintly. "How did he find out?"

"It was Stefan who found out, seeing us one day, as he said, *up
to no damn good*. He told us to run. He said Papa would kill us if
he found out. So we ran."

Marina wasn't looking at her. "Don't tell me anymore, Saika,"
she said. "I mean, *really*. I don't want to hear another word." She
stood up.

"Marina, sit down!"

Frowning, troubled, Marina crouched down.

Saika continued. "I guess after we ran away, Papa forced Stefan
to tell him where we were headed. And then he went after us.
After catching us near the Iranian border in the hut of a Tadjik
man who let us stay with him, he took Sabir and me into the
mountains."

Cursing herself, wavering on her haunches, Marina said, "Saika,
please . . . "

With her eyes not even lowered, Saika continued. "He took us
into the mountains, took off his rifle, put us up against the rocks
and asked us to tell him whose idea it was. We weren't sure what
he was talking about. To run away? Or . . . ? I said, it was Sabir's.
Sabir was Papa's favorite, and I didn't think Papa would hurt him.
I thought he would just beat Sabir, who was a boy and used to
beatings. So I stepped up. I said, 'It was Sabir's idea, Papa.' My

brother raised his eyes to me and said, *Oh, Saika*. And Papa raised the rifle and shot him."

Marina choked on her gasping.

"After he shot him," Saika went on tonelessly, "he took off his horse whip, and beat me, it's true, until I was half dead, and then slung me over his mule and brought me home. We left for Suki two months later when my back healed."

Saika fell quiet. Marina was mute.

"So what do you think? Too harshly or not? Just punishment or not? Appropriate to the crime committed? Was there *virtue* in the gravity of the retribution?" She smirked.

Marina half whispered, half cried, "I don't know what you're telling me, Saika! Why are you telling me these things? No wonder Tania . . ."

"Tania," said Saika, "is a witch. Personally," she added with a shrug, "I think my father was too harsh. I didn't see the big deal myself, still don't. Do you know what he said to me before he flogged me? Since you don't seem to be sorry on your own, I will make you sorry."

Oh. Marina emitted an inaudible gasp. What would Tatiana make of this—that despite the one and all-good universe in which the Kantorovs lived, the father still thought there were some things that required absolute justice. Yet Saika did not think so, and didn't seem to understand—or care—about one crucial thing: That there was no forgiveness for the unrepentant.

Marina put her hands over her face. "What time is it?"

"Two fifteen."

"Come on!" Marina exclaimed. "Two fifteen! Give me that watch!"

Saika handed it over. 2:15, the watch said.

Marina shook her head in disbelief. "We have to go back, Saika. She was supposed to find us right away. Something obviously went wrong."

"We're not going back. If we go back, we lose."

"Well, this *is* supposed to be a joke. What's fun about this?"

"Be a trooper. It's still fun. And she'll find us. You're the one who told me," said Saika, "that she is like a bloodhound."

"I didn't say bloodhound. I said hound. And even the hound first has to know it needs to look for something." Marina fell silent. "Why haven't we heard her calling?"

"How should I know?"

"Were the pebbles easy to find?"

"I hope so," said Saika noncommittally.

Another half-hour crept by.

The sky was overcast and had acquired a decidedly gray shade. Not just gray, Marina thought, but slate.

The white nights didn't quite reach Lake Ilmen—one too many degrees south from the Arctic circle. Dark did come here.

Hadn't Saika said they'd hide only a few minutes? They were going to play a prank on Tatiana because she always played pranks on other people. "It will be *so* funny." Marina had thought it would be funny, too. Tania yelling, yelling for them, and then they'd jump out from the bushes to scare her; oh, to see Tatiana's face. Everything had seemed so funny.

Except they had been crouching for nearly two hours! To Marina it suddenly began to seem that the joke was no longer on Tatiana. What had tempted her to agree to such stupidity? Marina was damp, and Tatiana wasn't coming. She climbed out from their covering and brushed the mud off her trousers.

Saika looked up. "What are you doing?"

"She's *obviously* not coming. I'm going to go find her."

In the same calm voice, Saika said, "No, you're not. Sit down."

"Forget it, Saika. It's not funny anymore."

"It'll be funny when she comes."

"She is not coming! Maybe she went another way, maybe we didn't hear her, but it's pretty clear, after two hours, that she's not coming."

"She'll be here any minute."

"Well, then, *you* sit and wait."

Saika stood up. "I said sit down, Marina."

Perplexed, Marina stared at Saika, who stood stiffly, the twinkle to her eye gone. Maybe it was too grey in the forest to see twinkles of any kind. Marina couldn't tell if there was anything pleasant in her own face; she didn't think so. "What's wrong with you?" she said. "Why are you getting angry?"

"I'm not angry. Who's angry? I'm not raising my voice. I just want you to sit down, that's all."

"She's not coming!"

"Marina!"

"Saika!" Marina was not afraid.

Saika stepped forward and pushed Marina down on the ground. Marina raised her eyes to a hovering Saika.

And then Marina was afraid. "What's *wrong* with you?" she said in a thin voice. "What's gotten into you?"

"I don't like to be thwarted," said Saika. "We're playing. You said you were going to do it, and I don't like my friends to go back on their word."

"My word?" Marina said slowly, getting up off the ground, "What about *your* word? All the words out of your mouth are lies. I didn't care before because I thought we were friends, but don't stand in front of me pretending there's something about *words* that has meaning for you."

"Talk all you want, you're not going."

"Oh, yes, I am. What are you going to do, push me again?"

Saika didn't just push her. She shoved her on the ground, and Marina staggered and fell back, crying out from landing on a stick. She tried to get up but Saika wouldn't let her. She forced Marina to remain down. "Loyalty in my friends is very important to me," Saika said, bent over Marina. "You are going to be loyal to me."

"Loyalty is important to you, is it?" Marina said, ripping away, reeling up. "Tell that one to your brother, will you? You sold him out in half a breath when you thought it would save your sorry skin!"

Saika went for Marina who ducked. Saika's fist glanced her temple; staggering, she hit Saika in the stomach. They fought, getting covered with leaves, with mud. They scratched each other's faces, they pulled each other's hair. They screamed.

When they separated, Marina was crying and panting. "I deserve this," she said with gritted teeth. What had Blanca said to her? *You are susceptible, because you can be swayed.* Now she knew the old woman had not been talking to Tatiana. Marina could hear Tatiana's mild but iron voice in her head. *Marinka, couldn't you have given at least a whimper before you handed yourself over? Did you have to be such a willing accomplice in your own corruption?* "I so fucking deserve this."

But before Marina could turn and run, Saika, also panting, reached down into her boot and pulled out Tatiana's knife. She said, "You're going to do as I say, and you *will* be quiet."

Marina stared in stupefaction at the knife. The sprinting short distance between the feelings of fuzzy friendly affection and naked hostility had been crossed so rapidly that Marina felt as if she had not taken the necessary long walk for such a quantum leap of heart regarding her friend, her intimate. She blinked in disbelief, but the knife blade remained in front of her, glinting, menacing, a meter away, held with intent. Marina simply could not comprehend the eyes filled with black malice that regarded her—it was as if Saika had been snatched and replaced.

She said faintly, "Saika, I don't want to play anymore."

"Marina, you think *you* decide when the game is over? That's like the mouse saying *that's it* to the cat."

"But I'm not the mouse . . . "

"No?"

"No." Marina frowned in her shaking confusion. "I thought Tania was the mouse."

"You know *nothing*." Saika shook her head. "Tania only pretends she is the mouse. But she is . . . forget it. I'm not going to explain these things to you. You're too small to understand."

Marina started to shake. "But she is not coming."

"No?" Saika smiled. "Perhaps you're right. And you know, it *is* getting late. It's three, and we told your mother we'd be heading back at four. We're still kilometers from the shore. I've got the compass. It's cloudy. It'll take us a little while, but you're so right. We really should head back."

"Head back where?" Marina whispered.

"Back to the boat, Marina. Where did you think?"

"Without Tania?"

"Well, I don't see Tania here, do you?"

Saika's face was shrouded in dusk. Marina could barely make out the shiny eyes. Trying not to get hysterical, Marina gasped, "You want to go back to the boat *without* Tania?"

"If we call for her, she'll win. How do we know it's not her pride that's keeping her from calling out for us?"

"What pride?" And before Saika could move toward her, Marina opened her mouth and screamed with all her strength: "TANIA!!!!"

Saika's hand went roughly around Marina's mouth.

Marina bit Saika's hand.

"Bitch! What did you do that for?"

Marina pulled away and continued screaming. "Tania! Tania, Tania, Tania!"

Saika slapped her. "Don't ever do that to me again or I'll slice your tongue out of your mouth with your Tania's knife, do you hear? Now come on, are you coming? Because in one second I'm going to go without you."

There was one thing Saika did not know about Marina, that Marina had no intention of sharing with Saika at this precise moment, and that was: Marina was terrified of the woods. The thought of being in the woods alone at night was more than Marina's heart could take. She was scared of Saika, but not as much as she was of crushing black terrors. Saika had the compass, the knife, the watch, and the matches. Saika was a paralyzed Marina's only path out. She had to follow Saika.

Biting her lip to keep herself from screaming for Tatiana again, tears rolling down her face, Marina slowly moved behind Saika as they began to make their way through the forest.

There were no sounds, just the occasional shrill whir of the large-winged cicadas.

From her pockets, Saika pulled out a handful of muddy pebbles and threw them on the ground. "Make my load a little lighter." She smiled with an easy shrug. "I thought the pebbles would make it too easy for her to find us."

The Second Largest Lake in Europe

Tatiana worried about them at first. She waited for them, yelled and yelled for them, not moving from the clearing where they left her. Soon the forest had lost the saturation of daylight. It didn't have that much to begin with, with so much cloud cover. The brush was broken in many places, every spoke out of the wheel of that clearing looked exactly the same, and the pebbles to help her find her way back were gone. She didn't know which way the three of them had come.

Belatedly realizing they were playing a prank on her, Tatiana finally left the clearing. She walked in one direction, calling for them, then in another. She did not hear them, not an echo, not a stirring of the lower branches. How far could they be? She walked and called for them. Then Tatiana started to worry. What if they were lost? The pebbles were gone for them, too; what if they tried to find their way back to her after they saw the joke had misfired, and couldn't?

Marina had fears about everything; if she was lost, she'd be scared, especially as evening was falling. But how far could they get from her? Tatiana called for them so loud and so long, she got hoarse and had to stop.

It got darker.

She started to hyperventilate. She had to sit down.

Night fell.

And now Tatiana was on the ground in a fetal position, afraid to move, to open her eyes, to unclench her hands. She heard noises in the forest, she couldn't see the sky, the stars, nothing. She imagined all manner of life around her, every nocturnal creature sending out signals that there was a member of another phylum among them. She tried to focus her thoughts away from the darkness, away from the forest.

When would Aunt Rita and Uncle Boris notice they weren't back? Let's say they weren't fighting; how much time would have to pass before they became worried?

And what could they do even if they did become worried? It was late now and dark. They'd say, we can't do anything tonight. We'll look for them tomorrow morning.

Oh, but to get through this night.

Why won't sleep come? What's bothering me here in the dark? It's not the badgers, it's not the snakes. What's bothering me? Something darker is worrying a hole inside me—look how my legs are trembling. Stop moving, Tatiana. That's how the carnivores find you, by the flash of life on your body, they find you and eat you while you sleep. Like venomous spiders, they'll bite you first to lull you into sleep—you won't even feel it—and then they will gnaw your flesh until nothing remains.

But even the animals eating her alive was not the thing that worried the sick hole in Tatiana's stomach as she lay in the leaves with her face hidden from the forest, with her arms over her head, in case anything decided to fall on her. She should've made herself a shelter but it got dark so fast, and she was so sure she would find the lake, she hadn't been thinking of making herself more comfortable in the woods. She kept walking and walking, and then was downed and breathless and unprepared for pitch black night.

To quell the terror inside her, to not hear her own voices, Tatiana whimpered. Lay and cried, low and afraid. What was tormenting her from the inside out?

Was it worry over Marina? No . . . not quite. But *close*. Something about Marina. Something about Saika . . .

Saika. The girl who caused trouble between Dasha and her dentist boyfriend, the girl who pushed her bike into Tatiana's bike to make her fall under the tires of a downward truck rushing headlong . . . the girl who saw Tatiana's grandmother carrying a sack of sugar and told her mother who told her father who told the Luga *Soviet* that Vasily Metanov harbored sugar he had no intention of giving up? The girl who did something so unspeakable with her own brother she was nearly killed by her own father's hand—and she herself had said the boy got worse—and this previously unmentioned brother was, after all, dead. The girl who stood unafraid under rowan trees and sat under a gaggle of crows and did not feel black omens, the girl who told Tatiana her wicked stories, tempted Tatiana with her body, turned away from Marina as Marina was drowning . . . who turned Marina against Tatiana, the girl who didn't believe in demons, who thought everything was all good in the universe, could she . . .

What if . . . ?

What if this was not an accident?

Moaning loudly, Tatiana turned away to the other side as if she'd just had a nightmare. But she hadn't been dreaming.

Saika took her compass and her knife.

But Marina took her watch.

And there it was. That was the thing eating up Tatiana from the inside out. Could *Marina* have been in on something like this?

Twisting from side to side did not assuage her torn stomach, did not mollify her sunken heart. Making anguished noises, her eyes closed, she couldn't think of fields, or Luga, or swimming, or clover or warm milk, anything. All good thoughts were drowned in the impossible sorrow.

Could Marina have betrayed her?

Tatiana failed to imagine the morning, with sunshine perhaps, with flowers. Tomorrow, there would be sun, and she would find the lake. How hard could it be to find a large lake that has swamps around it, that smells so strong of freshwater, a lake 27 miles long and 21 miles wide, the second largest lake in Europe after Lake Ladoga?

What if they had run, run gleefully through the woods, picking up the pebbles, run back to the boat, and rowed back home? Could the hapless Marina have agreed to lose Tatiana in the Lake Ilmen woods?

A womblike coil wasn't enough to hide from the black betrayal.

Honor Among Thieves

"Well, now what?" Marina and Saika had been walking for what seemed like a long while. Marina heard no other sounds from the woods. "Where's this lake, Saika?"

"Oh, be quiet. Can't you see I'm trying to find our way out?"

"Saika, you didn't pick up *all* the pebbles, did you?"

"Shut up with your pebbles already. Of course I didn't pick up all of them. They've disappeared." She paused. "Maybe Tania took them."

"Why would she do that?"

"Maybe the rabbits took them."

"The *rabbits*," said Marina, "took the pebbles?"

"I don't know. Can we just keep walking? I'd like to find a rabbit now. I'm hungry. And so thirsty." Saika tipped her flask, but there was nothing in it. A few drops dripped into her mouth.

It was impossible to tell how long or far they had walked. Saika kept glancing at the compass, which Marina might have found amusing under different circumstances. The tall pines and spruce obstructed the sky, and the underbrush was severe, slowing them down. There were fallen trees and rocks and uneven ground, but there was no break, and there was no lake, and there was no Tatiana.

"I don't understand," Saika muttered. "The compass is pointing northwest, which is the direction we should be heading, and I'm sure we walked as far as we did when we came this way, yet there is no lake. I just don't understand."

Marina laughed softly. "Are you relying on Tania's compass to get us out of here? What about the pebbles on the ground?"

"Oh, will you quit with the fucking pebbles!" yelled Saika.

Marina continued to laugh. In a minute she thought she would roll into hysteria. "There are two idiots in these woods," she said. "Give me that." Roughly she ripped the compass from Saika's hands. Turning it over, she grabbed the small steel square that was adhered to the bottom and yanked it off. The girls stared at the compass needle that turned sharply east, then sharply west, then spun around, stopping in a quiver between northeast and north. It did not move again.

"What *is* that?" Saika said.

"That," said Marina, "is what Tatiana thinks of your little directional." She flung the compass to the ground. "The compass is useless. Don't you remember Pasha telling you Tania spent last summer trying to make gunpowder?"

"What does *that* have to do with the compass? And what do you mean useless?"

"I don't know how I can be more clear." Marina laughed. "And now . . ." she said, more subdued but trembling, "I give you the rest of your evening, Saika and Marina. It's nearly eight o'clock. You have no compass, no rocks, no way out, no food, no light, no matches. And no Tania."

Short of breath, Saika said in a seething voice, "She did this on purpose."

"Did what?"

"Handed me the compass without saying a word, knowing it wasn't working."

"You didn't ask! You said, give me the compass. She did as you asked. How did she know you were going to ditch her? Perhaps had she known that, she would have kept her stupid broken compass. She would've been able to find her way out with it backwards and forwards, no matter which way the needle was pointing."

"Well, then perhaps she already did—even without it. Perhaps that's why she didn't call for us: she ran straight to the boat. Perhaps she rowed home," Saika said. "Left *you* here in the night woods by yourself."

Marina shook her head. "She got the leeches off *you*. She touched *you* when no one else would come near you. Tatiana would never row home and leave *me* in the woods."

"As a prank? She'd do anything."

"No, she wouldn't. That's not Tatiana." Marina stopped talking. "That's not her," she whispered after a moment.

"I'm glad you're so sure," Saika snapped. "All I know is, she was supposed to come looking for us, and she didn't. And you and I have a broken compass that *she* gave us. I think she's playing games with the mouse, Marina."

"Whose idea was it to hide? Hers? Oh, let's hide, Marina, let's hide, it'll be so funny!"

"Well, if you didn't think it was going to be funny, why did you do it?"

"I did it because I thought we would hide for a few minutes!" Marina exclaimed. "Because I thought we ran along the pebbles! Because I thought we were close to Tania, because I thought she'd find us, that's why." Breathing hard, she said, "I hid because I thought it was a *joke*. Because I trusted you."

"Why did you do that? Tania's been telling and telling you, I'm not to be trusted."

"God, I should've listened to her."

"Yes," said Saika, "you should've. But I am unrepentant. I don't care about her or you if you stand in my way. All I want is to get to the boat before it gets completely dark. Now are you coming, or are you going to stay here and rot?"

For a few moments Marina stood in front of Saika, motionless, haggard, hungry, thirsty in the coming of night.

Then Marina said, "I'm going to stay here and rot."

"Great," Saika said, and she turned around and began to walk away.

Marina pressed her trembling body against an oak, hoping to get some courage from the sturdy trunk.

A few minutes later Saika came back. "Don't be an idiot," she said. "Come on. Two in the woods is better than one."

"There are two in the woods," said Marina. "Me and Tania."

"So clever. Stop it and come with me."

"No."

"Come, I said."

"What are you going to do, drag me with you? I'm not coming with you. You don't know where you're going. Wherever you're headed I don't want to follow. Go ahead. Go, find the lake, row just yourself across, and then explain to my mother and father how you left Tania and me in the woods. You go on and be reconciled with your universe, Saika."

Saika stormed off. Huddling against a tree, Marina tried to focus on the feel of the bark, on the sifting leaves in her hands. The forest had gone dark. There were no human sounds in the woods.

Behind her she heard a voice again. "Come on, don't be stupid. Don't just stand there. Let's walk together, let's move forward."

"Saika, we've been walking for hours and have not found the lake. It might as well have vanished off the globe." Marina started to cry. "We have no matches. Do you even know how to start a fire so we can stay warm?"

"Without matches?"

Tatiana would know, Marina thought. She wished she were lost with Tania. There was a constant crackling, occasionally an owl hooted—and worse, there was a flutter of wings through the air.

Bats.

Marina shuddered. "What about a cave somewhere?" she said uncertainly. If there was a cave, there would be cover, and she wouldn't have to lie down in the dead leaves and spend a night on the damp ground in the open forest. Were caves safe for human beings? Marina didn't know. She wished she had read more. Tatiana would know.

"You want to go into a cave, Marina? What if there are bats there?" Saika smiled. "Flying rodents?"

Even with flying rats, thought Marina, as long as it was away from you. She groaned. If it weren't so dark, she would have covered her eyes. As it was, she remained stationary, the darkness of her clothes no longer discernible against the whiteness of her palms. She heard the flutter of wings again and a screech, and the fear of night became so intense she lurched forward.

"All right," she said in a lifeless voice. "I give up. Where to? Lead the way."

They found a small opening in the bedrock in the low part of the forest. Marina had been so brave talking about it, but when Saika motioned her to go in, Marina lost her nerve. Was it safe? She just didn't know. Who lived in caves? Robinson Crusoe. Who else? "You know what? I'd just as soon stay here."

"*You* wanted to find this damn cave!"

What was there to say? What if bears slept in caves? Or bats swung upside down? Bats and Saika in one small dark space? "No," is what she said.

"Fine, stay here by yourself." Saika crunched through the underbrush to the cave. Marina listened for noise. But Saika wasn't screaming, there were no flying objects, there was no flapping screeching. Saika's voice carried out muffled. "It's warm here," she said. "And it's quiet. It's fine. Come. There's nothing here."

Marina sank down against a tree. Night fell. The forest became black so suddenly once the last light left the sky. She could not see Saika, she could not see anything. Maybe morning would come soon in June. Maybe in a few hours Marina would be able to see again, and then they would get up and find the lake.

"Saika?"

"What?"

"Where are you?"

"I'm trying to get some sleep, that's where I am."

"Why don't you come out?"

"Why should I? It's warm here. It's nice."

Marina swallowed her fear, from the tongue to the throat where it remained lodged and prevented her from breathing and prevented her from sleeping.

She didn't know how much time passed. She was half asleep when she heard someone sink heavily down next to her.

When she opened her eyes, the silhouettes of the forest were marked in blue shadows. Morning had come.

Saika was slumped next to her. Daylight brought little relief for Marina. They could not find a clearing to see the overcast sky. They could not find a stream, or a meadow, just kilometers of tractless forest covered with underbrush and leaves, and lichen, and—

"This is ridiculous," she said as they wandered, miserable to the bones. "Wait until I tell Mama and Papa what you did. Just wait till I tell them, and they'll tell *your* mama and papa, and if you think you were punished before, just wait till this time."

Saika laughed. "You think this is worse than what I've been through? You think my father is going to care about *this*?"

Marina knew that Saika was right.

They spent a day in despair. Marina could have sworn she had seen the same felled tree several times in a row. She could have sworn she had seen the same clearing with the same pattern of white birches, black pines, taupe poplars. There were rocks and pebbles and debris from the forest, life organic to the forest, indigenous to the forest, essential to the forest. Marina and Saika were not essential, and as they meandered or sat to rest, it became very clear to Marina that the forest didn't particularly want them there, nor had any use for them. Certainly it was not going to give them clues as to how to get out.

She was cold. She was dirty, drained. She was hungry. She was thirsty. The blueberries she kept eating to quench the thirst irritated her stomach; she had to stop eating them.

Saika irritated Marina's whole *soul*. She had to stop listening to her. But Saika, seemingly having forgotten much of the past twenty-four hours, seemingly having forgotten showing Marina her true colors, nattered *incessantly* to an unlistening and sullen Marina. She was friendly, cheerful, indifferent to being lost, indifferent to not finding the lake. It didn't seem to Marina that she was even looking particularly hard. Saika just kept on and on, a barrage coming out of her mouth while Marina's chest wanted to claw out, *Help me! Help me! Please . . .*

"My parents must be going out of their minds," she said as the sky was darkening, another day coming to a close. "Tania's too."

Shrugging, Saika leaned over to grab a handful of blueberries. "How often do you stay overnight in the woods?"

Marina stared at Saika coldly. "Never."

"Oh. Well, if they're not too busy trying to kill each other, they might've noticed then." But she said it skeptically.

"What about you? Won't your parents be looking for you?"

That stopped Saika from eating blueberries for a moment. "How do they know I'm missing?" That's all she said.

Unbelievably, they spent another night in the woods. The mushrooms, so lovingly collected, had been thrown out long ago. The woods were noisier the second night and darker, and less inviting, if that were possible.

The Tundra and Taiga

The morning was cold and gunmetal. As it turned out, finding the second largest lake in Europe after Lake Ladoga proved difficult.

There was no sun. The sun meant Tatiana could tell time, could tell direction, could make a fire and cook mushrooms, and stay warm, and send smoke signals into the air. The sun was everything. *Everything.* Without the sun and without a compass and without a wind through the trees, with just a cloud cover and a chill to the air, Tatiana had nothing.

She waited what she thought was hours for the sun to come out but finally decided she couldn't stay in one place. She had long stopped shouting; she had lost her voice after yesterday's prolonged yelling. As Tatiana walked she looked for water and couldn't find any. She ate blueberries instead, which quenched her thirst a bit, making her wish for black bread and sunflower oil, and hot tea.

As she walked she kept getting the feeling that wherever she was, she wasn't in the right place. When she got that feeling, she would make a quarter turn and walk in a new direction. After getting nowhere, she would make a quarter turn again.

And again.

Tatiana tried to keep the turns in her head, but after hours and hours, the morning gone, the gray afternoon going, she thought she was closer only to nothing.

Nothing changed either in the trees or on the ground, or the smell. The conifers, the birches, the elms, the larch, did nothing to help her, to quell the alarm inside, the disquiet of being not just lost, not randomly lost, not accidentally lost, but *lost on purpose*.

As Tatiana made her way through the woods, she broke branches and threw them down in patterns—to leave a deliberate trail of herself behind, in case someone came looking for her. Aunt Rita and Uncle Boris—they might come across the twigs and realize the wood patterns were not random brambles.

She tried to think of poetry to comfort her. She couldn't think of a single verse. She tried to think of books she had read where the hero was lost. The hero or heroine was never lost alone. The heroine was always lost with someone, a friend, an enemy who became a reluctant friend, a family member with no mettle or too much mettle. *Together* people braved the South American jungle only to end up in an *African* slave village. Together with her friend, Dorothy braved dark wet tunnels only to find herself not in Kansas but under the Land of Oz. Maybe Tatiana could brave the Lake Ilmen jungle to end up—to end up where? Where did Tatiana Metanova, lost in the woods, want to end up when she came out on the other side?

Slowing down, she stopped walking, unable to take a step further, afraid it was in the wrong direction. What did Blanca Davidovna teach her? She said, no matter how far you've walked, if you've walked down the wrong path, it's always better to turn around, head back, and start all over—but this time in the right direction.

But what good were those words to her here? Every trail seemed to be the wrong trail. Every direction seemed to be taking her farther from the lake. Tatiana ate some more blueberries, the damn blueberries! She called out hoarsely for Marina, and she tried to remember how deep the Lake Ilmen woods were. She didn't know. She'd never seen a map of the area. She had no idea what was behind the woods to the south, to the east, to the north. Byelorussia, maybe? Without the sun, where was she?

Once she had read that taiga, the subarctic coniferous forest east of the Ural Mountains, was hundreds of kilometers long and when it ended, the tundra of the Central Siberian Plateau began.

Maybe the Lake Ilmen taiga ended there, too, in the Siberian tundra.

But who said she was heading east? She could be heading south to Moscow, or north to the Baltic Sea. Who knew? She was heading nowhere because she had stopped walking. After a while sitting on a fallen tree made her cold, and Tatiana got up and, with a sigh, began to walk again. It was *so* painfully slow getting through the woods.

Forgetting once again about shelter, she continued to struggle through the forest until night fell and it was too late.

Who am I near to, in the night? Tatiana thought, lying covered by twigs, by leaves. Do I feel alone? *Am* I alone? Where are the stars? The moon? Where is the sky, even the sky reflected in the lake, where is the mirror that contains plants, and algae and minerals and life? Where is life besides mine? My family? Marina? She is probably home right now in bed, looking up at the ceiling, giggling, thinking of me. What does she think happened to me, the second night alone in the woods? How far can I walk tomorrow under the cover of nimbus, of cirrus? If I walk far enough, will I be in Estonia? Will I be in Poland, in Prussia? Back in Leningrad, maybe? In the Land of Oz? Can this forest empty out into the Gulf of Finland and if I walk far enough, will I empty out into the Gulf of Finland, too?

How far will this forest take me?

How could the woods be so empty during the day, yet so *not* empty at night? They *felt* infested with living creatures, all waiting for the dark to wake up and begin their living while Tatiana tried in vain to sleep to shut them out. The hooting, the howling, the whining, the crying, the whinging—the scooping. She heard bats, she was sure she did. Time, distance, it all seemed to lose its meaning here. She could have walked twenty kilometers, but what did it mean if she were just spinning in one place, keeling over on her tilted axis?

Walking in circles, around the same stone, the same willow, the same cloud-capped clearing?

Yes, Tatiana thought, curling up—senseless, but not without purpose. There was always a purpose: to get ahead, to beat the night, to get to the lake, to a cabin, to another human being, to yell for help. The purpose was always to life. Because without life, all other values ceased to be. Blanca Davidovna said that, too. She said the earthly vessel was the temple in which resided the immortal soul.

Life was the first principle. And so you walked. Perhaps even in circles, painfully retracing your steps, but moving inexorably toward *something*.

If only she could find a small stream. Eventually it would lead her to a larger body of water, maybe a river, maybe even to the lake itself. If she got to the lake, she was saved, but she couldn't find even the smallest stream! Two days of blueberries, two days of no sun.

Tatiana tried to look on the bright side. At least it wasn't raining.

Honor Among Thieves Slightly Thinning

The next morning it was raining.

At first the rain was a blessing. Marina raised her face and opened her mouth and stuck out her tongue and let the droplets collect before she swallowed. Not very efficient. She got a large green leaf, held it slightly folded into the rain, letting it fall inside the groove and then when enough water collected, she drank it. Better. She did that until her thirst was slaked, and then she looked at Saika who stood under a tree, covering herself from the rain.

"Why aren't you drinking?"

"I'm not thirsty."

"How can you not be thirsty? We haven't drunk in two days!"

"So? Camels don't drink every day."

"Yes," Marina said impatiently. "But you're not a camel."

"I don't need to drink every day, obsessively like you," said Saika. "Besides, the blueberries I ate yesterday have water in them. And lastly, look at you, you're getting soaked."

Once Marina became wet and stayed wet without hope of warmth or of drying off, without hope of food, or rescue, she became so dispirited that she stopped walking and lay down in the wet leaves. "That's it," she said. "You go. Maybe if you find the lake and get across, come back for me. Try to remember my spot, will you, the way you remembered Tatiana's."

"Come on." Saika pulled on her. "It's just rain. It's not the end of the world."

"Oh, it is," said Marina. "It most certainly is."

Wiping her mouth constantly, Saika sat down on the ground and stayed close by Marina's side.

"Why are you wiping your mouth like that?"

"Like what?"

"Like that." Marina pointed. "All the time."

"I just don't want to drink, that's all."

"Are you afraid of rain water?"

"What the fuck are you talking about, afraid? Who's afraid, miss? Unlike you, I go into a cave by myself. I'm not afraid. I'm just not thirsty."

Marina had the feeling that if Saika knew the way out, and where the lake was, she would not hesitate to leave Marina in the woods. But Saika herself had nowhere to go. Marina hated her. She wished Saika would leave her alone, the way they had both left Tatiana, thinking the lake was just a couple of kilometers *that* way.

This is my punishment, Marina thought, closing her eyes, turning away from Saika. "My *just* punishment," she whispered, "for following you."

"And who is punishing *you*?" Saika laughed lightly.

"I betrayed my flesh and blood," said Marina. "I lied to her, I turned my back on her, and now what goes around comes around. Serves me right." She started to cry.

"But why am *I* being punished? I owe Tatiana nothing."

"You're not punished. Why would you be?" Marina said. "You're living in your own world. In your world there is no wrong, so how can there be punishment? In your world you thought your father was overreacting to your little childhood games. If you didn't feel remorse for Sabir, certainly you aren't going to feel remorse for my Tatiana. But you know what I think?" Marina jumped up. The thought was too terrible to contemplate in a position of even fraudulent rest. "I think you did this on purpose. I think you wanted to lose Tania, you wanted her to be lost. You removed the pebbles deliberately, you led us another way, off the trail, deliberately, so we couldn't find her, and she wouldn't be able to find us."

"You think so?" Saika said casually.

"I think so now. But this—being lost yourself—that didn't figure in your plans, did it?" Marina laughed a little. "You sure make a lot of plans, Saika, for someone who can't control a single minuscule thing, or as Tania would say, when you can't change a single black hair on your own damned head."

"You're delirious. I want to control nothing. I want to change nothing. I just want to get out of here."

"You're not getting out of here. Get it through your head. "Even

if someone did come looking for us—it's the deepest woods. No
one will ever find us. Tell me—was that part of your grand plan?"

"Oh, shut up already, it's getting so old."

"You're such a freak."

Marina fell silent. There was no more bedrock, no water table,
no caves. The remains of the day's rain were dripping off the soggy
leaves onto the sodden girls. Saika kept her head down as she sat
against a tree; she would not lie down and would not raise her
head. Marina had noticed that Saika too had become quieter. Her
incessant pointless chattering had stopped.

It fell dark again, their third night in the woods. The light had
left Marina's world, which now consisted of damp and gray cover
and a pervasive blackness next to her heart, walking step in step
with her, her guide, too.

Marina listened to Saika's breathing. The girl was holding her
breath. She would hold it for a few moments, then breathe, then
hold it again.

"What are you doing?"

"Nothing."

"Why are you fooling around with your breathing?"

"I'm not fooling around. I'm trying not to swallow," replied
Saika.

"By not breathing?"

"Yes."

"Why are you trying not to swallow?"

"My throat hurts. I think I'm getting sick."

"Do you have a fever?"

"How should I know? Do you want to touch me and see?"

Marina did not. "Is that why you haven't been drinking? Because
of your throat?"

"I told you already," said Saika. "I haven't been drinking because
I'm not thirsty."

Marina thought about something. "You stopped eating the blueberries."

"So did you. I'm sick of blueberries."

"You're not thirsty, you're not hungry."

"I'm getting sick, I told you."

"Does anything else hurt?"

"No."

In the middle of the night, Marina, who had drooped on her
side, woke up; rather she was woken up by Saika, who was fidg-

eting as she lay next to her. Marina said nothing at first, waiting for Saika to quieten down, but minutes passed during which Saika rubbed her back against the ground, and scratched her head, and tossed from one side to another, and finally Marina couldn't take it anymore; she moved away. And though she had finally managed to fall asleep, the sleep was restless and disturbed by the awareness of an uncalm and unquiet body shuddering close by.

It wasn't the rain in the morning that worried Tatiana. What worried her was knowing how impossible it would now be to smell fresh water coming from Lake Ilmen. What worried her was another day eventually turning into night again and her not having shelter, or food, or fire, or protection, or a way home again. Throwing the wet broken branches behind her, Tatiana resumed her trek. The ground was covered with twigs and rocks. It wasn't easily going to reveal her tracks if someone were looking for her. Though she didn't have a knife, she thought of making a mark on the trees, leaving her tracks on them. After judiciously looking, she found a rock with a sharp corner and managed to etch a small fine line in the tree bark, one small purposeful line to let another human being know she was here. And while it was easier than breaking branches, it was also harder to spot. Someone would have to be looking for the small scratch. Should she draw a ring around the whole tree?

Tatiana drew one. It took too long.

Though she certainly had the time.

Time.

It was just a human invention. Like numbers. Like measuring things. Just something humans invented to make life a little easier, to order life into manageable blocks, to ease their minds around unmanageable things, to help them with infinity. A minute, an hour, a day, a year, half a century, a millennium, two millennia since the dawn of man, five thousand years since the drawings in the caves, and fourteen years of a young girl's life. All divided neatly into little blocks. Tatiana went to school for nine months of the year, including Saturdays. She went to her Luga *dacha* for the other three. She lit the Bengal lights every New Year's Eve, at one minute to midnight, and counted down, and then counted up into another year, three hundred and sixty-five days of organization. And regardless of what Tatiana was doing, the sun relentlessly moved from east to west 360° in 24 hours, 15° an hour, a quarter of a degree a minute. Sun moved, man named. Degrees, hours, minutes, all to help himself to decode the workings of the universe. But what if you couldn't see the sun? What if you didn't have a man-made watch, or had no milk to get from the cows after pasture, and no potatoes to peel for dinner, and no dentist's office to be at by 9, and no Saturday night public bath to go to at 7? What if the libraries didn't close at 5, and the sun didn't set at a man-made-up 9:30? What if all of that fell away into chasms? What was left?

Infinite space left.

Tatiana kept time in the woods. She laughed at herself counting, and thought, I'm counting now in my desperate minutes to remind myself I'm a human being and not a beast. I'm counting to make sense of the nonsensical. To make order, so it's a little easier, even for me.

Oh, but this was perfect, just *perfect* for the girl who couldn't keep time, who didn't know the time to anything! Not when it was time to wake up, or stop reading, or milk the cow, or get ready to set the table for dinner. Tatiana didn't know what time the libraries closed, she didn't know when the cows came home. In Luga, in childhood, time had no meaning for Tatiana. She never counted, indifferently looking up at the cycles of the moon, at the arcs of the sun. She just did what she did until she started doing something else, or until someone yelled at her. To live as a child in a world without time—not in infinity, but in eternity, what joy. To never count your minutes. To just be—in the eternal present. What bliss.

And now she was counting—and growing up. Ten, twenty, thirty, forty. Was it one hundred and eighty, or one thousand and eighty, or one hundred thousand and eighty? How many blocks of her dying childhood did Tatiana count her third day in the woods?

It had rained all day and she had been unable to dry off.

I haven't been leaving enough of a wake behind me, she kept thinking as she etched Ts around the trees. She stopped with the rings long ago and now left her initial behind. A purposeful man-made line in the sand. A symbol for herself. Like time was a symbol for order. T for Tatiana. Still walking, still hoping, still believing, still living.

What to do? Stay in one place? Build a shelter? Can't start a fire without the sun and with the branches all soggy. There was nowhere to wash, nothing to wash with. Could she make soap from ash? Ash and what else? The ashes from the fire and a bit of . . . lard?

I'll make soap and clean myself with the ashes, and walk on, live on, fly on, covered with soot, unclean, unfound, just a speck in the woods, and soon I'll be so lost that I won't even find myself.

She called out feebly, Dasha, Dasha. She cried to heaven. *You who brought me here, bring me out, no other guide I seek.* She thrust out her arms in the coming darkness, she waited for a sound, she made one herself, she put down her hands and lay in the leaves to rest a while, covered with twigs, hoping she did not smell like a live thing that other live things could prey on.

Was this what Blanca Davidovna meant when she told Tatiana that her three main lines in the hand—her heart, her head, her life all beginning from one common root—were a harbinger for tragedy? Shavtala saw it, too; was this what she meant?

Tatiana didn't think so. They didn't say short life. They said irrevocable trauma. Meaning: struggling, suffering, agony—all values presupposing the requisite *life.*

Blanca didn't say death. She said *the crown and the cross.* The crown—the very best. The cross—the very worst.

Tatiana wished she had known nothing, nothing at all from the lines in her hand, from the leaves in her tea, from the Saturn line of fate that was etched like grief down the center of her palm.

Night was coming again, the third night.

What to do?

I was slain by false smiles.

One thing remained clear as the rainy twilight fell. Saika abandoned Tatiana in the woods to die. And Marina, blindly or willfully, followed her. Saika was Marina's guide. This wasn't lightning, or floods, or frostbite, or freak sledding accidents on the Neva. No. This was *deliberate destruction.*

Tatiana had been walking through the densest taiga-like forest for over two days trying to find the way out; she was emptied of strength. The truths about Marina and Saika had left her bereft.

The universe in which this was possible could make other things possible: the waiting with rifles on the outskirts of fields to kill men who stole wheat for their families. Keeping indecent company with your own closest blood relative without shuddering at the world. Moving from place to place, not just because the job demanded it, but because your own safety demanded it. Living a life in which you made only temporary arrangements lest the people you inflamed decided to take your life, because you took away all they had to lose. In comparison, being willfully forsaken in the woods to die was almost trivial.

Was that Tatiana's choice? If she survived and became an adult, would she have to live amid this random chaos of malice? Wasn't it better to have lived out her blissful but brief and ordered life and die rather than exist in the abyss of the other world?

She curled up more and more into herself. Then she got up and continued walking through the pathless forest.

No, Tatiana thought. Unbelievably—*no*. She wanted to live, that was all.

The Hole in the Ground

Tatiana had found a small clearing at deep dusk when she saw him. The woods were slowly emptying of light; the woods were emptying of color, too, the green leaves and brown trunks gray. All dark gray and the ground was brown-black, and Tatiana's hair was black, too, from mud and grime. She had come to a small natural clearing in the forest and as she was walking around looking for something to eat besides blueberries, maybe blackberries, or cranberries—though she knew that cranberries grew in meadows not forests—she stepped on a pile of leaves and branches that suddenly sank into the ground beneath her foot. Only her innate sense of balance kept her from stepping down with both feet. Tatiana wavered, tottered, spread her arms, and did not put a second foot down on the branches. After regaining her composure, she stepped away and examined the ground. The branches were strewn with a strange, haphazard purpose over an area about three meters square, much like the wake of branches she herself had left behind. She pushed with her foot. The branches gave way. Tatiana pushed them harder; they gave way some more. Tatiana found a long stick and prodded the leaves and the twigs until the lot of them fell into a deep hole below.

At first she thought it might be an uncovered grave. The branches had fallen deep into the ground. If there was something there, it was now covered with forest matter. She smelled the hole. A few times she had found decomposed rabbits in the woods, but this hole did not smell of putrescence like that. It smelled of grass and dirt and leaves and wood and pine cones. Whoever dug the hole out, took the dirt with them. Why? Then she saw—next to the edge, on top of the branches, berries were laid out: over-ripe, rotting blackberries, blueberries, pieces of apple. *Cut* pieces of apple.

It was a trap!

A trap for a very large animal, an animal that could fall into the hole and break something, and not be able to get back out.

But what kind of animal would be this big in these parts of the country? She couldn't think. A deer?

And it was then that she heard a noise behind her, and she was surprised at the noise, because it wasn't just a howl or a hoot. It was a respiratory noise. A noise of someone, of something breathing in . . . and then slowly breathing out.

Someone *big*.

She turned around.

Twenty meters away from her at the edge of the clearing stood a large, dark brown bear on his four legs. His head was tilted to her, his small eyes were unblinking, intensely alert.

Tatiana froze. She had never seen a bear. She didn't know bears lived in these woods. She couldn't remember if they were carni-vores, if they were peaceful, if you needed to make overtures or stand at attention, if you needed to offer them a piece of some-thing, which they would come and eat out of your hand. She didn't know. She thought any animal that was that wide, that hairy, that four-legged, and that watchful, could not be coming to eat out of her hand. Could a bear outrun her? A bear was not a tiger; could a bear even run? He looked so clumsy and immobile. And he *was* immobile. He was just standing flat-footed on all fours, his small head raised, his small eyes unblinking.

Tatiana smiled. She breathed though her open terrified mouth. Her heart was thundering. The bear breathed too, she could hear him. She didn't want to do anything to scare him, do anything that might be perceived as threatening. She didn't want to raise her hands, she didn't want to step back—or step forward, certainly. She did the only thing she could think of, the only thing she ever did when she didn't know how to make things better but when she wanted to calm, to comfort, to bring impossible things down to possible. She stood motionlessly and very slowly opened her hands, palms out, as if to say, *it's all right. Why such a fuss? Shh. Please.*

Bear-baiting. In Shakespeare somewhere she had read about dogs being loosed on bears, on a stage? In a cage? They were loosed until one or other perished. How many dogs, a pack? How many bears, one? Here, there was one matted brown bear and one matted blonde Tatiana.

She glanced sideways at the trees nearby. They were pines, with no low branches. Did bears scale trees? Why hadn't she read more about bears? Why did all her reading not once lead her to a bear? The pines were so useless! There wasn't even one suitable for climbing.

And so they stood in the middle of the woods, just Tatiana and a hairy (carnivorous?) four-legged, flat-footed giant mammal. There was a small startling cluster of sound from behind her, a twig falling under the weight of a bird. The bear seemed to smell her well, because he took a slow step forward. Tatiana took a slow step back. She was between the bear and the trap. Could she long-jump over a three-meter-wide hole in the ground? She didn't think so. Could the bear? She thought so.

"Easy, bear," she said softly.

The bear breathed.

"Honey bear."

Bear calmly breathing.

"Slow bear, hibernating bear, nice bear, turn right around and go away from me and from this hole that's meant to trap you. You don't want the trappers to come for you. They'll kill you for sure. Go. Save your life. Go away from me."

Slowly the bear moved toward her.

How fast could she run?

. . . *The trappers to come for you* . . .

Something echoed in her head. The trappers might come to check the trap for bear.

Tatiana made a choice. Lowering her palms, she turned away from the animal, held her breath, squatted and jumped down into the bear trap, as if she were hopping down from the cherry tree. It was about the same distance, two meters.

She fell on her side onto the prickly twigs. Falling from her bike while racing was worse. She was still on her side when she looked up to see the shadowy head of the bear leaning over the ditch to look down at her.

"No, no, don't come in here with me," said Tatiana. "You will never get out."

The bear didn't move.

Tatiana moved. She pushed off her right arm to get up. She pushed off what felt like a round metal plate. There was a releasing *ping* of a tempered steel coil spring and in the next irreversible half-second of *time*, her thought was *trap*, her instinct was *up*, arm flying upward to get away—flying right into the swooshing downward clasping heavy half-moon bracket. There was a savage blow to her forearm, a sickening snap of bone, a sickening shutting snap of a cast iron trap, and then searing, severing pain. One half second of *time*. Her piercing screams carried up to the fast running bear and echoed through the forest until she lost consciousness.

Tatiana didn't know how long she had been out. When she awoke, the first sound out of her was a prolonged wail. The agony in her arm was not going away. She couldn't hear the bear's breathing for her intense, unending crying. Her arm must have been snapped in two by the closing bear trap. Fortunately for her, the trap was big enough for a paw, big enough to incapacitate and hold a large animal two to three meters long with paws alone probably forty centimeters. It was not meant to incapacitate a human female adolescent forearm, twenty-five centimeters from thin wrist to small elbow. Disoriented, swooning, dizzy, moaning from pain, Tatiana pulled her limp swollen forearm out of the trap, and fainted.

When she came to, it was black inside the hole and out. She wasn't even sure she awoke. She was under a nightmarish haze of pain and had been dreaming of dull knives slicing into her arms, slowly carving her body to pieces, and she felt every nerve being severed, every blood vessel, every bone. Who was wielding that dull knife?

Awake, Tatiana realized the dream wasn't a dream at al. She had been and was still in the black with the knives. Her eyes were

open—rather, she *thought* her eyes were open—pain shredded her
from her fingertips to her shoulder blades, shot into the jaw, into
the throbbing eye, into her skull, and the blood pulsed under the
cutting blade. She couldn't even touch the sleeve over her forearm.
She could not make a fist with her hand, could not lift her arm,
could not bend it, could not move it. Tatiana had not had anything broken before, but she was certain nothing could hurt this
much and not be badly broken. In the dark, she felt for blood, for
bones. Tatiana licked her lips. She was thirsty. She wished she
could see something, a moon, a star, the tips of the trees, even
the bear's gleaming eyes would have been better than the void of
nothing.

Slowly she opened her parched mouth as she sat pressed against
the earth, and her dry throat moved to mutely form the words
she once could speak so well, words that Osip Mandelstam, the
man who no longer existed, wrote. *"You took away all the oceans
and all the room. You gave me my shoe-size in earth with bars around it.
Where did it get you? Nowhere. You left me my lips, and they shape words,
even in silence."*

Here are my words in silence. Dear God. I don't want to die
alone in the woods, in the earth, like I'm already in the grave.
Soon the leaves and the twigs and autumn will fall over me, soon
the hunter will come and move his trap elsewhere, and throw
fresh dirt on me, and I will be covered, I won't even have to move.

I don't want to die, cried Tatiana.

I don't want to draw my last breath in a hole.

I haven't lived, she whispered.

I barely even know who I am.

I have been much too young to see La Môle pass my way.

Please . . . don't let me die before once letting me feel what it's
like to love.

Tatiana in her desperation clawed at the ditch, in the dark.

Oh God. I'll do anything. I'll bear anything. Just let me live.

Help me . . . Dasha, Pasha, Deda, Babushka, please, somebody,
somebody help me . . . Lord of the earth, have mercy on me.

She fell into stuporous semi-consciousness, sitting up, her arm
propped on her stomach, her head tilted to the side, the prayer of
the heart at her lips, desperately in the deadfall.

Mononegavirales

On the morning of the fourth day in the woods, Saika and Marina found a narrow stream.

O joy.

Springing into the water, Marina drank. She put her whole face into the water and gulped to bursting. When she looked up, she saw Saika standing watching her with black eyes outlined by black shadows. Her face was in shadow though the air was sunny-bright and warm.

"Saika, look, fresh water. Come on, drink some. You'll feel better."

Saika shook her head. She was twitching.

"What's the matter with you?"

"Nothing." She rubbed her eyes. "I have a terrible headache."

"It's the lack of food and water."

"Oh, enough already. You're not my mother." Saika did not stand still for a moment.

After Marina took her time drinking and washing, the girls started to walk along the stream. Marina felt almost all right. She was not dry, and she was not fed, and she was not warm, and she was not found. But she felt hope walking along a rivulet. Who told her this? All the rivers flowed into the sea? Who said that to her?

What troubled Marina this morning was Saika. The girl was restlessly and slowly walking along the sloping banks, careful not to come too close to the stream. This was not the same Saika who had sat *motionlessly* for hours under boulders while waiting to trick Tatiana.

Out of the corner of her eye, Marina cautiously watched her, hoping whatever was bothering Saika would pass as the morning got warmer, brighter, and brought them closer to the lake.

Perhaps all hope was slightly premature. This was less a stream than a run-off from the rain. It drifted down the slope, but the slope was ending, and the run-off was pooling and puddling and ending, too. And Saika was pooling and puddling, slowing down so much that Marina, who had been wading in the stream holding her shoes had to frequently stop to wait for Saika to catch up.

Saika didn't catch up. Done with walking, Saika stopped and stood leaning against a tree. Suddenly she sank to the ground, turning from side to side, moving her arms and legs and running her fingers along her ribs, her hips, up to her hair.

Marina climbed up the shallow bank. "What's the matter?" Despite everything, Marina could not help but ask the question, could not help but feel a jitter of concern.

"I can't walk. My head feels like it's about to split apart."

"The lake shouldn't be too far. We'll just keep walking in this direction. Come on. Get up."

"Okay, let's go," Saika said, her voice weak. "Help me up. You lead, find the lake, find our boat. I'll be right next to you. Give me your hand. Just . . . don't leave me, Marina."

"What are you talking about? Come on already, let's go."

"Give me your hand, Marina," whispered Saika.

Marina stepped closer. "What's wrong with you?"

Saika screamed. Her body rolled from hip to hip, contorting from joint to joint. Then it stopped. She lay still. Her eyes were open, and she was blinking, swallowing with difficulty. "My throat," Saika hissed. "It's gone numb. At first it hurt, then it felt like there was something stuck in it. Now I can't feel it at all. I can't swallow. My tongue is numb." She spoke with difficulty. "My lips are numb. My face is going numb." Her mouth was spasming.

"Oh, what's happening?" Marina cried.

Saika was ashen. White foam formed around the edges of her lips. "The cave," she whispered.

"What cave?" Marina gasped.

"The cave . . . I must have stayed in it too long . . . "

"What do you mean?"

"Can't you see?"

"I can't see. What's wrong with you?"

"Mononegavirales," mouthed Saika, and closed her eyes. "*Vodoboyazn*. Fear of the water. Rabies."

"*Rabies*?" mouthed Marina in horror. *Now* she stepped away. Staggered away. *Now* she recoiled.

Saika tried to crawl to Marina. "I beg you," she whispered hoarsely, "don't leave me. Help me." She stretched out her hand.

"Saika, oh my God, let's get you home quick, get you to a doctor, don't worry."

Still crawling to Marina on her elbows, dragging her legs behind her, Saika opened her mouth. She looked like she were silently crying. "Oh, Marina. Don't you know *anything*? Ask Tania about rabies. She's around here somewhere."

"Where?"

"I don't know. Close." Soundlessly she moved her mouth, in laughter? In a cry? In a rasp.

"No! You weren't bitten. You said so yourself. You didn't touch a bat, did you? Nothing flew in that cave. It's something else. A little fever. We just have to get you home. We must go." But Marina wasn't coming anywhere near Saika, with a distressed and heavy aching watching the girl on her elbows creeping through the mire of the silt toward her. Marina backed a step away, then another step.

"Come near me, Marina," Saika said, stretching out her hand. "Come near me. Let me . . . "

Crying out, Marina tripped over her feet and fell. On her haunches, she tried to move away from Saika. Her legs had gone numb from terror. She couldn't breathe, she was suffocating.

"I don't want to be alone," Saika aspirated. "Come here, Marina. Let me touch you . . . " She opened her mouth, baring her teeth.

A crazed fear was in Saika's eyes. White foam and blood were dripping out of her mouth onto the ground. Saika was hissing and slithering closer.

Marina started to scream. And scream and scream.

Bearing Up

When Tatiana opened her eyes, it was morning, the birds were singing, the sky peeked azure through the tall pines, and the arm was throbbing.

She yelled for help but stopped quickly. She didn't want to expend her precious energy on useless acts. To get out from the hole was everything. What if the trappers were a week in coming? She couldn't wait. Once she was out, she would be better off than she had been; the sun was out. The sun gave her hope. Not merely because it was shining, but because with it, she saw all else. Other things became possible. She could make a fire, she could dry, she could get warm. To get out was first. The bear hole had tree roots sticking out from its sides. Tatiana grabbed hold of a root with one hand and pulled herself up by just her left arm. It was agonizing. The important thing was not to jolt her broken arm, because sharp pain would bring her unconsciousness, and she would fall back to the bottom, and who knew, maybe break something else, like her neck. Tatiana rested, her face against the moist dirt. The good arm was getting tired, threaded through the root. Her legs were resting on roots below her. She grabbed another root a little higher up and moved another quarter-meter. Another root, another quarter-meter. She rested again, touching the rock jutting out of the earth that was under her cheek. Then she lifted her face and stared at the rock. Rather, at the moist, glutinous, vascular green substance that covered the rock. Ah, she breathed in happiness. Moss!

She rubbed her cheek against it, she kissed it! She ripped off bits of it with her mouth and ate it. Moss!

Moss only grew on rocks close to the water.

She managed another root and another quarter-meter—but she couldn't hold on. The root gave way, the good arm gave way, and she fell back down into the twigs, onto the steel trap, to the bottom.

Time went by. Went by, went by.

Tatiana regained consciousness and tried again, much slower. She took her time because she had the *time*. Failure, falling back again was not an option. If she fell again, she would not get up. The sun was shining up above, a pale obelisk in the sky.

It was morning, perhaps ten or eleven. She found south, she found north and west. Perhaps she might find the lake after all. There was only one problem—Tatiana had nothing left for walking. The clearing, with the sun unobstructed by the damned pines, would have to be good enough.

The first thing she did after she crawled out was tie up her arm using the laces from her shoes and two sturdy short branches for a splint. She fainted only once, and finished tying it up while on her back on the grass. After stumbling up, she awkwardly collected some damp twigs and branches using only her left arm, and catching the sun with her magnifying glass like a concentrated hot beam, she managed to set some dry leaves on fire. It took her several attempts, but she did finally light a small twig with the burning leaves, and once she did, the rest of the twigs were blazing in a few minutes. She sat in the warmth, she couldn't move. On her good side she lay down in front of the fire and closed her eyes.

No sooner did she lay down than Tatiana heard screams—of terror worse than falling into a bear trap. But she wasn't getting up now that she found an open space with sunlight and built a fire. Going close to the woods? No—not a meter, not a centimeter.

But what to do? The screams wouldn't cease.

Reluctantly Tatiana struggled up and limped over to the edge of the clearing. Who was that screaming? Was it Marina? But Marina was home in bed under warm covers, wasn't she?

"God, help me! Help me!" a voice was shrieking. It sounded a *lot* like Marina.

Tatiana stood, supported by a tree. Finally she called out, "Marina?" She was hoarse; she called out again, and the voice stopped shrieking suddenly, and was mute. "Marina?" Tatiana said again, softly. There was a sobbing gasp, there were crunching, running, galloping footsteps through the woods. There was no more calling, just insane fear and relief in the whimpers and footsteps of another person.

A shape appeared in the trees, a shape that looked like Marina, except this haunted face, this wet, shaking body, black with mud, was not—no, it was Marina.

When Marina saw Tatiana standing at the edge of the forest, leaning against a tree, she completely lost control. She became so overwrought, Tatiana thought Marina was going to hurl onto her. She had to protect herself against a filthy wretch who dropped to the ground, sobbing. Marina stretched out her arms to Tatiana, who, with her body turned sideways to protect her arm, made no move toward her cousin.

"Oh, it's you," Tatiana said. "I'm surprised you're still here."

"Oh, Tania!" Marina sobbed cravenly. "Oh, Tania. I'm *so* sorry. But you have no idea what happened to me."

"And more to the point, I don't care," Tatiana said, holding her broken arm to her chest. She turned and walked back to the fire.

Marina hobbled close behind. "We're not far enough, Tanechka," she whispered. "We can't stay here. We have to get away."

"Get away from what?"

"From *her*," Marina whispered, flinching and glancing around. "Please, we have to run as fast as we can."

Calmly and slowly Tatiana sat down in front of the fire, threw some more branches on, some moss, some old berries. She wanted the smoke to be as black and acrid as possible, and to rise to the sky, and to emit a smell that could be detected from kilometers away. "I'm not moving from this spot," she said. "You can go though. Why don't you run along? But quick, Marina. Quick." She paused. "Like before."

"Tania! Please! I'm sorry. Tania, God! I know you're upset. I know you're furious. You have every right to be. But right now, please, we have to get away. She is going to find us, she's going to come after us."

"Let her come." Tatiana didn't even turn her head to the woods.

"She's got rabies, Tania . . . " Marina whispered with revulsion.

Tatiana glanced at Marina, slightly less calmly. "Ah," was all she said.

Marina jumped up. "Well? Are you coming or aren't you?"

"I guess, the answer would have to be," said Tatiana, "aren't I."

"Tania!"

"Stop," Tatiana said, her face only to the fire. She wasn't looking at Marina. "Stop. Sit down, or go away. Run or sit, but stop this nonsense. Stop your carrying on and take one look at me. Can you even see what's happened to me?"

"We found a stream, Tanechka," Marina whispered. "We found a stream, not too far in the woods. It will lead us to the lake, just like you said."

"*I* said that?" Tatiana shrugged. "I'm not going into the woods again. And isn't *she* by the stream?" She lifted her face to her cousin. The girls stared at each other. "I'm not going back into those woods, Marina," whispered Tatiana.

Marina started retching, retching and crying. "I'm sorry, Tania. It was supposed to be a joke. You were supposed to come and look for us."

"I was, was I? Well, I wish someone had told me what it was exactly I was supposed to do."

Babbling, rambling, shaking, Marina told Tatiana everything. She kept nothing hidden. She told of her own complicity and of her own realizations, and of Sabir and Murak, and of the days in the woods and of the crawling infected thing trying to get to her.

A slightly trembling but a preternaturally calm Tatiana pronounced, "Well, well," at the end of Marina's story, and then said nothing.

"Do you see why we have to run?"

"No." Tatiana sighed. "Don't worry about Saika anymore. Worry only about being found yourself."

"I *have* been found!" Marina cried. "But we're hardly going to get out of the woods sitting by the fire!"

"Go then," said Tatiana. "You've been walking three days in the woods, you haven't found a rock to help you. I've been walking three days in the woods. Where did it get me? But now we have a fire, and the smoke is rising over the pines. If somebody is looking for us, this will be what they'll be looking for. If they're not, well, then . . . I'm inclined to sit and wait. I don't have the strength I had at the beginning of this. But please, don't let me stop you. By all means"—Tatiana glared at Marina—"do what you like—as always."

As if Marina could move a meter from Tatiana. "Why do you think she won't be coming here?" she said, panting.

"Spinal cord paralysis," said Tatiana. "She might want to. She just won't be able to."

"Is it . . . " Marina paused, "*ever* curable?"

"No."

"So what's going to happen to her now?"

"Saika," said Tatiana, "is going to die in the woods. She's probably dead already. Like we still might be."

Marina lay down in front of Tatiana, in front of the fire. "I'm not alone anymore," she whispered, closing her eyes. "I don't care what happens now. I'm not alone."

They remained close together. Tatiana did not touch her.

"You're very upset with me?" Marina whispered.

"More than I have the ability to discuss with you."

"I'm sorry." But Marina's eyes were closing. "What time is it?"

Tatiana looked up at the sky. "One maybe. One thirty." Oh, that pale yellow sun. She wanted a life where the sun beat down on her three hundred days a year, not the miserly sixty-five in this northern neck of the woods. When she looked back down at her cousin, Marina was asleep.

She slept for forty-five degrees, while Tatiana sat awake under the sunshine and fed the fire and watched Marina slumber as if she were home in a comfortable bed.

Just as early evening was covering the land, she heard voices from the woods calling her name. "Tatiana . . . Tatiana . . . !" Not one voice, but a chorus of voices. Male, female, young, old.

She struggled to her feet. Marina woke up, jumped up.

"Taaaaaania . . . Taaaaaania . . . "

"Oh my God!" Marina cried. "You were right! They found you!"

Tatiana didn't have the strength to run, to shout, and Marina—who had the strength—didn't. She took Tatiana's good hand, ignoring Tatiana's flinching.

"Tanechka, I beg you," she whispered in a panic. "*Please* don't tell them. Please. It was just a joke gone horribly wrong. I learned my lesson. I almost died, too. I'll never do it again. But please don't tell them."

"Don't worry. It's just between you and me, Cousin Marina," Tatiana said without emotion, pulling her hand away. "It'll be our little secret."

Marina ran then, yelling. "Help! Here! Here! Help!"

Dasha came running through the clearing, crying, yelling Tatiana's name. Pasha was next to her, Babushka behind her, then Deda, and then Mama! That was surprising. Mama! Wailing, *Oh, Tania, Tania.*

Uncle Boris came too, for Marina, his only child. He looked very upset. "Who do we yell at around here?" he said, holding Marina to him. "Who is responsible for this?"

But Tatiana's family was so shocked at the state of their baby that they were not in the mood to be yelling at anyone. The broken arm horrified them. When Tatiana told them she had jumped into a bear trap, by the emotional reaction of her family, you'd think they had all jumped in with her.

"You did what?" said Marina with surprise.

Pasha looked away from Tatiana and toward Marina. "What do you mean, *you did what*?" he said suspiciously. "Where the hell were you that you don't know this?"

Dasha, too, stared unhappily at Marina, almost if they could tell something unholy went down that Tatiana wasn't sharing.

"Why would you do such a stupid thing as jump into a bear trap?" asked Mama.

"To save myself from the bear," quietly replied Tatiana.

Mama almost fainted.

Deda said, enough talking, all of you; she is in no state to be talking. He tried to pry Tatiana from their clutching arms. But they wouldn't let go of her. He gave her a flask filled with water. She drank, she swooned. Dasha held the flask to her mouth, and Tatiana drank in large gulps with the water running down her chin and onto her shirt. Deda asked if she wanted some bread; he'd brought bread. She took a grateful bite. Did she want some tea? He'd brought a Thermos of hot tea. Did she want some canned ham? He took out a small can and a can opener. "*Canned* ham?" Her entire family groaned with distaste, even Tatiana, who shook her head. The very *idea* of canned ham! Deda put the canned ham away. She didn't want anything. She had everything.

The lake was two kilometers due north. Deda had a good com-

pass and they had cleared a trail on which Uncle Boris carried
Tatiana. As they walked, Uncle Boris told the girls what had happened.

The morning after they didn't return, he telegraphed Luga and
Leningrad to notify the Metanovs. The family had been looking
for the girls for days now, in two boats, rowing across the lake
early in the morning and staying till night. They had found Tatiana's
twigs, they had found Tatiana's etchings in the trees. But they
simply could not find the girls. It was the fire that finally did it.

Deda said, "As soon as we woke up this morning and it was
sunny, I told everyone we would find you, because I knew with
the sun being out, you would make a fire." The girls were found
almost thirteen kilometers southwest from their boat.

Finally someone remembered to ask about Saika. Marina said
nothing, just shook her head. Tatiana said, "She and Marina
became separated from me." She paused. "We got very lost. Right,
Marina?"

"Yes, Tania." She lowered her gaze.

Deda said, "If Saika is still in the woods, we should go look for
her."

"No!" Marina cried. "She went into a cave at night and got
rabies."

"She went into a cave at *night*?" Deda repeated; even he sounded
shocked. "Who in their right mind goes into a cave at night?"

Tatiana spoke slowly, while carried by Uncle Boris. "It was
warmer for her, she felt at home there, she didn't like being out
in the open. She went in, scaring the bats, who flew away. She
didn't hear any flapping and thought it was safe. She forgot, or
maybe she never knew, maybe she didn't read quite enough, that
the rabies virus, in small confined, heavily infested areas also travels
by saliva particles in the air. It obviously found her."

"What a nightmare," Deda said. "What are her parents going to
think? Well, none of our business. As I always say: know your
business and stick to it. What is *your* father going to think? That's
our business. He's coming back next week." He tutted. "We have
to get you both back to Leningrad. Tania, you need to go to the
hospital immediately."

"I'm fine, Deda." She smiled. I'm fine now.

"You didn't go into a cave, did you, Tania?"

"I didn't go into a cave, darling Deda."

He kissed her head while Uncle Boris carried her. "I know your papa will bring you something nice back from Poland when he returns," he whispered. "It'll make you feel better, Tanechka."

"I feel all right already."

They got the girls into the boat, and Pasha got behind the oars, and said, with unsuppressed glee, "*I* am rowing across Lake Ilmen. Hee-hee, Tanechka. So really, *I* win."

Alexander laughed. Reaching up, he stroked Tatiana's face, then pulled her down to him and kissed her. "You say it like a joke, little Tanechka, but I know it's what rankles you most about the whole sorry episode."

Lightly Tatiana smiled. "Only because he was so annoying. I said to him, that's the only way you ever beat me, Pasha, when my arm is literally broken."

"Of course you did. And the Kantorovs?"

"When they found out Saika got rabies, they left without a word to anyone, without saying good-bye. They simply packed up and were gone. When I came back to Luga a few weeks later, they had already gone. Perhaps they looked for her. I don't know."

Alexander was thoughtful, contemplating the desert, the sky, the stars, the story. "If Anthony heard one word from your Lake Ilmen tale he would carry away from it two things. One: do not speak of your mysteries to your enemies. And two: have faith and stay alive long enough for someone to find you."

Tatiana said quietly, "My own husband learned the latter well."

"As you know, I need my mystic guide for both," he said, squeezing her and getting off her lap. He stretched his big long body and pulled out his cigarettes. Getting up and stretching herself, Tatiana picked up his Zippo lighter and flicked it on for him. Bending to inhale, he cupped her hand, as she looked up at him, and he looked down at her.

They came back to bed and took off their clothes. She pleaded with him not to hold himself up, so she could feel his whole body, all his bones, all his wounds and the marks of his life on her, his big arms, his smooth chest, the ravages of war, all of him on top of her.

"Tania," Alexander said when he was in her arms. This was their unimagined whisper. "I *have* to go to Vietnam to find him. Anthony won't come out of it by himself. Like I couldn't. Don't you feel it?"

She said nothing.

"Something's happened to him. You know it. I know it."

She said nothing.

"This is slow death for me." Glancing down at her, he said with a pained shrug, "Yes. I know. *You* did it. I let you go in Morozovo because I believed that you could bear anything. And I was right. But I can't bear this. I'm not as strong as you. One way or another"—a strangled breath—"I have to bring him back."

She said nothing.

"I know it's Vietnam. I know it's not a weekend in Yuma. I promised you I'd never go into active combat again. But I'll come back."

She said nothing.

"I have three other children. I'll come back," Alexander said. He had barely any voice left to speak the rest. "We can't leave our boy in the woods, Tania," he said. "Look at what's been happening to us. We can't continue living."

"Shura, I don't want you to go," she whispered.

"I know. Not even for our son?"

"I don't want you to go," she repeated. "That's all I feel." She wanted to say something else—and didn't. If she told him of her unspeakable fears, it wouldn't be free will. She pulled him close. But he was already as close as he could be. Two metal bowls fitted into one another.

"*Ordo amoris*, Alexander."

"*Ordo amoris*, Tatiana."

CHAPTER SIXTEEN

In the Heart of Vietnam

Aykhal

He couldn't give up the ghost. And now he was being sent away, all the way to outlying Aykhal, where she would never find him. He was told that the rules applying to him from hereon in were simple. If he was caught trying to escape, the guards who caught him were under strict orders to shoot to kill. They were done with him. And still he would admit to nothing, and he looked them in the face and denied his name. Past the fields, the Volga, the pines, the Urals. Through Kazan, across the Kama River, and his heart almost stopped beating while crossing it, remembering swimming across it, keeping his gaze back to make sure she didn't get carried away by the current. She never did. Any current was all right with her. Through the Urals, to Sverdlovsk, and past it through the taiga. They were on the Central Siberian Plain, and the steppe, and past that, too, and now they were on the North Siberian Plateau, in the frozen tundra, and it was there before the mountains, before the Ob and the Amur, before turning south to Vladivostok to China, to Vietnam, on the edge of nothing, in the middle of one road, one small indentation in the frozen earth known as the Rhone Valley, lay Aykhal. That would have been his ten years in exile after his twenty-five years in the Soviet prisons.

And he was going even farther than that now. Even farther than Aykhal.

Tatiana fretted over him before he left as if he were a five-year-old on his first day of school.

"Shura, don't forget to wear your helmet wherever you go, even if it's just down the trail to the river.

"Don't forget to bring extra magazines. Look at this combat vest. You can fit more than five hundred rounds. It's unbelievable. Load yourself up with ammo. But bring a few extra cartridges. You don't want to run out.

"Don't forget to clean your M-16 every day. You don't want your rifle to jam."

"Tatia, this is the third generation of the M-16. It doesn't jam anymore. The gunpowder doesn't burn as much. The rifle is self-cleaning."

"When you attach the rocket bandolier, don't tighten it too close to your belt, the friction from bending will chafe you, and then irritation follows, and then infection . . .

" . . . Bring at least two warning flares for the helicopters. Maybe a smoke bomb, too?"

"Gee, I hadn't thought of that."

"Bring your Colt—that's your lucky weapon—bring it, as well as the standard-issue Ruger. Oh, and I have personally organized your medical supplies: lots of bandages, four complete emergency kits, two QuikClots—no, I decided three. They're light. I got Helena at PMH to write a prescription for morphine, for penicillin, for—"

Alexander put his hand over her mouth. "Tania," he said, "do you want to just go yourself?"

When he took the hand away, she said, "Yes."

He kissed her.

She said, "Spam. Three cans. And keep your canteen always filled with water, in case you can't get to the plasma. It'll help."

"Yes, Tania."

"And this cross, right around your neck. Do you remember the prayer of the heart?"

"Lord Jesus Christ, Son of God, have mercy on me, a sinner."

"Good. And the wedding band. Right around your finger. Do you remember the wedding prayer?"

"Gloria in Excelsis, *please* just a little more."

"Very good. Never take off the steel helmet, ever. Promise?"

"You said that already. But yes, Tania."

"Do you remember what the most important thing is?"

"To always wear a condom?"

She smacked his chest.

"To stop the bleeding," he said, hugging her.

"Yes. To stop the bleeding. Everything else they can fix."

"Yes, Tania."

*   *   *

When Alexander arrived in Saigon on a military transport jet in November 1969, he thought he was dreaming someone else's diluvian nightmare. It was raining so biblically hard, the plane couldn't land. Alexander actually became worried they would run out of fuel, they were circling in the air so long. Finally they landed. So much for the hot and humid jungle. It was windy, cold and pouring.

Because the helicopter couldn't land in the wind and rain, they couldn't fly out to Kontum. Richter called, told him to sit tight. So he sat, smoking by the window of his hotel room, looking out onto Saigon Square, reading American newspapers. Mostly he paced the room—oh, he was good at that, pacing.

While drinking downstairs at the bar, a frazzled and wet Vietnamese woman approached him, told him she would give him boom boom for two American dollars. He declined. She told him he could sample for free but if he liked, he would pay. He declined. She offered him yum-yum for a dollar. He declined. She came back a few moments later, thrusting a small toddler into his face and saying, "My baby need food. Why you no give me piastres for yum-yum? I have to feed my baby."

He gave her twenty American piastres and sent her on her way. Five minutes later she was walking up the stairs with another man, baby in hand. Alexander ordered another drink.

Wishing for the rain to end.

The nights were long. But the days when the rain didn't end were even longer. He paced as if he were in his cell in Volkhov, in hell, pacing away what was left of his life. Despite all his presumptions at the time, a surprising lot had been left, which showed what he knew.

He wasn't in charge, he had finally learned that. Otherwise, he wouldn't be drumming out his son's life and his own life on the windowpane. He had telegraphed Tania, told her he'd arrived safely. He put his hand on the cold glass. Bar lights flickered down below in the wet night.

Why did you come? the weeping heavens seemed to be saying. It's bad out here. We won't let you pass.

There was too much time to think in his dark hotel room. He wondered if Tania could feel him from three continents away. He had not been in a hotel room alone . . . well, ever. He had been alone in many places—cold wet cells, on trains, in wet forests—but he had not experienced isolation like this since his solitary confinement in Sachsenhausen. It had been an instrument of torture and punishment. And he had not been alone since the door opened a crack, light streamed in, and a small slim shadow stood trembling in front of him.

After that, they lived in hotels and motels and rental homes and houseboats, and a mobile home that was preserved complete like a museum on the hilltop, and now they lived in a spotless stucco house that was clean and cool, where his bed was white and made, and she was always next to him. She never left him, except for those one hundred Friday nights—and somehow they managed to survive even that.

His hand remained fanned out on the damp, cold pane. Even now, in Saigon, he was not alone. Staggering comfort was always close, even in Vietnam, twelve thousand miles away from home.

He telegraphed her. "DESPERATE RAIN. STILL IN SAIGON."

Three more days of rain went by.

She telegraphed him back. "SUNNY AND HOT IN NOVEMBER. STILL IN PHOENIX."

She telegraphed him again. "HAPPY THANKSGIVING."

She telegraphed him again. "DECEMBER LADIES HOME JOURNAL. SEEK: 100 REASONS TO REJOICE."

He smiled. This is what he meant. She found a way even from twelve thousand miles away. In one of the news kiosks catering to the Americans, he found a December *Ladies Home Journal*, and the article she was referring to: "100 Places to Make Love," and spent one happy day, remembering some of those places.

Number 16, in a tent. Number 25, next to a fire; number 33, on top of a hill. At a rest area; on a picnic table; in a hammock; in a corn field; in a sleeping bag under the stars. On a boat on a lake; in a bath; in a barn; in the bed of a truck on a hot summer night. In the woods; in the woodshed; on the wood floor. During sunset and high noon. In the pool. On a beach, *almost* secluded; on a beach at night. In a car on a deserted road; at a drive-in movie theater. In a room with lit candles; in a big brass bed; in every room in your house; in a room at your friend's house during a noisy party; and once during a quiet dinner party right before dessert. On a porch swing; on the playground swings; on a bobbing houseboat deck; in the core of the Grand Canyon; in luminescent, lilac-heather, never-forgot Bed and Breakfast. And last but not least, on top of the Maytag washer when it was in spin cycle.

One happy day. Then he was clawing his hair out again.

Richter called. Alexander said, "I don't give a fuck if a tsunami comes and washes away the whole of South Vietnam. Tomorrow you're getting me on that slick."

Tomorrow it stopped raining. The sun shined as if it had never rained, as if the ground was just soggy with heavy morning dew. It got hot and muggy. Alexander choppered out with two young PFCs fresh from basic at Fort Bragg, plus two suppliers and two sergeants. The doors of the Huey remained open through the three-hour flight north. The young soldiers tried to engage Alexander in conversation, but he was looking down below him to the canopied countryside, trying to do Tatiana's thing, trying to feel for his son under the blanket of trees and ancient pagodas and broken beaten open churches and French Catholic palace ruins, trying to find that rising smoke signal. The green covering looked too thick to land the helicopter but then the jungle ended, and rice valleys began. A rectangular, orderly swathe of man-made clearing was laid out below surrounded by distant mountains. A large military base etched out in symmetry in the freshly cut elephant grass in the central highlands, that was the MACV-SOG Command Control Central in Kontum, the chopper distressing the grass and dust underneath as it came in to land.

Richter was waiting for him. Alexander hadn't seen Richter since Anthony's graduation four and a half years earlier. They were both in green battle fatigues, both with striped and barred officers' insignia at their shoulders, including sharpshooter badges, and rifle and machine-gun bars. Both had graying hair cut army short, Alexander's mostly black, Richter's mostly gone.

"I'm sorry to see you under these circumstances," Richter said. "But, man, am I happy to see your face." They shook strong hands, they smiled briefly. Richter's smile subsided. "Come, let's go have a drink, some grub," he said. "You must be exhausted."

"Exhausted from sitting around."

"I know. Not very good at that, are you, Major?" Richter shook his head as they started walking. "Look how much gear you brought. You're a lunatic. You know you can get anything you need here. Look at our supply points. Ground studies teams go out loaded for bear."

Alexander nodded in acknowledgment of the bear metaphor. "I had no idea you were so well equipped. But I have to talk to you and Ant's lieutenant ASAP, Tom."

"Come," Richter said, with a slightly resigned demeanor. They walked from the landing strip down to the row of well-maintained officers' barracks. "Lieutenant Elkins and Sergeant Mercer *are* waiting for you. They can't wait to meet you."

The base, its perimeter wrapped by a fence and barbed wire, was organized and functional: a landing pad, a landing strip, a hospital, a mail room, officers' barracks, enlisted barracks, command headquarters, many weapon sites, a training camp, all on flattened ground the size of three football fields.

In Richter's large, comfortable quarters—a desk, chairs, a conference table, maps, books, a cabinet full of liquor, obviously *home*—Alexander found two men. The small squat guy was the sergeant major of Anthony's Special Forces unit. His name was Charlie Mercer, and aside from a shortness and squatness of stature, he also conveyed a stubbornness he might call stoic but to Alexander it looked bloody-minded. Mercer said nothing. He barely spoke.

The other soldier, a young, slim, good-looking boy was Dan Elkins. Alexander knew of Elkins from Anthony's letters. For some reason, Elkins looked awfully young to Alexander, even younger than Ant. Too young to be in the army. His light hair was thin and stuck up, and his ears thick and stuck out. He chewed gum, popped bubbles, was instantly friendly.

"How old are you, Lieutenant?" Alexander asked.

"Twenty-seven, sir."

This boy that looked too young to be in the Army was older than Alexander had been when he returned to the United States after ten years of merciless bloodshed. Alexander lowered his head.

Elkins was all about eye contact. Mercer never made eye contact.

"What's wrong with that guy?" Alexander whispered to Richter.

"You are a legend around these parts, Major Barrington," Richter said, smiling, cleaning the conference table of papers so they could sit down.

"I am?" Alexander stared at Elkins and Mercer, who now *both* looked away.

They were brought snacks, drinks, smokes. Elkins said, "You don't mind that the non-com eats with us, do you, sir?"

"Of course not." In Poland and Byelorussia, his sergeants always ate side by side with him and his Lieutenant Ouspensky.

White teeth from one protruding ear to the other, Elkins said, "Mercer has been under Ant's command since Airborne. Anthony's the one who recommended him for SOG. Over the years, he—we all—have heard some serious shit about you, Major."

With a small nod, Alexander clicked his glasses with a nearly-trembling sergeant.

Elkins smiled. "Forgive us if we see a bit . . . um, flabbergasted—to finally meet you." The men stared.

Smoking intently, staring right back at Elkins, Alexander said, "You want flabbergasted? Well, how is this?" He swallowed a mouthful of his beer. "In his last letter home, Ant wrote that he married a Vietnamese girl. How's that for fucking flabbergasted? Know anything about that, Lieutenant?"

Profane surprise came from three throats.

"Hmm," Alexander said, taking an almost calm drag. "Guess not."

Richter, always a leader of men, asked to see the evidence. "Come on!" he said. "Let's see it. Don't tell me you don't have with you the last letter your son wrote. Let's fucking see it. Maybe there's something in it you overlooked and forgot to tell me. Maybe I'll be able to glean some other information from it."

"No matter how many times you ask me," said Alexander, turning away from Richter and toward Elkins, "I don't have it. Ant's mother has it. And as far as I know she's not here. But I do know what he said in it, and I'm telling you, he got married. What, you don't think I can read English? He said he married a girl he met last year near Hué, and that her name is Moon Lai."

It was at this point that Dan Elkins fell off his chair. Then he went wild. He had to leave the barracks for a few minutes to calm down. Alexander exchanged a glance with Richter. Mercer didn't speak, sitting like a hangdog. He reminded Alexander of someone; the faint familiarity was just out of reach. Something having to do with small kids.

When Elkins came back he was only *slightly* calmer. "It's impossible," he said. "It's fucked up *and* impossible. I'm shocked and I can't believe it. I have to see it in writing." He kept shaking his head. "I simply don't believe it."

"What did I tell you?" Richter said calmly. "Better cough up that letter, Major."

"Ant wouldn't do it," Elkins said to Alexander. "Your son is not fucked up like the rest of us. He doesn't do idiot things."

"Lieutenant, calm down," Richter said in his commander voice. "Do you know this Moon Lai?" They were sitting at the cleared rectangular wooden conference table, staring at one another.

"Yes, sir. Oh, yes, sir," said Elkins, banging his fists impotently on the table. "I most certainly do fucking know her. Which is *why*

I can't believe it." Elkins's blue eyes were blazing. "It's not true. It can't be true. Merce, do *you* think it's true?"

"I don't know," Mercer said. "I don't know her." He shook his head. "But with Captain Barrington *anything* is possible." The sergeant paused. "But why would he get married and not tell *you*, Lieutenant?" he said to Elkins. "You were friends. That's the part that doesn't make sense."

But Alexander, staring at the grain on the table, knew: a four-year love affair with Tatiana's best friend, in their house, under their nose, and no one suspected, not the estranged husband, not the prescient Tania. The most open boy was obviously also the most shut-in boy. With Anthony, everything was possible.

"Major, maybe you're mistaken," Richter said to Alexander. "Lieutenant Elkins here says it can't be."

"I didn't say it can't be, Colonel Richter," said Elkins. "I said, it can't fucking be. Meaning, it *can* be, I just don't fucking believe it."

"All right, Elkins, who is she?" Alexander asked.

"Who is she? Obviously that's the million-dollar question. Oh, the bastard! But not to say anything to me, not even a word, I mean how fucked up is that?"

Alexander waited until Elkins moderated himself down a degree or two.

"Ant knew I would've ripped him a new one, if I knew," Elkins finally said. "I wouldn't have let him do it. He didn't want to hear it from me. He's like that. When he wants to do something, he just doesn't want to hear it, the pig-headed West Point bastard."

"All right now, Lieutenant," said Richter. "The pig-headed West Point bastard is this man's son. Now tell us what you know."

Elkins finally told them what happened last year, the summer of 1968, in Hué. After Tet was over and Hué was destroyed—its civilians terrorized and massacred by the Viet Cong who were finally pushed out by the Americans—the U.S. soldiers were mopping up.

"We were a three-man killer team, silent and lightly armed," said Elkins.

"Security patrol, Elkins," corrected Richter.

"Oh, yes, I forgot. I apologize, Colonel," Elkins said dryly. "Security patrol. We wouldn't want to offend anyone by hinting there is a *war* on or anything."

"Lieutenant."

"Yes, sorry, Colonel. I'll continue. Well, we were patrolling the pachinko, hunting for—um, excuse me, *looking* for—Viet Cong; that was our mission, to find them and to, um"—he glanced at Richter—"to what, sir? To apprehend them?"

"Elkins, three hours in the stockade for you," said Richter, "if you keep this up. Just continue."

"Ah, yes, to *neutralize* them; *that's* the delicate word I was looking for!"

"*Six* fucking hours, Elkins!"

"Sorry, sir. Anyway, it was me, Ant, and our other buddy Lieutenant Nils; real good guy, he's not around anymore. Stepped on a mine two months ago," Elkins said, crossing himself. "Ant would be sad to hear it; they were tight." He sighed. "Anyway, we ran into a little situation." He coughed, rubbing his hands together. "We were on the outskirts of Hué, passing through a ravaged ville torched by the VC in their hasty retreat. And in this burned-out ville, in broad daylight, we found a South Vietnamese girl, very young, maybe fifteen? I don't know. Very young, very small, and very buck naked, tied to a tree. She had been beaten, had obviously been assaulted. No sooner that we lowered our weapons and approached her than from around the ruins a dozen Charlies opened fire, wounding me, Nils, and barely missing Ant. He was grazed in the scalp, bled like a slaughterhouse animal. He returned fire, hosing them down, then lobbed a frag grenade at them. He greased them, but unfortunately the grenade didn't spare the naked bird."

Richter said, "Lieutenant, what does this firefight have to do with . . . "

"I'm getting to that, sir. Well, she wasn't dead. Anthony untied her, took off his tunic, covered her, stabilized her. She'd lost an eye and two fingers. He bandaged her up, gave her morphine. We called for a medevac. Anthony kept asking her, where's home? At first she couldn't get control of herself, she was screaming. But just before the chopper came, she told us she was working in Pleiku, trying to support her—I don't even the fuck know—dying mother, sick sister? Point was, the medevac flew us all to a Pleiku hospital. As we landed on the roof, the little girl flung her arms around Ant's neck and pushed them both out of the hook and onto the ground. She was hysterical. After that she refused to leave his side. He stayed with her, helped her, got himself cleaned up. Nils and I convalesced at our leisure. I remember now, a few days later when we got leave, Ant went somewhere without us. We didn't see him until we got back to base for our next mission. That was a year ago. We never saw the girl again and Ant never talked about her. But now that I think about it, he never came on R&R with us after that. And he had had quite the . . . yen for the Asian ladies, if you know what I mean. We had some wild times together." Elkins broke off, staring solemnly at Alexander. "I mean, sir, you know, just normal guy stuff, sir, nothing too crazy—"

Alexander stopped him. "Just—continue." Why was it that the young were always convinced they had invented sex?

"Well, he stopped coming out with us. When he'd get a couple of days off, he'd disappear on his own. I know on his last trip in July he signed out to Pleiku."

Richter confirmed that records showed that Anthony had gone to Pleiku during each of his six leaves.

Alexander was thoughtful, considering Elkins, absorbing what he had been told, what it meant, and then he said, "And this young girl is Moon Lai?"

Elkins nodded. "This young girl is Moon Lai."

Alexander sat quietly, considering.

"Let's go and find her," he finally said. "Where in Pleiku does she work?"

Elkins was fixedly studying the wooden table and said nothing.

"Answer the major, Lieutenant!" Richter barked.

Elkins lifted his gaze to Alexander for a moment before he lowered it again and said nothing.

"Elkins," mouthed Alexander in disbelief. For a moment he thought he might have to leave the quarters himself. "Anthony did not"—he could barely speak—"marry a whore from Pleiku."

"Why do you think I've been cursing up a shitstorm?"

"No." Alexander shook his head. "It's some kind of a mistake."

"That's what *I* said!"

And then the four of them sat stunned, no one more so than Alexander.

Mercer finally spoke. "Hey, Major, don't feel so bad," he said. "Maybe she's a reformed whore."

"Oh, shut the fuck up, Merce!" exclaimed Richter.

"*Maybe* she's reformed?" said Alexander. "As opposed to what? Tom, in his letter, Ant said that not only had he married this girl but that she was expecting a child!"

Oh, the cursing from four hardened soldiers.

What was wrong with his son? God, where *was* he? "You see, there has to be some mistake," Alexander said to Elkins. "Because it's just *not* possible."

"That's what *I* fucking said!" yelled Elkins.

Richter spoke with authority. "All right, everyone, let's bring this down about a thousand. Alexander, this is the situation . . . "

"You have to tell *me* the situation?" snapped Alexander. Now it was his turn to bark. "My son, a commander of a Special Forces A-Team, a tight, highly trained, elite group of men, went on leave and did not come back. His weapon, his ruck, his gear, have not been not found. And now we find out he married and knocked up a yum-yum girl. Meanwhile, he's vanished off the face of the earth. Anything I forgot?" He was trying hard to think clearly.

Richter poured everyone another glass of beer. They lit up their cigarettes, they sat. "No, I think you just about covered it, Major."

"Hey, maybe his disappearance has nothing to do with Moon Lai?" Elkins said, brightening. "Maybe it's just a coincidence?"

The silent soldiers smoked skeptically.

Alexander's face was contorted in concentration. "Elkins, did you say the girl was South Vietnamese?"

"Well, yes," said Elkins. "Of course she was. What else?"

"What *else*?" said Alexander. "You three did walk into a *Viet Cong* ambush, did you not?"

Elkins looked puzzled and troubled. "Yes, but . . . I don't understand what you're saying. What are you suggesting? She was *assaulted* by them, Major. You should have seen the state of her."

"Elkins," Alexander said, "the girl sells herself to soldiers for money. I can imagine the state of her. What do you think she's not used to? What do you think she won't do? Get beat up a little? Look, I knew this when I came here—we need to find this Moon Lai, and we need to find her in a hurry."

"Oh, good luck finding her. That'll be easy," said Richter with a nod. "So easy. Why, I'm sure Pleiku has no more than one brothel full of young Vietnamese women. It won't be a problem."

"Yes," said Alexander. "But how many one-eyed, eight-fingered pregnant hookers does Pleiku have?"

"What are we going to do, go to each and every happy house until we find her?"

"If that's what it takes."

Richter laughed. Slapping Alexander on the back, he poured him another beer. "Absolutely, Major Barrington. Why don't I just telegraph your wife and tell her that her husband traveled halfway round the world so he can go to whorehouses for the next three months. I'll tell Tania it's for a good cause. I'm sure she'll understand."

Richter and Elkins laughed. Mercer did not allow himself such liberties. Certainly Alexander didn't laugh. "First of all, we don't have three months," he said, downing his beer. "We don't have five minutes. And second," he added with a straight face, "my wife is very understanding about whorehouses when it's for a good cause. We'll drive there tonight. How far is it? Fifty kilometers?"

"*Tonight*?" said Richter.

"At night the bars will be full." Alexander stared pointedly at Richter. "What, *you* don't know it's the best time?"

"Alexander, forget it, stay here," said Richter, glancing away. "I know how Tania feels about me with regard to my own wife. For this, she'll *never* forgive me."

"Enough talking, let's go." She forgives worse than this.

"She's going to think I ruined you. Forget it. I'll take on a division of Viet Cong before this happens under my watch. Stay here. Elkins and I will go. I'll bring one of our Yards, Ha Si, to translate."

"By all means bring him. I want to meet him. Which jeep are we taking?"

Richter rubbed his face. "I think we should talk about this . . . "

"Oh, for fuck's sake! Do you always do this much talking? It's a wonder anybody ever goes out on missions. Let's go!"

Alexander didn't leave Richter's quarters, not even for some fresh air. He smoked inside, stayed inside, and for dinner they had beef pho—Vietnamese thin noodles with beef broth—which Alexander couldn't get enough of. Richter asked Alexander if he wanted to rest, wash up, but Alexander wanted only for it to get dark so they could leave.

When it got dark, they drove to Pleiku. The road was unpaved but straight. It took them an hour.

As in any good capitalist city, the run-down bars—fronts for dingy brothels—were all located within a small stretch of delapidated streets in a squat, low-to-the-ground wet downtown, running along a muddy narrow river, overflowing after the rain. The whorehouses like ducks, all in a row, made it easier for the consumer in a hurry to make his inebriated choices. They certainly made it easier for the four men to look for Moon Lai. Alexander wished he had a picture of her, but at least he had a photo of Anthony to show around. They split up. Elkins and Ha Si, a Montagnard warrior, took half the bars, Alexander and Richter took the rest. From Ha Si they learned how to say in Vietnamese, "Does a young girl with eight fingers work here?"

Heads down, they walked from place to place, standing in narrow doorways, behind red curtains, in small smoky rooms, drinking a little beer, talking to the madams, quickly looking over the girls who hovered on chairs, waiting for customers like Richter and Alexander. There were dozens of establishments all laid out on these darkened unpaved streets, just mud and dirt from the rain. Alexander tried to wipe his boots before he entered the bars, but it was no use, the mud was slowly hardening into cement on his heels. Lights twinkled, men laughed, there was a sound of a fight somewhere. Alexander and Richter went to seven places with no luck.

In the eighth one, the madam, an older Vietnamese woman, smacked her chest and exclaimed, "Ah, Moon Lai! *Dien cai dau! Dien cai dau!*"

Richter whispered, "Dinky Dau. She's saying she's crazy."

"Tell her," said Alexander, "that's not as helpful as she thinks. She knows the girl?"

Apparently, yes, the madam knew the girl well.

"Where is she?"

They couldn't get that out of her. Alexander took out a hundred dollars. The madam started talking rapid-fire Vietnamese, interspersed with English words, grasping for the money, "I no see her! She go! I no see her! She go! I told you. *Dien cai dau!*"

"Tell her she doesn't get the hundred if all she's got is 'I no see her.'"

Alexander stayed behind while Richter ran to find Elkins and Ha Si. They needed Ha Si to talk to the madam.

While Richter was gone, the madam paraded her best-looking, youngest girls in front of a smoking and a politely inquisitive Alexander. "While you wait," the madam kept saying in broken English. "No take long. Thirty piastres." The girls—in various states of complete undress and what looked to Alexander various states of shocking underage—were trying to lure him with cheap prices for extremely advanced wares. "What the hell took you so long?" he said when the three men finally returned.

Ha Si talked to the madam. After he was finished, Alexander gave the nearly-fainting-with-gratitude woman a hundred

American dollars. They went out into the clear air and stood by the short wooden railing over the brown river.

"She knows little," said Ha Si, a tiny highlander, who stood still as a rock and had skin like ageless leather. He was their point man on missions, Elkins had told Alexander, because Ha Si was unde-tectable by the enemy until he was on top of them with his shiv in their throats. "She said Moon Lai worked for her for about two, three years."

"Two, three *years*? How old is she?"

"No one asks. No one would tell you the truth anyway."

Elkins said, "She could have been twelve. Or twenty-two."

Alexander shook his head. "Probably not twelve, if she worked for three years?"

Ha Si said nothing, unblinking and unfazed. Alexander groaned.

She was a quiet girl, Ha Si said, always did as she was told, never complained, never refused work, but had only a few repeat customers. She lived in the farthest, smallest room upstairs. The madam said even when Moon Lai had two eyes and was pretty, "the men did not come back for her." Except for one—and that was the soldier in the photograph, and he came back for her when she had just the one eye, and paid a lot of money for her so she could live in the room and not take other customers. He was very generous, madam said.

"She also said Moon Lai would sometimes disappear without notice for two or three weeks. Then she would reappear, ask for her old room back, and work without complaining. That is why madam said she crazy. She just comes and goes as she pleases. Last time madam saw her was in the early spring. Not since. Madam thinks maybe she die or become pregnant and could not work."

Alexander was thoughtfully smoking. Richter and Elkins milled around him. Ha Si stood still. He had not been released. "Where's Moon Lai from, Ha Si?"

"Madam was not sure."

"Are you joking?" Alexander exclaimed.

"I never joke, sir." Ha Si stood gravely little in front of Alexander.

"It's the only piece of info we can't leave Pleiku without. Go back immediately, take another hundred dollars, and don't come back out until the madam is sure. Go."

Ha Si slowly put up his hands. "Wait," he said reluctantly, not taking the proffered money. "Madam said she heard the fingerless girl talking about a ville called Kum Kau. Moon Lai's mother and sister lived in Kum Kau. Perhaps that is the place she went to every few months."

"Never heard of this Kum Kau," Richter said suspiciously. "Must be either very small or far away from here."

Ha Si said nothing.

"This is *so* fucked up," Elkins said, "Could Ant have gone with her to her stupid village? As a new husband? A father-to-be? To meet the in-laws, perhaps?"

"Let's say he did," said Alexander. "Why didn't he come back?"

"Maybe he tried," said Richter. "Maybe we've been looking for him in the wrong place. This Kum Kau—where is it, Ha Si?"

Ha Si did not reply, and was no longer unblinking. They asked him again, but he still did not reply. Richter raised his voice on the river street.

Very quietly Ha Si said, "You do not want to know, Colonel Richter."

"It's the only fucking thing we want to know!" Richter exclaimed. "It's the only thing we came here to find out. Stop fucking with us. That's an order. Now where is it?"

"Fourteen klicks north of the DMZ," Ha Si replied.

"It's in *North Vietnam*?" Richter said in an aghast voice.

"It's in *North Vietnam*!" said Alexander in a deathly voice, his voice inflecting, his heart falling.

Not speaking anymore to anyone, he barely finished his cigarette as he walked back to their jeep. With raised weapons, the men drove in silence for fifty kilometers through the dark countryside, back to base. *It's in North Vietnam!* was all Alexander kept thinking.

At Kontum, in Richter's quarters, Richter brought out the whiskey—beer was not strong enough. Ha Si was not drinking; he was sitting quietly in a chair; he was actually quieter than the chair. Alexander thought he himself had learned stealth well, but he was a jittery epileptic compared to Ha Si. Even now, the small man was imperturbable. Well, why shouldn't he be imperturbable? It wasn't *his* son who was missing in North fucking Vietnam.

"Do you see what I was getting at before, Elkins?" Alexander said finally. "You were ambushed."

"With all due respect, Major," said Elkins, "and pardon me for saying so, of course it was an ambush—that's clear to a duck—but what does an ambush a year and a half ago have to do with where Ant is now? Or with Moon Lai?"

Richter and Alexander exchanged a long whiskey-sodden look. Richter shook his head, pouring Alexander another glass from the carafe. They clinked and drank. "Don't worry, Major," Richter said. "Tomorrow I'll call Pinter, the commander of CC North. I'll ask him to send a recon team to the DMZ, up to where the fortress of Khe Sanh used to be. I'll ask him to send another RT to the Ho Chi Minh Trail in Laos. It comes down from North Vietnam and enters Laos about 30 klicks north of the DMZ. Let's see if they can scope out something there. I'll ask Pinter if he's ever heard of this Kum Kau."

Alexander's mouth twisted. He put his drink down. He put his cigarettes down, got up from the table and stood at attention, clicking his heels, looking grimly at Richter. "Colonel Richter," he said, very quietly, "can I talk to you alone for a minute?"

With great and visible reluctance, Richter motioned Ha Si and Elkins out and turned to Alexander, who was still standing stiff inside the barracks. "Look, I know what you're going to say—"

"You don't know what I'm going to say."

"Oh, I do, I do." Richter slumped in his chair.

"Tom, what the hell are you talking about, Pinter, his RT teams? I mean, whose benefit was that for?" Alexander started to pace in front of the long table.

"Only yours. Alexander, Pinter's men know that area by heart. You know my guys stay in the triangle." Richter poured himself another drink. "Want one?"

"Tom."

"Alexander!" The drink was slammed into the table. "There is something about this, I can see you just *don't* understand."

"Tom!" said Alexander. The fist was slammed into the table. "There is something about this *you* just don't understand."

Richter jumped up. "Listen to me! You do know that we are under direct orders not to go into North Vietnam? You do know that, right? Direct orders!"

"Oh, come on. I know how the SOG works. You tell your men where to go, they go where you send them. End of story. You're telling me Elkins won't go? Mercer won't go?"

"Alexander!" Richter's voice was lowered to a furious whisper. "You've lost your *mind*! It's not my area of operations! I'm here. My AO is in central South Nam, in Laos, in Cambodia. *Here*."

"Yes, and we're not supposed to be in Laos or Cambodia either, here, there, anywhere. You're not supposed to be sending your little excursion teams to the Trail. You're not supposed to be running SLAM missions into the Cambodian jungle to intercept their supply runners. Yet you are."

The two of them stood tensely across from each other. Two pairs of fists were clenched against the table.

"Fourteen miles *north* of the DMZ!" Richter said. "Not five miles from Pleiku, not ten miles from Kontum but *three hundred miles* from here in North Vietnam, where Abrams himself on express orders from Johnson said we could not set one toe so we wouldn't upset the Soviets and trigger an international incident that no one will be able to walk away from!"

"Give me a fucking break."

"Well, let me ask you, since you seem to have all the answers," said Richter, "what the fuck do you know about Kum Kau? Say we defy the commander of MACV and the President of the United States—your commander-in-chief, too, by the way—and we send our guys there, and we find out it's a nice little village where Vietnamese women in coolie hats stroll around with rice buckets on their shoulders and have babies. Say we find your son in that village, eating pho, helping in the paddies. Then what? Are we going to bring him back for a nice court-martial? Because it's been five months, and if he's picking his navel in a ville, he ain't coming back. You want us to bring back your son to be tried for desertion during time of war?"

"The answer to that is *yes*," Alexander growled through his teeth, "since you and I both know he is not sitting in *North* Vietnam picking his fucking navel."

"Fine," said Richter, also through his teeth. "Second question. So you think he met with foul play—"

"As you do, otherwise you wouldn't be all twisted up like this."

"Do you think he'd be sitting unsecured in some little civilian village?"

"We find Moon Lai, we'll know," said Alexander. "We find her, we'll know everything."

"Okay, we find her and then we're in enemy territory, and she kindly informs us that he is eight hundred miles up in the Hanoi Hilton or is part of the Cuban Program, at one of the POW camps deep near China, run in stealth by the Cubans from sugar cane country who come to North Nam pretending to be diplomats and then set up and run the NVA camps, brutalizing American men. Then what? You're going to walk eight hundred miles to Hanoi?"

"If that's what it takes," said Alexander.

"Holy Mother of God!" Richter was panting. "Okay, and that brings me to my fourth fucking question. We're in enemy territory, we get in an asskick situation, we need help. Where are we going to get help from? We usually have eight choppers on stand-by for support for this kind of mission. But for this? Anyone finds out we're in North Vietnam, and the shitstorm is going to be a lot worse than one missing boy."

"I don't fucking think so," said Alexander. "And you know what? Save it for another idiot, Richter, because you're forgetting who you're talking to. SOG has its own planes, its own helicopters, its own medevacs, its own hospitals, its own weapons. Clandestine, top secret, and *this* is precisely what they do. You're running Macvee's covert operations! This is SOG's whole point, otherwise they'd be fighting in open battalions with artillery support. They'd be the Marines. Do not, do you hear me?—do *not* try to sell this bullshit to *me* of all people!"

"I'm sorry I ever gave you a fucking G-2 MI job!" yelled Richter.

"Well, it's too late for sorrys. Now we have to go and get Ant."

"Oh my God," Richter gasped, "is *that* why you came here?"

"Why the fuck did you think?"

"I don't go into North Vietnam!" yelled Richter.

"You're going there tomorrow."

"Like fuck I am."

"The NVA have been breaking the rules and destabilizing supposedly neutral countries since 1954 to ferry Soviet-made weapons to South Nam so they can kill you," said Alexander. "Destabilizing Laos, Cambodia, Thailand, Papua New Guinea. Now you're worried about breaking a little rule? They've been arming the 17th parallel and the DMZ for fifteen years with their pretend civilian villages. You know that better than I do."

"That's right, but this isn't the DMZ, this is actual North Nam, and you do realize we have no information on Ant! We know absolutely fucking nothing! Why are you against sending a recon force there first? Pinter will send a seven-man team from CCN in Da Nang; at least then we might find out what we need. What if he's not there? What if we need a hundred men to extract him? What if we need just one, to carry his body? You did think of that possibility, did you not? God forbid, that he may be dead?"

"Alive or in a bag," Alexander said with a clamped everything, "we are bringing him back from North Vietnam."

"What if there is no Kum Kau, but I've sent twenty troops into enemy territory and they all get greased and I can't explain what the fuck they were doing there?"

"So you think if you send Pinter's men and they get greased, that'll make you feel better? You won't have Ant, but twenty of Pinter's guys will be dead. *That'll* be better?"

The two of them stood panting, facing off, two men, fifty years old, soldiers, fighters. The two of them at their wits' end, two men who could not believe it had come to this. But come to this it had, and now it had to be dealt with.

"You are thinking only of your son, Alexander," said Richter. "But I have to think of my whole command. There are a thousand guys I'm responsible for."

"Tom," said Alexander, "you *know* what the NVA and the fucking Cubans do to American soldiers."

"Kum Kau is near the DMZ. The Cubans are in Hanoi and near China. We're not going anywhere near China, are we?"

"North Vietnam has directly violated every sentence of the Geneva Convention, which, by the way, they signed. Our guys are turning up on the Trail dead, drowned, burned, mutilated beyond recognition because they can't be released alive to tell the world how the NVA treat their prisoners of war and you want to leave Ant there?"

"They can release them or not release them," said Richter. "Like the world gives a fuck how the NVA treats its prisoners of war. The world only cares what the Americans did at My Lai."

"Yes," said Alexander, "because *they* are judged mercifully for having no standards whatsoever, while *we* are judged harshly for failing to live up to our high ones. It's like Carthage being regarded more highly than Rome. I *know*. More is expected from Rome. But the point is," he went on, "you can posture all you like, with Elkins outside your door, but you know perfectly well that one way or another I'm going to Kum Kau to find out what happened to my son. I didn't come to Vietnam to go to cathouses with you. We're talking about Anthony. *Anthony!*" Alexander nearly broke down.

"I know who we are talking about!" Richter fought for his own composure. "I've taken care of him and protected him as best I could since he got here. He's had the run of everything. I barely asked him any questions, as long as the mission was accomplished, he could do whatever the fuck he liked. I did this for him because that's what he wanted."

"Good," said Alexander. "And this is what *I* want, just so we're straight. Either you help me like you're supposed to and meant to, or you stand there and give me five hundred more reasons why you can't, but Anthony is not going to remain in North Vietnam." Alexander's fists remained down at the table. "Not my son, and not one more day." He took a deep breath, not moving an inch, his shoulders up, the hair on his body standing on end.

Snarling in his naked aggravation, Richter stood down and backed away. Alexander did not stand down. He knew what Richter was going through. He just didn't want to hear it. And after five minutes and another glass of whiskey, Richter bowed his head. "What I don't understand is why *your* whole fucking life has to be a redux of Tatiana's commando mission in Berlin," he said, much quieter. "Why can't *your* life be about something else?"

"My life *is* about something else."

"Oh, I don't think so," said Richter. "I don't think so at all." After two cigarettes, Richter was finally calm enough to call Ha Si and Elkins back into his quarters. A groggy Elkins ran to wake up Mercer. It was well after one in the morning. The four men stood at attention. Richter, in his agitation, forgot to release them.

Circling around the Montagnard he said, his eyes boring into him, "Ha Si, you know *this* terrain like the back of your hand, I know that, but . . . let me ask you something, and I want you to think very carefully before you answer. That ville, Kum Kau, is far from here, far from your area of expertise. After all, you come from Bong Son, and that's nowhere near there. Wait, don't interrupt. Perhaps, just perhaps, do you think Kum Kau could be *west* of North Vietnam? Could it be a klick or two *inside* the Laotian border, in that mountainous Khammouan country? Maybe you made a tiny mistake. Hmm? *Think* before you answer."

Ha Si thought before he answered. "I think," he said slowly and quietly, "you may be right, Colonel. It could be just inside Laos. That border is very tricky through the mountains, and I don't know the parts as well as these. I spoke too quickly. Thank you for giving me the opportunity to amend. It *is* in Laos."

"Good," said Richter. "Because you know Ha Si, we can do many things, but we cannot under any circumstances go into North Vietnam. If Kum Kau is there, we can't at the outset define that as our mission parameters and go there to find this Moon Lai, and perhaps find out where our Captain Barrington is."

"Yes, sir. I understand, sir." Ha Si glanced at Alexander. "It's definitely in Laos."

Richter nodded. Finally, he put the men at ease. The five of them sat huddled together in his quarters, smoking, thinking, plotting.

"What I'd like to do—my preference," said Richter, "is to send a small recon unit there first." Alexander opened his mouth, but Richter cut him off. "But I know this better than anyone at this table"—he glared at Alexander—"if our men are detected, we're goners. If there is an actual Extraction and Escape and Evasion situation in Kum Kau, we can only go in once. They don't expect us; the element of surprise will be our greatest weapon. On the other hand, if we get into a position we can't defend, we're fucked. We simply can't bring enough men to both escape detection *and* engage a superior enemy force. So this is what we're going to do: we're assembling an A-team and going on a top-secret, location classified and undisclosed, long-range recon mission to Laos. Do you hear me? Laos. We're not calling it SLAM. Is that clear? We're calling it recon. A little intel gathering. Maybe some supply disruption."

"Understood, sir."

"We go in unmarked. You know what that means. If you fall in North Nam, no one will find you. You will remain unidentified. I suggest you make all appropriate phone calls and write all appropriate letters before we move out. Personally, unlike Major Barrington, our intelligence advisor straight from Fort Huachuca in Arizona, I think Kum Kau is just a regular village."

"Well, unlike you, gentlemen," said Alexander, "I haven't been on the ground since 1946, and I'm sure things have changed since then. And Colonel Richter may be right, having so much experience in this area. But let's just approach it as if it's a booby-trapped, mined, heavily-armed enemy camp. All the means with which we hope to achieve our objective, we have to bring with us. While I'm certain that all Vietnamese villagers are nothing more than innocent civilians, let's just in fucking case bring enough ammo to raze Hanoi, not torch a mud hut."

Richter glared sideways at Alexander. Everybody else glanced sideways at Richter.

"I'll charter a hook to take us into Laos," Richter said. "I'll get us a medevac crew. That way it inserts us, flies back down south to refuel and waits for our call. There's an SOG supply base just south of DMZ, I'll get our support gunships to wait there, plus two extra Hueys if we need them, and a medic slick. But remember, even our classified mission is parametered to Laos. Six fucking snakes cannot fly to North Vietnam—because that would no longer be called combat support, it would be called a fucking invasion." Snakes were Cobra helicopter gunships. "Everybody all clear on that?"

Everybody was all clear. Mercer was mulling. "Excuse me, Colonel. You keep saying, *we*. Are you . . . thinking of going, too?"

Alexander looked down at his hands so as not to see Richter sit defeated in front of his men.

"Damn it all to hell," Richter said. "I'm way too fucking old for this. But I'm going in because it's my ass if bad shit goes down in North Vietnam. There will be twelve of us. A six-man Yard team plus us. I'll get Tojo to come, if he doesn't have a heart attack first when he finds out I'm going. Elkins, Mercer, Ha Si, I'm assuming you're all volunteering to go?"

The three men nodded and then turned to stare at Alexander.

"What the fuck are you all looking at?" he said. "Without me, you'd still be getting laid in Pleiku, eating cheese sandwiches, and lobbing grenades at the fish in the river. Of course I'm going."

The men were quiet.

"Maybe you should stay back, Major," Elkins said. "You did just say you haven't seen active combat since *1946*."

"Active combat with a Donut Dolly doesn't count," Richter added bitingly.

Alexander said nothing. Richter obviously felt the need to have the last word.

"Does the colonel need to upgrade your security clearance?" Elkins pressed on. "Because that can take a month."

"My security clearance has long ago been upgraded by the Military Intelligence commander in Fort Huachuca, thank you for your interest, Lieutenant," said Alexander. The conversation was over. "Tom, can you walk me to my hut? I need sleep." The other men stood, saluted them, and they left. Alexander turned to Richter. "Are you going to be able to get your shit together by tomorrow?" he asked as they walked to his hut.

Richter didn't think so. "And we call it hooch, Alexander."

"Hooch, hut, who the fuck cares. We've waited long enough, Tom. We have to go."

"We'll need a couple of days," Richter said. "I have to commission a Chinook, we have to get our supplies, our weapons. You know better than anyone, we have to be ready. We get only one chance at this."

Alexander agreed they needed to be ready. He knew they got only one chance at this.

When they stood outside Alexander's barracks, Richter lit a smoke and said, "Alexander, you do know how small our chance of success is?"

"So you're confident then?" In a more relaxed mood, Alexander patted Richter's arm. "Tom," he said. "You understand you're talking to the wrong man about odds."

"Don't I fucking know it."

"What were the odds of a five-foot-nothing woman who never shot a weapon in her life getting into Soviet-controlled territory not knowing where I was, or even if I was there, or alive, and then finding me—there *and* alive?"

"Better than ours," said Richter.

Alexander shook his head. "One unarmed woman in a Gulag camp with machine-gun sentries every five inches," said Alexander, nearly reverentially. "Not twelve guys, carrying more ammo than their combined body weight. And yes, the NVA are bad motherfuckers, but the Soviets weren't ladies having finger sandwiches at the Kentucky Derby. They brought their artillery, too. And yet she found me and got me out. So sleep well." But he couldn't help thinking of what Tania had once said to him. We can rail all we want. *But sometimes what we do is just not enough.* He knew something about that. He tried to push the thoughts from his mind.

Richter sighed, blew smoke from his cigarette, attempted a smile. "I'm surprised you and Tania have never used your abilities to beat the odds to your benefit."

It was the first time since July 20, 1969 that Alexander laughed out loud. "Tom," he said, lowering his voice and briefly putting his friendly arm around Richter. "Who says we haven't?" A wide smile was on Alexander's face. "It's Las Vegas twice a year for us, baby," he said happily. "The kids think we're getting R&R in Sedona. As soon as we get there, we gamble for twenty straight hours. My wife is a roulette and blackjack queen."

Richter's mouth nearly fell open. "We're talking about *Tania*?" he said. "Tania, your *wife*, at the blackjack table?"

Alexander nodded. "And Tom—she needs to be seen to be believed. We've been getting a complimentary penthouse suite at the Flamingo for seven years. The hotel gives her free chips, free food, shopping vouchers, it makes no difference—she simply does not lose. If she is cold, she doesn't play. We went just a month ago to cheer ourselves up a bit, but she was cold, so we stopped playing. She kept getting dealt the queen of spades and busting. But that was an anomaly." He broke off, then lowered his voice. "The dealers don't see her coming. She sits at their tables, sips a little wine, dresses in pink, lets her hair down, jokes with them, and all their defenses are gone. They stand no chance. She is unbelievable." He recalled her fondly. "Me, I'm a different story. I play poker. I win, I lose. She comes and stands behind me and cools the rest of the table, while I heat up. We do all right. But she *loves* to do it."

Richter listened with wide eyes, and then laughed. "Unbefuckinglievable. You come here and in ten hours my world is turned upside down. I, a lieutenant-colonel, am taking orders from a fucking major, Anthony is having Vietnamese babies with whores, we're single-handedly and without authorization invading North Vietnam, and *Tania* loves Vegas. Is there anything else you want to shock me with?"

Instantly brought right back to earth, Alexander stopped smiling. "No," he said, giving him a careful pat. "Nothing that comes to mind."

Richter also grew serious. "Alexander, do me a favor. When we go in, don't talk to me like we've been friends for twenty years."

Alexander saluted him. Richter saluted him back.

"Good night, Colonel Richter," said Alexander.

"Good night, Major Barrington."

In his one room hooch, Alexander undressed and fell down on his bed. He lit a cigarette, smoked it down, lit another one, and smiled, staring at the ceiling.

"Ant, come here, I want you to play dominoes with your mother."

"No! Why? I never win." Anthony had just come home from his first year at West Point. It was June 1962.

"Well, I know," said Alexander, *"but I'm going to watch you two play. You play your mother, and I will watch her and figure out how she cheats."*

"Don't listen to your father. I don't cheat at dominoes, Ant," Tatiana said. *"I use all of my vital powers. That's different."*

"Just draw the tiles, Tania."

"Yes, just draw the tiles, Mom."

There were twenty-eight domino tiles. Seven went to Anthony, seven to Tatiana. Fourteen remained in the draw pile.

Alexander watched her. She sat impassively, putting her tiles down, drawing new ones, humming, looking at her son, at her husband. Soon all the tiles were gone except what remained in Anthony's hand, and in Tatiana's. Five to seven minutes each game. Each one won by her.

"Have you figured it out yet, Dad?"

"Not yet, son. Keep playing."

Alexander stopped watching the tiles. He didn't watch what went on the table, he didn't watch what was drawn, nor what was put down, not even who won or lost. He was intently studying only Tatiana's cool, unflappable face and her bright, clear eyes.

They played again and again and again.

Anthony complained. "Dad, we played thirteen games, all of which I lost. Can we stop?"

"Of course you lost, son," Alexander said slowly. "Yes, you can stop."

Thus released, Anthony fled the kitchen, Alexander lit a cigarette, and Tatiana calmly collected the tiles and stacked them back in the box.

She raised her eyes at him. His mouth widened in a grin. "Tatiana Metanova," he said, "For twenty years, I have lived with you, I have slept in your bed, I have fathered your children." He lowered his voice to a whisper and leaned across to her. "Tania!" he said exaltedly. "I almost can't believe it's taken me this long to figure it out. But—you count the tiles!"

"What?"

"You count the fucking tiles!"

"I don't know what you mean," she said blankly.

"When the draw pile is gone, you know what's in Ant's hand! You keep track, you know what tiles are left! At the end of the game, you know your opponent's move before they can breathe on a domino!"

"Shura—"

He grabbed her, brought her on top of his lap, kissed her. "Oh, you're good. You are very good."

"Really, Alexander," Tatiana said calmly. "I simply don't know what you're talking about."

He laughed, so joyously. Letting go of her, he went to the cabinet and pulled out a deck of cards. Rummaging around, he found two more decks. "Guess where you and I are going next month for our twentieth wedding anniversary, my little domino counter," he said, sitting at the table and shuffling the three decks of cards, with a cigarette dangling from his mouth.

"Um—the Grand Canyon?"

"Viva Las Vegas, baby."

And here in Kontum, in the midst of chaos and misery, not knowing if his son was alive or even saveable, Alexander, usually reminded so painfully of his own humanity, this time was reminded blissfully of it, as only humans can be—finding one strand of comfort amid a covering quilt of anguish.

A package came by express delivery for Alexander. He was surprised; he'd been in the country barely two weeks; who would be sending him a package already, and why? When he got to the post barracks, he saw a long and heavy box. It was from home. Elkins and Mercer were even more surprised as they tried to lift it.

"Some care package," said Mercer. "What's in here, bricks?"

They had to open it on the ground, in the dust, in front of the mail room. It was too heavy to carry. Inside Alexander found a very long letter from Tatiana that began, *"O husband, father of small boys, one of your sons has lost his mind."* And inside the box were sixteen punji sticks, each five feet long, carved out of round planed wood, notched at the tip, and sharpened like needles on both ends, for easier insertion into the ground, and greater penetration. The letter taped to them, in block handwriting said, *"Dear Dad, You are going to need these. Insert diagonally into ground at 45° angle. Also Mama says watch out for bears. Your son, Harry."*

"Your *kid* made these for you?" Mercer said incredulously.

"Can you believe it?"

"And your *wife* shipped them express mail?" said Elkins. "That I can't believe. She must have had to mortgage your house to do it. I don't know who's crazier, the son for making them or the wife for shipping them."

"How old's the boy?" Mercer asked.

"Ten on New Year's Day." Harry was born on the first day of the new decade.

Mercer and Elkins whistled and stared into the box. "Ten. Well, that's something. These are nearly perfect," said Elkins.

"They *are* perfect! What the fuck do you mean nearly?"

Tatiasha, my wife,

I got cookies from you and Janie, anxious medical advice from Gordon Pasha (tell him you gave me a gallon of silver nitrate), some sharp sticks from Harry (nearly cried). I'm saddling up, I'm good to go. From you I got a letter that I could tell you wrote very late at night. It was filled with the sorts of things a wife of twenty-seven years should not write to her far-away and desperate husband, though this husband was glad and grateful to read and re-read them.

Tom Richter saw the care package you sent with the preacher cookies and said, "Wow, man. You must still be doing something right."

I leveled a long look at him and said, "It's good to know nothing's changed in the army in twenty years."

Imagine what he might have said had he been privy to the fervent sentiments in your letter.

No, I have not eaten any poison berries, or poison mushrooms, or poison anything. The U.S. Army feeds its men. Have you seen a C-ration? Franks and beans, beefsteak, crackers, fruit, cheese, peanut butter, coffee, cocoa, <u>sacks</u> of sugar(!). It's enough to make a Soviet blockade girl cry. We're going out on a little scoping mission early tomorrow morning. I'll call when I come back. I tried to call you today, but the phone lines were jammed. It's unbelievable. No wonder Ant only called once a year. I would've liked to hear your voice though: you know, one word from you before battle, that sort of thing . . .

Preacher cookies, by the way, BIG success among war-weary soldiers.

Say hi to the kids. Stop teaching Janie back flip dives.

Do you remember what you're supposed to do now? Kiss the palm of your hand and press it against your heart.

Alexander

P.S. I'm getting off the boat at Coconut Grove. It's six and you're not on the dock. I finish up, and start walking home, thinking you're tied up making dinner, and then I see you and Ant hurrying down the promenade. He is running and you're running after him. You're wearing a yellow dress. He jumps on me, and you stop shyly, and I say to you, come on, tadpole, show me what you got, and you laugh and run and jump into my arms. Such a good memory.

I love you, babe.

Deadfall in Kum Kau

Two days later, barely at dawn, all saddled up, Alexander, Tom Richter, Charlie Mercer, Dan Elkins, Ha Si, Tojo, and a six man Bannha Montagnard team, one of whom was a medic, twelve Special Forces soldiers in all, flew out in a Chinook with a large red cross on its nose, three hundred miles north into the Laotian jungle.

They were escorted by two Cobra gunships from Kontum. They had to refuel once. They brought long dehydrated rations, regular C-rations, heat tabs, water, plasma, and arms for a hundred men.

The insertion point was barely a meter inside the Laotian border, seven kilometers west from the mapped-out location of Kum Kau. The hook flew high through the mountain pass, because just last week a Huey slick was flying too low above a valley and was fired at by an RPG-7. It went down; the pilot, the co-pilot, the gunner, and two of the Indians were killed. So this time Richter ordered the chopper to fly above cloud cover to escape detection and not take any short cuts through valleys.

They were inserted without incident in Laos, and then set off to walk through the jungle in the north central highlands, a thousand meters above sea level, deep in the high plateau of enemy territory. On the chopper, they had drunk coffee, smoked, talked bullshit, cut up, joked, but here in the woods, everyone became somber and silent, not speaking, weapons raised, trying not to disturb the fern. Richter made Ha Si walking point, Mercer slack man, Alexander third, and Elkins fourth. Tojo, the Bannha who was nearly seven foot tall, was the drag man at tail—he, apparently, was always at drag because he was like a stone wall. In front of Tojo was Richter, constantly and quietly on his radio, and in front of Richter walked six more Bannhas.

The trail they laid was just noticeable enough for them to make their way back. It was an early December morning, dry and a little cool. The jungle was tall and verdantly dense. After hovering over the men in a holding pattern until they disappeared, the chopper flew thirty kilometers south to the SOG base that was the standby reaction center for the mission. Six Cobras waited there and a medic slick—just in case. The pilot told Richter not to get into trouble for an hour. After refueling, he was ordered to wait for further instructions.

The troops were dressed in jungle camouflage battle fatigues; even their steel helmets and lightweight nylon and canvas boots were camo. Over his tunic, Alexander wore a combat vest stuffed to bursting with 20-round cartridges. The bandolier over his waist was filled with an assortment of 40mm rockets that flew farther than hand-thrown and were most useful for close combat. He had on a demolition bag of miscellaneous rounds for his pistols and extra clips for his rifle. He wore another bag holding three Claymore mines, plus clackers and tripwire. The M-16 was in his arms, with the rocket launcher already affixed below the rifle mount. He had with him his lucky Colt M1911, plus the regulation Ruger .22 with the silencer attached. He carried an SOG recon Bowie knife and an excavating tool that could also be used as a piercing weapon. His ruck was filled with medical kits and food. He had on at least 90 pounds of ammo, weapons and supplies on him, and he was 50. In the mountains of Holy Cross he was 25, and carried 60 pounds of gear. That was a physics problem worthy of Tania herself. And he wasn't even carrying Harry's heavy punji sticks or extra rounds. The Montagnards were carrying those, plus the awe-inducing 23-pound M-60 machine gun with a tripod, *plus* their own 90 pounds of gear. Without the Yards, the never-complaining, silent, helpful, mountain people of South Vietnam, who were trained by the SOG to be efficient killing machines and who fought alongside the Americans, search and rescue missions would have scarcely been possible.

It had been twenty-five years since Alexander led the 200-man penal battalion for the Red Army through Russia, through Estonia, through Byelorussia, through Poland and into Germany. Back then they had no food and barely any weapons or ammo—he didn't know why his gear had weighed as much as 60 pounds. His men had been political prisoners, not Special Forces commandos; his men were not trained; many of them had never held a rifle. And yet somehow they managed to get all the way into Germany.

And before Holy Cross, Alexander defended Leningrad. For two years he defended it on the streets, across the barricades, and across the Pulkovo and Sinyavino Hills, from which the Germans bombed the city. He defended Leningrad on its rivers, and its Ladoga Lake. He drove tanks across the ice, he shot down German planes with surface-to-air missiles. And before that, he fought against Finland in 1940, underfed, underclothed, undersupplied and freezing, armed barely with a single-bolt rifle, never dreaming that one day he would be walking through the triple-canopy jungle in Vietnam searching for his son while carrying a weapon that could fire 800 rounds a minute, discharging each round at over 3000 feet per second. Yes, the third-gen M-16 was an unbelievable rifle.

But he had liked his Shpagin, too, the Red Army standard-issue for officers. It was a good weapon. And the men under his command, they were good men. His sergeants, even in the penal battalions, were always fighters, always brave. And his friends—Anatoly Marazov, who died in his arms on the Neva ice. Ouspensky. They had been fine lieutenants. Ouspensky protected Alexander's hide for many years, even as he was betraying him, fiercely protected the man who was his ticket out.

Except for Richter, Alexander didn't know the men he was going into the heart of the jungle with—and wished he did. He wished he had heard their stories ahead of time, before they reached the mountains of Khammouan. He knew the lives of all of his lieutenants and sergeants in the battalion. Yet he had no doubt about any of the men with him now. Because they were Ant's men. And he knew his son, and had no doubt about him. Mercer, Ha Si, Elkins—they were Ant's Telikov, Marazov, Ouspensky.

Alexander was glad he had continued to train at Yuma, that he had kept himself rated to enter active combat at any time. He trained even when he was supposed to be translating military intel documents. He didn't want to tell Tania this, but he had always quite liked the weapons, and the Americans made weapons like no one else. So he went to Yuma, put on the ear protectors, fitted the silencers over the M-4 machine guns and spent the afternoons at the range, keeping his sharpshooter rating permanently on the whetstone. Then he returned to the married quarters at night, took a scalding shower to wash the traces of gunpowder off his body, and lay down with Tania. He touched her with the hands that not two hours earlier had been loading 40mm grenades into the breech of his rocket launcher and pressing the trigger, and then, satisfied in every way, returned to Scottsdale to be at work by Monday, and spackled and pounded wood, and lifted tile, and drafted at his table, smiling while using the nail gun as if he were born to it, having just fired a sniper rifle in Yuma as if he were born to it. And perhaps it was this, his well-hidden true self, that he couldn't help communicating to his youngest son, who wanted nothing more than to make his dad happy. Such a good boy.

It was getting warmer. Not much like the tropics here: the air was dry. The twelve-man team crunched through the golden cyprus and bamboo jungle in a single file, practically stepping into the forward man's boots as they looked out for snakes, for mines, for booby traps, for poison, for punji sticks. Ha Si, who saw everything, cleared the bush, held the relief map, the compass, the watch, keeping an eye out, weapon always pointed. It was as if he had six hands.

"He's fucking dynamite," Alexander said, leaning forward to Mercer.

Mercer nodded. "Rumor is," he said quietly, "he used to be on their side. That's why he knows everything, can do anything. But we don't ask. We're just glad he's ours."

"No kidding," said Alexander, marveling at Ha Si's innate sense of direction through these impassable parts. Tania should have had him with her when she was lost in Lake Ilmen. Plus a little razor-sharp Bowie knife, a C-ration, Richter's command-only VHF radio, and a Zippo lighter with the engraved words, *"And the Lord said, let there be soldiers, and the fish rose from the sea,"* and she would've been all set. Alexander smiled. Somehow she had managed, even without.

They walked for three hours. When they were on the sixth kilometer, Richter radioed in. He had found a tiny clearing at klick six, just enough for a landing zone into the man-high elephant grass, and gave the pilot the coordinates of the clearing, so that if they had to get out in a hurry, they wouldn't have to hump seven uphill kilometers and four hours through enemy terrain to get extracted. "Make sure the turrets are overloaded with ammo, though," Richter told the pilot. "Because I don't want anyone else here but you. The asskick will have to be completely SNAFU before I call in the snakes to North Nam."

Finally they reached the end of the forest, at the crest of a mountain, and came out onto a long and narrow mesa maybe six hundred feet up over a grassy gorge, at the bottom of which, nested between steep and rising ranges, on the banks of a brown stream, a ville was laid out in the flat, like an enclave. The mountains covered it on all sides, themselves covered in elephant grass and rocks and short pines. A dozen rice paddies were staggered in stair formations cut into the side of the mountain across from the A-team.

"*This* is Kum Kau?" asked Alexander, looking carefully.

"Yes, according to my specs," replied Ha Si. "What, too small?"

The village *was* small, one-sixth the size of their base at Kontum. It was maybe fifty yards on its two longest sides, and twenty to twenty-five yards on the shortest. The thatched huts were built symmetrically—on straight pathways—as if the area were designed by a Parisian architect and sprung all at once, except for the slight arc that followed the curve of the river. It was quiet and no one was out. It looked abandoned.

Alexander watched it for five more seconds before he put down his binoculars. "All my training may have come from a small office in Yuma, Colonel Richter," he said, "not the ground, like yours, but this below us is no village. It's a decoy. It's a fucking army base."

Richter was doubtful, picking up own binoculars. "The NVA build gray hooches to hide in. These look like regular civilian huts." They were so high up, they could talk without fear of being heard down below. Still, they moved a step away from the slope, hunkered down.

"It's noon," Alexander said. "Where is everyone?"

"How the fuck should I know? Sleeping? Jacking off?"

"That's what I mean. It's a *village*. The rice paddies are overgrown and waiting. Why isn't anyone out tending the crops like they're supposed to? Colonel Richter, in a normal village, in the middle of the day, people are out. They plant, they wash, they cook, they take care of their families. Where is everyone?"

Richter looked through the binoculars. "There. There are women. They're washing in that mud they call a river."

Alexander looked. "There are forty huts, and all you see is three old women?"

Ha Si—without binoculars—quietly said, "Colonel Richter, six hundred feet below us, at the base of this southern hill, a dozen men in coolies drawn over their faces, are lying on the ground, hidden by bamboo."

Alexander nodded. "The sentry are spaced fifteen meters apart, like they were at Colditz Castle, the highest security POW camp the Germans had. A civilian village, Colonel?"

"On the plus side," Ha Si said conciliatorily to a grumpy Richter, "the sentry *are* sleeping."

Alexander glanced at him. "I thought you didn't joke, Ha Si?"

Ha Si was straight-faced. "I'm not joking, sir. They are actually sleeping." The black irises in his narrow black eyes twinkled a little.

Ha Si had excellent command of English, which the other

Bannhas did not speak nearly as well, all except for Tojo, who was apparently fluent in English (and Vietnamese and Japanese, being half-Japanese himself). However, he chose not to speak.

Alexander suspected that while the village slept during the day the place turned into Las Vegas at night. They would have to wait until night to see if his inductions proved correct. Ha Si certainly thought they would: he didn't take a step without his weapon in hand. Whatever the status of the village, this was Kum Kau. They had to stay long enough to find out if Moon Lai was here.

They scoped out a good central location, cleared a little bush for monitoring activities, found rocks and nice high grass for cover, broke camp, ate. They couldn't smoke, which made twelve men crazy, but the Vietnamese smelled nothing as well as Western cigarettes. You couldn't take a puff without the wafting wind blowing it into the nose of the enemy. Alexander said had he known this he might have reconsidered coming.

Ha Si said, "I thought you didn't joke, sir."

"Who is joking?" Alexander had not been this long without a cigarette since Berlin. Nothing to do now. Cigarettes or a search for his son.

It was around noon and too warm. They thoroughly cleaned and inspected their weapons and then sat and tapped on their knees in the coarse yellow grass. The grass was thick, growing to ten feet tall in places, its razor-sharp edges making it almost impossible to penetrate. Richter, who hated to sit still, went himself—the height of foolishness—with three of his Yards to scope out the hill and help clear a swath through the grass down to the village, in case there was trouble and they needed to run back up in a hurry. Of course, if they could run up the trail, the Charlies chasing them could also move up the trail. So Ha Si and Alexander—who *could* sit still but hated to—planted Harry's punji sticks into the ground halfway up. Then they quietly moved through the grass down almost to where the sentries were snoring and Claymored the lower portion, stretching the thin tripwires fifty meters across. "The Charlies step on this wire," whispered Ha Si, crouching not five meters away from the slumbering men, "and for a hundred-meter radius they are eating small steel balls for breakfast." He almost smiled. "We will stagger the mines uphill, too. If this lower pass does not get them, the one ten meters up will, and then will come the punji sticks, and then we will set up the rest of our Claymores up top."

"We should really mine the entire perimeter," Alexander said, looking across the grassy hill and around the village.

"We do not have enough mines."

"You're right." Alexander was getting carried away. "One every hundred meters along the bottom of this hill will be fine. We'll need five. And then four more, ten meters up. And then three more at the top of the hill, near our trail. We have enough."

"We will forget where we put them," said Ha Si.

"Better not." Alexander winked.

"We do not have enough tripwire."

"Stretch it as far as you can."

"Many precautions, no?"

"Yes."

Ha Si nodded. "Preparing for the worst, Commander?"

"Preparing for the worst, Ha Si."

It took them two hours of stealth and great care—in case the hill was already booby-trapped—to do it.

After they meticulously marked the location of the tripwire, they cleared a separate, secret path through the elephant grass and, pleased with their work, went back to their encampment, sat down and had a drink. But not a cigarette. Alexander would have given up drink for life to have a cigarette. At least one pair of binoculars remained trained on the ville at all times. It was quiet: only sporadically did some women, young and old, creep out to the thick slow river to wash and quickly return to their huts. None of the women looked like the woman the soldiers were looking for—though two had been maimed: each was missing a leg. The guards below continued to sleep peacefully, with their Kalashnikov semi-automatic rifles in their hands and their hats covering their faces from sunlight.

At three in the afternoon, Ha Si said, "Heads up. Major Barnington, take a look. Could this be the one?" And he didn't even have binoculars!

They looked.

A small white shape emerged from a far hooch on stilts near the river and walked toward them, to the row of huts closest to their side of the mountain. She was wearing a white coolie and a white dress. She was small and thin—was easily overlooked, like a peony. But she was pregnant. Alexander noticed that first—how very pregnant she was. She had a white patch over her right eye.

"Bullseye, baby," said Elkins.

Bullseye indeed. Alexander could not look away from her belly.

Carrying something, she made her way down the path in front of the sentries, stopped, stood for a few moments as if getting her bearings, and then disappeared inside the last hooch in the row. The U.S. soldiers waited, Alexander nearly not breathing.

She reappeared twenty minutes later, still carrying something, and made her waddling way back. Through the binoculars Alexander could now see her right hand—missing the pinky and ring fingers. To him she looked heavier than when she went in, as if suddenly acquiring gravity that pressed down not on her belly but into her shoulders, sloping her to the ground from which she did not—or could not—lift her eye.

"If we don't hurry," said Elkins, "she's going to have the kid right in front of us."

Alexander wished he didn't have to look at her to make such an assessment. He watched her walk across the four rows of huts to the river and rinse the things she had been carrying. A small child of two, maybe three, ran up to her. She helped him in the water, splashed him a little. They sat by each other. They were alone.

Richter, Elkins, Mercer, Ha Si watched her quietly, sitting by Alexander's side. "I'm sure that's not her kid," said Richter, glancing anxiously at Alexander. "It's probably her sister's kid. Sister's dead, now she takes care of him."

No one spoke then.

Alexander did not speak most of all. He turned away from the village, from the girl, he turned his back, he leaned against the rock, and said, "Richter, man, if I don't have a fucking cigarette, I'm going to die." He closed his eyes.

Alexander didn't have a cigarette and hours later night fell.

Richter ordered his men into sleep and sentry. Two Yards were on watch, everyone else was sleeping, except Alexander. The camp transformed. Bugles blew faint reveille, lights went on, men appeared, moving in and out of huts, there was motion, activity; there was carrying, organizing, adjusting; even the perimeter guards awoke. They relieved themselves where they stood and some of the women (who now numbered in the dozens) brought them food and ate with them. Alexander watched it all through his green-eye StarLights, the night-vision goggles that magnified light up to 10,000 times, but even without them it was plain to see that in this place, in Kum Kau—night was day, and day was night.

Attaching the silencer and the StarLight to his rifle, Alexander leaned over the rocks in the blackness, aiming the muzzle at the perimeter men. The rifle was steady in his hands.

"What are you going to do?" whispered Richter, who had woken up to change sentry and crawled next to Alexander. "Pick them off one by one?" He leaned against the rocks, rubbing his face.

"If you say so, Colonel Richter," said Alexander. "I never disobey my commanding officer. One by one, tomorrow, while they sleep. It'll take me fifteen seconds. No one will even notice."

At two in the morning, a chopper lifted off from just beyond the village, having been camouflaged in daylight, and thup-thuped away.

"Well, looky at that," said Elkins, who had also woken up. Richter had ordered the men to rest, but most of them were now stirring, as if they were not supposed to be sleeping either.

"Nice Soviet Kamov helicopter they've got there," Alexander said to Richter. "I didn't know that friendly, women-run Vietnamese villages had much need of Soviet military aircraft. But then what do I know? I'm only in MI, not on the ground, like you fellas." He refocused his rifle sight.

Elkins pointed at something else through his green-eye. "Look over there," he said. "At the back of the camp, there's nothing but sandbags on that low flat rectangular roof. Missed it during the day. But what do you think they're keeping under those sandbags?"

Alexander thought of the sandbagged statue of the Bronze Horseman and smiled to himself.

"Same thing we keep under ours in Kontum." That is, heavy artillery in the ammunition supply points. "What's interesting about theirs, though," Alexander said, "is how long the sandbag roof is. In Kontum, ours are maybe fifteen feet. Theirs runs probably forty-five feet across. That's not a supply point. It's a supply dump."

"What the hell is going on with this place?" said Elkins.

The men stayed low, StarLights to their faces. At four in the morning, the Kamov returned. It was Ha Si, who, without any night-vision goggles, crouched next to Alexander and Richter and said in a calm voice, "Do you see what I see?"

"No, what do you see?" Richter exclaimed with impatience.

"What can you *possibly* see? You aren't even wearing the green-eyes! Go the fuck to sleep."

"Yours are obviously malfunctioning, sir," said Ha Si. "Green-eyes, that is. Because I just saw six uniformed, heavily armed Viet Cong jump off the Kamov."

Richter stared through his. "Oh, shit," he said, peeling the StarLight off his face. "We are in so much fucking trouble."

Alexander remained unfazed. "Nah," he said calmly. "I've got some HE rockets that in three seconds will blow up that Kamov faster than they can say, what the fuck. We have at least ten thousand rounds between us, plus the waiting Chinook is loaded up. Say there are two hundred men down there. Ten thousand rounds for two hundred Charlies. What, not enough?"

"No," said Richter, just as calmly. "Not nearly."

"And, we're on top of the hill." Alexander—who had spent two months at the *bottom* of the hill in the forest of Holy Cross, with barely any ammo and certainly no M-60 machine gun with armor-piercing rounds reaching nearly four kilometers—stayed unconcerned.

Elkins and now Mercer lay down close to them.

"Colonel, I'm going to have to agree with Major Barrington," said Elkins. "I know you're worried about their RPG-7s, but there are twelve of us here, each with our very own, American-made rocket launchers. Two hundred and fifty 40mm buckshot grenades, plus some high explosives for good measure. I don't know what you're so worried about."

"You're a fine one to talk, Elkins," said Richter. "You couldn't smell trouble during a Viet Cong ambush."

And Ha Si said, "Those men aren't Charlies, by the way, they're Vietminh. North Vietnamese Army. The Viet Cong don't rate Kamov choppers."

Alexander and Richter watched the village. "You know where they live?" said Richter. "Underground. They live like rats in tunnels, in dark caves. The huts, I will bet you your Las Vegas dollar, are almost all empty. Now *those* are decoys. Most of their ammo, their men and their women are all hidden beneath the earth."

"Like they're living already in the grave," said Alexander.

Richter was silent a moment. "Well, what do you plan to do, Major Barrington?" he asked. "Fight a war underground with twelve guys?"

"We're not going to fight a war underground," said Alexander. "We are going to get the girl."

"You don't think Anthony's here, do you?"

A small shudder was Alexander's only reply.

"Oh, Major!" said Richter. "He's been gone nearly half a year. He's probably been taken to Hanoi, to Hoa Loa." He paused. "Please, *please*, for a second, entertain that possibility."

"I don't want to entertain that possibility," said Alexander, "because Hoa Loa is far to walk—at least today. We'll get the girl. Once we get her, we'll know where Ant is."

In the darkness, the green human shapes, like aliens, flapped around, the flapping exaggerated by the green-eyes.

Ha Si was silent. Alexander thought he was *heavily* silent, like he had something to say and wasn't saying it. That was good because Alexander didn't want to hear it. He turned to Elkins instead.

"Elkins," he said. "the one-eyed Moon Lai, do you think she is a prisoner of the NVA in that camp below? Does she move about like a prisoner down there?"

"No, I don't think she's a prisoner, Major," Elkins said, hanging his head.

"Commander, if she is one of them," said Ha Si, finally speaking up, "she is not going to tell you a thing. We will get her, but we will not get a word out of her. She will die first."

They groaned to acknowledge the truth of this. Only Mercer was quiet, because he'd fallen asleep where he sat, and Tojo, because he never said anything, let alone groaned. Alexander said, "I appreciate what Ha Si is saying. I don't necessarily disagree. But we have to get the girl." He paused. "She is our best chance of finding Anthony. Don't you agree, Ha Si?"

Ha Si was quiet. "I think," he said, "you have decided to get the girl. Therefore, we are going to get the girl."

Alexander looked intently at the Yard. He wanted, *needed* Ha Si's help. The Vietnamese did not disappoint him, saying to Richter, "Sir, the perimeter is guarded zealously only at night." They had observed the sentries, awake and on high alert. "Perhaps they only expect trouble at night, but I think there are supposed to be guards on duty during the day, but are not. Personally I think they have gotten careless. Which is very good for us. So I think we should go in broad daylight."

"Don't fuck with me, man!" said Richter. "We're not doing an E&E in daylight!"

"Ha Si is right, though," said Alexander. "We must."

"You're both fucked up," said Richter. "Forget it. Our mission was to find and extract one man and escape without being detected. But now our mission parameters have changed since the entire fucking Vietminh army is headquartered down there."

The soldiers stood silently.

"We don't have enough men for this!" Richter hissed. "You all want to be dead?

"We're going to have to make do with what we have," said Alexander, adding, "Colonel."

"How many fucking times do I to have to tell you? What you're proposing will require a hundred men! To go underground? You don't know what you're up against. And you have to assume the worst. We will have to req at least two, probably three Snakes."

"The Cobras will hurt our mission, Colonel." That was Ha Si, and he spoke low and with respect. "The Cobra is not for clandestine work."

"Oh, and us, here on the plateau, building fires like fiery placards: if you want us, here we are, come and get us! What do you call that?"

"We build no fires," Alexander said defensively.

Ha Si stretched out his small hand. "You are right, Colonel. Theirs does seem a large-scale op—like a crucial base of operations between the NVA and VC. The river is probably used to transport their supplies downstream on barges. If they have any prisoners, they will be kept underground in bamboo cages." He turned to Alexander and said, eyes steady, "They torture them with rats. If your son is here, are you ready for that?" He blinked—less steady.

"I don't have much choice, do I?" Alexander was less steady himself. "We should go in tomorrow. At three. When Moon Lai goes into that hut."

Ha Si disagreed. "No, three is too late. The sentries have had a long rest, they are up. No. We have to go in no more than an hour after they have gone to sleep. Then they will be groggy, still exhausted, drunk possibly. I have something to help them sleep a little longer." He took out his blowgun, a simple aluminum tube, smiling lightly. "Muzzle velocity of three hundred meters per second, a little opium dart into their neck. Not bad?"

"At three hundred meters per second," said Alexander, "that opium is passing through their necks and exiting the other side. You might as well shoot them with my Colt."

Ha Si smiled. "Your Colt is very loud, sir. *Quietly*, I shoot into the back of their necks or their shoulder blades. They sleep. But we do not yet have sufficient knowledge to go in. Today we saw the girl at three in the afternoon. But she might pay her first visit early in the morning. We need to stay put one more day, watch for her early, see how the whole camp operates from morning till night. We will know when the best time to go in will be."

Richter glared at them both. "Are you two quite fucking done? We are not going anywhere. How many Charlies you think are down there? I guarantee you, a lot more than twelve. No, I'm calling for a Hatchet force to come help us," he said. "That's thirty-five more guys. I don't give a fuck anymore that we're in North Nam. We're going in with more men," he continued, "we're blowing the motherfuckers away and torching their whole fucking village. By the time anyone will come around to ask any questions, they'll be ashes, and we'll be back in Kontum. We'll say we got lost. The compass broke. We went the wrong way, thought we were in hilly Laos, stumbled on this."

Alexander put his hand on Richter. "Colonel," he said steadily, "let's just wait a day. One day. Your operational in charge of CCC while you're away knows what's happening. He'll get you your Hatchet team in three hours. But first let's just see if Ant is here."

"Alexander!"

"Let's wait." His intense eyes bore into Richter. "Please."

Richter grumbled that he was not Japanese and did not like kamikaze missions. *That* made Tojo speak! He said that he *was* Japanese and didn't like them much either. Richter radioed his sleeping pilot down at the SOG base, to ask how much ordnance they had in the Chinook. Turned out plenty. The pilot had listened well. Richter told him to fly to their insert position in Laos first thing tomorrow morning and three of the Bannha would go back and retrieve more ammo.

They fell asleep where they sat and woke up in the dew two hours later as the sun was barely coming up. It was cold in the morning in the mountains, low forties, Alexander figured, wrapping himself in the trench cover. Not much tropical humidity here in the winter months. The ville had quietened down. The men had disappeared and the women appeared. Dozens of young women with their babies and their old mothers came out of the huts and ambled to the foggy basin to wash their clothes and clean their pots in the sediment run-off. Though where were they cooking? Underground? Perhaps the smoke exhaust was emptying out into the fog, undetectable.

After watching this bucolic scene for a while, a defeated Richter and a grim Alexander stared despairingly at each other.

"So, Colonel Richter, are you going to send in a Hatchet force?" Alexander asked. "To torch all the women and children?"

Richter spat on the ground. "The bastards are hiding behind them," he said impotently. "And this is why we die, and this is why they're going to win this fucking war. Because they don't give a fuck about their own women, while we're supposed to."

"Yes," said Alexander. "More is expected of Rome."

Richter spat again. There was to be no Hatchet.

While the women worked, the guards on the perimeter had already fallen asleep in the growing bamboo. At eight in the morning, the small dark woman, all in white with a white patch over her eye came out from her hut looking fresh from sleep. Alexander's binocular gaze was zeroed in on her like the crosshairs of his rifle sight. Her belly protruding, she sashayed along the length of the huts, past the sleeping guards, carrying what he now saw were clean white gauze bandages, and disappeared into the farthest hooch. He waited. Twenty minutes later, she reappeared, holding unclean bandages in her hands.

Alexander's binoculars slipped for a moment at the sight of those unclean bandages.

When she was back by the stream, Moon Lai helped an old woman to the outhouse latrine. Perhaps it was her mother, since she touched the old woman gently, and the old woman rubbed Moon Lai's belly. Afterward, she carried two babies to a tub of water. The small boy was by her side again. The only activity on the base was near the murky soup of a river. The day got much warmer.

Alexander turned to Richter. "First of all," he said, "I can't think straight until I get a smoke. Second," he continued, "scientific evidence may still be deficient in deducing the workings of that girl's cross purposes, but our second empirical observation has told us a little bit more about her." He paused for the inhale of his invisible cigarette. "The *first* thing Moon Lai does when she wakes up in the morning—before mothers, before babies, before washing herself—is disappear into that hut. And comes out twenty minutes later with filthy rags."

"It's probably not your son, Major Barrington," said Elkins by way of comfort. "One-eyed, eight-fingered NVA whores are very fickle. It could be another injured john."

"Elkins, for fuck's sake!" said Richter. "Is this the time for jokes?"

"I wasn't joking, sir," Elkins said feebly.

But Alexander couldn't help it. He was tormented by the sight of the pregnant young woman. His judgment was failing him. In her actions, in her movements, in her posture, in the sweet expression on her face, no matter how hard to see, to decipher through the distance and the distorting magnifying lenses—she reminded him of Tatiana. A half-blind, mutilated Vietnamese Tatiana. Where was Anthony? Was Alexander wrong about everything? He was weary and troubled—and in the throes of grim nicotine withdrawal. He didn't know what to think. What would Tania think?

Miserably he watched the camp all morning and then said to Richter that either they had to go in to get Moon Lai now and not a second later or he needed to go have a cigarette now and not a second later. Richter was amused, mockingly inquiring what in the world did Alexander do in the past, when he was, say, in prison and was denied cigarettes for weeks at a time as punishment. Alexander, who was not amused in the least, unmockingly replied that unless Richter wanted to string him up by his ankles and hang him naked and upside down for eight hours, he would let him have a cigarette. Richter solemnly considered both options, but finally gave Alexander and Elkins permission to walk two kilometers into the woods. Elkins, rifle in front, could barely keep up. Deep in the jungle, Alexander sank onto his haunches in the wild bush and gratefully smoked down three cigarettes before he uttered a word. He found it only mildly ironic that he had gone nearly four years without a woman, yet could last barely twenty-four hours without nicotine.

"What's up, Ant's father?" said Elkins, smoking happily, and not nearly as desperately. "Worried about the snatch?"

Alexander shook his head. "I am, but that's not it." He dragged his smoke out because he couldn't drag his words out.

"What? You can't believe your son and my best friend fell for someone like her?"

Another cigarette. "That's a little more along what I'm thinking."

"Major Barrington," said Elkins, patting him comrade-like on the arm. "I'm assuming you don't know this, but to say you've fallen for a young Asian beauty, even a crippled beauty, is redundant. The

Asian girls are too heady for the white man. We have no weapons against them. That Anthony fell in love with that girl is now becoming quickly secondary to our main problem. What we want to know is—did he fall for the Mata Hari? Did she lure him here, her new husband, a soon-to-be-father, and then betray him?"

Alexander smoked. "Elkins," he said, "that *is* what I'm thinking. But what I don't understand is how he could have continued with her *beyond* the DMZ."

Elkins shook his head. "You're not seeing things anymore. It's okay. You don't have to." He paused. "You forget how you scolded me for not seeing that we were ambushed by her eighteen months ago in Hué. I had no idea what you were talking about. Well, now I do. If she was part of that ambush, and he was blind to it then, even before he fell for her, he would've easily come with her quite far north after he had."

Alexander nodded. That's what he thought, too. But *this* far? What confounded him was the observable change in Mata Hari's movements as she walked to that hut and then crawled back. Alexander couldn't reconcile what he had observed of her as contrasted with the things he suspected of her. He sat on the ground, thinking and smoking, and didn't tell Elkins any of his worst fears about Anthony's fate at the hands of the NVA.

Alexander smoked eight cigarettes before he staggered back, much slower on the return, and collapsed next to Mercer, feeling woozy and addled, but a little better having smoked, and better still, sitting next to Anthony's friends, as if by being near them he was a little closer to his son. Exchanging a look with Elkins, Mercer cleared his throat.

"What, Sergeant?" Alexander said. "Don't be shy. Say anything. We're in this together."

Diffidently, Mercer said, "I just wanted to say, sir, Ant was full of stories about you at war. How you escaped from Colditz. I think the entire SOG ground studies group in all three command controls knows your Colditz escape story."

Smiling a little, Alexander nodded, allowing himself to be pleased with his boy.

"Tell me, sir, is it true?" said Mercer, his breath bated, "did you really scale down ninety feet of wall and cliff in sixty seconds in the dark?"

Alexander laughed lightly. "No, I think the last forty-five feet we scaled after the sixty seconds were up."

"But no one escapes from Colditz, that's what we heard."

"Well, no, some escape. They're just all caught later." Alexander paused. "Like I was caught." He lowered his head, feeling a singe of himself sitting on the frozen February ground with Tatiana's dead brother in his arms, waiting for the German guards to come and catch him. His mouth twisted as he looked away from Mercer. Not all of it was just stories.

"But what about the Gulag camp? Didn't you get yourself and your wife to Berlin with a Soviet army following you?"

"I did," said Alexander, "and you know what, gentlemen? The Soviets themselves may have a hard time letting go of that last one, which could be the reason we're all here. Now if you'll excuse me." He moved away to sit next to Ha Si who mercifully didn't ask him any questions.

Alexander spent a long time cleaning and inspecting his weapons.

The day ticked slowly by.

They had to decide right away, did they go in first thing the next morning? Ha Si wanted to wait another day. Richter growled, Alexander growled. But the ungrowling Ha Si maintained that unless they had an indication from Moon Lai of a punctual morning pattern, they were dooming themselves to failure, and with odds already so long, Ha Si thought they should do everything to make them a little shorter. Richter and Alexander grudgingly agreed, and so they waited out the rest of the tortuous day and another awake and active Martian night, during which the Vietnamese men came and went as if at a Saturday bazaar in New York City, a bazaar with Soviet-made helicopters coming and going, dropping off armies and supplies.

It settled down finally, and then promptly at eight in the morning, Moon Lai emerged from her hut and started to her destination. Ha Si, not even looking at her anymore but only at his watch, said he was satisfied. Alexander said, "What, now that you know she is as punctual as a German, you feel better?" He smiled.

"I do not understand what you are talking about, Major Barrington," Ha Si said seriously. "I do not know any Germans. But yes. I feel better. Tomorrow morning, we go in when the guards are asleep. I will help them sleep. They will remain knocked out half the day."

"Let *me* shoot them, Ha Si," said Alexander, lifting his rifle. "They'll be knocked out a little longer than that."

"As you wish, sir." Ha Si smiled. "The girl goes inside the hut, we go in behind her. A word of warning—we are probably going to have to go down into the tunnels. Down there better not to shoot, better to use the knives, but if we shoot, we shoot only with our silenced Rugers. The sound of a charge going off is like an explosion."

Richter refused to let Alexander go with Ha Si to capture Moon Lai. "That's an order. That's final. No. We have nine other guys who can go. You're *not* going. One of the Yards will go. They're still like death."

Alexander was barely listening to Richter, as he was getting his ammunition ready. "Colonel," he said, "I'm also still like death."

"You haven't stopped pacing for five days!" exclaimed Richter. "You can't sit for five minutes without a cigarette. I said no."

"And yet," said Alexander, "I managed to survive six days with six men in one foxhole. And months in the woods. And in a cell in isolation for eight months. I'll be fine."

"That was twenty years ago! And in the meantime, sneaking up and scaring your mouse of a wife half to death on Halloween does not count as honing your recon moves."

"Anthony told you that?" said Alexander, disgusted.

"I don't think that boy can keep his mouth shut about any-thing," said Richter, staring at Alexander in a peculiar way that made Alexander look away.

Elkins said, "Let him go, Colonel. Mercer, Tojo and I will have his back from the trench. Ha Si will send us a sign if he is in trouble and needs help."

"*What* fucking trench?" Richter said, nearly yelling.

"The trench we're going to dig as soon as we get permission to dig one, sir."

Richer gave permission for Elkins and Mercer to go dig a trench directly across from Moon Lai's hooch, and then took Ha Si aside. Glancing over at Alexander, Richter said, "Promise me you'll watch his back." He paused, and added quieter, "the way you watched his son's back."

"Will do, Colonel," said Ha Si. "But hopefully better than I watched over his son. The boy *is* missing."

"You see how wired he is?" said Richter. "He's thinking only of his son. He's going to get reckless. All right? Take Tojo with you. He can help you."

Shaking his head, Ha Si said, "Three is too much. And Tojo is a Sumo. He is very good in a fight, but we want no noise. Major Barrington is almost as quiet as I am." That was the highest compliment Ha Si could pay.

They waited out the rest of the night hidden in the grasses and the rocks. They slept briefly and badly, from anticipation of the morning, and from fear that snakes would come out, smelling food and men. Alexander kept watch with Ha Si and Elkins. Then he went and sat by Richter. Nobody could sleep, even though they had to, even though they had been ordered to. Alexander thought his own freefalling anxiety was enough to keep all of Saigon awake.

"Don't worry about the men, Alexander," Richter said. "You worry about nothing but yourself, do you hear me, about nothing but yourself, and you regret nothing. This is Ant's team. He's their commander. They will go into the fire for him. The Yards, too." Richter paused. "Ha Si especially." When Alexander gave him a quizzical look, Richter nodded. "Ha Si was close to your Anthony. I'm almost surprised Ha Si didn't know about Moon Lai." After too long and heavy a pause he added, "This business with Moon Lai is nasty. I feel it."

"You should worry less, Tom." Alexander was worrying plenty for the twelve of them.

Richter shrugged. "Can't help it. What if they have more of our guys? Then what do we do? They're so well situated here."

"They're fucking idiots," said Alexander. "What kind of fighter builds his base in a hole in a valley surrounded by high ground, where an attacking force can entrench on top of a hill and with hardly any men grease them one at a time? Tom, you know this better than anyone—you who nearly single-handedly flattened North Korea until there wasn't a building standing, you who firebombed them into submission—if only we had invaded North Vietnam proper, the war would be long over and we wouldn't be in this predicament now."

"Let's try to find Ant first, all right?"

Alexander smiled, palming and smelling his cigarettes. "All I'm saying is he who controls the highlands controls everything."

"Don't forget to radio me every five minutes, Major Control," said Richter, "give me a heads-up."

"I don't even have to call my wife every five minutes," said Alexander.

"If shit starts flying, you radio me instantly, I won't care how much noise our chopper makes; it's coming in, and we evacuate.

You have to get up the mountain and just one klick in, to that little clearing. Ten minutes, so we just have to pray we can outrun them."

"We will outrun them."

"Thing is, soldier," said Richter, "you can't run forward and shoot backward at the same time."

"Watch me."

"One klick, Alexander."

Alexander studied Richter. "Tom, what's the matter?"

Richter shook his head. "They have some heavy shit down there. The place is lousy with Sappers." Sappers were NVA demolition commandos. "Vikki is already so upset with me for losing Ant in the first place. I keep telling her I didn't do it on purpose." He coughed. "I'll feel better if we find him. But if things go south, I can only take so much grief."

"And then a little bit more," said Alexander.

They sat. Richter asked, "You lived like this for ten years. You miss the mad minute?" He smiled. "Do you keep hearing the far drums beating the long roll? Our Supreme Allied Commander MacArthur heard them all his life."

"And not just him," Alexander said, smiling at Richter's sheepish expression before admitting, "I do miss the good men. Occasionally the idle bullshit. And I don't mind the weapons." He nodded sheepishly himself. "But . . . as for the rest of it, you won't believe it, but I hate to be wet, hate to be filthy, hate to bleed, hate to lose my guys, and I quite like my wife."

Richter smiled in assent, was thoughtful. "I liked my wife, too," he said, pausing. "Still do a little bit."

Alexander was not looking at Richter.

"I can't defend myself, Alexander. This here is my life. Once it mattered to Vikki, but now she is very much over me." He sighed. "It's funny, but the older I get, the more I wish she weren't quite as . . . over me." He struggled with something. "I'm not explaining well."

"Don't need to explain anything, man. Really. Not a thing."

"God! Whenever I think of her now, the thing I come back to is that first time I saw her, back in 1948. She had come to DC to meet you guys; she was disheveled and harried, running to Tania and Anthony. Her black hair was flying, she was crying, and she was scooping up your boy into the air, suffocating him with her arms and her loud kisses. I think that's when I fell in love with her—right then and there, watching her love on him." An anguished cry left Richter's chest. " She was so . . . emotional and Italian. *Apassionata*. I liked that. I needed that." He broke off for a long while. "We were so strong once, but now it's just for show," he said quietly. "I do what I want. She does what she wants." He hung his head. "Not really a marriage, is it?"

"No," said Alexander. "Not really."

"Yes," Richter whispered, "but I know that when *I* cross the river, the last breath on my lips won't be the Corps and it won't be this."

Alexander lowered his head in his mute, conflicted compassion.

"Everything good with you and Tania?" Richter asked much later when they were still reluctantly tensely awake.

"Yes, man," said Alexander, staring below into the black valley with the little green men like Martians, invading earth. "Everything is what it's always been."

"That's good." Richter said. "That's very good."

They fell asleep eventually, against the rocks, next to each other.

Then it was dawn. At seven in the unseasonably warm and cloudless morning, Ha Si and Alexander, armed, helmeted, ready, moved down the hill single file, with Elkins, Mercer and Tojo behind them. Richter and his six Yards had spread out and hid at the top of the hill amid the boulders, setting up their M-60 machine gun on a tripod. Ten 100-round bandoliers lay close, plus two extra barrels when the grease gun started smoking from the heat. Despite all their precautions, the white men couldn't help it: they were all nervous about a high-stakes mission without the cover of night. On the plus side, the crisp morning was dazzling and visibility was good.

From slightly above, Ha Si shot his opium darts one by one into the backs or shoulders or necks of the sleeping guards. *Whoosh*— and then he moved through the elephant grass to the next one. *Whoosh*. Behind him, Alexander went up to the guards and emptied their AK47s, throwing the banana clips to Elkins and Mercer in the trench. He left the weapons with the slumped-over guards because he didn't know how observant Moon Lai was. They jumped into the trench to hide until she came.

At eight, Moon Lai slowly walked down the path with clean bandages and came to the last hut barely thirty feet away from the troops. Opening the door, she disappeared inside. As soon as she was in, Alexander and Ha Si, silent like tigers, made their way to the hooch. They stood, stood, and then flung open the door and in one movement were through.

Inside was empty—a grassy space, perhaps twelve feet square, and no Moon Lai. Ha Si pointed to the secret trap door in the ground. Had they not known to look for it, they never would have seen it. The huts *were* decoys, empty of life.

Ha Si pulled the grass hatch open slightly to see which way it hinged. Turned out, it just lay on top like a manhole cover. The ladder faced away from the back wall of the hut and that's where Alexander and Ha Si planted so that Moon Lai's back would be to them when she ascended the ladder.

Twenty unbearable mute minutes crawled by. It was damp and fluid and sticky in the hooch, it was stifling and sweaty. Though Alexander listened, there was no noise from below. "Are you a Buddhist, Ha Si? An animist?" he whispered, pulling up and kissing his cross.

"No," Ha Si replied, kissing his own cross. "I'm a good Catholic boy like you and your son, Major Barrington."

A slight creaking of the ladder alerted them. They both crouched, got ready, barely breathing. The manhole cover was lifted by a small, crippled hand. She struggled, having a hard time pulling herself and her belly up onto the straw floor. Her back was to them. Alexander smelled the sulfur of medicine, he smelled the salt of blood, he saw the empty opium vials she put on the ground next to the bloodied rags. Whoever she was taking care of was not only hurt but in pain.

Alexander and Ha Si waited two more seconds.

She was barely out and still on her haunches when Alexander, not giving her a chance to stand or to see them in the peripheral vision of her eye, sprang on her, knocking her down on the ground, his arm over her arms, his hand over her mouth. Instantly Ha Si pulled the manhole cover closed so no one could hear them from below. Holding her very tightly, Alexander leaned to her ear and whispered, "Where is Anthony?"

The woman went into convulsions in her struggle against him. She tried to scream, to turn her head, he had to hold her so firmly it must have hurt her, but she fought anyway and flailed her legs until Ha Si grabbed hold of them, while Alexander gripped her around her chest with one arm, keeping the other over her mouth.

She tried to bite him. He had to snap her jaws shut. Turning her head to him so she could see his grim face, he said, "Stop moving. Stop fighting." He gave her head a yank. Since he didn't think she understood him, he jerked her head again to get her to stop her frenzy. A stick-on bandage covered one eye, but her other, seeing eye, very near his face, was black and round with—what *was* that? Strangely, it didn't look like fear. Despite the pressure on her neck, she kept trying to bite him, kept shaking her head, kept trying to free herself from him.

"*Dâu lá* Anthony?" Ha Si said in Vietnamese, while tying her feet together with rope. "*Où est* Anthony?" he asked in French.

She kept shaking her head in Alexander's hands. Shaking or trying to free herself?

"Where is Anthony?" Alexander asked in English. "*Gde* Anthony?" he whispered in Russian. She blinked. She blinked at *Russian*?

Alexander couldn't let go of her mouth until he was sure she wouldn't scream, because if she screamed they'd have to kill her and run, and their op would be finished before it began, and they still would know nothing about Anthony. "Should we take her into the trench?" Alexander asked Ha Si, panting.

She groaned, shaking her head against his hand.

Alexander looked down at her. "*She* understands me?"

She nodded. Recognition was in her eye. She was looking at him as if she knew him.

"Are you going to scream?" he asked.

She shook her head.

"You speak English?"

She nodded, but he couldn't trust her. What if she screamed? One of her hands had gotten loose from Alexander, and she reached over and grabbed the dirty bandage lying on the ground and waved it up and down—like a white flag.

After exchanging a look with Alexander, Ha Si pulled out his SOG knife and stuck it into Moon Lai's neck. "Listen to me," he said. "He will let go of your mouth, but if you utter one sound above a whisper, the knife is going into your throat, do you understand?"

She nodded. Alexander still held her head in a twist. "Even before he gets to you with his knife," he said, "I'm going to break your fucking neck if you raise your voice. Do you understand *that*?"

She nodded.

"Do you know where Anthony is?"

She shook her head.

"Do you want us to take you into the woods?" said Ha Si. "Two men to take you into the woods and keep you there until you tell us where he is? Because that's next for you."

Alexander frowned at Ha Si. Were these kinds of threats really necessary against a pregnant woman? Moon Lai saw his ambivalence. Ha Si, ignoring him, was undeterred. "Stop looking at him. Look at *me*. Where is Anthony?"

She shrugged again, struggled again. Alexander's hand remained over her mouth.

"If you don't tell us," Ha Si said, "we'll snatch your mother. And the little boy. Nod if you understand."

The girl nodded.

"Where is he?" Alexander asked in a milder tone than Ha Si, despite his firm hold on her fragile throat. He applied extra pressure. "Is my son down there?" he asked her. "Is he in the hole?" When she did not reply, Alexander yanked her neck back. She gasped against his palm but did not reply. She was a pregnant woman! This was *insane*. "Please," he said to her, moving off her body, no longer straddling her, letting her lie on her side. "Please. I don't want to hurt you. I just want my son. Tell me if he is down below, that's all I want." Taking a chance, Alexander let go of her mouth.

She just lay on the ground, panting and limp, not trying to get away, saying nothing, her brown eye moist and knowing, blinking at him. Ha Si backed away a few inches, his knife still trained on her, and Alexander moved away three feet—to get away from her heaving belly. He wished he could close his eyes and not look at her. His instincts were about to fail him, looking at a tiny woman so heavily pregnant, in a physical fight with two armed soldiers. It was too fucked up. "Please," he said, "just tell me where he is."

Moon Lai opened her mouth and spoke softly in halting but very good English. "You know," she said, "he assured me you would never find him. But I told him you would find a way."

No closing of eyes now. Eyes were opened wide. "*What?*" Alexander whispered.

"It won't do *you* any good to pretend to be surprised," she said.

"Who is surprised? He is alive?"

"I do not know," she said in her spare voice. "He was barely alive when they took him from here."

Took him from here! Alexander couldn't speak. He almost cried.

"You are too late. He is near Hanoi now," she said. "Soon they will take him to a Castro camp near China. And then USSR."

Groaning, exhaling, Alexander sank into the earth.

She was watching him unblinking. They were all on the ground, Moon Lai near the manhole, half-lying down. Alexander aghast and against the wall, legs spread out, Ha Si close to her, gripping the pointed knife.

"I know where he is. I will take you to him," she said. "You come with me. He was alive when he left here. But we do not have much time."

Alexander had lost his power of speech.

"You are a fucking liar," said Ha Si. "Whose bandages are you changing twice a day?"

Moon Lai smiled softly. "This is a transit camp. We have other POW here," she said. "I help them, too, the way I helped him." Sitting up, she straightened out and brushed the straw off her face.

"Keep your hands in front of you," Ha Si said, moving closer.

"Okay, okay." She put them on her belly and cringed as if she were in pain. She was trying to control her breathing.

If Alexander didn't listen to her words and looked at her mute, she was just a young *pregnant* girl pleading for compassion from men. Perhaps pregnant with Anthony's baby. Oh God. If one didn't look at the patch over her face, you could see how fresh she was, how small and pretty. "How old are you?" he asked numbly.

"Seventeen."

His heart nearly gave out. He glanced at Ha Si for strength.

Ha Si, emotionless, his eyes brutal, shook his head at Alexander, as if to say, buck up, soldier. "You are not seventeen," he said. "Maybe a hundred and seventeen. Do not lie to the major. How old are you?"

"Twenty-six," she said. "Born in 1943. Like his son."

Alexander was surprised; she looked young like a child. "Are there guards down there?" he asked, frowning at her lies.

"Many. Guarding the POW. But what does it matter? He is not here."

"Armed guards?"

"Heavily."

They were quiet.

"You lay in wait for the American patrols in Hué," Alexander said. "You lay in wait for my son."

"I was just bait," she said with a shrug. "Usually we killed them then and there. Not your son. He is some warrior. He is the reason I am half blind."

"Ah," said Ha Si, "but in the country of the blind, the one-eyed man is king."

"I do not care for your insults about my country," said Moon Lai without looking at him. She spoke in a gentle, non-inflammatory tone. Her manner was subservient. "It is your country, too, Bannha." She never once looked at Ha Si. Her eye was trained only on Alexander. "In Hué, Anthony thought he was saving me. He was so noble and decent. Such an easy mark, your son," she said softly. "The easiest. Just a few days and he was wholly addicted." Her eye smiled approvingly at Alexander. "But really, I must tell you, you did not teach him very well. He is too trusting. Though, of course, it is probably the only reason he is still alive today. Because I was going to kill him like I kill them all—kill him with opium, with deadly vipers." She had a lilting voice, sweet. "But he started telling me such interesting stories about his life! I waited to listen. He told me a little at a time, but when we married, he told me *everything*. I was just a Vietnamese whore he saved, a simple village girl desperately in need of his protection." Her eye glistened and shined as she spoke of him. "He told me so much, thinking I barely understood. And I sat and listened. He told me about his mother, the Soviet escapee, and about his father, the American who came to the Soviet Union, who had served in the Red Army, who escaped twice, who killed Soviet interrogators and NKVD border troops, who escaped from a maximum security Soviet prison and was now in U.S. military intelligence." Moon Lai looked as though she were tenderly reminiscing. "He was so thorough, we barely even had to go to your files to confirm his stories."

"Oh, my God, who *are* you?" Alexander whispered, his hands shaking.

"I am his wife," Moon Lai said in her most pleasant voice. "I am his pregnant wife and I was his nurse."

Alexander was grateful he was sitting. Once he had given *all* of himself away, the same reckless way, to a small, soft, very young Soviet factory girl, whom he had barely known, sitting on a bench under the summer elms in the Italian Gardens in Leningrad. Pale and trembling, watching this girl, he asked, "How did you get him to come with you all the way here?" He was looking for something from her, a small tremulous clue to one thing and one thing only: Where was Anthony?

Moon Lai shrugged. "He came peacefully. When he got suspicious, a few miles south of the DMZ, I helped him go to sleep, and when he woke up, he was here. It was not even a fight."

Alexander was mute, struck dumb by the vision of his son, waking up to find himself here.

Moon Lai continued in a murmur. "But once here, Anthony suddenly needed so much persuasion to keep on talking! Which is when all our trouble with him began. Because when he did talk, he told us the most damnable lies about the American military positions. He sent us on crazy missions that ended in large losses for us; we kept walking right into ambushes and booby traps. And he kept trying to kill our guards, succeeding three times, twice while he was still shackled! He became very dangerous. We had no choice but to incapacitate him and then to transfer him."

Incapacitate him? mouthed Alexander.

"Every *other* word out of your mouth," said Ha Si, "is a fucking lie. He is down there right now."

"No, he is not," Moon Lai said without argument. "But there *are* fifty guards there with the prisoners. You two want to take them on in the dark tunnels by yourselves? Please—go right ahead."

"Fifty guards?" said Ha Si. "How many prisoners do you have down there?"

Not answering, Moon Lai said to Alexander, "Tell your Bannha to take his weapon from me, Commander. I am your daughter-in-law. This child could be your grandchild. The knife comes off my neck *right* now."

After a frayed moment Alexander motioned to Ha Si who, with supreme reluctance, moved himself and his weapon away and behind Moon Lai.

"Is it . . . Anthony's child?" Alexander asked haltingly.

Her one eye stared right back at his two, all three brown-hued, a telescoping triangle playing for keeps, all unblinking and unflinching. "Commander, what are you asking me? You came to Vietnam, abandoned your family, put your own life in mortal danger, all to see your son again. I am about to help you do that, if you will be reasonable, and you are sitting here asking me about"—she pointed to her large belly—"this? What does it matter?"

Now Alexander flinched and blinked. "What does it *matter*?" He exhaled. "It matters a great, big, fucking deal. Don't evade me, don't defraud me. Can you say one fucking thing without dissembling? It's a simple question. Yes or no. Is it his child?"

She bowed her head as if she were praying. "Alexander Barrington," said Moon Lai, lifting her steady gaze to him, "what do *you* believe in? Do *you*, of all people, not know that your new country is at war with your old country? You are in the middle of a very hot war; shouldn't *you*, of all people, care about this most? Who cares about babies? What do you think is going on around here? Do you know that your country is also at war with *my* country? We are fighting for the very soul of Vietnam! Vietnam will be *one*. One Communist Republic of Vietnam. Nothing you Americans—or the stooges you call your South Vietnamese allies—can do to change that. We will not rest until you go. Southeast Asia: Laos, Cambodia, Vietnam, they are not your business. They are our business. Instead you come here and pretend to fight." She laughed easily. "You call this fighting? We call it losing."

"We are not losing," said Alexander. "We have not lost one single fucking engagement against you since this damn war began."

"You are losing regardless. Do you know why? Because you're wasting your time dumping bombs from safe air, going on recon missions like this one, and fucking whores."

"Like you?"

"But you know who *is* fighting?" she went on. "We are. The Soviets train us, and teach us, and educate us, and arm us. They teach us your language, Commander—Russian, English, and the language of war—which is the only language *you* understand. We fight with their old weapons and the new weapons you leave behind. We fight without boots and without helmets and without C-rations. You burn us with napalm? We bandage ourselves and keep going. You kill our crops with Agent Blue? We eat grass and keep going. We do not care about your bombs and your chemicals. We do not care if we die. Because we are fighting for our life, for our very existence—the way the Red Army once fought Hitler. Victory was the only option. That is the way Americans fought in World War Two, and for the first few months in Korea. But here in Vietnam, what you are doing is pretending to fight. That is why you will never win, despite having the most disciplined, best trained, best equipped force in the world. Because you are unwilling to sacrifice even fifty thousand of your men to defeat communism in Indochina, while we will sacrifice our man to the last one to defeat *you*. We will sacrifice *millions* of our men, tens of millions, not a lousy fifty thousand! No price is too high to pay, no sacrifice is large enough. We believe in this war, and you do not. *You* yourself do not believe in it, your *country* does not believe in it, your jodies at home do not believe in it. Your politicians and your journalists *certainly* do not believe in it." Moon Lai smiled warmly. "In fact, they do so much of our vital work for us, destabilizing the will of our American enemy. And once you leave, the South Vietnamese, despite all your training, will not last a week."

She spoke so softly; her voice was melodious; it never rose above a purr; words fluttered like butterflies off her tongue. She smiled! But these were the words she was saying. A poem, of all things, came back to Alexander. When she spoke what a tender voice she used . . . John Dryden, how had it gone? . . . Like flakes of feathered snow, it melted as it left her mouth. But her words were incongruous. Alexander wanted to say, I don't understand a word you're saying; speak English.

But he understood.

He was imprisoned by her voice and her large belly. She looked like Tania when she was eight months pregnant, when she could not get off the couch or the bed without Alexander's help, when she could not turn over without rocking and rolling, when he walked around after her with his hands constantly out, in case she tripped or slipped or wavered.

Alexander wavered. In response to what he had just heard, the only thing he uttered was, "The South Vietnamese also believe in their war, no?"

"No. They are weak, and they are led by the nose by you. Vietnam will be one despite them, and despite the mercenaries you send here to help them."

"My son is not a fucking mercenary."

"Your son was not, no," Moon Lai said, motionless and calm. "He was one among half a million men." She paused and blinked. "But do you know what? He did not believe in this war either. Oh, he thought he did. Until he met me, he thought he did. And when he married me, he still thought he did. But he never even asked me if I was South Vietnamese! He married me instantly when I told him I was having a baby, and he never even asked if it was his."

Alexander, his fists clenched, compassion for her draining out of him, said, "Yes. Because he believed in *you*."

Moon Lai shook her head. "Only superficially. When he opened his eyes here in Kum Kau and saw where he was and pleaded for me, the interrogator brought me to him, pregnant and roped up and told him to speak. Anthony spoke all right, but do you know what he said?" She took a breath. "'I don't give a fuck what you do to her,' said your son. 'And that baby isn't mine. They say that a wife is only for one man. But sometimes she is for two men, and sometimes for three. And *my* wife fucked every American soldier from here to Saigon, lying on her back trying to ambush them with her pussy like she ambushed me. She may as well have had razor blades in it. Kill her in front of me. I don't care.'" Moon Lai smirked casually even as a tremble passed her face. "Needless to say, of course, they did not kill me. But my point to you is made. He did not believe in me."

"Believe in you? What the fuck are you talking about, believe in you?" said Alexander, gratified that at that terrible moment Anthony finally saw the truth—Anthony, who once thought all the world was good. "My son finally learned he had found something lower than a two-dollar whore," said Alexander, "and he wanted you to know it."

"Yes, that is right," she said. "So love was not completely blind, was it?" Moon Lai composed her mouth. "You should be grateful to us, because it was here in Kum Kau that your son finally found out what he himself believed in. It was not the war against communism, and it certainly was not me. Until he found out what he believed in, we could not make any progress with him. Nothing we could say could convince him to confide in us. We threatened him with a transfer to the Castro camp. We brought in our best interrogators, we used our strongest methods—"

Alexander flinched and flinched again.

"—Nothing was making an impression on him. He cursed us in English, Russian, Spanish—even our own. He told us to kill him. We kept him in water, we deprived him of water. We beat him, we starved him, we burned him. We kept him with rats, we did . . . other things to him. And then I would come and minister to him." Her voice was soothing. "I ministered so *thoroughly* to him. I was his only friend, and his *wife*, and he was chained and naked and had no way out. He had to let me *touch* him. What punishment that must have been for him, what *torture*." Her hands were tensing slightly, lying less languidly on her stomach. "You are recoiling, Commander, why?" Moon Lai relaxed her hands. "Finally we figured out a way. Pretending to give up, we said to him that we have kept him hidden long enough. He was no longer of any use to us. We were going to notify his government that he was still alive and an NVA prisoner. Maybe they would negotiate for Anthony Barrington."

Alexander paled.

Moon Lai smiled. Her teeth were dazzling.

"Exactly." She nodded. "You are very good, Anthony's father. You see things. We said, your parents will be so glad to know you are alive, a POW in North Vietnam. But Anthony did not seem to think so at all. He said he would tell us everything, to keep his name from appearing on the POW rolls, and you from finding out he had been taken prisoner. How much valuable classified intel he gave us then! After all," said Moon Lai, looking straight at Alexander, "he knows you are a wanted traitor and deserter, who killed sixty-eight of our men to escape his just punishment."

Our men?

"And so now, Commander," said Moon Lai, "are you coming with me? Because your son is waiting. Is your wife here, too, with you, perhaps?" She waited for his answer and when Alexander did not speak, she whispered, "What a pity."

"Who *are* you?" Alexander whispered, inaudibly, trying not to gasp.

Her voice finally catching and breaking, Moon Lai said, "I want you to know I couldn't help it. I *loved* him." Her eye filled up, spilled over. "He was so . . . open. But you ask me who I am. Your son taught me this. Ask yourself these three questions, Moon Lai, he said to me, and you will know who you are. What do you believe in? What do you hope for? But most important, what do you love? And I will tell you. I am a Vietnamese Communist. That is what I believe in. That is what I hope for. That is what I love."

Before she was finished speaking, before Alexander could move, could draw breath, a shiny sickle flashed in Moon Lai's small hand, a splint blade that swung forward and plunged hilt-deep into Alexander's inner thigh. She aimed straight at his femoral artery. He jerked in a half-inch, half-second reflex and she missed— just—but she was lightning swift, and in the next inhale, without losing her balance, she pulled the blade out, ready to thrust the knife into Ha Si's face as he moved on her. But Alexander grabbed her wrist, and Ha Si had his own knife well in hand. She opened her mouth to scream and Ha Si yanked her head back and sliced his blade deep and wide across her throat. He pitched her on the ground away from them, and with her gurgling sounds behind him, dropped his knife and grabbed Alexander's leg.

They both struggled with their hands over the red river, fighting to cover the deep wound. With one hand Ha Si pulled out a QuikClot coagulant out of his first-air pouch. It was painless, sterile and worked by physically absorbing the liquid from the blood. Alexander pressed it into the wound; grabbing a vial of silver nitrate from the pouch, Ha Si poured an unconscionable amount over the leg and yanked out an emergency kit. He laid the primary bandage on top of the QuikClot, strapped the pressure bar against Alexander's thigh, tightened with adhesive and pulled the cords. He wrapped the secondary dressing twice around. All of this took no more than thirty seconds.

"I can't believe I wasn't more careful," Alexander breathed out.

"You were plenty careful," said Ha Si, dripping more silver nitrate over the bandages. "Your son got hooked and never saw the sickle until it was too late."

"You wrapped it like a tourniquet," said Alexander.

"The blood has to stop, Commander," Ha Si said quietly.

"The blood will stop but I'll lose my fucking leg." Alexander loosened the dressing.

"You will have your life," said Ha Si.

"I need my leg," Alexander said. "He is down there and we have to get him immediately before someone notices she's missing. And easy with the nitrate."

They waited a few moments to see if the blood would stop. "How do you know he's down there?" asked Ha Si. "I was bluffing her." He paused. "But I told you. She would be dead before she gave anything away."

"She gave it away," Alexander said, holding his leg, his hands red-gluey, sticky. "She couldn't help what she is either. He's down below." He broke off, glanced behind Ha Si, breathed hard, stared down at his leg to *retain* his composure, stared down at his profusely bleeding leg to keep his voice and his face, so that he could speak his next words to the Yard. "Bannha," Alexander said, with his head down, "could you—turn her away from me? Could you—turn her so her back is to me? Please." He didn't look up as Ha Si crawled across the straw. Alexander heard him flip Moon Lai's pregnant body away. He breathed out.

"It is all right, Commander," said Ha Si. "Do you want some morphine?"

"Get the fuck out of here, morphine. I won't be able to get up."

"You think you are going to get up now?"

"Just stop the bleeding, will you?" The room, so hot before, was not just hot now, the air was wet with floating red particles and the hooch began to smell like rust, like magnetic metallic compounds, like they were sitting in a blood smelt. It was suffocating. They were breathing in four quarts of Moon Lai's iron—and some quarts of Alexander's. Silently they held their bandages and clothes and hands and silver metallic poisons against the slick thigh, and waited out the seconds.

"You forgot there are no civilians on the other side," said Ha Si. "They are all enemy combatants. It is war, and you forgot even as her vicious words were reminding you. Her pregnancy was such a powerful weapon against you. She knew Ant had to learn it from somewhere. You did get careless."

"Wrong," said Alexander. "Rather, you're right—I wasn't listening to what she was saying. I didn't give a shit about her principles or beliefs or whatever other fucking thing she was telling me. And I've heard so many vicious things in my life, that frankly it's just water off my back. I was listening for one thing and one thing only—whether I had been right in what I had observed of her, walking into this hut and walking out with lead on her shoulders. That lead was love. Every time she went down she was devastated from seeing him." The opium vials told Alexander more than he wanted to know. "Once I knew she loved him, I knew she wouldn't let him go into the Cuban Program. I knew he was down below."

"Yes, but once you knew it, she had to kill you," said Ha Si. "She sacrificed her own life, her baby's life, to kill you."

"Did she kill me?"

"I cannot stitch this," said Ha Si. "The wound is deep. You need—"

"Ha Si," said Alexander. "I know what I need. To get my son. Now stop my fucking leg from bleeding and let's get to it."

Ha Si held him tighter. The seconds ticked. One minute became two. "You are lucky," he said. "She pulled the knife out too quick trying to kill me. Look, the blood is already thickening. Let us wait five more minutes." He gave Alexander some water.

Gulping it down, Alexander said, "We don't have five minutes.

We don't have five seconds. Let's go." He got up and fell down. He couldn't stand on his numb leg.

"Oh, we are *fucked*," said Ha Si. "We have to get out of here, ASAP."

"No." Alexander flipped on his radio. "Viper, viper," he said into the VHF transmitter. "Come in."

In a moment, Richter's anxious voice sounded. "What's wrong?"

"Back-up now," said Alexander. "Mercer, Elkins, Tojo. Send them in, tell them absolute quiet. Now."

Ha Si was staring at him as Alexander continued to gulp the water. "I'll be fine," he said.

"*Five* of us are going down this ladder one at a time?"

"Well, you heard her. Something out of her mouth had to be the truth, no? She said many guards. She said other POW. Who's going to help them? Who is going to help Anthony? We need Tojo."

"If she was telling the truth, there will not be enough of us. If she was lying, there will be too many."

Alexander stared steadily at the Montagnard. "Ha Si," he said, "you are going to pull up the cover, you are going to jump in, we're going after you, we find Anthony, we get out." He held his leg tightly. "The guards are likely sleeping. Day is night here, or haven't you noticed? For the cave rats, too."

Ha Si opened his mouth.

"Bannha," Alexander said grimly, "this is absolutely not the fucking time to argue."

Shaking his head, Ha Si raised his compliant hand. "Yes, Commander. Every time you move your leg, you are reopening your wound, is all I will say."

"I have to get my son. You do understand that, don't you?"

"I do," said Ha Si, taking out his knives, his Ruger, his StarLight. "My son was killed by the Vietminh during the land reforms of 1956. He was twenty. And he was on their side. He was a Vietminh, too." He paused, his black eyes blackening. "Like I was."

Alexander and Ha Si stared at each other for an interminable moment and then Alexander closed his eyes, slumping against the wall of the hooch. "Was she right, Ha Si, my Vietminh friend?" he whispered. "Do we just believe in the wrong things to fight this war to victory?"

"She was right, Major Barrington," Ha Si said. "We believe in different things."

Seconds later, Elkins, Mercer and Tojo were inside the hut.

"Holy fuck!" said Elkins, seeing Alexander. He *was* quite a sight, his right leg soaked in blood from his thigh to his boot, his hands sticky red-brown, the rest of him spattered. Then Elkins saw the dead woman. "Please, *please*, don't tell me that's our girl."

Alexander confirmed it was their girl.

"Is our boy under us?" Such excitement was in Elkins's voice.

"We hope so. Our boy, other POW, maybe their guards. Now, all of you," said Alexander, "stealth, silenced Rugers only, hand-to-hand, but no noise."

"Got it," said Mercer. "But we have to hurry. You need plasma, Major."

Alexander took another drink of water. "I'm fine," he said, and with enormous effort heaved himself off the ground. Losing blood was a little like remaining under ice too long—and Alexander had too much experience with both. Little by little you simply lost all sense of the imperative.

They got Richter back on the radio. Alexander told him what was happening. Richter, pleading all deliberate speed, said, "Our hook is already in Laos, just seven klicks away. As soon you are ready to move out, call me. It'll be a klick away in thirty-seven seconds."

"Please, all of you," said Ha Si. "Quiet. I'm opening the lid, I'm going down."

But no one moved. Alexander was having trouble standing. Blood was oozing out of his wound. He poured more silver nitrate on it, wrapped another dressing around it.

The four soldiers were looking at him with worry. "How are you feeling?" asked Elkins.

"I'm fantastic," Alexander said, pulling the StarLight over his face. "Stop mothering me, and cowboy the fuck up. Let's go." His weapons were on him. Casting one last look at Moon Lai, he asked if anyone had something to cover her with. So Ant wouldn't see her if they brought him through here.

Tojo took the trench from his pack and threw it over her.

They stood over the lid. "Ready?" said Alexander. "And be quick. If you find any of ours, get them up, get them out, tell them to run up the hill. Watch out for the tripwire. Go."

Ha Si opened the lid and listened below. All was quiet. He took a breath, nodded to Alexander, crouched and jumped ten feet down; he didn't even need the ladder.

Alexander listened, heart pounding, breath stalled, as Ha Si went down into the darkness. There was no fire, but there was a grunting *whoosh, whoosh,* there were two silencer shots, a sound of a blade tearing into flesh, and rapid breath. Alexander went next, with his knife in his mouth, lowering himself by his arms to favor his leg and jumping the rest of the way, quickly grabbing hold of his knife and his Ruger. His StarLights took a few seconds to adapt to the dark. Mercer, Elkins, Tojo, came down after him. Before Alexander's eyes fully adjusted, a green figure with a bayonet jumped him from the side; he barely had time to raise his knife to parry him; but raise his knife he did. The man fighting him was smaller and weaker, it was not an even fight despite the equalizing bayonet; the man went down. After that, Elkins and Mercer stepped in front of Alexander and Tojo went behind him. Where was Ha Si? They were in a rectangular open area with four corridors spanning out. There was damp straw on the ground. Slick liquid pooled up in the corners.

They moved uncertain and slow. Finally they found Ha Si, just inside one of the corridors, struggling with a large guard who was hanging on to Ha Si's back and choking him. So someone was awake. Elkins yanked the guard off; Mercer shot him. But Ha Si was right—the noise of the silenced Ruger was too large for the cave.

"Don't shoot anymore—if you can help it," whispered Alexander. "Just find Anthony."

They were in a pack now with Ha Si at point; it got very quiet. Alexander thought it might be false quiet. Water was dripping somewhere. They went down one corridor without flashlights, just their StarLights, their .22s cocked, their blades drawn, the five of them, whispering, *Anthony, Anthony.* That was their only refrain around the putrid cramped burrow in the sweating earth. It was Alexander's only refrain. *Anthony. Anthony.*

He heard someone moan. "Ant, is that you?"

Another groaning sound.

"Anthony? Anthony?"

They found five unguarded U.S. soldiers huddled together in one messy pile on the floor of a locked bamboo cage. Five soldiers, a miracle! The men were bloodied and beaten. Ha Si broke open the lock; they rushed to the prisoners. *Anthony, Anthony.*

None of them was Anthony. Elkins and Mercer helped them up. One of them was dead. Should they leave him? He was someone else's Anthony. Alexander said not to leave him. "Quick, get the rest of them up and out."

Which of them was strong enough to carry a dead man? One PFC volunteered, crying.

"Tojo, help them up the ladder," Alexander ordered, "and if they can hold a rifle, give them a rifle, and come right back. But don't call Richter yet . . . not until . . . " He asked the POW: *Anthony, Anthony?*

They knew nothing. Three of them, including the dead man, had been captured just two days earlier. The other two had been here a week. They looked and sounded as if they could barely recite their name and rank for the captors.

"They were not at all well guarded," Ha Si said. "Fucking Moon Lai. Lie is right. The men who charged me were sleeping near the ladder. It seems to be all there is. I don't think they are expecting trouble."

"Don't get casual, Ha Si. The Sappers are sleeping but if we wake them, that'll be it for us."

Anthony, Anthony.

Ha Si went forward down a corridor, and disappeared in the darkness. Alexander tried to keep up, but had to walk deeply hunched through the tunnel and much slower. The corridor was coming to an end about forty feet in front of him. Alexander saw four guards leaning against the wall before a small bamboo cage. They were slumped in sleep. Alexander and Ha Si took a stealthy step, then another. But even damp straw crunched; they could be only so quiet on it. One of the men opened his eyes and, well trained, instantly reached for his weapon. Ha Si, also well trained, hurled his knife in the dark into the man's throat. The other three were already on their feet. One blowgun shot from Ha Si—because it was accurate and quiet—two Ruger shots from Alexander—accurate but not as quiet. They ran up close; Ha Si retrieved his knife. The blowgun victim grabbed Alexander's wounded leg and yanked him forward. Alexander grappled with him, his gunmetal knife blade slashing up and down in the dark like lightning. Finally Alexander threw him off while Ha Si was already unlocking the cage.

He opened the bamboo door, stood in front of it like a post—but didn't go in. Alexander tried to get around the Yard.

"Move, Ha Si!"

Backing away, breathing out in struggling breaths, Ha Si said to

Alexander in a stilted whisper, "I am going to call Richter and tell him we found Captain Barrington. I will be right back with Tojo to help you. See if you can get him up." He didn't look at Alexander again as he hurried away.

His head tilted under the low ceiling, Alexander walked in. In the small cage he saw Anthony, lying on his side on the black and bloodied straw. Alexander instantly saw that something was wrong, but what?

"Ant?"

He kneeled by him. He looked unconscious, but he was alive! He was barely dressed: prisoner pajama bottoms and an old Viet Cong shirt thrown over his torso. Alexander yanked off his green-eye and removed the shirt covering Anthony.

Then he saw. Anthony's left arm was gone. It had been severed just a few inches below the shoulder and was now poorly band-aged with clean gauze—Moon Lai had just been here. Trying not to gasp, Alexander turned Anthony on his back and in the dim-ness saw his other arm, the inside of the elbow and the forearm a solid black from pierced needle marks. If Moon Lai kept him alive, it was by penicillin and opium alone. He was unclean and had savage wounds over the rest of his body.

Alexander looked away. He could not bear it. And when he looked again, he was blinded. "Ant . . . " he whispered, his hands on his son's chest. "Ant." He shook him.

Anthony opened his eyes and stared dully into his father's face, and Alexander saw himself, a quarter century ago, lying in his own filthy straw, bloodied and without hope—waiting for the guards and the trains and the chains to come and take him, in his despair having refused food for days—and then opening his eyes and seeing his father, Harold Barrington, bending over him and whispering, *"Don't be proud, Alexander. Take some bread."* And he had said to his father, *"Don't feel sorry for me, Dad. This is the life I made for myself."*

And the ghost of his dead father, so close, his voice barely audible over his audible heartbreak, whispered, *"No, Alexander. This is the life I made for you."*

And now Alexander—not a phantom—was kneeling over his own son, the same age, in the same straw, near the same death, in the same absence of hope, waiting for the same people, and he said, his voice barely audible over his audible heartbreak, "Anthony, I'm here. You're going to be all right. I'll help you. But get up, because we have to go *right now* if we're going to make it."

Anthony blinked. His eyes were glazed and cloudy. He was heavily drugged. But what a clearing when he said, "Dad?"

"Get up, Ant."

Anthony started to shake. "Oh my God. I'm hallucinating again. Please go away. I know it's not you. God, what's happening to me?"

"You're not hallucinating. Get up." Alexander was trembling. Anthony's legs were in irons, his remaining arm roped and tied to a ring in the wall. Alexander cut off the rope, and Anthony, lying on his side, reached out with his hand and touched his father's very real face. He groaned. "Oh God. No, Dad. No . . . You don't understand. You *have* to get out of here."

"I understand, and we're both getting out of here." Alexander was fumbling with the key ring for the leg irons. He was having no luck. Coming back to Anthony's head, he leaned over him; his arms went around Anthony, leaving bloodied prints.

"I can't move," said Anthony. "Look what they've done to me." What would Tania say?

"*Anthony, Anthony . . .*" Alexander whispered, pressing his face to Anthony's head, lifting him off the straw to sit him up. "Can you hear me, son? You are my life and your mother's life. You will always be for me my three-year-old boy playing in the yard, cutting your hair to look like mine, walking like me, talking like me, sitting on my lap, bringing me ladybugs, bringing me joy, keeping me alive. That's what I see when I look at you. Remember fishing together, Ant, when you were little? You have no idea how much happiness you brought me. You've made me nothing but proud your whole life. Now come on, bud. You must get up and come with me. You will see, you will not fail—not you. You'll be all right, but stand up, son. Come on, stand up, Anthony."

The boy didn't move.

He gazed at his father, his suffering eyes filled with incomprehension, confusion, pain, and then he turned his face away. "My mother can't see me like this," he whispered.

"Your mother," said Alexander, "saw me like this in Sachsenhausen. Your mother wrapped her sister's body in a sheet and buried her with her bare hands in an ice hole. Your mother will be fine, I promise you. Now get up." Alexander kissed him. "Don't worry about anything, just stand up." When Anthony didn't move, he said, "You know who else is here for you? Tom Richter." *Now* Anthony turned his head. In his eyes flared a brief concession to regret and rapture beyond those two proper nouns.

Alexander, having no time to acknowledge anything, nodded. "Yes, that's right. Tom Richter. First time in the jungle since 1962 and he's here—for you. Elkins is here. Charlie Mercer is here. Ha Si is here. And Tojo, who is going to carry you on his back."

Anthony whispered something.

"Son, I can't hear you." Alexander bent very close.

Without saying a word, Anthony pulled the Ruger out of Alexander's front holster, and without moving his shoulders or legs, or straightening out his listing body, he cocked the weapon with one hand, aimed and fired twice behind his father. At the door of the bamboo cage, there was the thud of a falling man. Alexander turned around to look.

"There'll be more where he came from," Anthony said croakingly, giving the pistol back. "I'll need another weapon. One I can shoot from the hip and change the cartridge myself. Single-handedly."

"How about the M-60 with a hundred-round bandolier?" Alexander said lightly, straightening Anthony back to a sitting position.

"Perfect." Anthony almost smiled.

Ha Si returned, kicking the dead guard out of the way. Elkins and Mercer were behind him. "Oh my God, Ant!" Elkins cried out and turned away. "Look what those motherfuckers did to you."

Tojo came back. The U.S. prisoners were out, already heading up the trail. Alexander asked Ha Si for help with the leg irons. Ha Si right away found the key on the ring and unlocked Anthony. "Elkins, turn around and face me. You are so fucked up," Anthony said, trying to stand. "What the hell are you doing here, man? Mercer Mayer, is that you?"

That was the familiarity! Mercer Mayer was the children's book author. Anthony, was right, Mercer did share some of the same physical characteristics with the Little Critter character—short, squat, dogged.

Mercer could not look up at Anthony. "It's me, Captain," he said, his tears falling on the straw.

Anthony stood with help, propped up against the wall and flanked by Alexander and Ha Si. Alexander saw that Elkins and Mercer were so distraught by the sight of the grievously wounded Anthony, they were having trouble doing what needed to be done. "Soldiers, come on," he said. "Chin up. We found him."

"Right," said Anthony. "Cheer the fuck up. And somebody, give me a pair of their BDUs, so I don't have to wear these devil-spawn pajamas."

Alexander had extra fatigues in his ruck. Tojo had an extra combat vest in his, and immediately started to take off his own boots, while Alexander pulled off Anthony's NVA prison bottoms. Before the tunic went on, Ha Si properly wrapped a new clean dressing around Anthony's mangled stump, tightly supporting it across the diagonal shoulder.

Anthony stood naked against the wall, slowly blinking, coming around.

"Tojo, man," he said, "thanks for the boots, but what are *you* going to wear? Dad—oh my God, Dad—what happened to your leg?" Anthony own legs buckled from under him. "You're—"

"Don't worry about that right now," Alexander told him, pulling the tunic over him. "I'll be fine." He held up his son while Mercer and Elkins struggled to put the fatigues and the boots over Anthony's swollen uncooperative legs and feet. Anthony was groaning; he kept sliding down. Ha Si was holding him, Alexander was holding him, five grown men lifting up their son, their commander.

"Does it hurt, man?" Elkins whispered.

"I feel nothing," Anthony replied in a hollow voice. He stood up straight—but not on his own. Ha Si said he wished he had a shot of Dexedrine. They gave him bread instead, they gave him a drink, ripped open a ration, gave him some peanut butter, a cracker. He chewed listlessly, drank egregiously, swayed.

"What? What? What do you need, son?" Alexander kept saying.

Anthony's only arm was around his father's shoulder. "A fucking cigarette."

"God, you and me both. Let's get out of here so we can have one."

Ha Si's calm voice kept telling them that they desperately needed to hurry. But before they left, Anthony ordered Elkins and Mercer to set up two closely staggered Claymores in the main corridor leading to the sleeping quarters; when they went off one on top of another, Anthony said, the cave dwelling would be rent in half, as if earth itself were opening its jaws. They set up the Claymores, ran tripwires in all directions. Anthony ordered two CS smoke grenades ("to suffocate them") to be set up in front of the Claymores, and when he was satisfied, he said let's go, but couldn't walk.

"Have you not stood up during all this time?" Alexander asked.

"Oh, I've stood up," said Anthony with unveiled hatred. "They tie me up once a day and jack me up on a hoist while she comes and cleans me and . . . tends to me. *Nurses* me back to health." Black irony was in his voice. "Did you . . . see her?"

Alexander exchanged a glance with Ha Si. He didn't want to lie to his son, but he also knew they didn't have time for this discussion. "Oh, we've seen her, Ant."

Anthony was disoriented. What's the date today, he asked, and then became even more disoriented when they told him, trying to wrap his brain around how many months he'd been in captivity. My tour was over in August, he muttered. That was going to be it for me. I was coming back stateside. With her. There was something else he was having trouble getting out. He was having trouble. "It can't be early December." He paused, tried to find the words. "Her . . . baby is supposed to be born in early December—"

"Come on, Ant," said Alexander, prodding him forward, holding on to him. "No time to chitchat. Let's go."

"What month is it, really?"

"Let's just get to the hook. Later for talking."

Tojo carried Anthony to the ladder, but how were they going to pull Anthony up by only one arm? He was going to have to help himself somehow. Tojo was behind him, supporting him, but it was Anthony who had to grab on to the rungs. He didn't, couldn't. His hold slipped, he fell backward, was stopped only by Tojo.

Alexander went in front of his son, steadied him on his feet, took his head into his hands and looking straight into his face, said, "Anthony, your mother at fourteen climbed out of a fucking bear trap with no ladder and with a broken arm. And no Tojo propping her from behind. So fucking pull yourself up by your one arm. Got it?"

"Got it."

Alexander kissed Anthony's forehead and pushed him forward.

Before climbing, Anthony ordered Ha Si to set up two more grenades in the straw below the ladder and to place another CS smoke bomb next to it. "To choke them to death," said Anthony, "as they are being fragged apart."

It had been fifty-five minutes since Moon Lai left her hut. Alexander was tense like heavy crystal falling over and over on the marble tiles. At last they were all above ground. Anthony held on just tight enough for Tojo to propel him upward, rung by excruciating rung, and then Elkins pulled him up the rest of the way.

And there was Moon Lai—lying under Tojo's trench.

The five men quickly blocked Anthony's view of her, ushering him to the door, but the stench of decaying blood in the humid heat was overpowering, and there was no mistaking the shape of a small body, even under a trench. Anthony glared at his men blocking him and said, "I may not be able to tell my father what to do, but you are a different story. Move the fuck out of my way, and I'm not asking you." Reluctantly they moved out of his way. Pulling up the trench, Anthony stood over her. His legs shook.

He turned to his father, his black-and-blue face an impenetrable mask. Only his lips trembled. He looked at Alexander, looked at Alexander's red-soaked leg, collected his voice, swallowed, and said as calmly as he could, "She was a demon-whore. She twisted all truth, all the things I believe in, all the things I told her into fucking evil contortions. Think no more about her." Her pregnancy went unspoken. There was nothing anyone could say. Anthony turned to Ha Si. "Well, point man," he said coolly, "don't just stand there and gawk at me with your silent eyes. Tell me, is it safe to go?"

Ha Si stuck his head outside. "All clear, Captain," he said.

Anthony asked for Alexander's Colt.

Alexander gave Anthony the Colt. "Ha Si, let Tojo go first. Tojo, your only mission is uphill, one klick, and get Ant on the freedom bird home. Got it?"

"Yes, sir."

"Tojo, you're a giant among men," said Anthony.

"Captain Barrington, I actually am a giant among men," said Tojo.

Alexander called Richter, told him they had Anthony, were moving out and to call for the hook.

One two three. They counted time to order it.

Ha Si took one step outside, with Anthony, Tojo and Alexander following behind.

Alexander instantly saw two women about thirty meters away walking toward the hooch. The women saw them and started to *scream* and run toward the passed-out sentries. They must have been coming to see what had been taking Moon Lai so long because in three days, no one besides Moon Lai and the sentries ever came to this side of the village during daylight hours.

Ha Si raised his weapon, but before *he* could fire, Anthony from behind him fired unhesitatingly with the Colt. The noise was shattering. The women fell and stopped screaming. But they had been loud, and the two shots were louder. There was a tick of silent time passing and then a wailing siren pierced the camp, sounding just like a bombing siren during the siege of Leningrad. Perhaps they were reusing the same sirens, Alexander thought. It really did sound uncannily like the sirens from Leningrad.

What was good about Tojo was that in the five seconds transpiring between the opening of the hut door and the sound of the siren, he was already ten meters up the hill with six-foot-two Anthony slung over his back. And he was right to do it. They didn't have an extra second. "Watch the tripwire!" Alexander yelled behind him. He, Elkins, Mercer, Ha Si were behind Tojo running up their narrow trail, their heads mostly hidden by the elephant grass. Ha Si was now at tail, a role Alexander didn't think he was well suited for. They were running as fast as they could, but it was six hundred feet *up* through barely cleared grass, over rocks and uneven terrain, and Tojo could only move so fast, carrying a two-hundred-pound injured weight, and so the rest of the column had to keep Tojo's pace, with Alexander saying, come on, faster, Tojo, faster, even as the blood dripped from his own leg. But he knew the ironclad rule of warfare—anything standing gets hit. And when you're running uphill with the enemy behind you, you get hit in the back. He heard the pop pop crackle of the rifles going off and yelled, "Right to the hook, Tojo. It's an order. Don't stop for anything."

"Yes, sir." Tojo was panting.

When they were halfway up the hill, three hundred feet up, Ha Si looked back. Alexander heard him say with uncharacteristic emotion, "Oh *fuck*."

Those were his last words. A round hit him in the back and he fell. Mercer grabbed him, slung him over his shoulder, and it was a good thing he did, because another round hit Ha Si.

Alexander turned around. And with characteristic emotion, he said, "Oh, *fuck*." Though his view was impeded by elephant grass, he saw at least a hundred NVA soldiers still in their oxymoronic sleepwear, with Kalashnikovs in hand, pouring out of the village hooches and from manholes in the ground, running, flying to the hill, ignoring the razor-sharp grass and the single-line-formation rule. An unruly wave of men cut right through the grass even as it was cutting through them. Without helmets or boots they ran, rifled up and fired up.

Alexander sent everyone in his team up ahead, remaining at tail; he counted, one, two, three—and there it went. One barefoot NVA soldier *finally* tripped a Claymore wire. There was a loud spread-out popping burst and widespread screaming. Someone tripped another Claymore. And another. More popping, more screaming. That slowed the bastards down a bit. Alexander caught up with Mercer, who was struggling up the hill with Ha Si on his back. Alexander ordered Mercer to stop running; from his M-16-mounted grenade launcher, he blooped three arching rockets right into the confused, mined-up, fragged-up midst below, and the grenades slowed them and upset them. He took Ha Si from Mercer, slung him onto his own back and resumed running.

The bloopers slowed the NVA—but didn't stop them. Neither did the Claymores. Alexander kept glancing back. Shouting to each other, the NVA ran another ten meters uphill. Alexander, carrying Ha Si, heard the second tier of Claymores detonate. A few men broke through, running up parallel to Alexander on the decoy trail—running up right into Harry's hidden punji sticks. The men screamed, stopped running. Harry would have been proud. Alexander opened fire straight from the hip, shooting through the man-high grass with Ha Si on his back.

He himself was now three-quarters to the top. Tojo was almost at the top. Mercer, now at tail, would run, stop, turn, fire in short bursts, then turn and run again. Elkins, out in front, was emptying his cartridges, reloading, and running. Tojo cleared the hill, thank God, but instead of moving into the jungle, as he had been ordered, he set Anthony down.

From fifty feet below, Alexander yelled, "Go! What the fuck did I tell you? Go!" But Tojo didn't go. Instead he ripped the rifle from his back and opened sustained fire.

Alexander turned around to look and saw why Tojo decided to disobey a direct order. A small tick of panic crawled inside Alexander, got lodged in, and stayed. It was the Sappers. They were running, falling, crawling through the grass, on their bellies, still in waves. On their bellies, they tripped the Claymores and got greased, but the rest, though injured and moaning, continued to run up, to creep up. And there were more and more of them, tens, dozens, hundreds crawling out of the ground like small twisting asps, slithering out, creeping and running up the hill.

Dropping Ha Si to the ground, Alexander swung around, stood
in a straight line with Elkins, Mercer, and Tojo and they opened
up at the dark forms below. Richter and the six Yards remained
just off to the side, in a great position on very high ground. They
had been inflicting enormous damage with their propelled grenades
and the M-60—less a machine gun than a fire-breathing dragon.

Yet despite this, some of the NVA were a quarter-way up the
hill. Alexander could see their black helmetless heads flashing
through the yellow grass. He ordered his men to find cover, found
himself a rock and some nice vegetation to hide behind, set his
rifle on semi and began shooting the Sappers in short bursts, picking
them off one by one, not wasting his fire. They were so dark and
moved so slow through the light-colored grass, thinking they were
hidden, thinking Alexander couldn't see them, and then they tried
running, thinking he couldn't hit a moving target.

They were very wrong on both counts.

Forty seconds to aim and fire twenty rounds, reload in three—
and again. He did that five times. Did he get a hundred heads for
his trouble? Tojo, Mercer and Elkins were as desperately as Alexander
trying to ward off the advancing Sappers. Mercer too was picking
them off one by one, while Elkins was auto-unloading at the dis-
persing men, and Tojo was blooping rockets down below straight into
the village huts. No quiet escape and evasion here, no subtle extraction. Kum Kau was burning in a black, acrid battle for the order of
the universe. Did they get a hundred heads each for their trouble?

Richter and his six Yards were spreading out. At Richter's
entrenchment, two Yards were splitting the ascending Sappers with
grenades and the other three were pulverizing them with M–16
rounds. One Yard was the M-60, which Alexander knew any
second was going to run out of twelve hundred rounds of armor-
piercing ammo. Did they get twelve hundred unarmored North
Vietnamese for their trouble?

Alexander hoped so, because the M-60 ran out of ammo, and
the rapid fire went quiet. In a moment the selective M-16 fire
resumed.

The Sappers were not selective. They had their AK47s set on
automatic and were just hosing down the elephant grass as they
continued to run uphill.

"Where's Ant?" Alexander yelled without looking behind him
at the woods. "Tojo—could someone take him to fucking extraction!" No one heard him.

Richter called Alexander on the radio. "Hook's waiting. Abandon your position and retreat. Move out to the hook now." The radio went dead.

Here was the trouble—Alexander couldn't move out to the hook now. He and his men couldn't run five feet through the jungle, much less a whole klick, because as soon as they ceased fire, the Sappers quickened their pace and jacked up *their* fire, shooting Alexander's men in the back. The fucking NVA were not retreating; they were stampeding up that hill, and though they were falling to rockets, to mines, to the grease gun, more and more kept coming. As if in a nightmare, they were pouring out from the underground like nothing Alexander had ever seen. They were like the fucking Hydra, he thought, loading a high-explosive shell into the breech of his missile launcher and pressing the trigger. You kill them, and they just grow new heads.

Alexander's men couldn't move out, but they couldn't stay where they were either—because their position on top of the hill was in five short minutes going to become indefensible. Alexander's ammo would be gone before all the NVA were gone, that was becoming very clear. Before they were overrun by three battalions of barefoot men in pajamas with Kalashnikovs, Alexander's guys needed to get a kilometer into the woods to the helicopter, because no matter what else happened, one thing *had* to happen—Anthony had to be on that bird.

Alexander lobbed a CS smoke grenade for more black confusion below, more thick teary havoc, and backed away from his enclosure, running into the woods, where he found Anthony with Ha Si by his feet.

"How is he?" he breathed out.

"Not good," was Anthony's reply.

Alexander flipped on his radio to call for one of Richter's Yards, but Anthony stopped him. "Throw him on my back, Dad," he said, slowly standing up and putting the Colt in his leg pocket. "I'm not good for anything else. Let me help. You need the Yards for other things. Throw him on my back and push me in the direction of the trail. How far in?"

"One klick, but please fucking hurry," said Alexander, lifting Ha Si onto Anthony, who started to walk like a rambling drunk man, holding on to Ha Si's slumped head with his one hand.

Back at the edge of the hill, the situation had gotten only more desperate. The Sappers had so thoroughly dispersed up the sides of the mountain that Alexander realized they were trying to flank his men. And sooner rather than later, the A-team was going to run out of ammo and still be a klick away from the chopper. Someone said, yelled maybe, we're done for, retreat, retreat.

Richter called Alexander on the radio. "Fuck it all to hell," he said. "I called in the snakes and the Bright Light team. The critical SITREP: we are *not* getting out of this by ourselves. Just assess the fucking situation. This is prairie fire." There were three kinds of emergencies: team, tactical, and prairie fire—where you were engaged by a numerically superior force, surrounded and about to be annihilated.

"How long before the Bright Lights?"

"Thirty minutes," said Richter.

"Richter!" yelled Alexander. "We don't have *three* fucking minutes!"

One of the Sappers thought to bring an RPG-7. Alexander saw him. Tojo saw him and shouted, "Holy shit! Incoming!" and mowed the man down, but not before a launched rocket sailed through the air, landed twenty feet below Richter's rocky encampment and exploded upwards into gray sickening smoke.

The radio went dead.

For five seconds as Alexander was running to Richter, there was no sound.

Richter was down.

Three of the six Yards were down.

Tojo fell down and started to cry. "How bad, how bad?" he kept asking Alexander.

"All the fucking way, Tojo," said Alexander. Richter's leg was gone, his side gone, his neck had a grapefruit-size hole in it. For a moment Alexander couldn't speak. He held up Richter and made a sign of the cross on his forehead. Inaudibly Alexander whispered what he had whispered over a thousand men. *Lord Jesus Christ, most merciful, Lord of Earth, I ask that You receive this man into Your arms that he might pass safety from this crisis, as You have told us with infinite compassion.*

They had to go and go now. "Tojo," said Alexander to the weeping giant, "we have to move out ASAP or we're all fucked. They're going to flank us in the woods and cut off our retreat. I'll get Mercer and Elkins. Tell your Yards to pick up their fallen and order those who can to fire at tail. Now grab your commander and let's go."

Alexander's hand had remained on Richter's head. "You're going to be okay, Tom," he said. "Just hang tight, man." He pressed his lips to Richter's bloody forehead and whispered, "Hang tight, my good friend." Because there are many mansions in His father's house, and He is preparing a place for you. Then Alexander jumped up and ran, as Tojo, continuing to cry, lifted Tom Richter off the ground.

The Yards picked up their own. Mercer had gotten hit in the leg and was limping down the trail with Elkins covering him, Alexander covered Tojo, as they ran through the woods in a single file.

Tojo, with Richter on his back, flew down the trail first and fast, but for Alexander, never did one kilometer, three thousand feet, seem so agonizingly long. There were fewer Sappers following them through the woods because they got hosed by another three Claymores at the top of the hill. Those that got through dispersed, trying to flank the U.S. soldiers, and new ones continued coming up from below, but slower. Just not slow enough. The enemy hid in the vines, and Alexander's Yard at drag kept getting hit—once in the arm, once in the thigh—and falling down. Alexander had to keep coming back to help him up, to push him onward. Little by little, Alexander was getting left farther behind with his Yard, who was now bleeding from the arm and both legs, but still somehow managed to get up, run, crank off rounds. When the Yard couldn't walk and fire anymore, Alexander carried him through the bamboo, but he couldn't continue like this, he had to protect his men. He told the Yard to crawl to the clearing as best he could. Alexander alone remained tail gunner, covering his wounded men as they inched to the hook.

Where *was* that fucking hook?

Mercer got hit again, got up again, slowed down, but never stopped firing. He was very good, that Mercer Mayer. Dogged, stoic, bloody-minded, good. Anthony was right; even wounded, Mercer saw the enemy in the hazel bamboo, saw them and killed them. Elkins, too, but then he got hit in the shoulder and couldn't hold his rifle with two hands anymore, and became much less accurate. Alexander shouted at him to just bloop the rockets at the moving bushes and forget about sniper fire, and he did.

Alexander ran when he could, hid in bamboo when he couldn't, and walked half backward, half forward the rest of the time, firing in all directions, trying to weed out the overgrown flanks from the concealed Sappers. He threaded a tripwire like a tail behind him, and quickly set up one of his few remaining Claymores. When the NVA would get close enough for him to see through the foliage, he would lob a frag bomb at the brush; he lobbed three frag bombs, two of his HE shells; he set the woods on fire with his rifle—and still the Sappers kept bunching up; in small groups, hiding, running, shooting and coming.

Alexander thought he heard the sound of the turbine engine and the chopper blades up ahead; maybe it was just wishful thinking. He glanced through the woods. No, it *was* the Chinook, whup-whup-whupping only fifty yards away through the thick trees.

Alexander yelled for Tojo, whom he could barely see. "Tojo, who's on the hook?"

He heard Tojo's voice right next him as he grabbed and lifted the badly injured tail Yard. "Almost everyone's on, sir. I'm taking him in or he won't make it. You, too, let's go, Major. Run in front of me."

"No." Elkins wasn't on, Mercer wasn't on. "Go, Tojo," said Alexander. "Get him on and come back for those two. *Go*, I said." Tojo ran.

Forty yards.

Elkins and Mercer were helping each other up, bleeding, hidden by the trees, wavering, but still firing. They moved five camouflaged yards when Tojo was already back from the chopper.

"Tojo!" Alexander called, "is my son definitely on?"

A voice sounded right next to him. "No, Dad," Anthony said. "He definitely isn't." The M-16 was at his right hip. He was holding it with his one arm.

"Anthony!" yelled Alexander, glaring at Tojo and then at his son. "Are you fucking crazy? Get on that bird!"

"I get on when you get on," Anthony said. "So let's go. And leave Tojo out of it. He doesn't give me orders. I give him orders."

But there was no way Alexander could get on, with four of his men, *including Anthony*, still twenty yards away from safety. The remaining NVA men quickly staked out positions trying to move closer to the clearing. The Chinook, which was armed and had a crew, could not open artillery fire blind through the woods where American soldiers were fighting so close to the enemy, the enemy who in one burst of a moment was going to make the landing zone a hot landing zone, a *red* landing zone, and extraction was going to become exponentially more difficult, if not fucking impossible. And once the NVA got close enough to bloop a rocket at the Chinook, no one would get out. Alexander stopped moving forward and emptied his chambers backward to give Tojo, Elkins and Mercer—and Anthony most of all—a chance to get on the chopper. He got off the trail, hid in the cyprus trees, and fired on automatic without moving a foot to the helicopter.

Mercer and Elkins were finally near the edge of the clearing, slowly limping toward the hook, trying to stay by the vegetation and not come out into the open. Tojo, bleeding from his own neck wound, was moving, but all three remained under fire.

Mercer Mayer got hit again. He fell down and this time did not get up. Tojo returned to pick him up.

Hidden behind the trees, Anthony stood, shoulder to shoulder against his father, firing his rifle from the hip. When his ammo ran out, he dropped the empty magazine to the ground, flipped the weapon under his bandaged stump, muzzle down, barely holding it in place and, stretching out his right hand, said, "Clip, Dad," to Alexander, who passed him another 20-round magazine. Anthony jammed it up, slammed the catch down, switched the rifle back to his hip and resumed fire. The tracer rounds had been loaded very carefully and conscientiously by Alexander near the very bottom of the magazine with two rounds under them to signal when the clip was about to run on empty.

"Clip."

"Clip, Dad."

"Clip."

"Anthony," yelled Alexander. "Please! Get on the fucking slick."

"Clip." Anthony didn't even reply to his father.

"Are they on?" Anthony was blocking his view.

Anthony looked. "Elkins is on. Tojo is almost on with Mayer," he said. They were ten yards from the clearing. There were still dozens of NVA hiding in the fern leaves, spot-shooting at them.

"Motherfuckers," said Anthony. "Clip, Dad."

Shoulder to shoulder they stood in the bamboo.

"Is this like Holy Cross?" Anthony asked.

"No," said Alexander. Holy Cross had no bamboo, or my son in it.

"Ha Si didn't make it." Anthony emitted a small groan. "Clip, Dad."

How many were left? God, how many had there been? Alexander unloaded a grenade into the bushes. He couldn't see who he was shooting at anymore, and he nearly couldn't hear. Throughout his life, in battles like this, his instincts became wolf-like with the flooding adrenaline: he saw and heard and smelled everything with painfully heightened acuity. But he had to admit that the deafening noise from several thousand rounds of sustained fire and from the hook rotary blades was diminishing him.

Hidden by bush, a Sapper lobbed an RPG-7 rocket right into the clearing. The shell exploded fifteen yards from the chopper, which lifted off into the air for a minute before it could set back down in the flaming grass. The Chinook opened brief fire, but the Sappers were deep in the bamboo; you couldn't see them, you couldn't get them. They had two, three locations, maybe four. The Chinook gunner on the mounted weapons thought he was shooting at his own men and was forced to stop.

Anthony said, "Dad, rocket at one o'clock for the RPG bastard."

Alexander loaded a 40mm rocket into the breech, fired at one o'clock.

Anthony was quiet. "Try one more. One o'clock. Not two-fifteen."

Alexander loaded one more, fired. "That was the last one," he said, feeling through his vest and bandolier.

"That's all the motherfucker needed. That was perfect. Clip, Dad." Dropped the empty magazine, jammed in the new one, resumed fire.

Was there less return fire, or was Alexander just deaf? No, he wasn't deaf. He heard his son loud and clear:

"Fuck. Clip, Dad."

Very soon there would be no more clips.

Richter had been right. Tens of thousands of rounds of ammo was not enough.

Moon Lai had been right. They were willing to lose every man to the last, while Alexander wasn't willing to lose even one.

He had to hold them off long enough for Anthony to get on the hook. Grabbing his son and pushing him away from the trees, Alexander started backing him slowly out to the small clearing, while he continued to walk backwards, firing into the jungle leaves in three-round bursts. Take that, you motherfuckers. And that. Another three rounds.

"Anthony!" he yelled in desperation over the noise of the blades and his rifle. "Please! Can you just get on the fucking hook? Run, I'm covering you. Run. I'm right behind you."

"Yes, but who is covering you?"

"The gunner. Tojo from the hook. Go, Antman. Go." Pushing his son, shoving him with his body, continuing to fire. Finally, reluctantly Anthony went.

How long did Alexander's mad minute last? Fire on all burners at maximum intensity, at maximum velocity? How many magazines had he gone through, how many grenades? How many rounds did he have left before he ran on empty? Go, Anthony, go. Go, son.

Suddenly Alexander wasn't running. Just like that. He was standing, firing one second, and the next he didn't even blink and was on the ground. He wondered if he blanked out, blacked out for a moment, maybe got tired, lay down and didn't remember. He didn't know what happened. What the fuck, he said, and tried to get up. He could barely sit up. He felt something bubbling up in his throat. Frowning he looked down—and threw up. Blood poured out of his mouth onto his combat vest, oh no, and instantly he was wheezing for breath. He ripped open his vest, his tunic. Blood was coming out from a hole in his chest. Alexander opened his mouth, but he couldn't breathe; he was choking. His mouth and nose were full of blood he kept trying to cough out, to clear his breathing passage. He reached behind to feel his back. Bits of his battle fatigues mixed with blood and bone came off on his hand. The fucking round went right through him. Alexander became overwhelmed; his eyes clouded; he didn't know where his son was, if he was all right, if he was on the hook, where he himself was, where the Sappers were. He didn't know anything. He couldn't find his emergency kit, and he couldn't breathe, and he was seriously fucking bleeding.

And he panicked.

And it was at the moment that he was overpowered with fear and anxiety he could not control that from behind him he heard a soft calm familiar voice, a voice not a face—and as soon as he heard it, he said in his own calm, very loud voice, *No fucking way, no, Tatiana. Get away from me*, and started rummaging wildly for his ruck with blind man's hands pawing the ground, while her unrelenting voice from behind him blew her breath in his ear and whispered, *Alexander, calm down, slow down, and open your eyes. Just calm down, and open your eyes. And you will see.*

He crawled back on his haunches, hoping to find a tree to press his back against and tripped over his ruck! Instantly he stuck his hand inside, pulled out the field dressing kit, and with one fumbling hand, managed to get the pressure bar around his chest and pull the rip cord that tightened automatically. The kits were supposed to be worked one-handed by the wounded: that was their purpose in the field. The pressure bar was better than nothing. He pressed his back against a tree, gasping for breath. Suddenly he saw again—Anthony's desperate face. I've been hit but it's okay, son Ant, Alexander wanted to say. Please—just get on the fucking hook.

Now he knew what the most important thing was: to get on the hook. Everything else they could fix.

With one hand, Anthony was tying a plastic trench around Alexander's back and chest, wrapping gauze around him, screaming something, holding him up. Alexander thought he saw Anthony mouth to him: *Close your eyes, Dad, smoke bomb incoming.* Anthony covered Alexander's mouth and nose with wet gauze, there was a whooshing pop, and suddenly Alexander really couldn't breathe, and couldn't see Anthony for all the coal-tar suffocating tear gas around him.

Anthony *lifted* him up—how did he do this, with one arm?—lifted him and ran through the smoke! Oh, *now* he runs. Two hundred pounds on top of him—and now he runs.

Was that dimming sound the rotary blades? And wind? And sudden loud fire? Now that there was no one in the woods but the Sappers—Alexander the last man out—the hook opened some serious fucking smoke from the mounted M-60. And then— finally!—the boy was in the bird.

Alexander saw the gray interior of the chopper, saw Anthony above him, as if his head were in Anthony's lap, and though he couldn't breathe at all, he could almost breathe now.

Because his boy was in the bird.

And the bird lifted off, whup-whupped in the air with its rotary wings, tilted once toward §earth, once toward the bright sun, and flew away.

Alexander wished he weren't lying down, but obviously he could not sit up anymore or Ant would have sat him up. Anthony knew how much his father hated lying down. There were gravely tense faces around him, Tojo, Elkins, unfamilar faces, a medic. He was being turned over, something was being pressed to him, done to him, then he was on his back again, his tunic was being torn off. He felt great commotion around him.

But Ant was right above him. In such relief Alexander looked at his son's injured face, but when he turned his head again and opened wide his eyes, he didn't see Anthony.

Alexander saw Tatiana.

They stared at each other. Every ocean, every river, every minute they had walked together was in their gaze. He said nothing, and she said nothing. She kneeled by him, her hands on him, on his chest, on his heart, on his lungs that took air in but could not move air out, on his open wound; her eyes were on him, and in her eyes was every block of uncounted, unaccounted-for time, every moment they had lived since June 22, 1941, the day war started for the Soviet Union. Her eyes were filled with everything she felt for him. Her eyes were true.

Alexander didn't want to see her so *desperately* that he turned his face away, and then he heard her voice. *Shura,* said Tatiana, *you have young sons. You have a baby girl. And I am still so young. I have my whole life still to live. I cannot live another half my life on this earth without my soul. Please. Don't leave me, Shura.*

He heard other things, other voices. His arms were raised, sharp things prickled his forearm, something was dripping in. A sharp thin long thing went in his side, it felt like he was stabbed from his rib straight to his heart with an ice pick. He couldn't see anything, not even Tatiana. He couldn't close or open his eyes at all. They were motionless.

CHAPTER SEVENTEEN

Kings and Heroes

Heaven

Heaven, as it turned out, was noisy.

Clattery, clangy, fussy, strident. All accompanied by a nearly constant high-pitched detestable whistling very close to his head. And every time it whistled, the ice pick went right back in his heart. Heaven had unpleasant medicinal smells. Was it formaldehyde, to replace the lost blood in his veins and to preserve him as an organic specimen? Was it old decaying blood? Other bodily fluids? Was it bleach to cover it all up? Whatever it was, it was pungent and dreadful. He had always imagined heaven as a place like Tania's Luga, where in the chirping serene dawn of tomorrow, someone caressed his head, while his hands braided Tania's hair, who sat between his legs and murmured jokes in her harp of a voice. That was heaven. Perhaps maybe some comfort food in front of him. Blinchiki. Rum over plantains. Maybe a comfort smell or two. Ocean brine. Nicotine. Oh yes! Nicotine. Sitting, smoking, looking at the ocean, hearing the waves break, while behind him in the house, warm bread rose in the oven. Now *that* was heaven. *Rai*. And then perhaps other things, too, rooted in the carnal, yet elevated to celestial. Eros and Venus all in one.

But here in this heaven, not only were there none of these things but clearly the things that were here resembled more a mountain of purgatory than a meadow of serenity. *Ad*. There was cacophony everywhere and grating sounds: of slamming doors, of creaking windows, of hurrying feet. Of things being dragged and scraped on linoleum floors, of metal pans falling, spilling, of loud language accompanying them like carnage, coming from irritated, frustrated throats. "Oh hell! Can't you just once watch where you're going! How many times do I have to tell you! Look what you did! Who the hell is going to clean that shit up?" Flying flapping screeching bats.

He couldn't move his body. He could taste nothing. He couldn't open his eyes. All he could do was smell and hear. And his senses of smell and hearing told him he was not in the Elysian Fields. What had happened to him? He was uncorked, and condemned for eternity to listen to scurrilous inmates fight over bedpans. Perhaps there was some cholla nearby, too. Maybe they could stuff it in their throats as they fought over who was going to clean what. Was this his Temple of Fame? Is this how he was buried with kings and heroes?

And then—oh, no! It just never stops. More loud noises, only now a bitter argument. Alexander sighed, rippling the River Styx with his whistling sighs, rowing at the crossroads between the land of the living and the land of the dead. He wanted to tell them to shut the *hell* up. This argument was too close, almost next to him.

He wanted to open his eyes. Why couldn't he see in his hereafter? He couldn't see, oh, but how loud and clearly he was hearing!

"Coma, I tell you! I know you're upset, and I'm sorry about that, but he is in a *coma*! A deep and prolonged unconsciousness, very likely brain dead, in a persistent vegetative state, very common after a severe injury like his, coupled with hypoxia. Coma! We're doing what we can for him, to keep him comfortable. I don't know who you think you are, telling me *we're* not doing enough."

"Enough? You're doing *nothing*!" a voice yelled.

Ah.

This one was angry, was loud, was upset, but it wasn't grating and it wasn't cacophonous. "First of all, he is *not* in a coma. That's *first*. Perhaps it's easier for you to abuse your medical privileges while you pretend he's lying here beyond your help, but I'm going to tell you right now, you don't know who you're dealing with."

"He *is* in a coma! He's been in Saigon a week under my care. You're here five seconds. I've seen thousands like him. I've been a nurse thirty years. Not once has his pulse risen above 40, and he has almost no blood pressure."

"His pulse is 40, is it? Have you even glanced at the patient? Have you lifted your eyes, just once today, or in the last seven days, and taken one look at the patient? A 40 pulse?"

Alexander felt his wrist being lifted and circled by a small warm hand and then dropped back on the bed.

"When was the last time you touched him? His pulse is 62 right now. And without even putting a cuff on him, I can tell just from looking at his skin that his blood pressure is not 60 over 40 as you've conveniently listed here in your little chart, which, by the way, you have not initialed off since yesterday morning, but 70 over 55! That is not a comatose patient. Did you even go to school?"

"I have fifty of these men to take care of, not just him! I'm doing the best I can. Who do you think I am? Who do you think you are?"

"I don't care who you are. And you don't want to know who I am. What matters is that this man is a major in the United States Army, and he was critically wounded, and he depends on you to take care of him so he can live, and you're standing here with your bedraggled face and your insolent eyes, telling me you've got to clean out the water closet on the second floor, while a human being is lying in your bed with undrained air pressure in his lungs, and with dressing around his *chest wound* that has not been changed for at least twelve hours!"

"That is not true! That is simply not true! We change it every four hours when we decompress his lung!"

"Bullshit! Listen to his wheezing—that sounds like a recently drained lung to you? He can't exhale! Where's the decompression catheter? And his chest dressing—I don't have to go near him to smell that dressing, to know that it has not been changed or irrigated in over twelve hours. I don't have to go near him to see that the IV that drips fluids into his body—fluids without which he can't survive!—has slipped out of the vein and now his entire forearm has blown up to three times its normal size. What, you can't see that?" The voice rose and rose and rose until it was the loudest voice in purgatory. "Put the metal pans down, nurse, they're blocking your view, put them down and take a look at your patient! Smell your patient! He's got a five-inch stab wound in his leg that's now infected *only* because his dressing has not been changed, and the penicillin you're giving him to treat him is now dripping into his open arm cavity instead of into his veins, and you're telling me you're taking care of him? This is your best? A *healthy* man would go into a fucking coma under your care! Where is your attending physician? I want to see him right now."

"But—"

"Right now—and not a single additional word out of you. But you will get one more word out of me—I will have your job, if it's the last thing I do. You are not fit to wash bedpans in this hospital, much less take care of wounded soldiers. Now go get me a doctor. This man is not staying in your so-called care another minute. Another *second*. The NVA could take care of him better than you. Now go! Go, I said!"

His arm was being lifted up, his gown pulled away, a long thin sharp needle going softly and without pain deep past his rib, past his muscle, into the pleural space surrounding his lungs. *Shh, darling, shh, you're all right, shh, breathe now. Everything is going to be all right.*

Ah, thought Alexander, no longer wheezy, his body relaxing, his mind clearing, his hands, his fingers, his heart comforted . . . his eyes still closed, and though no nicotine, no ocean, no Luga, no blinchiki, no bread, no quiet, no harmony, still loud, still noisy, still strident, and yet . . .

Heaven.

There was no sound, no smell, no taste, no touch, but finally he thought he had sight because he opened his eyes, and in front of him on a chair sat Tatiana. She was so pale, she looked as if her freckles had vanished. She was unglossed, was wearing no makeup. Her hair was pulled back. Her lips were matte pink, her eyes mottled sage, a gray-green. Her unsmiling hands were on her lap. She sat silently and said nothing. But all he knew was this: the last time he opened his eyes, he saw Tatiana and the first time he opened his eyes in he didn't know how long, he saw Tatiana. She was sitting by his side and her eyes were softly on him. Around her, in what looked like a hospital room, he saw lilac sand verbena, agave and golden poppy in planters on the windowsill. On the table in the corner stood a small Christmas tree, all done up and twinkly with multi-colored lights. And next to him on the little table, standing against a small easel was a vivid painting not of lilac sand verbena but of lilac in the spring, like the kind that used to grow in the Field of Mars across from his Leningrad garrison barracks.

Alexander moved no part of his body, didn't move his head or his mouth. He tried moving his fingertips, his toes, his tongue. Something slow to let him know he was alive. Just a small sign before he opened his mouth. Can he hear her voice in his head?

Are there any memories he has that they share? Is she telling him things, like not to worry? Is she comforting him with words?

He didn't know. He didn't think so. He was afraid to move because she was not moving. She was just sitting looking at him, not even blinking. It occurred to him then that maybe he hadn't opened his eyes, maybe he was dreaming and his eyes were still closed. They couldn't possibly be open because *she* was not reacting to his open eyes. He closed his. And the moment he closed his eyes he heard—

"Mom, look, Daddy blinked!"

His eyes flew open.

Pasha was standing in front of him, somberly peering into his face. Leaning over, he kissed Alexander's cheek.

"Dad? Are you blinking?" A strong strawberry-blond head pushed up and forced itself in front of Pasha. It was Harry with crystal green eyes. Harry had new freckles. Harry leaned over and kissed him on the mouth, on the nose, on his cheek. "Mom, you have to shave him again, he is growing a beard. But he is not as pale today, don't you think?" A small hand lay on his stubble, rubbed it. Harry lifted up Alexander's SOG knife, inches away from Alexander's face, the gun-blue blade gleaming and said, "Dad, I have *never* seen anything this sharp. I could shave you myself with this. This is an amazing knife! Is this the kind that went into your leg? Did you know it's so sharp, it etched the metal on the crank of your bed? After lunch, I'm going to etch your name with it!"

Another soft grunting noise, a body pushing, shoving, another small head rising up, but this one lower to the ground, not over him, but trying to jump up to be seen, a blonde, brown-eyed, round-faced head that said, "Daddy, look, I cut my hair to look just like yours and the boys. Mommy doesn't like it. But do you like it, Daddy?"

Now Alexander moved. His fingertips moved and his hand moved and his arm lifted and touched the three heads in front of him. He pawed them with his palm, placed his hand right over their eyes and noses, and hair, like a bear. They stood motionlessly, their heads bent into his hands. They felt warm. Clean. Harry had a small black stitch in his cheek. Pasha was wearing glasses. Janie really had cut her hair to her scalp—obviously spending too much time with her brothers, and had a bruise on her temple to prove it. Alexander opened his mouth, put his tongue to the roof, cleared his throat, took air into his lungs (or lung? Was he like the cursed one-lunged Ouspensky now?) and said, "Anthony?"

"I'm here, Dad." The voice came from his left.

Alexander turned his head. Anthony, dressed in jeans and a dark pullover, his hair longer, his face clear and shaved and saved and unbruised, sat draped in the chair by his other side. Alexander blinked in relief and for a flicker of a moment, for a brief soaring flutter of swallow's wing, he thought, *Please, dear God, maybe it was all a dream, maybe none of it happened, our dreams, mine and Ant's, all our lives, of caves, of burning woods, of running, and this was yet another, and it was real bad, but now I've opened my eyes and maybe everything is okay and Anthony is okay.*

But the moment went plummet. The swallow was gone. A million flickering decisions, a million choices, a million bricks and steps and leaves and actions starting with his father's life, with his mother's life, with their train ride through the blue Alps from Paris to Moscow in December 1930, with his mother's money already hidden deep in her suitcases, hidden away from Harold, whom she loved, whom she believed in, but still—her ten thousand American dollars came with her in secret, just in case, for her only son, for her only Alexander, whom she hoped for and loved most of all. One train ride from Paris to Moscow and now, forty years later, Alexander's perfect son sat in a chair, and had no arm.

His eyes filling with some very *alive* things, Alexander turned quickly away because he couldn't bear to look at Anthony, whose own eyes were filling with some very *alive* things. *Tania*, Alexander whispered. *Where are you, Tania?*

The children had been ushered to the background, and though they still tried to stick their little heads in, they were unceremoniously pushed aside, and now in front of him, on the edge of his bed, near his rib, sat Tatiana. His hand rose and lay in her lap. He turned his palm down to feel her skirt, it was soft—cotton jersey or cashmere. He felt her thighs underneath. Ah, density. He glided his paw up her sweater, also cashmere soft, over her breasts—ah, weight—up her throat, to her face. Yes. It was Tatiana, not spectre but matter. She was measurable. His little Newton had mass and occupied space. A small finite matter in infinite space. That is what math gave him—principles of design that tied together the boundless universe. That is why he measured her. Because she was order.

Her arms went around him. Alexander smelled her lilac soap,

her strawberry shampoo, faint coffee, musk, chocolate, faint bread, sugar, caramel, yeast, such familiar comforting smells, like refuge, and he was pressed into her neck, his jaw against her breasts and her silken hair was in his hands. He was alive. She said nothing, sighing so heavily, rippling her own River Styx as she held him, her struggling palpitating heart at his cheek.

But he said something. He whispered to comfort her. *"Babe, how can I die,"* he whispered, *"when you have poured your immortal blood into me?"*

And late late late when he thought they had gone—or he had gone—to sleep maybe, to a place inside his head where they couldn't reach him, in the dark, he opened his eyes, and next to him sat Anthony. Alexander shut his eyes, not wanting Anthony to see all the things he was carrying, and Anthony leaned deeply in and lowered his forehead onto Alexander's bandaged chest.

"Dad," he whispered, "I swear to God, you have to stop it. You've been doing this for weeks now, turning away every time you look at me. Please. Stop. I'm hurt enough. Think of yourself, remember yourself—did you want my mother to turn her face from you when you came back from war? Please. I don't give a fuck about the arm. I don't. I'm not like Nick Moore. I'm like Mom. I'll adjust, little by little. I'm just glad to be alive, to be back. I thought my life was over. I didn't think I would ever come back, Dad," said Anthony, raising his head. "What are you so upset about? It wasn't even my good arm." He smiled lightly. "I never liked it. Couldn't pitch ball with it, couldn't write with it. Certainly, unlike you, couldn't shoot fucking Dudley with it. Now come on. Please."

"Yes," whispered Alexander. "But you'll never play guitar again." And other things you will never do. Play basketball. Pitch. Hold your newborn baby in your palms.

Anthony swallowed. "Or go to war again." He broke off. "I know. I have some adjusting to do. It is what it is. Mom says this, and you should listen to her. She says I got away with my life, and I'm going to do just fine. All we want is for you to be all right," Anthony said. "That's all any of us ever wanted."

"Antman," said Alexander, his hand on his son's lowered head, his wounded chest drawn and quartered, "you're a good kid."

*   *   *

"I fucked things up so badly," said Anthony on another night perhaps, though all nights and days drifted, hung suspended, seemed like one. "I never listened to a word my mother told me. All our mysteries went straight to the enemy. I'm really sorry. I trusted her so completely."

"You've been like that your whole life. So open."

"I didn't see it. I really fell for her. I thought she was Andromeda, and she turned out to be the Gorgon Medusa, and I never suspected a thing until it was much too late." His voice was unsteady. "I don't know what I'm more staggered by—the depth of her abandoned heart or my own stupidity."

"You know what, Ant?" said Alexander. "Self-flagellation is unnecessary. You've suffered enough." He wanted to tell Anthony that even in Moon Lai's unholy world, where black was white, and white was black, and Alexander's twenty-five-year sentence for a fraudulent surrender and desertion charge was *just punishment*, and Anthony's heart was the taipan's plaything, and babies were nothing and meant nothing, the Gorgon Medusa still crept to the cellar door twice a day to change Anthony's bandages and give him opium to ease his pain.

"I'm sick about Tom Richter," said Anthony, his voice breaking.

"Yeah, bud," said Alexander. "Me too." They sat, unable to talk about him. Alexander turned away. He might have even cried. He was getting too soft in his hospital bed; he had to get on his feet.

Anthony told Alexander that back in 1966 Richter had called him into his quarters before Ant was moved up to SOG, and said that before he could put Anthony under his command, there was one thing he needed to know and get straight. Richter said that he had been legally separated from his wife since 1957, and so the time for recriminations had long passed; but there was one small question niggling him that he needed answered. After the Four Seasons graduation celebration, as they were all in the vestibule waiting for their cars, Anthony had been looking for his lighter and Vikki came up to him, flicked open hers and brought it to his face. The only reason Richter was mentioning this at all, he said, was because in the seventeen years he had known his wife, he had never seen her light a cigarette for anyone.

"I told him," said Anthony, "that I had no idea what he was talking about, that I didn't remember the incident at all. I apologized if it was improper, and Richter said that *that* was not the improper thing. I replied that there was nothing else and nothing to think about. And so we left it at that and never spoke about it again."

The father and son's heads were low, staring into their separate distances and Alexander wanted to say that sometimes even bad husbands saw things, and then, because they were great men, did the right things, and sometimes the impossible did happen, and cigarette lightning struck—where it was clearly not supposed to— a wild girl in New York, a wild soldier in Leningrad—and then wanted to ask but didn't if Vikki was going to continue to light Anthony's cigarettes.

Alexander closed his eyes while Tatiana tended and nursed him, wrapped and rewrapped him, washed him, embraced him, and fed him from her hands, as he slowly recovered, his glass becoming smooth with her ministrations and the constant metronome of the symphonic noise of his family.

"Darling," Tatiana said, touching his feet to see if they were cold, adjusting his blankets, "do you know what your youngest son built for his science project this year? A replica of the atomic bomb." She paused. "At least I hope it was a replica."

"It was, Mom," Harry unconvincingly assured her, sitting on his father's bed. "Dad, I showed everyone how it worked—from splitting the atom to launching the missile. It was so good, it won the Arizona state prize!"

"Yes, son," said Tatiana. "Congratulations. But afterward your mother was called into the principal's office with a school psychologist and asked if she would consider putting her youngest son under observation—wait, or was it . . . surveillance?"

Alexander laughed lightly. His chest still hurt every time he let out a breath. "Science project," he then said slowly. "It's not January already, is it?"

"It is," said Tatiana, squeezing his feet.

Alexander stretched out his hand. "Harry-boy, come here. Did I miss your tenth birthday?"

"Yes, but Dad, now you've got three *more* scars!" said Harry happily, coming to his father. "And one of them is in the chest! That's stupendous. My friends can't believe it. I told them you got shot in the heart and survived. I'm the most popular kid in school. I think your fame is rubbing off even on Pasha."

"Sticks and stones," said Pasha, calm and unfazed. "I don't need the approval of the masses to feel good about myself." He took his father's other hand. "Dad, for *my* science project, I made a replica of the human lung under the stress of tension pneumothorax."

"Yes, and it did not win first prize," said Harry.

Pasha ignored him. "Now that one of your lungs has undergone tension pneumothorax," he continued to Alexander, "will you at least consider not poisoning it anymore with nicotine?"

"Pasha, leave your father's few joys alone," said Tatiana. "He'll be as good as new soon." She was passing by Anthony with a drink in her hand and almost without stopping, brought it to his face, and he, barely looking away from his folded-over newspaper, bent and drank from the straw, because he could not hold the paper and the drink at the same time; and so he drank from his mother's hands, glanced casually at her, and then leaned slightly forward and kissed her hand and she moved on, almost without a stagger.

Alexander took Pasha's arm. "Nicotine isn't bad for your lungs, son," he said. "You know what's bad for your lungs? Acute lead poisoning from machine-gun fire."

Pasha, his hand still in Alexander's, turned to his older brother. "Ant, does your stump twitch?" he asked. "I read in one of my science books that you'll still feel your phantom arm for years because all your severed nerve endings will feel it."

"Thanks for that info, Pash. For how many years you think?" Anthony briefly lifted his amused eyes to his brother.

"Pasha," said Alexander, pulling his son to him, "what *have* you been reading? What the hell is tension pneumothorax?"

"An acutely collapsed lung brought on by trauma," replied Pasha, looking so happy to be asked. "Seriously life-threatening. In your medevac they had to do an emergency decompression puncture on you. But in the hospital, Mommy got them to place a plastic tube into your chest through an incision under your arm, and this tube expanded your lung and kept draining the unexhaled air that built up in the pleura and drained it until the hole in the lung healed."

Shaking his head at both his son and his wife, Alexander smiled. "So has *that* been my problem? A hole in my lung?"

"No, Dad," Pasha said soberly. "Most of your problems stemmed from systemic and pulmonary blood loss."

"Pasha!" That was Tatiana. "That's it. I'm forbidding the

children to speak until their father is discharged in a few weeks. Until then, they can just sit and look cute. Pasha, *no*." Dragging him away from Alexander, she pointed a finger at him. Eleven-year-old Pasha was already two inches taller than his mother. "No more," she said. "Don't even *think* of opening your mouth."

Alexander smiled at his chastised son, and even more so at his son's lioness mother, pretending to be mad but so bosomy and hippy and petite, wearing clingy raw cream silk, her hair in satin ribbons, her full mouth in sheer gloss, her slim legs in seamed nylon stockings, which meant tight accessible open girdles. He stretched out his hand to her, stirred and dilated, aching, alive.

"Daddy!" said Janie, jumping up and down. "I learned how to pee standing up, just like the boys. Are you proud of me?"

"Very proud. But I already have three sons. I need a baby girl, Janie."

"Anthony," said Jane, kicking Harry off Ant's lap and climbing on herself, kissing her brother deeply on the cheek, "Aunt Vikki was crying out on the deck the other day, and I asked her why she was crying, and she said because she lost her husband, and I said I was sorry for her but glad Mommy didn't lose Daddy, but then I started to cry for your arm because Mommy is so sad about it, and do you know what Aunt Vikki said? She told me not to cry, because even though they've cut the silver strings of your guitar, they have not taken away your whisper, and your lips shape words even in silence, and you can still sing, in *five* languages— and she said that was all right with her."

"Aunt Vikki said that, did she?" said Anthony. In a silent triangular vortex of exchanged and strangled glances, Alexander and Tatiana and Anthony had their years flicker before them in quavers, Bethel by Scottsdale, Luga by Leningrad, Moscow by memory as they looked down at the fascinating linoleum floor, hoping to find the solace there.

"Tatiana," said Alexander suddenly, "am I back stateside?"

"Of course, darling."

He opened his eyes. His wife, his babies were around him. Anthony was in his chair. "Am I back in Phoenix?"

"Of course, darling. You're home."

He looked at her. Stared at her. Glared at her. "Tatiana," he said. "Oh my God. Please, in front of my children, *tell* me, swear to me that you did not admit me to the root of all evil, submerge me in Hades, tell me I am *not* in Phoenix Perdition Memorial!"

There was no answer.

"Oh, for the love of all that is holy! Get my kids out of here before they hear their father say things no children should hear. Ta-TIA-na!"

The Son and the Father

The President of the United States in the name of The Congress takes pleasure in presenting the Medal of Honor
To:

Captain Anthony Alexander Barrington
March 13, 1970
5th Special Forces Group
1st Special Forces MACV/SOG Republic of Vietnam
Entered Service at West Point, NY
Born June 30, 1943, Ellis Island, NY

Citation:
> Captain Anthony Alexander Barrington, United States Military Assistance Command Vietnam, Studies and Observation Group was a battalion leader of a long range reconnaissance unit responsible for covert operations in Laos and Cambodia. On July 8, 1969, he went missing while returning to active duty. He was found by a search and rescue Special Forces squad of twelve men in an NVA POW camp, army base, and training ground that masqueraded as a civilian North Vietnamese village Kum Kau near the border with Laos. The team extracted Capt. Barrington and five other POW. Capt. Barrington, having been tortured, beaten and wounded, having lost his left arm during his imprisonment, despite his serious injuries, engaged the enemy in heavy fire after being pursued for a kilometer and a half flanked on three sides. The team escaped up a steep mountain into the woods, trying to make their way in enemy territory to a helicopter extraction. Despite suffering heavy losses, they inflicted grave damage on the enemy, killing all but a handful of the NVA. Separating from his troops, Capt. Barrington fought off the attackers in an attempt to let the rest of his injured men move closer to HEP. Though severely

injured, he carried two wounded men on his back, one by one, to the extraction point. One of the men was a decorated Montagnard Special Forces soldier, Ha Si Chuyk, and the other Maj. Anthony Alexander Barrington, Capt. Barrington's father. His gallant and intrepid actions during this time earned him the highest honor the U.S. Army can bestow.

Major Anthony Alexander Barrington
March 13, 1970
5th Special Forces U.S. Army Training Advisory Group
MACV/SOG Republic of Vietnam
Entered Service at Fort Meade, MD
Born May 29, 1919, Barrington, MA

Citation:
    Major Anthony Alexander Barrington, United States Army Reserve Corps, came to Vietnam in November 1969 to find his son, missing and presumed dead. He led a highly specialized and heavily armed Special Forces squad into North Vietnam to Kum Kau. Though Maj. Barrington was already critically wounded after hand-to-hand combat with the enemy, he found and extracted his son, Capt. Anthony Alexander Barrington, and five other U.S. soldiers who had been captured by the North Vietnamese Army. While escaping through the jungle to a helicopter extraction point, Maj. Barrington and his men came under heavy enemy fire of small arms, automatic weapons, mortar and rockets. Eleven Special Forces troops under Maj. Barrington's command fought a vastly superior division-size force of 550 North Vietnamese soldiers. During the battle, six of his men were killed and five were seriously wounded. The six fallen men included Lieutenant-Colonel Thomas Richter, commander of the MACV-SOG headquarters in Kontum, and Squad Sergeant Charles Mercer, plus four indigenous mountain warriors who had fought alongside the U.S. army since 1964. Despite heavy blood loss, Maj. Barrington carried three of his wounded men through enemy fire, and then stayed in the rear continuing to engage the enemy to let his men get further ahead to the HEP and not be overrun. Maj. Barrington and his son became separated from their troops and stayed

off the attack, throwing the NVA forces into disarray by grenades and machine gun fire long enough to let their comrades make it safely to extraction. This heroic action allowed seventeen injured and fallen men to be brought home. Maj. Barrington was still repelling the enemy when he fell nearly mortally wounded to an AK47 Kalashnikov round. His extraordinary leadership, infinite courage, refusal to leave the fallen behind, and concern for his fellow men saved the lives of a number of his comrades. With complete disregard for his personal safety, Maj. Barrington's courageous gallantry above and beyond the call of duty were in keeping with the highest traditions of military service and reflect great credit upon him and his unit and the U.S. Army.

CHAPTER EIGHTEEN

Crossroads

SDI

In March 1985, Anthony had news that was too big for the telephone. Tatiana asked if she should make some blinchiki—and he didn't say no! He flew home for the weekend, made sure Pasha was not on call, made sure Harry could fly up from MIT in Boston, and in the evening, when all was quiet and the lights were dimmed in the white kitchen, when they were all gathered and collected in their weathered jeans and jerseys, they sat down at the granite island, the five of them: Tatiana, Alexander, Anthony, Pasha, and Harry. Jane was away in Cabo San Lucas. Tatiana warmed up her blinchiki, and brought out bread and olive oil, wine and cheese, and tomatoes; they sat on high stools and ate, all except her, because when she was anxious she couldn't keep still, and so she paced and pretended she was tending the troops.

On one of her passes, Alexander took her arm, leaned to her from the stool and whispered, "Sit down. Can't you see? Until you calm down, he won't tell us what's going on."

"Really, Mom," said Anthony, "I'm not going to war again. Please sit. I have news. Good news and bad news."

She sat. "Give me the bad news first," she said.

A smiling Anthony handed her and Alexander a release from the office of the Press Secretary of the White House. "As in many times in life," he said, "this is both."

FORMER SPECIAL FORCES CAPTAIN NOMINATED BY PRESIDENT REAGAN TO BE THE CHAIRMAN OF THE JOINT CHIEFS OF STAFF.

"The Chairman of the Joint Chiefs of Staff!" Tatiana and Alexander exclaimed. For a moment they didn't speak; Tatiana's jaw fell open. "How is that bad news?"
Anthony smiled. "Keep reading."

General Anthony Alexander Barrington, a career officer in the U.S. Army has been nominated by President Ronald Reagan to serve as Chairman of his Joint Chiefs of Staff of the Armed Forces of the United States. If confirmed, Gen. Barrington will become the youngest Chairman ever to serve a U.S. President.

Gen. Barrington has had a long and illustrious career in the U.S. Army. A West Point graduate, he served four distinguished tours in Vietnam and was taken prisoner by the North Vietnamese in 1969, resulting in serious battle wounds including the loss of his left arm. His heroic actions during a well-documented intrepid escape led to his subsequent Congressional Medal and have contributed to his meteoric rise in the post-Vietnam era.

Anthony Barrington was promoted to lieutenant-colonel and was commander of Fort Bragg in North Carolina, then commander of a Mountain Division in Fort Drum, New York, and three years ago was moved to the Pentagon where he was promoted to general to chair the United States Special Operations Command. He has also been the honorary chairman of the POW/MIA Committee, at the forefront of multinational efforts to find and return all the missing coalition soldiers from Southeast Asia.

Ronald Reagan, in announcing his nomination, said, "General Barrington fought for a truly noble cause for which he nearly gave his life. The war he fought in Vietnam has not been lost; it did not begin in Vietnam, it has not ended in Vietnam. The war continues. I have said this before and I will say it again, unless we take serious measures, it will be five minutes to midnight for the United States. Gen. Barrington understands this. He has been fully engaged in the ongoing fight for freedom, and I for one am very pleased to have a man like him in my column. I also appreciate and am grateful to have his stalwart advocacy for an operational strategic defense system that I believe will be instrumental in our endeavors to bring peace to the world. Like myself, Gen. Barrington does not believe that holding people

hostage to the threat of a nuclear nightmare is a civilized way
to live. I cannot think of a more qualified man to be the principal military advisor to this President, to the Secretary of
Defense and to the National Security Council."

The good crystal and Cristal was brought out. Tatiana knew
Alexander was saving the champagne for their anniversary, but he
opened the bottle gladly tonight, as they clinked and drank and
congratulated their son and brother. Tatiana's feeling for Anthony
was unaffected by such things as pride in his new achievements.
No accomplishment of his added or detracted from the unsplittable
irreducible atom of what she felt since the moment she leaned
over her wounded husband in that Morozovo hospital made so
distant by time, and said: "Shura, we're going to have a baby. In
America." Anthony was conceived in the ashes and under the stars,
on doomed frozen soil and yet in hopeful fire. Nothing Anthony
did with his life could stop Tatiana from believing that there was
nothing Anthony could not do with his life. But looking at
Alexander's face, Tatiana smiled with pleasure, for Alexander was
unconscionably and embarrassingly proud of his firstborn son.
    Anthony himself, however, was only ostensibly pleased by the
proferred chairmanship, muttering that of course he was honored
to serve the President in any capacity, and yes, it was on the
surface a tremendous achievement, and yes the responsibilities
would be astonishing . . . but he was muted in his enthusiasm.
Looking conflicted, he sat at the head of the wide multiangular
island; Alexander and Tatiana sat across from each other so they
could fully see each other's faces. Harry was next to Alexander;
Pasha was next to Tatiana.
    "So where's the bad news, Ant?" Pasha asked.
    Anthony sighed. He said that next week would begin the closed
Armed Services Joint Session hearings into his confirmation. He
thought the hearings would present big problems for him and
would cast clouds of doubt on the success of his nomination.
    "You guys are not paying attention," he said. "Did you read the
press release? The part where the president is lauding my support
of SDI? Operational Strategic Defense system, ho ho, ho." He
coughed. "Do you not see the one small problem?"
    "You don't know what SDI is?" said Harry.
    "Shut up." Anthony cleared his throat. "I think SDI is a big
bunch of flaming bullshit."

They laughed and said, "Ah." They expressed surprise. Since the beginning of the eighties they had talked at length about the failing nuclear disarmament talks with the Soviets, but had not talked about the space shield.

"See my problem?" said Anthony. "The press and many people in Congress despise and criticize the President's ridiculous idea, while the President is grateful I'm on his side. But in my heart of hearts I agree with the people who mock his plan. Quite a pickle, no?" He smiled. "And once I get inside that room, as Dad well knows, it'll be very hard for me to hide my true feelings. I'm firmly with the President on every other policy on his agenda. But they'll ask me two *sua sponte* questions about SDI and they'll know where my abundance of the heart lies. Right, Dad?"

"Anthony, refuse to answer *sua sponte* questions, that's all," said Alexander. "But what the hell is wrong with you? Have you not been following what's been going on with the Soviets? Have you not been reading any of my reports?"

Alexander was still pulling at least five days a month in Army Intelligence. The homebuilding business was running so smoothly, with managers and foremen and accountants and two architects and Tatiana overseeing the bookkeeping that Alexander was able to devote quite a bit of time to the nuclear question since the ABM treaty of 1972.

"Of course I've been reading them," said Anthony. "But can I help it that I think SDI is a joke?"

Harry was shaking his tousled, strawberry-blond head. "Anthony, Anthony, Anthony."

"Harry, honestly," said Anthony. "Now is *so* not the time for me to listen to your crazy theories about impulse accelerators and rotary motors of zero curvature. I need to know in the next seven days if I can or should hide my heart on this issue."

"Ant," said Harry, "rotary motors is what it's all about. If you knew about them, you wouldn't have to hide anything. So if you don't want the job, just thank the President and refuse the job."

"That's just it—I do want the job!" Anthony exclaimed. "Chairman of the Joint Chiefs of Staff? I do want the fucking job— excuse me, Mom, sorry. I just don't want to defend this Star Wars crap. Nuclear disarmament, absolutely; conventional weapons reductions, yes; containing the Soviets everywhere they have their little grapple hooks in, bring it on, I'm your man. But Star Wars? No, thanks."

"Anthony," said Tatiana, "next time you get an urge to agree with the journalists, take a short trip to Vietnam."

"Mom, you're right," said Anthony. "Vietnam is extremely clarifying. Out of balance and unreconciled to the universe." He smiled. "But *that's* exactly my problem with Star Wars. We *should* be dealing with Vietnam—and El Salvador, and Nicaragua, and Angola—not playing with laser guns in space. I can't hide my skepticism. The President is going to withdraw his nomination as soon as he sees what a fraud I am, and I will have disgraced myself and my family."

"You're being too hard on yourself, Ant," said Pasha, always conciliatory.

"You're not being hard enough on yourself, Ant," said Harry, never conciliatory. "You *will* disgrace your family if you don't wrap your head around the possibilities of a nuclear deterrent that does not involve the Soviets developing new ICBMs and nuclear subs."

"Ant," said Pasha, "in this one instance, and *only* this one, I might listen to Harry. He knows nothing else but this."

"Pasha, I treasure your vote of confidence," said Harry, "but a defense system must be developed—"

Alexander put his hand on Harry's forearm. "Son, excuse me. You're missing the point."

"I'm not missing the point," said Harry. "That point is all the difference."

"Yes, it is," agreed Alexander, "but for completely different reasons than you think."

"Well, wait, Dad," said Harry, not raising his voice. Tatiana smiled. Confrontational with everyone—except his father. Harry did not argue with Alexander. Nonetheless . . . he had a quiet but vociferous opinion on the space shield. "In the beginning of his first term," said Harry, "the President wanted to know if a system could be developed that would locate and destroy the Soviet nuclear weapons as they left their silos. He was told it could be, and would be."

"It's the most far-fetched thing I've ever heard," said Anthony.

"What's far-fetchedt?" asked Harry. "What about a dropped bomb exploding two sub-critical atomic masses in a microsecond and converting one gram of harmless mass into an equivalent of 20,000 pounds of deadly energy? *That's* not far-fetched to you? You have been nominated to the highest military position in the United States and you have decided to draw your line not at titanium-armored vehicles that will stop a round fired point blank traveling 3000 feet per second, but at SDI's multi-megawatt space nuclear power program with its open-cycle reactor concepts and terminal ballistics? Dad is right, what the hell is wrong with you? Frankly, I don't think we should be judging SDI by your belief system. You still can't believe the Spruce Goose flew!" Harry laughed.

"Oh, Harry, give me a break!" Anthony exclaimed. "Just look outside your box for a second. A computer network runs a series of detection systems that controls lasers and hypervelocity guns in space?"

"Yes!"

Now Anthony laughed. "A *computer* detects hostile missiles going off thousands of miles away and then space lasers intercept and destroy the missiles in flight? A *computer*? I can't get my tax refund from last year because the computers keep going on the blink every five minutes!"

"Go ahead, yuck it up," said Harry, completely unintimidated, "but the computers *will* detect enemy nuclear missiles and then superconducting quench guns will attack them from space and destroy them."

"Ant, listen to Harry-boy," said Pasha. "He knows his quench guns."

"Forget it," said Anthony. "Billions of dollars spent, billions of man hours invested, on an unsustainable, insupportable, nonsensical defense system, and all the computer has to be is in restart mode and the whole thing is moot. And this is *exactly* where the committee will catch me and yank me out of the water with a hook in my throat. Hence my conflict. You know," he went on, "originally when I said I supported the President with respect to SDI, I meant, I agree with the President that the Soviets have been recalcitrant in negotiations and overweeningly militaristic, hellbent only on the concept of mutually assured destruction and nothing else. I agreed wholeheartedly that something needed to be done. Just not this." Anthony nodded as Tatiana poured him another glass of champagne. "Thanks, Mom. I know very well what our President has been going through. I know it pisses him off that the Soviets hide their military expenditures in pseudo-civilian manufacturing. I know he hates their vast superiority in conventional weapons and nuclear weapons, which they continue to build up without incurring international wrath. I just think that this is the wrong thing to invest our resources in."

"I read in the paper," said Pasha, "that the Soviets spend three to four times more on their conventional forces than we spend on ours. Is that true?"

Anthony glanced at Alexander and shook his head. "Don't read the paper, Pasha, read one of Dad's reports. The Soviets are spending much more than that. Every single steel plant and factory in the Soviet Union produces guns and ammunition and bombs and tanks. And we know this not just because we have inside information from our mother, the Kirov factory Soviet bomb-maker." He smiled lightly at his mother. "They make them in Kirov and then sell them to their little Vietnams the world over. Dad, do you know what was the NVA's second weapon of choice behind the Kalashnikov? Your 1941 Soviet-made Shpagin sub-machine gun."

Alexander whistled.

"That's some serious economies of scale," said Tatiana, ironically impressed.

"Indeed, Mom. And furthermore, Dad estimated last year that the Soviets spent 60% of their GNP on defense and not their stated 14%. While we spend 6%."

"Ant, look," said Harry, "their GNP is a hundredth of ours. They have to spend more to keep apace. But stop deluding yourself with conventional weapons expenditures. Shpagins, Kalashnikovs, Studebakers left over in the Soviet Union from Lend-Lease that are now being pedaled to Angola and Vietnam. It's just small fry. It's the nuclear threat that worries the President most of all. Every time the Soviets say they're going to think about arms reduction, they go and build a new nuclear sub. Our last negotiation in the sixties gave us ICBMs. The ABM treaty in the seventies increased both our arsenals by twenty percent. That's what keeps the President up at night. He wants to prevent nuclear war, in which— in the *best case scenario*—a hundred and fifty million Americans will die. And he is right when he says that mankind has never invented a weapon that they did not use sooner or later. That's his fear and his argument for SDI—that in 1925 the world got together and banned the use of poison gas. But we still kept our gas masks."

Pasha nodded, looking quite favorably across the island at his younger brother. "Personally *that* alone is enough for me to weather the doubts regarding SDI."

"Yeah, well, maybe you should've been nominated instead of me," said Anthony. "In the meantime, while Harry mocks me, I'm going to have to sit in front of those men and defend something I can't, despite his particle physics bombardment."

During most of this Tatiana and Alexander refrained from speaking. While their sons squabbled, they listened, sat, drank their champagne, considered each other. Reaching across for Tatiana's flute, Alexander poured her what was left of the champagne and got up from the island.

"Dad, where are you going?" said Anthony. "We're not close to done."

"Don't I know it," said Alexander, and left anyway.

Tatiana turned to Anthony. "Ant," she said, "you know how you can tell what your father thinks of your nomination? Because he went to get another bottle of Cristal." She nodded. "He really believes. Now, do you want to smoke? You can smoke in the kitchen, it's fine. I've put the filter on."

Anthony gratefully lit a cigarette. He'd become quite proficient at functioning one-armed, including lighting his own cigarettes. "Why are you and Dad so quiet? You don't agree with me?"

Tatiana didn't say anything at first. "Let Dad come back," she said softly. "He'll talk to you."

They sat quietly until Alexander returned, popped the cork and poured everyone another glass of the best champagne ever made. They raised their flutes, and Alexander said, "Anthony, this one I drink to you. All our chosen roads, your mother's and mine, and yours have led you here to where you now stand. I want you to stand tall, and say with no hesitation, Thank you, Mr. President, it will be my honor and privilege to serve you. And so we will drink to the clarity of your purpose, which seems to be so sorely missing."

Anthony put his glass undrunk on the island. "*My* clarity of purpose is missing?" he said, bristling.

"Oh, yes," said Alexander, himself less abrupt, but no less direct. He drank fully. "In this it is."

"Dad! I've been working with the President on ratifying SALT II for the last three years!"

"Well, then, you haven't been paying attention to what's been going on with SALT II in the last six months," Alexander said calmly.

"Are you kidding me?" said Anthony, slightly lowering his voice.

"You absolutely have not. There have been twenty nuclear disarmament talks with Soviet Union since 1946—twenty, Ant!

And to the one, they were all ended by the Soviets, who refused to make a single concession, a single even cosmetic reduction in their nuclear arsenal. The only thing we agreed on even in the lauded ABM is that we wouldn't make any more defensive missiles to protect our East Coast from their offensive missiles!

"That's right, but because of our efforts, SALT II has a very good chance of being signed!" said Anthony.

"Being signed is not arms reduction," interjected Harry. "But whatever. One of the reasons SALT II has a good chance of being signed is because this President approved the deployment of the MX missile and the installation of the Pershings in Europe to bring the Soviet Union to the negotiating table by telling them in no uncertain terms that their arms build-up was not going to fly with him. Four wars this century was all this President was going to go for."

"The MX and the Pershing were instrumental, Harry," said Alexander. "They brought the Soviets to the table. But the SDI is what's making them stand on this table on their heads."

"Oh, what does SDI have to do with SALT?" Anthony exclaimed, struggling to keep his voice low.

"This is what I mean by completely missing the point!" returned Alexander, not keeping his low at all. He put his glass down and turned to his son. "Don't you get it? SDI is everything! And it's not about what Harry thinks about SDI, or what you think and your journalist supporters think about SDI, or even what our President thinks about SDI. It's only about one thing—what do the Soviets think about SDI?"

"Who the fuck cares? Sorry, Mom." Anthony barely apologized—as if she needed it, having lived with a soldier for 44 years.

"Anthony." This was Tatiana and her voice was mild, and Anthony took a breath, and took a drink and, shaking his frustrated head, turned his face to his mother. "Don't get defensive. You're not listening to your Dad. Listen. He is saying it doesn't matter if *you* think SDI can't work—no, Harry, let me finish," she said across the island to her son, who was already opening his mouth in protest. "I know *you* think it can. I'm saying that for Anthony's purposes, it doesn't *matter* if it can. The only thing that matters," said Tatiana, "is whether the Soviets think it can." She gazed at Alexander across the island. "Shura, tell me, do the Soviets think it can work?"

"Fuckin'a they think it can work," said Alexander, slapping the island with the palm of his hand. "The Soviets have panicked so thoroughly, it would be funny if it weren't so shocking. Ant, the Soviet Union has bent over to accommodate the United States with regard to SALT II. Just in our preliminary discussions, they have agreed to dismantle a whole range of their atomic weapons, which as you know they have not agreed to do in forty years. They have agreed to move their ICBMs out of Europe! I mean, that's fucking astonishing," said Alexander, not apologizing to anyone for anything. "They've agreed to almost all of our other demands with respect to reducing their nuclear arms. And do you know what they want in return?" Alexander paused and stared intently at his son. "*All* they want in return it that we do not pursue SDI." Alexander laughed. "I mean, come on! I have never heard of a louder bell ringing for supporting anything."

Tatiana laughed, too.

"Yes, Dad," said Harry, "but just one small addendum—"

"Yes, son, I know, I know," said Alexander, putting his paternal, affectionate arm around Harry. "Our resident nuclear physicist thinks it will work. That's great. It doesn't matter. The Soviets think it will work, and that's *all* that matters."

Anthony sat quietly. He smoked. He finished his drink. Alexander poured him another. He looked at Pasha, at Harry, who mouthed to him, *It will work*, rolled his eyes, and said in a thoughtful voice, "I'm hearing something from you here that I'm not quite sure I'm understanding." He looked at Alexander. "Tell me this. SDI is slated to be a defense system, right, but this is the part I don't get: how is development of *our* nuclear defense system supposed to promote *their* nuclear *disarmament*? How is SDI going to help spur the Soviets to want to disarm? I would think it'd be just the opposite. They'll just be developing new weapons that can penetrate the shield, no?"

Alexander was very quiet. Tatiana was very quiet. They looked only at each other. Then it was Tatiana who spoke. "No. They'll just be trying to build their own SDI, Ant."

"Excuse me?"

"Son," said Alexander, "do you know why the Soviets are so frantic? Because they think we are not building a defense system but an *offense* system. That we're hiding behind words like disarmament, and SALT, and treaties, and accommodation, just as they hide behind their civilian steel plants while using those plants to produce a hundred thousand tanks to invade Afghanistan. They think that we're going to hide behind the shield of SDI and nuke them back to the stone age as soon as it's operational. This is why they want us to abandon working on it. If they didn't think it could be successful, they wouldn't care how much money we poured into it. But they sense our imminent superiority of nuclear weapons systems that their pride and sense of self-preservation simply cannot allow—the same way that at the end of World War Two they killed an additional million of their men to get to the enriched uranium factories around Berlin just days before the Americans did, and then engaged in feverish espionage to develop their atomic program." Alexander narrowed his eyes at Anthony. "And you know I know something about *that*, having been at the forefront of those million men, pushing my penal battalion into Germany."

Alexander poured everyone the rest of the champagne. "The Soviets have asked our President to stop, and he said no. SDI will continue. In their panic, the Soviets are at this very minute figuring out a way to plunge every resource they have into creating an SDI of their own." He spoke slowly and very deliberately. Tatiana knew he wanted Anthony to understand fully what he was saying. "But how do you think the Soviets will manage this? Where are they going to find the money for SDI?"

"Where are they going to find the money for SDI?" Anthony repeated incredulously.

"Yes, ask your mathematically-minded mother, Ant. What is her opinion? We'd like to know." Alexander smiled at Tatiana. "Tell your son, Tatia—to achieve perceived offensive nuclear parity with the United States, will the Soviets risk *bankrupting* their country, or will they do the prudent thing and not pursue crazy scientific notions, but instead believe our President—who has pledged that once he develops the technology, he will share it— disarm their missile heads and *save* their country?"

Tatiana smiled and said nothing. "Your father is just presenting all sides, Ant, all actions, reactions, weights, counterweights, measures, countermeasures, points, counterpoints. He is balancing the scales for you. It is your choice entirely what you do."

Anthony groaned, his father laughed, his brothers laughed.

"Tatiana," said Alexander, "don't be coy. Don't tell him the choice is his. Answer my question. Help your son."

"I think, and I could be completely wrong," said Tatiana—her palms down on her granite island that her husband built for her so they could sit around it and discuss matters of their life, large and small, like this—"that the Soviets will bankrupt their country to develop their own SDI."

In disbelief, Anthony shook his head. For a minute or two he didn't speak. "Look, you're my mother," he said at last, "and I—forgive me if I remain skeptical. You can't tell me that the Soviet Union, one of the richest-resourced industrial countries won't have the money for a little research and development! They have plenty of money. And if this is important to them, they'll come up with the money, the way they came up with it for the atomic bomb during Dad's time. They didn't go bankrupt then. They'll just do what they have to; they always had, they always will. They'll rearrange their priorities, they'll divert their resources, as all countries do—including our own—to pursue their agenda."

"Ant, son, they can and they absolutely will do just that." Tatiana looked at Alexander. "But you know, *perestroika, glasnost, solidarnost*, they all cost money. And I'm not saying they don't have the money." Tatiana paused. "I'm saying they're going to have a hard time coming up with it." She paused again and then said, "They'll have to *divert their resources*."

Anthony was quiet himself. "What are you two are telling me?" he asked. "Just so we're straight here. Are you telling me to stake my career and reputation on the belief that the Soviets will break their country to develop their own SDI?" He stared at his mother.

"We're just laying it out in front of you, Ant," said Tatiana.

Anthony, looking exasperated with his mother, turned to his father. "Dad, I'm going to be the principal military advisor to the President of the United States. He is going to need my head to be on straight if I'm going to counsel him to relentlessly develop SDI. You know how I feel about it. Do you think it's viable for the Soviets to pursue their own? And if they do, is Mom right? Will it matter in the long run?"

"Those are very good questions, son," said Alexander. "I'll try not to be as oblique as your mother. She really has been beating around the bush too long. Tania, you must learn to be more direct so your children and husband can understand you." He grinned at her, and turned his face to Anthony. "Let's see," Alexander said. "Yes, I think the Soviets will pursue developing this unfeasible system. Harry, please!" he exclaimed. "What I meant was, this feasible, workable, fabulous system. Is it viable for them to do it? Viable? That I don't know. Probably not. They're already stretched to the limits in the war in Afghanistan they've been fruitlessly fighting for six years. Not just stretched to the limits, but they've been borrowing from World Bank to pay for their little war. They owe more money to the World Bank than 172 other countries. There are only 175 countries in the world."

Everyone laughed.

"On top of the Afghani war," Alexander continued cheerfully, taking a drink of champagne and lighting his cigarette, "they are heavily subsidizing *all* their Eastern satellites—East Germany, Poland, Czechoslovakia, Romania, Hungary, Bulgaria. Plus they are funding a standing army of millions of Soviet men across the breadth and width of Eastern Europe. They're paying for the Czech wall and its guards, they're paying for the Berlin Wall and its guards. They're paying for the guards around Lech Walesa's prison cell, for the guards to keep the Poles out of churches. Is it viable for them to divert their resources from this, Ant? Away from the Berlin Wall and into SDI?" Alexander shrugged and smiled. "Perhaps it is. Perhaps that's where they should divert their resources from. If they can't defend it, the wall is coming down, Walesa is free, and the Catholics attend Mass in Krakow. The Soviets are having a very hard time keeping Christ away from Polish Communists. But they are also funding every new rebellion in Africa and South America, and subsidizing Cuba and Vietnam. And insurgencies in Angola, Ethiopia, Nicaragua, El Salvador, Grenada. Creating chaos throughout the world doesn't come cheap, you know." Alexander's eyes were glazed over Tatiana, as if he were remembering something, perhaps about chaos in the universe where all was one, where all was all right, and all was reconciled—and then he went on. "In 1979," he said, "the Soviets paid for the Vietnamese invasion of Cambodia and to help them repel the Chinese invasion. The same year they overextended themselves into invading Afghanistan. They continue to fund and supply the Vietnamese Army, one of the largest standing armies in the world. Why do they do it? And what does Vietnam still need an army like that for? Laos, Cambodia, Vietnam, they're all *one*." Now he smiled at Tatiana. "The Soviet Union produces *nothing* of value except gold and oil, and with the Gulag machine disassembling, labor, cheap as it is, is no longer free. The criminal prisoners alone are not enough to prop up the command economy of the Soviet state. So Anthony Barrington, my son, your third question is, you want to know if I think—with their hands already

so deep in every pot—the Soviets should spend hundreds of bil-
lions of rubles they don't have on the stupidest thing *you* have
ever heard of?" Alexander laughed. "But of course, I say. They
must!"

Coda

"Farewell, queen," said he, "henceforward and for ever, till age and death, the common lot of mankind, lay their hands upon you. I now take my leave; be happy in this house with your children, your people, and with king Alcinous."
[Homer, The Odyssey]

One

Many years passed since the seagulls in Stockholm, Sweden, and the hospital in Morozovo and the hut in Lazarevo; and many more still since the granite parapets in the finite twilight of the Northern sun.

It was Thanksgiving 1999.

While two turkeys were peaceably hiding in two ovens, the house was a zoo. Five opinionated women were in the kitchen, five loud cooks to spoil the broth. One was making mashed potatoes, one was making green bean casserole, one was cooking sweet potatoes. The loudest of all was adjusting her nursing bra, making milk, and the quietest of all was making bacon leek stuffing and yams with rum and a brown sugar glaze. Seven preadolescent and teenage girls were flung over the kitchen table gabbing about music and makeup, toys and boys. Next to them was a small infant seat and in it a small infant. The young girls were impatiently waiting for their grandmother to finish the leek stuffing and make the preacher cookies she'd been promising.

Across the long, sunny gallery, in the den, five mature professional men were cursing at an inanimate rectangular object on which the Cowboys were being carved up by the Dolphins. A toddler sat on his grandfather's lap with his grandfather's large hands over his ears.

Four boys were running in a pack around the house, at the moment playing ping pong polo. Three boys and one gangly twenty-year-old were playing basketball outside. Music piped through the speakers. The house was so loud that when the doorbell rang no one heard.

It's the end of November, and outside is 72 degrees. They're all going in the heated pool after dinner.

The freshly repainted walls are covered in memories. The beds are made. The fresh flowers are in vases. The mirrors have no streaks, the hardwoods are polished. The California golden poppy, orange fiddleneck and desert lavender bloom winter wild across the hills and by human design in their bedroom garden.

The dining room is banquet hall sized—because the one who built it had been thinking generationally. It has space for two long wooden tables pushed together. The tables are clothed in gold and scarlet and are set in crystal and china for twenty-six people: four grown children, three of their spouses, fifteen of their children, and two guests.

One mother.

One father.

At the head of the room, above where he sits, a small plaque reads, "*He brought me to his banqueting table and his banner over me was love.*" Under the plaque stands the gangly basketball player, a stranger to this house, staring at the walls and the photographs.

In her madhouse of a kitchen, Tatiana's sea-foam eyes shine in her round face as she shows her granddaughters how to make preacher cookies. "All right," she says. "Preacher cookies. Watch and learn. Half a cup of butter. Two cups of sugar. Half a cup of milk. Boil, boil boil." Her soft flaxen hair comes down below the nape of her neck. Her makeup is light. She has gained weight in her breasts and her hips but remains trim, and as if to prove it, wears a form-fitting, short-sleeve, jersey-knit, periwinkle dress. Her shoulders and the bridge of her nose are dusted with freckles. Her face is smooth, her skin plump and filled out. She swims every day, dives still, rides trail horses in Carefree, walks through the desert, plants flowers, lifts her smaller grandchildren in her arms. She has aged well.

"When it boils," Tatiana says, "you add three cups of quick oats, a cup of powdered unsweetened cocoa, and then, at your discretion, either half a cup of coconut, half a cup of walnuts, or half a cup of peanut butter."

Here ten different voices give their ten opinions. Tatiana sighs theatrically and puts in half a cup of coconut. "Your grandfather likes it with coconut, so that's how I make it. When you're in your own house, you can make it how you like." She stirs until the oatmeal is cooked, for about a mushy minute, maybe longer, and then takes it off the stove, and immediately spoons out glops of fudgy cookies onto foil. "They'll be ready in an hour," she says. Really, she might as well be speaking Russian because the older girls, the younger girls, the teenage girls, and even their chuckling dressed-up mothers all take a ball, hot on napkins, and pop them ah-ah-ahhing in their mouths.

There is frightening noise from the crystal-clad dining room. Tatiana is sheepishly told that Tristan and Travis, Harry's 10-year-old twins, are playing football with their two older brothers who should know better. No one wants to mention that the football they're playing around her banqueting china is not touch but tackle.

Rachel and Rebecca, Anthony's 19-year-old girls, both sophomores at Harvard, are gossiping loudly at the table with chocolatey red mouths. Rebecca has brought a boyfriend for Thanksgiving—a first for her, a first for the family—and is now giving her younger, open-mouthed cousins the loud, G-rated low-down on him, in full hearing of Tatiana, as if hoping Grammy will hear and approve. Rebecca's boyfriend finally appears in the kitchen after playing basketball and touring the house, and is introduced simply as Washington. He is tall, lanky-awkward, long-haired, laconic and unshaven for the holidays. When he speaks, Tatiana, with a small disapproving frown, notices a ball of silver flash on his tongue.

"Grammy, Washington is a math major!" Rebecca effuses, hanging on to Washington. "Aren't you impressed? Grammy *loves* math majors, don't you, Grammy? And Washington is *brilliant*!"

Tatiana smiles politely at Washington, who tries to look brilliant *and* nonchalant. He pastes a return smile for Tatiana, analyzes her face intently, looking for something, excuses himself after ten seconds and goes to get a drink without asking Rebecca if she wants one.

Rebecca, twinkling like a comet, says in a low voice, "Grammy, I think he is my first real love. Though truthfully, when you're this young, can you even tell?" She glances longingly after Washington.

"No, honey," Tatiana says to Rebecca. "You can't tell anything about love when you're young."

"Grammy, you're being ironic with me, and I simply won't stand for it," Rebecca rejoins, her chocolate lips puckering on Tatiana's face. "I'm going to write a book about you and then you'll be sorry."

"I give them till Christmas," Tatiana says quietly to Anthony, who has just walked in, heading straight for the preacher cookies.

"That long?" he says, swallowing the gooey ball.

A small dark delicate-looking boy trails behind him. "Dad," he says, "can I go to Grandpa's shed? We were making a chess board last time I was here. He said I could finish it."

"Don't ask *me*, Tomboy," says Anthony. "Ask Grandpa. Though you might want to wait till half-time to ask him anything." With his hand on his son's shoulder, he turns to his mother. "Mom, are you still collecting blood for Red Cross?"

"Who wants to know?" Tatiana smiles. "As President of the Phoenix Chapter, I think I must. We have a blood drive next week. Why, you want to donate a pint?"

"Why just a pint?" Anthony says. "Take the whole armful." And he grins back.

Pushing her small brother out of the way, Rebecca steps up to her father, taking him by his one arm, which he disengages from her, trying to take another cookie. She grabs him again and says petulantly to Tatiana, "Grammy, ask Daddy what he thinks of Washington. Ask him."

"Becky, honey, your father is standing right here. I give you permission to ask him yourself."

"He won't tell me!"

"What does that tell you?" Anthony says. "Let go. I have to go back for the disembowelment of the Cowboys. Tom, you coming?"

"That kid Washington plays pretty decent basketball," says ten-year-old Tommy. "If that's worth anything."

"Dad," says Rachel, coming up to his left side and poking him in the rib, "why don't you tell Grammy what I just heard Grandpa shouting at the TV in full hearing of the two-year-old." The model-tall girls, identically made up, identically attired, identical, stunning, flank their father, their identically affectionate gazes on him.

Anthony winks at Tommy. "We won't tell her, will we, bud?" He stares at his daughters. "Will you two let go of me? Tom, where's your brother? Uncle Harry wants him to watch Samson until Grandpa calms down."

"Grandpa was *standing* in front of the TV," whispers Rachel with a big grin but in a low voice so the young ones won't hear, "and yelling at his team, 'Hey, *girls*! Why don't you Cowboy the fuck up?'"

"Shhhhh!" exclaims Tatiana. "Rachel Barrington!"

"What? He's *your* husband!"

Shaking her head, Tatiana takes Tommy by the hand and the last two preacher cookies on a napkin and walks from the kitchen, through the long wide gallery with plants and pictures and floor-to-ceiling windows, to the family room, where she stands behind the couch and leans over a white head.

"Shura," she says quietly, her hand with the preacher balls extended, "be good. Don't teach the toddlers all you know just yet."

Alexander, without taking his eyes away from the TV, reaches over, takes one of the cookies, pops it into his mouth, leans his head slightly to her, and says in his rasping baritone, "I *was* good. I covered his ears. And if you saw the defensive line—God, when's half-time? I need a cigarette."

Tommy loiters by the side of the couch. "Grandpa, what about my chess board? Can we go finish it?"

"What a good idea, Tomboy," says Alexander. "Let's go right now." Standing up, he turns to Tatiana. Though his hair is white, and thinner, it is not gone from his head. Tatiana cuts it herself every month with her electric clippers. There are many physical things that age has not taken from Alexander: his height; his straight posture; his hands—with the iron handshake, still like a vise, and with softness still like feathers; hands that still work in his shed, whittle chess pieces, trim bushes, hold reins and children, shoot basketballs, touch his wife. His arms that do the frontstroke in the pool and support his weight in bed; his lucid eyes, still twinkling peace under his black-gray eyebrows, his caramel eyes—that suddenly narrow.

"Hey!" he shouts at two boys rolling in from the dining room. "Yes, you, Tristan, Travis—secure that! How many times do I have to tell you? Not one more time, you hear me? No horseplay in the house on holidays. Take the life-threatening games outside."

Before Pasha even has a chance to get up from the couch and glare at his sons, they instantly and silently and in an orderly fashion hightail it outside. Alexander smiles at Tatiana, and Tommy reaches for his hand. "Just for a minute, though, bud," says Alexander. "I've got a houseful today. But you're staying the week; I promise, we'll finish the set, okay?"

"Okay, Grandpa."

"How has your brother been treating you?"

"Terrible."

"Ignore him. He's in a bad mood."

"He's been in a bad mood since the day he was born."

During merciful half-time, Alexander gathers with his sons on the patio: him and Anthony and Harry—who has supposedly quit—for a long smoke, Pasha for a cold beer.

Alexander's sons are tall. Harry, the slimmest and tallest, is taller even than his father, a fact for which he jokingly blames his mother for allowing him to nurse until he was two and a half. ("You're depending on a two-year-old to wean himself? Grown-ups can't wean themselves!" Alexander had said to Tatiana). Harry and Pasha are blond. Anthony's pepper is slowly salting.

Pasha now likes to call himself Charles Gordon Barrington. His wife, Mary, always so proper, calls him, "Chaaarles." As soon as she turns her back, his brothers mutely imitate her. "*Chaaaarles*," they mouth. To his family he will always be Pasha, except to Jane, who, to tease him, calls him *Chaaarles* now, too. Not *exactly* like the sainted warrior of Khartoum; at 41, Charles Gordon Barrington is the U.S. Army chief surgeon at the Hayden Veterans Medical Center right on Indian School Road in Phoenix. His mother comes to have lunch with him once a week. His father continues to persist in his lifelong aversion to hospitals, so father and son play golf instead. Since Alexander left the hospital back in March of 1970, just in time to receive his Congressional Medal, he has never been back. Whatever ailments befall him, he's got his own nurse, right around the clock, and a son who anxiously observes his condition twice a week from holes one through eighteen. The son looks for signs of heart disease, emphysema, old age. Alexander is eighty. He figures any time now, Pasha might see the last. But not while the son demands golf twice a week, and makes Alexander walk the eighteen holes. Every few months, Alexander gets to play golf with two of his three sons.

Anthony doesn't play golf.

Pasha was the last of the four kids to marry, gallivanting intemperately through his twenties, and finally falling for another doctor when he was thirty and in residency; in 1988 they settled into an overworked life, and together they, organized, temperate, efficient, had twins in 1990—a girl, Maria, whom they call Mia, and a boy, Charles Gordon—and were done, and their family was ordered and quiet, and they each worked sixty hours a week. They now

live in Paradise Valley, in a house Barrington Custom Homes built
for them, and they come over on Sundays to spend the day. Except
Mary is pregnant again at 41, inexplicably, and they don't know
how to tell anyone. It is so unlike them not to plan. Pasha advises
Mary not to go anywhere near his mother if she doesn't want the
whole family to find out.

   Harry Barrington, 39, is a U.S. Army nuclear, biological, chem-
ical and conventional defense specialist. As Harry likes to point
out, "I'm not *a* weapons specialist. I'm *the* weapons specialist."
After getting his doctorate in nuclear physics from MIT in 1985,
he has been working for the Department of Defense at Yuma
Proving Ground. His career was made at the end of the eighties
when he had been experimentally designing a long tube that was
19 feet long and only 14 inches in diameter. His brothers called
it, "just a souped up punji stick." Suddenly Iraq invaded Kuwait
and Harry and his team of scientists had to work around the clock,
and in record time designed a guided bomb unit that in its final
form weighed nearly 5000 pounds and was fitted with over 600
pounds of explosive.

   Alexander said, "Harry, my son, if the bomb weighs 5000 pounds,
does it even need to explode?" Apparently, yes it did. It needed
to penetrate concrete Iraqi command centers deep underground
before it detonated. It was called a bunker buster. It was such a
rush job that the initial bunker busters were constructed out of
the army's old artillery material.

   Harry married a tiny girl named Amy in 1985, when he was
25, and his generous wife gave him one boy after another, after
another. They had Harry Jr. in 1986, Jake in 1987 and then the
twins Tristan and Travis in 1989. In one final last ditch attempt
for a girl, they produced Samson in 1997, who is enough boy for
four. Now all five sons trail like puppies after Harry and he teaches
them what he knows. The rest of the family loudly fears for the
fate of the world. They drive up from Yuma once a month to spend
the weekend at the house. Amy and Mary are good friends.

   Jane had the opposite problem from Harry. In 1983, barely
twenty, just finished with her registered nurse credentials, she married a boy she had known since birth—a fine man named Shannon
Clay Jr., Shannon and long-gone Amanda's oldest son, who runs
Barrington Custom Homes for both families now that Alexander
and Shannon are semi-retired. In 1985, Jane and Shannon Jr. had
a girl, Alexandra, another girl, Nadia, in 1986, another girl, Victoria,

in 1989, and yet *another* girl, Veronica, in 1990. The 1980s were baby boom years for the Barringtons—especially 1989, when six of the sixteen next-gens were born just as the Berlin Wall was coming down. That Harry had five sons is somehow cosmic, but that Jane, the tomboy of the family, in an ironic twist of fate had four daughters—Sasha, Nadia, Vicky and Nicky—when what she and Shannon both desperately wanted was just one little boy, is cosmically unfair. Harry advised them to learn from him and quit at four, because five was so unmanageable as to be comical. He said five was like war. "That's only because your fifth one is named Samson," Alexander said to Harry. "Teaches you right to call your son that." But Jane—afraid not only of another girl but of her mother's latent twin gene, which so far passed her by—heeded Harry's procreational advice up until the end of the millennium. Now her newborn *son* has five mothers, like cooks. He sleeps in the noisy kitchen, adored but unnamed—like a monarch. They're tortured over his name. Shannon wants his own, and Jane wants her father's.

Janie and Shannon live just downhill on Jomax in a spectacular pueblo house. Janie is always over.

Anthony, despite great pressures in Washington, tries to coordinate his own visits with Harry's from Yuma, so that at least a few times a year, their mother and father can have what they love best—all their children in one noisy house.

Anthony, who is 56, is currently a deputy advisor for the National Security Council. He has served three presidential administrations beginning with Ronald Reagan's. The Communist Party of the Soviet Union has gone quiet, as have all the rebellions it was stirring in Africa, across the breadth of South America, and in Southeast Asia—as if once the Gorgon Medusa's head was severed, all the serpents on it shuddered and died. Now Cuba, Angola, Cambodia, Laos, Vietnam remain some of the poorest countries on earth. And though Alexander has finally resigned his commission—deeming his work finished after the fall of the Soviet Union—as far as Anthony is concerned, the world remains unfixed. Old troubles are brewing on top of new troubles in the Middle East. And new troubles are brewing on top of old troubles in North Korea. There is some intel indication that the North Koreans are not sticking to their end of the agreements against nuclear weapons development. While dealing with them, Anthony has continued to wage his thirty-year-old battle to locate the 1300 still missing soldiers in Vietnam. In the same vein, he has just returned from Russia, where he met with government officials from Moscow and St. Petersburg to see if they could fix more firmly on the fate of 91 American servicemen missing in Russia since the end of the Second World War.

Over the years he has steadfastly refused a prosthetic; a functional device was impossible with his degree of injury and one for purely cosmetic reasons was insulting. He continued to feel the burning, stinging pain for years and still feels the electrical nerve impulses in his phantom limb whenever he is stressed.

He feels the electrical nerve impulses constantly.

And while there are some things he cannot do (golf, play his six-string, carve turkey), for the most part he manages just fine, and the people who know him stopped noticing the missing arm in the seventies. The people who don't know him, if they're in the service, don't ask, because Anthony is a general, and no one asks a general anything unless they're invited to, and Anthony does not invite them to. Civilians sometimes ask. In stores, on the street, during Alexander's VE-Day parades, they'll say to Anthony, "Hey man, what happened to you?" And he replies, "Vietnam." They whistle, shake their heads; usually, "Vietnam" is enough. Sometimes they want more. "Did you get shot?"

And then he tells them. "No," says Anthony. "I was a POW, and the NVA cut off my arm piece by piece starting with my fingers because I kept killing the guards that were torturing me."

And after that, there is not even a single follow-up *breath*.

In 1979, Anthony married an Indonesian woman named Ingrid, who was Janie's twelfth-grade music teacher. Janie introduced her 36-year-old brother to the 24-year-old piano-playing Ingrid at a winter concert. Janie had talked him way up—where he fought, how many tours he had, how many medals he got, how many times he got wounded. She even mentioned in oh-so-casual passing that her brother had only one arm and liked to sing. Ingrid was exotic, musically gifted, and impressed. Anthony married her four months later, and his girls, Rachel and Rebecca, were born in 1980. To their protégé mother's great disappointment—though they are both at Harvard—Rachel is immersed in Russian studies and Rebecca in English. They are raven-haired Eurasian beauties, combining their father's height with the vivid Italian-Russian-Indonesian markings from their parents. Few who meet them can see beyond the drama of their looks. In their freshman year, they made a calendar to raise money for the families of the Vietnam MIA/POW. The R-rated calendar was called "The Ivy Girls" and was the number-one-selling calendar in Cambridge. They said their father was too old to see it. This year, back by popular demand, they had to put out a new edition. That is how Washington first laid eyes on Rebecca: he bought the calendar.

In 1985, after two miscarriages, Ingrid finally gave Anthony a son, Anthony Alexander Barrington III. One more miscarriage followed before another son, Tommy, was born in 1989.

Of Anthony's four children, it is ironically Anthony Jr. who has his mother's gift for music and his father's voice; ironic because Anthony Jr. would rather be boiled in oil than touch an ivory or let a lyric note pass his lips. He used to play and sing when he was younger, even played guitar; but no more.

After he came back from Vietnam, and they buried Tom Richter in Arlington, Anthony lived with Vikki. She stopped working, stopped flying around the world; she traveled with him, stayed with him. Since Vikki was a troublemaker, her favorite thing to tell people in response to their slightly nosy, perked-up question, "And how long have you two known each other?" was, "Oh, we've been together—on and off—since the day he was born." And to an even more impertinent, slightly suggestive allusion to the absence of his limb, she would say, "Don't you worry, the man is still a quadruped."

They were together until 1977 when she got breast cancer at the age of 54 and died. Anthony was with her until the end. One of the last things Vikki said to him was, "Antman, because of you, *comé un fiume tu, adesso lo so—questro é amoré. Ti amo*, Anthony. *Ti amo. Quale vita dolce ho trascorso con te.*"

Vikki never knew her father, and her mother had been lost to her since childhood. She had been raised by Travis and Isabella, her Italian grandparents—who after a Tristan and Isolde inauspicious beginning were married for over seventy years, and were now long gone. Since in death, Vikki had nowhere to go, she was brought to Phoenix and cremated, her ashes scattered over Tatiana and Alexander's saguaro desert land, and a garden of colt-like ocotillos, red around a yellow *sole mio* palo verde, planted in her name, *ex animo, ad lucem.*

Alexander, Anthony, Gordon Pasha, and Harry come back inside and continue their half-time conversation in the dining room, standing like pillars against the white linen walls in their dark sweaters and dark trousers, holding their beers and discussing the latest crazy thing Anthony is doing that Harry needs to build something to protect him from, and Pasha saying, how long am I going to keep mopping up after you? Harry is in charge of the Ballistic Missile Defense Organization that used to be the Strategic Defense Initiative Organization. He oversees the deployment of the National Missile Defense designed to protect all fifty states from an attack. His interest in it has always been to design a robust and virtually perfect defense system to counteract a large threat, as well as counteracting, with conventional weapons—which he also designs. As he keeps saying, he likes to play both defense and offense.

He researches and tests ground-based lasers, space-based lasers, and automated space vehicles while continuing to play politics with the Energy Department over the costs of nuclear power systems in space. He tells his father of the unbelievable resistance he has encountered to his proposals for certain space-based directed and kinetic energy weapons that he admits do happen to have significant power requirements attached.

"How significant?" asks Alexander.

"Well . . . significant," says Harry. "But see, I build the defense systems, because that's *my* job, and they're supposed to deliver the energy system, because that's *their* fucking job. I don't ask them about plasma arcs of metallic railguns, do I?"

"I think it's just as well," says Pasha.

They're so absorbed they don't even see they're blocking Tatiana's path to the dining room table, to which she is trying to deliver her own energy system—homemade butter yeast rolls.

"Hmm," says Alexander, taking one warm roll, as she tries to squeeze past them with the tray. Stepping in front of her, he rips the roll into four chunks, gives three to his sons, takes the tray from her, puts it on the table. She moves this way and that, but they won't let her pass, surrounding her on all sides, Alexander in front, Pasha and Harry flanking her, Anthony behind her. Periwinkling, she vanishes inside their navy chests, looking up at her husband and her sons, from one face to the other and finally saying, "What? Do you four have nothing better to do than stand idly while I run around with thirty of you to feed?"

"We're not standing idly," says Harry. "We're discussing the fate of the free world." He bends nearly in half to kiss his mother's cheek.

"Mom, how's your burn?" says Pasha, taking hold of her forearm and turning it over. "I see you've taken off my dressing." He touches the wound.

For a moment, the five of them stand mutely together. Tatiana pats Pasha's hand and says, "Burn is fine. Free world is fine. And you've been watching too much football, stop blocking me." She turns around and lifts her eyes to her firstborn son whom she's not touching, and who's not touching her, but who's watching her silently. His eyes are not peaceful. His limb twitches. He wants to communicate something. But he says nothing.

Jane comes in from the butler's pantry with her baby in one hand and cranberry jelly in the other and says with exasperation, "Will you step out of her way, can't you see she's busy?" She tuts when no one listens. "Anthony, please—you at least, can you go open the door? The doorbell has been ringing for an hour."

"So if you heard it, why didn't you go open the door?" Anthony says to his sister.

"I don't know if you've noticed, but not only am I cooking, I'm lactating, too. What are *you* doing? Exactly. Go open the door, I said. You're not a general in this house. I don't have to salute you nineteen times like my brothers do. Now go."

As Anthony obediently goes to answer the front door, Alexander pulls Tatiana away for a moment into the empty gallery, where he presses her against the wall, lifts her face up and kisses her in brief seclusion before Washington's eyes peer at them from under palms and photographs.

The person outside is a pretty, very small, blonde woman in her early thirties, dressed nicely and smiling nicely for the holidays, holding a blueberry pie in her hands and a bouquet of blue irises. She introduces herself as Kerri, and says that she is Victoria's fourth-grade teacher and a good friend of Jane's, who apparently has invited her for dinner, since Kerri's family is out East. "You must be Anthony," she says, looking slightly flushed and intimidated.

Anthony wonders what Janie and Vicky have been saying about him. He lets Kerri through, taking the flowers from her hand. "Blueberry pie," he says. "My favorite."

"Really?" She looks pleased, relaxes.

In the kitchen, Anthony Jr. was cornered into a wall by his sister Rebecca who said, "TO-nee, you vile beast, tell me right now what you did to Washington or I'll tell Dad on you." Anthony had braved

a place he proclaimed he hated ("full of clucking women") to grab
a warm roll, but he hadn't been quick enough walking back out.

Pushing Rebecca off him, he said, "Like I care. Tell away—and
stop calling me Tony." At nearly fifteen Anthony was a six-foot
reed, an inch taller than his sisters. He was dark and Eurasian; all
angles and bones and eyes and lips because his hair had been
shaved off except for the thin Mohawk line running from his forehead to the back of his neck. He was dressed forbiddingly in black
for Thanksgiving, like a Visigoth, and was grim like one, too.

"What did you do to him?" Rebecca repeated. "He's walking
around this house like an apparition, gazing at walls. He won't
even go and watch football with Dad and Grandpa. He hasn't said
one boo to Grandpa, you know how Grandpa hates that. How is
he ever going to get to know them?"

"Maybe if you stopped calling me Tony, I wouldn't have had to
take matters into my own hands," said Anthony Jr.

"Anthony, then, OK," conceded his sister. "Now tell me what
you've done to my Washington before I wring your neck. Did you
scare him?"

"No," said Anthony Jr. "I mean—if he got scared, that's *his*
problem."

"Oh, *no*! What did you say?"

"Nothing." Anthony Jr. paused. "Nothing. He is very nosy, won't
stop asking questions about Dad. He asked me to show him something from Dad's Vietnam days."

"Oh, no! What did you show him? His SOG knife?"

"He wouldn't still be in this house if I showed him that. No. I
showed him the most innocent thing. I'm telling you, Beck, if your
slam of a boyfriend can't take a Zippo lighter, he's got no business
in this family."

"Which Zippo lighter?" Anthony's old Special Forces Zippo
lighters were engraved with all manner of bestial sayings and rude
drawings. "What did it say?" She covered her eyes. "Please don't
let it be . . . "

"This Zippo read, '*Yea, though I walk through the valley of the shadow
of death, I fear no evil*,'" Goth-like Anthony Jr. said, lowering his
voice only slightly in his grandmother's children-filled
Thanksgiving kitchen, not noticing Anthony standing next to Kerri
in the doorway, "'*for I'm the baddest motherfucker in the valley*.'"

"ANTHONY JR.!" That was Rebecca, Tatiana, Jane, Rachel, all
over him.

"Get the hell out of here, will you, and stop causing trouble like always." That was an unsmiling and unamused Anthony. Kerri was smiling and amused.

As he was being shoved out of the kitchen, an unfazed Anthony Jr. was telling Rebecca, "Like I said, if that silly boy can't handle a little Zippo, what the hell is he doing with *you*?"

"Please don't concern yourself with that, TO-Neeee!" Rebecca taunted his departing back.

Anthony smiled politely at Kerri. "Kids these days," he said, passing the flowers to his mother. "Jane!" he called. "Your friend is here."

Dinner was as out of control as only a Thanksgiving dinner could be with fifteen children, all squabblingly bunched together at their own table. Two china plates were broken, five drinks were spilled, the mashed potatoes were almost cold, and someone cut himself with a butter knife. Good thing there was a doctor in the house.

Alexander carved the two birds. At the table, no one, not even the young ones, put food on their plate until Alexander helped himself to his first forkful of turkey. He poured Tatiana drink, he stood to make a toast, he even said Thanksgiving grace over their abundant table, looking at her. *"All that we have is a gift that comes from You."*

And there was Washington, watching him, watching her.

The wives sat next to their husbands, all except Anthony's wife, who wasn't there. ("Where is Ingrid, Mom?" Jane had asked. "We don't know and we don't ask," replied Tatiana. "You hear me? We *don't* ask." To which Janie, in her inimitable Dad-like style, said, "Good fucking riddance. I hope she never comes back. I'm sorry I ever introduced them. She's been nothing but trouble. All she does is make his life harder.") Kerri sat next to Jane, and Anthony sat between his daughters, who mothered him, ladled food onto him, cut his turkey and poured his drink. By deliberate and careful omission, no one mentioned the absent Ingrid. Anthony's two sons—one chafing at being lumped with "the GD babies," one disquietingly quiet—sat away from the adults and any possible questions about their missing mother.

Their plates scraped clean of food (oh, they learned, they all learned), the kids were done with dinner in twelve minutes, and a truculent Anthony Jr. was asked to watch Samson in the pool while the adults sat a little longer. He loudly protested. Harry said not to worry, Anthony said, no, he *will* do it. Tommy pulled at his brother, saying I'll help you. Anthony Jr. said he didn't want to leave the table yet like he was a child, and Anthony said he wasn't being given a choice, to which Anthony Jr. got up with a snark, to which Anthony got up with a clench, which prompted Tatiana to jump up before Alexander got up and things got really out of hand. "Anthony Jr." That's all Tatiana said, and the boy fled from the table. Anthony sat back down; everything calmed down. The adults sat another hour. Never mind, said Harry. It's that age. Ask Dad what you were like when you were fourteen. A small glance passed between Alexander and Anthony. Alexander said, "He was always a good kid. But besides, headbutting was not allowed."

"It's not allowed with me either," said Anthony. "There's still headbutting."

To change the subject, Washington said that at fourteen he used to give his own mother a hard time when his dad was not around—which was most of the time.

To change the subject *much* further—because Anthony himself was not around most of the time—Janie asked Tatiana how long she should nurse the baby. The men at the table—particularly the three grown, mature men once nursed by Tatiana—groaned.

To expand on the favorably changed subject, Mary asked Tatiana if she had any complications having Janie at thirty-nine. Anthony wanted to know if it was *possible* for women, even *doctors*, to talk about things other than breasts and childbirth at the Thanksgiving table. Yes, let's talk about quench guns instead, said Harry. No, Tatiana replied to Mary, no complications—and then stared at Pasha until he rolled his eyes, turned to Mary, and said, "What did I tell you earlier? You don't listen, do you?" They were forced to tell everyone they were expecting a baby. The family was surprised and pleased. Alexander opened another bottle of Napa wine.

Washington was completely tongue-tied. (Perhaps it was the tongue piercing, Tatiana thought.) He could do no better than answer the family's questions in mono-syllables. Even shiny-eyed Rebecca became frustrated. They left him alone and asked questions of Kerri instead, who was a much better public speaker, was soft-spoken, laughed easily and was pleasant to look at.

After a protracted throat clearing, Washington did finally speak. "Mrs. Barrington—"

"Please. Call me Tatiana."

An impossibility. Washington didn't call her anything when he continued, "Rebecca, um, told me you both, you two, you and your husband, um, were from Russia. Have you, um, gone back since—all the, you know, changes there?"

Tatiana told Washington that for their fiftieth wedding anniversary gift seven years ago, the children did pitch in and buy them two white night weeks in St. Petersburg, but they ended up not going.

"You didn't, um, want to go?" asked Washington.

Tatiana didn't know what to say. *Eto bylo, bylo i proshlo/vse proshlo/ i viugoy zamelo* . . .

It was Alexander who answered Washington. "We almost went," he said, "but we'd already been to Leningrad, you see, and we heard about this place, right in the United States, that also had protracted nights and shining lights—but also rivers that ran through hotels, and circuses and jumping tigers, and indoor roller-coasters, and—what else, Tania?"

"I don't know. Free drinks? Indoor smoking? Cheap food? Interesting things on television?"

"Yes, and poker." Alexander smiled at his kids. "The thought of their mother in that cauldron of decadence was a shock to our grown children, but we thought we'd try it once, just for a lark, so we exchanged Leningrad for two weeks at the MGM-Grand." And then he smiled at Tatiana. "Tania didn't do too bad, did you? Beginner's luck, they say."

Tatiana assented. "Las Vegas is a fascinating place," she said casually. "We're thinking of taking a little trip back." She glanced at Alexander. So what if they take that little trip once a month? Las Vegas makes her smile and forget the remorse and the impossibility of seeing with old weakened eyes the streets of their once life that have become diminished by time, but which their old weakened hearts still see undiminished. All they have to do is close their eyes. For it is Leningrad, the death of everything, that was also the birth of everything: every ocotillo and wolfberry they plant today was borne out of the bombed-out sunlit streets of the city yesterday that the soul can't bury, can't hide, can't drive away.

Washington whistled. "You know, I've never met anyone who's been, um, you know, married fifty-seven years," he said. "I'm quite . . . impressed. My mother has been married for twenty-five years." He paused. "But to three different husbands, with several boyfriends and some breaks in between."

"I told Washington, Grammy," Rebecca said with a giggle, "that it was love at first sight with you two, and he said he didn't believe it because he doesn't believe in love in first sight."

"I didn't say that," said Washington. "I think it's something at first sight, just not necessarily love—" And broke off suddenly, turning deep red. The table went quiet. The grown children glanced at their parents uncomfortably; Tatiana and Alexander glanced at each other with amusement; Anthony glared at Rebecca who glared at Washington.

Tommy came back and asked Washington if he wanted to go— and Washington jumped up and flew out—". . . swimming," finished Tommy.

Rebecca apologized and said she didn't know what was wrong with him. "He is so twitchy tonight. He is usually very sweet."

Alexander coughed fakely. Under the table Tatiana kicked him. To her daughter, she said, "Janie, your friend Kerri must know quite a bit about us because she's not asking us any of the usual questions." Where did you meet? How did you escape? What happened in Vietnam? And she didn't peer into their faces as though looking for traces of things that could not be politely asked for, which is what Washington had been doing all day. Kerri didn't do any of that.

Kerri, rosy and pretty, blushed and chuckled. "Both Jane and Vicky have told me a bit," she admitted. "The lore *is* quite intimidating. I mean, I'm just a schoolteacher. I know Little League dads and librarians."

"Little League dads can be very intimidating," said Tatiana. "You've never met our friend, Sam Gulotta."

"How is he feeling? Perhaps, he'll fly up for Christmas?" asked Jane. "Kerri can meet him then."

"I don't know generals, or presidential advisors, or POWs," Kerri continued, clearing her throat, looking slightly faint of heart. "But for what it's worth," she said, "not being a Harvard alum and all, I'm not a cynic yet. I believe in love at first sight."

This made everyone fall in a pause, but not for long because Jane exclaimed happily, "And Kerri plays a *fantastic* guitar!"

Even Anthony laughed. "Does she indeed?" he said, with great amusement staring at a befuddled and embarrassed Kerri.

Rachel and Rebecca studied Kerri. "Does she indeed?" they said.

Before Anthony's open smile was analyzed further—or God forbid returned—by Kerri, Tatiana stood from the table signaling the end of dinner, and to her daughter whispered, "Child, you have absolutely *no* shame."

"That's right, Holy Mother," said Janie. "None whatsoever."

The men were dispatched to play pool, or poker, or watch TV, and Rachel and Rebecca, reluctantly trying to be adults, went into the kitchen with the women to clean up. Tatiana wasn't cleaning. No one would let her lift even her own plate. They sat her down, gave her a cup of tea, and she directed the Tupperware and the plastic wrap over the leftovers. The kids were all wildly in the pool, all except for Samson, who was in the kitchen climbing wet into Amy's arms, and for Washington—who was now dressed and sitting damply at the table next to Tatiana.

Rebecca, already bored with cleaning up after five minutes, threw herself over the table and said, "Grammy, Washington really likes your photographs."

Washington, who was sitting two feet away from Tatiana, said nothing.

"Well," said Tatiana, "tell Washington thank you."

"He is very observant, and he pointed out you had all kinds of photos but no wedding ones of you and Grandpa. He wanted to know why that was."

"Washington wanted to know this, did he?" Tatiana said, her bemused eyes on Washington. "Has Washington been to every wall in my house? And if so, ask him what he was doing in my bedroom."

Washington, as red as the spring barrel cactus, stuttered and said, "No—that's right—perhaps—I'm just saying—yes, perhaps there."

"They're not there either," said Rebecca. "I know. I told him it was because the camera technology didn't come to Russia in the eighteenth century when you got married."

"You know so much," said Tatiana.

"But do you know what *he* told me?" With a big mischievous smile, Rebecca lowered her voice. "He thinks it's because you and Grandpa never actually got married."

"He thinks this, does he?"

"Isn't that simply *delicious*?" Rebecca exclaimed.

"Becky," said Washington, "do you always have to tell everybody absolutely everything you're thinking?"

"Yes!" said Rebecca.

"So let me understand," said Tatiana, "not only does Washington think my husband didn't love me when he met me, but that he also didn't marry me. Is that right?

"That's right!" Rebecca said joyously. "Well, why should he have married you? He didn't love you!" She pinched Tatiana, poked her, tickled her. "Come on, Grammy, save your family's honor. Prove to Washington Grandpa loved you *and* married you. *Or* give us something to really gossip about."

"Yes," said Tatiana, "because usually you have absolutely nothing to say." She was infinitely amused by the delectable Rebecca.

Alexander and Anthony walked into the kitchen, smelling of cigarette smoke. "Mayday, Mayday!" Jane said. "Men in the kitchen during clean-up."

"I just wanted to make sure you haven't moved from the table," Alexander said to Tatiana, patting her shoulder as he walked past. "I know you." He picked up Jane's sleeping baby from the infant seat and sat next to her.

Rachel turned to Anthony. "Daddy, did you hear? Beck's new boyfriend thinks you were an illegitimate child."

"Oh, isn't he a prize," said Anthony.

Alexander twinkled at Tatiana, and everybody hooted it up, except for Washington, who now looked mortified *and* terrified, sinking into the chair.

Rachel and Rebecca were egging Tatiana on. Amy, Mary, and Jane were cleaning up and egging Tatiana on. Kerri was helping get the dessert out and saying nothing.

Alexander said lightly, "Anthony, go restore your mother's good name. Go get the pictures for the girls if you want." He glanced at Tatiana. "What? Do you want them all to think I didn't make an honest woman out of you?"

Rachel and Rebecca yelped with excitement. "I can't believe it, we're going to see your wedding photos!" squealed Rachel. "I take everything back, Becks. Washington *is* brilliant. It's all because of him and his insinuating provocations. No one has *ever* seen the wedding photos. We didn't even know for sure they existed!"

Now the infant was awake, and crying.

"I just want you to know, Grammy," Rebecca said mock-solemnly, "I defended you; I told Washington you and Grandpa had a crazy love once. Isn't that right?"

"If you say so, dear."

Rebecca threw her arms around Alexander. "Grandpa, tell me, isn't that right?"

"What are you, writing a book?"

"Yes!" She laughed. "Yes, I am. A book about you and Grammy for my senior thesis." She smothered Alexander's head. "I'm going to fill it up with things you think we're too young to know," she whispered, then smothering Tatiana, practically sitting on her lap. "If you're very good, Grammy," she murmured affectionately, kissing Tatiana's face, "and show this aspiring novelist the nice wedding photo to fire up my fervid imagination, I'm going to tell you what Washington really said about you and Grandpa, and he is going to help me write my book of love."

"A book of love?" said Tatiana. "Well, I for one, can't *wait*."

After loud overtures from his daughters, Anthony finally left the house and went up the winding path to the "museum," to the mobile home where he and his parents had lived from 1949 to 1958.

It has been left untouched. The furniture, tables, the paint on the walls, the 50s cabinets, the dressers, the closets, are all unchanged, remaining as they once were.

And in her closet in the bedroom, past the nurse's uniform, far away in the right-hand corner on the top shelf, lies the black backpack that contains Tatiana's soul.

Every once in a while when she can stand it—or when she can't stand it—she looks through it. Alexander never looks through it. Tatiana knows what Anthony is about to see. Two cans of Spam in the pack. A bottle of vodka. The nurse's uniform she escaped from the Soviet Union in that hangs in plastic in the museum closet, next to the PMH nurse's uniform she nearly lost her marriage in. The *Hero of the Soviet Union* medal in the pack, in a hidden pocket. The letters she received from Alexander—including the last one from Kontum, which, when she heard about his injuries, she thought would be the last one. That plane ride to Saigon in December 1970 was the longest twelve hours of Tatiana's life. Francesca and her daughter Emily took care of Tatiana's kids. Vikki, her good and forgiven friend, came with her, to bring back the body of Tom Richter, to bring back Anthony.

In the backpack lies an old yellowed book, *The Bronze Horseman and Other Poems*. The pages are so old, they splinter if you turn them. You cannot leaf, you can only lift. And between the fracturing pages, photographs are slotted like fragile parchment leaves. Anthony is supposed to find two of these photographs and bring them back. It should take him only a few minutes.

Cracked leaves of Tania before she was Alexander's. Here she is at a few months old, held by her mother, Tania in one arm, Pasha in the other. Here she is, a toddler in the River Luga, bobbing with

Pasha. And here a few years older, lying in the hammock with Dasha. A beaming, pretty, dark-haired Dasha is about fourteen. Here is Tania, around ten, with two dangling little braids, doing a fantastic one-armed handstand on top of a tree stump. Here are Tania and Pasha in the boat together, Pasha threateningly raising the oar over her head. Here is the whole family. The parents, side by side, unsmiling, Deda holding Tania's hand. Babushka holding Pasha's, Dasha smiling merrily in front.

Someday Tatiana must tell Alexander how glad she is that her sister Dasha did not die without once feeling what it was like to love.

Alexander. Here he is, before he was Tatiana's, at the age of twenty, getting his medal of valor for bringing back Yuri Stepanov during the 1940 Winter War. Alexander is in his dress Soviet uniform, snug against his body, his stance at-ease and his hand up to his temple in teasing salute. There is a gleaming smile on his face, his eyes are carefree, his whole man-self full of breath-taking, aching youth. And yet, the war was on, and his men had already died and frozen and starved . . . and his mother and father were gone . . . .and he was far away from home, and getting farther and farther, and every day was his last—one way or another, every day was his last. And yet, he smiles, he shines, he is happy.

Anthony is gone so long that his daughters say something must have happened to him. But then he appears. Like his father, he has learned well the poker face and outwardly remains imper-turbable. Just as a man should be, thinks Tatiana. A man doesn't get to be on the President's National Security Council without steeling himself to some of life's little adversities. A man doesn't go through what Anthony went through without steeling himself to some of life's little adversities.

In this hand Anthony carries two faded photographs, flattened by the pages of the book, grayed by the passing years.

The kitchen falls quiet, even Rachel and Rebecca are breathless in anticipation. "Let's see . . . " they murmur, gingerly picking up the fragile, sepia pictures with their long fingers. Tatiana is far away from them. "Do you want to see them with us, Grammy? Grandpa?"

"We know them well," Tatiana says, her voice catching on some-thing. "You kids go ahead."

The grandchildren, the daughter, the son, the guests circle their heads, gaping. "Washington, look! Just look at them! What did we tell you?"

Shura and Tania, 23 and 18, just married. In full bloom, on the steps of the church near Lazarevo, he in his Red Army dress uniform, she in her white dress with red roses, roses that are black in the monochrome photo. She is standing next to him, holding his arm. He is looking into the camera, a wide grin on his face. She is gazing up at him, her small body pressed into him, her light hair at her shoulders, her arms bare, her mouth slightly parted.

"Grammy!" Rebecca exclaims. "I'm positively blushing. Look at the way you're coming the spoon on Grandpa!" She turns to Alexander from the island. "Grandpa, did you catch the way she is looking at you?"

"Once or twice," replies Alexander.

The other colorless photo. Tania and Shura, 18 and 23. He lifts her in the air, his arms wrapped around her body, her arms wrapped around his neck, their fresh faces tilted, their enraptured lips in a breathless open kiss. Her feet are off the ground.

"Wow, Grammy," murmurs Rebecca. "Wow, Grandpa."

Tatiana is busily wiping the granite island.

"You want to know what my Washington said about you two?" Rebecca says, not looking away from the photograph. "He called you an adjacent Fibonacci pair!" She giggles. "Isn't that *sexy*?"

Tatiana shakes her head, despite herself glancing at Washington with reluctant affection. "Just what we need, another math expert. I don't know what you all think math will give you."

And Janie comes over to her father who is sitting at the kitchen table, holding her baby son, bends over Alexander, leans over him, kisses him, her arm around him, and murmurs into his ear, "Daddy, I've figured out what I'm going to call my baby. It's so simple."

"Fibonacci?"

She laughs. "Why, Shannon, of course. Shannon."

The fire is on. It's dark outside and still. They've had dessert; Kerri's blueberry pie was so good that Anthony asked for seconds, and not only did he ask for seconds but he asked what other kind of pie she made and if she played acoustic or electric guitar, and whether she knew how to play his favorite: "Carol of the Bells." Amy and Mary wanted to know where she bought the pie crust because it was delicious, and Kerri turning red said she made the crust herself. "You made the pie crust *yourself*?" asked an incredulous Amy. "Who does that?"

The family settled in to louder pockets of familiarity. From the other rooms of the house came noise, of smaller children fighting, a pinball machine, of a pool cue being thrown as a javelin, of tickling, of baseball card trading, of glasses falling on the floor, of older girls maternally screaming, "If you don't stop it this instant, I swear, I'll . . . ."

Finally the fifteen long-haired young collect in the gallery around a karaoke machine and while their parents and grandparents and guests sit in captivity and cheer, they belt out song after song with glee, indifferently out of tune, ecstatically out of time. Rachel and Rebecca put on quite a show shouting at the top of their voices they want to be young the rest of their life, how good it feels to be alive, and they want to be eighteen till they die.

Everybody loves the karaoke; Alexander and Tatiana used to delight the grandkids—and their own children—by together singing "I Walk the Line" and "Groovy Kind of Love" (everyone's favorite), and Alexander alone singing to loud howls, a lá Leonard Cohen, that if Tatiana wanted another kind of love, he'd wear a mask for her, and all three brothers, like the Animals, boisterously singing the naughty, chest-tugging "When I Was Young." But now the machine belongs firmly to those twenty and under.

And then Anthony, Jr. picks up the microphone, his black eyes on his father, and without music, without a beat, without any accompaniment, puts away the Goth and the snark for three minutes of an astonishing a cappella rendition of "The Summer of '69" that fills the house, shows his extraordinary but deeply hidden gifts, leaves them *all* speechless—even the ten-year-olds—and after the final *those were the best days of my life*, forces Anthony to leave the room, with Tommy trailing him, asking, "What's the matter, Dad? He was *so* good, what's the matter?"

Alexander sits in the corner of the small sofa by the window watching them all, slightly away from the hullaballoo, though two of Janie's youngest girls, Vicky and Nicky, are nestled around him.

Tatiana comes and stands behind him, leaning over. "You okay?" she whispers. "Loud in here? Go inside, lie down. You're tired."

She can't have a *whisper* with him without her children, who are watching, pipe up with, "Dad, really, go lie down, you're exhausted." "It's been such a long day, how are you feeling?"

"Daddy, go ahead, don't stay up for our sake, you know what night owls we are."

He laughs. "Stop mothering me. I'm fine," he says. "But can you see Pasha and Harry are getting that home movies look about them? Now is a *very* good time for me to take a long walk." He turns to Tatiana. "You coming?"

His is a rhetorical question. He knows she likes to skulk nearby while they dissect the seconds of time past. Not him; not anymore. Taking the baby from Janie, Alexander goes for a stroll in the lit-up agaves with the newly named monarch, Shannon Clay III while Tatiana hides inside.

The kids do this every Thanksgiving after karaoke—the custom of the holiday. The lights go out in the den and a crowd gathers, the teenage girls, the Harvard girls, this year even the aloof boyfriend, and the petite and curious fourth-grade teacher. With Tommy by his side but Anthony Jr. nowhere to be seen, Anthony cranks out an old 8mm projector, and soon choppy black- and-white images appear on the cream wall capturing a few snapshots from the canyon of their life—that tell nothing, and yet somehow everything. They watch old movies, from 1963, 1952, 1948, 1947—the older, the more raucous the children and parents becoming.

This year, because Ingrid isn't here, Anthony shows them something new. It's from 1963. A birthday party, this one with happy sound, cake, unlit candles. Anthony is turning twenty. Tatiana is very pregnant with Janie. ("Mommy, look, that's you in Grammy's belly!" exclaims Vikky.) Harry toddling around, pursued loudly and relentlessly by Pasha—oh, how in 1999 six children love to see their fathers wild like them, how Mary and Amy love to see their precious husbands small. The delight in the den is abundant. Anthony sits on the patio, bare chested, in swimshorts, one leg draped over the other, playing his guitar, "playing Happy Birthday to myself," he says now, except it's not "Happy Birthday." The joy dims slightly at the sight of their brother, their father so beautiful and whole he hurts their united hearts—and suddenly into the frame, in a mini-dress, walks a tall dark striking woman with end-less legs and comes to stand close to Anthony. The camera remains on him because Anthony is singing, while she flicks on her lighter and ignites the candles on his cake; one by one she lights them as he strums his guitar and sings the number one hit of the day, falling into a burning "Ring of Fire . . . " The woman doesn't look at Anthony, he doesn't look at her, but in the frame you can see her bare thigh flush against the sole of his bare foot the whole time she lights his twenty candles plus one to grow on. *And it burns, burns, burns . . .* And when she is done, the camera—which never lies—catches just one microsecond of an exchanged glance before she walks away, just one gram of neutral matter exploding into an equivalent of 20,000 pounds of TNT.

The reel ends. Next. The budding novelist Rebecca says, "Dad, who was that? Was that Grammy's friend Vikki?"

"Yes," says Anthony. "That was Grammy's friend Vikki."

Tak zhivya, bez radosti/bez muki/pomniu ya ushedshiye goda/i tvoi sere-bryannyiye ruki/v troike yeletevshey navsegda . . .

So I live—remembering with sadness all the happy years now gone by, remembering your long and silver arms, forever in the troika that flew by . . .

Back even further, to 1947 he takes them. "Look at how funny Grammy is!" the grandchildren peal. "Is she *arm wrestling* with Grandpa?" All you can see through the unsteady camera are her two thin white arms over a man's strong dark forearm upright and motionless on the picnic table. "She was always running around chasing you, Ant." "What a knock-out she was." "Still is," says Rebecca. "Daddy, look at you, sitting on her lap, being kissed by her. It's so weird! How old were you here?"

"Um—*four.*"

"Where is Grandpa? You've been showing us all these reels for years, and we've never seen anything of him."

"Well, he was the one holding the camera, wasn't he? You saw his forearm. What more do you want? It's just for him. She was always performing for him," says Anthony.

"Come on, you don't have a single reel with him?"

"I don't think so."

"Come on, Dad. You must have something! Come on, show us something. Show us Grandpa, Dad, Ant. *Please.*"

Reluctantly Anthony rummages in the cabinet where the reels are kept. Unwillingly he spools one on, impossibly adept with his one arm, and in a moment, to a collective inhale, flickering on the cream wall, as if by ghostly magic, a young dark man appears near the swimming pool, putting on a tank top to cover his scarred back when he sees the camera on him. He hops up on the diving board, arms out, body straight, about to dive in. The blonde woman is in the water. Click click click, the projector whirrs. His white teeth, his wet black hair, his long-legged, muscular frame fill the wall. The vague shapes of his dark tattoos are visible. He's been roofing, his chest is broad, his arms enormous. He dives in, far and strong, in an arc, and pulls the woman by her treading feet under the water. When they come up for air, she is trying to get away, but he won't let her. Only when they're in the frame together can you really see how large he is and how tiny she is. Soundless, whirr, whirr, just the two of them flinging their bodies against each other, kicking, splashing, and then she jumps into his hands and he lifts her above his head as she straightens up, in a little bikini, arms out, and sways, sways to balance, and for a moment they stand straight, she in the palms of his hands, with her own arms outstretched, right above him. And then he flicks her, sending her falling wildly back, the camera is shaking from laughter, and he is shaking from laughter, and when she comes out of the water she jumps on his back and covers his neck and head with kisses as he turns to the camera and bows and waves, a smile on his face. Click click, whirr whirr, the spool unspools, the wall goes white, and the only sound in the room is the vibration of the projector.

"They were so young," whispers Rebecca.

"Like us," says Washington.

The children sit. Somewhere soft the music plays. The children's wives and husband are asleep. The children's children are asleep—even the teenagers who got tired of air hockey and ping pong and basketball and board games, even the Harvard students; it's late even for them. The math major is sharing a room with Tommy and Anthony Jr., he and his piercings far down the hall from pristine and protected Becky.

Up on the heights by the mountain, the four of them sit at the island, in the house where they grew up. They've brought out the midnight food. Cold leek and bacon stuffing, pieces of turkey straight from the Cling Wrap. They drink old wine, they open new beer.

They sit, winding down. On this Thanksgiving they sit just a while longer, for comfort, for peace, for family, for memory, for the blissful childhood they all shared that flew by and ended much too soon. They sit in the oasis and eat their mother's bread. During the day in front of their wives, their husbands, their children, they talk about sports and kids, and politics, and weapons, and work, but at night on holidays they never do.

Harry and Pasha talk of going out on the boat with him at sea, possibly the Biscayne Bay, when they were small. They both remember palm trees, green water, hot, remember him massive between them, themselves just fingerlings. No Janie, no Ant. He put the boys on the bench and showed them how to wrap a stay-sail. He gave them fishing rods and hooks and worms and they sat flanking him, with their lines in the water. Their mother sat at the rudder. *Come with me and I will make you fishers of men.* He was smoking, yanking on his line once in a while, and they were imitating him and yanking on theirs. The fish ate the worm around the hooks but were never caught. Then Harry got very interested in his hook. What else could it catch? Could it catch a piece of clothing? Wood? A good chunk of Pasha's thigh?

"Harry, so there was something wrong with you from the very beginning, do you see?" says Janie.

Pasha says, "Yes, but I pulled the hook out of my leg and admin-istered first aid to myself, so there."

"Well, you are your mother's son," says Harry. "And *I* showed you that—and never a word of thanks. We all should be so lucky as to know who we are from the very beginning."

"We all knew who we were," says Jane Barrington. "From the very beginning." She turns to Anthony. "Did he ever go fishing with you, Ant?"

"Once or twice," replies Anthony.

And just a few feet away, in the long darkened butler's pantry between the banquet dining room and the kitchen, there is a small alcove between the wall and the cabinets. In this alcove stands a small stool, and on this stool sits Tatiana, her eyes closed, her head back, pressed into the wall in her little hiding space, shaking a little bit, nodding, listening to his children carrying him on their grown-up voices.

Alexander comes out looking for her, and Tatiana, though herself sleepless, undresses and lies down with him. She wants to talk about the day, but he is tired and tells her they'll debrief in full tomorrow. She waits until he is asleep, and then disengages and in her robe comes back out to the now solitary kitchen and makes herself a cup of tea. The hums of the house soothe her. She knows what floorboards creak and where the grease stain from a sticky little finger is. She knows the corner of the living room area rug shredded by Janie's ratel of a Labrador. She knows the drips of the faucet and the smell of garlic each time she walks past the *garlic tomb* as she calls it—a spherical clay pot with holes on top, a kind of scented candle in reverse.

The house is *all*.

In solitude she reflects and comforts herself. She doesn't want the day to end.

She makes bread.

She mixes a little warm milk with sugar and dry active yeast and puts the cup under the hot lamp to bubble up. She sits on her high stool, sipping her tea, and watches the yeast mixture slowly fleck with bubbles, rising in a creamy froth. After swirling it with a spoon and making it all liquid, she sits and watches it bubble up again.

After fifteen minutes she gets out the flour, melts her butter and warms another two cups of milk. She separates her eggs, and beats the whites until they are firm and foamy. When she turns around, a bleary-eyed Anthony is sitting watching her from across the island. "I can't believe you're still up."

"I can't believe you're still up."

She makes him a cup of tea. "So what do you think of your daughter's new paramour?"

Anthony shrugs. "I don't have to sleep with him, do I? What do I care? I'd prefer he didn't parade his tongue jewelry in front of her family, but no one asked me."

"Rebecca says he's her first real love," says Tatiana.

"At eighteen it all seems like real love," he replies, and breaks off, and then they glance at each other and say no more. Indeed it does, thinks Tatiana. And sometimes it is.

Spread over the island, Anthony watches her. Wherever she goes, his gaze follows, as she combines the flour and sugar and eggs and milk and yeast until it all holds together and then she kneads it, adding melted butter a little at a time until it is all soaked through.

She took a piece of black cobble-hard bread and cut it into four pieces the size of a deck of cards each. Then she cut the deck of cards into half again. One half she wrapped for morning. One half she put on four plates. She put one plate in front of her sister, one plate in front of herself, one plate in front of Alexander, and one plate in front of their mother's chair. She took a knife and fork, and cut a small piece from her share. A drop of blood from her mouth fell on the table. She ignored it. Putting the bread into her mouth, she chewed it for minutes before finally swallowing it. It tasted moldy, and faintly of hay.

Alexander was long done with his piece. Dasha was long done with her piece. The sisters would not look at their mother's bread or at their mother's empty chair. All the chairs were empty now except for hers and Dasha's. And Alexander's. Another drop of blood fell onto the table. What did her sister teach her to say a few days ago, kneeling in front of their mother who had died? Give us this day our daily bread, Dasha said.

"Give us this day our daily bread," said 75-year-old Tatiana in her home in Scottsdale, Arizona.

"Amen," said Anthony. "I have memories of you making bread that go back over fifty years. You don't realize what a complete food bread is until you see all the ingredients that go into it."

Tatiana nodded, lightly smiling. "Yes," she said, opening her palms and bowing her head before the kneaded dough. "Cottonseed, or hay. Cardboard. Sawdust. Linseed. Glue. A complete food, bread."

After she buttered a large ovenproof dish she placed the kneaded dough into it, covered it with a white towel and put it into the dark oven. Now the bread had to rise. She sat by her son; they sipped their tea. It was so quiet in the house, just the faucet dripped.

"Mom," he said, "you do know that we know you sit there and listen to us, don't you?"

She laughed. "Yes, son," she said fondly. "I do." She caressed his face, she kissed his cheek. "Tell me about Ingrid. She's no better?"

Anthony shook his head. He stopped looking at his mother. "She's worse than ever. She told the doctor it's all my fault. I drove her to it. I'm gone all the time. I'm never home." He pressed his lips together in sharp disappointment. "For fifteen years, she's been saying this. You're always on the road, Anthony. Like I'm a truck driver." He tutted. "I made her check into Betty Ford in Minnesota two days ago."

"Well, that's good. That will help."

He seemed unconvinced. "She's staying for at least eight months. I told her I don't want her back unless she is better."

Tatiana considered him. "What about your sons? Who's going to take care of them?"

"She doesn't take care of them now, Mom! That's the whole f— problem. Tommy's a good boy, but Anthony Jr. is always in trouble." Anthony sighed. "And I mean *trouble.* In school, with his friends. With the law." He shook his head. "I didn't want to say anything during the day, no reason to make everyone upset over this. But I've given the President my resignation. I have no choice.

I can't continue. I mean, honestly, what am I supposed to do? The boys . . . I can't leave them, and now she's gone." He paused. "We're leaving Washington."

This was monumental. Anthony had lived in DC for over twenty years.

"I accepted a new position—as commander of Yuma."

Yuma! Tatiana nodded, trying not to show her excitement.

"It's a three-year post," Anthony continued. "Intelligence, weapons, some travel. The boys will come with me, and I'll be mostly in one place. I haven't asked, but I'm sure Harry will help me out when I'm away; my kids won't know what hit them after a week with him."

"I'm sure Harry will help you out," Tatiana said carefully. She knew her son wasn't happy, and her own satisfaction was intrusive. This wasn't about her. "I know you don't think it's wonderful, son," she said. "But it *is* wonderful. Your sons will be better for having their dad. And Harry is going to go through the roof. Just imagine, both of you at Yuma. I want to wake him up and tell him." Her hand remained on Anthony's unhappy face. "You're doing the right thing. And you've done well. Buck up," she said softly. "Be strong. You have a lot to do. Perseus is only one man." She smiled. "He can't be everywhere at once."

"Thank you," he whispered, kissing her hand, leaning into it, and then said with deep regret, "Besides, how many Andromedas can a man have in his life?"

Their heads were together. Tatiana was hoping at least one more. "Have faith, bud," she whispered to her son.

Suddenly there was noise of familiar footsteps. Alexander appeared in the archway. His face was not amused. "What do I have to do around here," he said loudly to a sheepish Tatiana, "to get my wife to stay in bed with me? You have been up since sunrise, and it's three in the morning. What's next? Are you going to start bringing your chair to his front yard, too?" He turned and motioned for her. "Come," he said, inviting no argument. "Now. Come."

In their bedroom, she took off her robe and climbed naked into bed with him, into the old big brass bed they had shared since 1949. He was sulky but only for a moment, since he wanted to go to sleep and needed to touch her. "You couldn't stay in my bed, could you?" They lay face to face. "We were so nice, so warm. But no." He was caressing her back, her breasts, her thighs.

"I needed to make bread for tomorrow," she whispered, her kneading hands on him.

"Now that you've been in this country for fifty-six years, one of these days I will have to take you to a supermarket," said Alexander, "and show you this thing we have in aisle twelve—called *bread*. All kinds, all the time. No ration cards, no blizzards, and you don't even have to wait in line for it." He was relaxed now, warm, enlarged; he rubbed her back, murmuring to her something about Anthony Jr. being angry, and Tommy being sad, and the baby being cute, and the day being good, and not caring much for Washington despite his mathematical sycophancy . . . he murmured and nuzzled and she caressed him into relief and sleep.

Back over the years she flies, to Anthony's voice, learning how to accompany himself on the guitar. In their winter jackets, he and his dad sit on the deck called My Prerogative near the house called Free on Bethel Island in December 1948, Alexander holding both fishing lines while Anthony is showing him how to play and sing "Have Yourself a Merry Little Christmas," as Tatiana at her open kitchen window is cooking a ham with a brown sugar glaze for the holiday dinner, watching them out on the deck, struggling with the chords and the notes and the fishing lines, heads together, four-year-old Anthony holding his guitar in his two little arms, leaning into his smoking, twenty-eight-year-old father, as she listens to their chuckling voices, one deep, one soft, rising above the cold canals, drifting down the canopies . . .

> *Here we are as in olden days,*
> *Happy golden days of yore . . .*

Two

Soon the century has come and gone, from one sea to another and back again across the waters. Tatiana and Alexander have walked through the old world, they've walked through the new. They've lived.

But the mangoes are still ripe and sweet, the avocados are fresh, so are the tomatoes. They still plant flowers in their garden. They love to go to the movies, read the paper, read books. Once a month they drive up to Yuma to visit their sons and grandchildren. (Harry shows Alexander the latest weapons he's working on; Alexander loves that best.) Once a month they drive up to Sedona and the Canyon. Once a month they drive up to Las Vegas. They love

American television, comedies best. And other things that the penthouse suite up on the thirty-sixth floor of the Bellagio over Vegas Strip shows them.

"Tania, quick, come here, see what's on TV."

She comes. "Oh my."

"What a country. Bread—and this."

At home they sit on the couch late into the evening. The TV is off, and he can tell she is nearly asleep. The blanket is over their laps. She sits with her head pressed against his arm.

"Tatia," he calls for her. "Tatiana, Tania, Tatiasha . . . "

"Hmm?" she says sleepily.

"Would you like to live in Arizona, Tatia?" Alexander whispers, looking at the fire, "the land of the small spring?"

"Yes . . . " she echoes. "Yes, my horse and cart, yes, my soul."

He has his last cigarette sitting outside their bedroom, smelling the nightshade.

They swim in their pool every morning. Once, after they swam five laps and were resting, panting, holding on to the edge, Alexander said, "Did you know that when King David got old he was advised by his counselors to take in a young virgin to warm himself?"

Tatiana blushed at the unexpectedness of that.

"No, you *kill* me," said Alexander, pulling her to him.

"I think," said Tatiana, closing her eyes in his arms, "King David already availed himself of a young virgin."

"Yes . . . " His lips were over her face. "And she's been warming him for life."

He keeps telling her, the victorious do not surrender their weapons. They do not put away their swords, they sheathe and clothe them in scarlet and keep them ever at the ready. He keeps telling her, go easy on me, I'm not eighty-one anymore. And sometimes she listens to him.

She makes him Mickey Mouse homemade waffles for breakfast. When he is home for lunch, she makes him tuna with apples; in the afternoons they have a long siesta, and then Tatiana fixes dinner while Alexander watches the news in the kitchen, or reads the paper to her. They dine alone and afterward go for a long walk into the foothills before the sun sets. Sometimes they drive down to have ice cream and walk through the Scottsdale Common, sometimes they drive up a few miles north to Carefree to ride horses through trails in the mountains full of ancient saguaros and Corona de Cristo thorns. Their life is quieter for a brief lull before the next baby boom.

The wild grandchildren are growing up, becoming less noisy, flying away.

Anthony has not stopped working. Especially now, with the world going to hell in a handbasket, there is more to do than ever. When it quiets down, he'll retire. The time has not come. Anthony's son Anthony Jr. managed to shape up in Yuma, straighten out, and went to OCS right out of high school and then straight to Iraq. Tommy is still with Anthony. Ingrid got better, but belatedly, because in the eight recovering months that she'd been gone, Anthony recovered too, and moved on, and fell in love again. He divorced Ingrid and married Kerri, who accompanied his singing on her guitar for him, and baked every day for him, and adored him without pretensions or conditions, and got pregnant for him, and gave him a blonde Isabella.

Anthony's daughter Rebecca is having her first child next month. Washington, it turned out, had a permanent soft spot for Becks.

Could Rebecca really be having a baby? Because just a breath ago, an eighteen-year-old nurse was bending over Rebecca's father's father, a wounded soldier in a Soviet hospital, saying, yes, Shura, we are going to have a baby.

And now the father's father, the old warrior, sits on the raised deck in the Sonoran sunset and smokes.

And the nurse sits next to him and sips her cup of tea.

His arms are draped over the white rocking bench. It's in the 90s still, and the sun blazes orange over the saguaros and sagebrush, reflecting onto the rocky mountains.

Around her is the land that his mother's money bought for her— the land with such a price and without price. Behind them are Germany and Poland and Russia. Behind them farther down the meadows and the steppes is the great ancient city of Perm, née Molotov, and near it through a muddy track in the woods, a small fishing village called Lazarevo that they left in 1942 knowing they would never see it again, and never did.

Far, far east and steep south through treacherous jungle is the Hué River, is Kum Kau, is Vietnam. They don't face that way.

They look on the Western Mountains instead, at the McDowell Hills, at the sprawled valley over which the sun sets every night, they look on the uplands where they rode horses and saw their first saguaros bloom white, where Anthony found snakes and jack rabbits and Pasha dissected scorpions, and Harry chased Gila monsters with his punji sticks, and Janie deliberately put her hands on the cholla to show her father she could be as tough as the boys. They did well, their children, growing up in the creosote bushes. They did all right.

"I don't want this life to end," said Alexander. "The good, the bad, the *everything*, the very old, to ever end." His arm went around her. "It's fantastic here—the sunset over this great, gold and lilac desert and the million flickering lights in the frontier land of my mother and father." He kept his voice steady, kept it low. He pointed into the distance. "Do you see our 97-acre backyard?" he said softly. "Our own Summer Garden right past those Russian lilacs, where our Arizona lilac—the sand verbena, the phacelia, the desert lavender, the lantana—blankets the earth. Do you see it?"

"I see it." And the marigolds, too.

"Do you see the Field of Mars, where I walked next to my bride in her white wedding dress, with red sandals in her hands, when we were kids?"

"I see it well."

"We spent all our days afraid it was too good to be true, Tatiana," said Alexander. "We were always afraid all we had was a borrowed five minutes from now."

Her hands went on his face. "That's all any of us ever has, my love," she said. "And it all flies by."

"Yes," he said, looking at her, at the desert, covered coral and yellow with golden eye and globe mallow. "But what a five minutes it's been."

Rebecca's book of love for her grandparents is almost finished. But there are things Rebecca will not know and does not know and cannot know.

Tatiana is thinking of Fontanka and Moika canals, of Palace Bridge—and other bridges—oars and sandals, casts and dresses, fathers and brothers, one sister, one mother, on a Sunday long ago.

"Look, Tania. A new dress." Papa pulled out a package in brown paper. Tatiana perked up a bit despite her cast, which itched and hurt.

A tiny gasp escaped her and she forgot about her arm and her troubles and her lost summer. Oh, the dress! White and flowing with embroidered dancing crimson roses. It had satin straps instead of sleeves, and satin sashes criss-crossing her back, opening in a flowing skirt. The dress was soft and well made. "But, Papa!"

"But Papa!" he said, imitating her.

"Papa, where *did you get this?*"

Her hands were kneading the dress, turning it over, traveling to the tag sewed into the seam. "Fabriqué en France."

"You bought this in . . . France?" Tatiana breathed out. All she could think of was Queen Margot and her doomed beautiful soldier lover La Môle, rent with rapture in Paris.

"No," Papa replied. "I bought it in Poland. I was in a small town called Swietocryzst and they had a Sunday market there. Remarkable things. I found this and thought, my Tania would like it."

"Like it? Papa, I adore it! Let me put it on and we'll go for a walk."

Dasha said, "You're not putting on a dress like that with a broken arm."

Tatiana frowned. "If not with a broken arm, then when?"

"When you don't have a broken arm," said Dasha.

"But I need it to make me feel better now. Right, Papa?"

"Right." Papa smiled and nodded. "Dasha, you're too pragmatic. You should have seen the town I bought it in. The town, the dress, all for youth, for love. You'd wear the dress if you had no legs."

"Well, that's perfect for her because she has no arm," grumbled Dasha.

"Put it on, sunshine," Papa said to Tatiana. "Put it on, sweetness. Do you know what they told me in Poland? That your name means fairy princess. I never knew that."

"Me neither, Papa. How delightful. Fairy princess!" She twirled holding the dress to herself.

And so it was that Tatiana, for the first time, was allowed to borrow her sister's red, high-heeled strappy sandals that were too large for her. She tied them around her ankles, put on her new dress, and they left their cramped communal apartment on Fifth Soviet and went for a stroll. She did the best she could, every once in a while tripping on the Leningrad cobblestones, her brushed-out golden hair flowing.

That was a good way to describe her. She did the best she could. ·

They bought a beer, and with their hats on, in their Sunday shoes, smoking cigarettes, chatting idly, breathing in the dusty Leningrad summer air, they walked down to Engineer's Castle over the granite Fontanka Bridge and through the back gates of the Summer Garden. Down the paths and past the water fountains they strolled, shaded by overflowing elms. Couples were draped over the benches between the marble statues of ancient heroes: near Saturn eating his own children, near the doom of Amour and Psyche, near Alexander the Great, the commander of commanders of the ancient world.

The Metanovs ambled through the gilded iron gates of the Summer

Garden onto the Neva embankment, across from St. Peter and Paul's Fortress and walked the winding way along the parapets along a shimmering river, past the Winter Palace, past the Admiralty's golden spire to St. Isaac's Cathedral square, to the statue of the Bronze Horseman.

They had come a long way and they were tired. The evening was nearing, the amber shadows were lengthening. Tatiana's arm was still broken, but that was the only vestige left of a girl named Saika Kantorova. Everything else had been forgotten. Her name was never mentioned again by anyone in the family, even in passing.

It was as if she had never existed.

Dasha walked with her protective arm through Tatiana's good one, and Pasha was on the other side, bumping constantly into her cast, and Mama and Papa were arm in arm, talking intimately—such a rarity. Papa bought Tatiana a crème brûlée ice cream. They sat on a bench and gazed at Peter the Great's granite tribute, the Bronze Horseman, lit by Arctic light, gazed into the northern sun reflected in the halcyon Neva River.

"Papa, you said Holy Cross in Poland is a nice town?" said Tatiana. "But nothing can compare to Leningrad in the summer evening, don't you think?"

"Nothing," Papa agreed. "This is where I want to die."

"Here we are, enjoying our day and you're talking about dying," exclaimed Mama. "What's wrong with you?"

"He is so melancholic and Russian," whispered Pasha to a laughing Tatiana. "You're not going to turn out that maudlin, are you?"

"I'll try not to, Pasha."

"When I was in Holy Cross," said Papa, "it was also a Sunday, and toward evening I took a walk to the River Vistula running on the outskirts of the city. It wasn't the wide Neva, but it was blue and calm, and the bridge leading to the town was painted blue also. Couples and families strolled across the bridge in white hats, eating ice cream and watermelon, and children were laughing, and underneath the bridge, a young man was rowing his young lady."

"You see, Tania," said Pasha, "there are some cultures where it's appropriate, even desirable, for men to row."

She elbowed him.

Papa continued. "The man had put down his oars and the two of them just sat bobbing on the river. She was wearing a white dress and a wide-brim hat. In her hands she held a bouquet of white lupines. The sun glistened on them. I stood on the bridge and watched them for a long time." He sighed. "I felt happy just to be alive. I wish you could've seen it, milaya Tania."

"Don't you want milaya *me to have seen it, too, Papa?" asked Dasha.*

"And what about me, Georg? Don't you want your darling wife to have seen it while eating ice cream and wearing a white hat?" said Mama.

Somewhere in the near distance a troubadour was singing, his choral tenor spilling down the sidewalk, echoing off the glass of the iridescent river.

> *"Gori, gori, moya zvezda*
> *Zvezda lyubvi privetnaya*
> *Ti u menya odna zavetnaya*
> *Drugoi ne budet nikogda . . . "*

> *"Shine on, shine on, my only star,*
> *my star of love eternally,*
> *You are my sole and chosen one,*
> *There'll be no other one for me . . . "*

Snug between Papa and Pasha, fourteen-year-old Tatiana licked her ice cream on the bench with her family across from the Bronze Horseman, and saw with all her soul, felt with all her soul the white day, the stucco houses, the wide-brim hat and the young man with oars in his hands and a smile on his face rowing his white lupine beloved under the blue bridge that led to a small serene town in Poland named Holy Cross, saw with all her soul, felt with all her soul the life divine, the love divine.

Three

In the new millennium, Tatiana sits on a bench on a Sunday in a palm-covered Western-themed, art-gallery-filled, immaculate Scottsdale downtown, ecumenical, multi-cultural and yet deeply American. They have been shopping, they had lunch, they went to a bookstore, an antique store, a curtain store, a hardware store, a DVD store. It's now afternoon, around three, three thirty. She is wearing a hat and all white to reflect her from the sun, but the truth is, she *loves* that sun. She is perspiring and panting, and her breath is short; she doesn't care. She sits on the bench, thinking, if I stay here another minute, I'm going to boil away like burnt sugar. It's not a good time to be out, it's so hot, there is no smell except the smell of heat; she doesn't care. Alexander, who loves the heat slightly less, has gone to get himself a drink.

Tatiana sits under the palms and eats her ice cream. It's summer, it's June, her birthday is tomorrow. Under her hat, under her breath, she hums a slow sweet Russian song from long ago.

She blinks and looks up from her ice cream.

On the other side of the pavement, Alexander smiles.

A local bus heading to Phoenix downtown comes, obscuring his view of her. He moves his head, this way, that.

That was his moment in Leningrad, on an empty street, when his life became possible—when Alexander became possible. There he stood as he was—a young Red Army officer in dissolution, all his days stamped with no future and all his appetites unrestrained, on patrol the day war started for Russia. He stood with his rifle slung on his shoulder and cast his wanton eyes on her, eating her ice cream all sunny, singing, blonde, blossoming, breathtaking. He gazed at her with his entire unknowable life in front of him, and this is what he was thinking . . .

To cross the street or not to cross?

To follow her? To hop on the bus, after her? What absolute madness.

He comes around the bus; he only thinks he is running. He doesn't run anymore. He walks slowly to the bench where she is sitting. In front of her he stands and she raises her eyes to get a good look at him; she raises and raises them, for he is tall.

Her hair is fading white. Alexander blinks. It's blonde and long again. The lines are gone from her face. The green eyes sparkle, the freckles multiply, her red sandal toe bounces up and down with her crossed leg, and the strap of her white dress slips off her shoulder. Smiling, he says, "Tatiana, your ice cream is, as always, melting." He stretches out his hand to her—and wipes her mouth and fixes her shoulder strap.

"I am ridiculously hot," Alexander says, sitting down on the bench, opening his Coke and lighting a cigarette. "I can't believe I agreed, no, *chose* to come here. We could be in Bay Biscayne right now." He shakes his head and shrugs. Taking a long puff, he glances at her. They're sitting shoulder to bare shoulder. "Well? Thinking up another witty riposte for me?"

Tatiana turns to him, looks up at him, and smiles. "Do you know what a happy ending is to a Russian?" she says. "When the hero, at the end of his own story, finally learns the reason for his suffering."

Taking another swig of Coke, Alexander says, "Your jokes are getting so lame." He knocks into her with his stretched- out leg. She takes hold of his hand. "What?" he asks.

"Nothing, soldier," says Tatiana.

He is thinking of sailboats in distant oceans, the desert from dimmest childhood, the ghost of fortune, the girl on the bench. When he saw her, he saw something new. He saw it because he wanted to see it, because he wanted to change his life. He stepped off the curb and out of the deadfall.

To cross the street. To follow her. And she will give your life meaning, she will save you. Yes, yes—to cross.

"We'll meet again in Lvov, my love and I . . . " Tatiana hums, eating her ice cream, in our Leningrad, in jasmine June, near Fontanka, the Neva, the Summer Garden, where we are forever young.

The End

The End